SMALLVILLE™

OMNIBUS TWO

SMALLVILLE™

OMNIBUS TWO

Based on the Hit TV series

CONTAINS:

WHODUNNIT
SILENCE
SHADOWS

**Superman created by
Jerry Siegel and Joe Shuster**

www.orbitbooks.net

ORBIT

First published in Great Britain in July 2006 by Orbit
This omnibus edition copyright © 2006 by DC Comics

Whodunnit
First published in Great Britain by Orbit 2003
Copyright © 2003 by DC Comics

Silence
First published in Great Britain by Atom 2004
Copyright © 2004 by DC Comics

Shadows
First published in Great Britain by Atom 2004
Copyright © 2003 by DC Comics

A CIP catalogue record for this book
is available from the British Library.

ISBN 978-1-84149-500-2

Typeset in Times by Palimpsest Book Production Limited,
Polmont, Stirlingshire

Orbit
An imprint of
Little, Brown Book Group
100 Victoria Embankment
London EC4Y 0DY

An Hachette UK Company
www.hachette.co.uk

www.orbitbooks.net

CONTENTS

SMALLVILLE

WHODUNNIT

Dean Wesley Smith

For Kris, always
The mystery of my life

Clark Kent had to hide the strangest things. It was the hottest day of the spring, and he hadn't even broken into a sweat. Sweating wasn't something a guy could fake, no matter how many strange powers he found himself blessed with. So, instead, he kept a slight distance between himself, Lana Lang, and Chloe Sullivan, hoping that they wouldn't notice.

They hadn't walked far in the ninety-degree temperature, but Chloe and Lana looked like they had wilted. Initially, Clark had suggested that they wait until later to walk up to the Franklin farm, but Lana shook her head.

She'd already waited too long to find Danny Franklin. Lana had been assigned to work with Danny on a lab project, but Danny hadn't been in school for three days, and no one was answering the Franklin phone. So Lana had asked Clark to go along with her to the Franklin place.

"I'm relying on you, Clark," she had said. "I don't want to go to the farm alone."

Clark agreed, of course, and Chloe, who had been standing nearby, had offered to drive. Lana had smiled her gratitude to both of them.

She hadn't said why she was reluctant to visit the Franklin farm on her own; after all, she had been friends with Danny Franklin longer than anyone else had. But Clark hadn't asked. He didn't really want to know.

He would accompany her, no matter how silly it seemed to walk to a farm in the unusual April heat wave. He never could say no to Lana Lang.

The humidity made the air heavy and thick, dampening the sounds of their footsteps on the gravel driveway that led to the Franklin place. Trees shaded this part of the walk. Sunlight came through the leaves in beams, making the shadows dark and welcoming in their coolness. Ahead Clark could see where the gravel driveway crested over a slight hill. They only had another dozen steps in the shade, then the road would be out in the open sunlight again.

Clark had never been this deep inside the Franklins' property. He'd only been to the gate, which was about a hundred yards behind them.

Chloe's car was parked there, blocked from coming up the driveway by the metal gate and a padlock that looked rusted. Clark had no idea why someone would lock a gate across a driveway when there was no fence on either side of the gate. Just ditches and weeds marking the line between the road and the open fields. Any truck could easily bounce down through the ditch and go around the gate to get to the driveway.

Chloe had pointed at the indentation left in the weeds and noted that the gate looked like it had stood open for years and had only recently been closed. Clark did not like the sound of that.

"Maybe the Franklins had a family emergency in Metropolis," Lana said as she tucked a loose strand of hair behind her ear.

"That still doesn't explain why they would lock the gate," Chloe said. "No one in this area locks gates."

Clark nodded his agreement. There was a gate at the edge of the Kent farm that could swing across the driveway, but Clark couldn't remember a time it had ever been shut. He had cut the weeds around it more times than he wanted to count, but he had no idea why it had ever been built. And he had never asked. More than likely the driveway gates in this part of Kansas were more to show ownership of a road than anything else.

"Maybe the Franklins just shut the gate to let delivery people know they were gone," Clark said.

"Maybe," Chloe said. "But I still think it's weird."

"Everything in this town is weird to you," Clark said, smiling at his friend and bumping his hip against hers.

"True," Chloe said. "Weird keeps things interesting, that's for sure."

They came out of the shade and into the open sunlight. Clark could feel the heat instantly, but it didn't bother him, not like it bothered the girls. He didn't know why it worked that way, but on days like today, he was glad it did. He made sure his steps were slow enough to match Lana's and Chloe's, since both of them seemed to be fighting the unseasonably warm day, and he needed to at least seem like he was as well.

A slight breeze hit them from the south, but not enough to take away the thickness of the air and the strange feeling Clark was having that they were heading into trouble.

"I don't remember hearing we were going to have summer-like temperatures," Chloe said, wiping her hand across her forehead. "Hope they have the fans working at school tomorrow."

"We're just used to the cold," Lana said. "Makes it seem warmer."

Clark smiled. "Yeah, we're going to think this is cool in August."

"Not likely," Chloe said. "I'll sweat just as much then as now."

"I thought girls didn't sweat," Clark said.

"That's right," Lana said, laughing. "We glow."

"You can glow all you want," Chloe said. "I'm sweating, and I hate it. Someday I'm going to move to Alaska just to get out of this stupid humidity."

"And take pictures of bear and moose and piles of snow?" Clark asked, grinning at his friend. "You'd miss all the fun of Smallville."

"I'd miss the weirdness," Chloe said. "I wouldn't miss this heat."

They crested the top of the hill and stopped.

Below them, the Franklin farm filled the shallow valley. A large pond filled the right side of the valley, and the driveway skirted the left edge of the water, leading up to a turn-around area in front of the white house. Two large barns dominated the hillside behind the house. To the right a large area had been dug and tilled for a garden. There weren't any stakes, string, or iden-tifying markers at the end of the tilled rows, so Clark doubted it had been planted yet. Right now he knew his mom was starting to plant their garden, and when he got home he was going to have to help.

No car sat in the Franklin driveway, and the barn doors were closed up tight. Nothing was moving.

"Looks empty," Lana said. She sounded surprised.

Clark wasn't—and he finally figured out why. The silence. Working farms were never silent in the spring. He should have heard an engine roar from a tractor or voices as people worked the fields.

And the smells were wrong, too. Right now, the Kent farm was filled with the pungent odor of fertilizer. Clark's dad used manure—saying it was old-fashioned, but the best. Other farmers used chemical brands, but even those smelled as awful as the cow dung did.

Silence and no stench. Closed barn doors, and no cars. Something had gone wrong here. He could sense it. And now that he was thinking like the farmer's son he was, he realized that no farm family left home in the spring, unless there was an emergency.

"Did Danny seem distracted to you?" Clark asked Lana.

"Lately?" she said. "Sure. First he was worried about doing all his chores. Then his dad got laid off from LuthorCorp, so the family had financial worries."

"The Franklins always have financial worries," Chloe said.

"Yeah," Clark said. "Farm families generally do."

Lana gave him a sympathetic look, but he ignored it. He hadn't said that so Lana would feel sorry for him.

The Kents handled the financial troubles as best they could. But Clark could remember his father's reaction when Jed Franklin, Danny's dad, finally gave up full-time farming and got a job at LuthorCorp.

Do that, Clark's dad had said, *and you guarantee your farm's failure.*

But what choice does he have if they don't have any money? Clark asked.

A farm can always feed the family, Clark, his dad said. *Remember that.*

"Anything you can tell Mr. Phillips about the lab project?" Clark asked Lana. "Maybe get another partner to finish it?"

"It looks like I'm going to have to," Lana said. "I just wonder what happened. Danny didn't say anything about leaving town."

"Some people don't report to school when they go out of town," Chloe said.

"Danny talks to me," Lana said. "He would have mentioned something."

Clark fought the jealousy that rose in him. Danny wasn't Lana's boyfriend either. Whitney was, and he was off in the Marines. If Lana had been having a conversation about Clark, she probably would have said "He talks to me," in just that same tone.

But Clark had seen how Danny looked at Lana, had recognized it as a wistful look that often crossed his own face. Lana was a lot more popular than she ever thought she was, but part of her charm was that she didn't realize just how appealing she was.

Chloe glanced at Clark. He knew how attuned she was to his moods, and she could probably sense how deeply this worried him. She wiped the sweat off her forehead and frowned at the farm.

"Well," she said, "I'm about as pitted out as I can be. Another few yards won't make me any grosser. We might as well go knock to make sure no one's there."

Clark smiled at her choice of words. He nodded.

Lana shrugged. "Might as well."

They walked the rest of the way down the hill in silence. Chloe took her camera off her shoulder. She had that look that said she had gone into reporter mode.

Clark used the time to study the house and barns, looking for any danger inside them with his special vision. He couldn't see any problems, and he knew there was no one home. Everything seemed to be in its place. Yet still the sense of something wrong didn't leave him.

At the bottom of the hill, the road tucked in near the large pond before moving to the turnaround in front of the house. The hills, the nearby trees, and the fields behind the barns made this farm feel very isolated. Even the slight breeze they had felt on top of the hill didn't ruffle the smooth surface of the water.

The buildings were well kept and looked like they'd been

painted last summer. There was no trash in the yard and no tools left to rust. Tulips were starting to poke out of the ground in the front flower beds, and the small lawn was trimmed. Clearly Danny's dad ran a controlled operation here.

But Clark knew that money was really tight for Danny's parents. Since Jed Franklin's layoff, Danny's older twin sisters had taken part-time jobs around town to help out. Money was still so tight for them that Lana had even had to spring for the lab supplies she and Danny needed.

Since being laid off, Jed had been seen a number of times drunk and shouting nasty things about LuthorCorp. Clark had heard his parents talking about it a few times. His dad figured that Jed's anger would ease when the weather got clear enough to let him get back to work in the fields.

And from what Clark could tell from the neatly tilled rows, Jed Franklin had been doing just that. Only the tilling marks looked old and tamped down. Clark and his dad had started work a month ago, picking rocks, then tilling, and finally, just last week, covering everything in fertilizer.

Someone had clearly picked rocks and tilled, but the work had stopped there. And it looked like the Franklins had been on the same schedule the Kents were.

What would pull a farmer away from his farm right when there was the most work to do? It made no sense.

"Clark!"

Chloe's voice had a sharp bite to it. Chloe had stopped without him noticing, so he had to spin around.

Chloe was pointing into the water.

"What?" Lana asked, staring at where Chloe was pointing.

Something floated just under the smooth surface of the pond. At first Clark thought he was looking at a birch tree branch, the white bark almost luminescent in the brown water.

Then he saw blue fabric and realized that what he had taken for a branch was actually a white hand. It was about ten feet from the weeds bordering the road.

Someone was under the water.

Clark ran to the edge of the water and waded in. The water was shockingly cold, still holding its winter chill. The cold didn't bother him, but Clark hoped whoever was in the water hadn't been there long. He wasn't sure how much time the average person could be in water this cold and still survive.

The waves he created made the arm bob up and down. The hand peeked through the water's surface, mud-covered, dirt beneath the fingernails.

The water was chest deep and the mud on the bottom pulled at Clark's sneakers.

He reached the hand and pulled it upward. He knew at once the hand, and the body it was attached to, wasn't alive. And it hadn't been for a long time. The cold, slimy feel of the skin made him remember the time he had picked up a dead fish, kept too long in a cooler.

His stomach twisted, and he took a deep breath and held it.

He eased his grip on the slick skin and gently pulled. The body came to the surface right in front of him, facedown, bloated against the clothes it was wearing. Danny Franklin's blond hair floated around the head, brushing against Clark's chest.

"Oh, no," Lana said, sounding as if her heart had been broken. "Oh, no."

Blasted heat wave in the middle of April. Not only did it make a man uncomfortable, it also screwed up business in a hundred little ways.

Lionel Luthor adjusted his silk suit coat over his shoulders. Silk was not appropriate for ninety-degree days. He had summer suits for that sort of weather.

Not to mention all of the problems in the various buildings he owned around Metropolis. He had arrived at work this morning to find the heat still on. His secretary had called building maintenance, only to be informed that the maintenance supervisor was the only person who knew how to change over the system from heat to air-conditioning, and the supervisor was on a planned vacation until the following week.

It took two hours to find a way around that problem. Two hours in which Luthor cursed the old-fashioned building he usually loved. Even the windows in his office had swollen shut.

It was enough to make the most reasonable man cranky. And Lionel Luthor was not often a reasonable man.

He had business at City Bank and had spent the last three hours in their air-conditioned conference room. The cool air had taken the edge off his anger, fortunately, since an angry man was not a good businessman.

The meeting with the bank president had worked exactly as he had needed it to work. Lionel was leveraging a small-capital company named Stanley Feed and Grain into much larger capital. It didn't matter to him that in less than a month Stanley Feed and Grain would be shut down, its assets sold off, its long-term employees out of a job. This was business. The owners of Stanley Feed and Grain had sold him the controlling share of the company, and now he was going to use it.

If they hadn't wanted him to run their company the way he saw fit, they never should have sold him the controlling shares.

Of course, the idiots had had no idea why he had wanted those shares. They would soon understand.

Sometimes Lionel Luthor saw his job as simple education. He was teaching inept businessmen how successful people worked.

His sense of satisfaction left him, though, as he stepped through the revolving door in the lobby. The door opened into a small glass security enclosure between the bank and the street.

The enclosure was as hot as his office had been.

Beside him, Hank Bender, the current chief of security for LuthorCorp, sighed. Hank seemed even more uncomfortable than Luthor was, if that was possible. But Hank was a big man, strong and muscular. He often looked like he'd been squeezed into his suits.

Today he looked like he'd been squeezed into his clothes before they were dry.

"Fluky weather, boss," Bender said.

"Uncomfortable, yes, fluky, no," Luthor said. "According to this morning's paper, Kansas occasionally suffers high temperatures in April."

"Must be real occasional because I don't remember it."

Neither did Luthor. In fact, he always thought the best time of year in Kansas was the spring. Winters were too cold; summers were too hot. He did his best to be away from Metropolis when the worst of the heat hit.

The city's large population and all that went with it, the cars, the subways, the sheer hot air from too many conversations, seemed to increase the heat exponentially.

Bender pushed the glass door open for Luthor, and he stepped through. It felt like he was entering a steam bath fully dressed. Everyone seemed to feel that way. The crowd passing along the sidewalk struggled to maintain business dress. Most of the men carried their suit coats over one arm and had their sleeves rolled up. None of the women appeared to be wearing nylons, their bare feet swelling in shoes made for cooler temperatures.

Luthor shook his head. Through the crowd, he could see the limo, parked in the loading zone. The engine was running to keep the interior cool. Luthor had instructed his driver, Jerome

Jenkins, to do that every summer. Jenkins, good man that he was, remembered it in this heat wave.

Luthor's bodyguard, Tony Kodale, had already left the bank, checking out the area as he always did, before signaling that everything was all right. Sometimes Bender took that job, but Luthor preferred to have Kodale do it.

Kodale seemed to have eyes in the back of his head—almost literally. Once Luthor had actually looked. After all, he'd seen stranger things.

As Luthor started across the sidewalk, Kodale pulled the limousine's passenger door open. Standard procedure, although Kodale should have waited a few more seconds. He was letting precious chill air escape.

People streamed by, none of them in their usual hurry. The heat was so thick, it felt like water, slowing down everything in its path. Even Luthor was walking slower than usual.

Bender moved slightly ahead of Luthor, opening a hole in the crowd. A tall man in a heavy overcoat hung out on the edges, a winter cap pulled low over his eyes.

Now that was a determined person—one who wasn't going to let the realities of the day interfere with the way he'd dressed when he got up that morning.

Luthor shook his head as he stepped off the curb. The man in the overcoat bumped past Kodale, not looking at anyone. Kodale glared at him in irritation and started to say something, but his words sounded garbled.

Then Kodale's eyes rolled up, his shoulders slumped, and he dropped to the sidewalk, landing with a resounding crack.

Bender hurried toward him, then stopped as if he'd hit a wall. Slowly Bender crumpled to the sidewalk. There had been no shots, no sign of attack, yet two of his guards were down and out.

At that moment, the guy in the overcoat moved to the front of the car. He yanked open the driver's door. Jenkins toppled sideways. Apparently, he'd been unconscious the entire time Luthor had been walking to the car.

Luthor, knowing he was in trouble, looked over his shoulder for a way out. But the crowd had him penned in.

A hand roughly pushed Luthor in the back, shoving him at the open limo door. "Inside, Mr. Luthor."

Luthor stepped sideways, just the way his security team had trained him to do. Most people went forward or back, never to the side. He pushed against the crowd, hearing a man grunt as Luthor hit him in the stomach.

The hand grabbed Luthor's shoulder, holding him back.

Luthor tried to step away again, turning as he did so. A fine mist of spray hit him squarely in the face, stinging his eyes. He choked on the stench of orange—not like the fruit, but like orange soda pop left too long in the sun.

The world spun, the light of day started to dim. He tried to fight back, but his hands wouldn't move. His knees were giving way. He was going to end up on the sidewalk beside Kodale.

How could his security have been breached so easily? He had precautions for this. Safety net after safety net.

How dare these people attack him?

He struggled to maintain his consciousness, but he felt it slipping away.

Rough hands shoved him forward. His feet hit Kodale's sprawled body, and Luthor tripped, falling face first into the open limo door.

His face bounced against the soft leather seat. He tried to sit up, to move away, but he couldn't. He couldn't do anything. The sickly sweet stench of the spray seemed stronger in here.

Too strong.

The smell was the last thing his brain registered before he passed out.

It took Chloe nearly a minute before she remembered that she held her camera in her hands.

Lana was standing at the edge of the pond, hands covering her mouth. She'd cried out when she first realized that the body floating in the water had been Danny Franklin, and since then she hadn't made a sound.

Chloe was wondering if Lana was even breathing.

Clark still had ahold of Danny Franklin's hand. He was dragging the body to the side of the pond, ripples forming around them like rings.

Clark looked so heroic and so sad all at the same time, his tall broad form bent over the body as if he could protect it. The sun was behind him, making him glow, and he looked more than human, as if the light around him gave him an extra dose of strength.

That was what Chloe always relied on Clark for. His calmness, his personal strength.

The stench of rotted flesh filled the air, followed by something even fouler, like a swamp gas. Bubbles rose around the body, and now it was Chloe's turn to cover her face.

The smell was coming from Danny's corpse.

She wanted to throw up, and instead swallowed hard. If she was going to be a real reporter some day, she would have to be able to handle dead bodies, and everything that went with them, including the smells. Still, her stomach turned, and that was when she picked up the camera.

It was either look through the lens or lose the bland cafeteria pizza she'd had for lunch.

She focused the camera on Clark and took shot after shot, trying to get the effect of the light, thinking about Clark and not the boy he was pulling ashore, the boy she'd spoken to not a week ago—teasing him about his crush on Lana Lang.

How come everyone had a crush on Lana, anyway? All she

was doing was standing there, her long hair trailing down her back, her body shivering as if she were suddenly cold. She wasn't *doing* anything. Clark and Chloe, they were doing something. But Lana was just standing there. And it was beginning to bug Chloe.

"Hey, Lana!" Chloe said, surprised her voice sounded as normal as it did. "You got your phone?"

Lana's hand went to her book bag, then she turned, and Chloe thought she saw gratitude in Lana's eyes.

"Yeah." Lana walked away from the edge of the pond, digging in her bag as she did. "I guess we should call someone, huh?"

"The police," Chloe said. "We sure don't need an ambulance."

Hiding behind her camera, her finger clicking the shutter open and closed, the lens focused on Clark as he eased Danny's body to shore. Chloe felt stronger than she actually was. But if she brought that camera down, she'd have to face what she was seeing.

She had lost a friend. Not as good a friend as he'd been to Lana, but a friend all the same.

Chloe swallowed, and took a few more shots, glad she had her digital and not the school's expensive thirty-five millimeter. The digital gave her two hundred pictures, and she was probably going to use them all.

Lana had moved behind her. "Yes, this is an emergency," she was saying.

Clark had reached the shore, and he tugged the body past the reeds growing at the water's edge. Chloe took two more shots.

"It's Danny Franklin," Lana said. "He's dead."

Chloe's hand shook. She brought the camera down. Danny was wearing jeans and a denim work shirt. Had he been wearing that the last time she saw him? He didn't have a lot of clothes—or at least a lot of variety in his clothes—but he didn't wear the same thing every day either.

"I'm pretty sure he drowned. We're on the farm and he was in the pond and Clark just pulled him out . . . Clark Kent . . . I'm Lana Lang. Look, this is serious . . ."

Chloe made herself take a deep breath and really look at the situation. The pond wasn't that deep. Chest high on Clark who, admittedly, was outrageously tall, but still. Guys like Danny

Franklin didn't drown in their family's pond, not in the place
they'd grown up and played in and skated on and swum in.
Guys like Danny were competent and composed and—

"Clark!" Chloe yelled almost before she realized she was
going to say anything. "Clark!"

Lana stopped talking. Clark looked up. His face was pale,
and he looked ill. Chloe couldn't remember the last time she'd
seen Clark look ill.

"Don't do anything else. Don't touch him anymore."

Clark let go as if he'd been waiting for someone to give him
permission. He backed away from the body. His clothes clung
to him, and bits of algae hung off his jeans.

"What's going on?" Clark's voice carried across the pond.
He sounded as unsettled as Chloe felt.

Lana was still looking at her, hand over the cell phone. A
voice, faint and indistinct, squawked from the receiver.

"It's okay," Chloe said to Lana. "Get them out here."

Lana nodded and went back to talking on the phone.

Chloe walked toward Clark, clutching her camera at her side.
As she walked close to the pond, she caught a whiff of the
scummy water, mixed with that gassy odor she had noticed
before, all of it overlaying the smell of decaying flesh.

Her stomach turned again.

Clark watched her. He held his right hand away from his
body, as if he didn't want to touch anything else with it. Danny
lay at his feet, immobile, his flesh so pale that it looked like it
was made of ice.

"This is a crime scene, Clark," she said when she reached
his side.

"You don't know that," Clark said. "He probably hit his head
and fell in the water. He—"

"It doesn't matter." She should have thought of this before.
She wasn't yet a professional reporter, and she wouldn't be until
she did everything right. "He's too young to have died of natural
causes. The coroner and the police are the ones who determine
if this was an accident or not. And we just messed with it."

Clark closed his eyes for a moment, then opened them,
nodding. "I screwed up."

"No," Chloe said. "It's not your fault."

"I didn't realize he was dead until I touched him." Clark grimaced slightly as he said that last.

Chloe looked down at Danny's body. She had noticed how different it looked, but she hadn't thought about how it would feel. Slimy? Cold?

Dead. Definitely dead.

"And then all I could think was that I had to get him out of there." Clark was watching her, as if she was the one who was going to yell at him.

"That's just human, Clark. Anyone would do that. But we'd better not do anything else."

Clark nodded.

Then Lana folded her phone over and stuffed it in her book bag. "They're coming," she said. "They want us to wait."

Of course they did. Lana, Clark, and Chloe were witnesses.

The smell was stronger here. Chloe wasn't sure how long she could hold out against it—how long she could continue to ignore the fact that she'd liked Danny, who was now lying dead at her feet.

Chloe looked toward the house. Silent. Empty. The barn doors closed. She hefted the camera in her hand.

"We've got a little time before the police arrive," she said. "Anyone want to come with me? I'm heading down to the house."

"Chloe," Clark said in that tone of his. It was not quite disapproving, and there was fondness in it, but he was trying to stop her.

"Clark, I am a reporter," she said. Or she would be when she had her reactions under control. "And no reporter would pass up the chance to investigate just a little bit more. Especially since I have my camera."

"What do you expect to find?" Lana asked.

"Nothing," Chloe said, but she knew that she was lying. She had a hunch the farmhouse held a lot of secrets. She only hoped she would have a chance to glimpse a few of them before the police ordered her off the property. "Nothing at all."

◆◆◆

Lex Luthor resisted the urge to slam down the phone. Instead, he put the receiver gently in its cradle, then he stood and shoved his hands in his pockets.

Good thing he was alone in his study. He felt like yelling at someone, anyone, for any reason he could think of. He pushed his leather chair back, then walked to the window and gazed out at the garden.

Anyone who saw him would think he was calm. Lex had become good at looking calm, especially when he was angry. And right now, he was furious.

For three days, his father had been refusing to talk with him, always putting him off whenever Lex managed to reach him.

I told you that you were in charge of the Smallville LuthorCorp plant, Lex, his father would say. *That means the good and the bad.*

But Lex wasn't calling about LuthorCorp—not exactly, anyway. He wasn't even calling to ask advice. He wanted to let his father know about the growing unrest in Smallville.

Even though Lex's father claimed Lex was in charge of the LuthorCorp plant, his father still made the final decisions. And the layoffs that his father had ordered three months before were causing Lex great headaches.

Lex wanted his father to come to Smallville to see the trouble the layoffs had caused.

Somehow, his father seemed to know that, and was dodging Lex at every turn. And this afternoon was the worst. This afternoon, Lex's father wasn't even answering his cell phone when Lex called.

Lex would have to find a number that wasn't in his father's caller I.D., and try again. Then his father would have to pick up.

Lex leaned his head against the window. The glass was hot against his forehead, and he pulled back. He had forgotten the heat wave outside. The air-conditioning inside the mansion kept everything at a constant sixty-eight degrees year-round, just the way he liked it.

But outside the plants seemed to be struggling. The tulips he'd had specially imported from Holland were wilting, their colors almost bleeding into the ground. Even the trees, which had just started to leaf in the last few days, seemed exhausted.

If he hadn't seen the weather on a local station at lunch, he would have thought some strange Smallville anomaly was happening again. But this unseasonably warm weather stretched from New York to Denver. Kansans were suffering just like three-quarters of the nation.

Small consolation. Just as it was a small consolation that his father rarely answered anyone's calls. Until this afternoon, he took his son's even if they were fighting, which they usually were.

Lex turned back to his desk and sighed. The phone sat in the middle of the blotter, taunting him. He should call his father's secretary back and force her to put him through. She wouldn't be able to give Lex the same excuse twice, and if she tried, Lex would throw it in her face.

His father wasn't incommunicado. If there was anything Lex Luthor knew about his father, it was that Lionel Luthor was never incommunicado. The people who needed to get through to him did.

Apparently, Lionel Luthor no longer considered his son one of those people.

Lex shook his head. He should have known it was coming. He and his father had never been on good terms.

Lex moved the phone off the blotter, away from the center of the desk. He would handle the situation in Smallville himself. He had planned to anyway. He had just wanted his father to see how bad it had gotten.

But his father never liked to face the dark side of his policies—not for any reason, not for anyone.

Lex had no idea why he had deluded himself into thinking he had more influence with his father than anyone else did. After all these years, and all the times his father had proved to Lex just how little he mattered, it was amazing how badly his father's snubs still hurt.

Clark's hand felt like it was covered in slime. His clothes clung wetly to him, and his shoes sloshed as he walked.

He was trying not to think about how Danny Franklin's hand had felt in his own, how the skin had slipped over the bone as Clark tugged the body toward the edge of the pond.

Still, when he, Lana, and Chloe reached the first barn, he had to stop at the pump and rinse off his hands. Neither Chloe nor Lana said anything to him as he rubbed cold water over his fingers. He would have expected Chloe to mention the whole crime scene thing again, but she didn't.

Instead, she gave him a sympathetic look before she turned away, as if she were glad it was him instead of her who had fished Danny Franklin's body out of that pond.

Lana, on the other hand, stared at Clark but didn't seem to see him. He had a hunch she was in shock, and he wasn't sure what to do about it.

He wasn't exactly feeling great himself. He'd liked Danny Franklin. They hadn't been close friends, but they'd known each other for years. Sometimes they banded together—two of the only guys in Smallville whose chores prevented them from going out for the football team, even though that wasn't precisely true for Clark.

He didn't go out because his parents felt he would forget, and use his abilities to unfair advantage. And the one time he had the opportunity to be on the team, that had happened.

"I think we should spread out," Chloe was saying to Lana. "See if we can find anything."

Clark shook his head ever so slightly. Chloe was as shocked as he and Lana had been, but after a second in which Clark thought Chloe was going to lose her lunch, she gathered herself and went into reporter mode.

It didn't mean she was coping any better than Lana was. In fact, there were times when Clark thought this method—the I-Must-Have-As-Much-Information-As-Possible-Right-Now method—was even more dangerous than being numb. Chloe had a history of opening the wrong door, getting into the wrong situation, finding the wrong thing at the wrong time.

"Spread out?" Lana repeated, but she didn't seem to be listening. She was still clutching her cell phone in her right hand and was looking behind her at the pond.

"I don't think that's a good idea, Chloe," Clark said, splashing cold water on his face. That felt good. Maybe he had gotten hotter than he realized. "I think we need to stick together."

"You don't think whoever killed Danny is still here, do you?" Chloe asked.

"Killed Danny?" Lana blinked. The phrase seemed to bring her out of her shock. "I thought he drowned."

"We don't know," Clark said. "He looks like he drowned, but Chloe reminded me earlier that his death was not a natural one, so the police will deal with this like a crime scene."

There was a slight furrow in Lana's forehead.

"That doesn't mean," Clark added hastily, "that Danny was murdered. Just that his death is unusual."

"To say the least." Chloe shifted from foot to foot. "You done bathing now, Clark? Can we look around? I don't think we have a lot of time left."

And, he thought, there was that edge in her voice, the one she got when she was feeling overwhelmed, but didn't want to admit it—even to herself.

"Let's go." Clark let go of the pump and deliberately walked past Chloe. He was going to lead this search, and if he saw something he didn't like, he would stop it immediately.

"I think we should check the house first," Lana said. "Just like we planned. Maybe they're out searching for Danny. Maybe they don't realize . . ."

Her voice trailed off and she looked down. Clark put a reassuring hand on her shoulder, squeezed, and let go quickly. His wet fingers left a moist handprint on her shirt.

He didn't say as he passed her—he didn't dare—that if Danny Franklin had been missing, and his parents had been worried enough to look for him, then the entire school would have known about it. All of Smallville would have.

Because Smallville had such a bizarre history of strange goings-on, the police were pretty vocal in the first days of a search for a missing person. And there had been no notices in the paper, no flyers posted, no announcements in home room or at school.

In fact, no one seemed too concerned about Danny's absence,

except Lana. She'd spoken up about it long before their assignment was due. But the only way she'd been able to get anyone to take her seriously—Clark included—had been to mention the lab work.

He sighed and took long steps to catch up to Chloe.

"Did he have bruises on his head?" she asked. "You know, the kind of thing that would have happened if he bumped his head and then fell into the water."

Danny's face had been chalk white, with blue lines through it. Even his eyelids had been blue.

And that was odd, now that Clark considered it. Danny's eyes were closed.

Clark had never seen a drowning victim before, but he had a hunch that none of them died with their eyes closed.

"I didn't look that closely, Chloe," Clark said as carefully as he could.

He crossed the yard to the sidewalk. Weeds grew between cracks in the concrete. Up close, the detail work he had so admired seemed like work from a previous season. Between the daffodils and tulips were dead twigs, leaves, and the brown hulks of last fall's plants.

No one had cleaned up the flower beds when the snow melted. He doubted anyone had mowed the lawn either, although it was too hard to tell this early in the year.

The front porch floor was covered with winter dirt, and more leaves, piled in a corner. If he had left the fall leaves like that, his father would go after him. Leaves made good composting, and should have been in the compost pile long before winter set in.

"I would have expected this place to be a lot neater," Chloe said.

Lana was staring at the leaves, too. "It used to be. It used to be perfect. It would drive me crazy. Nell likes a clean house, but Danny's mother used to make their house perfect—and with three kids on top of it."

Clark gave Lana a sideways look. He hadn't realized she'd been to Danny's house before. Lana didn't notice his gaze, but Chloe did. She rolled her eyes like she always did when she thought Clark was mooning over Lana.

"Well, with a wraparound porch like that," Chloe said, sounding businesslike, "we should be able to see inside. I just need to look through that picture window and maybe get a few shots."

"I don't think that's a good idea, Chloe," Clark said. "After all, you don't know what you'll find."

And neither did he. He should have planned for this. He stopped on the sidewalk and made himself scan the farmhouse for bodies. He concentrated, and his special vision activated.

His vision passed through the walls into the main rooms proper. He didn't see anyone—alive or dead.

"I'm not suggesting we go in, Clark." Chloe started up the stairs, almost stomping in her impatience. "I just have a feeling that we might find something else here."

Clark had that sense too, but unlike Chloe, the idea of finding something else didn't attract him. He hurried to the steps and accompanied her up.

Lana followed, wiping her finger against the rail as if its dirt surprised her as well.

Chloe walked over to the picture window and pressed her face against the glass. Clark came up beside her and looked.

He didn't need his special vision to know that Chloe's hunch had been right. The couch was overturned, an end table was smashed against the wall, and a throw rug was bunched in the middle of the room. Other furniture had been flung aside, as if it had been in the way of something—or someone.

Lana stopped beside him. Chloe already had her camera out and was taking pictures.

Clark was glad Chloe was respecting the crime scene. That meant that as much as she wanted to, she wouldn't go inside.

"Do you think I'd contaminate anything if I just walked into each room, taking pictures?" Chloe asked as if she could read Clark's mind.

"Yes," he said.

Chloe frowned at the house as if it were the problem. "Maybe I'll just wander around the outside—"

"No, Chloe," Clark said.

Lana hadn't moved from the window. "The house never looked like this. If Mrs. Franklin were here, she'd clean it up, no matter what happened."

"I think it's pretty clear that they're not here," Chloe said.

"Or inside," Lana said. It was obvious what she was thinking. She was thinking there were more bodies in the house.

Clark didn't know how to tell her that he knew there weren't. It would be false reassurance anyway.

He had no idea what had happened to the Franklin family, but judging from the evidence, he knew it couldn't have been good.

CHAPTER 4

Lionel Luthor's shoulders ached. Perhaps "ached" wasn't the correct word. Perhaps "tugged" was. He'd had this feeling in his shoulders before, when he'd hung by his arms from the bar in his private gym, holding his entire weight off the ground.

But his hands weren't holding anything. They were behind him, their backs resting against the silk of his suit. His wrists were crossed and sore.

And he was tired. Very tired.

Nauseous, too. A swimming sort of nausea, the kind induced by too much drink (something he hadn't indulged in for decades) combined with movement.

Movement. Like a car, turning a corner too fast. And then another corner, and another, bump along a poorly paved road, hitting potholes, making his face bounce against the leather car seat.

Face, bouncing. Drool on the side of his mouth. Mouth dry, as if he hadn't had water for days.

His feet were asleep, his knees bent. He was on his side—and he was tied up.

His eyelids flickered, but he didn't open his eyes. He remembered—just in time—the crowd, the heat, the bank. The way his security people had gone down. His limo driver—his favorite employee—toppling over like a statue in the hands of a careless art patron.

The air-conditioning was on high. He was shivering now, where before he had been too hot. Maybe it was the effect of the drug that had knocked him out.

The car turned again, left this time, judging by the way he slid on the seat, and the nausea rose. He moaned before he had even realized he made the sound—no way to block it now. He just had to accept that he had let that one slip, and be vigilant. Ever vigilant.

"Hey, boss."

Bad old movie word, "boss." It needed to be spoken with a Jersey accent—or a Joisey accent to be more accurate. But this voice was calm, with a touch of Kansas—the prairies, not Metropolis.

Luthor kept his eyes closed, careful not to squeeze them shut. Still, his eyelashes fluttered. What had been in that drug? He didn't have complete control over his body—at least, not like he was used to.

"I think he's coming out of it."

"Give him some more." This voice was different, deeper. Another Kansas accent, prairie, not city, and something about the way the words flowed made Luthor think that "Boss" had less of an education than the first speaker, not more.

"More? Won't that hurt him?"

A third voice, also male. Same accent.

He didn't remember seeing a third player, but it made sense. It would have taken a lot of people to bring down his security team.

"What do you care?" Boss again.

"We don't want to hurt him," Third Voice said.

"We don't want to *kill* him," Boss said. "I don't care if he gets hurt along the way."

Luthor tried to remain motionless so that they'd continue to think he was out. He couldn't test the strength of his bonds because he wasn't sure how they were watching him. The limo had security cameras everywhere.

He had had them installed so that he could watch the driver or, if he chose to, he could sit in the front seat and see whatever happened in the back. If they were watching him from the front, they could see his every movement.

"A second dose won't kill him," Boss said. "Besides, we gave him less than his employees. They didn't die. Give him another dose, and he'll be no worse off than they are."

"How do we know they didn't die?" Third Voice asked. "We left them behind."

Luthor liked that piece of information. Their bodies alongside the road made the circumstances of his disappearance fairly obvious.

And when the most powerful man in Metropolis had been kidnapped, the police would scramble into action quickly. They'd have to call in the FBI, who always played well with Luthor's security team.

He'd get out of this, if he could keep himself alive.

"If we'd wanted to kill them, we would have killed them," Boss said. "Now shut up."

Maybe he could bargain with these men. They clearly wanted something from one of his companies—or maybe from him. If all they needed was money, he could provide that, and use it to catch them later. It would take very little, and he could be persuasive when he needed to be.

He had to start talking before they dosed him again.

He opened his eyes in time to see a small plant mister, held in a gloved hand, approach his nose. He looked up, saw an alien with a hose instead of a mouth, clear square eyes, a green face.

The gloved fingers squeezed the mister's trigger before Luthor could protest. He had his mouth half-open as the spray hit his face. Some of it landed on his tongue, filling his mouth with the rancid taste of spoiled orange soda pop.

As his consciousness started to drift again, he realized he wasn't looking at an alien at all. He was looking at a man wearing a military-issue gas mask. A man who was afraid the spray would get on him.

His dizziness increased, and he fought, just like he had the first time, even though he knew he'd lose.

Mist. They'd sprayed him in the crowd. And his security team. Had the kidnappers been wearing masks then? Probably. They'd kept their heads down. Which meant that not only Luthor's people had been knocked out. Others . . .

The thought trailed out of his head. He tumbled into blackness so deep he could no longer feel anything.

Not even himself.

The ambulance arrived first, its lights and sirens off. The drivers barreled down the gravel driveway as if it were an interstate. A sheriff's car followed right behind, its red-and-blue lights flashing.

Apparently, the locked gate at the end of the driveway hadn't bothered any of the authorities. Had they gone around it? Or had they figured out a way to open it?

Clark didn't know. He stepped away from the road, pulling Lana and Chloe back with him. Lana's face still didn't have enough color. Chloe had run out of room on her digital camera, and had been mumbling something about downloading to her laptop when the ambulance finally showed up.

"Why do they bring in an ambulance when someone's dead?" Lana asked.

"I don't know," Clark said. "They just do."

"Because they never know what they're going to find," Chloe said as if she knew. Maybe she did. "Sometimes people who seem dead aren't."

Lana looked over her shoulder at Danny's body. Clark couldn't help himself; he looked, too.

Danny was still sprawled facedown in the weeds, right where Clark had left him.

One of the paramedics got out of the ambulance. "Where?" he said to Clark, Chloe, and Lana.

"Over there." Clark nodded toward Danny's body.

The paramedics hurried down the slight incline toward the pond. When they reached Danny, they crouched.

Lana looked away.

"You kids the ones who called?" A Lowell County deputy that Clark did not recognize walked down the driveway toward them. Another deputy, also in plain clothes, joined the paramedics.

In the distance, sirens wailed. They were on the main highway and getting closer.

"I called," Lana said. She sounded stronger than Clark had expected her to.

"So you three found him?" The deputy looked suspicious.

"Clark did," Lana said. Apparently she hadn't heard the same suspicion in his tone that Clark had.

"You?" the deputy asked Clark.

Clark nodded.

"What made you go into the water? Skinny-dipping?"

Chloe's face flamed. "Of course not." She answered even though the question was meant for Clark. "We were down here looking for Danny."

"And you found him." The deputy's eyebrows went up, as if he thought the whole thing a miracle. "How amazing is that?"

Lana frowned. "It's not amazing at all. He was floating—"

"I saw him first," Chloe said over her. "Clark just pulled him out."

"It was—"

"Roberts!" The other deputy waved his arm from below. "Come see this."

"You kids stay right here," the deputy, who was apparently named Roberts, said. Then he trudged toward the side of the pond.

"As if we're going anywhere," Lana said under her breath. She had snapped out of shock and had clearly moved into annoyed. Not that Clark could blame her. That cop had an attitude, and he obviously didn't trust them.

The other sirens had grown a lot closer.

Chloe was watching the paramedics and the deputies. Her arms were folded over her camera strap. "They don't even seem to care if they're trampling the evidence."

"There's no way he could be alive, is there, Clark?" Lana asked softly.

Clark shook his head. No living person was ever that cold and rubbery feeling. Not to mention the way the skin had slid under his hand.

Clark shuddered, in spite of himself.

"Then what do you think they're doing?" Lana asked.

Chloe frowned. She took a step forward and squinted. "I think they might have found something else."

"What?" Lana asked.

But Clark knew. He had felt something brush against his leg as he stepped into the shallow water. Something cold and slimy, that touched him ever so lightly. Like fingers, tapping against his ankle.

He hadn't thought to look for another body. He had been so surprised to find Danny's. Clark had gotten Danny to shore, and then had planned to turn around, to look in the water for the cause of that frightening little touch, but Chloe had stopped him.

Chloe with her talk of crime scenes and contamination.

And murder.

Clark glanced at the house. Lana had said that Mrs. Franklin wouldn't leave it like that.

The car was missing, but Danny was here.

The barn door was closed, and the gate was locked.

Someone—or several someones—didn't want anyone to come to the Franklin farm. They had made it as uninviting as possible.

"What is it, Clark?" Chloe asked.

The sirens were very close now, so close they hurt his ears. He had sensitive hearing, too, always had, but it seemed even more sensitive at the moment. Chloe and Lana didn't seem to notice how loud the sirens had become.

He looked away from the house, back at the pond.

The paramedics were pointing at the water's edge.

Two more police cars jolted down the driveway, pulling to a stop in a haze of dust. The sirens shut off, but the lights continued to turn.

"Clark?" Chloe asked again.

"Put your camera away, Chloe," Clark said. He had to distract her, at least for a moment, so that he could check out his hunch.

"It's useless, Clark. I'm not getting rid of the pictures I have, and I'm out of memory. If I—"

"Put it away, Chloe," he said again, "or the police might confiscate it for evidence."

"They wouldn't. I'm a member of the press." Chloe said.

"I don't think the *Torch* commands as much respect as the *Daily Planet*," Lana said. "At best, you'd have a fight on your hands."

"I hate it when you're right," Chloe said, and bent over to pick up her book bag.

Clark focused on the water. He used his X-ray vision, boring through the murk. A lot of sand and silt, still stirred up from his trip through the filthy water. Sunlight filtered through, though, changing one area from black-brown to a light tan.

A hand bobbed gently against the muddy bottom.

Clark scanned the pond. The muddy water was hard to see through, but he could see enough.

The body near the edge was long and thin, hair floating upward, concealing the face. But the hand was a giveaway. The fake rhinestone-studded fingernails and rings on every finger.

He remembered how those fingernails had felt, scraping his scalp, when those fingers ruffled his hair just a week ago, the scent of bubble gum and vanilla perfume overwhelming him.

Wow, Danny, you didn't tell me how Clark had turned out, Betty Franklin had said. Betty was—had been—Danny's flirtatious older sister. Her identical twin sister, Bonnie, had given Clark a sympathetic smile that day, almost as if she had been apologizing for Betty.

Bonnie had never been as flamboyant as her twin, but the two of them were rarely apart.

Only they were now. Apart forever. Because Bonnie wasn't in that pond. No one else was. Just Betty.

"What's the matter, Clark?" Lana asked.

He swallowed, not sure how to answer.

Then the paramedics answered for him. "We got another one!"

And every person in the area burst into action.

The cops ran down the side of the hill, trampling weeds, and leaving footprints in the mud. A group of men had gathered along the water's edge, two of them—the paramedics?—wading in, and grabbing at something.

Chloe hurried down the driveway, stepping off the gravel in the same place the cops had. She had trampled innocently before. If she was going to contaminate a crime scene this time, she was going to do it the way the cops had.

Her fingers itched for her camera, but she knew better than to haul it out. Clark's warning had been a good one; the cops would confiscate her camera, and anything else she brought out, maybe even her notebook.

She would have to memorize everything. And she could do it. She'd done it before. What it took was simple: she had to write up her notes the moment she got back to the *Torch*'s office.

When she did that, she'd have a story good enough to get picked up by the local paper, maybe even good enough to sell to the *Planet*.

Clark was calling after her. He probably didn't want her down here. He was so protective, and so sweet, even if he didn't seem to share the crush she had for him.

But she wasn't going to listen to him. She had to be able to see what was going on.

The men thrashed in the water, creating waves. There was no smell this time, beyond that of stagnant water and algae. There was also no conversation. Everyone seemed to be working in complete silence, as if this were a routine that they'd all gone through before.

The paramedics were reaching into the water, pulling at something. An arm flopped out. Chloe could only see the elbow and the biceps, elegant and thin, unnaturally white. She finally understood what all those Victorian novels she read in English meant when they used the word "alabaster" to describe skin.

Although she suspected they didn't mean that the person with alabaster skin was dead.

Chloe felt light-headed, but she made herself take a deep breath. Professional reporter. Professional. Calm in a crisis. Noting the details.

No one had noticed her standing there yet, but it would only be a matter of time.

Two of the cops got behind the body and lifted it by the ankles. Water drained off the blue jeans and the sweater that covered the torso.

Long hair—dark, Chloe couldn't tell what color exactly— plastered against the face, hiding it. The body was female; that much was clear, but Chloe couldn't tell whose it was.

Until the arm flopped again, the hand trailing toward the water as if reaching for something in the murky depths. Rings on every finger, including a large fake turquoise one on the thumb.

Only one girl in school wore a turquoise ring on her thumb, and she was a senior. Flirtatious, difficult, extremely pretty. Danny Franklin used to shake his head as his sister Betty went by, saying she'd get them all in trouble.

Chloe used to think that was just an expression. Now she wondered if it meant something else.

"I don't think you should get any closer."

It was Clark, standing just behind her. Chloe hadn't even heard him come up, and she always noticed what Clark was doing. Always.

"I wasn't planning to go closer," she said, keeping her voice down. She wanted to be as unobtrusive as possible for as long as possible. "It's Betty Franklin, you know."

"I know," Clark said quietly.

"Oh . . ." Apparently Lana had joined them too. Chloe hadn't heard her either.

Chloe gave her a sideways look. Lana had a hand over her mouth. "Were you friends with Betty, too?"

Lana shook her head. "She was a senior, and way too popular to have time for someone like me."

Someone like Lana Lang, the most popular girl in their class?

Get real. Chloe normally would have said that, but this wasn't normal at all.

The men carried the body out of the pond. The water sloshed and moved, looking like a live thing.

Enough strange things happened in Smallville that the thought wasn't as odd as it seemed. Chloe resisted the urge to take a step back. She wasn't close enough to the water to have it touch her.

"Clark, you don't think that the water . . . ?" Chloe let her voice trail off, feeling like what she had been about to ask wasn't appropriate. Somehow, having a discussion better fit for the *Weekly World News* while the police took bodies of people she knew out of a pond didn't seem right.

But Clark was looking at her, those blue eyes intense. "The water what?"

Chloe shrugged, pretending a nonchalance she didn't feel. "Nothing."

"Do you think this is something for your wall of weird?" Lana asked. There was sadness in her voice, which surprised Chloe. Somehow she had expected anger. Lana hated the fact that Chloe put details of all the strange things that happened around Smallville on a wall in the *Torch* office. Since Lana's parents had been killed by the meteor storm that Chloe figured started all the weirdness, Lana found the wall insulting. After all, she was a centerpiece on it, her three-year-old face on a magazine cover the picture of grief.

"It just seems so surreal," Chloe said, deciding not to answer the question.

"It's only going to get worse," Clark said.

"What do you mean?" Lana asked the question so softly that Chloe barely heard her.

Clark got that worried weight-of-the-world look on his face. "Betty never went anywhere without Bonnie. And you're the one who mentioned that Danny's mom wouldn't have left the house like that."

"I did, didn't I?" Lana's mouth thinned.

Chloe felt a fluttering in her stomach. Nerves. It had to be nerves.

The paramedics set Betty down beside Danny.

"And no one leaves a farm like this, not in the spring, not a farmer who cares as much as Danny's dad." Clark was watching the cops, too. They were combing the pond as best they could without divers.

But Clark had already checked the pond. He knew that no more bodies rested in it.

"Do you think they're all dead?" Chloe asked.

Clark's gaze met hers. She was startled by the intensity in his eyes. "What do you think?" he asked.

"I think one dead teenager in a pond is probably a tragic accident. Two is probably something else, something deliberate." Chloe hadn't really realized she'd been having those thoughts until Clark dragged them out of her.

"That's my sense of it, too," Clark said.

"I can't believe the whole family is dead." Lana's voice rose.

Chloe shushed her, but the damage was done. The cop, the one who had been so unfriendly, waded out of the water and gestured at them.

"You kids," he said. "Back away from here. There's no more to see."

Clark put his hand on Chloe's shoulder just as she had been about to argue. "Let's go," he said quietly.

Another cop walked toward them. Chloe didn't move, even though Clark was trying to get her to.

"We have every right to be here," Chloe said. "We're—"

"The ones who found the first body, I know," the deputy said. He was younger than the other one, and familiar-looking. Chloe had seen him around town a lot since she'd taken over the *Torch*. He was one of the younger officers, and one of the nicer ones. "We'll need some statements from each of you, so you'll have to hang around, but Roberts is right. You don't need to see any more of this."

"Do you think there are more bodies?" Chloe asked.

The cop gave her a measuring look. Then recognition filled his gaze. "You're the girl who runs the *Torch*, right?"

"I'm the *person* in charge," Chloe said, trying not to bristle at the word "girl."

"Well, I can't give you quotes. Obviously, this is an investigation now."

"But you think you're going to find something else, don't you?" Lana asked. She had a way of making the question sound innocent, where Chloe always made questions sound like an interrogation. Chloe wished she could learn that trick from Lana.

"Let's just say there's a possibility," the cop said. He held out his arms, as if he were trying to physically protect the crime scene. "I'm going to walk you guys to the gate. Someone'll be there shortly to take your statements."

"We can just wait up by the house," Chloe said.

The cop shook his head. "There's already been enough activity around this spot. Let us do our job. When we're done, you can do yours."

Chloe sighed, but she knew he was right. And the time he was going to give her at the gate would give her a chance to make some notes about everything she saw.

"I like the Franklins," Lana said as the three of them walked up the driveway to the gate. "Why did something like this have to happen to them?"

Why indeed? Chloe didn't answer and neither did Clark. There was nothing either of them could say.

Smallville was cursed. Chloe knew that better than anyone else in town. But knowing that didn't make living through days like this any easier.

◆◆◆

Lex got the news through his e-mail. He had his e-mail program set up to alert him whenever there was breaking news that might affect the stocks he was watching.

The e-mail program pinged just as Lex was about to leave the study to go to his fencing lesson. He had planned to be particularly aggressive that afternoon, to work off some of the anger his father had provoked.

Lex almost didn't go back and check the alert. But he had done that in the past and had missed some great buy opportunities on stocks that were going through an "adjustment."

He walked back to the desk. The alert icon was flashing in the top right of his screen. He tapped the mouse, opening the e-mail.

LUTHORCORP STOCK PLUMMETS

His breath caught. He'd checked the stock thirty minutes ago. It was fine.

He made himself concentrate on the article.

```
. . . LuthorCorp stock suddenly finds itself
subject to heavy trading as analysts try to
digest this afternoon's late-breaking news
involving LuthorCorp's founder Lionel Luthor.
Luthor's security guards and driver were found
unconscious outside City Bank, along with
bystanders, all of whom collapsed on the
street.

Initially, authorities believed the mass
fainting had been due to some kind of reaction
to the terrible heat, but within the last
fifteen minutes, it has become clear that the
attack on Luthor's people was deliberate.
   Lionel Luthor, last seen outside the bank,
is missing, and so is one of the company's
limousines, a black stretch model with the
vanity plate LUTHOR 1 . . .
```

Lex wasn't breathing. He made himself exhale and then inhale, his breath suddenly rapid. No one had called him. The entire staff of LuthorCorp—hell, probably the entire population of Kansas—knew that his father had been kidnapped, and no one bothered to let him know.

Lex's fists clenched. He stood, then froze.

Was this a ploy? His father wouldn't want the stock to plummet like that, but the Luthors—both Lionel and Lex— had enemies who would. Not to mention LuthorCorp itself. People hated its success, and always tried to destroy it from the outside.

Lex whirled, grabbed the phone off its cradle and dialed his father's cell.

It rang, and finally, the voice mail picked up. Just like before. Lex's stomach tightened.

The secondary line rang, and Lex grabbed it. "What?"

"Mr. Luthor?"

Lex didn't recognize the voice, but that didn't mean anything. His father often went through assistants so fast that Lex couldn't keep up.

"This is Lex Luthor."

"I'm John Harrison. I'm one of the deputy security chiefs for your father's company."

A deputy chief low enough on the pay scale that he got the job of calling Luthor's recalcitrant son to give him the bad news. A few years ago, Lex might even have made that comment.

He had learned control since then. He wasn't going to let on that he knew anything. Not yet, anyway.

"Yes?" he said, keeping his voice flat, disinterested.

"Um, have you heard the news, Mr. Luthor?"

"I don't know, Mr. Harrison. What news should I have heard?"

"Um, about your father."

"My father's always in the news, Mr. Harrison. I really don't pay a lot of attention. Unless there's something going on that I haven't been informed about?" Lex added just enough of an inflection on that last so that a smart person might realize that Lex knew more than he was letting on.

"Your father, sir." Harrison's voice was shaking. "We have reason to believe he was kidnapped."

So it was true. Lex gripped the receiver so tightly that his hand hurt. "Reason to believe?"

"Yes, sir. We haven't had any confirmation yet, but—"

"What sort of confirmation do you need?" Lex asked. "Either he was kidnapped or he wasn't."

"What I mean is that no one has called with a ransom demand yet."

"So you don't know if he's been kidnapped or murdered." Lex's fingernails bit into the receiver. He could feel the hard plastic dig into the soft skin of his fingertips.

"Well, sir, I wouldn't put it that way, sir. I mean, the body-guards are all right—"

"Really?" Lex let some of the anger he was feeling out. "Then they weren't doing their job, were they? They were supposed to protect my father, with their lives if need be."

"Yes, sir. But—"

"But?" Lex stood. "What else can you give me? Hmmm? My stupid e-mail stock updates gave me more than you have. My father was taken off a busy Metropolis street in broad daylight. Several guards and bystanders are down. My father was taken in his own car. What have you people done since you got the news? You certainly hadn't contacted me. I assume that was because you were too busy."

"We were trying to confirm—"

"Trying to confirm that something happened? While my father could be dying? Don't you know the first few hours are crucial? Get to it, man. Make sure the Metropolis police—ah, hell. I'll do it myself."

Lex slammed the receiver down so hard, the phone cradle shattered. He didn't care what he ruined. He was too angry. These security people were utter failures. They were just sheep waiting for someone to tell them what to do. Without a strong leader, they had no idea how to proceed.

Idiots. They were letting his father die.

Lex froze then. His father, dead. How often had he wished for that? Almost every day at the first boarding school. A little less as time went on.

And sometimes, Lex had no idea what he would do without his father, without that constant struggle for acceptance, without someone strong to push against.

His father kidnapped. Maybe dead.

Lionel Luthor, gone.

It wasn't possible. His father was indestructible. Or so it usually seemed to Lex. Even though that wasn't true. His father was just as human as the rest of them.

Just as vulnerable.

He could die, just like everyone else.

Unless someone competent did something. Unless Lex stepped in.

He reached over the desk, punched the computer, turning

off the screensaver, and then shut the computer down. He grabbed his cell phone and the keys to his Porsche.

By the time he was across the room, he was on the phone with LuthorCorp's private jet service. He was clear about what he needed: when he reached Smallville's tiny airport, he wanted a corporate jet fueled up and ready to take off.

He wanted to be in Metropolis within the hour. Because, thanks to imbeciles like Harrison, there wasn't time to waste.

"What an awful tragedy." Clark's mother put both of her hands on his shoulders, and leaned against him, pressing her cheek against the top of his head. "I can't imagine what it would be like to lose one child, let alone two."

The kitchen table was piled with food. His father had hauled the grill out of the garage, a spring ritual that they hadn't gotten to do earlier this year. The chicken smelled terrific, and Clark's mom had finished off the meal with baked beans, potato salad, and corn bread she had made the day before.

Usually a spread like this would have cheered Clark up. But the day's events disturbed him. He kept feeling like he had missed something. If he had only known something was wrong sooner, he might have been able to save them.

Of course, he didn't say anything like that to his parents. They'd had this conversation many times. His parents would tell him he wasn't responsible for other people's actions and that sometimes, no matter how many abilities he had, he wouldn't be able to stop bad things from happening.

Clark knew deep down that his parents were right, but that didn't change how he felt. Sometimes he wondered what all his miraculous powers were for if he couldn't help people he cared about.

His father took a barbecued chicken leg off the platter in the center of the table. He glanced at Clark—a warning look of some kind that Clark didn't entirely understand. Something about his mother and the way she worried, but his dad always worried about that.

"We don't know what happened up there, Martha," his dad said. "The police aren't saying."

"Well, we know what Clark told us." His mom squeezed Clark's shoulders, then moved away from him, grabbing a plate of day-old corn bread off the kitchen counter. "At least two of the Franklin children are gone. Who knows what's happened to everyone else?"

"The farm looked pretty deserted." Clark grabbed the stoneware pot filled with baked beans. An hour ago, he would have thought he couldn't have eaten anything. But his stomach was rumbling just like it usually did.

If only he didn't think about Danny and Betty Franklin.

"But the fields were tilled?" his dad asked for the second time.

"Tilled but no fertilizer. It was like everything stopped last week," Clark said.

"If a body'd been in the water more than a week, then—"

"Enough," his mom said as she sat down. She put the corn bread on the table near the potato salad. "We're having dinner."

Usually Clark hated it when she limited dinnertime talk, but he was grateful tonight. He didn't want to think about bodies any more than he had to.

"All I was saying, Martha, is that it sounds like the work stopped before the tragedy. Tragedies." His dad took the baked beans from Clark's hand. "This is the wrong time of year to stop work on a farm, no matter what's going on."

Clark's mom used tongs to take a thigh off the platter. "What do you think happened?"

"I don't know," his dad said. "If the house was as messed up as Clark said, then maybe some stranger came in and tried to rob them."

"Killing Betty and Danny?" his mom asked. "What about the rest of the family?"

"We were trying to figure that out." Clark took a chicken breast and a piece of corn bread. He couldn't quite face the potato salad. The eggs made him uncomfortable in a way he didn't want to examine. "I used my special vision to look in the house and I didn't see anyone. Before we left, I checked the two barns, too. There was nothing."

"Was there anything strange about the water, Clark?" his mother asked.

"Not that I could see." Clark took a bite of chicken. It was good. He had forgotten how much he liked the first grilled meal of the season.

"No nearby meteor rocks?"

"No," Clark said. "And I was close enough to notice."

"We're awful proud of you, son," his dad said. "The way you went right into that water."

"I'd feel better if I could have found Danny before he drowned," Clark said.

"I thought the police weren't sure how he died." His mom stopped buttering her corn bread. She studied him, holding the butter knife upward as if it were a weapon.

"They aren't," Clark said. "I guess I'm just hoping it's something innocent. You know. Some kind of accident."

"I think we can guarantee that it's not something innocent," his dad said. "Two people don't just die like that, not around here, and not in ponds that shallow, especially when there aren't roads nearby."

"You don't think they were drunk and fell in?" Clark's mom asked.

"Danny didn't drink," Clark said. "He was a good guy."

"Everyone makes mistakes sometimes, Clark," his mom said.

"And we don't always know people as well as we think we do." His dad finished the chicken leg and reached for another.

"I know, Dad," Clark said. "But drinking's not something kids hide, at least from other kids. Danny didn't do that. I don't know about Betty. She ran with a different crowd. But Danny, he was a lot more interested in grades and school and stuff than hanging out with the drinkers on Friday night."

"I don't think he would have had time for that anyway," Clark's mom said. "A lot of the farming chores fell to him when his dad went to work. And Danny didn't have Clark's abilities."

"I know." Clark's father sighed. "The problem is, Martha, crimes are usually pretty logical things. Two dead kids and a trashed-up house doesn't bode well for the missing family members."

"The car's missing, too," Clark said.

"Yeah, and anyone could have taken it after killing the Franklins and messing up the house. I'm sure the police are looking into that angle."

Clark's mom put her napkin alongside her plate. "I would

think it would be difficult to murder an entire family, Jonathan, particularly since all five of them were full-grown."

"You're thinking of only one killer," Clark's dad said.

"A gang of killers?" Clark asked. "Isn't that a bit farfetched for Smallville?"

"This place isn't as innocent or safe as we'd like it to be, Clark," his dad said. "The whole country has changed in that way."

"Still," his mom said, "you'd think someone would have escaped, and gotten help."

Clark hadn't even thought of that. He had done his best that afternoon, but he had been as shaky as Lana and Chloe. It was hard to look into the face of a dead friend.

"There's a lot of woods around there," his mom was saying. "Someone who knew the area could hide out for days."

"Without getting help?" his dad asked. "I'd think by now we would have known."

"The weather hasn't been that good until today, Jonathan. And if the person was injured, there might be a possibility that they're still out there."

"Maybe I should look," Clark said. "I should have done it when we were there before. Chloe wanted to, but I didn't think it was safe."

"You had the right instincts, Clark," his dad said. "Besides, I'm pretty sure the authorities have already thought of this. They've probably searched the woods."

"But they don't have the advantage I do," Clark said. "I can see things no one else can."

"I don't think that would be a good idea, Clark." His dad pushed his plate back. "Let the authorities handle this one."

Clark's mom frowned. "You're not saying everything you're thinking, Jonathan."

His dad pushed his plate away. "I don't like what I'm thinking."

Clark took a sip of milk. It was cold and fresh. It tasted good. "What do you mean, Dad?"

His dad shook his head.

"You brought it up," Clark's mom said. "You may as well finish. We'll be wondering otherwise."

"Jed Franklin's been under a lot of pressure, that's all. And sometimes people under a lot of pressure do strange things." Clark's dad pushed his chair away from the table. He picked up his plate and carried it to the sink.

"You don't think—?"

"I'm sure I'm not the only one considering it, Martha," his dad said. "You mentioned yourself how difficult you thought it would be to kill an entire family."

Clark's mom shook her head. "I never thought Jed Franklin could hurt anyone. He seemed like such a gentle man."

"Push a man to the edge, and he might just fall off," Clark's dad said. "Jed Franklin has been on that edge for years. The last time I saw him, he was saying some mighty nasty things about LuthorCorp, things I never expected to come from Jed Franklin's mouth."

"It's a long way from hating LuthorCorp to killing your family," Clark's mom said.

"Besides, you'd have to be crazy to do that," Clark added.

They all stared at each other for a moment. His dad's silence was eloquent. Clark shook his head, just a little. His dad had a good sense of people. If he felt Jed Franklin could snap, then maybe he could.

Clark's dad grabbed the coffee pot, poured himself a cup, and came back to the table.

"Let's just hope I'm wrong," he said.

His neck hurt. His chin rested on his chest, and his lips were so chapped that they stung. His mouth was open and dry. More than thirst. Whatever they had sprayed on him, whatever they had used to knock him out, had left a terrible cottony flavor on his tongue.

Lionel Luthor kept his eyes closed and forced himself to take stock. He'd lost his advantage the last time because his kidnappers realized that he was awake.

He wouldn't make that mistake again.

Obviously, he'd been out for some time. His shoulders still

ached, only this time in a different place. He was sitting up on a hard chair. He wasn't dizzy, and he had no sense of movement. Apparently, they had arrived at their destination.

He wondered where it was. By keeping him unconscious, they'd ruined his sense of time. He had no idea if he was close to Metropolis or not, if they'd flown him somewhere, if they'd merely driven him in circles.

He wouldn't be able to help anyone find him—provided he got free.

They didn't have his mouth bound. That was a bad sign. It meant he could yell all he wanted to, and his kidnappers thought no one would hear him.

He couldn't think of any place in Metropolis like that, a place where a person would be absolutely certain no one could hear. Even the best soundproofing let an occasional loud noise out.

If he were a betting man—and he was not; he believed in making fortunes, not squandering them—he would wager he was in the country somewhere, somewhere with a lot of wide-open space around him, no neighbors and no busy roads.

Kansas had a lot of places like that. Come to think of it, so did much of America.

He was back where he started. He could be anywhere.

He suppressed a sigh and went back to his inventory. His hands were tied behind him, the bonds so tight that they cut into his skin. His feet were separated, his knees open, and his ankles were tied to something—probably the legs of the chair he was sitting on.

The room smelled of dust and mold, and carried the remaining heat of the wretched April afternoon. Luthor caught no food odors, no pet scents, no garbage smells.

The place had been abandoned, or was little used. Maybe a garage or a storage building, a hunting cabin, something far away from the road.

Somewhere nearby a man was snoring. Deep rumbling snores, punctuated by grunts and an occasional snort. The sound of someone in a sound sleep. Luthor didn't hear footsteps or a television. He couldn't hear ambient road noise or any other sound from outside.

Just the snoring.

Could his captors be that careless? Could they have brought him here—wherever here was—and left him with a sleeping guard?

Or were they testing him, trying to see if he was as ingenious as everyone said he was?

Ultimately, it didn't matter. In the end, these guys would kill him. That's what kidnappers did. Even if they weren't planning to initially, they would come to the realization that Luthor knew too much about them, that he no longer had any value to them.

If the ransom was paid, they'd return his corpse.

If it wasn't—and those were the instructions he always gave his subordinates, not to waste wealth on sentimentality—then his kidnappers would get impatient and kill him.

Escape. Survival. They were both up to him.

He opened his eyes enough to peer through his eyelashes. A small light burned on a teetering end table. On a ratty couch, a man sprawled, his arm over his eyes. The snorer, wearing ragged blue jeans and a flannel shirt that was too heavy for the day's weather. His boots, covered in mud, rested on the couch's arm.

Luthor couldn't tell if he'd seen the man before or not. The man was a type—thin face, a few days' growth of beard, scraggly hair in need of a cut. All the man needed was a pickup truck and a mangy dog, and he'd fit Luthor's definition of "redneck" perfectly.

The only thing missing was the empty beer cans on the scuffed wooden floor.

Luthor held his breath, wishing the snoring would stop. He couldn't hear anyone else breathe or even move, but he didn't trust his ears. The snorer was a symphony of noise—sound after sound, often without a pause.

Still, Luthor hadn't seen anyone else. The light from the single lamp was dim. He could risk opening his eyes all the way, if he didn't move his head.

He eased his eyes open, and found himself staring at the scuffed wooden floor. Mud caked it. Not all of the mud went to the shoes of the snorer. Some of it trailed around Luthor.

More of it was gathered around the door, as if people had tracked it in and out.

The mud was still black, too. Not dried yet. He didn't like the looks of that. It meant he was as far out in the country as he thought. A lot of roads off the main highway were either dirt or gravel, and most driveways definitely were. People who lived this poorly usually didn't put concrete sidewalks in either.

He definitely wasn't in Metropolis anymore.

The cabin was small, with a low ceiling and cracked windows caked with filth. The door was improperly hung. He could see light through the frame—a thin electric light, probably some kind of porch light.

So, the snorer was waiting for someone.

Or the cabin was so deep in the country that a single outdoor light wouldn't attract any attention.

Luthor raised his head slowly. The back of his neck cramped and he winced, biting his lower lip so that he didn't cry out in pain. The snorer snorted, sighed, and rolled over, his face colliding with the back of the couch.

He didn't seem to notice.

Luthor looked around. One main room, poorly furnished. A handmade table and chairs stood near the open kitchen. To call the area a kitchen, though, was to give it more dignity than it had. There was a sink, a refrigerator older than Luthor himself, and a small stove, with a coffeepot on top. It had been decades since Luthor had seen a coffeepot on a stove top. He almost felt as if he had gone back in time.

A thin pink throw rug covered the area in front of the sink. And filthy, threadbare towels hung from a rack hanging on the wall beside the refrigerator.

The sink was spotless, though, and so was the stove. No dishes sat out, and no crumbs covered the meager counter. Either no one had used this place in a long time or someone was neat.

Which didn't explain the mud.

Luthor glanced over his shoulder. An open door led to a small bathroom. Another door opened into what appeared to be a bedroom. He thought he saw the edge of a bed in there, but he couldn't be certain.

An open closet, with a curtain hanging over a bar in place of a door, stood across from the kitchen. There were no other doors in the room. Only the cracked windows and the main entrance.

To get out, Luthor would either have to walk past the snorer or break a window.

Provided, of course, that he could get himself untied.

He wiggled his swollen fingers, feeling the pins and needles creep up his hands. Even though he could touch whatever bound him, he couldn't tell what it was. He didn't have enough feeling in his fingertips.

He looked down at his feet. They were bound with a thick rope. He assumed that his hands were bound the same way.

The thick rope was to his advantage. It wouldn't tie as tightly as a small rope, and he might be able to wriggle free.

The snorer gulped, snorted, then rolled over again. Obviously, his dreams weren't pleasant. Luthor watched, waiting for the man to wake up. When the man didn't, Luthor pulled his hands as far apart as they would go.

The rope dug deeper into his skin, but he thought he felt a bit of give. Just enough, maybe, that if he worked it, he might be able to free himself.

He had no idea how much time that would take.

He had no idea how much time he had.

But he knew he had to act quickly and decisively. It was the only way to get free.

The door to the *Torch* office stood open, and the lights burned at every desk even though full morning light poured in the windows. The sunlight hit the Wall of Weird, turning photographs of the meteor rocks a luminescent green.

Clark walked in. He was worried. He hadn't seen Chloe all morning.

She had even missed first period English, the class she loved the most.

"Chloe?" he called.

Her book bag rested against a desk. Her purse hung from the side of an empty chair. Her camera was hooked up to one of the computers, which had a sign on its screen that blinked, *download completed, download completed.*

Clark's stomach clenched. It wasn't like Chloe to be so silent. After losing Danny and Betty Franklin yesterday, Clark was beginning to believe that anyone could disappear.

"Chloe?"

"She's down in the girls' locker room." Lana's soft voice behind Clark made him jump.

He turned. Lana was leaning against the door, hugging her books to her chest. She wore a loose long-sleeved shirt, hip-hugger blue jeans, and sandals, in deference to yesterday's weather. It wasn't supposed to be as warm today, but it hadn't been supposed to get that hot yesterday either.

"The locker room? What's she doing there?"

"Cleaning up." Lana stepped inside the *Torch* office and leaned on one of the computer desks. "She spent the night here."

"Doing what?" Clark asked.

"Looking up stuff on the Franklin case. She was checking disappearances off that property in the past, looking for ghosts, you know the basic stuff." Lana's eyes twinkled, but there were deep circles under them. Even though she seemed better than she had been the day before, she was clearly still bothered by Danny Franklin's death.

"Did she find anything?"

Lana shrugged. "I have no idea. I found her here this morning. She'd fallen asleep. So I loaned her a fresh shirt from my locker, and she went down to take a shower."

"She left her purse," Clark said. Seeing the purse had made him panic. Girls never left their purses behind.

"I know. I was coming up here for it." Lana walked around Clark and picked up the purse. "I was supposed to lock up the *Torch* office, too."

"Probably a good idea," he said.

"What is?" Pete Ross peered around the door, his familiar face squinched in a frown.

"Locking up," Lana said.

"Where's Chloe?" Pete asked, coming inside.

"Long story," Clark said.

"I got some of it from the local news. The day I decide to stick around school to finish my lab project is the day you guys stumble on some excitement."

"It wasn't excitement, Pete." Lana's voice got even softer than normal. "It was horrible."

Pete bit his lower lip. "I'm sorry, Lana. I didn't mean it that way. I just meant—"

"We know what you meant." Clark smoothed over the moment as best he could. Pete hadn't known Danny Franklin as well as Lana had. Clark had a hunch that Pete and Danny had had a run-in a few years ago. They never spoke. "Why're you looking for Chloe?"

"Actually," Pete said, "I was looking for you. Did you hear about Lex?"

"What about him?" Lana asked before Clark could.

"His dad's been kidnapped." Pete didn't sound too distressed about it. But Pete wasn't too fond of the Luthors. "Lex flew out of here yesterday afternoon."

"To Metropolis?" Clark asked.

"Yeah. His dad was taken from there. In front of a bank, of all things. They took his limo. You really hadn't heard?"

Clark shook his head. He hadn't paid attention to the news, and he'd been thinking about the Franklin murders. He wondered how Lex was doing. Lex and his father didn't get along, but it was obvious Lex cared about his dad. This had to be really difficult.

"I would've thought you were going with him," Pete said to Clark.

"Why would I have gone with him?"

"Because you two are friends." Pete made the statement sound casual, but they both knew it wasn't. Pete had been feeling left out of Clark's life lately, mostly because of Lex.

"I was a little busy yesterday," Clark said. "I hadn't heard about Lex's dad at all."

"What happened?" Lana asked.

"No one knows, exactly," Pete said. He obviously paid attention to the whole story. Pete had never liked the Luthors. He felt that they had betrayed his family when they bought the creamed corn factory from Pete's dad years ago and turned it into a fertilizer plant. "No one's talking either. I don't even know if they got a ransom note."

Clark swallowed, not sure if he wanted to ask the question that popped into his mind. But he had to know. "Are they sure it's a kidnapping?"

"And not a murder?" Pete said. "They're saying kidnapping. But it sounds suspicious to me."

"Poor Lex." Lana hugged her books even tighter. "What must he be going through?"

"Hell, I'd bet."

The three of them started. Chloe was in the doorway. Clark hadn't heard her approach either. Proof that he had a lot to think about. He usually noticed everything around him.

Chloe had stepped just inside the room and pushed the door closed behind her. Her hair was still damp, giving it some extra curl. The shirt she wore seemed too frilly for her. Even if Lana hadn't told Clark that she had given Chloe the shirt, Clark would have known that the shirt didn't belong to Chloe. It didn't suit her at all.

But it did give him a sense of a kinder, gentler Chloe, the

person she might have been without that fierce drive, incredible intelligence, and willingness to go the distance for any news story.

She picked up her purse and shook it at Lana. "I'm glad I didn't wait for you."

"I'm sorry," Lana said. "Pete was just telling us about Lex."

"I heard," Chloe said. "The whole school is talking about it."

"Not Danny Franklin?" Clark felt a twinge of sadness, as if Danny couldn't get any attention, not even in death.

"Oh, no," Chloe said. "They're talking about him, too. People are wondering if it's all linked, you know. Bad things happening to anyone connected with Smallville. The usual."

It was usual, that was the sad thing. Clark used to deny it, but he couldn't any longer, not with Chloe's Wall of Weird facing him.

"Do you think they're linked?" Pete asked Chloe.

"I'm not ruling anything out." She slung her purse over her shoulder, then paused at the computer that had been downloading the photographs from her camera. She moved the mouse, clicked off the alert, and backed up the pictures on a CD.

"That makes sense." Pete leaned on a nearby desk. "Wasn't it Sherlock Holmes who said there is no such thing as a coincidence?"

"I think the phrase is more modern than that." Lana moved toward Chloe, watching her work. "But I don't remember offhand which detective coined it."

"I thought it was Holmes," Pete said without rancor.

"Trust Lana," Clark said. "She's read everything, it seems."

She gave him a warm smile. "Not everything, Clark. Although that's one of my goals."

"Impossible goal," Chloe said, moving toward her main computer. "They keep publishing new books all the time."

"I'm just trying to get through my parents' collection of old paperbacks. With a side journey for the occasional new book that catches my eye." Lana leaned forward, squinting at Chloe's computer. "What're you doing?"

"Calling up information on the kidnapping. I didn't hear where it happened, did you?"

"Metropolis," Pete said. "Outside City Bank. It was a pretty big deal."

"Metropolis," Chloe muttered. She clicked the mouse a few times. Clark saw screen after screen of information appear on the computer. "Well, that's frustrating."

"What is?" Lana asked. "I don't see anything."

"He was abducted in his own limo." Chloe sat down in the wooden desk chair behind the computer.

"So?" Pete asked. "What were you expecting?"

Clark came forward, setting his books on a nearby desk. "She was hoping that there would have been a one-ton pickup involved, preferably a red one, about ten years old."

Chloe gave him a quick grin over her shoulder. "No moss grows on you."

"Huh?" Pete asked.

"I don't know," Lana said, "but I'm guessing that the pickup belongs to the Franklin family. Chloe was hoping for an obvious connection."

"I'll still settle for this one, though," Chloe said. "I think it's suspicious that the crimes happened on the same day."

"Good thing you're not a cop," Pete said. "You'd try to link a purse-snatching in Los Angeles to a bank robbery in London just because they occurred on the same date."

"If I were a cop," Chloe said, "at least one of those would be out of my jurisdiction."

She continued to type as she spoke, the keys making clicking noises that echoed in the room.

"Has there been any word on the rest of the family?" Clark asked.

Chloe shook her head. "And the police are searching everything. No one has any idea what's going on."

"It's just so sad," Lana said. "I'm trying not to think about it. But I keep wondering who'll take care of Danny. You know, the funeral and everything."

"There's other family," Pete said. "They're just out of state. I'm sure they're on the way here."

"If they're not hiding Mr. and Mrs. Franklin and Bonnie," Chloe said.

"I sure wish we knew what happened," Clark said.

"Well, I know what's going to happen to us if we don't make third period," Pete said. "You skip more than one class with Mr. Gates, and you get detention."

"I've never skipped a class with Mr. Gates," Clark said.

"You're not the one I'm worried about." Pete flashed him a grin. "Let's go."

He headed for the door, but Clark didn't follow immediately. As he grabbed his books off the desk, he said, "You're going to class today, aren't you, Chloe?"

"As soon as I find what I'm looking for," she said.

"You know that Principal Kwan won't let you continue with the *Torch* if your grades go down."

"My grades won't go down, Clark," Chloe said. "I've already read all my textbooks. Sometimes I feel like I could give the lectures myself."

Clark shook his head, but he knew better than to push her. He joined Pete in the hallway. Lana followed.

"Sometimes I wonder why I study so hard," she said, "when things come so easily to Chloe."

"They don't grade life on a curve, Lana," Clark said, leading the three of them down the empty hall. Second period hadn't let out yet, but the *Torch* office was pretty far from the chemistry lab.

"I wish they did," Lana said. "At least then I'd understand the rules."

She peeled off and headed for her locker. Pete stared after her. "What did that mean?"

"I have a hunch she was thinking about Lex's dad and Danny Franklin," Clark said.

"I don't think what happened to Danny had anything to do with rules," Pete said.

Clark nodded, but he found himself thinking about that comment all during Mr. Gates's chemistry lab. Something didn't fit. But Clark wasn't sure yet what that something was.

◆◆◆

Lex Luthor stood in the loading zone outside of City Bank. The area wasn't cordoned off—too busy for that kind of nonsense, the obnoxious police detective had told him—but Lex had gotten some of the security people to keep crowds and traffic away.

He wanted to see the place for himself.

He'd already seen it on the bank security tape. Several video cameras filmed the loading zone, the sidewalk, and the parking areas as a matter of course.

He had spent the night viewing the tapes, reviewing the events, and waiting for the kidnappers to contact him with a ransom. The police and the FBI were there as well, with their phone-tapping equipment and their instructions.

Lex had been ignoring the so-called authorities. They weren't relevant to him. The statistics—with or without police involvement—did not favor his father. Most kidnappers killed their victims within the first forty-eight hours.

Twenty-four of those forty-eight were nearly up, and no one had made any progress.

Lex scanned the area. It looked so different than it had the afternoon before, and not just because the security tapes were in grainy black-and-white. The limo wasn't there, of course, and the crowds seemed thinner. A lot of people were stopping to gawk. Apparently they knew who he was. They probably wondered what he was trying to do.

Too bad no one had watched when his father was kidnapped. The police had canvassed the area, tried to identify faces off the security tape, and had released pleas for assistance from the general public.

As usual, no one saw anything. At least, no one who saw anything was coming forward. If Lex had to, he would find a way around that. Money always talked.

He walked the short distance from the bank doors to the loading zone. So easy. It only took him a few seconds. The crowd watched him, unusually silent. His security people—or rather, his father's security people—watched as well.

They apparently had no idea what he was doing. He wasn't about to enlighten them.

He checked the ground for glass vials, spray canisters, anything that could have caused three grown men to hit the ground in a matter of seconds. The bystanders also got hit, which meant that whatever the kidnappers had used to knock everyone out—and they were knocked out—had been airborne.

No one had been seriously injured, at least from the knockout gas (a few people had been trampled after they fell, and a few others had hit their heads rather hard), but medical personnel couldn't identify the chemical used.

It was making treatment difficult, or so they told Lex, because they were afraid of drug interactions. They found no strange chemicals in the bloodstream of the people who went down. The doctors also took nose and throat swabs, and they were hoping to get something from that.

But those results might take days.

Lex knew his father didn't have days.

Lex rubbed his eyes. He hadn't slept all night. He reviewed the surveillance tapes, went over his father's files, looked through the threatening letters and e-mails that his father constantly received.

Even though he knew his father had enemies, Lex was stunned by the vitriol his father received day in and day out. It was a wonder that his father wasn't more cautious than he was. With that much hatred coming at his father, it was a wonder that his father went outside at all.

But it did explain his father's complete lack of interest in the unrest at the Smallville facility. The stuff that Lex had been calling him about every day was nothing compared with things his father had dealt with in Metropolis alone all month.

Brown glass winked against the curb. Lex crouched and examined the shards. They were thick—the kind of glass used in beer bottles. After a moment, he saw the neck of the bottle, farther down the curb, resting uncomfortably over a sewer grate.

Nothing. No evidence that anything had happened here.

He was at loose ends and he felt like he was fighting this alone. His father's security people didn't seem to know what they were doing. The police and the FBI were following the official handbook, taking everything one worthless step at a time.

They might find the kidnappers, but they would do so long after Lionel Luthor was dead.

Lex stood and surveyed the small stretch of road where his father had vanished. Large stone buildings that had stood on that site since the end of the nineteenth century faced him, their windows barred off so that no one could break in from outside. Around the corner, a taxi stand, and a little farther beyond that, a bus stop.

He would wager his entire inheritance that no one thought to canvass people on the other side of the street.

He signaled Harrison. The man, with the burly look of an ex-football player going slowly to fat, lumbered over.

"Mr. Luthor?"

Lex pointed at the buildings. "See those windows over there?"

"Yes, sir."

"I want every person with a view out those windows to be interviewed about my father's disappearance. I want the interviews to cover the three days previous to the disappearance all the way through this morning. I want to know everything that happened, however trivial. If some squirrel dropped a nut down that sewer grate, I want to know about it. You got that?"

"Yes, sir." Harrison had been amazingly humble since Lex had arrived, as if he were afraid of being fired.

Lex was withholding judgment on firing his father's people. If they could redeem themselves by finding his father, he would let them keep their jobs.

But he didn't trust that they would. He had his own network here in Metropolis. Younger guys, people he had befriended in boarding school, people whose characters weren't as pristine as his father would like.

Lex also had feelers out with them. If they heard anything, they would let Lex know. They knew he could match or double any amount anyone else would pay for silence.

Lex would find his father, one way or another.

The only worry that Lex had was whether or not he would find his father before it was too late.

Lionel Luthor had worked maybe a quarter of an inch of give into the ropes that bound his hands when the snorer woke up. The man snorted, choked, and sat up, clutching his forehead as if it hurt him.

"Honey?" he said, his voice deep and raw.

Luthor didn't move. He kept his hands as far apart as they would go so that it didn't seem like the ropes were loose.

The man didn't seem to notice him. Not right away. The man blinked, then rubbed his eyes with the heel of his hand.

For a moment, Luthor thought the man might lie back down, but he didn't.

The man had slept later than Luthor thought he would. The sun had been up for some time. Light poured into the windows behind Luthor, revealing the filth and the mouse droppings that mixed with the mud on the scuffed wooden floor.

No one else had arrived at the cabin, and Luthor couldn't see out the windows in front of him. He had no idea if there was a car or any other mode of transportation out there.

He had no idea what he'd do once he got free of his ropes.

After a moment, the man pivoted, put his feet on the floor, and groaned. Then he got up, adjusted his blue jeans, and started toward the bathroom. Halfway there, he saw Luthor.

Their gazes met. The man looked defeated, as if he were the prisoner instead of Luthor.

The man skirted around the chair without saying a word. Luthor waited until the man reached the bathroom door before saying, "You know, I have to do that, too."

The man sighed, leaned his head forward, and somehow managed to look even more defeated. "That's not my problem."

"It will be," Luthor said. "I am known for my rigid control, but after a while, even the most rigid control gives way to the inevitable."

"Whatever." The man went into the bathroom and closed the door.

Luthor closed his eyes in frustration. If he could get the man to undo at least one of his hands, he might have a chance. He wouldn't be able to push much, though. He was, after all, the one with the disadvantage.

He would just have to find a way to turn that disadvantage into an opportunity. He'd spent his life doing that. Turning a man like this one—clearly the flunky of the three who kidnapped him—shouldn't be hard.

If he had the time to finesse it.

Luthor glanced at the windows. Still nothing from outside. And then the water turned on in the bathroom. A shower? The man seemed awfully trusting of Luthor.

Luthor smiled for the first time that day.

Maybe gaining an advantage would be easier than he thought.

Chloe hadn't shown up for geometry. Clark finished the last problem on the pop quiz, then double-checked his work. Since this geometry class was in the last period of the day, the teacher let the students turn in their quizzes and leave.

Pete had just finished, too. He stood up, took the quiz to the front of the room, and handed it to the teacher. Clark followed.

Lana wasn't in this class. She had geometry earlier in the day. Her final class of the day was social studies, and that teacher rarely let anyone leave before the bell.

Pete waited for Clark up front. They left the classroom together, sliding into the wide, empty corridor, before saying anything. Even then, they kept their voices down. If they got caught talking too loudly, their open-classroom privileges would be revoked.

"Chloe's going to be really cheesed that she missed a pop quiz," Pete said.

"Maybe she can make it up," Clark said.

"No makeups if you attended other classes that day, remember? We got her to go to chem."

"So she's going to be upset at us," Clark said. "And here I was going to suggest we go to the *Torch* office to see what else she found."

"It better be the news story of the century," Pete said, "because the 4.0 she's been working on this quarter just got shot."

Clark nodded. He wondered if Chloe would even think about that—at least at this point. She'd notice later, when the story was over.

He and Pete moved silently through the hallways. The classroom doors were all closed, and through the small square windows in each, Clark could see teachers moving back and forth near their desks. In some rooms, students sat attentively in the front rows, and in others, chaos seemed to reign.

As he passed the social studies room, he saw Lana hand a note to a friend, who read the note, looked over at Lana, and grinned.

"You're hopeless, you know that?" Pete slapped a hand on Clark's back. "Let's move on."

He was hopeless. He did know that. And sometimes he thought Lana actually noticed how interested he was and returned that interest. Then he'd listen to her talk about Whitney and what he was doing in the Marines, and realize that she still thought of Clark as nothing more than the boy next door.

He and Pete arrived in the *Torch* office a few minutes later. Sure enough, Chloe was at her favorite computer, pounding on the keys.

"Any developments?" Clark asked as he set his books on a nearby desk.

Chloe jumped half a foot and put a hand over her heart. "Jeez, Clark. Hello would be nice."

"I don't think you would have heard me if I was polite," Clark said.

"Yeah," Pete said, pulling a chair beside Chloe. "I suspect someone could have told you any old thing, and unless it was related to the Franklin case, you wouldn't have noticed."

"I'd have noticed if there was anything on the Luthor kidnapping." Chloe started typing again. She was on the Internet. An ad flashed on top of her screen, followed by lots of text.

"So nothing's changed?" Clark asked.

"For the Luthors or the Franklins?" Chloe asked, not taking her gaze off the screen.

"Luthors," Clark said as Pete said, "Franklins."

"No," Chloe said. "Nothing's changed."

"For which?" Pete asked.

"Luthors," Chloe said. "There hasn't even been word of a ransom note."

"That's not good." Pete no longer sounded pleased about the Luthor kidnapping.

"No, it's not," Clark said. He wondered if he could get ahold of Lex. Of course, if he did manage to speak to Lex, he had no idea what he'd say. From this distance, there was really nothing he could do.

Besides, this was one of those cases where Clark agreed with his father: The authorities were better off handling the kidnapping. At least until they had a suspect. Then maybe Clark could find a way to help that wouldn't be noticed.

The past twenty-four hours had been very frustrating to him. He hadn't been able to help Danny or Betty Franklin, and right now, there wasn't anything he could do for Lex either. Yet he felt like he should be able to do something.

Clark grabbed a chair and pulled it up to Chloe's other side. "What are you doing?"

She leaned forward so that she blocked his view of the screen. "Working."

"I figured that much out. On what?"

She was too thin to hide the screen from both Clark and Pete, and she knew it. She looked first at Clark, then at Pete, and sighed. "Go close the door, one of you, okay?"

Pete was closest. He got up and pushed the door closed.

"Okay," he said as he walked back to his chair. "Spill."

"I've been monitoring the news reports." Chloe lifted a small Walkman from inside her purse. The movement made a tiny cord that she had hidden under her blouse move so that Clark could see it. The cord led to her left ear. "They've got a theory about the crime."

"The Franklin thing," Pete said, "not the Luthor thing, right?"

"Right," Chloe said. She put the Walkman back and grabbed the mouse. She hit "sleep" so that the screen she had up completely disappeared.

"And?" Clark said. "What's the theory?"

"They think Jed Franklin killed his whole family."

Clark started. His father had said the same thing last night.

Pete made a face. "Why would a guy do that?"

"I don't know the whys," Chloe said. "Just that they have some reports of him acting suspicious before the bodies were found. And someone claims to have seen him after the official time of death for Danny."

"Someone?" Clark said.

Chloe gave him a sheepish look. "I was in French."

"In other words, you missed it," Pete said.

"I missed it," Chloe said. "I figure it'll repeat."

"Meanwhile, you were looking for the same story on the Internet," Clark said.

"Not exactly." Chloe crossed her arms. "Look, if I tell you guys what I was doing, we could all get in trouble."

"I don't care about getting in trouble," Pete said. "Do you, Clark?"

Actually, Clark did. Whenever Chloe had such concerns, she had done something very wrong. Sometimes against-the-law kind of wrong.

"What did you do?" he asked Chloe, dodging Pete's question.

"Have you ever met Jed Franklin?" Chloe asked, dodging Clark's question.

Apparently, no one was going to give straight answers this afternoon.

"Not that I remember," Clark said. "Lana said he seemed nice. My mom called him gentle."

But Clark's father thought he'd seen darkness in Mr. Franklin. Only Clark didn't tell Chloe that.

"That's how I always felt about him, too. If anything, I got the sense that he wasn't strong enough to stand up to people. And that included Mrs. Franklin."

"Guys like that snap," Pete said. "You got to watch out for

the quiet ones. You know, like our buddy Clark here."

Clark felt his cheeks warm. "I'm not quiet."

"You're not loud either," Pete said. "Sometimes getting a read on you is difficult."

"But that's my point," Chloe said. "Clark's gentle, too. And he wouldn't do anything like this."

"You hope," Pete said.

"I'm being serious, Pete." Chloe frowned at him.

Pete studied her for a minute, then nodded. "Sorry. I'm not handling all this stuff too well. It's easier to joke about it."

"A lot has happened the last few days," Clark said.

"I don't like any of it," Pete said.

"And that's my point." Chloe grabbed the notebook she kept beside the computer. She opened it to a page covered with her handwriting.

Clark stared at it. Chloe hated taking notes by hand, considering it very old-fashioned. She did it when she had to, but she tried to avoid it at all costs.

"Their theory of the crime," Chloe said, still paging through her notebook, "is that he did it. Mine was that the family was on the run."

"Was?" Pete asked.

Chloe held up a finger to silence him. "According to my source in the sheriff's office—"

"You have a source?" Pete asked.

"A deputy who thinks she's cute," Clark said. "Hasn't she told you that?"

"That she's cute?" Pete asked.

"That she flirted her way out of a ticket and has been using the poor guy ever since."

Chloe elbowed Clark in the side. "Stop it. I'm trying to be serious here."

"Just catching Pete up on the facts."

Pete grinned at Clark. "Facts a man can use."

Clark nodded.

"Guys," Chloe said. "This is important."

"Sorry," Pete said, and leaned forward. "Go on, Ms. Woodward."

"I think in this mood, she's Bernstein," Clark said.

"*According to my source*," Chloe said, talking over them, "the police have some information that we don't have."

"That's a surprise," Pete said.

"*Like*," Chloe said with even more force, "the fact that Mr. Franklin was seen in Smallville as recently as two days ago."

"By the mysterious someone," Pete said, clearly becoming serious again.

"You said that was on the radio," Clark said.

"Part of it was," Chloe said. "But not the part about Smallville, and not the fact that it was a reliable witness—and no, I wasn't able to get the name. My source also says that Mr. Franklin was arrested three times in the last month for being drunk and disorderly. He actually tore up a bar."

"I thought you said he was gentle." Pete was frowning.

"I pushed on this point, and it turns out that 'tore up' means he knocked over some glasses and a table when he passed out. Of course, he'd been shouting before that about how much he hated LuthorCorp, and that really upset a lot of people, but there's no more than that." Chloe still hadn't looked in her notebook, although she'd stopped thumbing through the pages.

"They're basing the idea that he killed his family on that?" Clark asked.

"And a couple of other things," Chloe said. "Apparently Danny and Betty didn't drown. They were both strangled, and Danny had a lot of bruises on his hands and arms, as if he'd been pummeling someone, trying to get free. Neither of them was bound or gagged, and they weren't suffocated with a pillow or anything. Whoever killed them used his hands."

"You'd have to be pretty strong to do that," Pete said.

"Not to mention determined." Clark shook his head. He was strong, and he couldn't imagine killing anyone in that way. "This doesn't make any sense. To do that, you'd have to be looking your victim in the face."

"One point for the psycho-killer theory," Pete said.

"I've been doing some research on the Internet," Chloe said, "and there's been a lot written on this topic, especially lately because there's been so many instances of a parent murdering the entire family. Besides that woman in Texas, there've been cases in Georgia, Oregon—"

"We do follow the news, Chloe," Clark said gently.

She nodded, but barely took a breath before continuing. "Anyway, what all of these killers have in common was that they thought they were sending their families to a better place. It was, for them, an act of love."

"Yeah, right." Pete stood up. "That's a bunch of—"

The door opened, and Pete stopped. Lana looked in. "I thought I'd find you guys here. Is there more news?"

"We're trying to find that out from Chloe," Clark said. "It's turning out to be surprisingly difficult."

Lana grinned.

"Come in or stay out," Chloe said, "but either way, close the door."

Pete whistled. "You are uptight, girl."

"I've got more to tell you," Chloe said, "and I really don't want the entire school to know."

"Sounds serious." Lana came inside, closing the door tightly behind her. She pulled a chair over and joined the group. "So what have I missed? I need all the gossip."

Chloe's mouth was a thin line, and she was tapping her right foot.

Lana looked at her, then glanced at Clark, eyes twinkling.

"Yeah, Clark and I tried the gossip thing already," Pete said. "Chloe's having none of it, even if it was her cop boyfriend we were talking about."

"You have a boyfriend who is a policeman?" Lana asked. She sounded impressed.

Chloe shot Pete a dark look. Clark wondered why she hadn't aimed it at him. After all, he was the one who spilled the secret.

"He's a source, that's all."

"Is it that deputy?" Lana asked. "I've seen him around. He's cute."

Chloe's eyes narrowed. Clark recognized the expression. She was going to blow soon.

"Where were we?" Clark asked, to avoid more fireworks.

"Some idiotic theory about people murdering their families out of love," Pete said.

"Ick." Lana frowned. "They think Mr. Franklin did it? I don't believe that. He's so nice."

"I don't even remember why you were making that point, Chloe," Pete said.

"Because," Clark said, "I mentioned that to kill someone that way, you'd have to look them in the face. I didn't think a father could do that. But if he did it out of love—"

"No." Lana shook her head. "Mr. Franklin isn't crazy. There aren't a lot of people who love their families as much as he did. He would never do something like this."

"Someone did, Lana," Pete said.

"I don't think it was Mr. Franklin either," Chloe said.

"Yeah." Clark glanced at her notebook again. "You said you had a different theory of the crime."

"I think 'had' is the operative word," Pete said. "She was using past tense."

Chloe nodded, then graced Pete with a smile. The smile relieved Clark. It meant that Chloe was calming down.

"I did have a different theory, and I found some stuff that disproved my theory and the police's." She glanced over her shoulder at the door. "That's why I didn't want us overheard."

"Because of your theory?" Pete asked.

"No," Chloe said. "Because of the work I did to disprove it."

"You'd better catch me up," Lana said. "I'm not sure what your theory was."

"I hadn't told them yet, either," Chloe said.

Lana looked at Clark. He nodded his agreement.

Chloe stood up and checked the windows, talking as she moved around the room. "I developed part of the theory while we were at the Franklin farm. Remember, I said that it seemed odd to me that the car was gone. I was hoping the other three members of the family escaped."

"You're using past tense again, Chloe," Pete said.

Chloe nodded. She checked the closet door, then stopped in front of the Wall of Weird. She put a hand on it as if it gave her strength.

"After I talked to my source—"

"The cute deputy," Clark said.

"—I decided to do some digging." Chloe glared at Clark.

He got the message. He would remain quiet. But he felt like Pete had; he couldn't take the seriousness. He needed to lighten the mood just a little. Otherwise, the facts of the last day might overwhelm him.

"I figured if the family was on the move, I'd be able to track them," Chloe said.

"How?" Lana asked.

"They'd have to get money somewhere. I figured there'd at least be a big withdrawal from their checking account. Maybe they'd even use checks or their credit cards. But nothing turned up," Chloe said.

"Chloe." Clark spoke before he could stop himself. "That's illegal."

She raised her eyebrows at him.

"Hence the closed door," Lana said.

"How'd you know how to do that?" Pete asked.

"I wish I could say it was hard," Chloe said.

"Don't you think the police would do the same thing?" Clark asked.

"After they got warrants and orders and legal stuff, sure," Chloe said. "I suspect I'm ahead of them."

"And you didn't find anything?" Pete asked.

"Nothing." Chloe sat down. She picked up her notebook. "Their accounts are a mess though. They have less than two hundred dollars combined in their checking and savings account. Their credit cards are maxed, and the bank canceled their line of credit."

"That had to create a lot of pressure," Lana said.

Chloe nodded.

"If everything's maxed," Clark said, "then they wouldn't be able to use their credit cards."

"I did find a gas card that Mr. Franklin had been using for the farm equipment and his truck. That card wasn't maxed, and it would have gotten them quite a ways out of Smallville. It hasn't been touched at all."

"They could have been using cash," Pete said.

"From where?" Chloe asked. "They haven't made a withdrawal."

"A lot of farm families in the Midwest got into the habit of keeping their money in a safe at home. My grandfather says it went back to the Depression," Pete said.

"That was a long time ago," Clark said. "We're a farm family. We use the bank like normal people."

"I don't think they had money in a safe at home or under the mattress or whatever fantasy you want to concoct," Lana said. "It was really clear to me that Danny was panicked when we were assigned the lab experiment. We had to buy lab equipment, and Danny couldn't afford lunch every day. Remember, Clark? That day he was kicking the candy machine?"

Clark nodded. The candy machine in the lunchroom had eaten a dollar and not given Danny the candy bar he'd wanted. He kicked the machine so hard it dented.

Lana had talked to Danny, while Clark surreptitiously repaired the dent with his super strength. He didn't want Danny to get into more trouble than he would already be in.

That day, Lana had shared her lunch with Danny. Clark wondered how many other times she had done that.

"He was pretty upset about losing a dollar. I can't imagine him being that way if the family had a stash," Lana said.

"Provided he knew about it," Pete said.

"I think he knew everything there was to know about the family money," Chloe said. "He was the one managing most of the farm stuff while his dad worked at LuthorCorp. That was pretty clear from the financial records, too."

"Maybe they pawned stuff," Pete said. "The Franklins have lived in that house for generations. When you live someplace that long, old junk turns into collectibles after a while."

Chloe shook her head. "If they had stuff to pawn, they would have done it a long time ago. When the bank cut off their credit, or something."

"That makes sense," Clark said. "They had to pay for seed and fertilizer and gas just to keep the farm running. Usually the bank fronts that stuff and the farmer pays it back later. If they didn't have a credit line, they had to get the money from some-where. Those fields had been tilled. You don't do that if you have nothing to plant."

"Okay," Lana said, leaning back. "I'm confused then. Where does that leave us?"

"With two incorrect theories of the crime," Chloe said. "I don't think Mr. Franklin did it—after all, he'd need money, too."

"But Chloe, it's easier for one person to run than three," Pete said. "Maybe he's been stealing to survive."

Chloe shook her head. "The police have his car description and license plate number. They've gotten no hits on it so far, and they've publicized that part to pieces. They've had a few false positives on the truck, but when they checked it out, it was pretty clear that they didn't have the right one."

"The family couldn't have split up?" Pete asked.

This time, Clark shook his head. "Not if something this trau-matic happened. Think about it, Pete."

"I have been." Pete crossed his arms. "I have been ever since I heard about it. I don't like any of it."

"Me, either," Lana said.

Chloe looked at the Wall of Weird. "Just when you think you've seen everything—"

"But this isn't something for the Wall of Weird, is it?" Pete asked. "I mean this happens other places, not just Smallville."

"The first true crime novel ever written was about the murder of a family in Kansas," Lana said. "It's called *In Cold Blood*."

"What happened?" Clark asked.

Lana's gaze met his for just a moment. "That's the sad thing. It was so senseless. These two thieves heard there was a lot of money in this farmhouse, so they broke in, and killed the entire family, but didn't find any of the money they were searching for."

"Do you think that's what happened here?" Pete asked.

"It's a possibility," Chloe said.

Clark frowned. He stood up and walked to the Wall of Weird. Mutated frogs, meteorites, green rocks. He could deal with all that. He was having a lot of trouble with senseless violence.

"If that's what happened," he said, "then why hide the bodies in the pond? Why not just leave them where you killed them?"

"And why strangle them instead of shoot them?" Pete asked.

"That's the key," Chloe said.

"Strangling them?" Lana asked.

Chloe shook her head. "Hiding the bodies. That's why the police think it was Mr. Franklin. They thought he wanted to hide his crime."

"Makes sense to me," Pete said.

"But hiding the bodies is the act of a rational person, not an irrational one," Chloe said. "Most of these family murderers kill everyone—"

"With a gun," Lana said.

Clark looked at her in surprise.

She shrugged. "I read a lot. And for a while, I read a lot of true crime. It felt like an escape from all the strange stuff in Smallville."

"Some escape," Pete said.

"But Lana's right," Chloe said. "Usually these guys—and for the most part it is guys—shoot their entire family, and then shoot themselves. But there's no evidence of a shotgun blast in that house."

"And there's no way Mr. Franklin committed those murders if he was rational," Lana said. "I don't care how much evidence someone gathers. I'll never believe that."

"So," Pete said. "What kind of rational person would murder two teenagers and hide them in a pond?"

Clark frowned. "Someone who felt he had something to gain from it."

"What do you gain from murdering high school students?" Lana asked.

"Leverage," Chloe said.

Pete nodded. "If you want a man to do something, threaten his family."

"But who would do that to Mr. Franklin?" Lana asked.

"It goes back to the money," Chloe said. "It always goes back to the money."

"You think he borrowed from someone he shouldn't have?" Pete asked.

"I can't believe there's a mobster-style loan shark in Smallville," Lana said.

"Maybe not Smallville," Clark said, thinking of all the shady things Lex had told him about. "But I'll bet there's a lot of them in Metropolis."

Chloe walked back to her desk and picked up her notebook. "If someone was doing that to Mr. Franklin, he'd leave a trail. He'd be all over Smallville searching for money, for help any way he could get it."

The group was silent. Clark glanced again at the Wall of Weird. Something didn't fit. There was some piece that none of them had looked at, some aspect that they knew about but weren't seeing.

"Then we're back to square one," Pete said.

On the side of the Wall of Weird, Chloe had tacked a map of Smallville and the surrounding areas. She had pushpins stuck all over it in various colors: a large green one where the meteor went down; smaller green ones where meteor rocks had been found; different colors for some of the stranger news stories that had come out of Smallville.

She hadn't marked the Franklin farm yet.

"What are you looking at, Clark?" Lana asked.

He didn't answer her. Instead, he took a step closer to the map. "Is this a current map, Chloe?"

"Last year's," she said. "Why?"

"Did the police search the entire farm?"

"Of course," Chloe said.

"Including the second pond?"

"What second pond?" Chloe asked.

Clark pointed to the map. Hidden in what was now a forest of trees was a small pond. It wouldn't have been visible to someone who didn't know the terrain. It was clear, though, that the second pond had been the main pond back when the farm was smaller.

Chloe came over beside him and studied the map. "I didn't even realize that section was part of the farm."

"Me either until I looked at it," Clark said.

Lana joined them. "It's fenced off. I remember seeing that. Why would that section be fenced off?"

"Farmers fence things a lot, either to keep animals out or to keep them in," Clark said. "I can't tell you how many fences I've helped my dad build trying to keep the deer from my mother's vegetable garden."

"I'll bet the police haven't looked there," Chloe said.

"So maybe we should call them," Pete said.

Chloe shook her head. "Let's check it out ourselves first. We don't want to bother them."

"Not even the cute cop in traffic?" Clark said, only half-teasing.

"Not even him." Chloe was already across the room, gathering her purse and two different cameras. "Come on, you guys. Let's go."

CHAPTER 9

Even now, Lex could not bring himself to use his father's office as command central. Lex wasn't ready. Maybe someday, if—*when*—he took over LuthorCorp, he would take over this office.

Not until then.

And not in circumstances like these.

Lex passed the door to his father's inner sanctum and went to the large office he'd been using since he arrived in Metropolis. The office was supposed to go to his father's second-in-command. But in all the years that Lex had been paying attention to LuthorCorp, his father never had a second-in-command.

Once upon a time, Lex had thought the office was waiting for him to grow old enough, and experienced enough, to use it. And, if he hadn't known his father better, he might have thought the offer his father had made a few weeks ago—the offer to bring him back to Metropolis—was for the position of second-in-command.

Of course, it hadn't been. It had been because his father was seeing a new side to Lex, a side that had always been there: the dark ruthless side, the side his father had trained into him with all of those years of mind games instead of love.

Lex went inside the office. The room was large, with a standard company desk and a leather-backed rolling desk chair. Empty file cabinets stood against the wall, and a phone with multiple lines sat on the blotter.

The view was spectacular, of course. His father had the best building in one of the highest-rent cities in the world, and the best building had the best view. All of Metropolis spread out before him. Lex could almost imagine himself the Emperor's son, surveying the Empire he would once inherit, should his father die.

Lex clenched a fist. He had been uncertain yesterday, but when he arrived here, he knew his heart. He didn't want his father to die. Not like this. Not kidnapped, powerless, humiliated.

Lex wanted his father to live. Lex wanted to prove to the old man that he could be bested—by his own son. Lex wanted to show Lionel Luthor that underestimating his child was the biggest mistake of his life.

If revenge was a dish best served cold, it was also one made with exquisite care. These kidnappers had interrupted Lex's revenge, petty as it might be.

And if these people turned out to be murderers instead of kidnappers, then they would foil Lex's attempt to worm his way into his father's affections, by proving to his father that he was worthy of his father's love.

Lex allowed himself a small, bitter smile. Self-awareness wasn't all it was cracked up to be. He knew why he was taking these actions; he understood all of his own motivations; and still he despised them. The basis for them all was a childish desire for attention and an even older wish for love.

Sometimes he thought that if he had been raised with parents like Clark Kent's, he wouldn't be this twisted, brilliant man who still hadn't figured out his place in the world. He would know what his place was, and he would feel confident in it.

For even though Lex played at confidence, he lacked it deep down. And even though Clark seemed uncertain at times, he had twenty times the confidence Lex could ever have.

Lex went to the window and looked out. The buildings spread before him like worlds to be conquered. His father was out there somewhere, alive with any kind of luck. All Lex had to do was find him.

With so much money at his fingertips, it was a shock to Lex that he couldn't use it to gain more information. Even his underground connections had nothing.

Well, they had something. They agreed to a person that whoever concocted the scheme to kidnap Lionel Luthor had balls and also that that person was not involved in the Metropolis underworld. No one there wanted to call that kind of attention to himself and his operation.

The theory was that the kidnappers had come in from outside. And, as person after person pointed out to Lex, they had come in prepared.

He walked back to the desk. Even though this office wasn't his, it bore his stamp after twenty-four hours of work. Several empty cappuccino cups, a half-eaten Danish, the remains of a pizza ordered in the middle of the night. Crumpled papers lined the wastebasket, and the blotter was covered with his doodles.

Not to mention the laptop he had placed at the edge of the desk. The computer was one he brought from home. He had several recent models, all of them with programs he needed to scour the Internet for information not on the surface.

Some of his connections in Metropolis were doing the same thing, looking for anything that might link to the kidnapping — a leak of moneys, a passing remark in a chat room, a seemingly innocent query about Lionel Luthor's personal habits. So far, Lex hadn't gotten any reports, but the program he'd set up to do the same thing hadn't come up with anything either.

The silence frustrated him the most and, if he had to be honest with himself, also worried him the most. Kidnappers with an agenda revealed that agenda. Kidnappers who had no real desire to release their victim often didn't send out ransom notes either.

He sat down at the desk and, with the flick of a thumb, knocked the computer out of sleep mode. An envelope blinked on the side of the screen.

He had missed the alarm notifying him that he had e-mail. He reached for his pager and double-checked it. Nothing there, even though he had set it up for the notification.

His scalp prickled. He supposed if he actually had hair on the back of his neck, it would have risen.

With one shaking finger, he double-clicked the mouse, automatically opening his e-mail program. He had fifty new messages, most of them garbage — reporters, weirdos responding to the news reports, a few internal memos.

But one did catch his eye.

It was from LL, and the message header was also LL. The message had a red exclamation point next to it, marking it as urgent.

Lex realized he was holding his breath. He let the air out slowly, remembering the yoga calming techniques he'd learned at one boarding school or another.

The e-mail had an attachment, and it had gotten through his firewall. Still, he didn't trust that it was virus-free.

He silently cursed himself. He should have brought the e-mail in on a completely clean computer, not one he was running other work on. He could forward it, he supposed, but he decided to take the risk. He would open it.

But first, he ran his antivirus program. It didn't delete the e-mail, so he clicked the e-mail open. It read:

```
Lex Luthor:
   For $30 million you can have your father
back.
   Payouts like this:
   Ten million cash up front.
   Twenty million moved to a numbered account
which we will give you later.
   When the money is safely in our hands, we
will deliver your father to a spot of our
choosing.
   Do not answer this e-mail. We will contact
you.

   P.S. The attachment is proof of our good
intentions.
```

Before clicking on the attachment, Lex disconnected the computer from the office network and unhooked the modem. If the attachment did have a virus or a worm, he wasn't going to send it cascading through the entire corporation.

Once he finished that, he opened the attachments. The first contained several jpeg files, all of them photographs of his father.

The first few came from the limousine, as his father was pushed inside. The next was of his father sitting against a white curtain, his legs sprawled before him, his eyes open but blank.

Lionel Luthor's eyes were never blank.

Lex made himself swallow hard. He needed to get these photographs to someone who could tell him if his father was dead or if he was just doped up. He needed to resolve this—

Then he opened the last attachment. It was a small piece of video. His father, tied to a chair in a darkened room, the camera tight on his face and chest. This morning's *Daily Planet*—the edition that came out just after midnight—was pinned to his shirt. His father's eyes were closed, his head bobbing up and down like that of a man trying to sleep on an airplane. His chest rose and fell as well.

At that point, at least, his father had been breathing.

Then the video ended. Lex played it again, trying to see anything that might give him a clue as to where his father might be. He didn't recognize anything, but that didn't mean that someone with the proper equipment couldn't find details that would help in the investigation.

He would take this to the computer labs here at LuthorCorp, as well as to some of his shadier friends. They'd find parts of it that he wouldn't be able to see—a clue, a hint, something.

In all of that material, there had to be something.

Lex saved the e-mail to disk, then closed the laptop. From now on, he would consider it contaminated. He would have to use the backup he had at his apartment to continue the web search.

He slipped the disk into his pocket and stood.

"Mr. Luthor?" His father's secretary stood in the doorway. She was a timid thing, younger than Lex liked, certainly not the standard executive secretary material.

Of course his father had someone else—an older, wiser employee—do the actual office management. Lex had the uncomfortable and unspoken opinion that his father hired pretty secretaries as eye candy or something more.

He didn't want to think about the something more.

"What?" he said in a tone that let her know he was very busy and didn't appreciate the interruption.

"We just got this fax in, sir. I thought you'd want to see it." She extended her hand. In it was a plain sheet of paper. The paper shook.

He grabbed the laptop, slipped it under his arm, and walked over to her. She leaned against the doorframe like a soldier afraid to leave her post. He snatched the fax out of her hand.

The print was slightly blurry—the fax machine needed fresh toner—but the words were easy enough to read.

Lex Luthor, Check your e-mail

He looked at the sheet, searching for the originating fax's I.D., but there was nothing obvious.

"Thanks," he said to the secretary.

She raised large brown eyes to his. He saw both fear and worry in them, and he thought it amazing that someone could have those feelings—real feelings—for his father.

"Aren't you going to look at your e-mail?" she asked, her voice shaking.

"I already have." He gave her his warmest smile. "But thanks."

Then he slipped past her, taking the fax with him. Halfway down the hall, he stopped.

"Which fax machine did this come off of?" he asked.

"The one in Mr. Luthor's office."

Of course. Lex nodded. "Make sure no one goes near that machine until I do."

"Yes, sir." She had moved away from the door. "What about the FBI, sir?"

"I'll take care of them," Lex said.

After he took care of other things himself.

Clark sat in the front seat of Chloe's car and stared out the window at the passing trees. Pete and Lana sat in the back, not speaking. Chloe drove carefully for once, perhaps remembering Clark's comments from the day before about cars going into the water.

Amazing how much difference a day made. The weather still hadn't returned to normal, but the intense heat of yesterday afternoon had dissipated. So had Chloe's caution. Instead of parking outside the gate, as she had done the day before, she bounced the car through the ruts left by the police cars and emergency vehicles.

Weeds and rocks scraped the car's undercarriage, but Chloe didn't seem to care. She drove like a woman possessed, convinced that she'd get a scoop yet again.

The pictures in that afternoon's *Torch* had been impressive. To Clark's dismay, the main photo on the front page had been of him pulling Danny's body from the water. The only good part about it had been that the sunlight was behind Clark, putting a halo around the back of his head and placing his face in shadow. Still, anyone who knew him would recognize him.

He hated the notoriety. No matter how much he told Chloe that, she didn't seem to understand it. The story was the story was the story to her. She never thought about the consequences of what she printed.

The consequences in this case would be more than Clark's notoriety as a local boy who did an occasional good deed. The consequences also had to do with his parents, who liked the publicity less than he did.

They wouldn't like him coming out here again either. They would probably have told him to call the police.

But he didn't want to send the police on a wild-goose chase, and part of him didn't want to be right about the pond, either. The fact that he, Lana, and Chloe discovered the first two bodies could be seen as coincidence. Finding the second set—or at least knowing where they were—might put them under suspicion.

Calling in a hunch and having it be wrong might do the same thing.

The Franklin driveway was filled with potholes from the chilly winter. One of the first things Clark's dad did every spring was repair the road. That way, he said, the equipment would remain in better shape year-round. Better to spend a few dollars up front than pay for it all later on.

Clark watched the house go past as Chloe followed the driveway between the barns. Yellow police tape held the house doors closed and the barn doors as well.

"Chloe," he said, his voice sounding loud in the quiet car, "did your source say anything about the barns?"

"No." She was frowning as she stared at the road. Her car wasn't made for these kinds of conditions, and she was obviously beginning to realize it. "Why?"

"The police tape on the barn doors," Clark said.

"I suspect this whole place is cordoned off as a crime scene,"

Pete said, "whether they found anything inside or not."

"Maybe." But Clark didn't like it. Maybe there was more evidence in the barns, more reasons for the police theory.

"Do you think we should check it out?" Lana asked.

"When we're done at the pond," Chloe said.

"You think we're really going to find anything there?" Pete asked.

"I hope not." The tires caught in a rut, forcing Chloe to struggle with the wheel. Clark fought the urge to reach over and help her. He'd done that once, and she'd been furious at him.

"So maybe the barn would be a good idea," Lana said.

"I want to see where this pond is first," Chloe said. "It bugs me that the police missed it."

"If they didn't mention the barns, maybe they didn't mention the pond either," Clark said.

Chloe shook her head. "I asked specifically where they'd searched. They mentioned the farm itself, which anyone would know included the barns. And they said they looked over the rest of the property. But if Clark's right and that fence looks like the area is fenced off, they might not have thought of that as property."

The car jolted again. Clark's knees hit the dashboard. The taller he got, the more he hated small cars.

The road kept going straight, leading toward the fields. But on the left side, Clark saw faint lines, indicating the old road. The lines were hidden by thick weeds and brush, but it didn't take X-ray vision to see through that. Just experience with farms and old, abandoned roads.

"Stop here," he said.

Chloe slammed on the brakes. The tires caught and held, sliding the car on the gravel. Dust rose behind them, as if they'd been caught in a horrible wind storm.

"Jeez, Chloe," Pete said. "You could've eased to a stop."

"When you have your own car, you can ease," she said, tucking a strand of hair behind her ear. She popped the door open, sending clouds of dust inside.

Clark coughed and got out, standing up so that his head rose above the dust cloud.

Pete climbed out after him. "I don't see anything."

"Wait until the dust clears," Lana said from the other side of the car.

"I always wondered where that saying came from," Clark said.

"That's not what I mean," Pete said. "I mean, I didn't see anything to make us stop."

"Me, either," Chloe said. "But Clark did, and he seems to have this X-ray vision lately, so I trust him."

Clark felt his cheeks heat up. But he didn't say anything, knowing that Chloe was just turning a phrase.

Still, it came awfully close to the bone.

The dust was settling. Down in this hollow behind the farm buildings, the air was thick and close. It also smelled faintly of loam, rotting vegetation, and stagnant water.

"I see it." Lana stepped toward the faint tracks that Clark had seen. "This was a road once, notice?"

Pete and Clark stepped around the car. Chloe was staring at the tracks.

"I wouldn't have noticed that," she said.

"Living on a farm," Clark said, "you tend to notice the land."

"Yeah, well, it's creepy down here." Pete rubbed his left arm as if it ached. "You guys came down here yesterday?"

"No," Lana said. "We were up at the top of the driveway. That's when we saw the—you know. Danny."

Pete nodded.

"It doesn't look like anyone's been down here," Chloe said. She was studying the gravel road. Her car's tracks appeared to be the only ones made recently.

"The police should have checked this out," Lana said. "It's awfully close to the house."

"But it does look unused," Pete said.

Clark shaded his eyes with his hand. From the back of the house, he had a hunch this dip in the road didn't look like much. The graveled area made it all seem like extra parking instead of an actual road.

"I think the police are more focused on finding the Franklins' truck than on searching the property," Chloe said.

"What if the rest of the family is alive somewhere?" Pete asked.

"I don't think they'd be hanging around here." Lana had walked deeper into the weeds. "These tracks go into that underbrush."

Her movements sent up a cloud of gnats. She swatted at her arms absently.

A mosquito circled Pete. He slapped at it. "Isn't it early for bugs?"

"It was the heat yesterday," Clark said. "Better hope for one more good freeze."

"You're a sick man," Pete said. "You know I hate winter."

"I thought you hated bugs more," Clark said as he walked toward Lana. She had stopped just at the edge of the underbrush.

"See?" Lana said. "I don't think anyone's been in there for a long time."

"Someone has." Chloe pointed toward a bit of material hanging off a twig. The material was green flannel, almost hidden by the buds that had come out in the warm weather.

Chloe had slung both cameras around her neck. She picked one up, and took a picture.

"I don't see how anyone got through that tangle," Pete said.

Clark pointed to a dark space, hidden in shadow. "Deer bed," he said. "There's a thin animal trail through there. That's how someone got in and out."

"We can't go that way," Chloe said. "We'll contaminate the crime scene."

"We have no idea if it is a crime scene." Lana sounded prickly, which was unusual for her.

"I can smell stagnant water," Clark said. "Can't you?"

Lana sniffed. "Brackish. Yeah, I can."

"That's where your mosquitoes came from," Chloe said to Pete.

Then she walked past all of them and ducked into the dark space that Clark had seen. Somehow she managed to avoid the flannel.

"Wow," she said, her voice sounding far away. "Shades of Middle Earth."

"What does that mean?" Pete asked.

"I'm not sure I want to know," Clark said.

"Haven't you read Tolkien?" Lana asked, ducking in the space after Chloe.

"Saw the movie," Pete whispered to Clark. "Does that count?"

"Probably not to Lana," Clark whispered back.

He started to follow when he heard Lana whistle.

"Not Middle Earth, Chloe," Lana said, her voice strangely faint. "More like *Alice's Adventures through the Looking Glass.* All we need is a giant caterpillar and a hookah pipe."

The brambles caught in Clark's hair, and something bit the bare skin on the back of his hand. It almost felt like that something spit the hunk of skin out before flying away.

Clark grinned. He didn't get bitten by bugs very often, and those that did bite him always seemed to react like they'd tasted something bad.

"I'm getting eaten alive here." Pete was just behind Clark. Even though he was smaller, he was really shaking the underbrush.

"It's your cologne," Chloe said. Her voice sounded closer now. "Didn't anyone tell you not to wear cologne in the woods?"

"I wasn't planning to crawl around in the woods when I got up this morning," Pete said. "And it's not cologne. It's aftershave."

"Oops, sorry," Chloe said. "Forgot about the mysteries of shaving."

Clark stepped out of the bramble into an area touched with darkness. Giant mushrooms grew around the base of a nearby tree. Here the air had the smell of perpetual damp. The ground was marshy.

Chloe stood near the tree. Lana had taken a few steps farther, leaving footprints in the muck.

Pete burst out of the bramble, stumbling on a rotting log to Clark's left. "Wow," Pete said. "It almost feels like we're not in Kansas anymore."

"We have votes for Oz, Alice, and Middle Earth," Lana said. "You want to add an allusion, Clark? We're taking literary and movie-related, apparently."

But Clark didn't want to add anything. This place was making him very uncomfortable. Not because there were meteor rocks—there weren't—or anything obviously dangerous, but because it felt so isolated.

He looked at the ground, saw that the tracks were long gone. A small pile of dirt had gathered near the tree. It was probably quite cold back here in the winter, and the last of the snow might have melted only a few days ago.

That wasn't good for tracking. Neither was the marshy aspect. Lana's deep footprints were already filling with water, disappearing almost as quickly as she had made them.

"I don't see a pond," Pete said.

"That's because we're standing on the edge of it, unless I miss my guess." Chloe took one picture for good measure.

"This isn't a pond," Lana said. "This is a marsh."

"That's why they made their own pond," Clark said. "They couldn't control the water here, and it probably got contaminated real easily."

"Besides, who would want to come here regularly?" Pete asked, and shuddered.

"It looks like it gets deeper up ahead." Chloe pointed to an area around the tree.

Clark stopped near her. His shoes were getting wet. The ground was saturated here.

"This is the perfect place to hide bodies," Chloe said. "If Mr. Franklin did kill his family, wouldn't he have hidden them here instead of the other pond?"

"Probably another point in the argument against him doing it." Lana was the farthest forward. She raised up on her toes and scanned the area in front of her. "Although I don't know how anyone could have gotten much farther in here without getting really wet himself."

"Could always clean up back at the farm," Pete said. "Was there mud inside the house?"

"Not that we could see," Chloe said.

"There's still an old pump outside," Clark said. "I used it yesterday. Anyone could have cleaned up there."

Pete nodded. "How're we going to search this?"

"We're not," Lana said. "Not without the right gear. It gets deeper just ahead of me."

"I'm going to use the telephoto," Chloe said. "Sometimes it shows me a lot."

She brought the camera to her face and adjusted the lens as if it were a telescope.

Clark walked over to Lana. He sank deeper in the muck than any of them, but he was bigger and weighed more. If anything had been thrown back here, it would have been very hard to find.

Lana kept looking, moving her head, just as Chloe was.

Clark stood next to Lana and looked, too. The sun dappled through the trees. Flies buzzed ahead, and small pools of gnats rose like they were a single creature.

A lot of the surrounding trees had rotted, and moss grew on their sides. The brackish smell was thick, but not quite overwhelming. It was an odor of the land, something that Clark had grown up with.

He could see why the Franklins never used this part of the land, and why the map showed it fenced off. He had a hunch the fence had rotted away long ago. The land was too saturated to use as farmland. There was probably a creek nearby, close enough to feed this marshland—or perhaps there were underground springs.

Whatever caused the water to seep through the ground like this must have made this area hell in the summer, with the heat, the smell, and the bugs.

"I think I see some flannel up there." Chloe pointed toward an old oak that looked like it had been split by lightning a generation ago. She kept her camera to her face, then adjusted the lens. "I'm pretty sure."

"Let me see," Lana said, reaching for the camera. Chloe handed it to her, and Lana put it up to her eyes.

Clark couldn't see anything from this distance. But he would be able to see in the water.

He used his X-ray vision, scanning first the water ahead of them, and then moving toward the split oak, little bit by little bit.

The marsh was deeper than he expected, and filled with tiny bones, most of them from birds or animals that had gotten caught in the water, or perhaps prey that had gotten eaten there. Little pointed skulls, from some kind of rodent, littered one entire section like someone was keeping a collection of them. But the skulls were scattered enough that he knew the collection was an animal's not a human's.

When he got to the split oak, the water grew even deeper. The tiny bones he'd seen closer in were missing here, as if this was too deep even for the animals to mess with.

"I think I see something," Pete said. He was crouching, looking through the underbrush. Everyone turned in the direction he was pointing.

Another ripped piece of flannel and broken branches, a lot of them. The breaks looked pretty recent.

"Do you think it's shallower over there?" Chloe asked.

Lana brought the camera down. "You'd either have to test it or have local knowledge."

"I wouldn't want to test anything in this place," Pete said.

Clark scanned that area with his special vision and saw nothing as well. He returned his gaze to the oak, looking at the area around it. It took a moment for his eyes to readjust to the X-ray vision, but when they did, he saw what he had missed before.

Two hands, entwined, caught in weeds along the bottom. The hands were attached to arms, but Clark couldn't see how far they went, or if there was an actual body behind them.

"Well, Eagle Eyes," Chloe said to him. "Do you see anything?"

"I don't know," he said. "Can I have the camera?"

Lana handed it to him. Clark put the camera to his eyes, and adjusted the lens. It did work like a telescope. The oak tree was much clearer. He could even see the damaged bark.

Something clung to that bark—not just flannel, but strands of brown hair, too long to belong to anything but a human being. And, near the tree's roots, a footprint big enough to be his own.

"Yeah," Clark said. "Some hair near that flannel, and a print near the base of the tree."

Pete slapped his arm and everyone jumped, looking at him

in surprise. "I told you," he said. "I'm getting eaten alive back here."

Chloe took the camera from Clark and looked where he'd been looking.

Pete slapped his arm again.

"And," Clark said, not sure how much he should stretch the truth. "I thought I saw something else."

"What?" Chloe was adjusting the lens. "I see the hair—it's really fine. Nice work, Clark."

"Near the print. See that thing along the edge of the water? Is that a sleeve?"

He knew there were some leaves floating along the surface. He hoped she would misread one.

"It could be," she said.

Lana looked up at him, her eyes wide. "Are you going to check it out again, Clark?"

"In that water?" Pete said. "He'd have to shower for a week to start smelling like a person again."

Clark blessed him silently. "The last time, I went in because I had the mistaken thought that Danny was alive. I don't see any reason to go in this time."

Chloe took a few shots, then eased the camera down, holding it in one hand. "Especially since the police aren't going to be happy with us coming here today."

"Even though we might have found something."

"Especially if we found something," Chloe said. "Discovering another body? Or two? Or three? That's going to look some-what suspicious."

"You're not suggesting we just leave, are you?" Lana asked.

Chloe shook her head. "Not at all. I'm just warning you all that this is going to get ugly if there truly is someone there."

Pete slapped his arm a third time. "Well, can we make our decision near the car? I'm not enjoying providing dinner for a whole host of baby mosquitoes."

"That's mama mosquitoes," Lana said.

"I don't really care," Pete said. "I'm getting welts."

"My phone's back at the car," Chloe said. "I'm going to get a few more pictures. You want to call the authorities, Pete?"

"You mind if I crawl inside and close the doors and windows while I do it?"

Chloe gave him an absent smile. "Not at all."

"Then I'm all for calling the authorities." Pete slipped back through the brambles. As he went through, he cursed once, then cried "ouch!" followed by another slapping sound.

"I'll go help him," Lana said. "There's nothing more we can do here."

Clark stayed while Chloe took even more pictures. He walked along the edge of the deeper water, using his special vision to see if he could see more of the bodies. He had nearly reached the section where the other flannel was when he could see farther.

The arms were attached to two bodies. He'd been half-hoping that the arms were remains washed into the marsh from an old graveyard or something. But the bones didn't look old, not like some of the animal bones.

And these bodies were entwined together, almost as if they'd been wrapped together. Too deep to be seen from the surface.

Clark hoped his lie would hold—at least well enough for the police to bring in divers.

And, at the same time, he hoped he was wrong about the newness of the corpses. Because if they had been dumped here recently, then he was looking at at least two more Franklins.

The rest of the family might have been hidden in this marsh. Only with the help of the police would anyone know for sure.

CHAPTER 10

So far, this day had been one of the worst of Lionel Luthor's life—and it looked like it had just gotten worse.

Luthor was tied even more tightly to the chair than he had been before. That morning, he had taken advantage of his captor's shower and managed to slide his chair toward the kitchen. With the give in his ropes, Luthor figured he could find something sharp in there and cut the ropes off.

But he hadn't counted on the uneven flooring. Just as he reached the middle part of the room, one of the chair legs hit a raised floorboard. The chair toppled precariously for a moment, then fell to its side.

Without his hands free, there was no way he could break the fall. He landed, hard, on his left elbow. The cracking sound he heard and the pain shooting up his arm probably had nothing to do with the cheapness of the rotting wood flooring.

The sound of his fall reverberated through the entire place, and the shower shut off. No matter how hard Luthor tried, he couldn't get his chair upright again.

Still, his captor's reaction when he stumbled out of the bathroom, hastily pulling a pair of pants over his wet frame, was "Oh, crap, Mr. Luthor. We can't let them catch you like this."

Them, as if *they* were someone other than this scrawny captor with his beady eyes, two-day growth of beard, and nervous tics. Luthor figured this guy was the dumb one, the cousin or the brother who had thought he was going along for a good time and a lot of beer, and instead got stuck with all the heavy work.

The man managed to pull Luthor's chair upright—this captor was amazingly strong for such a scrawny man—but he was shaking as he did so.

"Mr. Luthor, you don't understand what you're dealing with. This isn't some movie. You get outta here, and you'll just get lost outside. Then they'll shoot you. Better to stay put, hope that your son comes up with the money, and then we can all go home."

Luthor let him talk, hoping the man would say something a bit more revealing, but he never did. Over the space of the day, they did come up with a rhythm of sorts.

When it became clear that something had snapped in Luthor's arm—the swelling and bruising told them that much—the man decided he could untie that hand. As a result, Luthor was able to feed himself—awkwardly (the arm was truly injured)—and drink liquids.

He was also able to use the facilities—with the man tying his good arm up to a towel rack first. Luthor tried and was unable to untie the hand with his injured arm. Reaching across his stomach to the tied hand was one of the most painful things Luthor had ever done in his life. Still, he did his best, and nearly passed out as a result.

His captor spent most of the afternoon monitoring a computer in the back room, and not speaking a lot. Luthor heard the warning bells, the sound of fingers against keys, and an occasional curse, but little more.

Luthor had just been about to see if he could talk his captor into some sort of lenient treatment—something that might give Luthor an advantage—when he heard the sound of tires on gravel. Through the windows in front of him, he saw a large truck pull up outside.

The truck had once been red, but had faded in the harsh Kansas weather to a dirty rust. Dents on the side of the bed showed that the truck had been heavily used.

As the truck wheeled to a stop, Luthor realized that he hadn't seen the limo. He wondered what they had done with it. These captors were smarter than he originally thought. They knew the limo would give them away, and they hadn't kept it nearby.

His captor came out of the back room, saw the truck, and actually turned pale. Luthor thought that was interesting. He had employees who were afraid of him, but they only had that reaction when they had done something wrong.

Had this man done something he shouldn't have?

Luthor didn't want to contemplate it.

His captor came closer and put his hands on Luthor's shoulders. The gesture was both comforting and menacing at the same time. Luthor wasn't used to someone in his personal space, but the man's grip was light, almost friendly.

"Mr. Luthor, these guys here, they're not nice men. Don't piss them off, whatever you do. They still haven't decided what to do with you after the money comes. They're pretty—"

Footsteps on the porch made his captor shut up and back away. The hands left Luthor's shoulders, and a chill ran down his spine.

When the door opened, letting in sunlight and the smell of new spring grass, Luthor made himself breathe easily. This could all be a game they were playing to make him reveal something.

Well, he knew game theory better than anyone, and he wasn't going to play by their rules. He was going to invent his own.

The two men who came in the door looked familiar in that same archetypal way that the first captor did. Luthor wasn't sure if he'd actually seen them before, or if they were just the standard rednecks from central casting.

These two seemed even more true to type than his captor. They were large, square, and solid. They had full beards that hid most of their features, and they wore John Deere hats pulled halfway down their foreheads. All he could see were eyes, surrounded by sun-reddened skin. Blue eyes, watery, and yet full of menace.

The first time he saw the leader's eyes and their malicious intent was the first time Luthor truly believed he might not make it out of this situation alive.

"Look how the mighty hath fallen," said the second man as he stomped into the room. His boots left more dried mud on the hardwood floor.

The first man remained silent, his gaze never leaving Luthor's face.

"Don't got nothing to say for yourself, Lionel?" the second man said.

"I'm not one for pleading," Luthor said, "and I doubt a polite request to leave will get me anywhere."

"You got it in one." The second man laughed. He walked away from the door, heading into the kitchen, and opened the refrigerator, pulling out a can of beer.

Luthor's original captor watched this with more trepidation than Luthor felt. "How'd it go?" his captor asked the first man.

The man finally broke his gaze away from Luthor's. Luthor felt its loss like the loss of a physical presence. "Dunno. That's up to the kid."

"I hear the kid hates his dad," the captor said.

"That true, Lionel? Can't even get your own kid to warm up to you?" The second man grabbed a chair, pulled it over, and sat down, legs spread. He clutched the beer in his left hand.

"What does Lex have to do with this?" Luthor asked, even though he had a hunch. He simply figured the more he could get these people to speak to him, the better chance he had of understanding them. The better he understood them, the easier it would be to play them.

If the ache and swelling in his arm, and the headache they were creating didn't interfere with his powers of concentration too badly.

"Only everything." The first man spoke for the first time, and Luthor recognized the voice from the limo. The one he'd thought didn't sound as educated as one of the others. Was his captor the educated one then? Or was it all an act?

"Think the kid cares enough to pay for you?" the second man said. "Because if he don't, we're all screwed."

"No, we're not." The first man cuffed his partner's head hard enough to dislodge his John Deere hat. The hat tumbled into his partner's lap, and as he bent forward, Luthor noted that he was balding on top. Not as young then as Luthor had initially thought.

Luthor waited in silence. He wanted to know how they wouldn't be screwed if Lex failed to pay the ransom.

"C'mon. I thought this was about the cash," the second man said.

"It's about revenge." Luthor's captor spoke from behind him. It almost felt like his captor was watching his back, but that couldn't be. There was a dynamic here that Luthor didn't entirely understand.

He felt that dynamic was the key to his survival. He would watch, listen, and work it out.

"Revenge?" he asked. "For what?"

"For everything, Lionel. You do so much crap to people you forget everything you done." The second man took another sip of his beer. Then he put the cap back over his bald spot. "See, if you was just a bad man instead of a truly evil old fart, you'd have an idea what's got us so riled up. But you've done so much horrible stuff over the years, we could be getting you back for any old thing. In fact, I think it's better you don't know. You can imagine lots worse stuff than we can ever come up with."

That was probably true—at least of the second man. He didn't look like someone with a lot of imagination. But that first man, the man of few words, the obvious leader, he seemed to have imagination to spare.

"What've we got so far?" Luthor's captor asked. "Any word?"

"Not from LuthorCorp, directly." The first man took a root beer out of the refrigerator. No hope then that they'd all get drunk and stupid. The first man wasn't going to allow that.

"What about indirectly?" Luthor's captor asked. He sounded eager. Maybe he wasn't as nice a guy as Luthor had initially thought.

The first man smiled. It was a slow, cold smile. "Stock's down ten points, and still plummeting. Seems the entire country thinks LuthorCorp can't survive without you, Mr. Luthor."

Stock spirals happened. If Luthor got free, the stocks would recover. If he didn't, and the first man's analysis was right, then everything Luthor had worked for his entire life would be lost, lost because he was.

He didn't let his dismay over that show on his face. If there was one thing he learned in the field of business, it was how to keep his emotions off his face.

"So," said Number Two. "Tell us about your kid."

"What do you want to know?" Luthor asked.

"How come he hasn't responded to our note yet."

"I trust you gave him a way to respond," Luthor said, careful to keep the hope out of his voice. If they had given Lex a way to respond, then there would be a way to trace these miscreants. The day would be simply that, a bad day, easily forgotten.

"Not directly." Number One smiled. He had a chipped bottom

tooth, right up front. His teeth were coffee-stained, the chip worst of all.

"Then how can you be certain he hasn't responded?" Luthor said.

"No financial activity in the accounts," Number Two said. "He should be gathering the funds now."

Luthor's stomach clenched. "Well, it sounds to me as if you've made getting funds difficult for him. You know most corporations don't have a lot of cash reserves, and our lines of credit are tied to our stock price."

"English, Lionel. Speakee English," Number Two said.

"He is," said Luthor's captor. "He's saying that you screwed yourself."

"We screwed ourselves, friend," Number One said, and in that moment, Luthor knew that they were smarter than he had originally given them credit for. *Friend*. They weren't going to slip and admit names.

Although it did bother him that they allowed him to see their faces. That didn't bode well for him. Perhaps they didn't want him to know names because they were going to let him talk to Lex on the phone, and perhaps they didn't care if he saw who they were because they planned to kill him once they had the money.

That's what he would do if he decided to stoop to something as mindless as kidnapping.

"You think that makes sense?" Number One was asking Luthor's captor.

His captor shrugged. "Big business isn't my forte."

"Well, money's money, and you can't tell me that one of the largest corporations in the world doesn't got enough assets to cover ten million in cash."

Luthor's throat tightened. Ten million? They were only asking ten million for him? And then he felt a faint amusement at himself, worrying how much criminals—criminals who just admitted they had no idea about big business—thought he was worth.

"You sure that kid of yours'll come through?" Number Two asked again.

Luthor realized he hadn't answered the question, and not because he was dodging it. He truly didn't know the answer.

He had no idea what Lex would do.

He would hope that Lex would use all the resources at his fingertips—and Luthor had left him with a lot of resources—to find this place, rescue him, and take care of these three men. Luthor also hoped that Lex was savvy enough to pretend to play their games.

But Lex was becoming more and more of a mystery. He wasn't making the mistakes that he used to, and he was thinking more on his own.

The thoughts he had unnerved Luthor. Lex had tested off the charts in intelligence and, it seemed to Luthor, never used that brainpower, until recently. Someday Lex would realize that he was smarter than his father, smarter than everyone around him, and he would take advantage of that.

The conversation they'd had a few weeks ago suddenly floated through Luthor's mind. He could actually hear Lex's voice in his head:

You know what those emperors you're so fond of talking about were really afraid of? That their own sons would become successful and return to Rome at the head of their own armies.

When Luthor had queried him about that, asking if Lex was going to come to Metropolis with his own army, Lex had dodged the question.

Now he didn't need an army. All he had to do was sit on his hands, wait, and his dad's head would be delivered to him on a silver platter.

Perhaps literally.

Luthor shuddered. The day had definitely grown worse.

◆◆◆

It took the sheriff's office an hour to arrive, and then it was only one car, unmarked. Clark felt nervous watching it come down the driveway, kicking up dust as it weaved its way toward them.

The four of them were leaning against Chloe's car as they

waited. Lana had made a second call just to make sure someone was coming, and she'd been about to make a third, when they'd heard the car's wheels squeal around the gate in front of the house.

The single car bothered all of them, and without speaking to each other, they gathered next to each other for support.

"This is the police, right?" Pete asked.

"Anyone with the right technology can listen in on cell phones," Chloe said.

"What does that mean?" Lana asked.

"It means Chloe isn't sure," Clark said. "But I am. That's deputy Roberts driving."

Deputy Roberts had arrived at yesterday's scene. He hadn't treated them well, but he had, once he realized the seriousness of the situation, handled the crime scene as well as possible.

Another man sat in the car with him. As the car fishtailed its way down the hill, Pete stood up.

"I've watched too much TV," he said.

"What does that mean?" Chloe asked.

"It means I'm not willing to believe these guys are good guys just because they're police. Shouldn't we have some kind of contingency plan? I mean, what if they did the killing?"

"Why?" Lana asked. "What reason would they have for killing Danny and Betty?"

Pete shrugged. "That's why they call these kinds of cases a mystery."

"We'll be all right," Clark said, but he was braced as well. He didn't think Roberts was involved in anything illegal, but now that Pete had put that thought in Clark's head, Clark was not going to let anyone harm his friends.

"Oh, yeah?" Pete said. "They got guns. We don't."

"If they did this, they're not going to use guns," Chloe said. "Danny and Betty were strangled."

"The police didn't do anything," Lana said. "You guys are just paranoid."

The sheriff's car skidded to a stop in front of them. The dust cloud continued forward, enveloping them in dirty brown air for the second time that afternoon. Clark's eyes stung. Next to him, Lana coughed and Pete made spitting sounds. Only Chloe remained quiet.

The car doors opened and slammed shut. It took a moment for Clark to be able to see clearly. Roberts and his partner, the same man who had spoken to them the day before, whose name they had not gotten, walked toward them.

"You guys just like hanging out down here or you got some kind of agenda?" Roberts asked.

"We're friends of Danny's," Lana said.

"Strange way you got of showing it. Snooping around where you don't belong."

The partner hung back and watched. Both men were in street clothes again.

"Did you check out the marsh?" Chloe asked.

"Why?" Roberts asked.

"Because if you did," Clark said, "we bothered you for no reason. But if you didn't, there's something down there you might want to see."

"Something you kids put there?"

"No," Pete said, sounding very perturbed. "We're being good citizens here. What's your problem?"

The partner stepped forward, putting a hand on Roberts's arm. "We're not used to young people taking an active interest in an investigation."

"We're not used to losing friends," Lana said.

The partner's mouth twitched, and Clark could have sworn the man was suppressing a smile. "Well, then—"

"I'll take it, Davies." Roberts took one step closer to them. He seemed to be trying to intimidate them. It wasn't working with Clark.

But Roberts didn't stop in front of Clark. He stopped in front of Chloe. "I didn't appreciate those pictures in the *Torch*. We need your film for the investigation."

"I didn't use film," Chloe said. "The pictures are digital. You want me to e-mail them to you?"

"Listen, young lady, you're already in trouble for being at this crime scene. You don't want to compound it."

"She's a reporter," Clark said. "She's doing her job."

"She's a high school student," Roberts said, "and she's butting in."

"Without her, you wouldn't even have a case," Pete said. "Her and Lana and Clark. And they're doing your work for you. Stop blustering and listen to them. We saw something in that marsh. You guys need to check it out."

Roberts's mouth thinned. He obviously didn't appreciate the criticism. But Davies stepped beside him, clearly taking over this part of the investigation.

"How'd you know there was a marsh there?" he asked.

"There's an old plat map in the *Torch* office," Clark said. "I was looking at it, and saw a pond marked on it and a fence line. We figured most people wouldn't have thought it was part of the Franklin property—"

"And we couldn't remember seeing any other pond or fence for that matter," Chloe said. "We thought if we missed it, you might have."

"So you came to investigate yourselves," Roberts said. "You coulda called it in."

"Look how long it took you to respond to our call today," Lana snapped. Clark looked down at her in surprise. She had color in both cheeks. She was angry at the treatment the group was getting. "Imagine how you would have responded if we had asked you to look at the marsh without knowing if there was anything to our hunch."

Roberts's gaze flattened, but this time, Davies smiled. "Point and set to the lady. You convinced me. Now someone show me this stuff you found."

"I'll do it." Chloe led him toward the dark opening in the bramble.

"I'll go with you," Clark said. He wasn't going to let Chloe go alone with anyone into that area, not after the little speech Pete gave. It was just enough to make Clark extra cautious— and a little paranoid.

He stumbled under the brambles, felt the gnats attack again, and then the brackish stench of standing water hit him. Chloe and Davies were already standing at the edge of the marsh, Chloe pointing at the split oak tree.

Davies was taking her seriously. He used the telephoto lens she offered him and looked at the bits of fabric. He didn't see any body, of course, or the fingers Clark had mentioned, but that didn't matter.

As he handed the camera back to Chloe, Davies said, "We should've checked this out yesterday. I even came down here. I had no idea that this was more than an uncrossable thicket. We'll radio for some divers."

Clark shuddered at the idea of going into the water, but he knew it was their job. He just wished they'd hurry up about it. He didn't like being the only one with the knowledge that there were at least two more bodies in that marsh.

And he wanted to find out who they were.

In a tiny room behind the Club Noir in one of the seedier neighborhoods of Metropolis, Lex stood, his hands behind his back. He'd been cautioned years ago not to touch anything in here, and he never had.

The room had fluorescent overhead lights, which he had never seen on. Instead, most of the light came from a dozen computer screens of various shapes and sizes. Over one desk, a small halogen lamp burned.

The stale air smelled of Cheetos and mochacinos, along with the faint scents of alcohol, perfume, and cigarettes filtering in from the club. Three teenage boys whom Lex only knew by their screen monikers—DeadMan, Terror, and Aces—sat with their backs to each other, their fingers working the keyboards.

An old schoolmate, whose real name Lex had vowed not to repeat, sat at the largest screen working the digital images. He was a year older than Lex and had dropped out of boarding school when the FBI came after him for hacking. His real name, Phil Brodsky, didn't have the menace it should have.

Brodsky could open any file, find any piece of information, dig through any encoded system he happened to stumble across.

And he stumbled across a lot of them.

Lex liked keeping him around. Brodsky had taught Lex everything he knew about computer hacking and then some, but Lex didn't have the natural talent for it that Brodsky did. Brodsky was almost an idiot savant. It was as if he became the code.

Lex had to think his way through each and every piece of it. Hacking, while logical, was too much like homework for him. Lex preferred to work with people, to get them to reveal their weaknesses, instead of finding those weaknesses hidden in some obscure part of the Internet.

"Not very sophisticated really," Terror said. He'd been assigned to trace the e-mail. The other two kids were working on the video images and the photographs.

Brodsky had the tough task. He was going through the security tape, frame by frame, searching for something, anything that would help Lex find his father.

"They used *A Luddite's Guide to Computer Hacking*. It's pretty clear." Terror leaned back and cracked his knuckles. He was the one who lived on Cheetos. The orange stains on his fingertips appeared to be permanent.

"You mean *An Idiot's Guide*?" Lex asked.

"Nope," Terror said. "I mean *A Luddite's Guide*."

"Would modern Luddites even know what that word means?" Lex asked.

"Not if they were, like, you know, our age. But if they're old," DeadMan said. "Those kinda books usually appeal to old guys anyway. Most guys who really want to do this stuff, they learn by doing, you know."

"And they're computer oriented," Lex said, "so they download their information."

"Exactamundo, dude," DeadMan said.

Of Brodsky's three sidekicks, DeadMan was the one Lex liked the least. He wasn't as talented as the other two, and he always had a chip on his shoulder when Lex appeared. Lex knew that DeadMan was posturing, putting on the hacker persona straight out of Hollywood, but Lex also knew that DeadMan didn't have enough of a personality to hide behind the persona.

"This *Luddite's Guide*," Lex said, "it actually lays out how to send an untraceable e-mail?"

"In 1999 terms," Aces said. His fingers continued to move across the keys as he spoke. He had taken a single digital image and refined it, so that now he was looking at a tiny section of it. Lex was too far away to know what it was a section of.

"How different is it now?" Lex asked.

"There's a million better ways to do it," Terror said. "This one is so by the book. I mean, I could trace it with my eyes closed now."

"Put it this way," Aces said. "No one does it this way anymore."

"When it hits print, man, it is so beyond passé that it's like Henry Ford material." DeadMan stood, tossed his paper

Starbucks cup over Lex's head, and missed the wastebasket. He didn't go over and pick up the cup.

Neither did Lex, although he was tempted. He preferred the world neat.

"So where did this e-mail originate?" Lex asked.

"Metropolis," Terror said.

Lex had expected that. He would have been surprised if the e-mail had originated anywhere else.

"Where, exactly, in Metropolis?" Lex asked.

"An Internet café about five blocks from here. I know the guy who runs it. We got a time code on the e-mail. He might remember who sent it."

Lex doubted that the owner would remember, but it was a start. "Give me the information. I'll send one of my people."

"No offense, Lex," Brodsky said, "but he won't talk to one of your 'people.'"

"I'll go then," Lex said.

"No need," Terror said. "I already e-mailed him. I expect a response any minute now."

Lex shouldn't have been surprised at the swiftness of all of this—after all, he was raised in a computer-driven world—but he never sank deeply into the lifestyle. He wished they hadn't e-mailed. He wanted to see the guy's eyes, know if he was lying, if he'd sent it himself, if he was covering up.

But right now, Lex would take what he could get.

"What about the fax?" Lex asked.

"Tougher," Aces said. "Shoulda brought us to your dad's office, let us work with the machine."

"Some things even I can't do," Lex said. Or wouldn't do, for fear that his father might come back in the middle of everything and not understand the measures Lex was taking.

Then there was Lex's smaller fear, the one he hadn't voiced to anyone, that his father was somehow involved in the kidnapping, that it was a ploy to test Lex (and if he ever discovered that, he'd quit trying to rescue his father right then and there) or that it was designed to shake up the market a little, find out how the market would respond if something happened to Lionel Luthor.

Lex liked to think his father wasn't that devious, but he'd be lying to himself. His father was that devious. So far, though, Lex couldn't find an obvious reason to fake a kidnapping.

"I know, bro," Aces said. He had a smaller window on his screen, running code. On the main portion, he continued manipulating the digital image he'd been working on for the past fifteen minutes. "Had to hack into the phone company. Your dad's office is tight."

"He means that in a good way," Brodsky said. "The phone company's easier."

"Way easier, dude," said DeadMan, in a tone that let Lex know that they'd tried to break into LuthorCorp before. DeadMan was trying to get a rise out of him, so Lex ignored him.

"And?" Lex asked. "What's the phone company tell you?"

"Fax came from a copy shop on the other side of Metropolis, a good five, six miles from the Internet café. And the fax came in at the same time as your e-mail."

"The copy shop could have sent the fax at a prescribed time, right?" Lex asked.

"Doubtful," Aces said. "The shop would've left its coding on the fax. Didn't do that."

"How hard is it to wipe off the sending number?" Lex asked.

"Not that tough if you've got a manual. Tougher if you don't. And weird in a place like that, where the code's damn near hardwired in. You got a real technogeek on your hands, Lex," Aces said.

"Two of them, I think," Brodsky said. "At least."

Three. This merely confirmed what the security tape showed. Two men working the technological corridors of Metropolis this morning, and one man (person?) guarding his father. At least that would be how Lex would do it.

But Lex knew how treacherous his father was. He'd have someone keeping an eye on the old man all the time. Most people underestimated Lionel Luthor, thinking him a crude bully.

Lex would never make that mistake.

Although there was yet another option. All three players were in Metropolis, sending out video e-mails and hidden faxes, while his father lay dead in a ditch somewhere.

A computer pinged.

"Got an answer," Terror said. "With pictures. Come look."

Lex stepped closer to Terror's machine. Terror's e-mail program was open. An e-mail from the Internet café filled the preview window, with an attachment indicated.

The e-mail started with no salutation or preamble, as if the two men had been carrying on a conversation instead of writing letters to each other.

```
Your guy's a weird dude. Worried me, so took a
couple pictures from a few different angles.
Got mostly nose hairs on the computer's cam,
but got some good ones when he paid. Take a
look. Wouldn'ta even thought he knew what e-
mail was. Guess it takes all kinds. Tell your
buddy no one's used the keyboard since. I'll
detach, put on a new one. I don't want any
obvious Feds in here, but I'll hand it over to
a nonobvious one. Lemme know.
```

"That's kind of him," Lex said, wondering what was in it for the café owner. Did he expect a payout?

"Dude, he's not being kind. He just doesn't want trouble, and he understands chain of evidence because he's had some experience with it, if you know what I mean." DeadMan had whirled his chair around and was staring at Lex pointedly.

"I suspect we've all had experience with chain of evidence," Lex said, feeling a bit defensive. If they wanted to compare arrest records, let them try. He'd have them all beat. Conviction records were another matter. They didn't have fathers with friends on the force.

Fathers with influence.

Fathers who might be dead.

Lex crouched behind Terror's chair. He was getting tired of standing. Being awake for more than thirty-six hours was beginning to take its toll.

"Let's see what your friend considers a weird dude," he said.

Terror opened the attachments. The first few were too close

to be valuable, just like the café owner warned. If a man could be identified by a single eyebrow and a few open pores, then maybe Lex could've used them. But there wasn't enough information there to help.

The other photographs, taken at the desk, were of a broad-shouldered man who wore a John Deere cap and a beard that might or might not have been fake. His flannel shirt, obviously dirty blue jeans, and work boots marked him as someone who didn't come to Metropolis often.

"Whoa," DeadMan said, doing a respectable Keanu Reeves imitation. "Redneck alert."

"No wonder he didn't want this guy in there," Aces said, looking over Terror's shoulder.

"Why?" Lex asked.

"Scare off the regulars. You gotta figure if this guy knows enough about computers to send e-mail, he's not writing to Granny. He's doing a Timothy McVeigh or something. Not something any respectable café wants to be involved in," Terror said.

"Are you saying that if he'd come in looking like one of you guys, no one would've noticed?" Lex asked.

"Damned straight," DeadMan said. "You don't get farmers in places like that unless they don't want their minister to figure out what they're doing. It's either bombs or kiddie porn, neither of which is good for some café's future."

Lex nodded. He stood up. His knees cracked. "This is a good start, then. Can you print up some of those pictures?"

"Doing it now," Terror said. "Figured you'd want them."

"And there's no coding on our stuff either," Brodsky said. "So your FBI buddies aren't going to find anything here."

"They aren't even going to look this way," Lex said. "Why do you think I came to you in the first place?"

Brodsky nodded. "Give me another hour or so. We'll have the images analyzed. I'm sure we'll have more information for you by then."

Lex took the pictures Terror offered him. "What we've got so far is good. Tell your friend at the café I'll send over a plain-clothes FBI guy. He'll show a badge—discreetly. Maybe the fingerprints'll tell us something."

"If the guy's got a record," Brodsky said.

"As smooth as this operation's been going," Lex said, "I'd be surprised if he didn't."

◆◆◆

Chloe could have kissed Pete. He was being absolutely wonderful, very supportive, and helpful. He managed to turn Detective Roberts's attention away from her when the divers arrived, so that she was able to sneak back into the marsh and photograph them working.

She'd already gotten several good shots of them going into the murky water, and coming out empty handed. Her shoes were full of water, she had mud between her toes, and her feet were freezing while the rest of her was too hot, but she didn't care. She was getting more on this story.

By the time she got done with these last two days, she'd actually have a clipping file big enough to show the *Daily Planet* for that summer internship they offered.

She slapped absently at a mosquito and watched a diver go down in the water again. She felt guilty thinking about the internship in connection with this story. When she was dealing with Smallville's weirder side, she never had this sense of obligation mixed with sadness.

She also knew it didn't hold the same kind of career opportunities. Stories about the effects of meteor rocks, Nicodemus plants, and mad scientists might be better served for an internship at one of the checkout stand tabloids instead of a respected paper like the *Planet*.

But the sadness—and much of her drive to cover this story— was coming from her friendship (if she could call it that) with Danny. He'd been a nice guy, and she'd noticed that he was having a tough time lately.

She just hadn't done anything about it. She hadn't even covered the story of Mr. Franklin's layoff like Danny asked her to. The conversation played over and over in her mind as she tried and mostly failed to sleep the night before.

Danny, I'm sorry that your dad got laid off. But this

stuff happens. It's business news, but not the kind of thing the Torch *covers. I mean, we'll put an article in, but it won't be much.*

Chloe, employees were targeted for this. Not just my dad, but other people, people who had finally gotten a second chance—

I'm sorry, Danny. People get laid off all the time. I don't mean to sound harsh, but it's not really news.

What she'd meant was that it wasn't really news to her. It didn't make her pulse pound and her fingers move across the keys. She wasn't going to be a reporter so that she could cover City Council meetings and layoffs and other evergreens that hit the newspaper as seasonally as Christmas advertising.

Maybe she should have listened to Danny, though. He had a human angle on the layoffs, and she had ignored it. Maybe if she had talked to Danny's father, things might have gone differently. Or maybe, if she had listened, she might have learned something else, something that would have given the last twenty-four hours some meaning.

The first diver's head popped out of the water. He had some kind of weed draped over his diving mask. He didn't even seem to notice. He gestured at the second diver, then went back down.

"They got anything?" Clark had come up behind her. Chloe didn't jump—she had more self-control than that—but her heart rate increased. He had the ability to move as silently as a cat.

"I don't know," she said. "They just went under again. This time it seemed urgent."

Clark nodded. He seemed subdued. Maybe it was because Lana was so heartbroken. Chloe had never realized how close Lana was with Danny; apparently Clark hadn't either.

Chloe glanced over her shoulder, but couldn't see around the tangle that marked the entrance to the marsh. Lana was out there with Pete, talking to Detective Davies. Detective Roberts was near the divers, looking annoyed.

"What is it?" Clark asked.

"You know," Chloe said slowly, "Danny said something to me last week that I kind of ignored. Now I wish I hadn't."

"What's that?"

"He was talking about the layoffs. He said certain people were targeted, and they lost their second chance."

"Like his dad?" Clark asked.

Chloe frowned. "That's what I thought when he mentioned it, and I felt bad for him, but I knew there wasn't anything I could do. I mean, we've all seen it. The layoffs, the changes. When LuthorCorp first came in and shut down the creamed corn factory, we saw a lot of people lose their jobs then."

Clark moved his palm up and down, in a kind of "be-quiet" gesture. "Pete's never really gotten over that. His parents had some kind of agreement with LuthorCorp that when they sold the factory, the employees would get to keep their jobs."

Chloe nodded. "I remember. And if I didn't, Pete would remind me of it often enough. But LuthorCorp set up a whole new factory, so the agreement didn't apply."

"You think that's what Danny was referring to?"

"No," Chloe said. "I've been thinking about it all day. Danny grew up here, like the rest of us. And I know this was personal for him, but he never came to me with a story idea before. It was like there was something else going on, something that had him worried."

"About the layoffs." Clark sighed and looked past her, staring at the spot where the divers had gone down. She doubted that he was really looking there. He seemed to be seeing something beyond all of them.

"What?" she asked.

"Lex," he said. "He didn't want the layoffs either. They came from his father, and Lex got pretty steamed about it. He said that if his dad wanted him to run the factory, then he should let him run it his way."

"That wasn't the first time that his father interfered," Chloe said.

"No," Clark said. "And each time it's had to do with employee relations."

Both divers popped to the surface again. One of them swam toward the oak. The marsh had to be very deep there. Chloe was glad she hadn't followed her instinct and tried to walk over there. More than her feet would have gotten wet.

The diver spoke to Roberts, who nodded throughout the whole conversation.

"I'd talk to Lex if I could, but this thing with his dad is going on," Clark said.

"Have you called Lex in Metropolis?"

Clark shook his head. "I imagine he's got enough to do without his friends calling him every fifteen minutes. I left a message on his voice mail, letting him know he can call if he needs to, but I doubt he will."

"Even if he does, you don't want to ask him about the lay-offs in the middle of this personal crisis." Chloe knew Clark well enough to know he felt that way. She would have no qualms about it, but she was short on tact anyway.

It was, she hoped, one of the things that would make her a good reporter.

"Don't you think it's odd," Clark said slowly, "that Lex's dad is kidnapped the same day that we discover Danny's body?"

"No." Chloe didn't even need time to consider the idea. "Crime goes on all the time, Clark. What's unusual about this is that we just happened to know the people involved."

"I suppose." He didn't sound convinced. "I thought you were the person who didn't believe in coincidences."

"On the same case," Chloe said. "This is clearly not the same."

"I thought we didn't know what this was," Clark said.

Chloe bit her lower lip. She had said that, or something similar to it.

But she was saved from saying any more. The divers came out of the water, carrying something between them. She grabbed her camera and zoomed the telephoto lens on the scene by the oak tree.

The divers were carrying a body—a woman's body. Chloe could tell by the long hair hanging down. The body was covered in a brownish muck.

"It's Bonnie," Clark said.

Chloe wondered how he could tell. He was just as far away as she was, and he didn't have the benefit of the telephoto lens.

But he was right. She knew he was right the moment he said

that. Bonnie's profile came into focus, her face pale in repose.

Chloe snapped photographs, stunned that she had almost forgotten to do so. But this case had unsettled her from the first. She got some fairly good pictures of the divers bringing the body ashore, and she hoped that Roberts wouldn't confiscate her film.

She'd have to find a place to hide it before he came back over here.

Almost as if he heard her thoughts, Roberts looked in her direction. He still seemed suspicious of the three of them. Chloe was glad Lana was still by the car. She would be upset at Bonnie's death and at the fact that Roberts was blaming them.

The divers set the body down and went back into the water.

"Oh, God," Chloe said. "There's more?"

"Maybe the whole family," Clark said softly.

"And to think all of Smallville's been blaming Jed Franklin." Chloe shook her head. She brought the camera down for a moment. "He might be there with the rest of his family."

"We don't know anything yet, Chloe."

"I know," she said. "The more that happens, the less confident I feel about what we do know."

Roberts was crouching near the medical examiner, who had come out with the divers. They were leaning over the body, and they seemed even more distressed than they had been the day before.

"I wonder what's going on," Chloe said.

"I could slog over there and find out," Clark said.

She shook her head. "We'll learn soon enough."

Clark gave her a sharp look. "That's not like you, Chloe."

She shrugged. "I don't have the stomach for this one, I guess."

He got that familiar studious look he had so often, as if he could see deep down inside her. "I would think this story would fire you up more than the others."

"What do you mean?" she asked.

"You knew everyone, and there's a mystery here. You've been at the crime scene twice. This is your story, not anyone else's. You've even scooped The *Daily Planet*."

"They don't usually cover your average murder case," Chloe said.

"This isn't your average murder case," Clark said. "It's clearly something more. And you've got the inside scoop, Chloe."

She nodded. "I guess I do."

"Investigative reporters search for good stories, Chloe, and this one just fell in your lap. You've got to run with it, figure out what's going on."

"How do you know so much about investigative journalism, Clark?" she asked. She had never noticed his interest in journalism before, but then, Clark kept many sides of himself hidden.

"I think there's nothing more important than a good journalist, Chloe." He put a hand on her shoulder. "And I think you're one of the best."

The divers finished up at twilight. They scoured the bottom of the marsh, getting covered in weeds and muck. Clark used his X-ray vision as well, and saw nothing else down there, even though he still couldn't get as close to the split oak tree as he wanted to.

One of the cops drove Pete and Lana home around suppertime, but Clark decided to stay with Chloe. He knew she wouldn't leave until the police did—especially not after the speech he'd given her.

He wasn't sure what possessed him to say all of that. It was true he admired her determination, her willingness to go after every important story that came her way. But he also saw what kind of a difference she made around school and sometimes even around Smallville.

He was beginning to realize what kind of an impact a good journalist could make. Chloe had the kind of logical intelligence that made for a good investigator, and she was an excellent writer. She also had a nose for digging out the stories that people wanted hidden.

She was the one who had pushed all of them to come back out here. He wasn't sure he would have done so without her.

At her request, he pocketed her film before Roberts came back to their side of the marsh. That way, when he asked for her film, she could honestly tell him the canister she gave him (of mostly shots of Clark and the marsh) was the only can of film she had.

She would gather the rest from Clark later.

Roberts hurried past them without a word, but Chloe managed to corner one of the divers before he made it back to the cars. The medical examiner was still near the oak, dealing with the bodies. Some of the other officers were helping him.

Davies apparently was scouring the area, looking for clues they'd obviously missed.

The diver walked toward Chloe and Clark, pulling off his mask as he came. His skin was red from the pressure of the mask, and he still had some weeds and algae along his chin.

He seemed a lot younger than Clark expected him to be. It made Clark wonder if the diver was actually a police officer or just someone they'd gotten from around the area, someone who knew how to use a tank and search under-water.

Chloe hurried toward the diver, going ankle deep in muck. "Excuse me," she said. "I don't mean to bother you, but—"

"I'm not supposed to talk to anyone," the diver said. He sounded weary. His voice cracked as he spoke.

"I know," Chloe said. "But we're the ones—"

"You're the ones I was warned against," the diver said. "The detective in charge said you were nosy kids."

Chloe's back straightened, but she didn't bristle like Clark would have expected her to. "We're not nosy," she said. "Clark here is the one who found Danny. He went into the pond up at the top of the property without a mask or diving equipment, and he pulled Danny out."

Clark felt his cheeks heat up. The diver raised his head and looked past Chloe at Clark. The diver's expression was cool, as if he thought what Clark had done was ridiculous.

"You pulled a body out?" the diver asked.

"I thought he might still be alive." Even to his own ears, Clark sounded sheepish.

The diver nodded. "I've done that once or twice. Kind of a shock when the skin's so cold, isn't it?"

"And slimy," Clark said. "That's really what got me."

"Did it move on you? Slide over the bone? That sensation comes to me in dreams sometimes."

Chloe shuddered. She opened her mouth as if she were going to say something, then changed her mind.

Clark extended his hand. "I'm Clark Kent."

The diver took it. "Mike Hawthorne. I'm just a volunteer, you know. Lowell County doesn't have the dollars to keep a diver on staff. They could use a few other folks who've got the experience."

"I've never done diving," Clark said.

"I could train you. Lord knows, I don't want to do this all the time." Hawthorne sounded weary.

"I hear you," Clark said. "I don't think I'll ever get past seeing Danny like that."

"He was a friend of yours?"

"I've known him most of my life," Clark said.

"Harsh." Hawthorne walked past Chloe as if she wasn't even there. She trailed after him. "I can't believe you thought he was alive, though. Not with his skull messed up like that."

"His skull wasn't messed up," Clark said. "He looked pretty normal—except, you know, the bruising and his skin color."

The image of Danny's bluish white skin rose in Clark's mind again, and he had to forcibly make the image disappear.

"Normal? You're kidding, right? I thought the other two bodies were from the same crime as these."

"I don't know," Clark said. "All we could tell was one of them looked like it might be Bonnie from a distance. You know, one of the twin daughters."

Hawthorne nodded. "Her and her mother. Both shot in the head."

"Shot?!" Chloe exclaimed, then put her hands over her mouth.

Hawthorne started as if he'd just remembered she was there. "I shouldn't be talking about this."

"Danny wasn't shot," Clark said. "Neither was his other sister."

Hawthorne glanced behind him, at the oak tree and the medical examiner, still working over the bodies. Clark wondered what the examiner had to do that took so long. Probably photograph their condition and make some kind of preliminary report before getting them back to his lab.

"These two were definitely shot," Hawthorne said. "You can sometimes miss the entry wound, but exit wounds like that . . ."

His voice trailed off, then he shook his head.

Chloe was still looking at the tree. Clark recognized her expression. She wanted to go over and photograph the bodies. She didn't dare. They were in enough trouble already.

"I didn't tell you any of this, by the way," Hawthorne said. "You didn't hear it from me."

"I didn't hear anything," Clark said. "But thanks for talking to us."

"Wish I could say it was my pleasure. You know, when I got my certification, I never figured I'd be doing stuff like this." He trudged off, ducking beneath the opening in the underbrush.

Chloe slogged toward Clark. He finally reached out and helped her onto firmer ground. Her legs were brown below the knees and caked with mud from the ankles on so badly that the only way he knew she was wearing shoes was by the shape of her feet.

"Shot," she said softly. "I can't believe it."

"It caught me by surprise," Clark said.

"Well, that shows there was more than one killer," Chloe said.

"It doesn't show anything, except that the killer was determined." Clark kept his voice down. He didn't want to take the chance of Roberts overhearing them and yelling at Hawthorne for giving out the information.

"I don't see it, Clark. Two different locations, two different methods of killing."

Clark pulled Chloe closer. She was shivering. He had to get her home. "I'm not an expert, Chloe. But it seems to me that one guy could have started out using his hands, kind of unplanned. Then his wife or daughter walks in on him with a gun, he grabs it away, and shoots the remaining members of the family or whatever."

"I thought you thought that Jed Franklin didn't do this."

"I thought you thought that," Clark said.

"I thought you thought the same way I did," Chloe said.

"I usually do," Clark said.

She nodded. "Then you should be confused by this news."

"I am." He sighed. "I have no idea what's going on. I just know that an entire family is gone."

"Except the father."

"Who has been under suspicion from the start."

"Don't you find that odd?" Chloe asked. "I mean, women kill their families, too."

"Only we know now that Mrs. Franklin didn't do it."

"Yeah, we do know that." Chloe looked down. "Man, am I a mess. Not only am I going to be late for dinner, I'm coming home a total wreck again."

"I thought you called your folks."

"And got the machine," Chloe said. "Let's just hope they checked it before Mom set the table."

Clark nodded. He had spoken to his mom, who had urged him to come home. He had told her, though, that he wanted to stay with Chloe, and his mom agreed that that would be a good idea.

The dappled sunlight had long since disappeared from this section of woods. The light had a whitish cast that Clark knew was a prelude to twilight. It would get dark faster in the marsh than it would anywhere else.

A mosquito buzzed past him, not landing on him as usual. Bugs swarmed around Chloe. She wiped a hand over her face, leaving a trail of mud.

"I hate being a wreck," she said.

Clark smiled at her. "You're fine."

She shook her head and trudged past him, her shoes making sloshing sounds. Mosquitoes trailed her as if she were the best meal they'd seen in weeks. Pete would have been happy to note that she was now getting that treatment.

Clark hurried to keep up with her. She went through the hole in the brambles as if she'd been doing it all her life. He followed, the branches barely tickling him as they had done before.

He was happy to be leaving this place. It had such a feeling of loss and sadness to it. Whoever had chosen to hide the bodies here couldn't have picked a better spot.

The way the bodies were hidden was one of the many things about this case that bothered him. Now he could add the fact that two bodies were shot and two were strangled. Two were placed in one pond, which was easy to see, and two were placed in a marsh no one but the family knew about.

The house had been trashed, the truck was gone, and there was still one family member unaccounted for.

None of it made any sense.

Clark came out of the tangle and nearly ran into Chloe. She was standing right in front of the opening, Deputy Davies beside her.

". . . didn't realize you were still here," Davies was saying to her.

Clark stood up behind her. Davies looked up at him.

"Both of you," Davies amended.

"We wanted to stay until we knew what was going on," Chloe said.

"Do you now?" Davies asked.

Chloe shook her head. "I can't speak for Clark, but I'm more confused than ever."

"We won't know what's going on until we have all the forensic evidence," Davies said. "We're working off too many theories right now."

"All of them having to do with Jed Franklin?" Clark asked.

Chloe looked at him sideways—her approving look. Apparently that was the question she would have asked.

"Frankly, it wouldn't surprise me if we found his body in the woods nearby—or in his truck not too far from here," Davies said.

"You think someone else murdered him, too?" Chloe asked.

"Self-inflicted gunshot wound, right?" Clark asked.

"You got it," Davies said. "We'll be combing this area all night. We owe a lot to you kids."

"I wish Detective Roberts would realize that," Chloe said. "He's been rude right from the beginning, as if he suspects us."

"You guys check out," Davies said.

Clark felt a shiver of surprise run through him. Chloe frowned at Davies. "You checked us out?"

"Of course we did," Davies said. "Alibis, school history, everything. We'd've been remiss if we hadn't."

"And we checked out," Clark said dryly.

"Checked out on the alibis and on the personality traits." Davies grinned at Chloe. "I believe Principal Kwan said that you were 'persistent' when you felt you had a story, and that your friends were always quite helpful in making sure you got that story."

"Leave it to Principal Kwan," Chloe muttered.

"Hmm?" Davies asked.

Chloe shook her head. "So we're not in trouble with Roberts?"

"I don't think you ever were." Davies looked around as if he were scouting for Roberts.

Several sheriff's cars were parked all over the yard, and deputies, many in uniform, were going into the wooded areas nearby. Clark didn't see Roberts, but that meant nothing. The man had the ability to appear out of nowhere.

"Then I don't understand," Chloe said. "Why's he been so mean?"

Davies looked at her in surprise. "Mean?"

"He hasn't believed us from the beginning. He's accused us of all kinds of things, and he was really angry this afternoon when we found the marsh."

Davies shoved his hands in his pockets. Clark took a step closer to Chloe. For some reason, he felt like he needed to protect her back.

"He's not mean," Davies said after a moment's consideration. "He's frustrated, and probably angry at himself."

"Why?" Clark asked.

"He was the one who got the files after Franklin's arrest last week. He was supposed to follow up. He never did."

Clark could feel Chloe snap to alert. "Franklin was arrested last week? How come that wasn't released?"

"It was." Davies gave her a sideways smile. "In that thing most reporters ignore, the weekly arrest report. It rarely hits the paper outside of small towns."

"Does the *Torch* get that?" Clark asked.

"No," Chloe said. "If you have someone on the police beat, they get to look at it or make a copy or something. But there's no one on any beat. Just me."

And Clark heard her unspoken thoughts: normally, she thought such things like police beats and city council reports beneath her.

"What was he arrested for?" Chloe asked.

"I don't remember," Davies said. "Disturbing the peace, drunk and disorderly, something."

"That wouldn't require a detective's follow-up, would it?" Clark asked.

Davies shook his head. "I don't know the details. I'd tell you to ask Roberts about it, but the subject's a sensitive one at the moment."

"He's blaming himself for this?" Clark asked.

Davies nodded. "If he'd followed up, maybe none of this would have happened."

"Or maybe he would have died, too," Chloe said with her usual practicality. She put a hand on Clark's arm. "C'mon, Clark. The mud's drying here, and pretty soon, I won't be able to move my legs."

"You want me to drive?" he asked, a little worried at the clip she would take going home, considering the new information.

"I'm fine," she said, and headed to the car.

Clark stopped by Davies. "Thanks for talking to us."

He nodded, looking beyond Clark at the farmhouse. "Figured we owed you guys something," Davies said. "We'd've been wondering about the wife and sister for a long time if you hadn't found the marsh. We'll do a more thorough search this time. I'll see to it."

Clark nodded at him, then went to the passenger seat of the car. As he folded himself in it, he realized that he was covered with mud as well. It flaked off him, landing on the seat and the floorboards.

"Sorry about that," he said to Chloe.

But she stared at it for a long moment, not saying a word. "There hasn't been rain for nearly four days now," she said after a moment.

"So?" Clark asked.

"There was rain last week. Imagine how muddy the marsh was then."

"And how covered with mud the killer got," he said.

She nodded, then started the car and put it into gear. She

spun around the gravel turnaround, and headed up the road, the car bouncing the entire way.

"I thought you weren't going to drive fast," Clark said.

"That was before I had two new pieces of information." Chloe grinned at him. "We might be able to crack this case yet."

Darkness had fallen across Metropolis, but the city was never dark. It had an ambient light, composed of streetlights, neon, and spots, that made the entire city seem to glow from within.

Lex had forgotten about nights in the city, forgotten how they lured him to leave the building, drink his troubles away, dance with women he'd never seen before, and invent new troubles, just to irritate his father.

His father. Lex turned away from the wall of windows in his father's office. There had been no word from the kidnappers all day, and that worried Lex. As the FBI guys said, the kidnappers weren't following the script—and any deviation from that script did not bode well for Lionel Luthor.

Word had leaked to the news media, of course. The banner headlines around the square just a few blocks away proclaimed in large red letters: KIDNAPPERS SILENT . . . NO WORD ON LOCATION OF FINANCIER LIONEL LUTHOR.

The front page of the *Daily Planet* ran one of the pictures of Lex's father, and asked people to identify the location, if they could. Other newspapers followed suit, and the local all-news channel had been running the digital clip ever since the police leaked it to them.

The police or the FBI. Either way, Lex was not happy about it. He didn't want any word of this case in the press, and now it was the day's main story.

That and the decline of LuthorCorp stock. The stock had plummeted dramatically again, and no amount of speechifying by Lex or the board of directors seemed to make a difference. If this decline continued, there wouldn't be a company for Lionel Luthor to come back to.

If, indeed, he was coming back.

Lex turned away from the windows, surprised to see a diminutive man standing in front of his desk. The man hadn't been reflected in the glass; for one fanciful moment, Lex thought him a vampire.

But the man's reflection showed up in the other wall of windows. He had just been standing behind Lex so that Lex hadn't been able to see him.

Crafty. But not as crafty as Lex could be.

"Who let you in here?" Lex asked.

"The secretary." The man had a Boston Brahmin accent. Lex couldn't tell if it was real or fake. The man's hair had been cut in the Kennedy style, short in front and long around the ears, and he wore a conservative black suit that could have come out of the early sixties.

Even his tie was too long and narrow.

"Well," Lex said, "she made a mistake. No one's supposed to be in this room."

"Not even you, right, Lex?"

Lex made his eyes go flat. It was a look that usually cowed people. It didn't seem to bother this guy. "I don't believe we've been properly introduced."

The man took a step forward, and extended his hand. "Reginald Dewitt. I'm the lead FBI agent assigned to your father's case."

Lex looked down at the offered hand. It was manicured, the nails buffed and groomed. Not your average FBI agent, but then, Lex knew the FBI culture in Metropolis was different than the rest of the country. At the upper echelons, this was considered the dream assignment, and a lot of guys took the perks.

Apparently this guy did.

"Identification?" Lex said.

Dewitt stared at Lex for a moment, then withdrew his hand. He reached into the pocket of his suit coat and removed a golden shield with the FBI logo. Lex took it, studied it, resisted the urge to bite it, the way people did in movies to see if gold was real.

He'd seen a lot of FBI badges in the past. This one was legit. He almost wished it wasn't.

"How come I didn't meet you yesterday?" Lex asked.

"Yesterday, I was in London," Dewitt said.

"Not working on my dad's case." Lex handed him back the badge.

"Believe it or not, there are other things we do."

"Oh, I believe it." Lex walked behind his father's desk, made sure the drawers were closed, and nothing revealing showed on the running computer screen. "I'm just wondering why they didn't keep you at your post and let the original guys handle this."

"I have more experience with high-level matters," Dewitt said. "A lot of people are concerned about your father's case."

"Who called you in?" Lex asked. "Because I know I sure as hell didn't."

"Given your experience with law enforcement, that's not a surprise." Dewitt could make his eyes go flat as well. Impressive, for someone who wore a designer knock-off suit and drew a government paycheck.

"I don't like dancing with someone I just met," Lex said. "Are you going to tell me who brought you in, or am I going to get security to throw you out?"

"You're probably going to call security anyway," Dewitt said.

Lex reached for the phone.

"Let's just say some very important people have investments in LuthorCorp, and after the other stock market debacles these past few years, they're not too keen on having another."

"Sounds like they're panicking," Lex said. "When my father gets back—"

"We both know that the longer these kidnappers remain silent, the less chance there is for your father to get out alive. Our people have been looking at the video and the photographs. We've got a line on the place the fax was sent from, and we hope to know where the e-mail came from shortly. We're going to take care of this, Lex, and get your father one way or another."

"Are you telling me or asking me? Or just blowing smoke?" Lex asked. He kept his voice calm, but he gripped the side of the desk so hard his fingers hurt. He had all the information that the FBI was just beginning to get. They were probably interfering with his investigation, although he didn't want to tell Dewitt that.

"I'm telling you," Dewitt said, "because I believe that part of the problem here could be you."

Lex felt his cheeks heat. He shouldn't have come into his father's office in the first place. He always felt inadequate in here. "Oh?"

"I understand you have been contacted by the kidnappers with a specific sum of money, yet you've done nothing to assemble that money."

"I thought you don't give kidnappers what they want," Lex said.

"Making a pretense is a good idea," Dewitt said. "My techs tell me these guys have some knowledge of computers. They might be able to monitor LuthorCorp accounts, to know if you're assembling funds. You haven't done anything today except go clubbing, talk to the press about LuthorCorp, and hole up in the office."

Lex felt anger, as cold as a midwinter wind, run through him. Clubbing? So they were following him, but apparently they hadn't gone inside Club Noir. Perhaps they thought Lex had kidnapped his own father.

That would explain the discussion now.

And, given Lex's background, it wouldn't be that farfetched, although it was a bit—Roman emperorish—for his tastes.

"Perhaps I have access to funds you people know nothing about," he said.

"We know a lot," Dewitt said.

"Have you run the fingerprints yet? The ones from the Internet café where the e-mail was sent from?"

Dewitt started. "What are you—?"

"This afternoon, we sent over one of your guys to an Internet café five blocks from where my father was kidnapped. The owner was saving a keyboard for us. The keyboard had been used to send the e-mail. I know your guy brought the keyboard back. I even know that the prints were taken, and sent to the FBI database. What I don't know is if they had a hit."

It was Dewitt's turn to flush. "No one told me—"

"Of course not," Lex said, "because you're committing an end run around someone else's investigation. Has no one told you that this is the worst way to handle a case like this? Because if your subordinates won't, I will. I want you out of here."

Dewitt frowned at him. "I'm here by orders of—"

"I don't care if you're here by orders of God," Lex said. "You can leave. We're handling this on our own."

He punched the intercom on his dad's phone system. "Send security in here. Have them escort Mr. Dewitt out of the building, and make sure he does not gain access again."

"Yes, sir," his father's secretary responded.

"Mr. Luthor, you're going to regret this. I have expertise that no one else—"

"Mr. Luthor?" Lex asked. "A moment ago, it was Lex."

"My mistake," Dewitt said. "You're going to want my help. The financial matters alone will be tricky, and while the team we have downstairs is a good one, they haven't worked as many of these cases as I have."

Lex heard the main doors outside the office open. "Tell me, Mr. Dewitt. Of all the cases you handled, how many of the victims came back alive?"

"Enough," Dewitt said.

"How many?" Lex asked.

"Five," Dewitt said.

"Out of?"

"One hundred."

"So the Big Cheese, whoever that might be, sent me a guy with a 95 percent failure rate? Fascinating. Maybe I should start investigating the FBI and see if they're behind this thing with my father."

"Mr. Luthor—"

The doors to the office opened. Two burly security men that Lex didn't recognize walked in, followed by Hensen, the FBI man who had been in charge up until now. Hensen glared at Dewitt, and Lex noted the hatred in both men's gazes.

"Mr. Luthor," Dewitt said, turning away from Hensen and the guards, "none of the companies was hurt financially in any way, and there were no leaks to the press. To this day, most people do not know what happened. I managed to keep the situation under wraps and to protect the assets involved better than any other man in the field ever had."

Lex let his gaze go flat again. "You think the assets are the most important thing to me?"

"You're not touching them. There has to be a reason for it."

"Perhaps because I've read the FBI playbook as well. I know that giving kidnappers what they want is no better than failing to give them what they want. The best thing to do is quick forensic work, figuring out where the victim is, and sending in a team to rescue him."

"That hasn't worked either, Mr. Luthor. In all such cases, the victims die when a team goes in."

"Then the team screwed up." Lex waved his hand at the guards. "Get him out of here."

"Mr. Luthor, I wasn't brought here by you. The director of the FBI personally made certain that I would be the one in charge. You can't change that." Dewitt held his ground.

Lex smiled at him. Lex made certain the smile was cold. "You're right. I can't change that. But I can make certain you have no access whatsoever to this building, my people, or any information that we obtain first."

"I wouldn't advise you to get involved—"

"And I am making it clear what I think your advice is worth. Gentlemen, I'm not telling you again. Get him out of this building, or I'll find someone who will."

The guards grabbed Dewitt, who shook them off. He headed for the door, still glaring at Hensen. Then he looked at Lex. "You'll—"

"Regret this?" Lex shrugged one shoulder. "I doubt it. A man who can't be more creative on his parting shot is not worth my time, and is certainly not someone who should be in charge of this case."

The guards pushed Dewitt out of the room. Hensen started to follow.

"Mr. Hensen," Lex said. "Any progress?"

"You know where we stand, sir." Hensen pushed the door closed.

"I got you those fingerprints this afternoon," Lex said.

"Yes, sir. We've sent them to the database, but there's a queue—"

"Jump the queue," Lex said. "If the director of the FBI is personally worried about LuthorCorp, then he should be able to authorize a rush order on those prints."

"Yes, sir, although they're not going to be happy that the request comes from me. Not after this." Hensen looked over his shoulder at the closed door.

"It doesn't come from you, Agent Hensen." Lex spoke softer than he had before. He always spoke softly when he was angry. "It comes from me. I'll speak to your boss directly if I have to."

"I'm sure that won't be necessary, sir."

"Good." Lex sat down at his father's desk. The chair was uncomfortable—built for his father, and not for Lex.

Hensen waited.

"That's all," Lex said.

Hensen left, pulling the door closed behind him. Lex put his hand over his face and closed his eyes. It was all a bluff to him. He had no real idea what he was doing. All he knew was that he didn't want to get caught in some government agency's power plays. Besides, Dewitt wouldn't have allowed Lex to run things his way. Hensen was easy to manipulate.

The computer screen before him flickered to life. He'd had his e-mail routed in here, and now an envelope blinked on the screen. He opened it.

It was from Brodsky, although it didn't say that. There was no address in the From category, and the subject line read "Noir."

There was no message, just four jpeg files. The first was a black-and-white photograph of three men, loitering near City Bank. The men held hats in their hands, and two of the men had spray canisters. They all had thick beards that partially obscured their faces. The third man looked familiar—and not because he was the guy at the Internet café.

Lex had the feeling he'd seen that man before.

The men were white, burly, and overdressed for the heat of that day. The third man was looking toward the street, a frown on his face.

Lex wondered what Brodsky thought was so important about

the photograph—besides the fact that Brodsky believed the men to be the perpetrators of the kidnapping. If Brodsky had this photo, he had others as well. They were frames from the bank's security video. There was some other bit of information in the frame that Lex should see, but didn't.

He closed that file, vowing to come back to it, and opened the next. It, too, was from the security video. It showed a red truck, brand-new, with Kansas plates, parked in the handicapped parking spot in front of one of the buildings across the street. The license number was obscured, but Lex got part of it.

He would be able to use that.

Then he went to the third photograph. It was a section of the curtain that had been behind his father in the still photograph. A hand hung there, as if it had gotten caught in the picture by accident.

The hand was reddish and dark brown. A spring sunburn over skin that normally tanned. On the ring finger, a plain gold wedding band, scratched and worn with time.

Again, information that Brodsky saw that Lex didn't. He'd have to think about it. Or maybe the fourth photograph would put it all into perspective.

He opened the last file. The photograph came from the digital video of his unconscious father. His father's ear and the top of his skull were fuzzed in the front of the frame. In the back, in focus, was a window. Outside the window, trees. Just trees.

So they had him in the country.

Lex looked again at the other photographs. Kansas plates, men who didn't belong, and that sunburned hand. Someone who worked outdoors. Maybe it was his property. If Lex found out the license number of the truck, he would find the men.

He glanced at the first photograph again. That was it. Not just the faces, but the boots. No one wore work boots in Metropolis. Only out-of-towners and young men trying to make a political statement. These men weren't young, and they weren't making that kind of statement.

They were after something else.

A knock sounded on his door. Lex sighed and hit the intercom. "I don't want to be disturbed," he said.

There was a moment of silence. He realized that the secretary was away from her desk. He sighed. He had the urge to fire her, but he kept thinking of his father, wondering if he wanted the eye candy gone.

His father, who might never come back.

Then the intercom beeped. "Sir, it's Hensen. We have a match on the print."

"Bring it in, then," Lex said.

The doors opened, and Hensen came in. His suit didn't pretend to belong to a high-end label. It was off-the-rack, ill fitting and brown, certainly not something that belonged in Metropolis.

He was carrying a sheet of paper.

"His name is Thomas Porter," Hensen said. "He did time for a number of things. His record extends back to some sealed juvenile counts. But as an adult, he started with robbery, then armed robbery, and then he moved into high-tech crimes, which put him on a watch list of ours. We had no idea he was in Kansas. Last we heard of him, two years ago, he was in Florida."

"Is this a mug shot?" Lex asked, extending his hand.

"Several," Hensen said, handing him the paper.

Lex brought the paper up and studied it for a moment. Five different mug shots, all from various parts of the country and from various years. The one at the top, the most recent, also showed Porter with a goatee. The man looked somewhat like one of the three standing outside the bank.

Then Lex's gaze fell on the bottom shot, the first mug shot, taken when Porter didn't have any facial hair at all. He gazed directly into the camera, and it almost felt like he was in the room.

Lex had seen that gaze before. He'd actually felt it in person. The anger he'd been feeling since Dewitt invaded the office—actually since Lex's father disappeared—rose up again.

"This man's name may be Thomas Porter," Lex said quietly. "But he worked in the Smallville plant under the name J. B. Bynes. My father ordered me to fire him three months ago."

"Why?" Hensen asked.

Lex set the paper carefully on his father's desk. "Bynes was an agitator. I had other plans for keeping him quiet, but my father believed that agitators should be thrown out quickly. It was the first volley in what would become a serious round of layoffs."

"The layoffs you and your father quarreled about."

Lex looked at Hensen. The man seemed nervous.

"Does everyone in the FBI suspect I'm behind my father's kidnapping?" Lex asked.

Hensen took a deep, nervous breath. "I don't think so, sir."

"But that's why they brought in Dewitt."

"Yes, sir."

One point for Hensen. At least he didn't lie. Lex reached over to the computer, turned on the printer, and printed up the photograph of the three men and the photograph of the truck.

He handed them to Hensen.

"Bynes is clearly involved," Lex said. "Let's find him. I suspect this is his truck. Let's track it down, too. He was in Metropolis as recently as this morning. And if he's the man I remember, he's not the trusting type. He'd have my father nearby so that he can check on him and his guards."

"In the city?" Hensen asked.

"Too suspicious. Too many witnesses." Lex wasn't about to tell Hensen that he knew his father was being kept in the country. "Let's check the countryside first. Use a copter, see if you can see that truck from the air. And start in the areas between Smallville and Metropolis."

"You think he's been planning this for a long time?"

"I don't think it, Hensen," Lex said. "I know it. He wouldn't have come to Smallville in the first place if he weren't. So all of his plans would have focused in that area. We're going to focus there, too."

Hensen nodded. He took the photographs and left the office without waiting to be dismissed.

Lex leaned back in the chair. His stomach twisted. He knew this man, had actually defended him and his job, and had thought of offering him a position that would have used his raw strength and oddly magnetic personality.

Maybe if he had been allowed to do that, none of this would have happened.

Maybe.

But there was no use looking backward. They had a name, they had a face, and they might even have more than one motive.

Now all they had to do was find J. B. Bynes and his hideout.

There was a lot of countryside between Metropolis and Smallville—not all of it cultivated farmland. Bynes was smart. The hideout would be difficult to find.

But that wasn't what worried Lex the most. What worried him the most was Bynes's—or Porter's—rap sheet. The man's criminal activities had escalated his whole life. It wasn't a large step from armed robbery to murder.

And Lex had a hunch that was precisely the direction J. B. Bynes had decided to go.

The lights in the *Torch* office were low. Chloe took a handful of M&M's from the bag that sat beside her computer. She ate the candies one at a time, savoring the chocolate.

She had closed the blinds so that no one could see in. Clark would probably yell at her for being here, but she felt time pressure on this case.

Time pressure mixed with guilt. She had a lot more in common with Roberts than she wanted to admit. If she had listened to Danny, then maybe none of this would have happened.

Chloe and Roberts, missing signals. She wondered how many missed signals happened in cases like this where entire families died—how many friends and people in authority looked back and wondered what they could have done differently to prevent it all.

Her hand was shaking slightly. She'd had too much caffeine already, and the night had just begun. Going two days without sleep wouldn't be the brightest thing she ever did, but if it resolved this case, she'd feel vindicated.

She had gone home, taken a shower, eaten the warmed-up dinner that her mother had left for her, then sneaked back out to the *Torch* office. Her parents thought she was in her room asleep, but she had more important things to do. If they needed her, they would know where to find her.

They hated the way she worked so hard on what they considered to be a school project, but at least she wasn't getting into trouble. Or typical trouble anyway—boys, drinking, petty crime.

Even though she wouldn't mind getting into trouble with boys—one boy in particular. If only Clark would take his gaze off Lana long enough to realize that he and Chloe had a lot more in common.

He had startled her when he had shown that he knew so much about investigative reporting—and when it became clear how much he admired people who did it well. Her cheeks still burned when she thought about that.

She sipped the double tall she'd gotten on the drive over. The coffee was cold now, but still useful. She'd been digging through arrest records, Internet files, and old news reports, looking for information on Jed Franklin.

What she'd found had been unexpected. In his youth, Jed Franklin had gotten arrested a number of times for protesting things like proposed nuclear waste sites here in Kansas, and actions of LuthorCorp outside of Smallville, long before the corporation bought the creamed corn factory from Pete's parents.

Then Jed Franklin's father died, and Jed inherited the farm. He dropped out of college and took over the Franklin property, shutting off parts of it that had always drained resources—like the marsh—and made the farm a viable enterprise. He got married, had a family, and except for the marriage and birth announcements, dropped out of the news.

Until three months ago. Three months ago, he had been laid off from LuthorCorp. He felt that he and a group of others had been dismissed because they were talking to some union representatives about improving working conditions at the plant.

He accused Lex Luthor of lying to him. Lex, according to Franklin, had seemed amenable to talking about making changes that would benefit the workers. Lex didn't want to unionize the plant, but he would do what he could to keep the workers happy.

Franklin had left the meeting feeling optimistic. Two days later, however, he got word that he and the others who had attended that meeting—in fact everyone whose name had been mentioned in connection with possible union activity—had been laid off.

The layoff notices had come from LuthorCorp offices in Metropolis. The story made the papers—including the *Torch*—and Chloe remembered talking to Lex about it herself.

He had promised to do right by those employees, saying darkly that it was against the law to fire someone for starting union activity. But the next time Chloe contacted him about the layoffs, Lex had said that the decision had nothing to do with unions, and gave her a number in Metropolis to call.

"Just put in your paper that this wasn't my decision," he had said. "My father and I have very different ways of doing things. Unfortunately, I have to follow my father's methods right now."

She had written that, and everyone had said it rang false. But it hadn't sounded false when Lex mentioned it.

Jed Franklin had stopped giving interviews, too. But he spent a lot of time getting drunk in neighborhood bars, talking about how easy it was for money just to disappear. First his farm, then the job he got to save his farm. Now he had no idea what he would do to take care of his family.

No idea at all.

Those words had been part of a puff piece the *Daily Planet* had done on area layoffs—not just at LuthorCorp, but all over the state as the economy went sour. Most people didn't sound as bitter as Franklin; they seemed to have the attitude that they'd get another job.

But Franklin claimed that LuthorCorp was making it impossible for him to get another job, telling anyone he interviewed with that he was a troublemaker and they might think twice about hiring him.

Chloe sipped from her double tall again, only to find the give-away all-you-can-drink cup from the Talon was empty. She would either have to make herself instant coffee using the tiny microwave she had bought for the *Torch* office, or she'd have to switch to Mountain Dew.

Somehow Mountain Dew didn't seem all that professional to her. But instant coffee didn't sound appealing.

She left her desk, found some old tea bags and a ceramic mug, and microwaved herself some tea. She carried the steaming mug back to her desk and read the last of the files she had found.

Two weeks ago, Franklin assaulted a shift supervisor from the Smallville plant in one of the local bars. The police were called, but the supervisor declined to press charges. Later in the week, Franklin got charged on two different occasions with being drunk and disorderly.

Up until then, he'd been known as one of Smallville's most upstanding citizens. This had to be when the police chief assigned Roberts the Franklin case, maybe just to quiet Franklin down or maybe because the chief believed there was some merit to Franklin's accusations, that LutherCorp was trying to blacklist him.

Chloe found nothing else in the public files. But about ten days ago coincided with the conversation she'd had with Danny. She'd made some notes after they had spoken, force of habit mostly, but sometimes those notes got her future stories.

She took a few more M&M's and found that week's notebook. She thumbed through the pages until she found the page with Danny's comment.

DF says no one understands what's going on there. Thinks his dad has lost it, but not just because of the plant. Because of two of the guys he's been involved with. Danny doesn't like them, says they're the ones who led his dad down this wrong road. Danny thinks they provoked the Luthors just to start a fight, and that this was about something bigger, but he won't say what.

Chloe turned the pages in her notebook, but found nothing else. No other references, no more notes. Nothing about that desperate look in Danny's eye when he spoke to her.

When she had brushed him off because layoffs simply weren't news.

She hadn't been listening to him, even though she'd recorded his comments. She had assumed he'd been talking about the layoffs, but it sounded like something else, something different.

She went through the news stories, but Franklin's name was the only one that appeared in connection with the layoffs. No one else's.

She needed to find out who else was laid off, what people Danny might have been talking about. Lex was in Metropolis dealing with his father's kidnapping, so Chloe couldn't contact him. But there might be other people at the plant who would be willing to talk. Maybe even that supervisor who refused to press charges. Clearly he had some sympathy for the things Franklin was going through.

All Chloe had to do was find out who he was.

Clark sat in his favorite chair in the loft, his feet on the windowsill. He balanced the chair on its two back legs, staring out at the night sky.

He didn't feel like looking through the telescope tonight. Reflecting on his real parents, where they had come from and what they must have been thinking when they put him into that spaceship didn't seem like idle speculation anymore.

He was looking at the dark side of parenthood now, where people weren't saints, and things could go horribly wrong. He'd always known that, he supposed, but it never hit home to him, at least not until earlier in the year, when his father—a man whose integrity Clark admired beyond all else—had pointed a gun at him.

Granted, his dad hadn't been in his right mind at the time. He'd been under the influence of the Nicodemus plant. But even then, when his father realized who he'd been aiming at, he had stopped—even under the influence.

There was nothing good about the Franklin case. The weight of the additional two bodies felt like something from a dream. The fact that they'd been killed differently seemed worse, somehow. It made the killings seem less random to Clark, even more deliberate. And he couldn't put his finger on why.

"Hey," his father's voice came from the loft stairs. "Mind if I come in?"

Clark turned. His father was carrying a tray with one hand. On it were two soda fountain glasses his mom had gotten at a garage sale.

"Remember when we used to sit up here, look at the stars, and pig out on your mom's famous root beer floats?" his father asked.

Clark brought his chair down on all four legs. "Is that what you have?"

"Two special floats, the right amount of root beer, the perfect amount of ice cream, and, as a special treat, homemade whipped cream."

"Wow, she went all out." Clark grinned at his father. "I guess that means you can come in. But be careful. I'm going to expect this all the time."

His dad chuckled and sat in the other chair. He handed Clark one of the root beer floats and kept one for himself. Then he set the tray on the floor.

The float had a sugary root beer scent. A long-handled ice tea spoon stuck out of the glass along with a straw that bent. His mom had gone all out.

"She's worried about me, huh?" Clark asked.

His dad, taking a bite of ice cream mixed with whipped cream, shook his head. "I think she's feeling lucky and guilty."

"What?"

"Lucky that we have you. Guilty because we have you."

"You're still not making sense, Dad."

His father nodded. "The Franklin thing. I think it has shaken every parent in Smallville. We're all counting our blessings and realizing how close to the edge things can be at times."

His dad didn't remember the gun incident, and Clark had never told him. Clark had never told anyone. So he knew that his dad wasn't thinking of that.

"You're still thinking that Mr. Franklin did it?"

His dad shrugged. "I don't know what to think anymore, Clark. The whole case doesn't make sense."

"Dad," Clark said, taking a spoonful of ice cream. "Don't tell me what you told Mom."

His dad smiled sideways, but kept looking at the stars. "I think he did it, Clark. I think it happened just like you told Chloe. He got caught halfway through and used more extreme measures."

"It still doesn't explain why he hid the bodies," Clark said. "Chloe's been looking this stuff up on-line, and most of these folks don't move the bodies at all."

"I don't think you can say there's any typical killing, Clark. Everyone's different, and everyone snaps differently." His dad's spoon clanked against the glass. "I think this case does show how callous Smallville has become."

"What do you mean?" Clark took a sip of root beer. The float tasted as good as always, but lacked something. Maybe the sense of festive occasion that usually accompanied this treat. He didn't like it being associated with sadness. Still, he drank it anyway, knowing his mother would be disappointed if he didn't.

"I mean since the meteor, and the strange things that have happened because of it, and since the Luthors have come back to town—"

Clark frowned.

"—I know you like Lex, Clark, but he's part of that family, and they seem to set the tone for the town. We're a lot more insular than we used to be. We used to do things for each other, not gossip about each other. I can't help thinking that maybe we should have done more for the Franklins. Maybe if we'd been more of a community, this wouldn't have happened."

"Just yesterday, Dad, you were saying that nothing can be done when people snap."

His dad nodded, then set his float aside half-finished. "I've been rethinking that. It bothered me when I said it. I'm not sure if we could have made a difference with Jed Franklin, but maybe his family wouldn't have felt like they were alone with their problems. Maybe we could have helped his wife and kids find a way out."

"You don't think they were taken by surprise?"

"I don't know," his dad said.

"The police at the farm said that Mr. Franklin had gotten in trouble with the law in the past two weeks. Did you know that?"

"I knew that Jed Franklin was spouting crazy stuff since he got laid off, something about plots to destroy LuthorCorp, drunken speeches mostly. No one paid a lot of attention."

The root beer stuck in Clark's throat. He made himself swallow. "Plots to take down LuthorCorp?"

His dad nodded. "I overheard one of the rants when I went to the feed and seed store about ten days ago. It was crazy stuff, Clark."

"Don't you think it odd though that Lex's dad got kidnapped at the same time as all of this has been happening?"

His dad looked at Clark. "I hadn't considered it."

"Losing Lionel Luthor would hurt LuthorCorp, right?" Clark asked.

"It already is," his dad said. "Stock prices are going down. There's talk of some kind of audit. The board of directors is getting nervous, especially with the idea that Lex'll inherit his father's voting shares. It's all over the business pages, and it's not pretty."

Clark nodded. "What if this has nothing to do with Jed Franklin? What if this is about LuthorCorp?"

His dad sighed. "Why would the family be killed and not Franklin? If he knew something about a plot, then why not take him out?"

"Maybe they did," Clark said. "It took a while to find the family's bodies. Maybe they just haven't found his yet."

His dad stood and rested a strong hand on Clark's shoulder. "I admire your way of thinking, son. But usually the least complex answer is the correct one."

"How is this plot any less complex than a man killing his entire family?" Clark asked.

"One, unfortunately, is pretty common. I think every state in the nation has been touched by it in the last ten years," his father said. "But taking out a family because one member knew something—that sort of thing went out with the gangsters of the 1930s."

Clark had no response to that. Maybe his father was right. Maybe Clark preferred to think of a conspiracy instead of a single man destroying everything he loved.

But the idea was one they hadn't looked at. One that he and Chloe might be able to investigate tomorrow.

◆◆◆

Lionel Luthor wasn't sure if beer was his friend or his enemy. His captors had had a lot of it, and were pretty drunk. No one seemed to notice that he had worked his bonds loose again.

The effort had been a difficult one with the extreme pain in his elbow. Sweat had beaded on his face. If the men hadn't been drinking, they might have noticed that and found it suspicious.

Instead, they were sitting at three different points in the room, arguing about what to do with him.

The leader—the big man with the beard—wanted to kill him. Luthor had sensed that from the beginning. For the leader, Luthor's death seemed almost seductive.

Luthor's original captor was arguing against it, saying the money was worth more to them than some obscure financial disaster. And the third guy, the one who had come in with the leader, was silently listening, drinking beer after beer until his eyes got glassy.

He was the first to pass out.

The other two didn't even notice, as involved as they were in their argument. Luthor noted, though, that even though they were drunk and in the middle of a heated debate, they managed not to use each other's names.

He wished they'd pass out like their friend. When that happened, he knew what he would do.

The truck keys sat on the filthy kitchen counter, next to one of the John Deere caps. He would sneak across the room, grab the keys, and hurry outside, making no noise at all. Then he would start the truck and drive out of here as fast as he could, doing his best to make sure they didn't follow him.

A cell phone or a gun hidden in the truck would be too much to hope for, of course. From the moment he got free of the ropes until he arrived in the nearest town, he would be on his own.

He knew he'd have to be careful. One mistake, and he would lose what might be his only opportunity.

But he'd never been a man who waited for anyone else to take care of him. If he had done that—if he had had that attitude—he would never have put together LuthorCorp, never have succeeded in business, never have achieved half the things he achieved.

A beer can toppled to the floor and rolled away from the couch. His initial captor had passed out, and apparently the can had slipped through his fingers.

The leader stared at the rolling can as if it were a grenade. He picked up the pistol he had laid on the table and pointed it at the can, tracking it across the floor.

Luthor watched, hoping that the leader wouldn't shoot the can. The man was too drunk to be thinking clearly. A can like that would explode and send shrapnel all over the room.

"Bang," the leader whispered, and then laughed. "Scare you, Mr. Luthor?"

Luthor didn't answer. He wasn't going to bait this man.

The beer can settled in the middle of the floor, rocking back and forth, the remaining liquid sloshing inside. The can had left a trail of foam that extended all the way to the couch.

"Don't want to admit how scared you are, huh?" The leader stood, swayed, and caught himself on the arm of the chair. "Think I'm wrong? Are you worth more alive than you are dead? Time to find out, huh? See if that kid of yours has been gathering my money yet."

"You're monitoring the accounts of my corporation?" Luthor asked.

"What do you think?" The leader walked across the floor to the tiny kitchen. His steps were steadier now.

Luthor hadn't been keeping track of how much the man had actually had to drink. Maybe he wasn't as drunk as Luthor initially thought.

"Because if you are," Luthor said, "and you're using that information to judge Lex, then you're making a mistake."

"I'll bet you think I'm making a bundle of mistakes, Mr. Luthor."

The leader opened the refrigerator and used the door to brace himself as he looked inside.

"Idiots never buy enough beer," he mumbled.

Luthor glanced at the other two. The initial captor was on the couch, in the same position Luthor had first seen him. The snoring was just beginning—little muffled grunts. Pretty soon, Luthor knew from experience, they would become full-blown roars.

The gun lay on the arm of the chair where the leader had been sitting. Careless. Deliberately careless to see what Luthor would do? Or drunk careless?

Luthor wasn't sure yet. But he would find out.

The leader closed the refrigerator door. He was holding another beer can. It took him a moment to get a grip on the pull tab. When he finally got the beer open, the can sloshed, spilling liquid all over the floor.

The entire cabin smelled of beer now, a scent Luthor couldn't abide.

"So," the leader said. "Tell me about my 'mistake.'"

"It's just that Lex has no access to those accounts. He needs cooperation from the full board or help from my CFO, who happens to be in Canada. Lex's hands are tied."

It was a lie. Luthor didn't have a chief financial officer. He didn't believe in having someone else run his money. The board was easily accessible, but the average person didn't—couldn't—know that.

"CFO?" the leader said. "I expect you expect me to ask you what that is."

Luthor remained quiet.

"I didn't think you had no CFO, Mr. Luthor. Thought you believed too many hands in the money stole the money."

That was one of his pet phrases. This man knew more about him than he had realized.

"LuthorCorp has a CFO," he said. "I don't know where you heard that we didn't."

"The write-ups in *Business Week* and *Fortune*, not to mention those profiles they do in the business section of the *Daily Planet*. They shoulda called yours Portrait of a Control Freak."

The man was probably right. Luthor actually found a bit of humor in the moment. "Then you understand the dilemma. Lex has no access to any real money. If you know my family's history, you know that my son isn't exactly—reliable."

"Hell." The leader grabbed a wooden-backed chair, and sat in it backwards, bracing the beer on his knee. "If I had a choice between trusting you or trusting him, I'd pick him any day."

"Would you?" Luthor was finding this conversation fascinating. Where had this man gained his opinions of Lex and LuthorCorp? He sounded almost as if he had personal experience.

"Sure. Lex seems to understand the working man. You never have."

Luthor shook his head. "You people fail to realize that I am a working man. I built my fortune from the ground up. I was once a man with no means, and I made myself into someone. People like you seem to think the world owes you money, owes you wealth. You don't want to work for it."

"'People like me?'" the leader said softly. "What do you know about me, Mr. Lionel Luthor?"

"Only that you believe breaking the law is the best way to make a dollar. And that you're probably a control freak, just like you accuse me of being. Except that you like having people in your control. People who are more powerful than you are."

The leader was across the floor in half an instant. He grabbed Luthor by the hair and pulled his head back, straining Luthor's neck. The man bumped Luthor's injured arm as he did so, and ripples of pain ran through Luthor's body.

"I got complete control over you, Luthor. Don't you forget it."

The man smelled of beer. His eyes were red-rimmed and his cheeks were flushed.

Luthor didn't say anything. After a moment, the man released him, shoving him forward. The chair tilted dangerously for a moment, then righted itself.

"You'll never have complete control over me," Luthor said. "You can beat me, hurt me, or kill me, but you'll never break me, and you'll never control me."

The man's eyes narrowed. "Don't give me a challenge like that."

"I feel rather safe in doing so," Luthor said. "You don't have the patience to defeat me."

The man slapped him across the mouth so hard that Luthor bit his tongue.

"'Violent delights,'" Luthor said, tasting blood as he quoted Shakespeare, "'have violent ends.'"

The man yanked him backwards, pulling him so close that their faces almost touched. Luthor's arm was pinched between the chair and the man's leg. The pain was exquisite.

"You ever wondered, Luthor, what happens to everything a man learns when he dies?"

Luthor stared up at those eyes, realizing that they weren't the eyes of a drunk at all.

"I think," the man said, "the knowledge just goes away. Poof! Vanished. Gone. Nothing left. It's why I never bothered to learn nothing that I couldn't use later—not to batter someone with words, but to actually put to use."

"Yes," Luthor said, his voice strangled by the position of his head. "I see how well this plan has worked for you."

The man shoved the chair away again, and this time it fell on its side. Luthor landed on the arm again, and the pain was so intense that his entire world turned white for a brief moment.

He blinked, then opened his eyes. The trail of beer ran past him like a tiny river. The man was crouched in front of him. When he saw that Luthor was awake, he kicked him as hard as he could in the kidneys.

Luthor's breath left his body.

The man grinned. "If I decide to kill you here and now, there's no one to stop me, Luthor. Those idiots are passed out. It's just you and me."

Luthor stared up at him, trying to not gasp for air.

"What I like best about it," the man said, "is that I can take my time. Rather like you do when you decide to destroy someone. I can do it one punch—"

And with that he brought his fist down on Luthor's neck, making Luthor choke.

"—and one kick at a time."

The boot found his ribs again. Luthor closed his eyes. He wouldn't give this monster the satisfaction of seeing pain, however involuntary.

Luthor braced himself for a long night of violence—and hoped that somehow he would survive.

Clark deliberately missed the school bus the next morning. He waited until the bus was around the corner before he used his superspeed to head into Smallville. Running that fast, faster than anyone could see him move, always gave him a thrill. While he was moving that fast his super-vision seemed to slow the world down around him, letting him place his feet perfectly, never missing a step. It was as if the entire world slowed down instead of him speeding up.

He stopped at the Talon, bought Chloe the House Caffeine Special, made with chocolate and a triple shot of espresso, and then hurried, again using his speed to get him past any distractions, and to school.

He knew where he would find her—and he was right.

She was asleep in front of her computer in the *Torch* office, the lights on low the way she had had them all night, and the blinds drawn.

Clark opened the blinds first, letting in the morning sunshine. Chloe groaned. He set down the coffee beside her, along with the pastry he'd picked up at the same time, then stood back.

"This is not fair," Chloe said. She wiped her hair out of her face. "Whoever invented morning should have been stopped."

"I hope you brought your own clothes last night," Clark said, "because I don't think Lana has anything else that she can loan you."

Chloe groped for the coffee, pulled off the lid, and took a sip. "Oh, Clark. You got me real caffeine."

"I got you a buzz that'll last until next week." He sat down. "I hope your work last night turned up something."

"It did." She took a bite of the pastry. "This is good too. You're a saint, Clark."

He felt his cheeks flush. "Don't get carried away."

"Don't mind me," she said. "I'm delirious from lack of sleep."

She took another bite of the pastry. Clark was glad he had

done this for her. He couldn't remember seeing her look so wan—at least not when she was healthy. It was more than lack of sleep. This case had gotten to her, just as it had gotten to him and his parents.

"Well?" he asked. "What did you learn?"

She chased the last bit of pastry down with some coffee, swallowed, and said, "I'm not sure what to make of this, but I have a hunch that somehow everything is tied to LuthorCorp."

Clark frowned. "I'm beginning to think everything in Smallville is tied to LuthorCorp."

"Well, it does seem that way." Chloe seemed to be gaining animation as the caffeine and sugar hit. "But I found some strange things."

She told Clark about her findings—Jed Franklin's arrest record, the fact that he once had made the farm a going concern, but somehow lost control of it, the work he did at LuthorCorp, and his strangeness the last few weeks, including his arrests.

Then she took a deep breath and drank some more coffee. Clark could tell she wasn't quite done with her story, so he gave her time to gather herself.

"Clark," Chloe said. "Danny Franklin asked me to write a story on the layoffs. He said they weren't what they seemed, that there was something funny going on. I blew him off . . ."

Her voice trailed away, and she looked down, but not before Clark saw her eyes fill with tears. So that was why she was fighting this story so hard. She felt guilty, too, just like Roberts did. Just like Lana did.

Had the entire community failed these people? Maybe Clark's dad was right. It certainly did seem that way.

"Anyway," Chloe said after a moment. "I'm wondering if we shouldn't check this out. There might be something to it."

Clark nodded. "Last night my dad told me he'd heard one of Jed Franklin's rants. I guess Mr. Franklin was talking about some kind of plot to take down LuthorCorp."

"Do you think he knew about the kidnapping?" Chloe asked.

"That's what I said to my dad, but my dad dismissed it. Said Mr. Franklin was spouting 'crazy stuff.' But I don't know. Maybe he wasn't."

"That still doesn't explain what happened to the family."

"Maybe someone came to kill Franklin and ended up getting everyone," Clark said.

"And they just haven't found Franklin's body yet."

"Exactly."

Chloe stood up. She seemed to be her old self again, energetic and interested. "We've got to track down this plot, Clark."

"We've got American Lit in half an hour, Chloe. I think the investigation can wait until after school."

"Can it?" Chloe asked. "What if we track down the kidnappers?"

"Now you're dreaming," Clark said. "At best, all we're going to figure out is what was going through Jed Franklin's mind in the past week. And I'm not even sure we're going to get that."

"I fell asleep figuring I needed to talk to some of the others who were laid off at the plant," Chloe said. "How about you go to American Lit and take notes, and I go to LuthorCorp to get names?"

"How about we both go to American Lit, and then we talk to this guy I know during lunch," Clark said. "He'll probably be able to tell us the names of everyone laid off from LuthorCorp since the plant opened here."

Chloe shook her head. "Why're you pushing class, Clark?"

"Because, Chloe. The *Torch* isn't the *Washington Post*, and you're not Woodward or Bernstein. You're not going to bring down a president today."

"But I might solve a murder and a kidnapping," she said, grinning at him.

"And then what?" Clark asked. "Most newspapers hire people who've graduated from journalism school, Chloe, and to get into the best journalism schools, you need good grades. You can't skip class whenever you're on the trail of something hot."

She grabbed her book bag. "If I didn't like you so much, Clark Kent, I'd be really annoyed at the fact that you're right all the time."

"So you're coming to class?"

"If you take me to this source of yours."

"I promise." She shook the book bag at him. "And yes, I did bring my own clothes this time. So I'll see you in class."

"I'm expecting you there, Chloe."

"Yes, sir, Truant Officer Kent. I'll be right there, sir." And, still smiling, she flounced out of the room.

Clark sat there for another minute. On days like this, he didn't like the restrictions of going to school any more than Chloe did. But he knew how his parents would feel if he cut class to follow a hunch.

Besides, he and Chloe were trying to solve murders, not save someone from dying. He had a hunch his parents wouldn't mind if he missed class to save someone's life. But to solve a case, that was entirely different.

Even though it didn't feel that way.

◆◆◆

Lex had gotten a few fitful hours of sleep on the couch in his office. He had vacated his father's office somewhere around midnight when he had the thought that working in there made him feel like his father wasn't going to come back.

Sunlight pouring into the wall of windows had woken him out of a dream in which his father was a Roman emperor, dying at the hands of his subjects, while Lex stood on a nearby hill and played the fiddle.

He didn't like it that his brain was casting him as the careless Nero. The message was one he didn't want to contemplate.

Lex had also sent an order to personnel to get him a real secretary, not someone who looked like she should grace the pages of *Playboy*. His father's secretary was still on the job — he had sent her home, though, at ten, making her promise to return at her usual time — but he really wanted a competent person who knew how to create office miracles.

The first miracle his new secretary had to perform was to get Lex a nourishing breakfast and more coffee than any human could drink. He wanted everything piping hot, and he also insisted on tasty.

Mrs. Anderson—reassuringly middle-aged and gray-haired—had managed that task with aplomb. He was eating eggs Benedict, and eyeing the stack of pastries that sat on his desk. The coffee, hot, fresh, and tasty, was the best he'd ever tasted in Metropolis.

He was looking at satellite photographs that Hensen had gotten from some government agency. They were photos of the areas between Metropolis and Smallville, taken just after dawn.

There were even more remote rural areas than he had thought. His impression of Kansas, the state he'd always called his home, was of flat prairies and rolling farmland. He had forgotten just how many wooded areas there were, and how many secluded rivers and streams ran throughout those places.

Kansas, though, had a bloody history of outlaws and fugitives. The James Gang had gotten its start here, not to mention the actual war fought on the land in the years before the Civil War started. They called the state Bloody Kansas then. The marauders had found a whole bunch of places to hide, and had never been caught.

Lex shook off the thoughts. They would catch the people who held his father, and they would get his father back. Alive.

Not that his father would reward him for that.

Part of Lex's complex emotional reaction to this entire ordeal was a concern—as time went on—that he would pull his father from near-certain death and his father, instead of complimenting him, would say, *Leave it to you, Lex, to take so long.*

Suddenly, the eggs Benedict didn't taste good any longer. Lex grabbed his coffee mug and stood. He went to his computer and saw that another e-mail was blinking for him.

He'd set Brodsky another task last night. He wanted Brodsky and his team of hackers to find out everything they could about Porter a.k.a. J. B. Bynes.

Lex clicked open the e-mail program. Sure enough, the e-mail waiting for him, amidst the e-lists he was on, the various business letters he got, and a whole slew of requests for e-interviews from reporters, was a note from Brodsky.

The e-mail note was short and to the point.

```
Our boy rents an apartment in Smallville, as
I'm sure you know. The address is probably in
your corporate database. However, he has no
real reason to rent since he owns some
property in the next county. County records
show a building on that site, but do not
register an owner. In fact, records indicate
that the owner is absentee, living in
California. Some research led me to the fact
that the owner, listed as one B.J. Ropter is
actually our friend Porter/Bynes.

Address listed below. Area map at this URL.

Have Fun . . .
```

Lex clicked on the URL. His Internet program opened quickly and he found himself staring at a piece of property large enough to hide several houses in. The property was off a county road. Survey work had been done for another road leading onto the property, but, according to the map, the road hadn't yet been built.

Lex checked the map's date. It was a year old.

If there was no development on that property, then there was no reason to put a road up there. In fact, the owners of the property might have fought it—particularly if they used the undeveloped land for hunting or other outdoor activities.

He grabbed the surveillance photographs, thumbing through them, looking at the marks Hensen or someone had made that showed where this was located on the grid.

The satellite photographs showed a heavily wooded area, filled in with young trees. The county road ran along the bottom of the photograph. That road was so badly maintained that potholes were visible.

Several fire lanes and driveways opened onto the county road. Through the trees, Lex could see the brown roofs of several buildings, all of them far enough from each other that they would seem isolated.

His mouth was dry, and the eggs Benedict churned in his stomach. He regretted them now. Or maybe it was the coffee that caused him to be unsettled.

Or maybe just the information itself.

He opened the top drawer of the desk, saw that it was empty except for a few pens, and cursed. Of course it was empty. This wasn't his desk from home. He punched the intercom, and said to Mrs. Anderson, "Get me a magnifying glass. Quickly."

She yessirred him, but he ignored it. He held all of the satellite photographs of that region up to the light, dismissing one after another, until he settled on the one whose place on the grid matched the map he'd found.

Something reflected morning light—something shiny and metal. A tin roof? They weren't uncommon in buildings finished during the thirties, forties and fifties, especially in rural locations. He squinted, saw overgrowth thick and so abundant that he could barely see past it.

He set the photograph on the blotter, got the photograph of an area adjacent to it, and slid it into place. There was a fire lane off the county road that might lead to the shiny thing, but he couldn't tell. The fire lane had been poorly maintained. Obviously, there hadn't been a lot of traffic on it—which made sense if the land was owned by J. B. Bynes.

Mrs. Anderson came into the office, clutching a magnifying glass. She set it on his desk and left without saying a word, something Lex appreciated.

He picked up the glass and ran it over the satellite photograph. The flash of light bounced off the roof of something smaller than a building. A truck, maybe, or a car.

Next to it was something he wouldn't have noticed without the magnifying glass. A moss-covered brown roof. Without the glass, it had looked like part of the woods.

"Found you, you son of a bitch," Lex said. "I finally found you."

CHAPTER 16

The phone call came in two hours later.

Lex had spent the morning sending out people to gather more information. He told the FBI guys just enough to get them out of his way. And then he assembled his own security team.

He was going to get his father, and deal with J. B. Bynes his own way.

Mrs. Anderson intercommed him just before he went back to the Club Noir to meet with the guys—old friends all—who were going to go with him.

"Mr. Luthor," she said in a tone of voice he'd only heard people use with his father. "You have a call."

As she said that, the door to his office opened and Hensen stood there.

"We think it's him," Hensen said.

"Then you should have him," Lex said. "You can trace anything nowadays."

"Except cell phones. We're not getting a reading yet, which leads me to believe this is one, but we will. If nothing else, we'll triangulate the signal."

"I thought you have to be close to do that," Lex said.

"We will," Hensen said. "Once we pinpoint the tower he's using, we'll get someone there to triangulate."

Lex resisted the urge to roll his eyes. He was so glad he wasn't one of those people who listened to authority and trusted their every word. If he did, he knew his father would die at these kidnappers' hands.

No wonder Dewitt the Expert had such an abysmally poor success rate. Attempting to triangulate a signal that could be coming from California for all they knew.

As if that would work.

"All right," Lex said. "You can leave now."

"I'm going to help you with the call," Hensen said.

"No, you're not." Lex put his hand on the receiver. "I'll risk letting him hang up before I talk in front of you."

Hensen's mouth thinned. In that moment, Lex realized that Hensen approved of him even less than Dewitt had. Hensen just hid it better.

But Hensen backed out of the door, and Lex picked up the receiver, punching the button for the line at the same time.

"Lex Luthor."

"Took you long enough." The voice was vaguely familiar, but Lex didn't know if that was because he expected it to be. He wondered what J. B. Bynes would do if Lex called him by name.

But Lex decided not to. He didn't want to scare the man off. "Do I know you?" Lex asked, his tone cold.

"Do you know me." The man laughed. "Good one. Nice try, Lex, old chum. You know exactly who I am, and you're toying with me, trying to keep me on the line so that your police buddies can trace this call. Tell them it's not worth their time. I'm not using a tower. I got one of them satellite phones—"

Something people often needed in wooded areas, because there weren't cell towers close enough, or the reception was too bad to use.

"—and they're not going to be able to track me down, ever."

"I see," Lex said, not surprised by this development. Bynes had shown amazing savvy thus far. That had surprised Lex, although it shouldn't have. Bynes had been a smart man. Lex still wondered if Bynes had planned this long before he even came to Smallville.

"You do, huh?" Bynes—or one of his henchmen—said.

"What I don't understand," Lex said, "is why you didn't e-mail me this time."

"Figured I only got one free pass at your friend's Internet café. Did I photograph real good? I tried to give you the best view of my nostril that I could."

So he had seen the small camera on top of the computer. But he hadn't known about the one behind the desk. Lex was going to keep it that way.

"Your pores need flushing," Lex said. "They're a bit enlarged."

"I'll do it when I got the money," Bynes said. "You are going to get me the money, aren't you?"

"You haven't told me when you want it." Lex picked up the satellite photograph. If Bynes was using a satellite phone, then he could be calling from this little spot in the woods right now.

"I figured you were smart enough to know I'd want it as soon as possible."

"You going to come here and get it?" Lex asked.

Bynes let out a bark of a laugh. "Nice try. I've got instructions for you. Ready to take them down?"

"No, actually." Lex leaned back in his chair, pretending to be relaxed, just like he would if he were talking to Bynes in person.

His words met with silence on the other end, and for a long moment, Lex thought Bynes had hung up. Then Bynes said, "No?"

"No."

"So it is true. You really do hate your father."

"How I feel about my father is between me and him," Lex said. "What I am unwilling to do is pay you money if you've already murdered him."

Lex regretted that phrasing immediately. *If you've already murdered him* left the door open for Lex paying Bynes, and then Bynes killing his father. In fact, it almost put the idea into Bynes head.

"He's alive," Bynes said.

"I have no proof of that," Lex said. "All you sent me were some photos taken shortly after you kidnapped him and a video taken God knows when. I've had nothing today. For all I know, you're not even the guy who has him."

"I'm the guy." Bynes sounded offended.

"There's no way for me to know that," Lex said. "Your *modus operandi* is different."

"My what?"

Lex smiled. "Your way of doing things," he said, making his tone deliberately condescending.

"You and your father have a lot in common, you know that?"

"Of course we do," Lex said. "He raised me, after all."

Bynes made a noise that sounded suspiciously like a Bronx cheer. "You want the instructions or not?"

"You can give them to me," Lex said, "but I won't follow them until I have definitive proof that my father is alive right now, as we speak."

"And if I can't provide that?"

Lex's entire body turned cold. He gripped the phone so hard that he could feel the plastic give. "Then you don't get your money."

"And you don't get your father back," Bynes said.

Lex took a deep breath, doing his best to sound calm. "If you kill him, we both lose."

"Do we?" Bynes asked. "Seems to me you stand to inherit a lot. You could share, you know."

Lex slammed down the phone, hoping he made the right choice. His father always told him not to negotiate with terrorists, kidnappers, or any other criminal who crossed his path. *It's always the wrong decision, Lex. They'll keep coming back.*

Still, hearing his father's voice on this did not reassure him. It made him feel worse.

He was gambling with his father's life. He knew it, and now Bynes knew it, but probably didn't understand why. If his father was alive now, he might not be shortly.

Or Bynes might call Lex's bluff and send photographs, something to prove that his father was alive.

Lex hid his face in his hands. He wouldn't wait for another contact.

He had to move quickly. He had no other choice.

Clark was on his way to American history class when he glanced out the windows in the hallway and saw a blond head bob through the cars in the parking lot. Chloe. She wasn't going to wait for lunch.

He should have known. She was too obsessed by this. She wanted the story too much.

He wondered where she was going. He had told her that he knew how to find out who had been laid off.

But of course Chloe had her sources, too, and she was going to talk to all of them—without him. Then she would go and get into trouble, and he wouldn't be able to save her. Not without knowing where she was.

"What's going on?" Pete stopped right in front of Clark. Lana was just behind him.

"Chloe. I promised to help her with the story, and she's leaving now."

"Now?" Lana asked. "We've got most of the school day to finish."

Clark nodded. "Look, I'm going to see if I can stop her—"

"You won't be able to stop her," Pete said.

"Well, then, I'll tag along," Clark said. "Make some excuses for us, Lana. Say that I had to drive her home sick or something."

"Clark," Lana said. "You shouldn't—"

"Me, too," Pete said.

"If you're all going, I'm going," Lana said.

Clark felt his heart sink. He couldn't keep an eye on everyone. "Look, guys. I don't think there's any reason for this."

"We're all involved, Clark," Lana said.

Pete was already heading to the exit near the windows. "I'll stop Chloe."

Clark bit his tongue. It would have been more effective for him to do it, especially since she had such a head start, but now he wouldn't get the chance.

He had no choice but to trail after Pete. Lana followed.

"It would be better if you just made excuses for us," Clark said.

"Not for me," Lana said. "It's better to be doing something than sitting around learning about people who did something."

Clark shook his head, holding the door open for her as she stepped outside. "Somehow I'm thinking you meant for that to make sense."

"You know what I mean, Clark."

And he did, too. That was the tough part. He let the door close behind them.

The air had a bit of a chill to it today. The heat from the previous days was gone. Clark started across the sidewalk, heading for the parking lot, tempted to take large steps so that he left Lana behind.

But she managed to keep pace with him. She seemed as determined as Chloe did.

Pete was already halfway across the parking lot, running and waving his arms. Chloe had driven toward the entrance, but she stopped, apparently having seen Pete. She stopped there, rolling her window down.

Clark could hear her voice, even though he was still half a parking lot away.

"You're not going to change my mind. I've got a lead . . ."

And then her voice faded. She must have turned her head. Pete walked to the side of the car. He was responding to her, but Clark couldn't hear him.

Then Pete grabbed the car door and pulled it open. He stood there, not getting in, and looked for Clark.

"Come on," Lana said. She ran between a group of cars until she reached Chloe.

Clark followed, wishing that there was some other way to do this. He knew it would be better to wait, but no one else was going to.

And he had a bad feeling about the entire project.

When he reached the car, Lana and Pete were already in the backseat. He looked at the passenger seat, remembering how his knees banged against the dashboard on the last trip.

"Get in, Clark, before Principal Kwan comes out here and I get into even more trouble," Chloe said.

Clark climbed in. "I'm pretty sure you're going to be in trouble anyway."

"So," Chloe said, as she took her foot off the brake, "where're we going?"

Clark pulled the car door closed. "You looked like you knew."

"I was heading for the plant. I figured I could wheedle the names out of someone. But you said you knew a person who could talk to us." Chloe looked at him. "You weren't just saying that to keep me in class, were you?"

He could have lied at that moment, although he wasn't sure it would have done any good. She was already out of class, already in her car, already determined. And she had a plan in case Clark didn't come through.

"His name is Bob Reasoner," Clark said. "He used to work at the feed and seed. Then he went to work for LuthorCorp. Now he's working at the gas station downtown. I saw him the other day, and commented on his new job. He said he was one of the unlucky guys who got laid off."

Chloe gave Clark a brilliant smile. "I knew you'd come through for me."

"It might be for nothing," Clark said.

"If so, then we'll all be back in class in an hour or two," she said.

Clark doubted that they would be back at all today.

Chloe drove down back streets to an apartment complex she hadn't even realized existed. She had never been in this part of Smallville. Nor, from their comments, had Pete and Lana.

Clark was being unusually quiet—even for him. He had gotten out of the car with her at the gas station so that they could talk to Bob Reasoner. Reasoner was a short, dumpy man with a perpetually bitter expression on his face, certainly not someone Chloe would have expected Clark to know.

Reasoner had also been rude when he found out why they were there.

"Look," he'd said. "I saw where talking about this got Jed Franklin. I'm not going to tell you nothing."

"You think Mr. Franklin killed his family because he was laid off?" Chloe asked.

Reasoner had given her a how-dumb-are-you look. "I think Franklin got mixed up with the wrong element, and when he tried to talk about it, things got worse."

"What do you mean?" Clark asked.

"I said, Clark, I ain't gonna talk about it, and I mean it."

Clark had given him that gruff apologetic look that Clark seemed to specialize in, then he'd walked back to the car. Chloe had stayed for an extra minute. Sometimes Clark's aw-shucks style was too soft for people like Reasoner.

"I'm going to find out what the problem is, Mr. Reasoner," Chloe said. "And when I do, I'm going to put your name in the *Torch* along with everyone else's. So you can talk to me now, or you can talk later, maybe to reporters from bigger papers, like the *Daily Planet*. It's up to you."

Reasoner's eyes narrowed when she had said that. "You ain't as nice as you look, are you, Missy?"

Chloe gave him a half smile. "Not even close."

He sighed. "I'll tell you one thing, then you'll leave me

alone. You won't mention my name, not now, not never. Got that?"

"Depends on what you tell me, Mr. Reasoner."

He seemed to weigh that. Then he started talking. "The problem started when a guy by the name of J. B. Bynes signed on at the plant. Troublemaker from the start. He tried to unionize, but I never thought his heart was in it, you know? He spent too much time talking about how much money the Luthors was worth, and how we deserved a piece of it. I think word got to Daddy Luthor, and those of us who was listening to Bynes, we all got fired."

"I thought you were laid off," Chloe said.

"Laid off is fired with benefits. We was told if we went quiet, we'd get the benefits."

"Mr. Franklin wasn't quiet."

"Nope. I think if word of that got back to Old Man Luthor, there'd've been trouble. But now even Luthor's got trouble, don't he?"

Chloe frowned. "You think that's related?"

"I think I done said enough, Missy." Reasoner turned his back on her and walked away.

"Mr. Reasoner," Chloe said. "One more thing. Where can I find J. B. Bynes?"

Reasoner stopped, and looked around as if he wanted to make sure no one else heard her ask the question. Then he walked all the way back to her.

"He's got an apartment on Oak Circle in that complex they built about fifteen years ago. Ground floor, first building, first apartment. You can't miss it." Then Reasoner had leaned close to Chloe. "I never did see you. I don't know you, and if you tell anyone you heard this from me, I'm gonna say that you're lying. You got that?"

He had actually unnerved her, not because she was afraid he would hurt her, but because he seemed so very frightened.

"I got it," she had said, and hurried back to the car.

At that point, she had offered to drive the group back to school, but they wouldn't hear of it. They made her tell about her conversation with Reasoner, and only Clark thought it sounded really strange.

In fact, that was when he went all strong-and-silent type on her.

"What's with you, Clark?" she said, as they approached the apartment complex.

Clark shook his head.

"Clark," Lana said. "You're being mysterious."

Usually when Lana butted in, Chloe got a little annoyed. But she was grateful this time.

Clark turned toward Lana. "I don't mean to be."

"Then what's bugging you?" Pete asked.

Clark shrugged and looked out the passenger window again. Trees that were half the size of the ones near the Kent farm grew near the curb.

Chloe willed him to answer.

"If it's that Reasoner guy," Chloe said, "I think he was just being dramatic. Guys like that—"

"Guys like that are usually straight up and honest, Chloe." Clark sounded almost annoyed at her. "I've never seen him like that, and I've known him for years. He never says much, but when he does, you listen."

Chloe sighed. "I did listen, Clark. That's why we're here."

She turned into the apartment complex's parking lot. The complex was one of those two-story things, with the lower apartments jutting out. The second-floor apartments had balconies that overhung the entrances to the first floor.

When it had been built, it was probably the best complex in Smallville. Since then, it had become run-down. So, apparently, had the residents. The cars parked in the marked spaces were several years old, dented, and rust covered.

Chloe stopped in front of the first building, just like Reasoner had told her to. She was surprised to note that two-car garages were attached to the buildings.

"I'm going to do this," she said. "I think it'll freak this guy if all four of us go to the door."

"You're not going alone," Clark said.

Chloe glanced around at Lana and Pete, who were both nodding.

She had known he was going to say that. In fact, she was

counting on it. Even though she didn't want to admit it to the group, Reasoner's comments had bothered her, too.

"All right," she said. "Just you, Clark."

She grabbed her tape recorder and stuck it in the pocket of her jeans. Then she picked up her camera. Clark was out of the car before she was.

He met her on the curb. Together they walked toward the first apartment, leaving Pete and Lana watching intently from the car.

Small, neglected shrubs lined the walkway. Tulips years past their first bloom shoved their spindly buds through the hard dirt. The steps leading up to the first apartment were cracked and filthy from the winter snows. Months' worth of advertising circulars had been kicked away from the door and left on the stoop to rot.

Clark went up first, peered at the name above the bell, and shrugged. "This is it."

Chloe took a deep breath. She shouldn't have been so pleased that Clark was helping her. One day she would have to go to places like this alone.

But something about this apartment, its darkness and obvious neglect made her feel more uncomfortable than she had ever felt approaching an interview subject. She glanced at Clark, who raised his eyebrows at her, as if he were asking her if she wanted to go through with this.

In answer, she punched the bell.

An anemic wheeze echoed through the apartment. No other sound came from inside. Chloe punched the bell again.

Nothing.

"He's not there." A woman's voice came from above them. Chloe had to step back, off the stoop, to see who was talking to her.

A woman in her late twenties, wearing a bikini despite the afternoon chill, her face covered with sunscreen, leaned over the rail.

"Where is he?" Chloe asked.

"Looking for work, probably." The woman shrugged. "Said he had a line on some good money."

Clark, after staring vacantly at the door for a moment, stepped back so that he was standing beside Chloe.

The woman grinned. "Thought I saw someone else underneath this balcony. Who's your friend, sweetie?"

Chloe wanted to say that Clark was in high school and should be left alone, but she had a hunch she would never hear the end of it.

"What kind of money?" Chloe asked.

"I don't know. He's not the most chatty guy." The woman leaned even harder on the rail. It didn't look too stable. Chloe wouldn't have put that much weight on it.

"So do you know when he'll be back?" Clark asked.

"Probably not for a while. He left for Metropolis about a week back."

"That's where he had this job lined up?" Chloe asked.

"You know, sweetie, you act like it's my week to watch him. It's not."

Clark gave her the brightest smile Chloe had ever seen him use. "I'm sure, though, you overheard a few things."

He was actually flirting to get information. Chloe never thought Clark would do anything like that.

"Honey, if you come up here, I'll tell you a few things."

Clark's smile got wider. "You did, didn't you," he said. "What'd you hear?"

"I heard him fighting with one of his buddies. The guy was screaming awful things about his family and everything else."

"Jed Franklin," Chloe whispered.

Clark nodded.

"J. B. said everything'd be fine in a week or so. Then he come back here a day or two later, with another guy. They were laughing, and going on like they were having the best time. That's when I called down to J. B., and he said he had one job to finish, and after that, he was getting out of here."

Clark's smile faded. "He said that?"

"Sure did. Don't like that, honey?"

"Just doesn't sound like him," Clark said, pretending to know the man.

"Oh, it sounds exactly like him. Don't know him well, do you?" The woman leaned over farther. Chloe wondered if the bikini top would stay on. "Want to come on up here? I could show you a few things."

"I'll bet she could," Chloe said under her breath.

"I mean, a few things of J. B.'s." The woman said, glaring at Chloe. Apparently, she had heard Chloe's comment.

"No, thanks," Clark said. "I'll just leave him a note."

"Best put it on his truck," the woman said. "If he comes back for anything, he'll come back for that."

"Which one is it?" Chloe asked.

"The one in the attached garage. I'm subletting it. He owes me three months, too, so I'm hoping he gets back real soon now, or that truck is mine." The woman pulled away from the rail, as if talking about J. B. Bynes's truck soured her on the conversation.

Clark glanced at Chloe, who shrugged. She hadn't expected a dead end like this. For some reason, she thought she'd run into J. B. Bynes at his apartment.

Lana and Pete had gotten out of the car. They joined Chloe and Clark as they walked to the garage.

"What was that?" Pete asked.

"Someone with too much time on her hands," Chloe said.

They reached the garage. The garage door hadn't been painted in years, and a large chunk of wood had broken off the front, probably where someone ran into the door. The windows were soaped, and Chloe tried the regular door to the left.

It was locked.

"Now what do we do?" Lana asked.

"Guess we head back," Pete said. "It's another dead end."

Clark walked to the regular door. "Let me try. It might just be stuck."

Chloe hated it when he did that. He seemed to have a magic touch with doors, an ability to open them even when she was certain they were locked.

Sure enough, he leaned his body into the door, grabbed the knob, and the door opened as easily as if it hadn't even been closed tightly.

"Someday you'll have to show me how to do that," Chloe

said as she walked past him into the darkened interior.

The garage smelled of old gasoline and mildew. There was another odor overlaying that, one that seemed both familiar and disquieting. Chloe took a deeper breath, but couldn't place it.

Clark came in behind her, followed by Lana and Pete. It took Chloe's eyes a minute to adjust to the dimness, but enough light filtered in from the soaped-up windows to allow her to see.

The truck certainly didn't look like something to come back for. It was old and dented, just like the ones outside. The difference was that this one had no rust on it, and looked like someone had tried to care for it.

"It smells like the marsh in here," Lana said.

"Thank heavens there aren't any mosquitoes," Pete said.

Chloe looked at Lana. That was the smell, exactly. The stagnant-water smell of the marsh.

"Chloe," Clark said quietly. "That's not J. B. Bynes's truck."

"How do you know, Clark?"

"Because," Clark said as he walked toward it, "that truck belongs to Jed Franklin."

Chloe took a good look at it. Clark was right; the truck was the one she'd seen in the police descriptions, down to the license plate.

The overhead light went on. Chloe turned slightly. Pete was still holding the switch, but he was looking at the floor.

Thick mud, still slightly damp, formed prints from two different kinds of boots. One set appeared from the driver's door of the Franklin truck; the other from the passenger side. They all went to the main door of the garage.

"Wow," Pete muttered.

"Wow is right." Chloe picked up her camera and took shot after shot, making sure she had enough light to get good pictures of the boot prints. "Don't anyone step on those."

"Two people," Clark said. "Two people came back from killing the Franklins."

"And they came here," Lana said. "That Bynes is involved, then."

"Maybe that plot thing my dad overheard wasn't so farfetched after all," Clark said.

Chloe worked her way toward the truck. She took pictures of it, too, the back, the sides, and the interior. Her flash illuminated papers strewn all over the seat.

"But we've hit that dead end," Lana said.

"I don't think so," Clark said. "The woman said Bynes thought he was coming into money. Maybe he's the one who kidnapped Mr. Luthor."

"And the Franklins found out about it?" Pete asked.

Chloe brought her camera down. The truck had a strong odor of mud and mildew and fertilizer. She fought the urge to sneeze.

"Found out about it, said they were going to report it, I don't know," Clark said. "Obviously, Mr. Franklin was involved."

"I didn't check the police reports this morning," Chloe said. "I don't know if they found his body."

"I'll bet they will if they haven't already," Pete said.

"All we have to do is let the police know that the truck is here," Clark said.

"Better make it anonymous this time," Lana said.

"I have a hunch if they find Bynes, they'll find Mr. Luthor," Pete said.

"Maybe I should let Lex know," Clark said.

Chloe was only half-listening. She reached through the open passenger window, and took a sheet of paper off the top.

It didn't look like a receipt for grain or gas. It looked like a scrap of writing paper, something someone would have in their kitchen for notes or scrap.

She held the edge of the paper between the nails of her thumb and forefinger.

"What's that?" Lana asked.

"I don't know," Chloe said. She carefully opened the crumpled sheet, and read:

Old County Rd. B about 10 miles to Fire Road 115423 (hard to see. Weeds). Turn right, follow 3 miles. Cabin on left.

"Directions," Clark said, looking over her shoulder.

"To somewhere obscure," Lana said.

Chloe nodded. "A cabin in the woods."

"The perfect place to hide something," Pete said.

Chloe shoved the paper in her pocket. "Or someone," she said.

The country road was as filled with potholes as it had seemed from the satellite photographs.

Lex sat inside the cab of a flatbed truck—riding shotgun as it were—heading down the road at seventy miles an hour. The potholes felt like caverns at this pace.

On the back of the truck sat an elite unit of men, specially culled from various areas of LuthorCorp and from Lex's old friends. All of them were dressed like firefighters—the kind who took care of out of control brush fires. The flatbed truck, rented from a place just outside of Metropolis, looked like it belonged on these roads.

Now, if no one stopped them, the truck and its passengers would seem like men going about their daily routine. If they did get stopped, all hell would break loose.

The amount of firepower alone on the vehicle was enough to hold off most armies. Lex didn't have the clout his father had, so he wouldn't be able to make any police officer or redneck county sheriff look the other way.

And Lex didn't even want to think about the number of guys with shady pasts sitting behind him. These guys might just bolt if the police stopped the truck, and then where would they be?

Which was why Lex insisted on a strict seventy-mile-per-hour pace, which was fast for this road, but not completely out of line. Anyone seeing the truck pass would think they were on the way to supervise a spring burn or to put out something caused by the heat of the past few days.

If the passersby thought about the truck at all.

Lex was counting on that, not getting noticed. It was important to his plan.

His plan was simple. He'd go into the cabin with enough men and firepower, overwhelm his father's kidnappers, and get his father out of there.

Lex was not running this show, however. For that, he had a

former Green Beret, who knew how to deal with situations like this. He had two sharpshooters, and several expert marksmen. If his luck held, the kidnappers would be dead before anyone even entered the cabin.

The truck bounced over several more potholes. There were no springs in the seat. Lex gripped his seat belt, glad he was inside instead of out. On the truck bed, the men were sitting on metal. They had no seat belts, and they probably got nearly bounced out of the bed each time the truck ran over something.

Lex was the odd man out on this trip. In fact, his men had suggested he stay back, that he might actually be in the way.

He would do the best he could to avoid being in the way.

But he had to be here. He had to see how this went. He was taking a gamble doing it this way, but gambling was the only way he knew to succeed.

Hensen had chewed him out after the phone call. Hensen had been listening on the other end. He was stunned that Lex hadn't taken the instructions, stunned that Lex had called the kidnapper's bluff.

But Lex hadn't told Hensen about this plan, and wasn't going to. When Lex left LuthorCorp's headquarters, he didn't tell Hensen where he was going. The FBI had been following Lex, and he would let them continue.

He headed back to the Club Noir, his cell phone on his hip like an Old West marshal's six-shooter. If the kidnappers called back, Mrs. Anderson had been instructed to put the call through to Lex, wherever he was.

So far, there had been no callback. That had him worried.

Hensen was checking Lex's e-mail, though, and perhaps the directions had come in that way. Or perhaps the kidnappers were having trouble finding a way to send more pictures and video without being caught.

The first time they had the element of surprise. This time, they knew people were looking for them. Going into an Internet café wouldn't be easy. Going home would be impossible, and setting up a line out here would be difficult.

Lex knew he had given them a hard task.

It also bought him time, and he'd been using that time as

best he could. He'd sent one guy out here already to scope out the area. Lex wanted to make certain his hunch was correct before he committed men and resources to the rescue operation.

His guy had gone out as soon as Lex made the connection between J. B. Bynes's property and the satellite photograph. The man's instructions were simple: Make sure the cabin is occupied; see if he could see the occupants; and try to ascertain if Lionel Luthor was inside. The guy was not to attempt a rescue all by himself, and to pose as a hiker if he got caught by the kidnappers.

But the guy hadn't gotten caught. And he had found a bonus clue, one that guaranteed Lex was on the right track.

He had found the limo, hidden off the fire lane. The limo was parked in a ditch, covered with leaves and tree branches, and impossible to see from the road or the air. Lex's guy—whose real name Lex never knew—hadn't seen the limo either; he had literally stumbled into it.

He also took a few digital photographs of it, including the dirt-covered license plate. LUTHOR 1. That had convinced Lex to go in.

But he was being extra cautious.

He left an envelope with Mrs. Anderson with the instructions to give it to Hensen if she hadn't heard from Lex by four o'clock. Inside the envelope were the information and some of Lex's plans for the rescue attempt.

That way Hensen would know what was happening, that something had gone wrong, and would be able to send the real authorities in. They'd botch it up, of course, but if Lex had already screwed it up, the authorities' mess wouldn't matter at all.

The fire lane numbers were only a few digits off the lane he was looking for. Lex's stomach clenched.

"Remember," he said to the driver. "We block the lane about a half mile in, and then we go by foot."

"We don't know what the acoustics are up there," the driver said. "A half mile might be too close. They might hear us coming."

Lex had already thought of that. "Fine. They still have about two and a half miles to walk from the cabin to that part of the fire lane. If they decide to check us out, that's all the better for us. It'll mean fewer people guarding my father."

"I just hope they don't have this place booby-trapped," the driver said.

Lex felt himself go cold. He hadn't thought of that. "If they did, we wouldn't have been able to scout the place out."

The driver gave Lex a sideways look, but said nothing. Lex felt the contempt, but he ignored it. J. B. Bynes was a career criminal, not career military. He didn't do large-scale operations. Kidnapping Lionel Luthor was probably the most complex plan Bynes ever had in his life.

And, judging by Bynes's past, his henchmen weren't rocket scientists. They all probably assumed that the cabin was too secluded to find. They hadn't counted on all of Lex's contacts, and the information age's resources enabling him to find out so much so fast.

Lex put a hand on his cell phone. It still hadn't vibrated.

He hoped his bluff worked.

He hoped he hadn't made it too impossible for Bynes to collect the money. He had a hunch Bynes would be content just destroying LuthorCorp itself—which could happen without Lex's dad.

But those unknown henchmen. Lex knew they wouldn't be satisfied with some intellectual goal. They'd want cold hard cash. And if Bynes even mentioned that it wasn't possible, then the henchmen might turn against him.

Lex closed his eyes for a moment and leaned his head back. So many scenarios, and no way of knowing if any of them was right.

He was going with his gut, and he knew there was a good chance of his gut's being wrong.

Chloe had missed Old County Road B on her first pass. Only Pete's shout from the back seat had convinced her that something had gone wrong.

The road was no longer a major artery, and the sign was

faded and pierced with birdshot. There was no official exit off the highway between Smallville and Metropolis, only an access road that led to a very active truck stop. Behind the truck stop was a road that ran perpendicular to the main highway. That road was Old County B.

Apparently B was one of those roads only the locals knew about. Potholes as big as craters made the road even more treacherous. A ditch ran along either side, so Chloe felt that if she swerved too much to avoid potholes, the car would topple over the edge.

"This is a great place to hide out," Lana said.

"Certainly is the end of nowhere," Pete said.

Chloe's hands stuck to the wheel. She was sweating, even though the windows were open and it was cool in the car.

Clark wasn't saying anything, having become the strong silent type again. Chloe had the odd feeling that he was planning something, but she wasn't sure what it was.

"Do we know what we're going to do when we see this Bynes guy?" Pete asked.

"We're going to ask him about Franklin," Chloe said.

"Chloe, how realistic is that?" Lana asked. "If he did kill the Franklin family, he's not going to tell us. And if he did, we could be in trouble just for mentioning it."

Chloe nodded. "We'll just play it by ear."

Clark shifted in his seat. His knees banged against the dash, but he didn't even wince.

"We're not far," Clark said. "The fire lane numbers are real close."

Chloe looked at him in surprise. She was beginning to get used to his silence.

Movement up ahead caught her eye. A truck was coming toward her, going very fast.

She hadn't seen any other car on this road. It made her nervous to see the truck.

"You don't think that could be them, do you?" Pete asked.

"Them?" Lana asked. "You mean Bynes?"

"Yes," Pete said.

"I don't know," Chloe said. "It's hard to tell."

The truck slowed, as if it were looking at lane markers, too. Then it almost stopped.

Clark glanced at it, frowned, and tilted his head. He looked surprised.

"What is it, Clark?" Chloe asked.

Clark shook his head slightly, and didn't say anything.

"Clark?"

The truck turned onto one of the fire lanes. As it turned, Chloe noticed a lot of men in the truck's bed. Maybe six guys, maybe more. None of them looked friendly.

"What do you think that's about?" Lana asked.

"I don't know," Clark said, "but it can't be good."

"Why?" Pete said.

"Because," Clark said, "unless I miss my guess, that truck just turned up the road to Bynes's place."

The fire lane was even more rutted than the road had been. Lex bounced along, feeling like his teeth would rattle out of his head. Dust rose alongside the truck. He was amazed the men in the back weren't coughing.

Lex turned his head so that he could see the odometer. He wanted to make certain the driver would stop at a half mile in. He didn't need to worry. It took almost no time to cover that half mile, and then the truck skidded to a stop.

The dust moved ahead of the truck in waves. Lex wondered if they could see the dust from the cabin, and if they could, what they made of it.

The muscles in the back of his neck ached from the strain. The inside of his right cheek hurt where he had bitten it without even realizing he had done so, and he was short of breath.

Behind him, he heard the scrape of metal against metal as half a dozen semiautomatics left the bed of the truck. Then the men jumped off.

Lex pushed the truck door open.

The men already had their heads covered, their faces painted so that they blended into the forest. They must have done that on the drive. He stuck out like a flashlight on a dark night. He could almost feel the sunlight reflecting off his very white, very bald head.

"My father comes out of this alive," Lex said. "You all understand that, right?"

They nodded.

He was just reminding them. He had already told them about the heavy penalties they would pay if any of them accidentally shot his father. If Lionel Luthor didn't survive this ordeal, it would be because he was already dead when the rescue team arrived.

◆◆◆

Just like the directions said, the sign indicating Fire Road 115423 was hard to see. Mostly hidden by weeds, it looked like it hadn't been maintained for years.

"Stop here," Clark said.

Chloe stopped. Clark stared at the fire road. Dust still rose off it from the truck.

"We have to have a new plan," Clark said. "You guys are not going down there."

"You guys?" Pete said. "Since when are you different?"

Since always, Clark thought, but didn't say. He had slipped up and he knew it.

"Did you see what was on that truck?" he asked.

"Lots of guys," Chloe said.

"Dressed either like paramilitary people or firefighters," Clark said. "And they all had guns."

He wasn't going to tell the three others that using his X-ray vision, he also saw Lex Luthor in the front seat. Clark knew what was happening now. Lex had brought in a team to rescue his father—and a lot of people most likely were going to be killed.

But not if Clark could help it.

He got out of the car.

"If we can't go anywhere, what are you doing?" Chloe said.

"I'm just going to walk a little ways down the road, and see if I see anything."

"We're waiting five minutes," Chloe said. "You had better be back."

"Wait until I say it's safe," Clark said. Then he made himself smile at her. "Who knows? You just might have stumbled onto another story. Now stay here until I give the all clear."

She started to answer, but he didn't wait for it. He slammed the car door closed and headed off down the fire lane.

The road was overgrown with weeds and dirt. Most of the weeds had been knocked down recently, though, suggesting a lot of regular use.

Clark walked normally until he knew he was out of sight of the car. Then he used his superspeed to hurry down the lane, letting the world around him go into that superfocus that happened when he was moving fast.

He stopped behind a tree when he saw the truck. It was parked about a half a mile in. Eight men, most carrying semi-automatic rifles, stood near Lex. Lex looked nervous.

Clark understood how he felt. This was the choice Clark would have made if his father were in trouble. Not that he would have brought in men with guns, but he wouldn't have paid any ransom. He'd have tried to rescue his father himself.

Lex didn't have superpowers, so he didn't have the option of going it alone. He had to go in with help. Unfortunately, he had chosen help with so much firepower that someone would get killed—and probably not the kidnappers.

Chloe had been on the right track. J. B. Bynes had something to do with the Franklin family and with the kidnapping. More than likely the Franklins had died when they learned what the plot was.

Lex seemed to be giving last-minute instructions.

This would give Clark the opening he needed. Somewhere up this road were J. B. Bynes and Lionel Luthor. If Clark got there first, he might be able to prevent a lot of bloodshed.

He decided to speed past the truck parked across the road. The men would only see him as a blur. They would have no idea what he was. And it was better than tripping on things through the trees—and maybe forcing one of these nervous hunters to shoot, giving their position away.

He sped forward, hoping that this part of his plan would work.

Something blue and tall zoomed past Lex in a blur. A streak of light and color, zipping around him and the truck as if they weren't even there.

Lex wasn't sure he saw anything until the sound followed— the kind of hiss a car made when it carroomed past a person going more than two hundred miles per hour.

Whatever had gone around Lex had gone faster than that.

The team saw it too. They had their rifles aimed almost before Lex could turn around.

The rifles were aimed at him and his breath caught. Then he realized they were aiming the rifles around him, looking for the cause of the blur.

"Let's not get trigger-happy, gentlemen," he said in as calm a voice as he could.

"What the hell was that?" one of the men asked.

"Probably some kind of bird," Lex said. "There must be wildlife here. Let's not put a hundred rounds into a rabbit just because it startles us, all right?"

The men brought their rifles back into position.

They weren't as disciplined as he would have liked, as he even thought they were, but they were all he had. Now was the time to make the decision.

Did he let them go in, take that risk, and hope that they did the job the way he'd planned it? Or did he abort and let the authorities take it?

Put that way, it wasn't even a choice.

"I don't want to hear any gunfire until we have Bynes in our sights, is that clear?" he said.

The men nodded.

Lex took a deep breath. Now or never.

He opted for now.

"All right then," he said. "Let's fan out."

Clark reached the cabin only seconds later. He stopped behind a parked truck, so new that its chrome still shone, except for the layers of dust on the mud flaps and wheel wells.

Two men stood on the porch. One of them was tall, with a beard, wearing a flannel shirt too hot for the weather and boots covered in marsh mud. The other . . .

The other was Jed Franklin.

Clark felt his stomach knot. Franklin was alive? He had killed his wife and children for this?

Clark couldn't believe it.

"What you're asking me to do," Franklin was saying, "is commit suicide. I'm not going to Metropolis. I don't know how to operate an e-mail, and I'm not going to ask someone for help, especially not when I have to add these pictures."

Clark turned his special vision onto the cabin itself. Two more people were inside. One was sitting down, head lolling to the side. That had to be Lionel Luthor.

"You don't go," the other man said, "and your family is dead."

A shiver of horror ran through Clark. Jed Franklin thought his family was still alive. He was cooperating with the kidnappers because he thought if he did, his family would live.

"What's the difference if I do this or don't?" Franklin said. "You already told me that if I get caught, my family will die. So you put me in an impossible position, J. B. If I don't do what you say, they'll die, and if I do what you say, I'll get caught, and they'll die."

J. B., so Chloe had that much right. J. B. Bynes was involved. No wonder Reasoner was afraid of him. Had Bynes threatened Reasoner's family, too?

Clark glanced over his shoulder. He didn't see or hear any of Lex's people, but that didn't mean they weren't on the way. He only had a few minutes to resolve this whole thing.

"Then you just gotta be smart enough not to get caught," J. B. Bynes was saying.

Clark scanned the entire cabin. There was a crawl space that went beneath the entire sublevel. That helped.

He needed priorities. The first thing he had to do was save Lex's dad. Then get Jed Franklin out of there. And maybe prevent the whole firefight.

He only hoped there'd be time.

"I don't like this," Chloe said, getting out of the car. "Clark has been gone forever."

"It's only been a few minutes, Chloe," Pete said. "It's going to take a while to go up that road. And you said you would wait five minutes, remember?"

"I hope he doesn't go too far," Lana said. "What if he gets seen?"

"We have no idea what he's walking into." Pete crawled out of the back of the car.

Chloe stared down the road. Nothing but wheel ruts, dirt, and broken weeds. No Clark, no truck, no mysterious J. B. Bynes.

"I'm going down there," she said.

"No, you're not," Pete said. "We're waiting for Clark, just like we promised."

Chloe sighed. Then she looked at her watch. "If he's not back in five more minutes, I'm heading down there, with or without you guys."

"If he's not back within five minutes," Lana said from the backseat, "we're all going down there."

So they were decided. And Chloe knew it was going to be the longest five minutes of her life.

Clark scanned the woods behind him, using his special vision. He could see seven people, heading toward him, guns in hand. They'd be here any minute now.

He ran using his super speed to the crawl space, and dug himself in under the house, then quickly turned around and pushed the dirt back so nothing would show. It smelled of mold and animals under there. He crawled over some mouse droppings. A spiderweb caught him in the face. He was in position, and it had only taken a few seconds.

"What was that?" Jed Franklin said.

"What?" Bynes said.

"I thought I saw something flash by."

There was a momentary silence, probably as Bynes looked, then the sound of boot heels on the wooden porch.

Clark held his breath and waited.

"I don't see anything," Bynes said.

Clark scooted into position under the floorboards. Using his X-ray vision, he could see the chair above him. The man in it wasn't moving.

"Look," Franklin said. "I'll do this last thing for you if you tell me where my family is."

"When you get back, I'll tell you," Bynes said.

Clark stuck his fingers in the cracks between the floorboards. Then he heard something that made him go cold.

The voice of Lex Luthor.

"Anyone in the cabin!" Lex's voice echoed over the valley. "You are surrounded. Come out with your hands in the air."

Clark scanned the area around the cabin with his special vision. Lex wasn't kidding. His men had gotten into position quickly and the cabin was surrounded.

The man inside the cabin scurried toward a window. Then, from the porch, came the sound of gunfire.

"What the heck was that?" Chloe asked.

"Gunshots, close by." Pete grabbed her head and forced her into the car. "Lie down. If we get hit by stray bullets, getting detention for skipping school is the last thing we've got to worry about."

More gunfire followed. Pete crawled in beside her, holding her down.

"You down, Lana?" he cried.

She didn't answer. Instead, Chloe heard the beep-beep-beep of buttons being pressed on a cell phone.

"Are you calling 911?" Chloe asked, thinking it was a bad idea.

"That seems to be my function these days," Lana said.

"They're going to find us here and—"

"Don't worry about it," Pete said. "I'm sure we're not the only ones calling."

"Besides," Lana said, "Clark's in there. I want help here if he gets hurt."

Hurt. Chloe hadn't even thought of him getting hurt. He seemed so solid, so indestructible somehow. But she knew it was a possibility. A very real one.

And all because she didn't have the patience to wait until the story came to her. She had to put herself in danger to get it.

Clark had said he admired that about her.

But the last thing Chloe wanted was for that admiration to kill him.

It sounded like World War III above Clark. Gunshots, over and over again, ricocheting everywhere, more bullets flying than he had ever heard in his life.

Above it all, Lex's voice, futilely shouting, "Stop! Stop! My father might be in there."

His father was in there, and he was in danger.

Clark, using his super strength, plunged his hands through the wood floor of the cabin above him, grabbed the legs of the chair, and pulled it into the crawlspace.

The chair fell on him in a shower of dust and debris.

Using his own body as a shield against any stray shots, he checked Lionel Luthor's pulse. It was strong, but the man was a mess. He'd been beaten and he was unconscious.

Above them, Lex continued shouting. Someone screamed, and Clark heard a thud. Then there was another thud, and the shooting stopped.

"You stupid bastards." Lex sounded more panicked than Clark had ever heard him. "If my father's dead, you'll all pay for this."

Clark wrapped his arms around the chair and the man in it, then, digging his heels into the dirt, pushed himself backwards, opening the crawl space as he went. As he did, he used his X-ray vision to look through the floorboards.

One of the men was sprawled near the window, another on the porch. The third leaned against the porch door.

Clark wondered if they were all dead.

He wasn't sure which would be better for Jed Franklin. Death or life. And he wasn't sure he wanted to find out what Franklin's sentence would be.

J. B. Bynes was dead, sprawled on the porch like a broken doll. The other man—who looked vaguely familiar—was propped up near the door, alive, one hand covering a wound in his leg.

Lex was shaking with fury. The cabin was riddled with bullets. He didn't care how good a marksman each of these guys was, they had screwed up just as bad as he thought the authorities would.

No one inside the cabin could have survived the gun battle. No one.

He walked down the hill. One of the men he'd hired tried to say something to him, but Lex shook him off. Lex felt like he'd been encased in a bubble. He could almost feel his father's disapproval surrounding him.

It's amazing to me, Lex, that a son of mine is so very inept.

Lex nodded, almost as if his father had spoken to him.

Lex mounted the porch, stepped over Bynes's body, and ignored the other man who was reaching out to him. Lex pushed the door open and stared inside.

A single body sprawled beneath the window. It was too tall and broad to be his father's.

Lex started shaking. Had he been wrong? Had he led a firefight in this remote location for nothing?

It took him a moment to see the hole in the floor. He held his breath and walked over to it, peering down. Disturbed dust, fresh marks of something down there.

Had his father been kept underneath the cabin? That wouldn't be the first time kidnappers had done something like that.

If so, his father might have survived.

If, of course, he was here in the first place.

Lex walked around the hole in the floor to the back of the cabin.

And there, on the weed-covered lawn, sat Clark Kent, untying Lex's father from a chair. His father was unconscious. Clark was holding him up with one hand as he untied ropes with the other.

Lex flung open the back door. "I'm imagining you, right?" he said, and he half believed it. How did Clark manage to show up every time Lex was in trouble?

Clark shook his head. "I'm real."

Lex walked down the back steps onto the lawn. Weeds grazed his jeans. In the distance, he heard sirens.

"Your dad's pretty beat-up, but he's alive."

Lex knelt in front of his father. He'd never seen the old man like this—hair filthy and tangled, blood on his face, his lips blue, eyes closed.

He didn't look as powerful as he should have.

"What're you doing here, Clark?" Lex asked.

"Actually, Chloe was tracking a story. She's just down the road, and I saw this truck come up here, so I was going to check it out, and—"

"Managed to rescue my father all by yourself?" Lex kept his tone light, but his face averted. He didn't want Clark to see how shook-up he was over his father's condition.

"No," Clark said. "He was tied up out here. I just knocked him over when the shooting started."

That, of course, didn't explain the dirt stains on Clark's back or the cobwebs in Lex's dad's hair. But Lex was going to overlook that for the moment.

The sirens were even closer now.

"You could have died," Lex said.

"If I'd known that," Clark said, "I wouldn't have volunteered to check this place out."

Lex smoothed the hair away from his father's face. It felt strange to touch the man. He so rarely did.

Clark stood. "I'll go see how Chloe and the group are."

Lex nodded, but didn't stand. He was reluctant to leave his father's side. Lex noted, with strange detachment, how unusual that feeling was for him.

Clark started to walk away.

"Clark," Lex said, turning slightly. Clark stopped. "I guess I owe you my thanks. Again."

Clark shrugged. "You know me, Lex. Wrong place at the right time."

And then he disappeared down the road.

CHAPTER 22

Chloe put the finishing touches on the last of the news stories she had to write. She leaned away from the computer and stretched her arms. Her hands were tired. She'd worked through another night.

Clark had already brought her the morning coffee and a cinnamon roll. She could get used to this kind of treatment, although she didn't tell him that.

He was sitting in one of the chairs near the Wall of Weird, reading everything she had written. Lana was beside him, reading the pages as he finished with them and passing them to Pete, who sat cross-legged on a desk.

"I can't believe this," Lana said. "Danny Franklin is dead because this Bynes guy wanted the big score."

"That's what Mr. Franklin told the police, and everything Clark said he overheard at the cabin confirmed it." Chloe leaned forward, saved the story in rich text format, and then opened her e-mail program. This would be her first statewide byline. Not only was the story going in the *Torch*, but it would be in the *Daily Planet*, too.

That was the only way the *Planet* would get the whole scoop. She wasn't going to let them interview her. She had a hunch from the way the editor reacted, she'd be rewritten and her stuff would probably be turned into quotes after all, but she didn't care. She had her first shot at the big time.

"The poor man," Lana said. "Losing his whole family that way."

"He got in with the wrong people," Pete said, giving Clark a meaningful look. "Stuff like that happens when you think the wrong people are your friends."

Clark kept his gaze on the papers. Chloe wondered how he could ignore that look from Pete. "At least Lex's dad'll be all right," Clark said.

"As all right as he can ever be," Pete said.

"Pete, stop," Lana said. "The man's been through an ordeal."

"He puts the people around him through ordeals all the time." But Pete picked up another piece of paper and started to read, showing that this part of the conversation was done.

"So Bynes and this friend of his, Rowen, they kill the entire Franklin family, and tell Jed Franklin they'd been kidnapped just to get his cooperation?" Lana said. "It seems like a lot of work."

"I think they might have planned to kidnap them first," Chloe said. "I think the first death—probably Danny's—was an accident. The coroner said he fought his attacker."

"It also explains the two killer theory that we had," Clark said. "There were two victims each, and they took care of things fast so that when Franklin got home, he would think his family had been kidnapped."

"Why'd they need him?" Pete asked. "He didn't have any special skills. Clark said he didn't know anything about high tech."

"They needed someone they could blame when it was all over," Chloe said. "And he heard about the plot. Remember he was making a lot of noise about it around town. He became their victim."

"They had a lot of victims," Lana said. "Too many."

She bowed her head.

"We're all going to miss him, Lana," Clark said softly.

"I know," Lana said. "And it's funny. I feel a little better about it now that I know his father was trying to save his life, not take it."

"Me too," Pete said.

Chloe nodded. "Small consolation for Mr. Franklin, though."

"I doubt there's going to be any consolation for him," Clark said.

◆◆◆

School let out early so that those who wanted to could attend the Franklin funerals. Clark went, then decided to walk home.

As he came up the drive, he looked at the farm. He'd spent his entire life in the white house, spent most of the last five years looking at the stars from the loft, and spent the better part of a decade learning how to work beside his father.

It could all have been lost in an instant.

The family truck pulled up beside him. His parents were wearing their best clothes. They had just come from the funeral, too, although they had stopped at a neighbor's for the small post-funeral meal. Clark hadn't been able to face it.

"Want a lift the rest of the way, son?" his dad asked.

Clark shook his head. "Dad," he said, asking the question that had been on his mind the entire walk home, "if that had been us instead of them—"

"It wouldn't have been us, Clark," his dad said.

"Why not?" Clark asked. "Because of my strength?"

His dad sighed, then looked at Clark's mom. "You want to drive the rest of the way? I'll walk with Clark for a moment."

She nodded.

His dad got out of the truck, and his mom slid into the driver's seat, pulling away slowly so that she didn't spray them with gravel.

"Clark," his dad said, "Jed Franklin made one mistake."

"Going to work for LuthorCorp?"

"Forgetting he had friends and a community. If he had gone to the authorities the moment he heard about this plot, none of this would have happened."

"But he was afraid," Clark said.

His dad nodded. "But that's not an excuse, Clark."

"I guess not," Clark said. "But you heard him talk about this. You said it was crazy talk."

"He was drunk at the time. Doesn't help credibility, and neither did his bitterness toward the Luthors. He seemed to think they were going to get what they deserved."

Clark took a deep breath. He didn't like to challenge his father, but he couldn't let this one pass. "You've said that about the Luthors more than once."

His dad looked surprised. "Guess I have. And you know what? I'm beginning to think I was wrong. No one deserves what happened this past week. Not the Franklins, and not the Luthors either."

Clark looked at his father.

"You know," his dad said. "Times like these, a man needs comfort food. We never did finish those root beer floats your mom made the other night. Maybe we should see if we can get her to make some again."

Clark smiled at the twinkle in his dad's eye. "Sounds perfect."

SMALLVILLE

SILENCE

Nancy Holder

This book is for the one and only
Rebecca Morhaim. Rock it, girlfriend

ACKNOWLEDGMENTS

With sincere thanks to the cast and crew of *Smallville,* in particular to THE PRODUCER/CREATORS and to Mr. Tom Welling; to my DC editor Rich Thomas; and to my Warner editor, John Aherne. To my agent Howard Morhaim and his assistant, Ryan Blitstein, thank you so much. Anna Robinson, Lily Gile, Laura Newman, and Michelle Taliaferro, thank you for being Rebecca Morhaim's good friends. Dal Perry and Matt Pallamary, thank you, boys, more than I can say. To Debbie and Scott Viguié, thank you for being my friends. My beautiful daughter, Belle, you are the answer to a mother's prayers. Finally, to Kym Rademacher . . . who walks the walk, and is showing me her moves: Thanks for the choreography lessons. I'm grateful beyond words for your generosity. And for her mother, Suzy, who knows how to treat a kid.

CHAPTER ONE

"'Listen, do wah do, do you want to know a secret?'" Chloe sang out as she sailed through the doors of the Talon with all its Egyptian–Art Deco fashion stylings. She loved the brilliant colors of the columns and the way the shiny mirrors bounced the light all over the busy room. It reminded her of Metropolis.

As she scooted around one of the beefy football players—*I think his name is Ty Something*—her reporter's brain automatically began searching for his last name, but stopped, realizing it didn't matter because at the moment, Ty had done nothing newsworthy. Not today, anyway.

She caught sight of Clark and Pete, and hurried toward them. She was beaming; she was euphoric. In her hot little hands, she held the mock-up of tomorrow's edition of the *Torch*. And in that mock-up, the most amazing scoop of her reporting life. It was like a dream, and the fact that she was wearing the new embroidered corset Lana had talked her into buying, and that she looked, well, *super,* just added to the mix. Heads were turning, male heads, and one never knew: where a few might turn, others—one in particular—could follow.

"'Do you promise not to tell?'" she crowed, ending her cover of the old Lennon-and-McCartney Beatles song.

She gave her short blond hair a shake as she made her way through Lana's noisy, crowded coffeehouse. The shiny copper espresso machine was steaming away, reminding her of a calliope in this circus of life. Accessorized with mugs, books, or cell phones, school kids were chatting in friendly groups, rehashing the day, dishing gossip, or hooking up. Right now she loved each and every one of them.

It's a great day to be . . . me!

Of her own friendly group, Clark saw her first. He raised his brows and gave her a pleasantly inquisitive smile as she approached, taking in her state of high elation. *Okay, not an oh-my-God-you're-here-at-last-my-darling* smile, but at least she rated a reaction from tall, dark, and not-hers. Not that it mattered, of course. She'd moved past her crush on Clark.

Right? Right! And so, who cares what I wear in front of him? Well, caring beyond having my personal dignity . . . as a girl and as someone he abandoned at the Prom . . .

"Hi, Chloe," Pete said for Clark and himself. "What's up?"

"Plenty." With a dramatic flourish, she displayed the mock-up of the *Torch,* stretching it between her hands. A banner headline in seventy-two-point font announced, *SH Teacher of the Year Caught in Drug Bust!*

"What?" Clark said, raising his brows.

"Read it and gasp," she said, holding out the paper.

Warily, Clark took the paper from Chloe and scanned her prize-worthy prose. She was sometimes amazed by how fast he could read. His eyes moving rapidly, he started to flip to page three, where the article continued, then jerked as if he had been caught doing something wrong. *Speed-reading is not a crime,* she wanted to remind him.

He looked up at her, and said, "This is pretty harsh, Chloe."

She was disappointed. *Harsh?*

"The words you use . . ." he continued, trailing off and flashing her a patented Clark not-trying-to-hurt-you grimace.

"Clark, I'm breaking a story," she ventured. "A big story. I have to grab the reader's attention."

He shifted, clearly not agreeing with her. Pete looked on, brows knit as he worked to read the paper upside down.

"Drug bust?" Pete echoed, shocked. His eyes widened. "Mr. Hackett? You gotta be kidding me."

"Not a bust exactly," Clark told him, shaking his head. "Not that bad."

"Not that bad?" she said. "Clark, you did start reading it, right?"

He moved his shoulders. "I'm sorry, Chloe, but it seems . . . severe."

She frowned as she took the paper back from him. "It's all true," she said. "Every word."

Clark looked uncomfortable. "Yeah, but . . . 'cover-up'?" He gestured to one of her columns of tightly written journalistic prose. "I mean, you wrote that Mr. Hackett is going to resign from his job. It's not as if he was going to get away with something."

With a look of complete astonishment, Pete extended his hand for the paper. "Resign? He's been here forever. What's he got until retirement, like a couple of years?"

"And now he's leaving? Just like that?" Clark asked, trying to process the enormity of what Chloe had reported. "He's such a great teacher. He deserved to be named Teacher of the Year. Even the kids who get in trouble all the time like him."

I am so right to break this story. Look at their reactions! This is big news.

"Yes," she replied with satisfaction, as Clark handed Pete the paper. "They did. He *was* good at his job. And he had less than two years until retirement. But he sold steroids to Jake Brook!"

"The new tackle?" Clark asked. "He's a big guy. I don't see him needing anything to beef up."

"And yet," Chloe drawled. She nodded at the two guys. "'An anonymous source' saw the transaction in the parking lot and reported it to Principal Reynolds. Reynolds confronted Hackett, and the rest is . . . on page three."

Pete took that in, or tried to. In his more idealistic world, school officials did not sell drugs to students. Showing him that his own reality was not conforming to the school reality at large was like telling a little boy that Santa Claus wasn't real.

Grinning at him, she clucked her teeth sympathetically and shrugged as if to say, *What can you do?*

"I was shocked, too. You would have never guessed he was such a scumbag. And I used to think he didn't have any school spirit," she added, chuckling ironically. "But here he was, helping the football team pump up the volume. What a guy."

"Chloe," Clark reproved. "It's not funny."

She huffed. "Excuse me, guys, but he's only getting his due. Hey, *I* wasn't the one selling illegal drugs to minors."

"One minor," Pete said as he turned to page three and read her stuff. "Chloe, this is hard-hitting stuff, but . . ."

"Are you suggesting I shouldn't run this story? You guys, it's *huge*."

Pete glanced first at Clark, then at Chloe. He pointed at the first paragraph on page three and began to read aloud. "'A closed meeting took place, with the aggrieved parties, Mr. Hackett, and members of the administration and the school board in attendance. The meeting was not discussed on any publicly disseminated agenda or memo between the administration and the school board. And yet, it occurred last Monday at 6 P.M." He looked hard at her. "How did you find out about it?"

"The public has a right to know," Chloe said, feeling confused. She did sense that now was not the time to admit she'd accidentally hacked her way into the digitally transcribed minutes of that off-the-record meeting—which had felt to her at the time like finding buried treasure. She had scarcely been able to stop herself from whooping aloud when she'd realized what she had found. Reporters dream of finding dirt like this on public figures. And in a small farming community like Smallville, one of the teachers at the only high school in town *was* a public figure.

"Hey, I didn't commit a crime," she snapped. "I'm reporting one."

"I don't know," Pete ventured, shuffling the mock-up back together. "It says Jake's parents consented to keeping it private." Pete nodded. "And I'm not sure you should drag his family into this."

Chloe was even more confused. "His family?"

"Mr. Hackett's family," Pete continued.

Just then, Lana arrived at their table with a tray in her hand. "Hey, Chloe," Lana greeted her housemate. "How'd the *Torch* turn out?"

Chloe didn't answer, and Lana had already started wiping off their table. Her long hair was pulled up, wisps tickling her jawline. She was obviously busy, but she looked great—which might or might not have explained the adoration on Clark's face. Then Lana smiled at the three friends, and added, "I just took some cinnamon buns out of the oven, and we're frosting them right now. They're fantastic. Any takers?"

"I'm not hungry," Chloe said grumpily.

"No thanks, Lana," Clark added.

Lana frowned as she looked around the table. "Is something wrong?"

"Clark and Pete think I'm a troublemaking muckraker." Chloe snatched the mock-up away from Pete and crisply folded the pages. Opening her cherry-appliquéd shoulder bag, she crammed them inside. Her treasured story seemed like a piece of garbage now. She was embarrassed and angry.

They're not journalists. They don't understand these things.

"Is this about the Hackett article?" Lana asked cautiously as she straightened and put her cleaning towel on the tray. Chloe was hyperaware of the look that passed between Clark and Pete.

Chloe grimaced. "Not you, too." Lana had stopped by the *Torch* office just after school let out for the day, and glanced through the parts Chloe had already edited and pasted together.

Lana hesitated. "Well, it was a little . . . strong."

Stung, Chloe scowled at the trio and said, "*Strong?* I can't believe you guys! We're not talking about coffee, Lana. We're talking about a grown man who sold steroids to a high-school athlete. Hello? If we were in college, this would be on the evening news."

Pete gestured at Chloe's purse. "It says that part of the agreement Hackett has with the school board is that he won't be prosecuted." He looked at the others. "No criminal charges have been brought against him. So I think, technically, he's still presumed innocent."

"Did you read my sidebar interview with my source?" Chloe demanded, her voice rising. Didn't her own friends understand that the public had a right to know what was going on in the world around them? "He saw Hackett selling Jake the steroids. Hackett admitted it. In other words, he's guilty, guilty, guilty."

Pete pondered her words, but still looked quite troubled. "Maybe you're right. It's just . . . Marshall Hackett's in my biology class. If you print this . . . everybody will know that his father did something illegal."

"*Wrong,* Pete," Chloe said for emphasis. Her frustration level was beginning to match the pressure inside the hissing espresso machine. "His dad did do something wrong, whether or not he's prosecuted for it."

She could see from his expression that Pete was moving to her side of the argument, so she decided to push him a little further over the line.

"And come on, guys, Marshall *must* already know. Something like this can't exactly go unnoticed in a family unit. What's his father going to tell him? 'Hey, kid, I decided to stop working all of a sudden. For no good reason'?"

"But what if Marshall *doesn't* know?" Clark asked. "What if nobody in his family knows this secret?"

"That'd be something you're familiar with," Chloe shot at him. "Secrets."

Clark flushed. Lana ticked a warning glance toward Chloe; Chloe knew she should back off. They'd often discussed Clark's own penchant for being secretive. It bothered them both, and they'd both told Clark that it was an issue. And yet, he was still all mystery guy on them.

Chloe ran out of steam and remained silent, considering the effect hearing about this from a third party would have on Marshall Hackett. Mr. Hackett's son was one of the nicest guys she vaguely knew. He had a wicked sense of humor, too. And fact of the well-known matter was, he flat-out worshiped his father. They had the kind of close relationship greeting card companies extolled every Father's Day.

"Mr. Hackett's been an inspiration to a lot of people with disabilities," Clark pointed out, as the uncomfortable seconds stretched into nearly a minute. "If you print this, it's going to tear him down in their eyes."

"Disabilities?" Chloe echoed, surprised. She gestured to the group at large. "Guys, he uses a wheelchair. That's all. No heroics involved. It's not like he . . . like he's some kind of victim who should be coddled and protected because he . . . he can't walk. Justice should be blind." She added, "Don't you think?"

The others said nothing. Chloe huffed. "Fine." She pushed back her bangs as she exhaled, frustrated, and said, "I'm . . . I'm going now. I have a paper to finalize."

As Chloe turned on her heel, Clark said gently, "Chloe, hey. Wait. It's just—"

Chloe waved a hand at them dismissively and moved away. Her face was hot; she was uneasy with the feeling that it was she who was in the wrong, not Hackett. Keeping secrets was not part of her job description. Exposing them was. She had every right to print this story. What if the teacher had sold steroids to other students as well? What if revealing the truth prompted just one other kid to come forward, tell his parents about it, get some help for whatever damage taking the drugs had done? The facts should come out, even if they did hurt a few people. After all, *she* wasn't the one hurting them. Mr. Hackett was.

I'm only doing what a reporter is supposed to do. Aren't I?

Without another backward glance, she shoved open the double doors and stepped outside. The fresh air helped her clear her head as she took a deep breath, then let it out.

The crack about Mr. Hackett and his wheelchair had come out all wrong. She wasn't an insensitive jerk. He *had* done a lot of things in the community for kids with disabilities. He'd spearheaded a drive to get wheelchairs to disadvantaged kids and worked tirelessly to ensure that all the public areas in town provided wheelchair access.

It was just that he'd always seemed so competent and . . . complete . . . that Chloe hadn't ever regarded him as someone with a disability. She'd stopped paying attention to his wheelchair long ago. And to be truthful, she hadn't considered that aspect of her story, either, until Clark had pointed it out.

Maybe I'm completely wrong, she mused, as she walked down the street. *And if I'm not, maybe I should have at least done a little more checking.*

The late-afternoon sun lengthened her shadow, stretching it into a Chloe she didn't know. Birdsong trilled from a lamppost, and, somewhere distant, a dog barked. A trash can beneath the lamppost urged passersby to *Keep Smallville Clean!*

The urgency of the exhortation, with the exclamation point and all, made it somehow endearing. Chloe felt an unusual twinge of tenderness for the town she usually despised. For all its own weirdness, Smallville was a place where real people lived. They had houses and pets and kids.

The story about Mr. Hackett was more than just a story about a crime. It was a story about a man. The school board had promised him he could resign without his wrongdoing—*alleged wrongdoing*—coming to light. But if she printed her story . . . there would be plenty of light shed on his actions. He would not be allowed to leave quietly.

But shouldn't I print the truth?

She pulled the folded pages of the mock-up from her purse and examined them. The headline was enormous. She had to admit that she had been gloating over her discovery. In her excitement, she'd forgotten about the individuals involved. It had all been about the story.

I'm not a social worker, she thought halfheartedly. *I'm supposed to go after gems like this. I'm supposed to find the stories . . . if reporters don't come back and inform the rest of the tribe about what's going on, how will they be able to protect themselves from the dark beyond the campfire?*

Secrets are bad. They almost always wind up hurting people.

Nevertheless, she walked slowly to the trash can and stuffed the pages into it. A penetrating sadness hit the pit of her stomach, and her eyes welled with tears. She felt defeated. She had worked very, very hard on the mock-up, and now she had to start over from scratch . . . minus her best story ever.

Then she reached forward, thinking to retrieve it. But no, this was the right thing to do. Deep down, she could admit that that was the real reason she'd gotten so defensive around her friends. They'd hit a nerve. She knew that if she'd been sure about the story, she wouldn't have lost her temper with them.

With one more lingering regret for the one that got away, she turned back toward the Talon to tell the guys that she'd decided to bury the revelations about Hackett after all. But just then, the streetlight winked on. Her dad would be coming home, and it was Chloe's turn to make dinner. She'd suggested pot roast, which would take a while to cook, and now she had to write another story to fill the issue on top of it.

I'll write it at home after I get dinner started, she decided, *and e-mail it to my school account. Maybe Lana can help me think up something.*

Damn. I worked for hours on that story!

Feeling virtuous, she took the crosswalk and reached her car, slid in, and started the engine.

At least I got Clark's attention, she thought ironically.

Maybe I won't be such a great reporter after all, she thought, as she signaled and pulled away from the curb. *Maybe I lack that killer instinct truly great reporters need in instances like this.*

Ahead, a pretty tortoiseshell cat dropped from the curb and began to saunter across the blacktop. Chloe slowed. As if in sync, the cat stopped walking. Languidly it stared at her from its territory of the middle of the road, then plopped onto its side and began to lick its left front paw.

"Excuse me, kitty cat, let's move it," Chloe said to the cat, although, of course, it couldn't hear her.

Unflustered and unhurried, it continued to groom itself.

Chloe drummed her fingers on the steering wheel, then turned her tires slightly to the left and put her foot back on the gas. She'd go around the cat, then.

As Chloe approached, the cat rose, stretched, and sashayed into her path once more. Chloe stopped the car and stared at it through her windshield. It stretched back its little head and yawned, flicking its little pink tongue in her direction.

"About that killer instinct that I lack," she said to the cat. "All I have to say is count your blessings, Nine Lives."

As if in reply, it lay back down and flicked its tail into the air with a certain insouciance that Chloe had to admire. She began to laugh to herself, and by the time the cat consented to allow her to get through the intersection, she was actually smiling.

Maybe I'll write about Smallville's escalating traffic problems.

She snorted, because that was a good one—and edged the car to the right before the cat had time to react.

"Well, that's *one* I win," Chloe murmured.

Glancing into the rearview mirror, she watched the cat rise and saunter the rest of the way across the street.

Game over.

After Chloe left the Talon, daily life there overtook the singular moment of high drama as Lana got back to work, and the conversation about Mr. Hackett eventually died out.

Then Clark glanced at Pete's watch. It was getting late, and Clark had chores to do. If he had been any other farm kid, he would have had to go home immediately after school to help with the family business. Because he was an alien from another planet, he actually had time for a social life.

But despite his otherworldly origins, he was part of a family now—a human family—and he had to go home and do his share. Working the land was a backbreaking way to make a living, but he understood why his parents loved it so much. The sense of accomplishment in a job well-done—growing things, springing them from the soil yielding new life as a result of the Kents' efforts—was hard to beat.

I understand what Chloe felt when she wrote that article, Clark thought. *When you do what you do well, it satisfies something in your soul. I'm sorry she's upset.*

I wonder what she'll do—print it or throw it away?

He knew Chloe well enough to know that seeds of doubt had been planted in her mind, and she wouldn't simply ignore them. Chloe had a lot of integrity. He admired her for that.

"I've got to go home," he said to Pete as he got to his feet. He picked up his books. "I've got chores. You sticking around?"

Pete nodded. "Uncle Howard is visiting. It's easier to study here."

Clark grinned sympathetically. He'd had experience with Uncle Howard. The man was a sales rep for a feed company, and he had a story for every mile he'd driven his shiny teal Lexus along the country roads of the Midwest. All his stories were entertaining, but there were so many of them. Going to dinner at Pete's when Uncle Howard was in town tired even Clark.

Sighing, Pete hoisted his backpack from the floor and unzipped the pouch section. He pulled out a calculator. "Might as well get the math out of the way. Then the rest will be smooth sailing." He grimaced. "Smoother sailing. Don't forget our history gig, Clark."

"Right," Clark assured him. Then he hesitated.

"Your part is looking around the farm for old farming implements," Pete reminded him. "I'm already finished."

"Yeah. History of pesticides," Clark said, trying to reassure Pete that he was hooked in.

Pete rolled his eyes. "It's pretty bad. What I have to say about pesticide use, I mean. Lex is going to love me if he ever gets a chance to read it."

"The LuthorCorp plant makes fertilizer, not pesticides," Clark observed.

Pete shrugged. "Sometimes it's hard to distinguish the two. Which you'll discover once you read my report," he added pointedly.

"Right," Clark said uneasily, not because he had forgotten to search for antique farm equipment at home, but because of Pete's tone of voice when Lex's name had come up. Clark and Lex were good friends, although that friendship had been sorely tested in the past, and probably would be again. Many people in Smallville didn't like Lex simply because he was a Luthor. Clark knew it wasn't that simple.

He also knew that his own father had had a hand in helping Lex's father buy Pete's family's creamed corn factory. Lionel Luthor had assured the Rosses that the factory would remain in operation. Today, the fertilizer factory stood in its place—to Jonathan Kent's everlasting shame.

It's one of those bad family secrets, Clark thought. On the other hand, Pete was the only one who knew his own secret, besides his mother and father. Lex didn't even know, although he had tried more than once to figure out what Clark was obviously hiding from him. *Pete knows. Lex doesn't. Does that make Pete my closest friend?*

"Hey, Clark, don't freak out or anything," Pete said, as he fished in his backpack. "I'm not going to start a fight with Lex or hold an anti-LuthorCorp rally or anything." He pulled out some pieces of paper from his pack. They were paper-clipped together, and there were some notes scrawled in the margins of page one.

Pete said, "This is the first draft of the report. Take a look, see what you think. There's nothing in here that can really hurt Lex. Not like Chloe's article on Hackett." He exhaled. "Man."

They were back to it. Clark took the pages from Pete, and said, "She was pretty upset."

"Yeah. But not half as upset as Hackett is, I'll bet."

Saying nothing more, Clark rose from his chair. Lana gave him a wave from behind the counter, and he waved back. Her forehead was furrowed; he guessed she was still thinking about Chloe, and he was glad the two girls had become such good friends. It was good to have someone to talk to, a sounding board for issues one couldn't discuss with other people. Pete had learned about Clark's secret by accident, but after the Kents' initial scare, it had proved to be a good thing. More than once, Pete had come to Clark's rescue specifically because he knew his secret.

Lana and Chloe both knew what it was like to lose a mom, and they had a few other things in common. *I like Lana, Chloe knows it; Chloe . . . well, she's over liking me that way. It's awkward now and then. Friendships bring their own complications with them.*

He told Pete he would read the report.

"Cool." Pete settled in to do his math.

With another nod at his friend, Clark turned to go. Pete settled in for math torture.

Then, through the din of the coffeehouse, Clark heard shouting outside. Another voice rose in what could have been anger, might have been fear. He was tempted to use his X-ray vision, but it was just as simple to push open the Talon doors.

Then he was outside. About ten feet away, beneath a lamppost, Marshall Hackett was yelling at another guy from the football team. His face was fire-engine red; spittle flew from his mouth as he screamed, "Give that to me!"

"Marsh, chill!" the other guy protested. It was Ty Westfall, dark-haired, and about the same height and build as Marshall.

Both were wearing their letter jackets, jeans, and running shoes. Jocks to the end.

Ty held a wad of paper in his left hand. Marshall flailed for it; Ty took a step backward and held them out of Marshall's reach. Marshall rushed him, and Ty easily sidestepped him, saying, "I just want to see what it says, man!"

"Give it to me!" Marshall shouted, flailing at him. Clark thought about how coordinated he was on the field. But right now, Marshall was so upset he couldn't control his movements.

Ty dodged Marshall again. "Is it true?"

"No!"

"But it says he's resigning," Ty persisted.

Uh-oh.

This time Clark did use his special vision; he zeroed in on Ty's hand; among the bones, the words *Drug Bust!* appeared in a negative image—the way Clark saw things when he used his X-ray vision—and Clark realized Ty had a copy of Chloe's mock-up of the *Torch.*

How'd he get hold of it? Chloe usually makes only one, and then she puts it in Reynolds's in box when she's finished. She never wants any spare mock-up copies floating around until the finished copies are distributed.

"Give that to me!" Marshall bellowed. Then he doubled up his right fist and slammed it into Ty's solar plexus. The force of the impact made Clark wince.

Grunting, Ty contracted around the punch. The tatters of the *Torch* mock-up flew around his head like a circlet of tweeting birdies in a cartoon.

With brutal force, Marshall slammed Ty against the trash can, so hard that Clark heard a crack. Clark took a step toward them, aware that guys did not bust up other guys' fights, but it sounded as if Ty had broken a rib. As he scanned Ty's torso, his X-ray vision caught sight of the remainder of the pages of the mock-up inside the trash can.

Chloe threw it out. And Ty and Marshall must have found it.

Marshall pulled his fist back to his ear and prepared to lay into Ty again when Clark said, "Hey."

The two looked up at him. Despite the fact that he was getting hurt and could use a hand, Ty was no more happy to see him than Marshall—Clark got that; it was an embarrassing situation—but Clark was glad to see Marshall unball his fist and take a step away from his teammate. Without another word, Marshall dropped to his knees and began grabbing up the shreds of the mock-up.

Ty remained where he was, his hand pressed against his rib cage. He muttered something about Marshall being a psycho, but eventually he said, "Marsh, it's cool, dude."

Marshall glared at Ty as he snatched up the pieces and cradled them against his chest. "Get the hell away from me."

An unwilling witness to his pain, Clark steadfastly looked away. Ty did the same.

The two stood in acute discomfort until Ty sneered at Clark, and said, "What you lookin' at, Kent?"

Clark knew he couldn't do anything to help, and the knowledge frustrated him. He wasn't friends with Marshall Hackett, and any attempts to step in would be highly resented at a time like this.

The papers in his arms, Marshall began to get to his feet without using his hands. He fell back. Ty reached to help, and Marshall shouted, "I told you to leave me alone!"

Retreating as if Marshall had socked him again, Ty shook his head. Then, as he watched Marshall dropping the same pieces and then picking them up again, he muttered, "No. No, I won't leave you alone."

"My dad . . ." Marshall breathed. "My dad, he couldn't have sold drugs to some kid. He wouldn't do that. He's a good man!"

"Marsh, it's cool," Ty said again. "She probably just made it up. It's in the trash because Reynolds told her it was bogus."

Then he narrowed his eyes at Clark and took a threatening step toward him. "Get the hell out of here!" Ty shouted.

Clark remained stoic and walked on by.

I've got to tell Chloe about this, he thought. *Talk about bad news.*

"My . . . father . . . didn't . . . do . . . anything!" Marshall Hackett screamed. "He wouldn't do this! I know my father! I know him! He's my *father!*"

His voice echoed down Main Street.

His agony came tumbling after.

CHAPTER TWO

Cap du Roi, a small village in Haiti

Maria del Carmen Maldonaldo Lopez had never run faster in her life.

Her short, spiky hair was slicked back with blood and sweat. Dressed in an olive tank top and khaki shorts, she was smeared with mango, mud, and sweat. Her arms and legs were slashed by the stalks of sugar cane as she raced through the field, the reedy stalks breaking off and acting as a medieval abatis—the pointed ends of the broken cane at the ready to run through anyone unlucky enough to fall on them.

Her field boots were caked with mud; her right boot was stretched tight over her swollen ankle as she staggered past the cane field and shuffled through a pitiful vegetable patch. She could smell the crops as she helplessly destroyed them—bean plants, overripe pumpkin, the overturned earth hot and thirsty. She slid over some fallen plantains, grinding them into mush. She knew how hard the villagers worked on their subsistence-level gardens, and that she had just wiped out a good portion of the village's food supply.

She couldn't help that now. She kept running. She ran as if her life depended on it.

It did.

She could hear her own breath as she flew through the thick night, the steamy air practically boiling on her skin. Salt mixed with the blood that dripped after her, leaving a delectable trail of odors for the nightmare that wanted nothing more than to rip her body open like a plantain and devour her.

She couldn't take a second to gauge the monster's progress. She didn't need to. The thing that was hunting her was a nightmare—tall, gaunt figure of a dark-skinned man, his face half-eaten away, his eyes bulged glassy and empty. His mouth hung open, as the mouths of the dead often do, but the jaw clacked shut at a frighteningly steady pace — *click clack click clack*.

Starving for her flesh, the creature was hunting her down. She had been running for what seemed like hours, and its pace had never slowed. It was like being stalked by the Terminator.

No, it's worse. This thing is real. It's a zombie, and it's real!

She burst into tears as she ran, though consciously she was unable to register any emotion to go with those tears. She was drowning in a numbing, free-floating terror, and yet some part of her brain demanded that she keep moving, past the intense pain in her ankle, past her exhaustion. It was a miracle to her that she had enough energy in her body to cry. That there was any moisture left in her body for tears. She kept seeing an image in her mind of herself half–eaten away but still alive. And that was her goal now — to get away from him before he ripped the flesh completely off of her bones. It was as if she didn't believe she could hope to get away unscathed, and that only if she kept running, kept praying, kept dodging it, could she manage to survive at all.

Beneath the moonlight, she saw at last the pathetic string of yellow lights that signified the perimeter of the AYUDO compound. *Home!*

Gasping, she reached for the lights; they were her lifeline. Inside the gate she would be safe from this monster . . . if she could only get to the gate before *it* reached *her.*

"Ayudame," she tried to scream. *Help me.* But nothing came. Any sound was strangled by her shallow panting. She was light-headed with fear and the desperate need to take deep breaths to fill her lungs; how on earth could she ever hope to scream?

"Ayu . . ." she tried again.

And then, in view of the watery lights, it grabbed her around the waist and flung her to the ground. She went facedown into the mud. And even though her nose and mouth were immediately plugged with mud, she could smell the foulness of the zombie as it straddled her. This was Haiti, and people died here; she had seen death and smelled it.

But this was worse.

This was the stench of hell itself.

Finger bones gripped her shoulders and dug deep, slicing through her flesh. Something hard pressed against the back of her neck; a sharp pain pierced her skin.

The zombie was beginning his feast.

She went rigid. Somewhere deep inside herself, she realized that if she didn't act now, she was going to die. Horribly.

I can't die. I'm a good person! I was doing good here!

The shock of actual words in her mind galvanized her. Though the zombie had a big frame, he wasn't as heavy as a normal person. Portions of his flesh had either fallen off or been devoured by the packs of wild dogs that plagued the village. Before arriving in Haiti three months before, Maria del Carmen had taken six months of self-defense classes. Three months of classes were required before joining the AYUDO Project; her parents had insisted that she double that amount of time.

Don't panic, Marica, she told herself, using the diminutive of her own name, as her family, friends, and coworkers did. *You're dead if you panic.*

But oh my God, I'm in a foreign country and a zombie is devouring me . . . piadosa Virgen Maria de Guadalupe, dale clemencia, amor y compasion a aquellos que te queieren y vuelan a tu proteccion . . .

She prayed to the Virgin of Guadalupe with all her heart and all her soul. She kept her mind on the words of the prayer, forcing down her terror as she willed herself to focus.

You can save yourself, she heard her interior voice whispering. *It's within your ability. Think of your self-defense classes. You can do it.*

It was as if the Virgin herself was speaking to her.

Marica listened.

And she remembered what to do.

She hadn't taken enough lessons for the movements to be automatic. But if she could manage not to completely lose control, and take a few seconds to work through her offensive postures, she might be able to survive.

The zombie bit into her again, and she grunted in horror. Blinded by the mud, she was pinioned tightly as the monster's jagged, broken teeth sank into her. Then she went strangely cold.

Am I going into shock? Is it injecting me with something?

Her panic level shot up; for a moment she could do nothing. Groggy from lack of oxygen, she sensed that if she didn't do something soon, she really, truly was going to die.

Marica . . . remember your training . . . execute putar kepala . . . putar kepala . . .

Sí!

She sprang into action.

In its eagerness to grab hold of her neck, the zombie had loosened its grip on her wrists. This was her only chance, heavensent. As she yanked her arms free, a fiery pain shot from her wrists to her shoulders, and she wondered if she had broken something. The monster didn't appear to notice that it had lost hold of her, so lost it was in its feast.

Miraculously, through the haze of white-hot agony, she managed to draw her hands toward the center of her chest. She balled her fists as best she could, although her strength was fading, and she was in danger of passing out.

In the semblance of a double fist, she anchored her hands together, then pushed up and to the right. The zombie stayed on easily, like a cowboy on a very sluggish longhorn.

Her arm muscles shook, but she propped herself up into a tripod by rolling her fists so that she was resting her weight on her palms. Then she rolled herself onto her hip, pushed again with her hands, and flipped onto her back, on top of the zombie.

It grunted, writhing and grabbing at her; Marica summoned reserves she didn't know she had and rolled off the zombie, scrambling to the right. Its flopping hand batted against her right ankle and she jerked out of reach, sobbing for breath. Throwing herself forward, she tried to crawl, and she scrabbled like a baby in the slippery mud.

The zombie sat up, teeth clacking, and dived for her.

She kicked her legs frantically, but it was no use. The zombie grabbed her, and this time, held her tight. She closed her eyes as despair washed over her.

Then she heard another shuffling sound and opened her eyes.

A pair of feet stepped into her field of vision, filthy, blistered, and caked with mud. She glanced up and saw rags covering strong, muscular legs and a well-defined torso and firm arms. It was a man in excellent physical condition. He had a little goatee, and he wore an earring . . .

. . . and his eyes were as sightless and unseeing as the zombie who, even now, was clacking its teeth at Marica's booted feet.

This new zombie before her opened its mouth.

The one behind her flung itself at her. The stench from its mouth was unbelievable. Its blank eyes stared right through her; it was like a machine as its teeth clacked, as if scenting her not from its nose but from its bloody maw . . .

It came closer, leering sightlessly at her, as the first zombie grabbed her around the neck. Instinctively, she grabbed at the bony fingers, pulling as hard as she could, trying to dig her heels into the mud for traction.

The second zombie gripped her forearms.

She screamed again.

Its mouth clacked at her; blood dripped onto her arm . . .

The world began to grow dark. She thought of her mother and father, who had begged her not to come to Haiti, calling it hell on earth. They had known what they were talking about. But the images and memories swam as the world sank away, sank away . . .

Don't let them eat me. Don't let my mother see that . . . merciful Mother of God, intercede for me . . .

A shot rang out.

A sharp pain erupted in her shoulder, and Maria del Carmen Maldonaldo Lopez prayed no more prayers, and made no more wishes.

◆◆◆

Field Operative T. T. Van De Ven and two other soldiers marched their zombie captives across the fields of cane, their heavy boots crushing ripe shoots rising beneath the earth-crunching noises. The two zombies staggered along barefoot, their feet covered with blisters. Van De Ven had no idea if the zombies were in pain. He didn't particularly care, either. His mind was on other things.

They got to the artificial boulder that housed the alarm system and the elevator. Van De Ven took off his skullcap and showed the retinal scan his left eye. Three clicks signaled that his scan had been accepted.

They went down in the elevator to where the real action was.

The two soldiers were new, and he could tell they were scared. He smiled grimly to himself.

They ain't seen nothin' yet.

The zombies stood silent, their mouths slack, their eyes vacant. To all outward appearances, they were the mindless hulks the Project had transformed them into. But that was now, after he had captured them and pumped them full of Thorazine. These zombies had gone AWOL, and they had wreaked havoc in a total frenzy that had impressed the war-hardened combat veteran. Gone completely wacko.

Ferocity was good. Aggression was even better. But it had shown up unexpectedly . . . and it was happening more often. There was something wrong with the doctored fertilizer the Project was receiving from LuthorCorp. The formula was incorrect.

The elevator doors opened, and Van De Ven turned his attention from the zombies to the soldiers. As he had anticipated, the stench hit them full force. The one on the left covered his mouth. The other blinked as his eyes began to water.

"Man," Watery Eyes gasped.

Zombies stank. No two ways around it.

"C'mon, boys," he said to the two zombies, who staggered out of the elevator. They began to walk down the tunnel.

A shriek pierced the air, and Watery Eyes swore under his breath. The other soldier made a comment about joining the military and seeing the *under*world.

"Thought I'd end up in Germany or something," he muttered.

Van De Ven was patient with them. Not everybody had the stuff, like him.

There was a second shriek. One of the zombies froze. The other one ran into him. Then the first one turned around very slowly. His vacant eyes stared at Van De Ven, moving just a little bit, as if he were trying to focus, perhaps even to communicate with him.

Interesting, Van De Ven thought.

Down the second corridor they went, deeper into the earth and into a complex of rooms. Van De Ven gestured to Germany, and he fished in his pocket for some keys.

He showed them to Van De Ven, and the quintet moved into the first of a dozen blocks of cells in which zombies were housed.

Some were in good shape—they had been the soldier volunteers, not quite clear on exactly what they had volunteered to do. They were the best results of the Project so far, the ones that made the failures worthwhile.

"In you go," Van De Ven said to the two zombies as Watery Eyes opened the door to an empty cell.

That matter dispatched, Van De Ven went to report to his superior, Colonel Adams, a craggy-faced older man, who looked up expectantly from behind his metal field desk and returned Van De Ven's sharp salute.

"At ease," he said.

Van De Ven assumed parade rest and debriefed as quickly as possible.

"They were wild, sir," he told the colonel. "Went completely crazy up there, nearly ate a girl."

The colonel took that in. "Local girl?"

"No, sir. One of the relief workers."

The colonel set his jaw. "Damn."

"I recommend we take them all out, sir. The AYUDO personnel, I mean, sir. Security has been breached. They're sure to get on those laptops of theirs and tell the world what's going on out here."

The other man shook his head. "Killing them will call even more attention to the Project." He smiled wryly at Van De Ven. "Let them look like idiots, trying to make people believe in zombies. They might as well add that they all got in their spaceships and took off."

"But, sir—" Van De Ven protested.

The colonel waved a hand. "I'll take it under advisement, son." He leaned on his elbows, and added confidentially, "Not everyone appreciates a military solution. You know we're working with a civilian."

"Yes, sir."

"And he likes to stay under the radar. So . . ." Col. Adams smiled. "For now, we watch. And wait. If the AYUDO workers get to be too much of a nuisance, you'll be the first one I send to take 'em out."

"Sir, thank you, sir." Van De Ven stood tall, proud, and eager.

"Meanwhile," the colonel said, sighing, "we have to figure out why this batch went so wrong. Thank God no civilians have any of this stuff. Can you imagine what would happen if they actually used it for fertilizer?"

Van De Ven could not . . . but it was an interesting question.

The phone rang while Chloe was checking her pot roast in the oven. Figuring it was Lana or her father, she left the oven door open as she picked up the cordless and said, "Hello?"

"It's Clark." Chloe nodded, warmth coming to her cheeks. The room behind Clark was very noisy; she figured he was still at the Talon.

She shut the oven door and turned her attention to the phone call, raking her fingers through her hair before she realized what she was doing—primping for a boy who couldn't see her—even when he was standing right in front of her, much less when he was talking to her on the phone.

"Before you start in on me again. I decided not to print the story, okay?" she informed him. "Because you guys had a point, and I—"

"Chloe, Marshall Hackett saw your article," Clark cut in.

Chloe was speechless. As his words sank in, she shut her eyes and felt a wave of guilt wash over her. An image of Marshall's reaction followed after.

Not good.

"Chloe?" Clark pressed.

Then she opened her eyes, and said, "I . . . I threw it away. I threw the whole mock-up out, and I'm going to start over."

"Yes. It was in the trash. By the Talon. I don't know how they found it, but they fished it out and read it."

"They?" she asked sharply. "They who?"

"Marshall and Ty Westfall."

"Oh, my God." She took a breath. "Did . . . Clark, did he know about his dad? He didn't learn about it from my story, did he?"

There was a beat, and then Clark said, "No, Chloe. He didn't know."

There was a sharp rap on her front door. She walked toward it.

"Chloe, listen," Clark went on. "Marshall's very upset. He was making threats. I'm coming over there."

"Threats . . ." she said slowly as she opened the door.

"Against you."

Marshall Hackett stood on the other side of the screen door. He looked terrible; his eyes were swollen, and he was very pale, like a vampire—and in his fist he clenched her mock-up, the pages torn and filthy.

"Hi, *Marshall*," she said anxiously into the phone. "Marshall who is at my door *right now.*"

"On my way," Clark told her.

"That would be good. Are you using a cell phone?" she queried shrilly. Her heart slammed against her rib cage. "Are you coming now?"

"Pete, I'm taking this," he said away from the receiver. "Chloe, I have Pete's cell phone. I'll stay on the line."

"You . . . *bitch!*" Marshall shouted at her. He yanked open the screen door; it smacked against the side of the house, making a noise like a rifle shot.

"Chloe, tell him to leave," Clark told her firmly.

"Go away, Marshall." Chloe's voice shook. *"Now."*

In a bizarre way, the guy was ignoring her at the same time that he was totally focused on her, his face contorted with rage. It was as if he wasn't seeing her. The phrase *blind with rage* snapped into her mind.

Looming over her like a giant, he stepped across the threshold and stomped into her house. Chloe backed away, clutching the phone and saying into it, "Clark, I need help!"

"What's going on?" Clark demanded. "Chloe, what's happening?"

Marshall loomed over her. Chloe gasped, and said, "Marshall, listen . . ."

"No, *you* listen!" he shrieked at her.

He smacked the phone out of her hand. It arced across the room and hit the wall, narrowly missing a framed picture of Chloe holding a copy of a newsletter called "Chloe's Room" she used to edit in middle school. Then it ricocheted off the wall and smacked the coffee table, hard.

Chloe held up her hands like an unarmed cowboy, backing away from him as she mentally counted how many minutes had elapsed between when Clark had called her and now. She came up with thirty seconds—far too early for Clark to come to her rescue. She was going to have to handle this on her own—and without any way to call for more backup. Nine-one-one might have been a good idea, but the next available phone was in her father's bedroom, and there was a hallway and a closed door to get through. She was afraid to turn her back on Marshall.

God, I'm scared, she thought. *I'm terrified.*

"Marshall," she began. All she had to defend herself was her wits. She knew she was well armed in that department, and she was grateful for her intelligence. But panic was beginning to overtake her. "I'm not printing the story. I buried it."

"Doesn't matter," he gritted at her, still moving toward her. "Now everyone knows."

"No. Nobody . . . very few people know. And they won't tell a soul. I promise."

"Ty's already told half the football team." He glared at her. "My dad's out of a job."

Westfall, her helpful reporter brain informed her. *Ty Westfall is his full name.*

Don't go there, she ordered herself. *Last names are unnecessary details. That is so not the point right now.*

"I'm so sorry, Marshall," she said, and she meant it.

"Not half as sorry as you're going to be."

He rushed her. Maybe his fury made him clumsy; maybe her adrenaline rush made her unusually agile. Whatever the reason, Chloe dodged him, and he stumbled forward, colliding with the coffee table with a grunt. He managed to stop short of flying over it and whirled around, his face contorted with even more fury than when he'd appeared at her front door.

Chloe went numb from head to foot, unable to believe that this was actually happening.

Hold on, Sullivan, you are *talking about Smallville, right? Guys have tried to freeze you to death, burn you to death, and throw you off a cliff. Having a guy break into your house and threaten to beat you up . . . hey, rolling off a log here . . .*

"Marshall, please, calm down." She tried to smile, but her mouth said *no way*. She tried to swallow. Also not possible.

She tried to run. That she managed, but it didn't matter. Marshall was a football player, and this time, he tackled her hard and flung her to the floor. The contact was rough, and it was hard to stay conscious, but Chloe's self-preservation instincts went into overdrive as she screamed and started kicking her feet into his chest as hard as she possibly could. She might as well have been kicking a bale of hay for all the effect it had on the burly ballplayer.

Grunting, she scanned the area ahead of her for something to hit him with. There were chair legs attached to chairs, and sofa legs attached to sofas, and that was about it.

If this were a movie or a TV show, she thought, *or even a badly written novel, I'd have conveniently played baseball with the gang sometime before Marshall showed up, and left my Louisville Slugger on the floor, within reach. Then I could whack him with it.*

It's really too bad that reality doesn't provide for contingencies that way.

"Marshall, this is stupid," she said in a rush. "Really stupid."

He said nothing in reply, only got to his feet and yanked her up as easily as if she were a feather. Dangling in his grasp, she looked up at him; his eyes were red and swollen. He'd been crying, and she detected behind the blaze of anger a very frightened, very wounded guy.

"I don't mean stupid," she said. "I mean, tragic."

For a second, she thought she was going to get through to him. Emotions warred across his features. Then he sneered at her and made a fist.

Oh, my God, Chloe thought. *He's going to hit me.*

"Marshall," she said desperately. "Marshall, please . . ."

His fist flew at her.

Behind her, a loud, wrenching sound covered her scream. Then before she knew what was happening, Marshall flew backward, arcing into the air before he slammed onto her sofa. The force of his trajectory was so strong that the sofa tipped backward and Marshall rolled over the back and onto the floor.

Then Clark's arms were around Chloe, and his face was inches from hers.

He stared at her hard. "Are you okay?" he demanded.

She nodded, and Clark released her, running to stand over Marshall in case he got back up.

How did he get here so quickly? Chloe wondered. She pressed a hand over her chest, trying to catch her breath.

As she turned around, Clark was helping her attacker. Marshall was red-faced; he didn't look at Chloe or Clark, only focused his attention on the floor.

"Marshall," Chloe tried again. "I'm sorry. I wasn't going to print the story. Honest."

"You . . ." He began, then sagged, utterly defeated. Still avoiding her and Clark's gazes, he lifted the sofa back off the floor and righted the piece of furniture. He appeared dazed, as if he was wondering what he was doing in the Sullivan living room.

"Would you like a glass of water?" Chloe asked gently.

He nodded. Clark took a couple of steps backward, giving Marshall some space. Marshall sat down on the sofa and buried his face in his hands.

Exchanging looks with Clark, Chloe hurried to the kitchen to get some water. She poured herself a glass, too, and chugged it down at the sink.

"Clark?" she asked.

"I'm good," he replied.

By the time she handed the glass to Marshall, he had calmed down. He took it and said in a rush, "You got it wrong, Sullivan. Wrong . . . and a little bit right.

"My dad wasn't selling steroids to Jake Brook because of football. Jake . . ." He shook his head and clamped his mouth shut. A muscle jumped in his cheek. His hands were shaking.

After a sip of water, Marshall stared up at Chloe. The look of despair on his face was far worse than the anger he'd shown her.

Chloe sat on the arm of the sofa and waited. She was a good listener, and she knew that the silence before someone's words was usually part of the message.

"My dad has MS," he said, and his voice was saturated with equal parts of sorrow, anger, and relief. Chloe's lips parted in shock, and she ticked her gaze to Clark. He looked back, equally surprised, and raised a brow.

The room was pin-drop silent while Marshall struggled to speak.

Chloe guessed that no one else knew what he was about to tell them. She wasn't sure Marshall even remembered that Clark was in the room. This connection was between her and him.

"Multiple sclerosis," Marshall clarified. "My father has multiple sclerosis."

Chloe's heart caught, but she stayed quiet. This wasn't about her reactions or her sympathy. This was his chance to talk it out.

"He's been on an experimental medication, but it didn't seem to help. You can't get it with a prescription. You can only get it as part of an approved medical trial."

She nodded to show that she was hearing him. She didn't know very much about the disease, but she vaguely recalled that there was no cure . . . and that over time, it usually got worse.

"Does Jake have MS, too?" Clark asked, his tone respectful.

"That's none of your business," Marshall said harshly. His moment of connection was over, and now he was pulling back. As he scowled at Chloe, she sensed that in that instant he had stopped seeing her as someone he could talk to; she was the enemy again.

"My dad's disease was none of your business, either." He balled his fist and brought it down on his thigh, hard. "Reynolds and the school board were to let him resign so he could get another job in the district. Jake's parents were going to cooperate.

"But now that you've blown it open, that is not gonna happen."

He took a hefty swallow of water and rubbed his forehead wearily. "And without a job, he doesn't have health insurance."

Chloe closed her eyes.

"And he has a preexisting condition, so it'll be next to impossible to get private insurance," she filled in. She felt sick. No wonder Marshall had gone ballistic.

"Maybe it *was* a cover-up," Marshall went on, his voice dull and sad. "Maybe what he was doing was wrong. I don't know. But he was trying to help somebody."

His voice lowered. He spoke so softly Chloe had to crane toward him to hear him. "All I know is that my father is a great teacher, and he had a lot to offer another school. No one's going to hire him now. He's finished. My family's finished."

"Marshall, no," Chloe said earnestly. "There . . . there are always options. There's a solution."

"Is there?" He stared at her. "Do you have a way to change that headline you wrote to 'Happily Ever After'?"

"If he explains to . . . to the education board or whatever it is, " Chloe ventured.

"We live in an age of lawsuits, Chloe. By the time this is resolved . . ." He shook his head in disbelief. "We can't afford a lawyer. All our money has gone for medical bills, even though we do have medical insurance. At the moment."

"I'll—I'll print a story about that," she offered. "I'll get a campaign started to reinstate him. We'll have a fund-raiser."

"Don't. You've done enough already." Marshall handed her the glass. "I'm going to go now," he told them both, "unless you want to call the police and press charges against me for assault."

Chloe's brows shot up. "Marshall, I would never do that."

He stuffed his hands into the pockets of his letterman's jacket. "It's hard to say what you're capable of, Chloe." He said to Clark, "No hard feelings?"

Clark shook his head. "No, man. Do you need a ride?" He was carless, but Chloe would let him use hers.

Marshall moved past them. Then he turned around and stared at both of them.

"When he was diagnosed, my dad told us kids to walk as much as we could, whenever we could. He told us that health is a gift, and we needed to do everything we could to take care of our health. Because in the good old USA, it's a really expensive gift.

"I don't need a ride, Clark. I need a time machine."

There was nothing Chloe could say, no way to make things

better. But in her mind, she was already surfing the net, searching for some way to help the Hackett family.

Chloe and Clark turned to watch Marshall leave. When he got to the threshold of Chloe's house, he gestured to the screen door, which Clark had ripped off its hinges and thrown onto the porch.

"Wow, dude. You really should try out for the team," he said, impressed.

"Been there," Clark replied.

Marshall nodded, stuffed his hands back in his pockets, and trudged away. His receding figure was hunched and lost.

Clark shut the front door.

"Oh, my God." Chloe began to shake all over. "Clark, what did I do?"

"You didn't know." He was at a loss to comfort her. "You thought it was a good story, and when you felt otherwise you tried to dump it."

"I ruined their lives." She burst into heavy, racking sobs.

Then Clark moved to her and put his arms around her. She closed her eyes and leaned her head on his chest, the pain of loving him magnifying her misery. She was lost in guilt and sorrow and hurt. And Clark was there for her, holding her close.

They stood that way for a couple of minutes.

Then Lana's voice penetrated the sound of Chloe's weeping, as she said, "My God, what's going on?"

Standing in the doorway, Lana was holding a Talon to-go box. The scent of cinnamon mingled with Lana's perfume as she tentatively walked toward them.

"What happened to the screen?"

Awkwardly, Chloe pulled herself out of Clark's arms. She realized that she was still holding Marshall's water glass, and that she had accidentally spilled water down the back of Clark's sweatshirt. Clark hadn't said a thing about it.

"Ty Westfall fished Chloe's mock-up out of the trash," Clark explained to Lana. "Marshall was there. I guess Ty's telling people all over town what happened."

"So, no quiet resignation." Chloe hugged herself, exhaling heavily. "Mr. Hackett's got multiple sclerosis, and Marshall figures he won't be able to get another teaching job. He'll lose his health insurance benefits."

"But . . ." Lana frowned. "They'll be okay, right?"

"They're not okay now," Chloe observed, her voice cracking. "They haven't been okay for a long time. Only none of us knew it."

Chloe fought back tears. "Mr. Hackett is sick, Lana. He's got a chronic, progressive disease."

"That's not your fault," Lana said firmly. "You didn't make him sick."

"It's okay, Lana. I have to accept responsibility for my part in this fiasco. I'm past the rationalizing," Chloe said, flashing her a faint, wry smile.

"But it's not rationalizing," Lana protested, reaching a hand toward her friend. "You threw it out, Chloe. It's not your fault that those two guys went rooting through the trash."

Chloe let that sail right past her. She pursed her lips together and shrugged, then said pleasantly, "I have a pot roast to check on." She gestured toward the box in Lana's hands. "Cinnamon buns?" As Lana nodded and held it out to her again, Chloe carried it into the kitchen.

Clark stood with Lana. There was a beat of silence between them, then he said, "Marshall was going to beat Chloe up."

"Oh, my God." Lana covered her mouth. "Did he hurt her?"

"No. I called her to warn her, just as he reached the house."

"And you miraculously got here in time to stop him," she said archly. "How do you manage it, Clark? All the great timing, I mean?" She turned her beautiful brown eyes on him. "And the rescuing?"

He raised his brows, realizing that the innocent look he cultivated had long ago stopped working on both Lana and Chloe. He didn't insult her intelligence by saying, "Just lucky, I guess," which he would have said—used to say—back when they were younger.

I wish my having a secret didn't bother her so much. I wish she could just let it go.

Finally, he said, "I ran into Marshall and Ty Westfall outside the Talon. I wanted to let Chloe know that Marshall had read her story, so I called her on Pete's cell phone." As if offering her proof, he pulled Pete's phone from his back pocket.

"It all happened really fast, but I was in on what was happening as soon as it started," he finished.

Flushing, Lana ticked a glance at the cell phone. She shifted her weight, and said, "I guess that sounded a little bit accusatory. I'm sorry. I didn't mean it to be." She hesitated. "I should go help Chloe. She's pretty upset."

"Yes. She is." He tucked the cell phone back into his pocket and headed for the screen door. "I'll fix this," he assured her. "Tell Mr. Sullivan that the hinge was broken. That's why it came off so easily."

"Sure. Thanks for helping her, Clark. We're both lucky to have you around."

She gave him a smile—his chest tightened in response—and Clark took off.

CHAPTER FOUR

It was a beautiful new day, and all was really, really good in the world.

Pausing at the sink with her dad's new LuthorCorp coffee cup in her hand, Rebecca Morhaim looked out at the brilliant wildflowers decorating her front yard. There were sunflowers and bluebonnets, and small magenta-colored blossoms whose name she didn't know, laid out like a magical road leading right up to their new ground-floor apartment. The sun glowed a warm, welcoming yellow. Sunbeams sparkled and capered over the breathtaking beauty. In the distance, a rooster crowed, and Rebecca giggled with delight at the reminder that she was living in the country now.

We made it.

She and her dad, the notorious jewel thief Thomas Morhaim, had finally escaped Metropolis, the mean, gray city she had come to despise. For them, there would be no more skyscrapers, no traffic, no pollution . . . and no one who knew that her father was a convicted felon.

He paid for what he did, but nobody in Metropolis would let him get past it. Daddy was a marked man, and there was no way anyone was going to give him a break, ever. We were outcasts, and we always would have been.

I'm not going to let a single person in Smallville know about our past. They don't need to know. And Mr. Luthor promised Daddy he wouldn't tell a soul.

Of course her father had had to check "yes" on the LuthorCorp job application that asked, *Have you ever been convicted of a crime?*

So many times, checking that box had ended her father's job search right then and there. But Lex Luthor had given him a chance.

"I've had some scrapes of my own," was all the young, bald-headed billionaire had said, and that was the last time he brought up Tom Morhaim's descent into crime.

She would be grateful until the day she died for Lex Luthor's faith in her father. Given the terrible economy, no one in Metropolis would hire a criminal when there were so many other, more deserving folks going without.

Now, down the hall, her father hit a high note as he showered and got ready for his first day on the job. He had always loved to sing in the shower. Even though she had been a preschooler when he had been sent away to prison, she remembered his Top 40 Shower Hits concerts. Sometimes, when she'd felt all alone in the world, she had closed her eyes and listened to his voice inside her head.

Sometimes, the memory of those songs was all that kept her going.

But when he'd gotten out fourteen months ago, the singing had not resumed. Trips to the welfare office, the unemployment office, and handing over food stamps at the market had kept her father very silent, very worried, and very ashamed.

That had all changed six weeks ago, when Lex Luthor hired him. Tom had sung "Bye Bye Love" the morning he had given their Metropolis landlord—*more like slumlord*—their thirty days' notice.

Now Tom tried another high note. It was more a raspy shriek, but she loved him for straining to reach it. As far as she could tell, this morning's selection was "I'm as Corny as Kansas in August."

She grinned broadly.

We're safe from all the gossip. We're going to start over. And we're going to have a life.

Everyone in their Metropolis neighborhood had known she was the daughter of the man who had gone to prison for shooting a security guard during the robbery of a Metropolis jeweler's. A hush would fall over the kids at school when he came to pick her up. And some girls' moms told them to stop hanging with Rebecca once they realized who her father was.

Over winter break, Rebecca had met a guy named Ryan Gile at the skating rink. He was sweet, a boy a year older than she, and he went to a different school. They went out a couple times, going to the movies, then making out like crazy afterward. She was thrilled; she'd never had a boyfriend before.

Then Ryan abruptly stopped calling her. When she called him to see what was up, he said in a strange voice, "I've just been busy. That's all."

But a few days later, Lily Newman told her that Ryan had heard about Rebecca's father, and he had decided that dating her was "just too freaky." His very words.

But here, in Smallville, I'll have a chance to be judged on my own merits . . . and my own drawbacks. No one will think I'm "just too freaky" because of my dad's mistake.

"Good morning, baby doll," her dad said, sailing into the kitchen. He was wearing khaki pants and a shirt with an embroidered patch with his name on it.

She tried not to think about how much it looked like a prison uniform. He was making slightly more than minimum wage—better than in prison, where he got a few cents a day for cleaning the laundry—but still not really enough to live on. But she knew that and had been trying to focus on the good. Things were going to have to get better.

The only reason they could afford their apartment in Smallville on top of their moving expenses was because Grandma Morhaim had died a year ago and left them some inheritance money. Rather than saving it—for college, as Rebecca had hoped—Tom had used it to finance the move, calling it "an investment in our future."

It had been tough going all her life, and he had reminded her over and over that there was no money to cushion a fall and no health insurance if something should happen to him. Then the grandmother Rebecca had never known left them some money, and things had eased up a little.

The foster families she had lived with hadn't stayed in touch with her, so it was just she and her dad. But being together made it a lot easier to face the future.

Things were going to get better. They already were, in fact.
I hope it lasts . . .

She smiled for her father, and told the ghosts in her head to shut up.

"Hey, Daddy. I made coffee and scrambled eggs," she told him. "A nice, healthy breakfast to start the day."

It was a momentous occasion, the first breakfast on his first day of work and her first day at a new school. It was also noteworthy because in Smallville, the Morhaims had not applied for food stamps. They had paid for this breakfast with their own money.

"We're not going to be the 'poor lowlife Morhaims' here," Tom had told her. "We're going to be a nice, normal family."

And we are, she thought proudly.

Back home, the local church had helped the Morhaims a lot— with a subsidized apartment, food donations, and access to good medical care from St. Theresa's mobile medical unit, a van that traveled to the homes of different parishioners.

It had embarrassed Rebecca to be one of the parish's charity cases, but as her father had once reasonably pointed out, doing good works was the church's job. While that might be true, she had flushed with mortification when one of the other girls in catechism class had sung out, "Oh, my God! Becca, you have on my little sister's sweater! I thought she threw it out!"

Rebecca tried not to become fashion-obsessed the way girls who were not poor could afford to be. Although she was tall for her age, she was very slender, and sometimes she could still buy clothes in the kids' section. That was one trick—kids' clothes usually cost less than juniors, even if the styles were the same.

Her thick, dark hair curled down to her shoulders, and she knew how to French braid it, bead it, and twist it into an elegant chignon, holding it in place with a chopstick or a lacquered decorative stick. Her father had once commented that she'd inherited her mother's artistic flair.

Rebecca wouldn't know about that. Her mother had died seven years ago.

"You look handsome in your uniform, Daddy," she teased him as he took his cup from her. She always put cinnamon in with the grounds. He liked it that way. She couldn't resist adding, "For an old guy."

"Hey, hey, easy on the 'old guy's' ego," he chided her, leaning against the counter as he sipped his coffee. His profile was to her; he was a good-looking man in a dad sort of way—silvery blond hair and silver in his beard. He had sharp features and a firm jaw. Despite having been in prison for so long, he looked young for his age, and well-groomed.

He moaned softly, closing his eyes with pleasure as he swallowed the coffee. "Good job on the java, Becs."

She beamed with pleasure. "Sit down. Have some scrambled eggs." She fussed over him, taking his cup from his hand and setting it on the table, indicating the simple plates heaped with fluffy yellow eggs, two slices for each of them of cinnamon toast, and orange juice. In the center of the table stood a plain clear-glass vase brimming with flowers that she had picked at sunrise.

"Well, this is beautiful," he told her appreciatively.

She pointed at the cinnamon toast. "I got it all on sale. I even snagged some day-old bread at the outlet next to the grocery store."

"Even better." He grinned at her. "A great cook and a frugal housekeeper. You're going to make some boy a great wife."

She snorted. "Yeah, if I go back in my time machine to the fifties and turn into Beaver Cleaver's mother. Then I'll spend all day vacuuming the house in high heels and pearls."

"Trade you. You go be the warehouse clerk at the fertilizer plant, and I'll vacuum the apartment." He waggled his sandy blond eyebrows. "Cuz, honey, I look *good* in those high heels."

"Dad, you are such a dork."

He shrugged with mock innocence and picked up his fork as she sat down in her own chair and surveyed the table with pride.

We're gonna be good here, she thought.

She added, "By the way, we're going to have to eat a lot of eggs, because they're a lot cheaper when you buy them in flats."

He grinned. "Don't mind a bit."

It's all good, she told herself happily.

About an hour later, Rebecca was not so certain of that.

Smallville High was a busier, larger school than she had anticipated. That was because a lot of kids were bused in from distant, rural farms—and there were a lot of those in the county. Agribusiness had not come to Smallville, and most of the farms were still small, family-run affairs. That made for more families. More families, more kids.

She could have taken Smallville High's busyness. She was used to going to a large urban school, so the number of students wasn't a problem. But she could see she was going to have trouble penetrating the cliquish, small-town attitude of the kids she was meeting—or rather not meeting. They weren't letting her in. These kids had grown up together, and they weren't used to having a stranger in their midst. It wasn't that they were particularly rude; they just weren't very welcoming or friendly. For Rebecca, who had dreamed of having a lot of friends once the onus of her father's past was safely buried, it was a little disappointing.

But that was until lunchtime.

She had stood quietly with her tray, anxiously surveying the throngs of talkative students, and wondering if she could just sneak away and find a quiet place to eat alone. She wondered if they could tell that her lime green mohair sweater was second-hand, and if her jeans were too worn for this school. She'd gone for green in a big way: her eye shadow was green, and she had on her green beads from Grandma.

Nervously twisting her thumb ring beneath the edge of her tray, she swallowed down tears—she had pictured this day so differently . . . and started scanning for the loser table. There always was one. She should know: With a dad in prison—and then recently released from one—she had been relegated to that table, along with the gamers and the geeky kids who had seen *The Lord of the Rings* way too many times.

Then a short, slender blonde with a killer haircut got up from her table and trotted over to her. She smiled, and said, "Hi, I'm Chloe Sullivan. You're new."

"Yes," Rebecca said, feeling shy. "We just moved here."

Chloe smiled. "Poor thing."

"No. It's all good." Rebecca ducked her head. "My dad got this job at LuthorCorp and—"

"No kidding," Chloe cut in, smiling even more brightly. "My

dad works there, too." She laughed. "Well, lots of kids' dads work for the Luthor empire around here. And moms, too. Clark's mom, for instance."

She glanced back over at her table, and Rebecca's mouth literally dropped open.

The most handsome guy she had ever seen was sitting there, idly munching an apple. He had dark hair and incredibly blue eyes beneath dark brows, and the way the sunlight hit him, it was like he was from another planet, he was so compelling. His jaw was strong, and he had great shoulders. He was wearing a blue T-shirt that set off those amazing eyes.

Seated next to him was a girl as striking as he was. She was so pretty that she, too, was almost unreal.

Figures, she thought wistfully. *Best-looking guy, best-looking girl.* Chloe was no slouch, either.

"That's Clark," Chloe said archly. "The one you're staring at. His mom works for Lex's dad."

"Lex?" Rebecca blinked at Chloe. "You call Mr. Luthor 'Lex'?"

"We all do." Chloe shrugged and gestured with her hand at the guy—Clark. "Clark is Lex's best friend. And Lex and Lana and her aunt own the Talon together. That's our local coffeehouse."

With a mischievous grin, she jerked her great haircut in the direction of the table. "Come sit down. You're about to drop your tray."

"Wouldn't want that to happen," Rebecca murmured, following as Chloe led her toward Clark and the girl. *Lana? Is that her name? She owns a coffeehouse?*

"We have another castaway on the island that is Smallville," Chloe announced to the others as she presented Rebecca. "A moment of silence for my new friend . . . um"—she chuckled—"shall we call you Poison Ivy?"

Because of all the green, Rebecca thought, wondering if it was too *much* green. Maybe she looked like a leprechaun. Maybe she looked like she was trying too hard.

But how can one try too hard in high school?

"I'm Rebecca," she told them. "Rebecca Morhaim."

"Hi, I'm Lana," the other girl announced. She gestured to the empty chair beside her, and for one small second, Rebecca considered taking the empty chair on Clark's left instead.

"Thanks," she said, and meekly sat beside Lana.

"I'm Clark," the adorably cute guy said, quickly swallowing down his bite of apple. "Kent."

"Hello." *Wow.* His gaze was so intense she could almost feel heat coming off it. He had a square, chiseled jaw and full lips. His hair was shiny and dark . . . but it was his eyes that kept drawing her in. She felt almost dizzy, he was so handsome.

"Hey." Chloe waved at someone. "Here comes Pete."

Rebecca was grateful for the chance to look elsewhere.

Another handsome guy strode toward them. His light blue shirt set off his dark skin; Rebecca found herself wondering if he had a girlfriend, too. Then she caught the look he slid Chloe's way, and figured that he did.

Which is okay, she's awfully nice.

"Guys," he said, ignoring her. His face was drawn, his eyes bleary. "Very bad news."

"How bad?" Lana asked.

"Is it about . . . the Hacketts?" Chloe asked, biting her lower lip. "Do I want to know this?" Lana leaned around and put her hand on Chloe's forearm in a gesture of solidarity, while Rebecca looked on curiously.

The guy named Pete sank into the chair beside Clark and leaned his hands on the table. He looked as if someone had dealt him a harsh body blow, and he was still reeling from it. He scratched the top of his head and sat silently, as if trying to figure out what to say.

"Pete," Chloe begged. *"What?"*

"Maybe I should . . . should I leave?" Rebecca whispered to Lana, assuming that he was hesitating because there was a stranger in their midst.

"No. It's okay. It's just . . ." She trailed off, her gaze on Pete. "Pete, please, you are pretty much killing us with the dramatic pause here."

Pete wiped his mouth, then lowered both his hands to the table.

"Ah, strange choice of words there, Lana. Mr. Hackett killed himself this morning," he announced in a rush, as if he were glad to be rid of the words. He drooped like a deflating balloon, hunching over his hands, shaking his head. "In his garage."

There was silence. Rebecca looked from one face to the other as the three friends tried to absorb the news.

Then Chloe bolted from the table.

"Chloe!" Lana called after her. She got up and ran after her. "Chloe, wait!"

That left Rebecca alone with Clark and Pete.

She had no idea what to say. She didn't know who they were talking about. But someone was dead.

The three sat for a moment. Then Pete looked over at her, and said, "Hey. Are you a friend of Lana and Chloe's?"

"I'm new," she told him, distressed. "We just moved here from Metropolis. My dad and me."

"We had a . . . a tragedy," he said awkwardly. He looked at Clark, as if for guidance on how to proceed. "One of the teachers got caught selling drugs to a student and . . ."

"That's not what really happened," Clark cut in, glancing sharply at his friend.

Pete nodded. "Yeah." He exhaled, looking frustrated and confused. "It's actually a lot more complicated than that. It was being kept silent. But Chloe found out about it, and she accidentally left a story around—

"In the trash," Clark pointed out.

"In the trash," Pete confirmed. "But the teacher's kid's friend found the article, and now it's all over the school."

"Chloe's the editor of the school paper," Clark told Rebecca.

"We got on her back about running the story," Pete added, sounding distant, a bit cool. "Told her not to do it, and she decided not to run it. But it got out anyway."

Rebecca felt as though she were watching a tennis match, the ball bouncing back and forth over the net. They were telling her far more than she had the ability to process. She didn't know anybody in the story besides Chloe, and she didn't really know Chloe yet at all.

"This doesn't happen a lot here," Clark said to her. "People dying."

"Sure it does." Pete frowned at Clark and shook his head. "This is Smallville, man."

"Wh-*what*?" Rebecca was thrown. "What are you talking about, 'people dying'?"

But just then, the bell rang, signaling the end of lunch. Chairs scooted back. Students reached for their heavy backpacks and polished off bits of french fries and the famed Smallville High cafeteria mystery meat surprise.

Above the noise, Pete said to her, "Ask Chloe to show you the Wall of Weird. That'll help explain what we're talking about."

"The Wall of . . . ?" She hoisted her backpack, feeling small and scared.

"Don't worry," Clark said gently. "I'm here and . . . I mean, we watch out for each other around here. Small town." He smiled reassuringly at her.

Watch out for each other . . . from what? she wondered. *What's a Wall of Weird?*

"Seriously, don't worry," Clark said, as they fell into the crowd leaving the cafeteria.

Pete's response was to roll his eyes. "Yeah, right," Pete grumbled.

Rebecca swallowed hard.

What have Dad and I gotten ourselves into?

Lionel Luthor had claimed some extended business in Metropolis, leaving Martha Kent back in Smallville. "In my absence, try to straighten out Lex, all right?" he'd asked her briskly but pleasantly. "See if you can transfer your business acumen into his skull."

She was sorry for the harshness of his words, but she'd grown to understand Lionel well enough to know that he didn't mean them precisely as he said them. He was very proud of Lex. He just didn't want Lex to know it.

It was a very complex and rather sad relationship.

In Lex's office in his palatial mansion, Martha hung up the phone and stared at Lex in shock. He was sitting at right angles from her, he behind his desk and she at the corner beside him, with a PDA flipped open and plugged in to a truly amazing laptop. In anticipation of Lionel's return, they were scheduling some meetings between father and son. They had been snacking on a fruit plate piled high with blueberries, one of Martha's favorites. They weren't as good as the ones she grew in her organic garden, though. In fact, they were somewhat bitter, and she had been dusting them with sugar when the phone rang.

She could scarcely believe what she heard.

"You look as though you've seen the proverbial ghost, Martha," Lex observed. "What's wrong?"

Reflexively moving her hair away from her temples, she said, "That was Jonathan. With very bad news. Do you know Samuel Hackett at Smallville High?"

Lex looked acutely uncomfortable as he shifted in the chair behind his desk. "Distantly."

She gave her head a little shake. "Lex, he's dead."

As Lex stared at her in silence, his lips parted.

"He ran his car in the garage," she added. "He was asphyxiated by the carbon monoxide."

Lex blinked, taking that in as well. Steadily, he said, "Does anyone know why? Why he did it?"

"Why?" She repeated the question as though he were insane. "Lex, does it matter why?"

"Of course it does." He regarded her steadily, but there was a flush on his cheekbones.

She moved her hands. "He was selling drugs to a student. Jonathan told me he was discovered, and . . ." She hesitated. "That's really all I know."

Lex pursed his lips and folded his hands on his desk. He was quiet for a few seconds, then he said, "Jake. Jake Brook. That's the student he was selling drugs to."

"You know him?" Martha asked. "This Jake?"

"In a manner of speaking. I know his disease." Lex sighed. "And it's a bad one, Martha."

"Jake's a drug addict?" Martha asked, trying to process all

the information he was giving her. "Mr. Hackett was a drug dealer? Oh, my God."

"No. Jake has a different kind of illness." He looked acutely uncomfortable. "As did Mr. Hackett. And LuthorCorp is trying to help find the cure."

"What disease . . . ?" she began, then trailed off, shaking her head. "I guess it's none of my business . . ." But actually, she did feel that it was her business. Her son went to that school. If someone had an illness, perhaps potentially infectious, she deserved to know every single detail about it, privacy or no.

"The family appreciates my discretion," he said simply.

She was monumentally put off by his evasiveness, and decided to let him know it.

"If that's the case," she said in a mildly accusatory voice, "why did Mr. Hackett have your experimental drug to sell?"

"That's a point of discretion as well." When she looked at him blankly, he said, "Hackett was also afflicted with the identical diagnosis, and he and Jake were taking part in a clinical trial. Jake was convinced he himself was getting the placebo, and he asked Mr. Hackett to sell him some of his dose. Jake's symptoms were worsening."

He added gently, "Jake's only sixteen. He's scared."

"Oh," Martha said. "Mr. Hackett . . . he was in a wheelchair. That's all I know. I always assumed he'd been in an accident."

"No," Lex said. "Not an accident."

She was trying to understand the situation. "But if they were both in the drug trials . . . why would Mr. Hackett give someone else his share of the medication if he was fairly sure he had the actual drug, and not the placebo?"

Lex sighed. "He was that kind of man, and his family is paying for his generosity. Some people feel too much, try to do too much."

He lowered his gaze to the polished wood of his desk, and added, "Rest in peace, Samuel Hackett." Then he added, "I hope this doesn't invalidate the medical trial. It would be a terrible shame at this late date. My investors will be screaming. We're at the fourth down with ten yards to go on this protocol. Millions will go down the drain."

She flared. "Oh, my God, Lex. How can you sit there so calmly and talk about this as if it were a football game?"

"Not much for football," he said calmly. "I'm more of a polo man myself."

"*Lex.*"

"Martha, I'm not without feelings," he replied, glancing back up at her. "But I am the head of a multimillion-dollar operation, and, as such, I have to think with my head first. Stockholders expect a return on their money. They want results."

He looked philosophical as he leaned back in his chair and crossed his ankle over his knee. "Clinical trials are very expensive. It's disappointing when they show that a promising drug isn't useful after all. But when a trial is halted due to possible side effects of the drug, we have to think about other factors as well. Such as lawsuits. It's a tough game, Martha. For the thick-skinned and the hard-hearted."

Martha decided to press. "What disease is it? What did he have?" She thought a moment, trying to picture any of Clark's classmates who used a wheelchair. "I don't think I know Jake Brook."

"Football team. For now." His eyes grew sad. "He's not doing very well. If he's lucky, he may last the season."

She glanced up sharply at him. He pushed away from his desk and stood, wandering idly to his bookcase, where he picked up a Roman coin from the days of Alexander the Great and scrutinized it.

"There are some very ugly diseases in the world," he said, running the tip of this thumb over the bas-relief of Alexander's profile. "Many of them are thought to be the diseases of aging. Arthritis, Parkinson's. MS. But they strike the young, too."

Lex looked sideways at her. "They're the modern plagues of our time, robbing victims of their memory, their mobility. No one wants these illnesses to exist. So they try to find out how people contract them. Scientists go through fashionable theories the way some women go through shoes, always chasing after that funding. Grants are hard to come by unless people think you're going to make some progress.

"Right now, it's businesses like LuthorCorp that are the scapegoats." He put the coin back down on the shelf and turned his back on it. "Everyone's blaming chemicals in our food. They're saying these plagues are caused by hormones injected into our poultry and the pesticides on our lawns. That we're coating our playgrounds with lethal antiemergents and killing ourselves in the process. That's what they say."

"There's merit to that argument," she cut in. "And a lot of data to back it up."

"Depending upon which side of the argument you're standing on," he said.

Martha reddened slightly. "I'm not naive, Lex. And I don't mean to be disrespectful to you."

"I make fertilizer, not pesticides." He shrugged. "To a lot of people, chemicals are chemicals. But I know what you're getting at. You're an organic gardener, and I applaud your efforts to keep your food as free of man-made additives as possible. I wish everyone could eat organic produce.

"But they can't. The food you grow is also expensive because of all the handwork you have to put in to raise your crops. Agribusiness can't afford to do it the way you do. They need some good fertilizers and some good pesticides. I make very good fertilizer. The best." He smiled wryly. "It's my claim to fame. And fortune, I might add."

Martha began to connect the dots. "And you were funding the drug because . . ."

He smiled. "In part, because I'm a businessman in a controversial field. You know what my father likes to say: 'Plan for the best, expect the worst, and always have a backup plan.'"

"And your backup plan . . ." She considered. "In case a connection is ever proven . . ."

He made air quotes, as if around a magazine headline. "'LuthorCorp scientists work night and day to find cures for terrible diseases, and they certainly would not want to make products that harmed people. They're in the business of helping the American farmer.'"

"I see," she said slowly.

"But we're off topic." He dipped his head. "And you're upset."

"Yes. I am. And so is Jonathan. Clark's coming home from school because Smallville High has been dismissed early due to the tragedy. That's why Jonathan called." She flicked her PDA closed and picked up her purse. "Lex, I need to be with my family this afternoon."

"Of course. I'll call Clark later myself, see how he is."

"A man he knew killed himself today," she said sorrowfully.

"Clark's had a lot of losses," he observed. "I'm sorry he has to go through another one."

"That's nice of you, Lex," she said. "Seeing as you lost your mother, too."

"Still got Dad," he said.

Martha pushed back her chair and rose. "I'll be in tomorrow."

"I'll look forward to that."

She excused herself and left the room. Lex watched her go, very concerned.

I wonder if Hackett's despondency was a side effect . . . he mused. *Or if it was a natural by-product of life. Which would not surprise me in the least.*

CHAPTER FIVE

Half a world away, in Cap du Roi, Marica groaned in pain as she shifted on her cot in AYUDO's makeshift infirmary. The night was hot, and her arm was on fire. Jean Claudine was her hero, but he insisted that what had attacked her was a couple of wild dogs, not zombies. And he refused to see her when she was by herself. She didn't understand it at all.

The hut was crude, but it was shelter nonetheless. There were a dozen such structures in the compound, used both for housing as well as an on-site lab and place for storing fertilizer, seed, equipment, medical supplies, and the bare necessities such as batteries and some gasoline for an emergency generator.

Miguel Ribero, the team's doctor and chief scientist, informed her that the bullet had missed bone, but not muscle. He was planning to have her transported to a "real" hospital in a few days, once he had made arrangements. She did not protest. She was in pain, but she was alive.

Her other coworkers checked on her all the time, teasing her that some people would do anything to get out of their rotation of helping the villagers with weeding the vegetable gardens.

"Not that there are many vegetables to harvest," Marica moaned. "I ruined most of the gardens when I was attacked by the zombies."

Anna Cruces leaned forward and put her hand over Marica's forehead. "Zombies. *Ay, chica, tienes fiebre.* You've got a fever. You're delusional."

Marica wrinkled her forehead beneath Anna's damp palm. "I saw what I saw. And don't I have bite marks on my neck?"

"Dogs, as Jean told us," Anna told her. "Marica, think about it. You were scared. Come on; zombies aren't real. They're for scary movies, *chavela.*" She giggled at the absurdity of it, and added, "And they certainly can't run after people and chase them. They drag along like mummies. The only way they can get you is if you fall down helplessly and twist your ankle."

She demonstrated, lurching across the dirt floor of the tiny hut. Marica wanted to laugh, but she couldn't. "Her" zombies had been nothing like that. They had been wild and crazy, and they moved as fast as ferrets.

"But I did twist my ankle," Marica insisted, pointing to her swollen leg. "And I did scream helplessly."

"You're right, Anna, about her fever. I was there," Jean announced, striding into the hut. "It was dogs and nothing more. *Grâce à Dieu*," he added, crossing himself. Then he walked away.

Marica sighed. "He's in total denial, Anna. He had to have seen them. Because . . . because they were there."

"Well, if you say so," Anna finally said. But it was clear she remained unconvinced.

Looking ill at ease, she sat beside Marica's bed, not speaking, and Marica began to doze, feeling comforted by her company, despite the fact that Anna didn't believe her.

After a little while, Anna announced that she, too, had to go. "I have to do your share of the weeding," she said in mock accusation. "Crazy lazybones."

She lightly kissed Marica's forehead. "Rest, Marica. You've had a terrible experience."

Marica accepted the kiss, nodding with resignation as she said, "Say hello to Mama Loa for me." Mama Loa was the matriarch of the village. It was she who had permitted the AYUDO workers to help her people, she who decreed after each week of service that the AYUDO team could stay for a little while longer.

Her name was bizarre. *Loa* were the Haitian equivalent of gods. It was rather like being called Mother Spirit. Equally unusual was her son's name: though sixteen, he was called Baby Loa. A bright, fun kid with a future, the team was arranging for him to attend a private school in Mexico City.

"She said she's going to bring you a healing tea," Anna added, making a face. "I just hope it doesn't have any boiled lizards in it, like the one she made for Jean."

"Why did she make him a tea?" Marica asked.

"He hasn't been feeling good," she said. "Lots of headaches. Nightmares."

"Because he's lying about what happened," Marica said hotly. "His conscience is bothering him."

"*Ah, sí*. The Devil has his pitchfork in his brain," Anna said merrily, demonstrating. Then she waved at Marica and left the hut.

After a time, Mama Loa arrived. She was dressed in her signature colorful dress and skirt, a kerchief around her head. She wasn't very old, and Marcia liked her very much. Sometimes it seemed she kept her poverty-stricken village alive through sheer force of will. Baby Loa adored her, and was always at her side, doing for her, making sure she had a sun umbrella, a cool drink—whatever might make his wonderful mother's life easier.

Marica had been dozing. Now she opened her eyes and smiled at the amazing, charismatic woman. Mama Loa smiled back, flashing brilliant white teeth in a face the color of freshly turned earth. She carried a small china teacup in her hand, and said, "*Pour toi,* Marie-Claire."

"*Merci, Maman.*" She took the cup and stared down at it. "Ah . . ." She was afraid to drink it. She spoke enough French to ask her what was in it, but not enough to be able to understand what Mama Loa would tell her.

The woman snorted and put the cup to Marica's lips. Then she poured it down.

To Marica's instant relief, it tasted delicious. Like berries. She swallowed it down, and smiled.

As she handed the cup back to Mama Loa, the woman grew serious. She narrowed her eyes at Marica and nodded very slowly. Then she whispered to her, "Zombie. *Oui.*" She laid her finger across her lips and jerked her head toward the open window of the hut. "*Oui,* Marie-Claire."

"I knew it. I knew I wasn't crazy," Marica said. She held out her hand to the woman. Mama Loa squeezed hers hard, then patted her.

At that moment, Baby Loa stuck his head through the doorway. He was very dark and very cute, with a special sparkle that made people grin around him.

He waved at Marica, and said in English, "Whas 'appeneen, sweetart?" Then he spoke to his mother in rapid-fire Haitian French, gesturing with his hands.

Mama Loa rolled her eyes and answered him, sighing with exasperation. She said something to Marica, but whatever she had put in the tea was already beginning to affect her. Marica's lids were closing, and everything was sliding away, becoming a blur of echoing sound and hazy images.

Mama Loa made the sign of the cross over her and rose. As she moved toward the doorway, the colors of her clothing jittered in Day-Glo hues. Then she left with her son.

Marica slept heavily, dreaming. She felt herself floating, then she was running through the cane field; the pain in her neck was excruciating . . . the crack of the bullet, the pain . . .

. . . *and the zombie, gliding silently through the cane. He was different from the two she had encountered—tall, and dressed in a ragged T-shirt and torn jeans. He was a man, his eyes glassy and unseeing. Looking neither left nor right, he shuffled along—not the monster that had attacked her, but something far more docile, almost helpless.*

"Vite," a harsh voice ordered it. Hurry. Then something came down against its back, and the zombie groaned.

As if she were a movie camera, Marica's gaze abruptly shifted to the figure behind the zombie. He was a man in soldier's gear, wearing a short-sleeved olive green T-shirt and baggy cammo pants. She couldn't see his face.

The thing that had come down on the zombie's back was a semiautomatic weapon. Though it looked like a compact toy in the soldier's muscular grip, she knew appearances could be deceiving. The damage to her arm was testament to that . . .

As she watched, the soldier pulled out a walkie-talkie and spoke into it. In English, not French. She couldn't quite make out the words except for the single phrase, "Number 320."

Number 320 . . .

. . . and then she was drifting away, drifting away . . .

In the morning, she wondered if she had dreamed it all. But she didn't say anything about it to anyone. She took Mama Loa's message to heart; no one wanted her to be talking about zombies . . . so she wouldn't talk about them.

After that, things started going very wrong for the team members of the AYUDO Project, and for those they were trying to help. Anna Cruces and Jean Claudine both left abruptly, their reasons—family problems, being needed at home—vague and unconvincing. Neither one contacted those still in the village to let them know that they had gotten home safely.

Was it because we talked about the zombies? Marica wondered, terribly frightened. *Did they leave of their own free will?*

Then Baby Loa went missing. Mama Loa went insane with worry.

Dr. Ribero took the matter up with the local authorities, greasing palms, as was the custom in Haiti. In return, the police assured him that they were searching everywhere for the sixteen-year-old. But Baby Loa did not return to the village.

Everything took on a different tenor after that; with guards stopping the AYUDO team members every time they left the village, demanding to see papers. They were rude and threatening, demanding bribes, which they described as "security service fees," and generally making the relief workers feel unwelcome. Most of the others took the hint and abandoned the project. After two weeks, there were only five workers left, including Marica and Dr. Ribero.

Although she continued to write home, at first she didn't tell her family what was really going on; they would insist that she leave, and she didn't want to leave Mama Loa until Baby Loa was found.

But two more weeks passed, making it a total of a month with no sign of Baby Loa and six weeks since Marica had been attacked by the zombies. Mama Loa sank into a deep depression, insisting that her boy had been turned into a zombie and that she would never see him again.

Taking a deep breath, aware that she might be putting herself in danger, Marica sent out queries about what was going on, but she received no replies. She wondered if someone was intercepting her mail.

She became increasingly afraid, listening in the night to strange shuffling sounds that crept throughout their little compound.

It is the zombies, she thought, terrified. *Are they coming for me?*

I came here to do good, Blessed Virgin, she prayed. *Did you call me here to help these people grow food or to save them from zombies?*

AYUDO had come to Haiti to help the impoverished villagers learn new agricultural methods so that they could increase their production and better feed themselves. Dr. Ribero, a Paraguayan professor of agriculture who had once taught at the Sorbonne in Paris, had joined them. He had been instrumental in equipping AYUDO with sturdy strains of rice and vegetables, and prevailing upon several large corporations to provide farming implements, microscopes, and lab equipment for finding ways to increase production.

Aside from his influence in the world community, Dr. Ribero knew how to negotiate the underground economy of the poor, oppressed country. From some gunrunners in Port-au-Prince, he had purchased some used Smith & Wessons, ostensibly for warding off the packs of wild dogs that terrorized rural Haiti.

He had also "lifted" several hundred pounds of the fertilizer destined for the vast cane plantations of some rich landowners. He left sufficient behind in the docking warehouse at Port-au-Prince so that no one would notice the theft. Besides, in Haiti, it was commonplace for anyone who had the means to steal something of value, to go ahead and skim a little off the top.

The fertilizer did miraculous things to the nutrient-hungry soil. Yams and greens grew in abundance. Cane began to grow where it had refused to grow before. The vegetable gardens doubled in capacity, bursting with lovely, sturdy shoots of beans and other vegetables.

But after Marica got attacked, everything fell apart.

With Mama Loa so despondent worrying about her child, the other villagers had stopped working in their gardens, rice paddies, and cane fields. The soil needed nurturing, but they skimped on feeding the plants, and the crops began to show the effects of nutrient starvation.

Her mood affected them all, and the villagers collectively gave up hope that they could do anything to improve their lives. They went back to the mind-set they'd first had when Marica had arrived in Haiti over a year earlier: that anything they did was doomed to fail.

As they grew hungrier, they grew more lethargic. All anyone had to do to believe in zombies was look at the villagers, who trudged through the long, hot days like the pathetic person Marica had seen in her dream.

She was devastated.

During her days at the University of Mexico, Marica had specialized in what she termed "crisis agriculture," and it had been her dream to help people help themselves in just the way AYUDO did. She had known there would be obstacles and difficulties, but she'd been willing to give the mission her all.

It had never occurred to her that despite being given tools, knowledge, and other forms of assistance, people who were starving would refuse her help. But that was what was happening in Cap du Roi.

At first, things had gone so well. In the year that she had been with the project, children had lost the distended, bloated appearance of starvation. Their eyes had begun to sparkle, and they had begun to laugh. Mothers who used to wake up every morning wondering how to feed their babies had worked diligently in their individual gardens and in the communal plots as well. Bonds of sisterhood had formed among the women.

But these days, they hardly acknowledged each other's presence. It was as if walls had risen up around their hearts at the same time that their spirits had been trampled.

Children were crying in the night for food, and Dr. Ribero predicted that even worse starvation than before would hit the village before the year was over—as a result of a better diet, more village women became pregnant. Also thanks to better nutrition, more babies were being born, and the elderly were living longer. These all added up to more mouths to feed. The villagers had worked hard on their gardens, and they had cane to sell to the AYUDO project, who in turn processed it at a local factory and sold it to churches and international benevolent groups.

Now there was very little cane to process. Perhaps even more frightening for Marica, the remaining AYUDO team members absorbed the prevailing mood of lethargic apathy as well. They began to neglect their huts in their compound, and didn't take the time to wash themselves or their clothing. Marshaling the wherewithal to help the villagers with their problems was something the team could no longer manage.

Marica and Dr. Ribero discussed the situation at length. They seemed to be the only ones who wanted to discuss it. Something was terribly wrong, and they had secretly agreed to find out what it was. They had taken the problem and analyzed it piece by piece.

For the last week, they had zeroed in on the fertilizer Dr. Ribero had taken, wondering if something so wonderful for crop production could actually turn out to be harming the people instead of helping them. It had come from a factory in the United States owned by LuthorCorp.

Marica had heard of the Luthor family; they were very wealthy. They had lots of business interests in Mexico, and her own well-to-do family traveled in the same circles. Interesting that Lex Luthor, close to her in age, had chosen agriculture as his way to make a mark on the world, just as she had done.

"Look at this, Maria del Carmen," Dr. Ribero said now as they sat in the lab hut together. All their scientific equipment had been housed in the ramshackle tin shed, and AYUDO paid two local teenagers less than pennies a day to guard it for them.

Marica moved swiftly to his side. He was seated behind their microscope, and he moved his chair in order to give her a better view. She glanced at him, puzzled, then gazed through the viewfinder.

Her heart literally skipped a beat.

"Dios mio," she murmured, crossing herself.

At first she was confused by the tiny particles of a strangely glowing substance. It was green; she wondered if it was some kind of chlorophyll.

But she ignored them as she realized that also present in the compound were molecules arranged in the same composition as several forms of datura, the compound assumed to be the active ingredient in the "magical powders" that Voodoo priests and priestesses—*houngans*—administered to their victims in order to turn them into zombies.

There was absolutely no reason for it to be present in fertilizer that had been processed in a plant in the United States.

She frowned at the doctor, who frowned back and gestured for her to take another look. His face was drawn and pale. He looked exhausted . . . and worried.

She peered through the microscope again.

It had to be datura. The green material . . . maybe there was a little Voodoo magic involved; some chemical that bonded with the datura in such a way that it took on interesting properties such as illumination.

She took a step away, realizing that her life had just changed forever. Voodoo, in some form, was real. She had proof. And the North Americans were providing it to the Haitian upper class in order to exploit the poor and oppressed.

If that isn't proof that Satan is real, then I don't know what is.

Her heart thudded in her chest, and she became aware of how hot and muggy it was in the lab. Outside, tropical breezes were threatening to burst into winds. Palm leaves rubbed against each other like big pieces of sandpaper. Tree trunks swayed and moaned like ship masts. Snakes slithered in the underbrush. The villagers' chickens shifted uneasily in their coop. A hillock away, a local pack of wild dogs yipped at the moon like Sonoran Desert coyotes.

Datura. The implication boggled her. Could it really, honestly be true that LuthorCorp, the American fertilizer giant, was providing the rich landowners of Haiti with the means to turn their plantation laborers into mindless zombies?

Sweat poured off her forehead, and she felt dizzy and sick. Dr. Ribero placed his hand on her left arm, indicating that she should sit down.

She did so, very clumsily. She was so shocked that she couldn't really even think. She kept her right hand grasped around the base of the microscope, as if anchoring herself to the scientific reality of what she had just seen.

It occurred to her that neither one of them was talking. As if he read her mind, Dr. Ribero pointed upward toward the bare lightbulb and tapped his ear.

We're being bugged? she thought, stunned.

His eyes were sad, his mouth pressed tightly in a frown. He moved to her and whispered in her ear, "Now that we know this . . ." He didn't finish his sentence. He didn't need to.

She swallowed hard. *Now that we know this, we're in terrible danger.*

Are we going to disappear as well?

"Now that we know this, it is the beginning of the end," she whispered back to Dr. Ribero.

Only God can save us now.

Marica was correct. Things got even tenser in Cap du Roi—if that were possible. She tried to find a computer to e-mail her parents but was told there were none. Their electricity was cut off. Then the police took the team's scientific equipment away from them.

Mama Loa went missing, too.

Two more AYUDO team members left. That left her, Dr. Ribero, and a young man from Italy named Marco Taliaferro. Dr. Ribero tried to get a message to the Mexican embassy to request an escort out, but it was no use. No one wanted to get involved with the plight of the foreigners. The locals had enough problems surviving; they had no resources to take on anyone else's burdens.

About a week after their discovery of the datura in the fertilizer, Dr. Ribero slipped into Marica's hut; he had a canteen around his neck and one of the Smith & Wessons slung across his chest.

"Marco saw something," he said. "We have to go. *Now.*" He pointed to her bed. "If you have anything you need, grab it."

"What?" She was speechless.

"They're coming. He heard someone talking on a walkie-talkie." His face was ashen. "Marica, we're 'targets.' That's what they said of us. In French. Marco translated it. They're coming for us."

Then the drums began.

She raised her head, listening. Low, insistent, the complex rhythms plucked the nerve endings beneath her skin. They stared at each other. Tears of fear welled in her eyes.

"In case," he began, and hoisted a fanny pack around his waist. Unzipping it, he showed her a couple of baggies of LuthorCorp fertilizer.

She nodded.

The drums sounded longer, stronger. He took her hand and began to lead her outside. Then he raised a hand as static and distorted electronic voices overlaid the drumming, very close by.

Too close.

"Wait," he told her. He unhooked the plastic tabs on the fanny pack, leaving it in her hand. Then he crept outside.

"No!" she whispered fiercely.

His boots crunched in the loamy soil; she watched him trot, hunched over, toward the next hut, about six feet away.

"Come back," she whispered to the retreating figure. Then he went inside the hut . . . and didn't come back out.

The wind picked up; she smelled smoke. She moved to the doorway and glanced out anxiously.

The zombies of Cap du Roi were walking.

The slack faces of perhaps eight people were illuminated by flashlight and torchlight as they shuffled toward the scattered huts. They were surrounded by a dozen or more men in military garb.

The zombies moved forward; as she stared at them, she cried out and crossed herself.

She was relieved to see that Mama Loa was not among them. But Baby Loa, Jean Claudine, and Anna were. They stared straight ahead, no light in their eyes. They looked completely dead. They looked like people who'd had lobotomies.

Moving, and yet dead.

The drums beat a thundering syncopation with the footfalls of the zombies. Smoke stung Marica's eyes.

They were torching the compound.

I'm going to die. They want to kill me. I know more than they want me to know.

Dr. Ribero . . . Marco . . .

He still didn't emerge from the other hut.

It was time to go, before the zombies and their guards figured out which huts were occupied.

I have the fertilizer. I have to leave now, with or without the men.

Her mind raced as she tried to formulate a plan. The police had all the team's passports locked in a safe inside police head-quarters in Port-au-Prince. Her French wasn't very good, and even if it were, it wouldn't be much help. Everyone in Haiti was used to their comings and goings being monitored, and one didn't just leave at one's own whim. One received permission to leave.

She stood in her hut, her attention momentarily snagged by a large lizard skittering across the wall. She watched it disappear into a hole behind her bed. She had never noticed the small opening before. She never had a reason to notice it.

But it didn't matter now. What mattered was getting out of the compound, away from the oncoming zombies, and finding an official who would listen to her story, investigate what was going on out here, and help her get back home.

Or else, simply running on her own.

That seemed the safer course. There was no one in Haiti whom she could trust now.

I'll try to get to Miami. Or Cuba.

And then she realized that she had waited too long to leave her hut.

For she smelled them, smelled the rank, fetid odor of decom-posing human flesh. Heard the scratching shuffle of their feet, which were too heavy for their thin leg bones to pick up and set back down. As the wind whipped the trees, she heard the crack of crushed branches, the odd noise as something was knocked over—garbage cans, a basket of silverware, a wooden bowl loaded with plantains.

The drums provided counterpoint; they were speaking to her in some macabre and incomprehensible language. Then they picked up speed. Their tempo shot from slow and sedate to anxious and threatening, and she felt her body responding with the fight or flight syndrome. She began to hyperventilate. Her mind raced.

The drums beat faster.

She grabbed the fanny pack.

Then firelight threw a sudden silhouette against the cracked, peeling wall: It was of a man walking toward the entrance to her hut. It was not Marco. There was nothing sinister about his shape, except that it was there. She had no idea if he was zombie or living human being, friend or foe, and she knew she couldn't find out.

She yanked the bed back to further reveal the hole in her wall of about two feet in diameter.

As she dived under her bed and scrabbled toward the hole in the wall, whoever stood on the threshold came into the room. Marica prayed that the noise from the drums would cover her escape.

She beat at the sides of the hole with the fist of her good arm. The damp, rotted wood easily gave way, and she kept crawling, feeling like a butterfly bursting from its cocoon. Her other arm was on fire.

Tears streaming down her face, she emerged from her hut and into a copse of trees. The undergrowth was thick and thorny, pulling at her clothes and hair, scratching her.

Her hut burst into flames.

The figure she had seen thrown against the wall emerged, carrying a torch. He was wearing fatigues and a black hood over his head. He was a soldier.

She put her hand to her mouth. She was sobbing, completely at a loss about what to do.

A flare hit Dr. Ribero's hut, and it, too, burst into flame.

Marica flattened herself against the ground, biting her lip so hard to keep from screaming that she drew blood. Throwing her forearm forward, then pulling herself up to meet it, she managed to put a bit of distance between herself and the two blazing huts.

She dived into the forest underbrush.

Footsteps came up behind her; foliage was pushed out of someone's path.

She froze, closing her eyes in an effort to boost her hearing ability. A voice called out, "*Mademoiselle* Lopez? *Est-ce-que vous êtes ici?*"

Miss Lopez? Are you here?

She clamped her mouth shut, lest she scream with terror.

Her hands were covered with cuts. *I have work to do here. Very important work. Something very, very wrong is going on around here. I have to let someone know about the datura, and the zombies. I have to stop them.*

She stayed hunkered in the darkness, her heartbeats counting off the seconds like a time bomb. She heard the click of a weapon, and she shut her eyes as tightly as she could. She began to list her sins, preparing herself for the moment of her death. She hoped that if she died, she would be given Last Rites in time by a priest. She had been a good Catholic all her life, and she fervently wished to die a good Catholic as well.

The searcher evidently gave up. Marica exhaled with a sob as his presence receded, then disappeared.

As the only home she had known for the last year was ransacked, Marica hid for hours, shivering like a rabbit. Moonlight washed over her, and she listened to the roar of a flash fire and the crackling of burning wood. Smoke burned her eyes; she struggled hard not to hack as the smoke filled her lungs and made her feel sick and dizzy.

She heard every building in the AYUDO compound burn to the ground.

At the end of it, the air was empty of sound. There were no drumbeats, no shuffle of zombie feet, nothing. It was as if the world had been frozen . . . the action halted for an unspecified amount of time.

Those who believe that silence is golden have never listened to the silence of the dead.

Marica let the tears flow, grieving for her friends. She had no idea where Marco or Dr. Ribero were. But she didn't let herself completely give way; she sensed that this reprieve was only the calm before the storm, and she had to get out of there before she was found.

She was exhausted and terrified, but she knew what she had

to do. She had to keep going, and she had to put an end to the zombie business.

With the rising of the new day, Maria del Carmen Maldonaldo Lopez slipped into the jungle and put as much distance as she could, as fast as she could, between herself and the murderers.

In the pack, she carried evidence . . . and secrets. She made a vow to the sweet and merciful Virgin of Guadalupe then and there that she would find out what the datura-like compound was in the LuthorCorp fertilizer . . . and make sure no one was ever harmed by it again.

She might not be able to now, but she would eventually expose this evil to the light of day . . . before she was silenced herself.

Mr. Hackett's funeral was scheduled to be held two days after he died, on Friday. That Thursday Principal Reynolds held an assembly in the gym, announcing that there would be no school the following day.

Nobody was tacky enough to cheer.

"I hope to see many of you at the service," he told the student body as he concluded his announcement. He looked shaken. As he gathered up his notes, Clark saw how badly the principal's hands were trembling.

"Man, this is so weird," Pete murmured. "This is unbelievable."

"I know," Lana whispered back. "I can't believe it's happening. It's like it's not real."

Clark, Pete, and Lana had sat together in the bleachers. Chloe was absent. Ever since the news of Hackett's suicide, she had stayed home from school, and Clark figured that made sense. Lana told the guys that Chloe needed some space, so he and Pete gave it to her.

That didn't stop Clark, however, from checking on her house every couple of hours or so. He'd occasionally put on a burst of superspeed and race away from the Kent family farm, run to her house, and make sure she was safe.

Because Marshall Hackett was staying out of school as well.

Clark had checked on the Hackett home, too. It was not a good place. The family was in shock; they were all moving silently from room to room in a daze, not speaking, not eating. Lights glowed in bedrooms at all hours of the night. TVs were left on in several different rooms, but no one was watching any of them. The mail was piling up. In the kitchen, a carafe of coffee had been sitting in the coffeemaker for days, and a sheen of mold coated the surface. Everyone trudged past it, and Clark figured Mr. Hackett must have been the family coffee drinker.

It was as if everyone had died, not just him.

Marshall was a mess. He mostly sat in his room and stared into the darkness.

When Clark told Pete about it, he shook his head. "That guy's going to need some serious therapy," he said.

They were now sitting in Clark's loft, supposedly working on the farm implement section of their history project while they waited for Clark's parents to drive them to the funeral. Pete's mom and dad would meet them at the church.

On the table sat some old rusty scythes and the remains of a wooden yoke worn by farmers while walking behind a mule when plowing. Pete's report on pesticides and fertilizers was there, too. Truth was, they hadn't touched any of it. School seemed amazingly inconsequential at the moment.

Martha was baking bread; the warm, homey smell permeated the loft, mingling with the fragrance of hay and flowers. She usually baked when she was upset.

Jonathan came up the steps and gave the boys a nod. Like Clark and Pete, he was wearing a suit. None of them looked comfortable.

"Okay," Jonathan said. "We're ready to go."

Clark and Pete nodded. They followed Clark's dad back down the stairs and out to the truck. As Clark and Pete climbed into the truck bed, Martha crossed the yard from the house. She was wearing a black dress and low black heels.

Jonathan helped her into the truck, and they took off for the center of town, to the small Methodist church the Hacketts had attended. They had been active in the church, and Principal Reynolds had cautioned the students that it would probably be standing room only unless they got there early.

As they jostled along in the truck, Pete and Clark watched the fence posts blur by. Portable sprinklers chittered in the fields, spraying the wheat and corn with water, fertilizers, or pesticides.

After a while, Pete said to Clark, "Do you wonder about it, Clark? Dying?"

Clark shifted uncomfortably. "Yes. I wonder if I can die," he said frankly. "Or how long I'll live. Maybe I'll burn out quicker than most people."

Pete grimaced. "Man, Clark, that's intense." He gazed at him.

"I mean, I hadn't thought of that. What if you're immortal?"

Clark shrugged. "I'm pretty sure the meteor-rocks can kill me." He grimaced, thinking about the devastating effect their poisonous green glow had on him whenever he came near them. "So I can die. I guess."

"Yes," Pete said. "But sometimes in Smallville, not even the dead can die." They were quiet for a moment, both thinking about the ghosts they had tried to exorcise in the Welles farmhouse and cornfield last year. The bones had been infused with radiation from the meteor-rocks, which seemed to have kept the spirits of the dead people bound to the earth. And their pursuit of Clark had nearly killed him.

Pete grew lost in thought as well. They sat silently, as the truck bounced down the road.

About ten minutes later, they reached the center of Smallville. At the far end of a U-shaped road, the Smallville United Methodist Church gleamed like a beacon. It was made of wood, and had been freshly painted. Clark recalled a picture in the *Smallville Gazette* of Mr. Hackett in his wheelchair, holding a paintbrush in his hand as the church pastor pretended to pour a bucket of paint over his head. Like Chloe, it hadn't really dawned on him that the man was confined to a wheelchair—that that may have been the reason the picture got printed. He had simply chuckled at the good-humored teacher being "threatened" by the minister.

All that is gone now, he thought.

"I wonder if that new girl Rebecca will show," Pete said. He shook himself. "Not that I'm hoping, to, like date her at the funeral or anything."

Clark gave him a faint smile. "I guess it's true what they say. 'Life is for the living.'"

Clark's dad pulled over to the curb across the street from the church. Clark took a breath and climbed out of the truck bed, careful not to get dirt on his suit. Pete followed after, and they joined Clark's parents on the sidewalk.

A small crowd congregated around the front of the small, white-steepled building. Outfits were somber. No one was smiling. Pete nudged Clark, and said, "There's Principal Reynolds."

"And there's Lana," Clark said, gazing at her.

She was wearing a black dress with jet beads at her neck. She had on small dangling earrings that grazed her jawline and her hair was pulled back into a topknot. She looked pale and tired.

When she saw Clark and the others, she lifted a hand. Martha waved back as Clark started across the street, glancing both ways for traffic. Although a car couldn't hurt him, it would certainly raise a lot of questions if Jonathan Kent's boy dented the front end of a car when it collided with him.

"Lana," Clark said when he reached her. He glanced over his shoulder and realized that Pete had hung back to give him a chance to talk to Lana privately.

"Hey." Her eyes glistened with tears. She pressed her lips together, and said, "I hate this."

There had been a few times when the two of them had held each other; and others — fewer still — when their lips had touched. But when Lana slid her arms beneath his and sank her head onto his chest, he felt as if she were coming home after having been gone a long, lonely time. As her soft cheek pressed against him, he was overcome with tenderness. Something loosened inside him, and a rush of emotion caught him off guard. He had to hold back tears of his own.

"It's so awful at the Sullivan house," she whispered. "Chloe's going crazy with guilt. She hasn't slept in days. Her father's upset, too."

"She has nothing to feel guilty about," Clark asserted, but Lana shook her head.

"You'll never convince her of that." She lifted her head. "I've never seen her so upset. She's shut down." Then Lana looked past Clark's shoulder, and said, "Hey, Rebecca."

With that, Lana gently broke from Clark's embrace. He was sorry . . . sorrier still that holding her was awkward for them both. But he had no idea how he could ever hope to be close to Lana if he didn't share his secret with her. And he wasn't ready to take that risk — nor saddle her with that responsibility.

"I hope it's okay that I showed," Rebecca Morhaim said. Her peasant-style dress was navy blue, and the embroidery on it looked frayed. And her shoes were scuffed. For the first time, it dawned on Clark that she and her father might be poor. "I mean, I'm new here, and . . ."

"You're a member of the student body," Lana said warmly. "The same as us. You belong here."

Rebecca exhaled, vastly relieved. "Thanks, Lana." She smiled weakly at Lana, then Clark. "This might sound weird, but I've never actually been to a funeral before. Mom . . . my mom died, but we didn't have a service. I'm pretty freaked."

"I have." Lana's voice was filled with pain. "For my parents. When I was three."

"Oh, my God," Rebecca breathed. "*Three?* How awful." She looked questioningly at Lana.

"It was the meteor shower," Lana answered, unwillingly pulling memories and images from the past. Clark knew the story well. Lana had been sitting in her Aunt Nell's flower shop; her parents had gone to the Crows homecoming game.

And the meteor-rocks had screamed from nowhere into the bright Kansas sky, the enormous, fiery boulders slamming into buildings . . . and the Langs' car, just as her parents had gotten out of it in front of the flower shop.

The meteor shower that accompanied my ship to earth, Clark thought, cringing inside. *The same one that turned Lex bald.* His father had told him to let that one go. There was nothing he could have done, nothing he could do now. But it made the burden of his secret even heavier to bear.

Rebecca looked too shocked to speak. Then she managed to say, "You saw it happen?"

"I only remember bits and pieces," Lana answered truthfully. "And it grows a little grayer every year." The thought clearly distressed her; Clark knew that Lana held on to her pain in order to hold on to her parents. She had said as much to him on several occasions.

His own parents, his genetic parents, had no hold on him, nor he on them. Why hadn't they put a message in his ship, tried to explain who he was and where he came from, and told him that they loved him? There was nothing for him to hang on to — no names, no faces. They could have at least left him a photo-graph of themselves — if they had such things as cameras on their home planet. They had to have had some kind of imaging equipment—Clark's ship was evidence of a vastly advanced technological society.

Why didn't they give me a past? I have no idea who I was . . . who I am . . .

"How's Chloe?" Rebecca asked, startling him out of his reverie. He felt ashamed that he was focusing on his own pain when Chloe was in such distress.

"Bad," Lana admitted. "It's like she's checked out. I mean, she's there—her body's there,—but Chloe's not home. She's just going through the motions. She wanders around the house like a ghost."

Clark was so sorry. He knew how hard Chloe would take something like this. She had a tremendous sense of integrity.

"Guilt's a tough gig," Rebecca murmured. Then she shook herself as if she were remembering where she was, and said, "I would never commit suicide if I had kids. That's so cowardly."

Lana sighed heavily. "I guess the shame was more than he could stand."

"No, it wasn't that." Pete said, approaching the group. As he drew near, he looked as if he were going to be sick to his stomach. "Apparently his symptoms had worsened with the stress. He could hardly move. He couldn't even make his wheelchair go. He got afraid that he was going to drag his family down."

Lana was horrified. "So he . . ."

Pete looked down at his hands, then up at his friends. "He took his own life to spare them. He didn't want to be a burden." He added sourly, "He had a lot of life insurance."

The three stared at him. "How do you know all that?" Lana asked him gently.

"Ty Westfall's blabbing it all over the place. They found a note," Pete informed them, shaking his head in disbelief. "In Marshall's sports bag. Mr. Hackett put it there because he figured Marshall would eventually find it. Turns out there were more secrets in the Hackett family than the drug sale." He paused. "Marshall was adopted. Mr. Hackett was his stepfather, not his biological father."

"Whoa," Clark said.

"Yeah." Pete shook his head. "Nice parting words. 'By the

way, I've kept something from you your whole life.'"

"Marshall didn't know?" Rebecca asked.

"How did that happen?" Lana asked. "I mean, why did they adopt him?"

Pete stuffed his hands in his pockets. "When Mr. Hackett was diagnosed with MS, he and his wife decided not to have any more kids. They stopped with one, Marshall's brother, Jeremiah. But I guess they wanted a bigger family. So they adopted Marshall. That's kind of nice, actually. Tells me they had hope for a future together, as a family."

"Isn't it a bad time to be telling your kid he's adopted, I mean, when you've decided to kill yourself?" Lana asked. "That's a huge revelation. I still have to deal with it, and I've known for years."

"He didn't want Marshall to worry about getting MS," Pete replied. "He wanted to let him know he wasn't genetically related to a man with such a terrible disease. Jeremiah's not so lucky."

"How's Marshall taking it?" Lana pressed.

"Not well. If it was supposed to make Marshall feel better, it did just the opposite. He's all messed up."

Rebecca thought to herself, *These are nice people. Something bad happened, and they're not judging everybody. They're trying hard to understand how it happened. If they ever find out my secret, I hope they're as kind to me.*

"Did Ty mention if Mr. Hackett told Marshall who his bio-logical parents are?"

"I don't think so," Pete replied. "I think it was a—what do you call it—a closed adoption. I suppose he can try to find them. Seems easy enough in this day and age, with the Net and all."

Lana looked troubled, and Clark remembered when Chloe had researched the identity of Lana's natural father—against Lana's express wishes. It had created quite a rift between them, and it had taken some time for Lana to learn to trust Chloe again.

I know how she feels, Clark thought. *If Chloe ever suspected I . . . that I'm more than what I appear to be, she'd probably start investigating me. If she hasn't already. And I don't know how I would stay friends with her after that. I don't know how Lana managed it. I'm glad she did, but that was one place Chloe should not have gone.*

"This must be so unsettling for you," Lana said to Rebecca. "Coming to a new school and having all this to deal with."

Rebecca looked mildly uncomfortable. "It's kind of nice, in a weird way. It takes the spotlight off us. I mean, me." She shifted her weight and put her arms around herself in a defensive posture.

Clark turned. A black limo rolled to a stop in front of the church. On the dashboard was slapped a white sign with black letters that read, "Funeral." The windows were tinted, but he used his X-ray vision to look inside. There were three figures in the stretch—a woman and two young men. Marshall was leaning against the door, gazing blankly at the church. His heartbeat was slow and dull.

They've given him something, he realized. *Something to help him through.*

A tall, thin man in a dark suit had been standing off to the left. He turned and gave a nod, and two more men joined him. They went down the brick steps of the church in a little clump, the guests parting for them. There was an air of professional sadness about them that put off even Clark.

"Funeral director," Pete filled in. "And his two sons." He made a face. "Not the kind of family business I would want to be in."

"How do you know who they are?" Rebecca asked him.

"Believe it or not, that man—" he gestured to the oldest-looking of the three men—"buys feed from my Uncle Howard. They raise beef cattle. Just a few head."

As they watched, the man reached Marshall's limo and opened the door.

A hush fell over the crowd as Mrs. Hackett emerged. She was wearing sunglasses, and her face was slack. She leaned heavily on the funeral director's arm, losing her balance as he guided her away from the limo door.

"She's on something to get her through this," Pete said. "I would be, too. Man, this is awful."

Rebecca turned away. Her face was ashen. She said, "I think I'll go inside. My dad's already here."

"Okay," Lana said. "We'll catch up with you."

Clark glanced curiously at Rebecca as she walked away and

started up the stairs. "She's really upset by all this."

"Aren't you?" Lana asked him. But it was clear from her tone that the question was rhetorical. She knew he was.

"Clark," his mother said, as she and Jonathan joined him, "You okay?"

"Hey, Mom." He gestured helplessly. "Um, not really."

There was a stir in the crowd, and Clark and Martha turned to see what had happened.

"Marshall!" someone yelled. It was Marshall's brother, Jeremiah.

After climbing out of the limo, Mr. Hackett's adopted son had fallen to his knees. Now the funeral director and one of his sons were attempting to help him up. But he was a burly football player—sagging and uncooperative because of the tranquilizer he was on—and they were having trouble.

Clark edged his way through the clump of onlookers and hurried to Marshall's side. He said, "Excuse me," to the funeral director, who relinquished his hold on Marshall and gave his place to Clark.

Clark wrapped his hand around Marshall's forearm and gently, carefully raised him to his feet. Using his strength, he held him up, keeping him balanced, although to the casual observer, he was simply giving him a steadying hand.

Marshall murmured, "Get 'way from me, Kent."

"It's okay, Marshall," Clark soothed. He looked over his shoulder at the church. "Can you go in?"

"Dad . . ." Marshall moaned. His eyes opened and closed. He was heavily dosed, and Clark was a little concerned. He listened to his heartbeat, which was slow but steady.

Then Marshall saw Lana. He slurred, "Did Sullivan show? Come to gloat?"

"No," Lana assured him. "No, Marshall."

"Good. I'm gonna get her." He shook his arm, trying to break contact with Clark. But Clark could tell that if he let go of Marshall, the guy would fall again. Clark wasn't going to let that happen to him.

So without saying a word, Clark began to walk him up the steps to the church. Marshall became as docile as a lamb.

Jeremiah came out of the limo next. He was trembling, and his eyes were so swollen from crying that they appeared to be closed. His demeanor was the exact opposite of Marshall's— where Marshall's emotions had been subdued with drugs, Jeremiah's were raw and unharnessed, and as he gazed up at the church, he burst into heavy sobs. His wails rolled up and into the church like physical things. He was so loud and so distraught that people began to murmur.

The pastor of the church came out. A young man with a goatee, he was dressed in a long black robe with a whiter, shorter robe over it. Gently requesting that people move out of his way, he hurried down to the Hacketts, straight past Marshall and his mother, and gathered Jeremiah in his arms.

The older son of the family sobbed openly. He clung to the pastor and practically screamed with grief. Meanwhile, the two other Hacketts made no reaction. It was eerie; as if they had no emotions left.

"Let's go in," Clark said to Marshall. He glanced at the son of the funeral director who was escorting Mrs. Hackett. The man nodded back at him and they each guided their respective mourner into the church.

The scent of chilled, dying flowers hit Clark as he entered the church. The pews were overflowing, and heads were turning in his direction. It was an awkward moment.

His mother and father had gone on ahead. Martha half waved, indicating that they had saved him a place. Pete had joined his own family. Lana was with Clark's parents, and Rebecca was sitting with an older man with blond hair. Clark figured him for her father.

Taking his cue from the man escorting Mrs. Hackett, Clark walked Marshall up the center aisle.

A closed coffin stood before the altar. It was made of brilliantly polished wood, with brass fittings along the side of the lid.

Marshall stopped and took a deep breath.

"You okay?" Clark asked him.

"Don't feel a thing," Marshall slurred. "Gave me something."

"Okay." Clark licked his lips as they walked past row upon row of curious faces. He was hyperaware of his surroundings:

the scent of women's perfumes mingled with the odor of the dying flowers.

Organ music began, playing the hymn, "Amazing Grace."

They reached the front pew, and the bearded man said to Clark, "Go on in."

Clark hesitated. He hadn't planned on sitting with Marshall during the funeral. He really wanted to be back with his own family, and with Lana. But Marshall was like a rag doll, unable to move under his own power. So Clark eased him into the pew, making room for Mrs. Hackett and Jeremiah, and reluctantly sat with them. He helped Marshall into a sitting position, rather like a ventriloquist with his dummy.

"Thanks," Marshall managed.

Mrs. Hackett was also eased in. She gazed dully at the coffin, as if she couldn't quite understand what it was. Clark was uncomfortable with how disoriented she seemed to be.

From the back of the church, Jeremiah's shrieks of pain shot loud and harsh, so out of control that he, not Clark, might as well have been from another planet.

Clark half rose to help the pastor with Jeremiah, when he saw his father leave his pew and walk toward the two men. Jonathan touched the minister on the back, talking to him for a few seconds, then put his arm around Jeremiah and walked him to the pew where Clark, Marshall, and Mrs. Hackett sat.

"My boys . . ." Mrs. Hackett's voice was breathy.

"It's okay, Mrs. Hackett," Clark told her.

"No. It's not." Without tearing her gaze from the coffin, she patted Clark. "You're a good boy." She didn't seem to notice that she was patting a stranger, and not her own son.

"Thank you, ma'am," Clark said.

"So polite."

The pastor walked toward the casket, moving to a podium beside it and looking down at what must have been an order of worship. He bent down, retrieved a glass of water, and took a sip.

"Dearly beloved, let us listen to the word of the Lord," he said.

Heads bowed.

Tears flowed.

And Jeremiah Hackett wailed with loss.

At the Scottish castle he called home, Lex, who had skipped the funeral, was seated behind his desk and watching the beautiful, disheveled woman as she paced the floor and yelled at him. She was small but wiry and beautifully proportioned; and her short, black hair and blazing eyes lent her an air of danger — an alluring combination of kickboxer and runway model.

"I fully believe that something sent me here to stop you," she said.

She was limping. Her left arm was bandaged; it had been in very bad condition, and Lex had had one of his own doctors clean and rebandage it. She was now also on an antibiotic protocol.

"Like an angel?" he asked her.

"You are not listening to me!" she shouted at him. "There is something in your fertilizer. In this!" She held a clump of what appeared to be dirt in her hand. "This killed people, Mr. Luthor! Friends of mine!"

"I am listening, Ms. Lopez," he said firmly. "Very carefully." He hadn't yet figured out her angle—blackmail money? A lawsuit? Lex was a Luthor, and therefore, quite accustomed to dealing with both.

And to think I was talking to Martha Kent the other day about this very thing.

Lex steepled his fingers, watching her. She was beyond exhausted, and she had told him an amazing story of hitching a boat ride filled with refugees from Haiti to Cuba. And then an old university friend wired her some money from Mexico City, so that her parents wouldn't find out and make her come home before she had completed her mission. And then . . . coming to Kansas to talk to him about poisoned fertilizer?

The timing after his conversation about fertilizers, pesticides, and diseases with Martha Kent was . . . curious. But the fact that LuthorCorp might have sold a foreign country some contaminated fertilizer didn't surprise him as much.

If what she's telling me is true, I'll bet my Porsche my dad's mixed up in it. In fact, I wonder if his leaving for Metropolis has anything to do with this.

Her next tirade was cut short by the arrival of Lex's assistant, Drew, who had brought them something to eat. He wheeled in a table. It was covered with a starched white linen tablecloth and a number of elegant silver-covered dishes. Also, an iced champagne bucket and two flutes. It was too late for lunch and too early for dinner, but Lex was not about to let his guest go hungry. From the story she had told, she had been on the run for at least a week, with rarely a chance for a decent meal, much less a good one. By her elegant carriage, she appeared to be the kind of woman who had been raised on the finer things of life.

He hoped she approved of his menu selections.

With a flourish, Drew uncovered the largest dish. A beautiful sliced London broil lay on the silver tray. The next dish revealed new potatoes, the third, fresh asparagus. A simple meal, beautifully prepared.

Lex got up from his desk while Ms. Lopez sank into a leather chair. She glanced around, got back up, and dumped her handful of LuthorCorp fertilizer—if that was what it really was—into one of the champagne flutes. Lex smiled to himself—*feisty, isn't she?*—and began unwrapping the champagne cork. He popped it expertly—practically the only useful thing he'd learned at a string of prep schools, and poured it into the empty glass. He carried it to her and stretched out his hand.

"*Salud,*" he said in Spanish. Health.

That seemed to defuse her. Shaking her spiky-haired head, she sighed, took the champagne, and sipped it. She closed her eyes and leaned back against the luxurious leather chair.

"Better," she said.

His smile grew. He hadn't expected her to apologize, and he was glad that she hadn't let him down.

"Thank you, Drew," he said to his employee, who silently withdrew. Then he picked up one of the plates and began to serve her, watching her as she quietly drank his finest champagne and began to relax.

"There's datura in it," she informed him. "The herbal poison that *houngan* in Haiti use to create zombies."

He said nothing, only finished arranging her meal, and carried it over to her. Before she took it, he fetched her a white napkin and held it out for her to wipe her hand off.

She did so, then handed him the champagne without a single word of thanks.

He liked that, too.

She cut the meat and took a healthy bite, chewing appreciatively. Her eyes flickered with satisfaction, and she cut another piece.

"Did you see any? Zombies?" he asked conversationally.

"Yes." Her look at him was fierce and angry. "I saw friends and colleagues changed into zombies. Their will drained, herded along like pigs . . . and crazy, like demons. And they . . ." She touched the back of her neck, where there was a thick bandage.

She shuddered and lifted her plate. "I've lost my appetite."

"If the *houngan* in Haiti use datura to create zombies, they don't need to buy my fertilizer to get it," Lex pointed out. "Otherwise, zombies would be a new thing in the world. And they aren't. At least the stories about them aren't."

"I am not making up stories!" she thundered. "Don't you patronize me. I risked my life to get this sample to you."

"I don't mean to patronize you," he persisted. "I'm simply thinking aloud, Señorita Lopez. Maybe my father's figured out a way to artificially create datura. With economies of scale, LuthorCorp may be saving the Haitian growers a lot of money."

She looked stunned. "You are admitting it?"

"No." A strange smile played over his mouth. "May I be frank, with the proviso that you will be discreet, at least for now? It wouldn't surprise me if my father was processing custom batches of fertilizer here in my own plant without my knowledge. He's done things like that before."

"And . . . you are your father's son," she said slowly. She sounded nervous, and Lex fell a little bit in love with her right then and there.

"Yes. But our relationship isn't what you might expect. It's . . .

complicated." He cocked his head. "He didn't send you here, did he?" *Is this some kind of test concocted by my father to see how I'll handle it? Or less euphemistically put, one of his traps?*

"So you are trying to blame this all on him?" she asked. "Come now, don't play the innocent with me. I'm not some little peasant from the mountains. My family has dealt with people like you before."

"Really?" He was intrigued. He leaned forward, smiling, and said, "Where? If we've met before—"

"—'you would remember it,'" she mocked. She picked up her champagne again and drank. Her hands were shaking and there were circles under her beautiful brown eyes. "All I'm saying, Mr. Luthor, is that I'm here to find out why everyone except me died in Cap du Roi."

"Died . . ."

"Men in uniforms," she said. "Bloodthirsty butchers! They slaughtered everyone. I hid."

"The *tonton macouts?*" Lex asked. "I thought they had been disbanded."

"You know an awful lot about the country," she observed, draining her glass.

He took it from her and began to refill it. "What's to know? It's a poverty-stricken nation with a penchant for ghoulish legends. I've never been there, but I've been known to watch a good zombie movie now and then."

"It's no joke!" she thundered at him. "You arrogant industrialist!"

He lifted a brow, stifling a chuckle. "I don't think I've ever been called that before."

"Don't think that because you're handsome and rich, you can be glib with me," she shot back at him. "I have been through hell. I'm not in the mood for banter."

She rose and set her plate down. "They were not *tonton macouts,* the bogeymen of the old regime, which I suspect you already know. I may have walked into the belly of the beast when I came to you, but I warn you, my family knows I'm here. If anything happens to me—"

"Nothing is going to happen to you. At least not that I have anything to do with," he assured her.

That gave her pause. She looked at him, and said, "Mr. Luthor, I watched people die. *De veras, hombre.* I saw zombies." She crossed herself.

"All right." He inclined his head.

She gave her head a shake, seeming to shiver all over as she raked her fingers through her hair, and said, "I need a shower, and I need to sleep." They were not requests. "Then I need to talk. If not to you, then to the authorities."

And which authorities would those be? he wondered, fascinated by her air of command. Women usually tried to get his attention through the gentle art of seduction, not by accusing him of turning people into zombies, then insisting that he give her a place to crash for the night. But Maria del Carmen Maldonaldo Lopez most certainly had his attention.

"Here's what I suggest," he said. "I will personally help you investigate the fertilizer. For all we know, there are more bags of it stamped with LuthorCorp labels sitting on pallets in my warehouses, already waiting to be shipped to Haiti. We can at least try to halt any scheduled shipments. And we'll figure out who's behind it, and stop him."

She blinked. "We may be speaking of your father. Your own father."

"I'm aware of that," he replied calmly. He gestured to her food. "Why don't you finish your meal, and I'll see to it?" he suggested, rising. "A bath. A nice bed."

"Bueno," she said. That seemed to appease her. She sat back down and cut herself another piece of meat, her appetite restored. She had obviously dismissed him.

Yes, I definitely think I'm in love, Lex thought, amused.

Without another word, he left the room.

At precisely the same time, just inside the Luthor compound, a tall man dressed in black adjusted his earpiece, having listened carefully to every word that was spoken in Lex Luthor's office. The man had successfully planted some state-of-the-art surveillance equipment in the Luthors' mansion the previous night, and it had been a lot easier to accomplish than he had expected.

First he disarmed the "A" bank of security lasers with a super-advanced high-tech device he'd first heard about back in prison. It not only detected the beams, but it distorted them so that they were rendered harmless against anyone who brushed up against them, or walked through them. After he'd been let out, he'd gone straight to a man he'd met in the joint who had worked in surveillance for years. The man had sold him some fantastic state-of-the-art equipment that he had boosted from a fancy new high-rise in Metropolis.

Once they'd been satisfied that it was in perfect operating order, the burglar had trotted it down to Smallville. *Time for payback for all those years I made nickels pressing license plates while bastards like the Luthors stole vast fortunes "legally."*

Eavesdropping on the conversation between Lex's visitor—one Ms. Lopez—and the rich boy himself, the thief had decided that he'd better steer clear of Lex Luthor's bedroom that night. He had planned to start there, robbing the rich boy blind, but it was beginning to sound as if someone else might be visiting there.

The rich get richer, even in babes, he thought enviously. *And this one sounds hot. 'Course, when you've been in the joint for a lotta years, any lady sounds hot. And when you're filthy rich, it's not hard to charm the ladies. What have I got? "So, what's your favorite meal at San Quentin?" ain't high on the list of successful pickup lines.*

I'm going to change all that. Smallville's the answer to all my prayers . . . and I've been praying steadily for ten long years.

He kept listening in for about another minute. This was too good to be true . . . there was some weird fertilizer in the mansion that he could snatch along with every single piece of gold or silver he could carry.

A subtle little ding on his handheld readout informed him that someone was using a LuthorCorp computer to access the Net. And that someone was trying to hack into LuthorCorp protected files.

Then she—for he figured it was the woman who had identified herself as Señorita Lopez—dialed in an e-mail account—

he immediately cloned her password—and wrote a message in Spanish which he was able to intercept. It read:

PAPA, MAMITA. I'M SAFE. I DECIDED TO TAKE A DETOUR HOME TO LOS ESTADOS UNIDOS (EL ESTADO DE KANSAS!) TO VISIT LEX LUTHOR! MORE LATER. TE QUIERO, MARICA.

Marica, the man thought, smiling. *Cute name.*

Then his remote device showed that she had abruptly disconnected.

"Your room's being prepared. There's an adjoining bathroom," Lex Luthor was saying to her. "I can have Drew escort you there." Then he said, more softly, "You're trembling."

"I'm very tired," she replied frankly. "I've been through a lot."

"Do you need something to help you sleep?" he asked.

"No."

"You could always ingest some of my fertilizer."

"I'm quite certain that I have." Her voice was frosty.

"And yet, you seem to have a will of your own," Lex pointed out. "No ill effects."

"You weren't there." Her voice dropped to a whisper. "Some of them did have wills of their own. They were . . . crazy."

There was a moment when neither spoke.

"I'm going to help," he said. "I told you that."

"And why should I trust you?" she demanded.

"I've given you no reason to. I understand that," he replied.

"God will punish you if you've been lying to me."

"Well, I would hate to anger God any more than I already have," he said dryly.

As the thief listened, he detected receding footsteps, two pairs of them. After fifteen minutes of silence, he thought about modifying his plans for the evening. He was still going to break into the Luthor mansion, but he was going after different loot . . . at least this time around.

Looks like I've got better things to steal than tiaras and old coins.

Payback is going to be a lot sweeter than I expected.

No one at the Kent home slept well the night of the funeral. Jonathan tossed and turned in his sleep. Martha eventually got up and made herself some tea.

Clark stared up at the layered indigo night sky through his telescope, wondering if his birth parents were dead; if anyone who had known him when he was a baby was still alive. And if so, how could he contact them? Did they know where he was? Were they looking for him even now?

Breezes rustled through the crops, waving tall stalks of corn and wheat like impatiently snapping fingers. Clark could practically hear the world demanding that life move on, that things happen. He knew that growth was like that. Nonfarmers saw either dormant furrows or cultivated fields brimming with crops. They didn't know about what went on between the sowing and the harvest, the molecules merging and separating, spores germinating, the earth giving up nutrients to millions of tiny units of life as they struggled to sprout and blossom. There was an awful lot of "during" between "before" and "after."

Mr. Hackett is part of that cycle now, Clark found himself thinking, and he hied himself away from the image, which more than bordered on morbid.

When I die, what will happen to me? To my body? To my soul?

Can I die?

Upset, he moved away from the telescope and took the stairs down to the ground. Wandering through the barn, he saw the light on in the kitchen and heard the kettle's insistent whistle, announcing that the water inside was boiling.

Clark watched, expecting his mom to appear to retrieve the kettle. But she didn't come.

The kettle kept whistling, the valve sputtering like the espresso machine at the Talon.

Clark made his way toward the kitchen, pushing the door open. "Mom?" he called. "Mom?"

There was no answer.

Puzzled, he took the kettle off the stove with his bare hand and placed it on a back burner. Then he walked toward the living room, wondering if she'd forgotten about her tea and gone back to bed.

"Mom?"

There was a shape in the darkened living room. Clark's heart jumped as he ran toward it.

Martha Kent lay crumpled on the floor, unconscious.

"Mom! *Dad!*" he bellowed, as he dropped to his knees beside her. He picked up her wrist and found a pulse. Her skin was warm and she was breathing.

"Mom, Mom, what's wrong?" he whispered, leaning over her. Then he yelled again for his father.

"Clark?"

Jonathan's hair was tousled and his eyes laden with sleep; he wore a T-shirt over pajama bottoms, and his feet were bare.

Then he saw his wife and raced to her. Clark moved out of his way as his father crouched over her, opening her lids and examining her eyes.

"Clark, call 911!" he shouted.

"Dad, I can carry her to the hospital faster—"

Jonathan vigorously shook his head. "We shouldn't move her. Call them. *Now.*"

Clark responded to the demand for action in his father's voice. He moved in a blur to the portable phone in its wall cradle, then forced himself to slow down as he jabbed in the numbers. Now was not the time to break the phone by employing too much strength.

"Emergency services," a male operator answered.

"Hello? It's Clark Kent, at our farm. My mom . . ." He took a breath and tried to calm down. "Our address . . ."

"Your address is on my screen," the man assured him. "It came up as soon as you dialed. Tell me what's going on, Clark."

"My mother . . . my mother is unconscious." *This isn't happening. It's happening too slowly. It's happening too quickly.*

I can't keep track of what's happening. His mind was racing. He took another, deeper breath.

"I just found her. She has a pulse. Her skin is warm."

"Her pupils are normal," Jonathan called to him. "She's breathing on her own."

Dazed, Clark repeated the information.

Clark heard the clack of the computer keyboard on the other end of the line. Then the man said, "I'm sending an EMT right now, Clark. Don't move her. Keep her warm. If she regains consciousness, don't let her get up. Do you understand what I'm telling you?"

"Yes." Clark glanced anxiously over his shoulder. "They're coming, Dad. EMT."

Jonathan nodded.

The man on the phone said, "Clark, I want you to stay on the line with me until they get there, all right? Keep talking to me. Let me know what's happening."

"Yes." Clark gripped the phone as waves of fear washed over him with a roller-coaster sensation. He was trembling. "Please hurry."

"Hang in there with me, Clark. They'll be there soon, son."

Clark closed his eyes, nodding, though of course the man couldn't see him.

"How's your history report coming?" the man asked.

Flustered, Clark opened his eyes and frowned quizzically. *My history report?*

"My son Dennis is in your history class. He said you and Pete are doing something about pesticides."

"Fertilizer," Clark murmured, his mind not at all on history papers and guys named Dennis. "It's . . . it's fine."

"Dennis still isn't done with his."

Clark vaguely understood that the dispatcher was trying to keep him grounded by giving him something to focus on. But it wasn't working.

"Clark, take one or two slow, deep breaths. But if you start to feel dizzy, sit down slowly and put your head between your legs, all right?"

Clark took a moment. Then he said, "I'm all right."

"Knew that. Good job, Clark." The man added, "Any changes in your mother's condition?"

"Dad, any changes?" Clark asked his father.

Jonathan frowned. "No. Tell him to get off the phone and dispatch that damn ambulance!"

"He already did, Dad," Clark soothed him. "It's on the way."

Taking that in, Jonathan looked back down at Martha. He had covered her with a blanket, and he tenderly tucked it under her chin.

"I just got a readout from the ambulance, Clark," the dispatcher said. "They should be there shortly."

Just as he said that, Clark heard the siren and hung up the phone.

Then time sped up, and there were lights flashing outside; a man and a woman in yellow jackets that read EMT flew from the front of the vehicle. In a precision dance, they took over the care of his mother, who still had not regained consciousness. His dad looked on helplessly. If there was anything Clark's father hated, it was not being in control, and there was nothing he could do for his wife, not even ensure that she was getting the proper treatment.

The portable phone rang in his hand, and Clark pressed the talk button and brought it to his ear.

"Hey." It was Lana. "I'm so sorry to call so late, Clark. Please apologize to your parents. It's just, Chloe's really losing it and—"

"Lana." His voice cracked.

"Clark, what's wrong? Is something wrong?" she demanded.

He told her what was happening, and she said, "I'll be right there."

As they were loading Martha in the ambulance, Lana and Chloe drove up. Chloe was wearing a sweatshirt over a pair of pajama bottoms with blue clouds on them, while Lana had on jeans and a white gauze peasant's blouse.

"Clark, what's happened?" Chloe cried. There were shadows under her eyes, and her face was streaked with tears.

He shook his head, feeling helpless, and so grateful that his friends were there.

"We don't know," he said. "She just collapsed . . ."

The female EMT said to Clark, "Do you want to ride with your mother, son?"

Clark hesitated as his father hurried out the door with a jacket in his hand. It looked to Clark as though there was room for only one passenger in the ambulance.

"We'll drive you to the hospital," Lana offered. "Your dad can go with your mother."

"Thanks," Clark said gratefully. He nodded at the EMT as Jonathan drew closer.

"Dad, they've saved room for you with Mom. Lana and Chloe will take me."

"Good." Without another word, Jonathan climbed into the ambulance. The male paramedic trotted to the driver's side door, opened it, and hopped in.

The siren squealed on, and Clark winced.

"It's okay. It's going to be okay, Clark," Chloe said. She seemed to be coming out of her own distress, as if by having someone else to focus on, she could let go of her stranglehold on pain.

The three barreled into her car. Chloe peeled out, following the ambulance, which was squealing down the dirt road off the Kent family farm and onto the road proper.

"Clark?" Chloe pressed, as she worked to keep up with the ambulance. "Did you hear me?"

He stirred, realizing he hadn't even noticed that she was talking.

"Do you think it might be asthma?" Chloe asked again.

"My mom doesn't have asthma." He looked at her in the rearview mirror.

She took a breath, ticking her glance away through the windshield and then back again. "Who was it who said, 'If I can name the monster, I can fight it'?" she asked. "Clark . . ."

"Not a heart attack," Clark blurted, and the sharpest, darkest fear he had ever known rose inside him like a huge shadowed beast. He shut his eyes. *Not my mom.*

"She's going to get the best of care," Chloe consoled him. "Everyone's going to do all they can. It's great that you found her. You've got good friends here, and we're going to help you."

As if to prove her point, she picked her phone up from its cradle above the dash, held it to her ear, and daemon-dialed a number.

"Yeah, hi, Lex. Chloe Sullivan here. Clark's mom is in an ambulance on her way to the hospital. Right. No, we don't know yet. Unconscious in the living room. Good. Thanks. I'll tell Clark."

She disconnected and replaced the phone in its cradle. "He's making calls."

Clark lowered his head, confused by his own reaction. On the one hand, he was glad she'd called Lex. But on the other . . . he didn't know how to describe it . . . embarrassed, maybe. He wanted to say to Lex and her, *We can take care of Mom ourselves.* But that wasn't true. He wanted Lex to make the calls, get the best doctors. But a small part of him insisted that this was Kent business.

After a time, he said, "Why'd you call me, Lana?"

Chloe shot Lana a look. Lana moved her shoulders, and said, "I was worried about Chloe."

Chloe huffed. "And Clark could fix Chloe? Fix what I did?" she demanded.

"No. I could talk to him about being worried about you," Lana said a little defensively. "That's all, Chloe."

They were tense. Everyone was. Too much happening, too much to deal with.

Without realizing what he was doing at first, Clark slowly began to shut down, as if, one by one, all his power switches were being turned off. He fell into the center of himself, tuning everything else out. He couldn't feel anything, not the jostle of the car, not his own heart pounding; he couldn't really hear Chloe mutter, "Great," when a flicker of lightning gave scant warning and a thundershower broke overhead. He couldn't really see anything, either. But in his mind, the image of his mother lying unconscious on the floor was all too clear.

It was very odd. He didn't feel connected by his senses to his surroundings. As if his whole world had shrunk down around him and gone inside his body.

At that image, his heart skipped a beat, and it was as though someone had pushed "reset." He shook his head. His vision was a little blurry, and he felt strange, almost as if he weren't quite *inside* his own body.

It's just nerves, he told himself, but he wondered . . .

Thunder rolled over the top of the car like a tank as the skies cracked open and rain pummeled the top of Chloe's car. The force of the downpour rocked the vehicle. Lana held onto her side armrest. Chloe muttered, "Just let's not have an accident."

Lana glanced over at Chloe. "I'm sorry I snapped at you."

"Me too," Chloe said tersely. "I mean, I'm sorry too. That *I* snapped at *you*."

The windshield wipers became the only sound in the car—they and the heater. They were comforting sounds, and Clark tried to concentrate on them, and on the fact that two of his best friends were with him.

"Should I call Pete?" Lana asked, turning to Clark. Her question startled him, and he nodded.

She gave Chloe a questioning glance. Chloe gestured to her phone and Lana picked it up.

"Daemon-dial," Chloe said. "Punch two."

Lana did, then said, "Hi, Pete. Listen."

Clark felt like a spectator on his own life as Lana filled Pete in. He lost track of the conversation until she hung up and turned to him, saying, "He'll meet us at the hospital."

"It's the middle of the night," Clark said weakly.

"Yeah, so?" Chloe retorted, giving him a patented frustrated look in the rearview mirror. "Clark, we're your friends. Your mother's in trouble."

Heart attack. He didn't want it to be something like that, something so serious that friends of his were calling each other to meet down at the hospital. He remembered an old saying, that bad things came in threes. First Mr. Hackett; now his mom . . .

"Clark, we don't know what happened yet, okay?" Lana asked him. Her eyes were luminous. She was truly the most beautiful person he had ever seen. Her features were soft, and there was a gentle, reassuring air to her words. He wished they were in a place relationship-wise where he could hold her, and not just for the sake of solace. But they weren't.

"We're almost there," Chloe told him. "Hang on, okay?"

I don't have much choice, he thought, then the temptation to shut down swept over him again. If only he could just stop everything for a while. Stop thinking. Stop worrying.

But he couldn't. This was his mom they were talking about.

When they got to the hospital, Clark marveled at the sense of unreality about it. Pitch-dark outside, bright lights inside. The thunder rolling and lightning snapping versus the squeal of soft-soled shoes on tile; the PA system paging doctors; now and then a little child yowled and someone else coughed.

"I hate hospitals," Chloe muttered. She pointed toward the reception area. "Come on."

She took over, asking about Martha Kent's whereabouts. The nurse ushered them through to the ER wing, which lay beyond her desk and to the right.

Clark took off with a jog . . . not a superfast run that would have alerted the others that he was something other than he appeared to be, just a regular-paced one, although it took everything in him not to move more quickly.

Curtains were draped everywhere like big sheets of ice; almost more by luck than chance, Clark found his mother's little sectioned-off area.

Martha lay in a hospital bed, a sheet draped over her up to her chest. She was still unconscious, hooked up to machines that blinked and beeped. A man in scrubs was examining her, and a woman also in scrubs stood by with a clipboard.

"Clark." That was his father's voice. Jonathan was shielded from Clark's view by the man in scrubs.

"Dad . . . ?"

Jonathan shook his head. "They don't know what's wrong yet."

"I'm guessing not an MI," the man in scrubs said to his colleagues. "Guys, you need to go to the waiting room, all right? I'll let you know how she's doing once we stabilize her. But we have to focus on what we're doing here."

Jonathan hesitated. Clark said, "Dad, he's right. Let's give them some room."

Reluctantly, Jonathan followed his son, still looking over his shoulder at his wife.

As they entered the waiting room, Chloe stood anxiously waiting. Lana had just finished filling the second of two cups of coffee from the vending machine, which she offered to Jonathan and Clark as they came in. Jonathan thanked her and took one, while Clark silently shook his head.

"They don't know what's wrong yet," Jonathan said. "But they don't think it's a heart attack."

"So we can't name the monster yet," Clark murmured, hardly relieved that it wasn't a heart attack. "Which means they can't fight it yet." He knew that in situations like this, seconds mattered.

Chloe came over and gave him a hug. So did Lana. Then Lana touched Jonathan's arm and said, "I'm sure she'll be all right, Mr. Kent."

He nodded gratefully. "Thank you." It was clear that he wasn't as sure about that as Lana was.

"When will they know what's going on?" Chloe asked.

"We don't know that either," Clark told her.

"Time to hurry up and wait," Chloe said. She gestured to herself. "In my pajamas."

The four sat. Clark fidgeted. His father's eyes were closed, and Clark wondered what was going through the older man's head.

A few minutes later, Pete walked in. He crossed over to Clark and clasped hands. "Hey, Clark," he said. Pete took the second cup of coffee that Lana had bought and joined the anxious vigil.

Clark nodded at him, grateful beyond words for his presence. Pete remained silent as well, but his company spoke volumes: Here was a truly good guy who cared about Clark and his family. He knew Clark's deepest, darkest secret, and he had kept and honored it.

Clark didn't know anyone else in Smallville he could trust like that.

Lana would never tell, he thought.

Then he felt a pang of sorrow.

But Lex might.

◆◆◆

On his way to the massive garage where he kept many of his finest cars, Lex paused before Maria del Carmen's door. He listened for sounds that might show that she was still awake. But there were none, and he moved on.

Martha Kent was in trouble.

He flipped open his cell phone and began punching in numbers, calling doctors and specialists. He wondered briefly if the ER doctor who had advised against his father's operation after the twister would be on duty. They'd gone out a few times, and it had been pleasant. But no sparks.

Now take Maria del Carmen . . . there's sparks, all right.

He smiled faintly. Then the reality of his evening's mission wiped the smile off his face.

Martha Kent is in the hospital.

◆◆◆

There, thought the thief, spotting the window of the guest room as he compared it against his map. The map was encased in a plastic sheet; it was raining, but he had come prepared.

Maria del Carmen was most likely asleep in that room, if he had triangulated her position correctly from the sensorial output he had received on his headset. Like Lex's office, he had managed to bug some of the rooms. This guest room was one of them.

He threw a grappling hook expertly into the ivy-covered wall, checked the tension, and started climbing. It was easy. He'd done this kind of thing dozens, if not hundreds of times, and thanks to the weight room in prison, he'd kept in shape during the long years of his incarceration.

He'd brought a glass cutter, but to his surprise, the window was ajar. All he had to do was push slightly, and it opened with ease. Gingerly, he climbed through it, collapsing his bulk into a ball to avoid making any noise.

One boot down, then the other, and he was standing in her room.

He drew a pair of night scopes from his black jacket and pulled them over his eyes. He could see everything in the room even though it was pitch-dark.

Pretty girl. Bit boyish. Got that short hair they like these days.

She was sleeping the sleep of the dead, completely out of it, in a large canopy bed fit for a princess. He wasn't too worried about her. In fact, he found this part of his mission exhilarating. The realization that he might get caught was a rush—always had been, always would be. He'd already planned an escape route, and he'd be out the window before she could do much more than let out a scream.

He continued to survey the area. She wouldn't have much with her; she'd been traveling like a refugee . . .

. . . . *Hmmm* . . .

On the ornately carved dresser lay a beat-up fanny pack, the only object in sight.

He picked it up and sniffed at the contents, rubbed some between the fingers of his latex gloves.

Bingo.

He was back out of the window in seconds.

Like a cat.

In her room in their small apartment, Rebecca Morhaim woke suddenly. She thought she had had a bad dream, but as sleep evaporated, so did the memories of any nightmares.

Still, it had been an upsetting day; she deserved to have a few nightmares.

And a bowl of ice cream.

Smiling in anticipation, she got up, slipped her feet into her slippers, and padded down the hall. She tiptoed past her father's door, not wishing to awaken him. His new job was going well so far, but he came home tired, didn't say much, and went to bed early.

There was a new half gallon of store-brand chocolate chip in the freezer of their small refrigerator. *Someday we'll be getting the expensive brands,* she promised herself. *But for now . . . it's the cheap stuff.*

She got out a bowl, a spoon, and a scoop. Carrying her bounty to the table, she had just pulled out her chair and sat down when the knob to the front door twisted.

She jumped back up, frightened.

Someone's trying to break in!

And then the door opened, and her father walked in.

He was wearing all black, like a ninja or something, and he didn't see her at first. She called out, "Daddy?" and he started.

Then he laughed. "Hey, sweetie."

"Where were you?" she demanded. "I didn't even know you had left!"

"Sorry. Insomnia." He shrugged. "I took a walk. I still have those dreams . . ." He left the rest unsaid. They were dreams of prison, of being caged up. When he had them, he usually woke up in a cold sweat and couldn't get back to sleep. He'd been to see a therapist courtesy of a Kansas state felon reentry program, and she had suggested that when it happened, he ought to go out, get some exercise, and clear his head.

"What are you eating?" he asked, coming into the kitchen.

"Food of the gods," she replied.

"Ice cream. Yum," He got out a spoon and a bowl. "Mind if I join you?"

"I'd love it."

Father and daughter got down to the serious business of life, each with a nice big bowl, each smiling at the other almost shyly. They hadn't actually known each other for all that long. Been in each other's thoughts, yes, but as for living in the same house, talking every day about things . . . Rebecca was still adjusting to that.

"How do you like your job?"

He kept his gaze on his ice cream. "It's all right."

"Kind of boring?" she ventured, and when her father smiled

up at her, Rebecca was a little surprised at how old he looked.

He had been in prison for so long. When she was nine, her mother had died, and she'd been placed in foster care. It had been horrible; her foster family hadn't wanted her, only the stipend her presence brought into their home. They'd finally decided that she cost more to take care of than they were bringing in, and "relinquished" her. It was put into her records that someone had brought her back, and that made her next placement difficult. When she finally was placed, that family moved out of state, and she bounced back into the system. The fact that she had two foster families in such a short amount of time made her look even worse.

Rebecca never wanted to be parted from her father again. Sometimes, she woke in the night in a cold sweat, worried that she had dreamt his return and that he was still in prison.

She would do anything to keep that from happening.

Anything.

It was nearly dawn, and day would break soon. Already, the sky over the fields of Smallville was beginning to lighten.

Ten minutes longer, and Field Operative T. T. Van De Ven would have scrubbed the mission and attempted it again the next night. He would have been far too conspicuous.

"Insertion complete," he said into the wafer-thin mic sewn into his balaclava. "Over."

"Roger that, sir," said the voice on his headset beneath the knitted mask. "Over."

"And out," Van De Ven said.

He unhooked the umbilical around his waist and gave it a tug. It began to rise as, above him, the helicopter glided upward, its blades whirring silently. The machine was state-of-the-art, the finest money could requisition.

He was dressed in black, but to-blend-in-with-the-civilians-black—turtleneck sweater, black jeans, and his boots were not standard issue. The only remarkable part of his appearance was the black balaclava over his face.

And the submachine gun slung over his shoulder.

He had authorization to shoot to kill if he was spotted. So far, it was everyone's lucky night.

He and his superiors had chosen a fallow field not far from the Smallville Hospital to infiltrate the small town. His fellow field operatives had traced Maria del Carmen Maldonaldo Lopez to its borders, and he was here to stop her from disclosing what she knew about the Project.

It had taken a while for Van De Ven's superiors to realize that she had not been eliminated in the shutdown of the AYUDO compound. Her remains had never been recovered—unlike those of Dr. Ribero and another worker named Marco Taliaferro—and another operative had traced her to Port-au-Prince, where she had successfully arranged transport off the island of Haiti.

They'd lost her after that, but then a colleague had intercepted a phone call made in Cuba to Mexico City. A friend wired her some money. That had gotten them back on her trail, although she seemed to have incredible luck staying one or two jumps ahead of them. Van De Ven doubted she knew she was being followed, but he did know she was afraid for her life, and that made her cautious. She was a clever woman, and he was sorry he was going to have to take her out.

But she knows way too much to be left alive.

He pulled off his balaclava and stuffed it into his black field jacket. Then he trotted from the field toward the hospital. He'd go in there, use the bathroom, then see if the cafeteria was open so he could get a bite to eat. It was one of the least conspicuous places he could go to reconnoiter—strangers were always going into and out of hospitals, no matter how small the town—and he needed to figure out where Maria del Carmen was. He had his suspicions, but they were yet to be confirmed.

If she had gone to Lex Luthor's mansion, the mission was already severely compromised. It might be necessary to take Luthor out as well.

He took a deep breath, savoring the fresh night air. He had grown up in the Midwest himself, and he loved to be among vast fields of growing things. It made him feel alive in a way that running covert operations never could . . . and his job was, to him, the closest thing to heaven that existed.

It was a pleasant early morning, far cooler than back in Haiti. It didn't stink like Haiti, either. Haiti was a hellhole, as far as he was concerned. He hated his rotation there, couldn't wait to leave. He had never seen so much grinding poverty in his life, and he had lived all over the world.

There was nowhere else the Project could be conducted, however. The cooperative *voudon houngan*—the local Voodoo priests and priestesses, as eager as any other Haitian to make some money and gain some ground with the ruling elite—had given the department invaluable information about how they created actual, living zombies. Some of them had wanted only money, while others lusted after the magic powder the department was using in its own zombie experiments.

They would have been surprised to learn that blended with

the datura was a common herb called milk thistle. The plan was to make the zombies more active, to give them strength and power so that they could become supersoldiers—secret weapons for the US Armed Forces. Milk thistle did that. The mixture was concealed in fertilizer that was being shipped to the vast cane plantation that was the cover for the Project.

How Dr. Ribero had heard of that fertilizer—much less stolen some—was a matter of utmost concern. Given Haiti's leaky economy and the many shades of gray that made up the market system, skimming imports was a way of life. But the Project had watched the LuthorCorp fertilizer like proverbial hawks at every juncture of transfer. No chain of custody had ever been more rigorously kept.

Yet, somehow, Ribero had managed it.

Too bad we killed him before we found out how he did it.

To complicate matters, the batch Ribero lifted had been bad. There was too much milk thistle in it, and the excessive amount had made the zombies go berserk after a while. First they were docile, like traditional Haitian zombies, then they slipped into overdrive. They became ravening monsters, their killer instinct outweighing everything else.

The two zombies who had attacked Maria del Carmen had reached overdrive. The third didn't go crazy until after Van De Ven had contained it. Its time had come on the way back to the lab.

Ribero might be dead, but the pretty AYUDO team member was not. And given the fact that she had done everything she could to get to Lex Luthor, it was likely she had discovered that it was something in the stolen fertilizer that had created a new kind of zombie—one that was fast-moving, aggressive, and unpredictable.

As soon as she had escaped, they were after her. Trouble was, she had a head start. Van De Ven had assumed she had died in the fire along with Ribero and Taliaferro, and it wasn't until two days later that the forensics specialists informed him that her remains were not among the ruins of the AYUDO compound at Cap du Roi.

It was very bad that she had come to Smallville. It was even worse if she had convinced Lex Luthor that fertilizer from his plant was being shipped to Haiti as part of a clandestine government plot to turn ordinary soldiers into ravening monsters.

Lex was not the Luthor who had authorized LuthorCorp's participation in the Project. Lionel Luther was . . . and he was in so deep that if he ever told a living soul what he had consented to doing, he would probably be assassinated before the next morning.

We'd be first in line for the kill if he breaches our security, Van De Ven thought angrily. *And we'd be justified.*

A lot of people in this world have no idea of the kind of evil we're up against, the things we have to protect them from. For the kind of commitment to freedom we have, we have to accept that there are going to be some casualties along the way. Necessary losses. But all those bleeding hearts—same ones we protect day in, day out—would throw up their hands in horror if they heard about the Project.

Same as if they ever saw one of the slaughterhouses where the leather to make their fancy shoes was retrieved . . . or a sweatshop where some six-year-old boy was forced to work a sewing machine for fourteen hours a day.

Lionel Luther understood these kinds of things—he wouldn't have become a billionaire if he didn't—but Lex . . . Lex Luthor was a loose cannon. It was hard to figure him out. He claimed to be an altruistic liberal, but lately, he'd been coming down pretty hard on the side of might. He bore watching, perhaps cultivating. But at the present time, he could not be trusted.

Especially given his love of the ladies . . . and Lopez is one lovely lady.

One lovely soon-to-be-dead lady, that is.

Farmers can't call in sick.

Cows need milking and chickens need feeding no matter how bad one feels.

So it was that Jonathan told Clark to go home and try to get some rest while he stayed at the hospital for news of Martha's condition. After some shut-eye, Clark would have to do all the chores—not that difficult a task for someone with special gifts like his.

Clark protested because he didn't want to leave his parents, but Chloe put her hand on his shoulder, and said, "Your dad's right. Besides, you two should work in shifts. While he's up, you should sleep. And vice versa, until you guys find out what's going on with Mrs. Kent." She looked at Clark's father for agreement, which he gave with a weary nod.

At least it's a Saturday, Clark thought. It was four in the morning, so, technically, they were into the weekend.

Sensing his surrender, Chloe said, "Lana and I will drive you home, and—"

"I'll do it," Lex said. He had arrived about forty-five minutes before. Jonathan's back had stiffened at the sight of him, but the older man had managed to remain icily polite to the younger one. They had an edgy relationship, Jonathan and Lex, with Clark planted firmly in the middle of it.

Lex gave Clark a knowing smile. "I drove my Porsche," he said, tempting his friend.

Clark glanced at his father, who muttered, "Just don't speed."

"If you hear anything . . ." Clark said to his father.

"I'll call you," Jonathan promised.

"I can give you my cell phone number," Lex offered.

"I'll call the house," Jonathan said to Clark. "You'll be home soon."

"Up to you, Mr. Kent," Lex replied. He fished in his pocket for the keys.

"Hey, Clark, you need company at your house?" Pete asked, half-rising.

"I'll be okay," Clark told him.

Pete looked a little hurt but said nothing, only nodded as if to say, *Can't compete with a Porsche.* "I'll be by later, help you with the chores."

"Thanks." Clark knew that Pete was aware that he didn't really need any help—that he would only be coming by to check on him.

He's a really good friend.

Lex and Clark walked outside to the hospital parking lot. Lex's car sat beneath one of the parking lot lights, gleaming like a beautiful spaceship. Pressing the key, Clark deactivated the security system while Lex observed, smiling, and the two walked around the car, Clark to the driver's side. He sank into the low-slung seat and put the key in the ignition. The vehicle purred, ready for zero to a hundred and sixty in sixty seconds, and they took off.

Lex gave him a look. "I should have asked if you're okay to drive."

Clark nodded. "Gives me something to think about besides my mom." He wrinkled his eyebrows and took his gaze off the road for just an instant.

"Can you think of anything she ate at your house that might have done this to her, Lex? The doctors can't figure it out."

Lex shook his head. "We had some fruit and cheese. Just like we always have."

Something in his tone caught Clark's attention. There had been a hesitation just before Lex had answered.

Does he know something he's not telling me?

Clark was shocked. He was so upset he missed a shift up and ground the gears. Lex was supposedly one of his best friends. He wouldn't hold back anything that would help his mother, would he?

"Clark, you want me to drive?" Lex asked, sounding a little nervous.

Clark shook his head. He glanced at his friend, "You'd tell me, wouldn't you, Lex? I mean, if something happened . . . if she accidentally ate something that was off . . ."

"You think that I'm not telling you something," Lex said slowly. He blinked. "Do you think I'm afraid you'll sue me or something?"

"It's my mom, Lex," Clark pressed.

"Clark." Lex kept his voice low, kind, and patient. "I don't know what's wrong with your mother. But whatever it is, I sincerely doubt it has anything to do with me, my house, or my food." He raised his hand. "I ate everything she did, and I'm fine."

Clark exhaled. "I'm sorry, Lex. I didn't mean to . . . I don't know what I'm doing."

"You're right there!" Lex shouted.

He grabbed the wheel and pulled hard to the left, where the road dipped off the tarmac into a cattle guard in a dry creek bed. The Porsche cornered beautifully, but the turn was too extreme, even for the precision machine. The sports car angled downward toward the cattle guard, hit something, and then rolled.

"Lex!" Clark shouted.

There was chaos inside as the car tumbled over and over and over. Clark was tossed hard like rag doll, but he felt no pain. He was certain Lex was not as lucky.

Finally, the car rocked to a stop. They were hanging upside down; with an easy yank, Clark freed himself and got to pulling Lex out of his harness. The odor of gasoline permeated the air like an oiled tarp.

His friend was unconscious. Clark shook his head to clear it from panic. *First Mom, and now Lex. Did someone curse Smallville or something?*

Lex came to as Clark was yanking the straps out of the seat. Realizing his friend was awake, Clark refrained from his next move, which would have been pushing the door off the hinges with a brush of his hand.

"Lex, I smell gas," Clark said urgently. "We've got to get out of the car."

"Oh, my poor Porsche," Lex said with irony dripping in his voice. He moaned. "Next time, I'm driving."

Clark got out of the car and ran around to the other side. Though the door hung open, it was slightly jammed. Clark gave it an extra pull—from his vantage point, Lex would never be able to tell that Clark had had to use his superstrength on it.

"Hang on, Lex," Clark said.

"I'm okay," Lex replied. "Do you smell all that gas?"

"Yeah. I'll have you out of there in no time," Clark assured him.

Lex broke into one of his enigmatic smiles. "I know, Clark."

Clark worked the seat belt, wishing Lex would slip back into unconsciousness so he could perform his rescue more easily.

For all he knew, the car was going to blow at any moment.

Maybe now he gets to find out about my secret, he thought. *If I have to let him find out who I am to save his life, I'll do it.*

"Who are you?" Lex slurred.

"Lex, it's me, Clark." Clark was concerned. Confusion was often the symptom of a concussion—a bruise on the brain, which could be life-threatening.

"No," Lex said. "Him."

Clark looked over his shoulder. In front of the car, a grim-faced man was sprawled on the ground. His face was illuminated by the headlights, and Clark saw with great relief that his eyes were open, and he was blinking. That meant he was alive.

Did I hit him? Clark wondered uneasily.

He finished easing Lex out of the Porsche, helping him to climb out and flop onto his stomach. Lex appeared to be in good shape, his eyes open and focused, his coordination good as he rolled back over.

"Thanks, Clark," he said. "I'm okay."

"Good," Clark replied. Then he hurried over to the other man, assessing the damage as best he could. "Are you all right?" he asked.

"Yes." The man spoke tersely, gritted out the one-syllable word. He seemed more angry than hurt, and Clark was confused. "No thanks to you, son. Out joyriding? You two boost a car?"

"No," Clark said, shocked at his question. "This is our . . . his car." Then he realized how strange it must seem for two young guys to have a car that cost over a hundred thousand dollars in rural Kansas.

Ouch. What a waste of a great vehicle. Of course, Lex can buy another in a hot minute.

The man appeared startled as Lex lifted his head. The car's headlights illuminated his features . . . and his bald head.

The man's voice stayed calm, well modulated. "Lex Luthor?"

"In the flesh," Lex said. "What's left of it. And you are?"

"Just passing through," the man said easily. "Now I can tell the grandkids I almost got run over by Lex Luthor in his Porsche."

Lex chuckled wanly. "That's a good title for a children's book. Or a Christmas carol. 'Grandpa Got Run Over by Lex Luthor.'"

The man squatted and looked inside the car. "Fine piece of craftsmanship."

"Used to be." He fished in his jacket pocket and brought out his cell phone. "I'll call for some help. You should get checked out at the hospital just in case. Clark, you okay?"

"I'm fine," Clark said quickly. "Not even a scratch."

"I insist." Lex was firm but pleasant. "Clark, have you got the number written down anywhere?"

He had been taking a sheaf of papers home for his father— when someone was checked into a hospital, there were enough papers shuffled back and forth to fill a file cabinet, all because of liability and insurance. And Clark figured that was why Lex was being so insistent about calling to make sure the man was all right. In a lot of ways, it was more complicated being as rich as Lex was. Clark could never get over how many lawsuits were filed against the Luthors, and many not even because billionaires did things that were . . . questionable. Some people saw suing a rich man the same way they viewed the lottery—a way to get rich, overnight.

"All the papers are in the car, Lex," Clark told him. "Why not call 911?"

"Good idea! Why didn't I think of that? Must be the blow to the head!" Lex said, and punched in the triple-digit number.

Just then a siren wailed in the background. Clark and Lex looked startled.

"Someone must have heard the accident and alerted the hospital," Lex guessed. He flicked the phone shut. "They should be here soon," he assured the man. "The hospital's just down the road, so it's not a long drive."

"I'm fine," the man said. "And I'm in a hurry."

Lex said to Clark. "I'll call for another ride home." He dialed a single number.

To the surprise of both Clark and Lex, the man got to his feet and began loping away.

"Wait!" Clark called to the retreating figure. "You might need help! You might not realize that you're hurt!"

The man waved a hand as if he had heard Clark but was dismissing him. Then the siren grew louder, drowning out anything the man might have yelled to Clark in return.

Soon a Smallville Fire Department truck screeched to a halt behind Lex's Porsche and four or five firefighters leaped out of the vehicle, one of them stumbling as he blurted, "Awesome car!"

One circled around to Lex and Clark and shouted, "Two males out!" He said to Clark, "Anyone else inside?"

Clark shook his head while Lex said mildly, "It's a Porsche. There's no room for anyone else."

"Hell." The firefighter stared at it. "What a damn shame."

"We're all right, too," Lex said. He gestured in the direction where the stranger had run off. "We swerved to avoid a man who was crossing our path. I told him to wait for you. He should be just up ahead."

"Stranger? Ran in front of you?" the freckle-faced firefighter said. "I'd sue his butt!"

Lex smiled politely but said nothing. Clark guessed that this was not the time for Lex to be talking about lawsuits.

"I'm not seeing any danger here," said another of the fire-fighters, this one wearing a name tag emblazoned with the word CAPTAIN. "Would you like me to call a towing company?"

"Got my own," Lex said.

The captain nodded. "Well, we need to fill out a few papers."

Clark silently groaned.

More papers.

Lex said, "Of course," and walked with the captain to the fire truck. More than once, Clark had watched Lex handle these kinds of situations with total calm and self-possession. He knew demons haunted his friend, but when he had on the Luthor "game face," no one would guess that Lex Luthor was anything but a self-assured billionaire with the world by the tail.

"Who was driving?" the captain asked.

"I was," Lex said quickly.

He gave Clark a look. Clark didn't like lying, but he remained silent. There was nothing to be gained by correcting Lex, and it wasn't important.

But one never knew, in the grand scheme of things . . . did maintaining one's silence on the little things become so habitual that it became the first reaction to whatever life handed one? To keep silent, pull back, see if someone else stepped forward? As someone with special gifts, Clark couldn't let that happen to him.

I have to remember that sometimes it's my duty to act, not react. I don't have that luxury.

"And that guy who just appeared?" the captain was asking Lex, frowning slightly. "Who was he?"

"I have no idea." Lex cocked his head. "Who called in the accident?"

"Let's see . . . it was anonymous. Cell phone." The captain shrugged. "It happens out in these fields. Someone on a farm hears a crash, phones it in, doesn't want to get involved for some reason. You know, country folk."

"I know," Lex said. "Actually, it's the same in the city. Hard to get citizens to get involved."

The captain looked appreciative that Lex understood the complexities of his job. "People get spooked. Don't know if they should say anything or stay out of it."

Clark raised his brows, wondering if the fire captain could read minds.

Then the man said, "Son, a word with you as well?"

"Of course," Clark said.

T. T. Van De Ven had jogged on ahead, then dived into a cornfield and carefully made his way through, an expert at making his presence nearly undetectable.

Except when I dodge out in front of my subject's luxury automobile, he thought, beyond irritated with himself.

Scowling, he turned on his headset and contacted the helicopter.

"Who the hell authorized you to contact the Smallville Fire Department?" he demanded, dispensing with protocol.

"Sir, we saw you go down. We thought . . ."

"You aren't paid to think. I am."

"Yes sir, I'm sorry. Won't happen again."

"Go back to base," he ordered the chopper. The Project had a secret base near Metropolis. There was one in each region of the United States.

"Yes sir."

"Over," Van De Ven snapped, and disconnected.

Moron.

Ought to be shot.

Stealthily as the helicopter, he made his way through the cornfield. Now he had to add an unintentional contact with Lex Luthor to all the strategies he planned from now on.

Then it dawned on him: for the time being, Lex was away from his mansion. If his target was there, he could take her out with a lot less fanfare than if the young billionaire was in residence.

I don't know if I'll make it there before he does, but I've got nothing better to do. Completing my mission is my only priority.

The zombies were marching. Torchlight flickered on their faces, drawn and confused . . . some were rotting and dead; but others were still alive . . . and their eyes were screaming.

Help me, help me, help me, I'm in hell . . .

Marica ran from them, ran for her life. But they were screaming.

Help us, help us, we're in hell . . .

She reached the edge of a cliff and looked over. Below, the thick tropical foliage of Haiti was blazing. Smoke boiled up from wave after wave of flame. Birds and animals screamed.

Help us, help us . . .

It was the cry of Haiti, a country brought so low that the rest of the world had given up on it.

The cry of the zombies left back in Haiti, people she had known like Baby Loa . . .

We're in hell!

Marica woke with a start. She bolted upright, confused for a moment about where she was. The things hanging down around her—*snakes! Hands!*

She lay back down, trembling, staring up at the hangings draping the beautiful canopy bed in one of Lex Luthor's guest bedrooms.

Only a dream.

A dream that had been the nightmare that was Haiti. That still was Haiti, for the people trapped on it.

She wiped tears from her eyes—she had been crying in her sleep—and rolled onto her side. What a strange journey she had been on. Last night she had hoped it would all end here, and now she wondered what strange compulsion had prompted her to confront Lex Luthor so fearlessly . . . and stupidly.

He claims he doesn't know a thing about the fertilizer. But if he's involved, he's not going to admit it to me. And if he is, he's not going to be happy having someone around who can point a finger at him.

People were murdered in Cap du Roi. Did I somehow assume that because he and I come from the same social class, that I would be immune to being eliminated if I pose a threat to what is going on in Haiti?

I don't even know if it was because of the fertilizer. I don't even know if it really did turn people into zombies. For all I know, Dr. Ribero had his own agenda, and he showed me a faked slide. I don't know anything, really.

I've been running on sheer terror.

She slung her legs over the side of the bed, smiling weakly at her long LuthorCorp T-shirt. Lex had offered her any number of exquisite nightgowns, explaining that he kept a few in the guest closets "in case someone decides to stay over." There had not been a bit of shame in his voice or his mannerisms; it was a known fact in the upper circles of society that Luthor men had . . . appetites.

Not my concern, she reminded herself. *I'm not here to begin a romance with Lex Luthor.*

Stiffly she stood, sore from her travels and her injuries. She hobbled over to the dresser where the fanny pack lay, and . . .

It was gone.

She whirled around to see if she misremembered where she'd put it . . . but it was nowhere to be seen.

She opened up all the drawers of the dresser, dropping to her knees with a grunt to look beneath the nightstand beside it. She crab-walked to the bed and lifted the sapphire dust ruffle, feeling around on the spotless hardwood floor.

Nothing.

She rifled through the other nightstand, then the closet. She raced to the bed and pressed her palms into the bedclothes, ripping them away. She picked up each of the large, goose down pillows and shook them hard.

When she stood in the center of the demolished room, she shouted, "Damn it!"

He had taken it in the night . . . or had it taken.

How could I have been so stupid? she thought to herself. *I walked right into the lion's den with a big chunk of fresh kill . . . and expected him to leave it alone?*

She threw open the door and stomped into the hall.

"Lex!" she bellowed.

There was no answer. Then Lex's assistant, Drew, glided down the hall like a windup toy and smiled at her politely. Despite the early hour, he was dressed in black trousers and a white T-shirt, ready for the day.

"Yes, Ms. Lopez?" he queried.

"Where is my pack?" she demanded, then shook her head. "Where's Mr. Luthor?"

"He's not home at the moment," he said, all smoothness and polish. "He should be returning shortly. Is something missing from your room?"

She wasn't about to go into it with the hired help. "Are my clothes finished?"

The man looked mildly apologetic. "Sorry, but they came apart in the wash. They were pretty worn."

That rang true. She really wasn't surprised that her old khaki shorts and the ragged T-shirt hadn't made it.

"Mr. Luthor pulled together an outfit for you," Drew continued. "I'll go get it. Would you like something to eat? There are fresh croissants."

"Fresh . . ." She was startled by the juxtaposition of her year in Haiti with the realities of life among the wealthy . . . no matter where they lived.

"There was something in my room," she began, then realized that it made no sense at all to go into this with him.

He looked concerned. "A spider? Would you like me to come check?"

She snorted and whirled on her heel, half-running down the corridor.

"Your room is in the other direction," Drew told her.

"I'm not going to my room," she announced. "I'm going to Mr. Luthor's office."

"It's also in the other direction."

"Oh." She turned back around. "Where's a phone? I need to make some calls."

"I'll bring you one," he offered. "Would you like me to bring it to your room? For privacy?"

She thought about the T-shirt she was wearing and the lack of clothing beneath it, but she didn't really care at the moment what he or anyone else thought of her.

"*Sí,*" she said imperiously. "With coffee. And one of the fresh croissants."

She raised her head and went back into her room.

She slammed the door and crossed to the windows. Pulling back the drapes, she stared out at the beautiful garden behind the house. So incongruous, this huge Scottish mansion in the middle of Kansas. It was like a fortress, an island to get away from all the cares of running a huge empire. She did not deceive herself; the life of the ultrarich was certainly comfortable, but it was not without its own set of stresses. It only looked that way from the outside.

But no matter how much stress there may be here, it's nothing compared to watching your child die of starvation. Or having your parent dragged away by soldiers in the dead of night to never come home again.

Or becoming a zombie . . .

Those are the stresses of Haiti.

She paced, furious with herself for being so trusting. She had let down her guard.

I have got to get my evidence back. What am I going to do?

Her mind raced, but she had no answers.

By the time Lex's assistant had brought her the phone and a breakfast tray, she had calmed down enough to realize that if she phoned home in the excited state she was in, her parents would insist that she return to them. In their world, such matters were left to others to deal with. The police and the politicians were looked upon as hired help, charged with keeping things going. They wouldn't dream of becoming involved in a situation such as she was in now.

So she took a long moment to compose herself before she took the phone and dialed her parents' estate in Mexico.

"*Bueno,* Residencio Lopez," came a voice. Marica smiled.

"Chana?" she asked the housekeeper on the other end of the line. "It's Marica."

"*Señorita* Marica!" Chana cried. "How are you? Are you well? Your parents were so glad to hear that you had decided to visit the Luthor family. Are they treating you well?"

Marica bit her tongue. Then she managed to say, without tripping on the words, "Oh, yes. Very well." She reached for her cup of coffee and sipped it. It was excellent. "I'm eating fresh croissants as we speak."

"That is wonderful. I'll go get your mother. They're so glad you're out of that terrible place. They'll be flying out to get you, and—"

"No!" Marica blurted, then caught herself, and said, "Ah, Lex is here, and we're off to go . . . to admire his fertilizer factory," she finished lamely. "I wouldn't want to keep him waiting."

"Well . . ." Chana sounded torn.

"I'll call back in a couple of hours, Chanita," Marica said playfully, taking advantage of the old housekeeper's affection for her. "Lex is so busy . . . he's taking so much time out just for me."

"Ah." The housekeeper's voice dropped. "Is he single, Marica?"

"For now."

The two women giggled.

"Take care, *mi hija.* You know those men, they are playboys."

"I know. I will take care. Don't worry. Give *besitos* to my mother for me. And keep many more for yourself." *Besitos* were

little kisses . . . and Chana had always loved receiving them
from her favorite girl in all the world.

"You're such a good girl, Marica." Chana sighed. "I'm so
glad that nonsense with Haiti is over. You were wise to leave.
You need to come home. Your mother is such a fine lady, helping
with the church orphanage. You can do things like that."

"Of course," Marica soothed.

They hung up, and Marica shook her head. Chana and her
mother lived in a different era, when wealthy Mexican women
did the kind of "good works" that did not interfere with their
endless rounds of teas, fashion shows, and shopping.

I'm a different kind of Mexican lady, she thought. *I can't tell
them what's going on here or they'll just make me come home . . .
or try to. And if I step outside this house . . . it's possible I'm
not safe. I don't know the whole story, but I do know I cannot
assume anything.*

I can't trust anyone.

*I'm going to have to be careful around here, monitor how
much I tell, and stop telegraphing my plans.*

She looked out the window again, feeling lost and afraid.

Supremely frustrated, T. T. Van De Ven lowered his field glasses
and took out his earpiece. There was far too much activity on
the Luthor compound for him to take out his target. He was not
pleased; and confirmation that the Lopez woman had lost possession of the fertilizer sample displeased him even more.

Sighing, he pulled out his secured field-worthy phone and
called his superiors. As he anticipated, they told him to lie low
and wait for further orders.

In his rathole apartment in Metropolis, Shaky wadded up the latest rejection letter, taking extra time to compact it tightly, the thicker paper from this one making even the simple task frustrating.

He took the paper and slammed it against the Formica top of his ancient steel desk, letting kinetic energy and the hard surface do the work for him.

—Wham, wham, wham, went the paper.

Dammit! I was sure I had this one.

The letter was the latest in a series. Shaky tossed it in a high arc over the top of his somewhat battered lab table, strewn with reports and beakers. The piece of paper bounced off the far wall and fell through a tiny basketball hoop he'd stuck over the huge wire basket he used as a bin.

He shoots, he scores!

Even with the bad news, his own abilities cheered him.

No biggie. There will be other grants.

The down-on-his-luck scientist tried to be optimistic. Yet even as he sat there, sweating slightly in his chair, his polyester shirt not wicking the sweat away as well as he would have liked, his mind added the score like beads on an abacus. *Tak-tak-tak.*

That was the last one.

He'd sent out seven letters, and he'd gotten seven rejections. No one wanted to fund his experiments, no one had a sense of *vision.*

He sometimes felt he understood what it might have been like to be one of the scientists in the old B movies he'd loved as a kid. The actors in their roles would bemoan about how no one understood them, how no one else could see what their works would do to benefit mankind. But he, Charles "Shaky" Copper understood what it was like to *be* the man they only pretended to be.

His ideas for immunotherapy treatment, his suggestions at

wakening latent psi powers through the use of chemicals and altered consciousness . . . those were only his less controversial ideas, and they still scared people too much.

You'd think people would be more daring in the twenty-first century.

But no. They were limited, blind idiots and only *he* could see. He stared at the pile of paper in the basket across the room. There it was: empirical evidence of their lack of vision.

Oh well. Things were bad, and he'd have to see what he could do. He still had that pad, didn't he? Shaky reached into one of the big side drawers of the desk, scrabbling past several candy-bar wrappers, some throat lozenges, and fast-food napkins.

Aha!

He still had it—the pad he'd swiped from the hospital, right before he'd been fired. He could write up some prescriptions, employ a few homeless men to get them filled, and through good sales technique, gain rent money and enough capital to keep operating for a little while.

Guess I'd better get on it.

He had a good work ethic, even if he applied it to strange ends, so he was hard at work on a prescription for a new name-brand muscle relaxant when he heard the knock at the door.

"Come in!"

Well! Business at last.

Shaky tried to think. What was the latest flyer he'd put out? Was it the "Spanish Fly for Real," advertising his own home-made roofies, or perhaps the "Memory Potion Will Help You Ace Tests—It Worked for Me!"

Periodically he'd plaster the local college with signs and had sold a number of tonics and knockout drugs to some of the more adventurous kids there. It wasn't much, but every little bit helped, particularly when things got tight. Some of his wilder customers had been involved in his prescription drug racket as well, which had been lucrative.

The figure in the doorway didn't look like a student, though. He wore a matching jacket and jeans, and he had a backpack slung over his shoulder. In his right hand he carried a clear plastic carrier full of . . . *dirt?*

Shaky gave it a try anyway. "How can I help you?" He'd spent a summer as the assistant manager for an apartment complex, working his way through school. He had loathed learning the people skills the job required, but they came in handy now: helped him sell himself—and get himself out of trouble. Too bad he hadn't learned how to *write* that well.

The stranger scowled. "I don't want any of your mumbo-jumbo crap. What I want is for you to help me with this."

He indicated the container.

He wants me to help him with that? thought Shaky. *Dirt?*

"Ah, I don't really work with earth. There is a potter next door who might be able to help you . . ." Shaky let his voice trail off, hoping the guy would get the picture.

He did.

A fresh scowl and another shake of his head. "Look, pal, I *know* you're the kind of guy to help me out with this."

Setting down the backpack, he reached inside his pocket and threw down several of Shaky's flyers, including some that he hadn't circulated lately—an old one talking about the juice of youth, and yet another about a superexfoliating foam Shaky had done some experiments with, hoping to be the next Ron Popeil of chemistry, with his own hour-long infomercials full of pimply teens.

But underneath them was a copy of the paper. The one that had been the beginning of the end of his time at college, the one that had separated the scientists with vision from those without. He'd been on the way to his master's degree and he'd written a paper called "Mad Scientists—Not so Mad?" The paper had focused on the concept of scientists as visionaries, as agents of change. One of the teaching assistants had thought it was so funny that he'd distributed a copy to his friends.

The fact that the paper had been backed up by several experiments—descriptions of providing electric shocks to dead animals, suggestions that the fictional character created by Mary Shelley in *Frankenstein* had perhaps not been so off base, or that Robert Louis Stevenson had been far ahead of time in his portrayal of Dr. Jekyll, reverting intellect to ancestral memories—had made the ridicule worse.

Shaky could tell that he'd made a mistake when he'd started hearing the snickering. Other students had called him names, had not *seen* what he was truly getting at.

The paper in the dirt-man's hand was well worn, and looked like it had been thumbed through many times.

"I don't know where you got that—" Shaky began.

"Hey, you don't have to worry about me—I've been a fan of yours for years." The stranger lowered his voice, looking around. "I'm here to give you a chance—a chance to work with the stuff that your wildest dreams are made of."

Shaky tried to keep his anger in check. Some guy coming in, messing with his mind, wanting him to play with *dirt* for Pete's sake. Saying it was some kind of weird science!

"Look, Mr. . . . Ah . . ."

The scientist waited, giving the pause some weight. People always wanted to leap into pauses, hated uncomfortable silences. This guy was no different.

But he surprised Shaky.

"Sorry, no names just yet. This stuff is too hot."

Shaky frowned. This idiot just wasn't making it easy. *Go away,* he thought. *I've got illegal drug prescriptions to write.*

"Look, I don't know who you are, but I don't play with dirt, haven't since I was a kid, and I'm not interested in running any soil samples for you."

Shaky expected the man to get tense, yell, or react strongly. Instead, he laughed.

"Okay, okay. Sure." He chuckled again. "You're a man of science! And you haven't seen any *proof* yet. I can dig that."

The man reached down and unzipped the backpack. He reached in and withdrew a tiny cage; within it was a mouse. Nothing special, just a little lab rat, nose quivering.

The man set the cage down on Shaky's desk, moving aside some old canary yellow paper pads that sat there. Then he put on a rubber glove and grabbed some of the soil from within the clear container, careful not to get it on his hands.

Shaky took a closer look at the stuff and could see that it was too processed—too refined to be just simple dirt; the stuff looked more like fertilizer.

His irritation notwithstanding, Shaky was curious. What was the guy going to do next?

It is that very curiosity that gives me vision.

Too bad it made him patient with strangers who were messing with his schedule, but then, who knew?

The man put some kind of clear liquid over the fertilizer. The stuff was pungent, smelling like old cheese.

"This is a chemical I learned about in . . . my last living situation. They put it in junk food. Makes animals—and people—eat just about anything. Boy, I love chemistry."

Shaky watched the man place the mixture in front of the mouse, who sniffed at the mixture, then began nibbling it.

"He hasn't had anything for a while; I wanted to keep him hungry."

The mouse finished eating, but was clearly still hungry. He kept looking for more, little head moving, eyes darting, animated whiskers quivering. He looked outside the cage, over toward the legal pads, then the other direction, peering up at Shaky.

Suddenly, the poor little thing went into horrible convulsions, twitching and jerking, then collapsed onto the floor of the cage.

Shaky grimaced. Though he was a scientist, he did have feelings. He didn't like to see anything suffer, despite the need for lab trials.

Then the mouse trembled all over, and slowly got to its four feet. And then it stopped. The little nose still quivered, the eyes still peered, but it was as if the mouse had been completely anesthetized, a veil of disinterest put between him and the world. There was no more *life* in his motions.

The stranger pulled a wedge of cheese from his pocket and put it in front of the mouse.

The creature didn't move. It stood there, alive, yet somehow *not* alive, dead to its own desire to eat . . . to survive.

Shaky felt a chill. This was eerie, *spooky*-cool. He couldn't take his eyes off of the rodent, which stood there, hungry, yet not going for the cheese.

It was as if its will had been taken away.

"Look, it's like this. This stuff"—Shaky saw him indicate the soil out of the corner of his eye—"has some kind of way—"

Here the man paused.

"—of creating zombies."

The scientist's eyes widened as he added the evidence he was seeing in front of him with the man's statement. Could it be? Was this guy messing with him, jerking him around?

"Ah . . ."

"It's real," the man assured him. "This isn't the first thing I tried it on."

Shaky stared at him in wonderment.

The man chuckled. "You're wondering why I came to you?"

"Yes," Shaky said, his eyes still on the mouse.

"It's worked on a cat, and a dog, and a couple of mice. But I'm running out of it. And let's just say I want some help extracting the, ah, *active* ingredient. Not everyone wants to eat dirt, you know.

"I'm thinking . . . more than one," the man continued. "I'm thinking you and I could make . . . several of these," he said as he gestured to the mouse.

A thrill ran up Shaky's spine. He pulled his gaze from the mouse and looked up at the man standing in front of his desk. He didn't look like a mad scientist, a world conqueror, or a man who wanted to create legions of zombies.

Zombies!

The very word resonated in his soul. To do this for *real*.

If it *was* real.

"This is commercial fertilizer," the man continued. "I stole it. It's got the zombie-making stuff hidden in it, so they could conceal what they were doing."

"'They?'" Shaky asked anxiously.

"Slave labor. Foreign country," the man assured him. "No one in the States knows I've got the stuff."

From then on, Shaky thought of the man as "the thief."

"It's for real," the thief continued. "Works great. But all I have is this little batch of it, and I can't get any more from my, ah, supplier. So I'm thinking, figure out the formula, distill it . . . and let 'er rip."

Let 'er rip.

Shaky started thinking about how he might analyze the soil,

run pH checks, put some in a 2:1 soil-to-water suspension, maybe see if he could get access to the U's gas chromatograph. He still had a friend in one of the lab guys there, got him a few bottles of pills now and then—

His eyes sharpened on the man. Maybe this guy was DEA, messing with him before he busted him. Or what if he was a nutcase and there was just some kind of dope on the smelly stuff?

A knock came at the door.

Both Shaky and the thief looked annoyed.

An elderly man stood there, dressed in a ratty old army coat. He had an anxious, ingratiating smile on his face.

"Sorry, boys, din't mean to wake yez," he said in a high-pitched, whiny voice.

Shaky relaxed. It was old Willie Thorpe, one of his partners-in-crime in the drug racket. Shaky would give him a prescription, send the old man to a local pharmacy, and wait outside for him to come out with the drugs.

Willie came by now and then to check and see if there were any more prescriptions in the offering, or if there was other work he could do. Once or twice, Shaky had asked him to deliver stuff, giving him a semireliable cutout in his drug delivery service; not that the old man wouldn't give him up if it came down to it.

The scientist hadn't used him for a while—there had been a matter of a few uppers going missing in one of the man's last errands. The kid who'd bought them had called Shaky on it, demanding his money back. Only two pills had been missing, but it had put the old man off Shaky's useful list for a while.

But now . . .

Now I need proof before I get involved. Mice are one thing. Men are another. If Willie counts as a man anymore in the state he's in.

So what are you, Mr. Thorpe, a man or a mouse?

Shaky hid a grin. "Sure, Willie," he said. "Glad you showed. I could use your help."

The old man's rheumy eyes brightened slightly, a smile passing across his face like a drop of water in the desert. Something was up—maybe it was his itch for some booze, maybe he was lucid enough to realize that he was hungry. Whatever it was, desperation had brought him to Shaky's door, and desperate men did desperate deeds.

Willie nodded eagerly. "Yeh, yeh, I hoped yew could."

"But first I want you to do something for me," Shaky said, holding up his hand. "Something you're peculiarly equipped to help me with. Because you know, Willie, there are times I need you."

The old man's face grew wary. He'd been on the street for years, had seen and had things done to him that Shaky didn't even want to guess at.

"What?" he asked. "What do you want me to do?"

"Try this new vitamin sample I've made," Shaky said offhandedly. "See if it tastes any good. My friend here, Mr. Smith, is going to try to sell it through health food stores. We're wondering if the taste is too off-putting."

He nodded at the thief, who looked back at him and grinned a cruel, thin smile. The thief took the fertilizer and put in on Shaky's desk.

"Running low," he said to Shaky.

"That don't look like no vitamins to me," said Thorpe. He had stepped forward to look at the sample, and was edging back, now, toward the door. "I dunno, Mr. Shakes. It don't even look like it would taste good. I don't think even them health nuts would eat it."

"Willie," said Shaky. "It's really, really good for you. You can't believe what a boost it will give your immune system. I think you owe it to yourself to try this."

The old man gave the guy a reproachful look. "I hain't done nothin to deserve any tricks, Mr. Shaky."

"But I know you have, Willie," said the scientist. "Like maybe taking a few of the goods we sent to the U?"

Thorpe looked scared and headed for the door.

"Do it, Willie," Shaky said. "And . . . maybe I'll forget the whole thing."

Willie paused.

Gotcha.

Shaky set the hook.

"But I tell you what. I'll give you this"—and Shaky held up the prescription he'd been working on—"and some cash to get it with, and . . ."

The old man's eyes were on him, wide. He hadn't gotten any deals that sounded like this in a while, ". . . you get a nice beer to wash the vitamins down with."

Thorpe hadn't survived as long as he had by being stupid. But he was thirsty. Very thirsty. His eyes raked across the so-called vitamins and the prescription.

"Where's the beer?" he asked, suspiciously.

Smiling, Shaky reached into the minifridge he kept to the right of his desk, under the printer. He pulled out a beer and felt the pull it had on the old man, who unconsciously licked his lips.

Shaky kept up the polite smile, setting the drink down on the desk next to the other items. He watched Thorpe's face as he did so, enjoying the vacillation between fear and lust. Oh, how the man wanted that beer.

And how he feared what Shaky might do to him for stealing the pills.

Finally, a look of sadness came over his face, a grim acceptance of his weaknesses, and the old man came forward, shuffling slightly.

"Yew drive a hard bargain, Shakes," he said, "but I'm a man that likes a bargain, so let's see what you got."

He grabbed the prescription, looked at the writing on it, and nodded.

Then he opened the beer and took an appreciative swig.

"Got to get my mouth a little wet 'fore taking your vites," he said, smacking his lips. This close, his skin was a patchwork of webbed veins and blocked pores.

Shaky kept his smile; his sense of curiosity was alive as he watched the old man eat the fertilizer, scooping it up with his knobby hands. He gulped it down in several fast chomps, doing his best not to taste it. Then, as Shaky had suggested, he took several pulls on the beer to wash it down.

"Tastes like *crap*," he said with a grin, confident that he'd gotten the better end of the deal. Sure he'd had to eat some dirt, but that was nothing. He had drugs on the way, and a beer to keep him company.

Shaky let out a sigh. "Yeah, we're working on that," he said. He raised his eyes at the thief, who gave him a barely perceptible nod.

Shaky turned back to the homeless man and looked. Thorpe was standing there, just looking straight ahead. The beer bottle was held cradled in his left arm, and the prescription in his right. His eyes stared at nothing.

Too damn cool, thought Shaky.

Then, like the mouse, Willie went into convulsions. He dropped to the floor and went fetal, his legs kicking backward, his hands balling against his stomach as he contracted and heaved. Shaky was so astonished he bent to help, but the thief waved him away.

So Shaky stood by and observed, taking mental notes. How long it was lasting, what kind of injuries Willie was inflicting on himself, and so on. He thought about grabbing a notepad, but he was too mesmerized, wondering if Willie was going to up and die in his apartment. That would be really bad. And if it happened, he was going to give the thief holy hell.

Willie was in such bad shape to begin with that the damage he inflicted on himself caused severe consequences—his nose began to bleed, and bubbly blood foamed on his lips. He made a strange, whirring noise like an overheated engine. His eyes fluttered open, then closed.

The thief began to look concerned. He determinedly avoided looking at Shaky, which scared the scientist.

He's thinking the old bastard's gonna eat it, too. What have I gotten myself into?

Strangely, his agony didn't affect Shaky the same way the mouse's had.

Then Willie went limp. Shaky heard him panting, then an odd groan.

He leaned over the old man, whose eyes were open, and very blank. So he was going to live after all . . . at least for a while. Shaky was flooded with relief. He had never had to think about how to move a dead body out of his place before, and he hoped he would never have to again.

He gave Willie a little longer to recuperate. Then he waved a hand in front of the old man's eyes.

Willie was still breathing, but he didn't blink. His lips parted slackly.

The man glanced at the thief, who gestured at him as if to say, *Be my guest.*

Shaky stared at him a moment. Then he said, "Willie, sit up."

Willie did so, raising himself off the floor with great difficulty. He hunched over, hands dangling in his lap, looking like a lumpy old stuffed animal someone had just plopped on the floor. It was a wonder he didn't sag right back over and collapse.

Shaky stared at the thief, who chuckled and folded his arms, cocking his head as if he didn't quite believe what was happening, either. Shaky's world was shifting upside down, and his mind was whirling. His heart pounded. This was too amazing! If he didn't know better, he would have sworn that the thief had set this whole thing up, paid Willie to knock on the door and go through with the charade. It was the kind of thing Shaky himself would do . . . if he had the resources.

I have the resources now, he thought. *Oh, my God, do I.*

He said more steadily, "Willie, stand up."

The poor old man had to work very hard to fulfill the command, but it was obvious that he really, really wanted to do it. It was all he wanted to do—he completely ignored the outstretched beer in Shaky's hand.

"So," Shaky said to the thief.

The thief waved an imperious hand at their . . . at their *zombie.* Shaky wanted to pinch himself. Their zombie!

"Pick up the bottle and the prescription, Willie," he said, indicating the desk.

Without acknowledging him, the old man did just that.

"Put them back down."

Willie complied.

Wow!

"You see?" said the thief. "You *can* see, can't you?"

Shaky felt his heart thudding in his chest as he nodded eagerly.

Oh yes, he could see all right. He could *see*! The possibilities of a psychotropic like this, of something he could use, learn, expand on . . .

He wondered how far he could take it.

"Go downstairs," the thief said to Willie. "And step in front of the next bus you see."

"Hey, wait," Shaky said, horrified. "Wait just a minute."

The man gave him a tired, cynical look. "You wait. This is my gig. Unless you're fond of the old guy? Sounds to me like he ripped you off. Don't you want to take it to the limit? See how far we can push him? Cuz if you ain't got the stuff, there's a dozen more like you. All I have to do is spin a dial and take my pick of partners."

"No, wait," Shaky pleaded. "But . . . they'll—they'll autopsy him. They'll find the . . . stuff."

The thief chuckled. "Not in this town, Dr. Innocent. They don't cut open homeless derelicts. They don't have the money or the manpower. Autopsies are expensive. Unless there's foul play involved, they'll throw him in a box, run it through the crematorium, and forget about him."

While they were arguing, the old man turned and walked toward the door, his eyes focused on a far-off place.

"Wait," Shaky whispered, but the thief held up his left hand. His right went into his jacket, and Shaky thought, *Oh, my God, does he have a gun?*

Willie turned the knob. The thief looked challengingly at Shaky.

Willie opened the door and paused on the threshold.

"Walk in front of the first bus you see," the thief repeated calmly.

Willie, don't do it, Shaky thought; but another part of him was urging Willie on. This whole deal was evil and exciting and beyond anything he had ever imagined in his life. It was exactly what he'd been writing grants about, trying to keep body and soul together with writing his stupid fake prescriptions; wondering each morning if he was going to get busted—*again*— and sent away—*again*—and never see anything more exciting than the cracks running down his walls and the cockroaches skittering across his floor.

Without a single look back, the old drunk exited, and the scientist heard him clumping down the stairs.

A thrill raced up his spine as he and the thief moved to the window.

In silence they watched.

Willie exited the building and walked toward the street. Shaky's heart caught. He found himself whispering, "Go, go, go," like an armchair quarterback glued to the set.

The bus that ran from the university to downtown zoomed around the curve.

Oh, God, no, don't do it. Don't, Willie!

He opened his mouth to warn off the old man. Just as spontaneously, he clamped it shut.

"Go," the thief whispered. "Do it."

The bus rattled closer. The old man stared straight ahead.

Shaky watched as the old man looked over and saw the bus coming.

As it neared the front of his building, Willie took a sudden step forward.

The bus hit him square on.

Willie's body was tossed forward like a baseball from a pitcher's hand. Then the wheels on the bus rolled over his old body.

The scientist let out a breath he didn't realize he'd been holding.

"Cool," the thief said.

Shaky turned from the window. True to his name, he was shaking.

He went to the fridge and bought out a bottle of vodka, which he liked to drink chilled. He unscrewed the cap and took a hefty swig, then handed it to the thief.

"Cool," Shaky agreed, trying very hard to smile. "Very cool."

About half an hour after the crash, Lex's personal mechanic rode along in the flatbed truck that came to pick up the Porsche and supervised the loading of the once-beautiful car with a crane.

A driver had come with a Mercedes—*one that has lots of metal,* Lex thought, amused. *In case we have another crash. When it comes to me and cars, it's safe not to make assumptions that lightning—or car wrecks—won't strike five or six times in the same place.*

Taking one look at Clark, who appeared to be drained and tired, Lex told the driver they would take Clark home first.

Clark protested mildly, but the truth was that he was exhausted, and he wanted to see if his father had phoned to report on his mother's condition. By the time they got to the Kent farm, Pete was there. He was milking Mary and Elizabeth, two of the dairy cows. A large woven basket of chicken eggs sat on the ground beside him in the barn.

"Hey," he said, as Lex and Clark walked up. "What happened, man? I thought you'd be here hours ago."

"We had a little accident," Clark began; then at his friend's look of alarm, added quickly, "but we're both fine."

"Well, I got the eggs, and I'm working on the cows," Pete said, wiping his forehead. "Takes me back to the days when my family had more livestock." He grinned. "And reminds me that I don't miss 'em."

Clark smiled.

Lex rubbed his hands together, and said, "I'll make some breakfast."

"That's okay," Clark said. Then he realized that Lex wanted to stick around, help out in some way. He hid a smile, unable to imagine Lex doing farm chores. "Thanks." Clark picked up the basket of eggs and handed them to Lex.

Lex glanced down at the eggs, then up at Clark. "Can't say

they're not farm fresh," he said. "An omelet good with you both?"

"Sure. Thanks," Pete said gratefully. "I've been working up quite an appetite."

"Okay. I'll get started." Lex looked at Clark over his shoulder as he began to walk out of the barn. "You wanted to check your phone messages?"

Clark paused, feeling a bit awkward. In an effort to save a few dollars—the farm, as usual, hovered on the brink of insolvency—his mother had canceled their voice messaging service and bought an old answering machine at the Smallville Hospital thrift shop. There was no way to listen to the messages without playing them back on the speaker. If his father made any reference to his special gifts on the message, Lex would hear it. On the other hand, Clark wanted to know if he had called in to report on his mom.

Unaware of Clark's dilemma, Lex glanced expectantly at Clark. Clark licked his lips, and said to Pete, "I'll be right back."

The phone machine was in the kitchen. The light was blinking, signaling that someone had called.

Lex set the basket of eggs down beside it and picked an egg up in his hand. He smiled faintly.

"Amazing," he said. "They're still warm. I had an omelet in France once that was to die for. My father bribed the chef to give us the recipe, and I swear he lied when he wrote out the ingredients. We could never duplicate it."

The phone machine sat waiting. Clark finally said, "Uh, Lex? I . . . I'd like to listen to my messages in private."

Lex blinked, then said, "Of course, Clark." But his voice was a little strained.

Uncomfortable and a little defensive, Clark mentally cataloged several times in the last month that Lex had wandered off with his cell phone while in Clark's company, taking and making calls.

I guess I'm not as important as he is, Clark thought, then caught how petty that sounded and flushed, as Lex wandered out of the kitchen.

Turning down the volume, Clark hit REWIND and waited while the answering machine chugged along.

Then he heard his father's voice.

"Son? It's Dad. She's a lot better. Sitting up . . . hold on."

"Clark? Hi." It was his mother. Warmth spread through his body, and he smiled as he listened to her weak but steady voice. "Don't forget Elizabeth's antibiotics. And we should probably throw away her milk."

He nodded. The vet had been out to see Lizzie, and declared that she had a bit of a bovine sickness that was not harmful, but needed seeing to.

"I'm better, honey. It was something I ate, apparently." She sounded almost chipper. "I'm on a liquid diet right now, so your father is going to sneak me in a sandwich from the cafeteria."

"Oh. I guess he's not home," she continued. Then she said away from the speaker, "But Jonathan, I'm starving!"

"Doctor's orders," his father said in the background. Then Jonathan said into the phone, "I guess you're out doing the chores. Call us, son. Your mother misses you."

The call ended. It was followed by another one . . . from Chloe.

"Hey," she said. "Your mom's better, so Lana and I went home. Take care. Give us a call."

There were no more calls. Lex must have been nearby, for he came into the kitchen and said, a bit brusquely, "So. All done?"

"Yeah. Thanks." Clark moved away from the phone machine.

"Good. Because I have an omelet to cook." He opened up a drawer and pulled out a wire whisk. "Any word on your mom?"

"She's awake. And much better. They still think it was something she ate."

"Not at my house," Lex said tersely. "Which reminds me, I have a call to make, too." He paused.

Private, too. Clark said, "Mom wants me to check on Elizabeth. Our cow." He gave Lex a wave and went back out the door.

The day was fresh and clean, the kind of day that made him

understand why his parents worked so hard to keep the farm going. Sunlight glittered on tidy rows of vegetables in his mother's organic gardens. The aroma of damp earth and fresh produce was heady and good. There was no city job that could compare with the sense of satisfaction one could get from walking on one's own land and seeing the efforts of one's labor. As his father liked to say, "It makes perfect sense to me that the Garden of Eden *was* a garden."

In the barn, Pete was hefting a pail of milk. Clark rushed over to him, and said, "Did you put both the cows' milk in there?"

"No. Your mom said something the other day about Elizabeth being sick." He handed the pail to Clark. "This is from Mary. So, how is your mom?"

"Talking. Razzing my dad." A wide smile split Clark's face. He hadn't really felt the tension in his body until now, when it was a little safer to relax. A suicide, a funeral, the hospital, a car wreck . . . everything had mounted up. But it felt as though the bad times were beginning to end.

"That's awesome," Pete said. "I'm really glad, Clark."

They smiled at each other. Then Clark said, "You know, with that phone machine my mom bought . . . I was worried that my father might say something . . . that he shouldn't."

"Got you." Pete walked back toward the barn door with Clark. "Especially with being up all night and so worried about your mom. He could have easily forgotten to be careful." He looked at Clark. "So, what happened with this car wreck?"

Clark flashed him a sheepish grin. "I rolled his Porsche."

"Get out!" Pete stopped walking. "His *Porsche*?"

"This guy was running across the road . . ." His grin faded. "Man, Pete, I could have hit him. Lex turned the wheel just in time."

"Whoa."

The reality that he might have killed someone this morning finally hit home.

There's a lot of dying in Smallville, he remembered one of them—someone in the group—saying to that new girl, Rebecca. She had looked really freaked out.

"Well, Clark, you *didn't* hit him," Pete finished. "And your mom's on the mend. It's all good."

"Yeah. Back to normal."

Pete slid him a sly glance. "Which means that you can spend today working on your farm implement report."

Clark winced and groaned. And then nodded.

They dumped Elizabeth's milk, washed up at the sink next to the barn, and ambled into the farmhouse.

Lex had just finishing scooping two halves of a fantastic-looking omelet onto two plates. As the guys sauntered in, he gestured to them, and said, "Your timing couldn't be better. *Bon appétit*."

"Aren't you joining us?" Clark asked.

"Can't," Lex replied. "I have a houseguest. She's waiting for me."

I'll bet, Clark thought, grinning to himself.

"Don't worry, Clark. Someday you'll have a 'houseguest' too," Pete drawled. He washed his hands and dried them on a towel.

"She's a good Catholic houseguest," Lex drawled.

Then, as Lex picked up his black leather jacket, which he had slung over one of the dining room chairs, he saw the wadded-up sheaf of papers that comprised Pete's first draft of his pesticides report.

"What's this?" Lex asked. He chuckled. "The word 'fertilizer' jumped out at me."

"Go ahead and read it. It's for a history project we're doing," Clark told him. It was only then that he caught Pete's anxious expression.

Lex looked interested. He bowed his head and began to scan, then frowned and read aloud.

". . . 'commercial fertilizers such as those produced at LuthorCorp's factory in Smallville release significant amounts of lead, cadmium, and arsenic into the ecosystem, causing equal or greater harm as is generally associated with pesticide use. But while the creation of the multibillion-dollar pesticides industry has received much criticism for the unhealthy effects of its products, fertilizer development has grown alongside it without as much public outcry. Yet the fact remains that commercial fertilizers can and do cause serious diseases in humans and animals.'"

He looked up at Clark. "Are you writing some kind of exposé piece on my factory, Clark?"

Clark's lips parted. He was shocked. Pete had assured him there was nothing in there that would slam Lex's business.

"I wrote it," Pete said.

"But it's got Clark's name on it," Lex said slowly. His eyes were clouded with questions . . . and anger, too. "And as for your research, it's faulty at best."

Pete reached out his hand for the report. He said, "I'm just reporting what I found."

"You've drawn some fairly dramatic conclusions," Lex argued. He looked over at Clark. "So, you're putting your name on this?"

"I . . . I don't know," Clark said. "I'll have to read it."

"I thought you had by now," Pete said irritably. "It's getting pretty close to the deadline for you to expect me to take another tack. And besides, this is what I found to be true." He frowned at Lex. "I didn't make up the statistics on page two, Lex. I'm sure you know by now that a lot of dangerous chemicals go into the process of making your fertilizer."

"There are standards, and we meet them," Lex shot back. He thrust the report at Pete.

As he slung his jacket over his shoulder, he said to Clark, "I thought we were friends."

"We are," Clark said, bewildered by the turn of events, the sudden, thick tension in the air.

"Oh," Lex said coolly.

He headed for the door.

"Lex!" Clark called after him. "Wait!"

Clark looked through the kitchen window at the retreating figure. He was very familiar with the hunched, squared way Lex was holding his shoulders, the way he was stomping across the field. Lex Luthor was pissed off.

He turned to Pete, and said, "You told me you're weren't going to get into his face."

"He shouldn't be surprised by what I wrote in there," Pete rejoined. "These are commonly known facts."

"You've said that about three times now." Clark turned away, not sure what to do or say next.

"There's no getting around the fact that the fertilizer factory isn't that great for our environment." Pete looked at Clark as if he were insane. "Or have you rationalized that because you like Lex?"

"That's just . . . strange," Clark said. He picked up his plate. "I'm hungry," he announced.

Pete followed him to the table. "Are you going to put your name on this? Because I'm not rewriting it, Clark. You've taken so long to get around to it, and—"

"I've been a little busy. My mom is in the hospital," Clark reminded him.

There was a long silence between them. Then Pete put the paper down on the table.

"Pete," Clark tried again.

Pete sighed heavily. "I guess I knew you wouldn't like it. That's why I got so defensive. But it's all true. You should read some of the environmental briefs that were filed when the town tried to stop the Luthors from building the plant. It's scary how toxic some of that stuff is."

"Not the whole town. And lawyers always exaggerate."

"Even if they did, they can't alter the basic facts." Pete held out his hands. "What do you want me to do, Clark, not tell the truth? Not mention things that might hurt Lex's standing in Smallville? Because it won't affect his bottom line. Nobody cares what kind of garbage he makes down at the plant, as long as the yield per acre stays solid."

We're having almost the same conversation we had with Chloe, Clark thought. *This is so weird.*

"I don't know," he said honestly. "Let's eat."

"Okay," Pete grumped.

The two friends sat down. Pete picked up his fork. Clark followed suit, and they both dug into the omelet.

It was incredibly salty. Way too salty.

Clark glanced over at Pete, and they both burst into laughter.

"Okay. If he'd been here, would you have told him his cooking sucks?" Pete demanded, cracking up. "Or said nothing and eaten it?"

"We'll never know," Clark said archly.

They both carried their plates to the sink. Pete leaned against the counter while Clark scraped their breakfasts into his mother's portable composter.

"Careful. There's so much salt in that stuff, it might hurt her garden," Pete said.

"I was just thinking the same thing," Clark admitted.

They both started laughing again, harder and harder. It was pure tension release, and it felt great.

Lex pondered Pete's report on his drive back home; he was still thinking about it when he let himself in.

Drew met him at the door, a sharp expression of concern on his face, as he said, "Mr. Luthor, there's been a burglary."

"Burglary!" Marica shouted as she stood on the stairs, gazing down at the two of them. She was wearing black leather trousers and a scarlet blouse, and she looked amazing.

As she came down the stairs, she launched into a barrage of Spanish, some of which Lex actually understood. He spoke passable French, and Spanish was in the same class of languages—the Romance languages—although it was clear she was not discussing anything good, she stomped toward him.

"I don't think it can be called a burglary when the man who owns this house took it," she said. Fuming, she planted her hands on her hips as she glared up at Lex. She was so close to him that he could smell the scent of French-milled lavender soap on her skin. He was distracted by her fresh beauty and the astonishing force of her indignation, and he simply stared at her for a few moments.

"You stole my fertilizer!" she snapped at him, and it sounded so comical he almost laughed aloud. But he understood that someone had actually gone into her room and taken it, and that was a serious breach of security.

Lex glanced at Drew, silently asking him if he had figured out the details. As Drew raised his brows and shook his head, Lex politely took Marica's arm and led her into the library.

He closed the door. "I didn't steal it," he said flatly. "Are you sure Drew didn't move it for safekeeping? Put it in the safe? Maybe it was the maid when she was cleaning. After all, it was just dirt." He avoided the temptation to remind her that he had suggested she put it in his wall safe, and she had demurred. She hadn't wanted to let it out of her sight. Without waiting for her to answer—his question was rather inane—he picked up the phone and called Security.

"Your guy already did that," Marica said over his voice as he instructed the two house guards to meet him in the library immediately. "And they said they couldn't find anything."

"That's ridiculous." He gestured for her to have a seat, but she remained standing.

"Someone came into my room while I was sleeping," she said, as if that had not occurred to him. "Was it you?"

"No, Señorita Lopez. I assure you it was not," he said. He thought a moment. "Tell me again what you told me last night."

She shook her head. "I will not," she informed him coldly. "You are not to be trusted. I will inform the authorities and . . ." She trailed off, looking confused.

"No proof," he said, practically reading her mind. Her eyes flashed, and he held up his hand. "Hear me out," he said, then gestured to two chairs by the leaded-glass windows.

There was a soft, polite knock on the door.

"Come in," Lex said patiently.

It was Drew. "Would you like some coffee?" he asked.

"Very much." Lex smiled at Marica. "Miss Lopez?"

"No, *gracias*," she snapped.

"Just for me."

"There are croissants," Drew added. "I'll bring some. Miss Lopez likes them very much."

He shut the door. Lex shrugged as if to apologize for his

staff, then folded his hands and made a steeple, thinking through what he was about to tell this woman, who was, for many intents and purposes, a virtual stranger. And someone, for all he knew, who had made up this entire story in order to extract cash or something else from the Luthor family.

"As I mentioned last night," he began, "my father and I have a . . . complicated relationship. And as you know, LuthorCorp is an enormous conglomerate. A lot goes on that I don't know about. But my father always knows about everything."

"And you admire him for that," she shot at him.

His smiled faintly, but didn't respond. "It concerns me greatly that someone came into your room without your permission."

There was another knock on the door, and Drew reappeared with the coffee. Two of Lex's burly security men were with him.

Without preamble, one of them came to Lex and asked to speak to him . . . alone.

Lex said to Marica, "Pardon me a moment," and walked with the guard to the window.

"The window in the lady's room wasn't completely closed," the guard said. "We're wondering if someone came that way. Scaled up the wall. There are no footprints in the mud, of course, with the rain."

"Of course," Lex said smoothly. "How about the doorknob? Could you find anything there? Any prints?"

They discussed their investigative methods at length; Lex was pleased to see that they had already gone through their paces, yet very angry that someone had walked into the room of a guest and taken her belongings. The other man appeared to read Lex's expression, for he stammered an apology before he left the room.

After the two men were gone, and he and Marica were alone again, Lex said, "When I was a boy, I had a pet spider monkey named Coconut. I don't think he ever stole fertilizer, but we did find a pair of my father's diamond cuff links in his bed."

Marica shook her head and began to rise. "There's no point in my staying here any longer," she said angrily. "As you pointed out, I have no proof, and without proof, there is nothing I can do to stop you from what you're doing."

"I'm not doing it," he said, gazing hard at her. "I swear to you. But if it was my father—and like you, I have no proof of that—I can tell you that he knows some very dangerous people."

"Are you threatening me?" she demanded, her voice rising.

"I'm *warning* you," he replied.

She looked at him, and he saw a flicker of fear.

"I think you're safer staying with me than if you leave here." He moved his shoulders, amazingly tired. "At least you have a home base here. And someone who believes you."

And even then, he wondered if she was setting him up in some complicated scheme.

"If you believe me, then help me look for it," she told him.

Lex poured himself a cup of fragrant coffee and grabbed a croissant. What he wouldn't give for a few moments to put up his feet and read *The Wall Street Journal.*

"Of course," he said. He carried the cup and croissant with him as they left the library.

They scoured the house, and the sample was nowhere to be found. Marica became increasingly angry as they searched, more than once threatening to leave, until Lex reminded her that she might be in danger.

Finally, they took a golf cart to the main warehouse in search of more of the doctored fertilizer. If it was coming from his plant, there was the off chance that the material was just sitting out on a pallet, awaiting shipment to Haiti. At least, that was Marica's hope. He was a bit dubious, but he was glad to accommodate her insistence that they begin a sweep of all the warehouses and outbuildings, just in case.

Turning the matter this way and that had been exhausting; now they began to move onto other topics as they spent the day together. Their current subject was relationships . . . which Lex figured was natural enough, given that they were both young, attractive people used to getting what they wanted.

"Well, there's love, and then there's tension release," Lex observed, as they whirred along in the cart toward the large metal building. The vehicle was an experimental prototype that ran on fuel extracted from corn, and he had high hopes for it.

There was a guardhouse in front of it, with orange-and-white-striped barriers over the entrance and exit for cars and trucks. Lex was having all the plant's security procedures reviewed. He'd never dreamed anyone would want to steal his company's product.

Now, if I ran a diamond mine, that'd be different . . .

"Tension release," Marica drawled. "How romantic."

He sensed that the way to this woman's heart was honesty, and he liked that. Shrugging, he smiled at her, and said, "More often than not, a relationship is really an excuse for the latter, don't you think?"

"Spoken like a man," she pronounced.

His smile grew. "It's true. You've seen the world. You know how it is. Would you rather people keep to the polite conventions, pretend it's always love?"

She had been grilling him about the amount and variety of clothing and grooming items he kept on hand for "overnight guests." He had offered her a choice of black leather pants or jeans, a slinky scarlet top or a peasant blouse. In a way, she found it rather gallant, but on the other, it spoke volumes about his interest in commitment.

She had opted for the black leather and scarlet. They both wore black hard hats, with LUTHORCORP painted on them.

"In my culture, men do keep to the polite conventions in these matters," she informed him.

He inclined his head as he steered the cart, one part of his mind assessing the prototype's performance on the fuel. Smooth ride, no glitches. He might have a winning product on his hands.

"Ah, yes," he said, sliding a glance her way. "The hidden mistress. Why do you women put up with that? Say nothing, and let it go on?"

"I didn't say I would put up with it." She had a faraway look in her eyes as she added, "and I wouldn't keep my silence. I'm rather religious, Lex. You must have noticed that."

"Yes," he admitted.

"I wanted to become a nun when I was a little girl. I've always been interested in helping people who were not as fortunate as I. Then I wanted to become a missionary at one point in college. My parents compromised and allowed me to work for AYUDO. So . . ." She smiled at him. "Just so you know, I won't be borrowing any of your nightgowns."

"My loss," he said. "Truly." Then he cocked his head and gave her an assessing once-over. *God, she's beautiful. I can't imagine her as a nun.*

I can, however, imagine her in one of "my" nightgowns.

"You're big on saying what's on your mind," he said. "I really think you should be careful until we know what's going on. It could get you into serious trouble."

Her smile faded. "It already has."

The moment was lost, the conversation too lighthearted for the matter at hand. He was learning how to read her, and she was more afraid than she was letting on. While that fear lent credence to her story, it made the break-in into her room even more alarming. He had already given Drew the go-ahead to replace the entire mansion security staff. When he and Marica returned from the warehouse, new people would be guarding her room tonight.

He gave the warehouse security guard a wave and the man tipped his own hard hat, raising the barrier across the vehicular entry for Lex's cart.

Then they drove from the bright Kansas sunshine into the dim warehouse. The smell of chemicals hit Marica's nose, and she sneezed. As she surveyed the vast warehouse in wonderment, she said softly, "If something's in here, we'll never find it."

I tried to tell you that, Lex thought to himself, but remained silent.

"Where to begin?" she murmured.

"Exports," Lex suggested. He hung a right and headed for the northwest quadrant of the warehouse. "You are aware that we have off-site fulfillment centers as well?"

"I have nothing better to do," she said, "and I don't care if you do."

Olé, Lex thought admiringly. *Maybe I really* am *in love.*

Row upon row of large plastic bags were piled all the way up to the ceiling. There were towers of fertilizer as far as they could see, and Marica was taking it all in with an air of mild astonishment.

Yes, it's all mine, he thought, with no small measure of self-deprecation. *I am the king of fertilizer.*

She looked at him with a little grin, as if she knew what he was thinking. Then, growing more serious, she said, "They could use this in Haiti. The good stuff, I mean."

He nodded, wondering if he could arrange some shipments as a humanitarian effort . . . after this current situation died down. It would be a nice write-off . . . and she would appreciate it.

"Do you ever think you'll go back?" he asked her. "Work on a different project in Haiti?"

She shivered. "I haven't even thought about it. I have a mission now. This is life and death, Lex."

I'm beginning to believe that, he thought.

He steered the cart around a corner, where he caught sight of someone run-walking from one aisle to the next in an almost furtive motion, and he gave the cart horn a little beep.

The figure stopped as if he had been pinned to the wall by a searchlight and slowly turned.

It was Tom Morhaim, the new hire with a police record. Was it Lex's imagination, or did the guy look guilty about something?

What's he doing in the warehouse? His job site's on the third floor of the main building.

"Hey, Tom," Lex said easily.

"Mr. Luthor." Tom gave his boss a nod. "Mr. Hamilton sent me to see if we have any spare fertilizer for your tiger orchids."

"Tiger orchids? What are those?" Marica asked.

"I grow them. As a hobby," Lex said. "I have a few specimens in my private office in the building. As a rule, they're only cultivated in Indonesia." So it made sense that Jack Hamilton had sent Tom to check in the export area.

Still, it's pretty interesting that we're looking for something that's been stolen, and we've come upon a thief . . .

"Have you seen any containers marked for delivery to Haiti?" Marica asked, bulldozing over Lex's authority. "Specifically Port-au-Prince?"

"No, ma'am," Tom said. Lex watched him carefully for signs that he might be lying. There were none.

"But I haven't been looking for any. I'm here for the stuff for tiger orchids."

She looked dispirited. "As if it would just be sitting out," she muttered. "This is ridiculous."

"That's often the safest place to hide something," Lex observed. "Out in the open."

She humphed and said nothing.

They drove around the stacks, but after an hour, she turned to him, and said, "Let's go back to your house."

I did have a full day of meetings scheduled, he thought. But instead, he said, "All right."

She looked around anxiously as the cart shuttled back out of the warehouse and into the sun.

"I'm a sitting duck," she said.

Lex replied, "Don't worry, *señorita*. I'll make sure you're safe."

She looked at him anxiously. "Will you really, Lex? Or should I be afraid of you?"

Their gazes locked. He found her an intriguing mix of real bravado, false courage, and an honesty that was rare these days. He really liked her.

"You have nothing to fear from me," he said. "I promise you. I'll protect you from whatever comes."

She looked unconvinced. "You didn't see what I saw," she told him quietly.

"And what was it that you did see?" he asked her.

She looked him full in the face. Her dark eyes were troubled; tears welled, and he was astonished at the misery written across her face.

"Hell, Lex. I saw hell." Tears slid down her cheeks. "I'm scared," she admitted. "So scared."

"Marica . . ." He took a breath. What was happening here? "Marica, I'm here for you."

She closed her eyes. "I've been so tired."

"I'm here," he said softly.

Clark did the best he could on the farm implements report, but he kept looking over the paper Pete had written. It was extremely critical of both pesticides and fertilizers, and it was well researched. Pete had worked hard.

Clark still couldn't help wondering if his mom had suffered some kind of reaction to something at Lex's house, something that had to do with his business. There were probably traces of chemicals in the mansion that Lex's system had gotten used to. She was known for her organically grown produce, and she had spoken many times against the amount of chemicals put into the earth by commercial agribusiness. She had not wanted the fertilizer factory, either, even though she had eventually gone to work for Lionel Luthor. When she married Jonathan Kent, she married the land he loved as well.

He finished the paper and did some more chores. He was about to call Chloe when his father came home, looking tired but far more relaxed than Clark had seen him in days.

"She wants to come home," he told his son, "but they're going to run a few more tests."

"Can I go see her now?" Clark asked.

"She can't wait," Jonathan said.

"Did you really sneak her in a sandwich from the cafeteria?"

Jonathan smiled. "Now, Clark, your mother and I have to have *some* little secrets just between us . . ."

Clark chuckled. "You didn't," he guessed.

Feigning innocence, Jonathan raised his brows, and said, "Ask her when you see her." He fished out the keys to the truck and handed them to Clark. "Drive carefully, son."

Clark decided that now was not the time to tell his father about rolling the Porsche. Feeling a little guilty about concealing it, he took the keys and headed for the door.

Clark drove to the hospital, remembering the man who had darted out in front of the car. *How would I feel if I killed some-*

body? he thought. *Because I'm strong enough to do it without sitting behind the wheel of a car. I'm going to have to be careful all the time . . .*

His gloom dissipated as he drove into the hospital parking lot and entered the hospital. On impulse, he stopped at the gift shop and looked around for something to buy her. He saw a picture frame surrounded by sunflowers on sale.

An older woman behind the cash register smiled at him. She said, "This for your girlfriend, honey?"

"My mom." He flushed.

She beamed at him and carefully wrapped the frame in pink tissue paper. She added a bow and handed the package back to him.

"She's lucky to have such a nice young man for a son," she said. Then her face turned wistful. "My grandson was diagnosed with multiple sclerosis recently."

He glanced down at her name tag. It read MATHILDE BROOK. Jake Brook was her grandson.

He swallowed hard, and said, "Thanks, ma'am. And I'm sorry."

She looked sad. "He's such a good boy. You wonder why these things happen . . . well." She changed her tone of voice, brightening up. "Go and give your mom a kiss."

"I will."

And he did, when he came into the room and found her reading a book about edible landscaping. Her glasses had slid down to the end of her nose, but she didn't seem to notice. When she saw him, it was as if the sun had risen in her face. She positively glowed.

"Clark." She held up a hand.

"Hi, Mom." He bent over and kissed her. Then he said, "I brought you a present."

"Oh, Clark. You shouldn't have." She looked enormously pleased. She looked at it for a moment, then handed it back to him. "Could you unwrap it for me? I'm pretty tired."

That scared him a little. The thing was only wrapped with tissue paper and Scotch tape. Concealing his unease, he smiled at her, and said, "Sure."

He unwrapped it and handed it to her. She beamed at him.

"Oh, honey, it's lovely." She held it against her chest.

"Dad told me he really did sneak you a sandwich," he tested.

She winked at him. "Now, honey, married people need to have a few secrets."

He was astonished. Sometimes his parents really were like two halves of the same person.

They talked for a while, watched a little TV together, then the nurse shooed him out because visiting hours were over.

It was dark. He was surprised so much time had passed, and he wondered if his father had been able to get the basic chores done without him.

He got into the car and turned on the radio, then decided to swing by the minimart to grab a soda. Soon he was trundling down Main Street, glancing over at the Talon and wondering if Lana was working, and remembering that he had never called Chloe back.

He hung a U to go into the drive-through when he noticed a flash of light in the alley next to the sporting goods store. Curious, he skipped the entrance to the drive-through and turned into the alley.

Someone was crawling into the store's transom window.

When Clark's headlights shone on the person's body, the man fell back out of the window and landed on his butt in a puddle.

It was Marshall Hackett.

"Hey," Clark said. He got out of the truck and hurried over to Marshall, who was trying to wipe muddy water off the sleeve of his letterman's jacket. His jeans were wet around the thighs.

Marshall glared blearily up at him. "Kent," he said with derision. "You in love with me or something? You're always around."

The smell of alcohol hit Clark full force. Marshall was very drunk. He said, "Let me help you up."

"Go 'way." Marshall flailed at the window. "Gonna steal a shotgun."

"Come on." Clark helped him to his feet and guided him toward the truck. "I'll drive you home."

"Oh, God, don' do that," Marshall pleaded, his face betraying panic and despair. He pawed at Clark like a wounded animal. "We're all dead there. We're zombies." He burst into tears.

"How could he do that? How could he?"

"I don't know," Clark said honestly. "I'm sorry, Marshall. I really am."

"Didn't he love us?" he wailed, stumbling. "How could he kill himself?"

Clark was at a loss. There were no answers, and saying he was sorry only went so far. Of course he was sorry. Everyone was sorry. But that didn't bring Marshall's father back to life, or make Jake Brooks well.

"Why?" Marshall asked again, stumbling. "Just tell me why!"

Then a voice behind them said, "Because he couldn't get past his own pain. It doesn't mean he didn't love you. He just hurt too much."

Clark wheeled around, taking Marshall with him.

Silhouetted beneath the streetlight at the other end of the alley stood a girl with her hair piled on top of her head. A decoration of some kind was stuck in it—like a Chinese chopstick, and she had on a black V-neck sweater and faded jeans. Heavy makeup, big earrings. She looked very arty and exotic.

It was the new girl, Rebecca Morhaim.

"Rebecca, hi," Clark said. "What are you doing out here?"

She hesitated, twisting her hands together until she seemed to realize what she was doing and dropped them to her side. "I . . . Chloe dropped me off and . . ."

Marshall stiffened. "It was because of *her.* That Sullivan bitch." He staggered; Clark kept him upright as he began to cry. "I'm gonna kill her!" He tried to push Clark out of the way. "Gonna steal a shotgun!"

"Marshall, you're upset," Clark said, restraining him, mindful of his own strength. "You don't know what you're saying." *And you shouldn't be saying it, at least not around strangers.*

"Be careful. Drunks are trouble," Rebecca said to Clark. Then she looked flustered, as if she realized she was in the middle of a situation that had nothing to do with her, and said, "I—I have to go."

"Wait." Clark glanced back at the truck, trying to figure out how to take care of both Marshall and her. He couldn't just leave her there without a way back. "Do you need a ride home?"

She hesitated, scanning the area. Beneath the streetlight she looked lost and alone. She was very small, and the harsh light gave her the appearance of being trapped in the glare. Without completely understanding his reaction, he felt for her, sensing that she was troubled about something.

"I'm . . . I was supposed to meet my dad here," she said. "Pretty soon. Um, he's . . . he'll be here soon, I mean."

In an alley?

Red-faced, as if she realized how implausible that sounded, she put her arms around herself and smiled weakly at Clark. Her black sweater was thin, and a slice of her belly was showing above her jeans. Clark was impervious to temperature, but he figured she must be awfully chilly.

"I don't think he'd want you out here by yourself," he told her. "It's getting late."

She looked left, right, and the expression on her face reminded him of a lost child. There was definitely something up with her. Then she said, "Maybe we got our wires crossed. Maybe he's waiting for me at home." She unwrapped her arms from around her waist, and said, "Yeah, maybe I would like a ride home after all. Thanks."

There was an edge to her tone that Clark didn't understand, but he led the way back to the truck, Marshall in tow.

They had to sit three abreast, Marshall shotgun and Rebecca in the middle. She smelled good, of makeup and perfume, and Clark thought of Lana.

Why can't I just move on?

Rebecca was checking him out, too; he could tell, could feel her eyes on his profile. He wondered what she saw, what she thought of him. He knew that if he turned his head now, their gazes would lock.

He kept his eyes on the road.

She's pretty, she's nice . . . what is it about Lana that keeps me there?

Then the moment passed. Marshall's head fell back, and he started to snore, and she and Clark chuckled. Rebecca gently nudged his head toward the window so that it wouldn't end up resting against her own head. She pressed her hand against his head for a moment, then pulled it away experimentally, apparently satisfied when it remained where she had put it. Marshall murmured something, then began to snore again.

"I thought about putting him in the back," Clark told her. "I'm sorry. I should have."

"No. This way, he's safe. In his condition, he might have decided to see if he could fly," Rebecca said. "I had a foster brother . . ." She caught herself. "I knew someone who saw *Mary Poppins* and jumped off the roof of his house with an umbrella. He broke his arm, but he was more upset that it hadn't worked like in the movie. 'It didn't work! It didn't work!'"

They laughed together.

Then she grew serious, and said, "What I said about drunks. That had nothing to do with my dad. I . . . I lived with relatives for a while, and one of them . . . he drank a lot. It was pretty scary."

He knew she had distinctly said "foster brother," and he knew that had nothing to do with living with relatives, but he didn't press for an explanation. He only nodded, and said, "That must have been tough."

"Yeah. I learned to handle myself around him." Then she gazed out the window for a moment, and said quietly, "Everything in my life is different now." She moved her arm to pat her hair, brushing his as he drove, and then she murmured, "Sorry," and put her hand in her lap. He ticked his glance over to her and saw her flushing in the lights from the dash.

I wonder what she thinks of me, Clark thought. *I wonder if Chloe and Lana have talked about me around her. If she knows about how things are among the three of us.*

Heck, I don't even know how things are among the three of us.

"Well, unless you're psychic," she said, "you don't know where I live."

"I'm not."

At least, not that I'm aware of. My powers have been developing as I age . . . Is that something I have to look forward to? Because from what I've seen of telepathic ability, it's not something I'd like to have to deal with.

Rebecca gave him directions, and he was still curious why she was waiting for her father in an alley instead of meeting him at home. The question hung between them, making him feel awkward, but he didn't ask it. It seemed like prying, and she was so edgy he didn't want to add to it.

She lived in a run-down apartment building in town, and it was obvious that she was embarrassed for him to see it. That might have explained her hesitation in accepting a ride from him. But on the street she had looked cold, tired, and a little frightened, and he figured those factors had mentally canceled out her shame, and so she had let him take her home.

He pulled up to the curb and saw that there were no lights on in her apartment.

He said, "Your dad's not home yet. Do you have a cell phone?"

She chuckled and said, "We can't afford something like that. He probably left me a message on the answering machine," she said, too brightly. "I'll bet he forgot he was supposed to meet me. You know how single dads are . . . Well, I guess you don't know. You have two parents." She sounded wistful, a little envious.

"I'm lucky," Clark agreed. He opened up the truck door. "I'll walk you in, make sure everything's okay."

He walked her to the door and stood by her while she fumbled with her key and finally got it into the lock. The screen door was ripped, and the hinges were rusted and needed to be replaced. He thought about how Marshall had terrorized Chloe, and for a moment anger and frustration swept through him that someone as nice as Rebecca had to live in a place like this.

After she opened the door, she reached around and switched on a light. Her look of discomfort spoke volumes: She didn't want him to see how she lived. Clark couldn't avoid a glance as she stepped inside, turning to face him as if to block his view.

"See? Everything's fine," she assured him.

He could see the living room. There was a big, ugly sofa, a cheap coffee table, and a TV on a stand. That was it. He compared the stark room to his own family's living room. His mother had worked hard to make it warm and inviting, and there were days when he walked into it that he felt the safety there, the sense of sanctuary. He doubted Rebecca felt that way in this room, especially when she had to come home to it alone.

"Want me to check the rest of your apartment for you?" he asked. Without waiting for her answer, he focused his X-ray vision and swept it through the other rooms. There was no sign of another person. No sign of much at all, in fact. The two bedrooms were very sparsely furnished, like the living room. He saw no pictures on the walls.

Well, she did say that they just moved here . . .

"No, that's fine," she answered, unaware that he had already searched her place for intruders. "But thanks. You're very gallant."

He smiled. "Chloe would probably say I'm a chauvinist."

"I like it," she admitted. Then she blushed again.

She likes me, he realized. He was flattered and embarrassed at the same time.

"Okay," she said, brightly. "I'm good." She kind of stood on the balls of her feet as if for emphasis, like a little cheerleader jump, and for a second he thought she was trying to kiss him good night. He wasn't sure what to do. She was so much shorter than he that he had to crane his neck to look at her.

Then the moment passed, and they were simply smiling at each other again.

"Okay." He nodded at her, waiting a beat. "If you're sure you're okay here by yourself."

For a moment she said nothing. It was almost as if she were holding her breath. Her eyes glittered, and her smile faded just a little as he took a step away. She wasn't okay alone.

If I didn't have Marshall to contend with, he thought, *I'd stay with her until her father got here. Maybe I should call Chloe.*

Then she said clearly, "Yeah, I'm sure. You'd better hurry. Marshall might decide he can jump out of there in one giant leap for mankind or something."

"True." He glanced over his shoulder at the truck. Marshall's head was back, his mouth tipped open. No doubt he was still snoring. "Well . . . see you Monday."

She gave him a little wave. "Thanks, Clark. If you see Chloe or Lana, please say hi for me."

He smiled at her in return. "Sure."

She waited until he was in the truck to shut the door, giving him one more wave. Clark put the truck in gear and drove off. Marshall was still passed out, still snoring, with his head tilted way back. Clark felt sorry for him, but he was also alarmed at what Marshall had said about getting a shotgun and going after Chloe.

I'd better tell Dad about it, see if we should get the sheriff involved . . .

As he was thinking about it, he saw a flash of white across the street. He leaned forward to peer through the windshield. There it was again, catty-corner, lurching past the minimart where Clark had planned to get a soda.

It was a very pale person, dressed in a navy blue sweatshirt and a pair of jeans. The way he was walking, Clark figured that, like Marshall, he had to be drunk.

It was none of Clark's business, and yet he felt strangely drawn to the stumbling man, so obviously out of control. The guy was disheveled and very disoriented, jerking forward, then stopping, then jerking forward again. He was like a battery-operated toy that was running out of juice.

Clark drove up abreast of him and looked out the driver's side window. It was dark on that side of the street, and Clark couldn't get a very good look at him. He considered using his X-ray vision but refrained, waiting to see if he could make contact by normal means.

"Hey," Clark said, rolling down the window.

The guy didn't react. He didn't even seem to notice that the truck was there. He just kept walking and stumbling on down the street. He looked drunk.

He's so white. He doesn't look real.

"Are you sick? Do you need to go to the hospital?" Clark tried again.

The guy shambled on, then jerked, stopped, and disappeared into an alley.

Okay, that was weird, Clark thought uneasily.

Then Marshall raised his head and muttered, "Kent, gonna be sick."

Great.

Marshall had the decency to wait for Clark to pull over and let him out; then Clark waited inside the truck. In less than a minute, Marshall was back inside, looking miserable.

After a few more minutes of driving, Clark pulled up to the Hackett residence, a pleasant gray two-story house with a wraparound porch. The porch light was off, but the streetlight glowed on weedy grass and a pile of newspapers beside the front door. It was as if no one had been living there. Perhaps no one was. Perhaps the best they could do was simply exist, make it from one day to the next, one hour to the next . . .

Clark was as reluctant to leave Marshall there as he had been to leave Rebecca at her house. But he hoisted the football player out of the truck and half walked, half carried him up the three cement steps, then to the front door, where he hesitated, reluctant to ring the doorbell.

Marshall slurred, "Key's in pocket."

Clark felt in Marshall's jacket and found a ring of keys. He searched through them, looking for a likely candidate, and came upon a small family photo encased in a plastic frame. From behind her husband's wheelchair, Mrs. Hackett was leaning forward, her arms draped around her husband's neck, her face pressed lovingly up against his. The boys were grouped on each side, apparently sitting on chairs. Portrait of a happy, loving family. He could almost hear the photographer ordering them around, telling them how to pose, hear the Hacketts laughing as they took their places.

Now all those faces were silent . . . and at least one of them would never laugh again.

Letting the picture go, he found the right key and opened the door, easing Marshall inside, half-expecting Marshall's mother to call out, "Where have you been?"

But there was no sound other than the *tick-tock* of a clock in the hallway. His and Marshall's footfalls provided a counterpoint as Clark turned to him, and said, "Where's your room?"

"'Stairs," Marshall slurred, and Clark walked him to the stairs. Expecting Marshall to negotiate them was hopeless, so Clark put his arm around him and did almost all the work himself by hoisting Marshall up, so that his feet barely touched the stairs. The football player didn't notice. In his condition, there wasn't much he would notice.

Clark's efforts made considerably more noise than if a single pair of footsteps had sounded on the stairway, and he kept waiting for Mrs. Hackett to call out. Growing more concerned, he swept the Hackett home with his X-ray vision, and found two figures in two different rooms. In the largest of three bedrooms, a woman sat, clutching a photograph and weeping. In the other room, a male figure sat at the window, unmoving. Mrs. Hackett and Jeremiah. Both were awake, and yet neither called out to Marshall.

Clark found that very sad.

"Left," Marshall rasped, and at first Clark thought he was saying that he had been left, as in abandoned. Then he realized that Marshall was indicating that the door on his left was the door to his room.

Clark pushed it open and Marshall lurched forward, falling onto the bed. Clark stood awkwardly, wondering if there was anything more he should do.

Then he turned and left, going back the way he came. As he walked down the hall, his elbow brushed a sideboard and knocked over a ceramic vase. It made a loud clatter. He grabbed it and righted it, thinking that surely now Mrs. Hackett would come to check on what was going on in her home. For all she knew, they were being burglarized.

Silence reigned through the house, except for the incessant ticking of the clock.

He thought of the saying, "Let the dead bury the dead." These people were not dead. They would come back to life, once their grieving was done.

At least, that was what he told himself as he went down the stairs and through the front door, vastly relieved to be out of the house.

When Clark got home, his father was in his robe, drinking a cup of tea and watching the news. He smiled at Clark, and said,

"Did Mom finally get tired or did they throw you out?"

"Dad, the strangest thing happened," Clark replied, filling him in about Rebecca, Marshall, and the pale man who had seemed to vanish before Clark's eyes.

"Smallville. You gotta love it," Jonathan said. Then he laughed wryly, and added, "Though I'm not sure why." He looked hard at Clark. "Do you think Marshall Hackett might actually harm Chloe?"

"I don't know," Clark said truthfully.

"That family's been through so much. I'd hate to put any more pressure on any of them." He sighed, then regarded his son with an intensity that caught Clark up short.

"If anything ever happens to me, you need to stay strong. For your mother," he said levelly.

Clark raised his brows. "Of course I will."

Jonathan ran his hands through his hair and sighed heavily. "When I saw her lying there . . . I never want to feel that way again." He looked away, lost in a mix of emotions. Clark swallowed hard, remembering the panic he himself had felt.

What if I hadn't found her? What would have happened?

"The Hacketts must have been under a lot of stress, keeping a family secret like that. Always having to be careful of what they said, doing their best not to let on." As if Jonathan realized what he was saying—and drawing the same parallels Clark was drawing—he smiled wryly, and said, "But I guess every family has its secrets."

Yeah, but rocket ships in the barn probably aren't on most people's lists, Clark thought.

"Marshall was really drunk," Clark told his father. "He probably didn't know what he was doing. He didn't even get inside the sporting goods store. He couldn't possibly have taken anything."

"Then maybe we can leave it alone," Jonathan ventured. "He'll probably have forgotten all about it when he wakes up."

Clark grimaced. "I wouldn't want to be him when he does wake up. He's going to have a terrible hangover."

"This just in from Smallville," said the news anchor on the TV. *"The police have reported a rash of burglaries that have*

swept through the center of this small farming community. Over a four-hour span tonight, all three of the town's jewelry stores were burglarized, with sizable amounts of merchandise being stolen from each store."

There was a shot on TV of Kendrick's, the oldest jewelry store in Smallville.

"In each case, entry was accomplished at the back of the store, through a transom window or, in one instance, by forcing the back door."

The camera traveled up the door of Kendrick's to show a small window above the doorway.

"That's how Marshall was trying to get into the sporting goods store," Clark told his father.

"Was he carrying any jewelry?" Jonathan asked his son. "Anything bulky?"

"Nothing," Clark replied.

They looked at each other. Jonathan sighed.

Clark said quickly, "Dad, we don't have any proof."

Jonathan's brow furrowed, and Clark knew he was weighing what to do. Clark's father had always stressed that justice must be tempered with compassion . . . and they had both learned that there was no such thing as black and white, right and wrong. The context of a situation could change its tenor; what might look wrong to one person could feel right to another. A military general might look upon him as a threat to national security—and on his parents as criminals for harboring him. But someone else . . . someone who loved him—would see them as Clark's true family.

On the other hand, if someone who loved him, or someone whom he loved, found out that he was an alien from outer space . . . would that person still love him? What context would she put her feelings in?

Chloe had felt that he had abandoned her at the prom to dash off on a hopelessly romantic quest to save Lana from the twister . . . when the truth was, he had been able to save Lana; if he hadn't left the prom when he did, she would have died in the storm.

"Do you want to watch any more of this?" Jonathan asked

Clark. When Clark shook his head, his dad clicked off with the remote.

"We'll talk about what to do in the morning. From what you told me, Marshall's not going to be going anywhere tonight."

"That's right," Clark insisted.

Jonathan sighed. "We're going to have to get serious about helping that family out, son. They're in distress. That boy is sending out SOS messages so loudly the whole town should be able to hear them."

"Then we won't tell the sheriff?" Clark prodded. "We won't say anything?"

"Now, I didn't say that," Jonathan reminded him. "But don't dwell on that tonight. Get some sleep."

"Okay, Dad. You, too."

But Clark sincerely doubted either of them would be able to stop worrying about what to do about Marshall.

A few hours later, the sun rose, tinting the walls of Marshall Hackett's room with rosy light. He woke up slowly, groaning. His head felt as if someone had ripped it off his neck, turned it inside out, and stuffed it back onto his body. Everything hurt; everything felt sick.

He couldn't remember a thing he had done. And when his mother told him that Clark Kent had practically carried him into the house, he was both humiliated and ashamed.

"I watched from my doorway," she said. "I saw him take you into your room."

"I'm sorry, Mom," he told her, looking at her tear-streaked face, her gaunt cheeks and hollow eyes. *You jerk,* he railed at himself. *She's going through enough without you screwing up, too.*

"I know, baby," she murmured, and she took him in her arms and held him tightly. They stayed that way for a few minutes.

Then his mother said wearily, "Drink some water and go back to bed, honey."

As he turned to go, she touched his face. "You know your

father loved you, don't you?" She searched his eyes. "Just as much as Jeremiah."

Even though I was adopted, Marshall filled in. He nodded, even though he was still reeling from the shock of the discovery. It was all too much: Chloe blowing their cover and his father telling him something in death that he should have told him in life.

"Why . . . why didn't you guys tell me?" he asked in a small voice.

She flushed. "Your father . . . he was afraid you would feel different. But I . . ." She let the sentence trail off.

But her unspoken message was clear: She had wanted to tell Marshall. She hadn't in order to please her husband.

Neither spoke of it, and Marshall realized with a start that there were still lots of secrets between them.

He drank the water and dozed. The afternoon shadows dragged across the walls of his bedroom as he lay still, listening to the dull thumping of his heart. Now and then, he imagined he heard his father's comings and goings. He could almost hear his voice.

He finally managed to eat some dry toast and drink some ginger ale—his father's prescription for nausea. Moving slowly, he was standing at the kitchen sink, munching on the toast, when he heard his mother weeping in the hallway.

"Monica, get your mommy, will you honey?"

She was on the phone with his little cousin in Arkansas. Monica's mother was Marshall's aunt Maryellen. Had she known that he'd been adopted and never said a word all those years? Had the whole family known? He thought of all the family gatherings he'd attended, assuming he was just a regular Hackett . . . how many of them had promised not to tell him the truth?

"Maryellen? They won't give us the life insurance money," his mother said brokenly. "Because of the way . . . because Sam killed . . ." She began to cry harder. "Self-inflicted."

Marshall went numb.

"I don't know what we're going to do. All the medical bills. The mortgage. I don't make anywhere near enough to carry it all." She sounded terrified and alone. "I'm so scared, sis . . ."

Marshall started to go to her, but he figured she would clam up and stop talking with Aunt Maryellen.

We're broke. We're going to be homeless, he thought. *I can't let that happen.*

He set his jaw.

I won't *let that happen.*

The thief smiled at his partner-in-crime, and said, "This town is too small. We're running out of places to rob."

"Guess that's why they call it Smallville," Shaky replied.

They were walking the streets together, casing various businesses to burglarize, when Shaky added, "I don't think it's such a good idea to pull any more of these right now. It's on the news. If someone sees one of our . . . creations . . ."

The thief laughed. "Relax. I've got someone right here in town I can pin the blame on. An old friend."

"Wh-what?" Shaky asked, even more freaked out. "What are you talking about? I thought we picked Smallville so we could test out the zombies. I didn't know you had something else to . . . deal with."

"An old score to settle," the thief said. He scratched his head, pointed, and said, "What about that electronics store? Let's do that one."

Shaky looked across the street at the place the thief had indicated. Beside a row of storefronts, an alley cut back into what he surmised was probably a parking lot. It was the standard configuration for commercial buildings in Smallville.

"I think we . . . we should lie low," Shaky said.

The thief just laughed.

Shaky hid his trembling. He was very, very sorry he'd hooked up with this guy.

Not that I had much of a choice.

That evening, Marshall didn't drink, but he did take a tranquilizer from his brother's new prescription. Since their father's death, Jeremiah had been put on so much medication he could probably open his own pharmacy.

At midnight, Marshall began to feel woozy, and he wondered

if he was going to be able to stay awake long enough to commit his crime.

He wasn't after a shotgun this time; he was after money. After his mother had hung up from her conversation with her sister, she had begun phoning all the places they owed. It had taken her a long time. She'd started arranging for ways to make the payments smaller, or to delay them for a while. Some of their creditors had been accommodating. But others had made his mother cry fresh tears.

He would not let that happen again.

With his father dead and his brother out of commission, it was up to Marshall to shoulder some of the burden of providing for the family.

I just never thought I'd do it like this.

In his pocket he carried the handgun Samuel Hackett had kept locked in a drawer in the desk in his study. It was a heavy, alien object. In his other pocket he had stuffed a ski mask.

His destination, an all-night grocery store, gleamed in the distance. Marshall's heart pounded at the sight of it, and more than once, he thought of turning around and going home. His mother thought he was at the Talon. He could be, within ten minutes.

The memory of the desperation in her voice strengthened his resolve.

He walked on for a few more minutes. Yawning, he tripped on a crack in the sidewalk and the world wobbled. He realized he was getting sluggish from the tranquilizer. Gazing at the moon, he saw it as a blur of nearly two moons. The streetlights were diffuse yellow globes that seemed to move as he ticked his glance to them.

He chuckled bitterly.

No way am I robbing anybody tonight.

He turned around to go home, glancing left and right, as if to assure himself that no one would guess that he had nearly committed a crime. Home was not that far away—nothing in Smallville was—and he hoped he could keep himself together until he got there.

Then, from the corner of his eye, he caught the movement of something white on the other side of the street.

Slowly, becoming more unfocused, he turned his head to check it out . . . and his mouth literally dropped open.

Am I seeing things?

It looked like a dead person. It moved like a mummy. Staggering down the street, staring straight ahead, it was dead white, its unkempt hair sticking out around its head like a fright wig.

As Marshall gaped, it was joined by a second one that lurched out of the nearby alley. It moved like a windup toy.

A man carrying a black leather bag came up behind the pair of nightmares. He sauntered along as if he hadn't a thing on his mind. There was something very wrong with his face . . . was it a mask?

Marshall spotted a Smallville community trash receptacle. With great effort, he crept behind it, lowering himself to a squat as he peered around it at the three figures.

Shortly after that, a van pulled up to the curb. The man skirted around the two white figures, pulling open the rear passenger door. Once they were inside, he slid it shut, opened the passenger door at the front, climbed in, and closed it behind him.

The van squealed away.

Marshall murmured, "What?" He was almost completely overcome by the drug he had taken. He fell to his knees, his head bobbed forward onto his chest, and he tumbled facefirst onto the pavement.

After a while, he became aware that someone was shaking him.

"Mom," he slurred. "I'm up."

"This is the Lowell County Sheriff's Office," a voice harshly informed him. "You're under arrest."

◆◆◆

Dressed all in black, T. T. Van De Ven sauntered into the Smallville Grille and was escorted by the hostess to a booth. A waitress made her way to his table, sparkling and eager to please. She flirted a little, and he smiled back. He knew she liked what she saw: He worked out, and he had big, dark eyes that drew women in and made them want to listen to his troubles.

Stay out of the limelight, he reminded himself. He didn't need any civilians remembering him later. He politely ordered a steak, and toned down the charm as he waited for his meal to arrive.

Then, as was his custom, he discreetly inserted his omnidirectional earphone into his left ear and started eavesdropping on those around him. The snippets he overheard painted the usual word pictures about the locals. Small towns were all the same. Hell, people were all the same: He heard businessmen cheating on their wives, people sharing worries about their jobs. The weather, the crops, what Lex Luthor was up to . . .

Hmm. He focused in on that, ignoring the other conversations.

". . . Luthor shouldn't have fired us," a man's voice was complaining. "For what? A bag of dirt?"

Van De Ven raised a brow and glanced idly around the room. Two burly men were seated approximately eight feet away from him, and by the looks on their faces, they were extremely upset.

"She probably lost it herself," the taller of the two men said to the others. "You know how rich chicks are. Think they own the world. They never keep track of anything. She probably threw it out and forgot."

Dirt? They had to be talking about the fertilizer. She had lost it?

"Luthor won't even write us letters of recommendation," the shorter one groused. "How are we supposed to get new jobs?"

"Guess His Royal Highness figures we should eat cake."

"Frickin' Lex Luthor," the short one grumped. "I'm gonna sue him for false termination."

"You and what lawyer?"

"Yeah."

Van De Ven was thunderstruck. They *had* to be talking about the sample Lopez had on her. The one he had been sent to retrieve.

It was *gone*? Who had it?

"It was probably Blanca," the short one said. "That maid from the agency? She's a kleptomaniac."

"Yeah. Probably so. Hell of a maid, though," the other one replied. But there was no real conviction in his voice. He was just helping his friend blow off some steam. "Man, I can't get over it. He fired us because of *missing dirt*."

"Yeah, well, I never liked him. The Luthors are rich snobs, and that's all there is to it," the short one rejoined.

They continued talking for about thirty minutes. T. T. Van De Ven listened to every word.

And then he walked outside "to have a cigarette," so he told the waitress, and contacted his superiors. His line was as secure as if he'd been inside Air Force One, but he was cautious all the same, avoiding using any names and keeping to their strictly enforced code.

"This will change your mission parameters," came the reply. "Stand by for further orders."

"Standing by, sir," Van De Ven replied crisply. He felt a small thrill; maybe instead of all this waiting-around crap, things were about to move into high gear. He hoped so. He was getting incredibly bored.

"Good." The man on the other end of the line disconnected.

And T.T. got back to his listening.

CHAPTER FOURTEEN

A week passed, and Rebecca grew more and more confused about what her dad was doing when he thought she wasn't looking.

He kept leaving, and she had only managed to follow him twice. Each time, he'd wound up here, at the cemetery. It creeped her out.

What is my father doing in the Smallville cemetery? Rebecca wondered, as she hid behind a tree and watched her father pacing among the headstones. *Why?* It was Saturday night, and all the other kids in Smallville were hanging out—Chloe and Lana had invited her to the Talon—but here she was, spying on her father in a boneyard.

She had been grateful to Clark Kent for giving her a ride home the other night, and even more grateful that he hadn't asked her any questions about why she was searching for her father in the middle of the night. She felt stupid now for lying to him about getting a ride from Chloe. All he had to do was mention it in front of Chloe to discover that she had lied to him. She'd actually been following her father on foot like a spy.

She didn't mention that she had long before lost track of him, and had gotten so lost that she'd wondered if she'd ever find her way out of the maze of the town. That in itself was embarrassing enough; Smallville proper was a tiny place. But she'd been so preoccupied with trying to keep up with her dad that she'd completely ignored the route she had taken.

Then he had turned into an alley and seemingly disappeared.

Something had happened to her father since they had come to Smallville, and she was scared. Tom Morhaim kept leaving when he figured she was asleep, and staying out for long hours at a time. If he was going on long walks, as his therapist had suggested, then he was more troubled than he had been back in Metropolis. Because the walks kept getting more frequent, and lasting longer.

. . . and now these walks are taking him to a graveyard. What's up with that?

She peered around the trunk of the tree. Her father kept walking up and down a particular row, staring down at the names as if he were searching for a particular gravesite. Fog was wisping along the ground, then rolling upward, wafting around his knees as he moved. More fog billowed behind him, like skeletal hands sliding up his back and resting on his shoulders. It was an eerie sight, as if ghosts were winding themselves around him and trying to pull him down into the very graves themselves.

She shivered. She was cold, and frightened.

He walked on. Then he stopped abruptly and shined his flashlight on one grave in particular. He stood motionless before it and dropped to his knees.

Rebecca craned her neck, but she was at the wrong angle to see much more than the top of his head and the glow from the flashlight, which was illuminating him from below. His features were cut into sharp sections of yellow light and muted shadow; he was like a jagged Halloween pumpkin. He was like a stranger.

His head dipped, and she could no longer see him. Her heart pounding, she moved around the tree, clinging to the trunk, and found a space between overhanging branches of lacy leaves to observe him. Part of her was deeply ashamed that she was spying on her own father; but another part was wounded to the core that he had not confided in her, told her what was troubling him . . . and what he was looking for among the dead of Smallville.

She took another step forward. He didn't hear her, only kept his head bowed, as if in prayer.

Is it someone he knows? she wondered. As far as she knew, he'd never been to Smallville before in his life.

She took another step.

And a distant step answered hers.

The hair rose on the back of her neck. She and her father were not alone.

"D-dad?" she croaked, but she was so freaked out that she couldn't make a sound. The word came out as a breathy whisper, nothing more.

Then there was another footstep, and the crack of a tree branch under someone's foot.

"Dad!" she called. But again, her voice was a sandpapery rasp.

Then a bone-chilling fear swept over her, an icy net that fanned over her body and caught her up; she was so afraid she went numb from head to toe.

Someone was standing right behind her, and ready to put a hand on her shoulder—

"Daddy!" she shouted.

Her father leaped up from the grave and whirled around.

"Becca!" he shouted.

She ran toward him, flinging herself into his arms. But he pushed her out of the way and raced toward the tree, pulling a gun from his jeans pocket as he did so.

"Come out of there!" he shouted.

"Daddy, no!" Becca cried.

Her father disappeared into the darkness; she heard him thrashing through the overhanging tree branches, and she covered her mouth with both hands and whimpered, not really aware that she was doing it.

Oh, God . . . please, don't let my dad get hurt . . .

She took a step forward, then another, then she was galvanized into action. She raced toward the trees, shouting, "Don't hurt my father!"

"Rebecca, stop!" he bellowed.

She didn't listen. She ran straight into the thick foliage, panting, flailing with her arms . . .

. . . until someone caught her wrist and dragged her back the way she had come.

To her relief, it was her father.

"Oh, Dad!" she cried, and threw herself against him. "Who was that?"

"Nobody. I don't know," he amended. "Probably just some homeless drunk." Then he looked at her strangely. "What are you doing here?"

"It felt . . . evil," she said. She glanced in the direction of the trees and felt her stomach do a flip.

"It was just some guy," he said again. "Rebecca, I asked you why you're here."

"I . . . I followed you," she admitted. Then she looked up at him. "I'm sorry, Daddy. It's just . . . you've been going out so much, on these walks. I was worried."

He frowned at her. "Then why didn't you just tell me? Why did you sneak around behind my back?"

"I—I don't know," she admitted. She looked down, embarrassed. "I'm sorry."

"No need to be sorry." He cupped her cheek. "We have to be honest with each other. We're all we have, you know?"

She blinked back tears as she gazed up at him. "It was so hard, while you were . . . away. Mom . . ."

He swallowed hard. "That should never have happened," he said. "Your mother was a good person. I know it was hard on you, baby."

She closed her eyes as grief washed over her. The loss of her mom was a wound that still hadn't healed.

"It was hard on you, too," she said.

"She died believing in my innocence," he told her. "I know you were awfully young when it happened . . ."

"She told me about it," Rebecca said.

"I was only there to drive the car." He sighed and shook his head. "I certainly didn't expect anyone to get hurt."

"You were young," she said loyally.

"Thank you, honey," he said.

He pulled her against his chest and leaned his head on the crown of her head. She could hear his heartbeat and listened to it, finding refuge in its calm steadiness. This was her father, her only living relative. This was the man who had come for her when he'd gotten out of prison, like a knight in shining armor . . . her father.

"We have a chance to start over here in Smallville," he told her. "I know you had a rough road too, honey. Bouncing around from foster home to foster home . . . it's hard to trust anyone. And it shouldn't have happened.

"There are nights it upsets me so badly that I can't sleep. So I go on walks."

"But . . . why here?"

He sighed, and shook his head. "It's a little weird," he warned her. Then he took her hand and walked her toward the grave she had seen him kneeling in front of.

On the headstone were the words, MICHELLE MADISON, BELOVED WIFE AND MOTHER. 1935–1978.

She caught her breath. Her mother's name had been Michelle, and the double-M initials had been her mother's, too.

He said softly, "This lady was only forty-three when she died. Pretty young. So it was a little like visiting with your mother." He gazed at the headstone, sorrow sharpening his features.

"Oh, Daddy." She sniffled.

"I didn't want to upset you," he said. Then he flushed. "I actually thought you might worry that I'd gone a little nuts."

"No." She shook her head sadly. "I have a doll that doesn't look a thing like her except that it has blue eyes, like Mom did. And when I miss her a lot, I get that doll out. I was embarrassed to tell you that. I mean, I *am* in high school now."

His features softened. "It's not fair, what you've gone through. I'll make it up to you, Rebecca. I promise. Right now we have it tough. I have a low-paying job and we live in a dump."

"Oh, Daddy, it's not that bad," she cut in. "And we're together."

"You deserve a lot better," he insisted. "And you will have a lot better." He cupped her chin with his hand and gazed into her eyes. "But you're going to have to trust me, all right?"

"All right." She smiled at him. "I'm sorry I didn't tell you I was scared."

"In prison, you learn to hide your feelings from other people," he said. "You wall yourself in and learn to take care of yourself. I'm still pretty rusty at letting you know what's going on with me." He gave her a wink. "But I'll do better on that score, too."

As they hugged, she remembered that he had gone into the stand of trees with a gun. He was not supposed to have a gun. It was a violation of his parole.

Be honest with him. Ask him about it, a voice inside her head prodded her.

"Let's go home," he said, taking her hand.

But she didn't want to lose the warmth between them, this special moment where after so long, they had really connected. They had a lot of time to work out the kinks, figure out all the details . . . not for *anything* would she say or do something to shatter the mood.

She smiled back at him . . . and kept her silence.

They went home, had some hot chocolate, and watched a little TV together. As they were gazing in companionable silence, she snuggled against her dad and thought about all the burdens he was trying to carry—still adjusting to life outside prison, working a job, trying to pay the rent and buy food, and taking care of her. All she had to do was go to school.

I'll get a job, she decided. *An after-school job, so Daddy won't worry about me being alone, and I can make friends, and make my own money.*

Shaky was having a nightmare.

In his anxious, fevered mind, buses zoomed back and forth; buses flew; buses honked and slammed on the brakes; but each one of them hit Willie hard enough to shatter him into pieces that spun and danced like comets. The wheels boomed as they spun in a rhythm like heartbeats, then like a death march prior to an execution.

Willie was dead, and the wheels pounded words inside Shaky's head, *Your fault, your fault, your fault.*

Then another bus hit Willie and his head shot off his body, soaring into the air, end over end; until it floated toward Shaky, and that ruined mouth opened and said, in the snaggle-toothed old man's voice, *You did this to me!*

Shaky woke up with a start; and from the other room of the thief's Metropolis apartment, the thief himself appeared at the threshold in a pair of sweats and a T-shirt that said, ironically, "DARE to keep kids off drugs."

"Would you stop that?" he snapped. "Night after night you go into this routine . . ."

Shaky raised a hand to his damp forehead, and said, "Sorry."

The thief grunted in disgust. "Medicate yourself or something. We need to be fresh for the morning. We got business down in Smallville."

More robberies, Shaky realized. He felt sick and tired and scared. His partner was crazy. And evil.

"Okay," he said, and wondered how on earth he could ever get himself free—free of the waking nightmare, and free of the guilt.

I killed that old man, as sure as if I'd shot him.

"So, no more moaning?" the thief said, regarding him closely. "Right?"

"No more," Shaky murmured. Tears welled in his eyes. "No more."

The next morning was a Sunday, but Rebecca had already noticed that all the shops on Main Street were open on Sundays. She went down the rows of stores asking for job applications.

When she got to the Talon, she discovered another world inside—this was where all the kids from school hung out—and Lana Lang was behind the counter.

Rebecca approached her shyly, and said, "Lana, I was wondering . . . if you need any new waitresses?"

"As a matter of fact, I do," Lana replied, smiling pleasantly as she put several frothy cups of coffee on a tray. She sprinkled some chocolate on top of one of them and added nutmeg to another. "Are you looking for a job?"

Rebecca licked her lips. "Yes. I don't . . . I have a little experience doing waitress work . . . well, no, I don't. But—"

"Do you know how to run an espresso machine?" Lana asked, gesturing to the ornate brass object glittering against a larger mirror that reflected back the bustling interior of the coffee-house.

"No," Rebecca admitted, discouraged.

"Would you like to learn? It's really cool when the steam kicks in."

Lana was grinning at her. A little shy, a little eager, Rebecca said, "I've always wondered what the difference between espresso and cappuccino really is."

"Espresso is black—cappuccino's got steamed milk. You're not a coffee drinker, I guess? That's okay. Around here, you'll catch on quick," Lana told her. "What schedule were you thinking of? After school? Can you do the occasional weekend?" She laughed. "Well, most weekends? Especially after football games?"

"Sure. I'm not exactly doing anything else at the moment." She took a breath. "So, do you think you could use me?"

Lana beamed at her. "I know I could." She held out her hand. "Welcome to the Talon."

Rebecca was thrilled. "Thanks, Lana."

Lana hefted her tray. "My pleasure. I was just about to advertise for more help. You saved me the effort."

"Thanks so much," Rebecca blurted, still amazed that someone so young was running a business . . . especially a thriving business like this one.

She looked around, impressed. *She's probably making more an hour than my dad is. She seems so happy. Life can be good. It really can.*

"It'll be great to have another pair of hands around here," Lana added kindly. "We've been shorthanded this semester. A lot of family farms are really struggling. The kids have to pitch in."

She smiled, and said to Rebecca, "Well, let me take this order to its final destination and I'll help you fill out your paperwork. You can start today, if you want."

Rebecca was stunned. And moved. "Thank you . . . for your faith in me," she said, having a little difficulty getting the words out. She wasn't used to things turning out like this. "This is great."

"Hey, guys." It was Chloe, who came up to the counter holding a newspaper. It wasn't the one she edited at school, but the regular Smallville paper, the *Gazette*. "There were two more burglaries last night."

"What?" Lana frowned at Chloe. "I thought Marshall Hackett had been arrested."

"He was." Chloe opened the paper and showed Lana and Rebecca the headline.

SMALLVILLE CRIME WAVE.

"The bookstore and that little store, Fair Notions, got hit," Chloe continued.

"Fair Notions." Lana shook her head. "I don't know that store."

"The new yardage shop. They've got that cool Goth fabric I made my Halloween costume out of last year. It's over by the cemetery, fittingly enough." Chloe considered. "The bookstore's over there, too." She made a scary face. "We're being robbed by ghosts!"

Rebecca blanched. She had found her father by the cemetery, and he had had a gun with him. What if the person in the bushes had been a security guard, searching for him? Or a cop?

Trying not to be conspicuous, she sank down on one of the barstools. Her legs simply wouldn't support her.

"You okay?" Chloe asked.

"Yes," she said brightly, covering up her reaction. "Guess what! Lana just hired me to work here!"

"Oh, cool," Chloe enthused, her green eyes sparkling. "Congratulations! You're on the caffeine train now."

"By the way, you get to drink all the free coffee you want," Lana said. "And at night we usually divvy up the pastries that are too old to sell."

"Wow, that's great," Rebecca continued, smiling a huge fake smile.

"It says here that some woman saw one of the burglars. She said he was dressed in white, or glowing, or wearing a mask or something." Chloe bobbed her eyebrows up and down. "That should be helpful."

"The ghosts of Smallville," Lana said.

"It's probably true." She smiled in Rebecca's direction. "I still haven't shown you the Wall of Weird, have I? Why don't you come to the *Torch* office after school tomorrow . . . unless you're working?" She gazed questioningly at Lana.

"How about you start at four?" Lana suggested.

"Great," Rebecca said again. Then she blurted, "My dad's going to be so proud of me."

It was a little bit of a geeky thing to say, and she was immediately mortified. But the other two girls just smiled at her, sharing her victory, and she thought, *Wow, they really are nice. Maybe we'll become good friends. Friends I can confide in . . .*

Then the walls her father had been talking about went up. There was no way she would ever tell a soul in Smallville about what had happened to her father back in Metropolis. More than once, a girl had assured her that the fact that her father had been to prison didn't bother her in the least; that of course she loved being friends with Rebecca. But after a time, that girl—and the next girl, and the next—stopped hanging out with her.

It bothered most people that he had been convicted of a terrible crime. And it bothered them even more that back in Metropolis, a man who had once supported five children, a wife, and a mother-in-law on a security guard's salary was now stuck in a wheelchair for life, collecting disability. The last mayoral race, the victim had been on TV in a political commercial endorsing the candidate who was toughest on crime. That had dredged everything back up, and school had become unbearable.

"Oh, we're going to have Punk Day on Friday," Lana told her. "We're all going to do our hair the way they wore it back then, and dress up." She wrinkled up her nose. "It's going to be a lot of fun. Do you think your mom might have anything in her closet you could wear?"

They don't know about us. They really don't. I'm safe.

"My mom passed away," she said, using the old-fashioned term because it seemed just too harsh and pathetic to say, "died."

"Oh, I'm sorry, Rebecca," Lana said. "I didn't know."

"That's okay," the girl replied, feeling even more uncomfortable now that she'd told them the truth. "It happened a long time ago."

"We don't have mothers, either," Chloe said. Her voice was edgy, tinged with bitterness. Then she relaxed a little and added, "We take care of each other."

She smiled at Rebecca, and so did Lana; and Rebecca thought,

If they ever find out about Dad, I'll just die. I couldn't stand not having friends again.

◆◆◆

When Rebecca got home from the Talon, there was a note on the table that said, *"Gone to the store. Back in a bit."* Rebecca set it back down on the table and wandered to the fridge. She got out a diet orange soda and moved to the well-worn sofa they had purchased from the Salvation Army and sat down. She turned on the TV and something caught her eye.

". . . woman told police who arrived on the scene that she had discovered a man with slack features and a pale complexion loitering in the supply room of Smallville Drugstore near the locked cabinet holding controlled substance medication."

The screen showed a woman with blue hair and enormous, frightened eyes. She said, "He just stared at me. I told him to leave or I was calling the police, that's what I said, yes sir!" She had a heavy Southern accent. "He didn't move a muscle. I swear he was on something.

"Then when I went to call y'all, he turned around and left. Just like that!" She snapped her fingers.

Then it wasn't Dad after all, Rebecca thought, and she was ashamed for thinking it might have been.

◆◆◆

Howard Ross, Pete's uncle, was coming back from a nice evening at the Smallville Pizza Palace, where he'd eaten some pie and swapped some tall tales with a few of the farmers he sold feed to. The men around here were anxious—family farming was a tough way to make a living—but they were honest guys, and friendly, too.

Of course, Howard made friends wherever he went. He liked people. Liked to yak with 'em and yak at 'em. Drove his nephew crazy with all his yakking.

He chuckled, thinking fondly of Pete. The kid didn't know it, but Howard was considering giving the boy his teal Lexus when Pete graduated from college. Hell, he could afford it. Even when times were tough, farmers still needed to buy feed for their livestock. Couldn't exactly skimp on that.

He motored along, admiring the way the moon hung in the clouds, whistling along with the radio.

Then, to his right, he saw a clump of white figures staggering out of an alley. He raised his brows; they looked terrible. They were the palest, whitest people he had ever seen.

Must be the light, he thought. *Maybe they're in a punk rock band or something.*

He drove on.

Yeah, he thought, switching radio stations, his mind returned to the Pizza Palace and his customers. *I think Pete will get this car. Man needs a fine automobile once he's grown-up.*

In the middle of the night, the zombies of Smallville walked. Six of them, they swayed on holy ground, the dead of Smallville slumbering beneath their feet.

These zombies—homeless men no one would miss—were in better condition than the zombies of Cap du Roi. The poison that had distorted their nervous systems and harnessed their wills was more refined than what had been used on the living dead of Haiti. If the Project had had Shaky on their team, it was likely that no one would have ever learned of the Project. At least, that's how the thief saw it. He'd done a little background work starting with the information the Latina had given Lex Luthor—information he had heard over his headset prior to stealing the sample. He knew what the government was up to . . . and who was involved.

He hadn't shared this information with Shaky. There was no need. They were partners, not friends.

The thief had no friends.

Fog boiling up around them, the zombies stared at the face that filled their souls, giving them the only direction they had. Beneath their seemingly mindless attentiveness, their silent voices were screaming, *Help us! Save us! We're in hell!*

But the thief held some terrible power over them, as surely as if he had some kind of remote control hidden in the pocket of his navy blue windbreaker. As he looked on, surveying their condition, they were forced to stand stock-still as he instructed each of them on their tasks for the evening: more burglaries, with just enough mayhem thrown in to distract anyone who got in the way of successfully lifting credit card numbers and cash from the tills of the businesses of Smallville.

The scientist was dressed similarly to the thief, in jeans and, in his case, a burgundy sweatshirt.

Though they usually kept the zombies rounded up in an abandoned warehouse just off the interstate, the two men had assembled their zombie patrol in the cemetery, which seemed a good place to begin the night's wild work. They had agreed that if anything went down—such as the law catching up with them— they would simply leave the premises, abandoning their creations. If anyone figured out what was going on, that would be tough luck for the creatures who would have no way to describe their captors, nor to explain that somewhere inside the apparently mindless shells of their bodies, their conscious minds were drifting below the surface, struggling for release.

But these zombies weren't going to be talking anytime soon. They couldn't even speak if they were tortured—the thief had already experimented in that direction, and he was positive of that. They were silent witnesses, and silent accomplices. Their lips were sealed—with drugs and maybe even a little Voodoo magic somehow loaded into the formula.

"By the way, do you need any more lab equipment?" the thief asked Shaky. "You mentioned a lab supply store in Metropolis that you like. We could take some of these guys up there, snag whatever you need. Want an electron microscope?"

Zombie eyes watched. Zombie eyes listened. Shaky shook his head. His dark eyes were troubled. He pulled out a cigarette and lit it, taking a deep drag. The zombies stirred, the smoke stinging their eyes. Shaky took no notice, but as he began to pace away from them among the headstones, they found relief. They still breathed, still needed food and water.

And they needed marching orders. They needed to be told what to do . . . or they would stand in the cemetery all night, without volition, without direction. That was the real curse of the living dead.

"We need to cool it," Shaky said. "There's been too much news coverage. We're doing too much, committing too many burglaries. There have been sightings."

The thief shook his head. "You're wrong. We're safe as houses."

Shaky flicked ash from his cigarette on a headstone and took another breath. "If anyone connects us to Willie back in Metropolis . . ."

"He was a bum," the thief said, snorting with derision.

"That case was closed the minute they found his body. No one gave a damn about him while he was alive, and no one gives a damn now. The Metropolis Police Department has far better things to do than look into the death of a piece of societal debris."

"I can't take any more risks. I got in a lot of trouble when I was younger," Shaky protested.

The other man sneered at the scientist. "You've been clean for years. You've fallen off the law enforcement radar as well, my friend."

"That never happens," Shaky argued. "Once you've been in the system, they never forget you. Especially now, with databases. You're never free. You have to walk their walk until you die. Just like these guys. We're all zombies." He was getting agitated.

"You should be more careful," he went on. "You're fresh out of prison. They're probably watching you."

The thief chuckled. "Calm down, Shaky. It's been over a year. I check in with my parole officer. They have no idea what I'm up to."

Shaky moved his head, and said desultorily, "Everyone leaves a trail. We're not even zombies, man. We're hamsters on a wheel."

"You are really getting boring," the thief said irritably. "You with your nightmares and your whining. I try to be nice, try to get you stuff you need. Listen, do you want out?"

Shaky looked startled. He tamped out his cigarette on the headstone, letting the butt fall into some flowers that were growing in a pot atop the grave itself. His eyes glittered. "Out? How am I going to get out? How are you going to 'let' me out? We're both in this for good."

"'Til death us do part?" the thief mocked.

Shaky had begun to pace again. His back was to the other man, and he was scared. "Something like that."

"Then . . . you could always die," the thief said reasonably. He looked over at the group of zombies.

Shaky raised his brows, backing a step away. "Hey, hold on," he said. "You just wait a minute."

Then the thief reached into the pocket of his windbreaker and pulled out his Anschütz .22.

He said to the scientist, "I wouldn't move if I were you. But then again, I would never be you in a million years. Never let myself be what you've become. I take the next right step, and you just stagger around. And this, my friend, is the next right step."

"Hey!" Shaky shouted. "Don't do this, man!"

The nearest zombie was grizzled and gray-haired, toothless and rheumy-eyed. The thief said calmly to him, "Kill him."

"Hey! Wait a minute!" Shaky cried. "Help!"

The zombie began to advance, raising his hands just like in the old movies, shambling slowly forward. It would have been simple for Shaky to outrun him . . . if the thief wasn't aiming a gun at him.

"Listen," Shaky said, "this is crazy. There's going to be a body if you kill me. There's been enough bodies, man. That's traceable evidence . . ."

The thief considered. "True," he said. "Very true." He reached into the pocket of his windbreaker and produced a vial. It was the distilled zombie formula Shaky himself had devised. There was plenty inside the vial to take away Shaky's life from him . . . and never give it back. In fact, there was enough in the vial for another dozen zombies, at least.

Right now, however, the thief was interested in creating only one.

"Open your mouth," the thief ordered.

Shaky stared at the vial. "Don't do this to me, man. Don't do it! We're partners!"

"C'mon, Shaky," the thief said, grinning. "You know the old saying about there being no honor among thieves. I'll bet you had something planned for me, too."

"No. No, man," the scientist insisted, his face betraying his lie. "No way."

"Hold him," the thief ordered the zombie.

The zombie moved toward Shaky, who waved his arms in terror. The thief advanced on him with the gun, pointing it straight into his face, and Shaky continued to shake while the zombie grabbed him.

"Open your mouth." He waved at Shaky with the gun. "Open it, or I'll have another one of these guys do it for you."

"Oh, God, please, no," Shaky murmured. Tears and sweat streamed down his face. "Please, no."

The thief unscrewed the top and walked toward Shaky. The other man's eyes bulged, and he struggled in the arms of the zombie.

"I'm the only one who can make the formula," he said desperately.

"Wrong, chucko. It's all on the hard drive now. I figured your password out easy. 'Shaky' is not terribly original."

Shaky flushed hard.

He gestured around himself, at the headstones, at the graves. "I don't need you anymore, Shaky, although I was willing to keep you on, at least for a little while longer. Until I was sure I could handle the operation on my own. But you're done. I see that now. As my old man used to say, 'the graveyards are full of indispensable people.'"

The zombies stared at the unfolding drama, heartbeats slow and lethargic, brains unable to process what was happening. They had been given their orders but not given leave to fulfill them, and they were getting anxious and restless, behind their quiescent exterior of passivity.

"Damn it, Shaky, open your mouth," the thief said. "This is the last time I tell you. Next time, I blow a hole in your head and pour this stuff into your brain."

Shaky glanced down at the gun. Seeing that it was equipped with a silencer, he must have realized that his former partner was telling him the truth.

With a groan of utter panic, he opened his mouth.

The thief began to pour the liquid into his mouth. The bitter taste hit Shaky's taste buds, and he hacked, hard, sending the vial spinning into the air. It landed on the nearest grassy grave mound, but did not break.

The thief grabbed the vial, advanced on his victim, held open his mouth, and poured the poison down Shaky's gullet.

Shaky went into a fit of convulsions. The zombie held him fast, since he had not been told to let go of him, and the thief watched in awe . . . and no small measure of amusement. He liked watching the transformation, liked knowing that when it was complete, he'd have another lackey at his beck and call . . . and this one had been somebody once upon a time. In terms of victims, he was moving up in the world.

One day folding blankets in the prison laundry; just a few days later, turning people into mindless followers.

I'd think of myself as a mad scientist, but Shaky had that honor. Until now. Now he's just another dumb jerk who didn't have the sense to give me some respect.

Like the Gadsen flag says, Don't tread on me.

The people who do pay for it . . . one way or another.

The scientist's head slumped forward, and his knees buckled. The thief waited, but Shaky didn't change right away. Sometimes the transformation was rapid. Sometimes it took a few hours.

He looked idly around the graveyard and spotted a crypt on the opposite side of where he was standing.

"Follow me," he said to the zombie who was holding Shaky.

Eerily, the zombie moved forward. He lost his grip on the unconscious scientist and seemed to be unaware of that fact as the man tumbled to the ground. Then he stepped hard on Shaky's arm. The thief heard a crack; Shaky's arm had just been broken.

"Easy, buddy," he said to the zombie. "Stop."

The zombie stopped.

"Pick up your burden."

The zombie bent over and grabbed Shaky by his broken arm. The limb was bent at a bad angle; it cracked again as the thief winced sympathetically.

Was that a jubilant gleam in the zombie's eye?

I wonder if somewhere in there, this guy knows exactly what he's doing, he thought, scrutinizing the zombie. *Maybe we didn't mix this batch right.*

He felt a little uncomfortable . . . until he reminded himself that he had a gun. He wagged it at the walking zombie, who had no reaction at all as he dragged Shaky along after him like a rag doll. He lost his grip again, and Shaky's ruined arm thudded onto the grass.

"Help him," the thief told the others.

Slowly, painstakingly, the others moved forward and glommed on to Shaky's arms and legs. They carried him like a big raft across the graveyard as clouds scudded across the moon. In the distance, a crow cawed, and something rustled in the bushes. The thief was tempted to shoot into the undergrowth, just in case. But just as he aimed his Anschütz in that direction, a possum ambled out, licking its paw without a care, and ambled away.

One of the zombies turned its head in the direction of the possum and clacked its jaw a couple of times. A couple of the others imitated it. The thief watched, intrigued. So far, he and Shaky's experience with the zombies they'd produced was that they were docile, compliant guys who ate regular food and had none of the violent, flesh-eating tendencies like in the movies. Neither one of them had been surprised, chalking all that up to Hollywood invention.

"C'mon, boys, let's go," he said.

They turned back around and shuffled after him, he their mother hen and they, his fast-moving chicks of the damned.

◆◆◆

It was almost dark by the time Rebecca's father came home "from the store." She had fallen asleep watching TV, and when he opened the door, she roused herself and smiled in his direction.

"What did you buy?" she asked eagerly.

"Oh. Not much," he replied vaguely. He was carrying a paper sack, and he reached in and pulled out a couple of apples, a quart of milk, and a loaf of bread.

"That's it?" she asked. He had been out for hours.

He paused, then admitted, "I didn't have enough money to pay for the rest of it, Bec. I had to put it back."

"Oh." She felt an anxious tightening in the pit of her stomach. Then she remembered her good news, and said, "Not to worry. I got a job! At the coffeehouse. You said I was good with coffee, and I got to thinking about that, and I got hired!"

He beamed at her. "That's terrific, honey." Then he frowned.

"You won't let it interfere with your schoolwork, will you?"

"No. It's with my new friend, Lana," she added proudly. "She kind of owns it with Lex Luthor."

"That guy's got his hooks into everything, doesn't he?" Tom murmured. "Must be nice."

"Daddy?" she asked.

He shook himself. "Sorry, honey. I'm really happy for you. For us both." He grinned at her. "We'll be eating filet mignon before you know it."

"I don't care if we have meatloaf as long as . . ." She trailed off shyly, and added, "I'm glad we're here, Dad. Together. I like Smallville."

"A change of scene has been good for both of us," he confirmed. He held out his arms. "I'm so proud of you. My smart, pretty girl! This place . . . what's it called?"

"It's the coffeehouse, the Talon." She took his hand. "I'll show it to you tomorrow. I have my first shift then. If that's okay . . ."

"As long as you can manage it all," he said firmly. "Education is your ticket out of this, sweetie. I'm going to make sure you have a good life."

She sniffled a little, glad to have a father around to give her some boundaries and care for her, the way she dreamed he would back when he was still in prison.

We're gonna be all right, she thought.

But that night, her father went out again. She heard him go; she was half-asleep and dreaming about Clark Kent's eyes and his smile and how cute he was. But she was roused by the sound of the door opening and closing, the lock clicking.

She sat up yawning and glanced at the clock. It was almost two in the morning.

When I get my first paycheck, I'll buy him a treadmill, she thought, half-joking. But her stomach was churning. Where did he keep going? Was he really that troubled? Was their situation more dire than she realized?

She lay back down and tried to go to sleep. After a while, she succeeded.

The next morning, as she and her dad ate a quick breakfast of toast, coffee, she idly flicked on the TV. The local news was on.

". . . burglary attempt . . ." the young female news anchor was saying. *"This time, Brian Cienci interrupted what had obviously been an attempt to open the safe of the Smallville branch of Jackson's Auto Body Shop. He saw no suspects, but he did notice muddy footprints on the floor. Local forensics experts are examining the footprints. Police say this hard evidence represents a break in the case."*

Rebecca's hair stood on end. She couldn't help it. She didn't want to think what she was thinking.

But as her father got up to pour himself another cup of coffee, she checked out his shoes.

His muddy shoes.

Then he said to her in a lighthearted tone of voice, "Oh, guess what. My supervisor's wife does beading. She had this neat earring. I thought it would go nice in the new hole you got."

He fished it out of his pocket and handed it to her.

She swallowed hard. *Oh, Daddy, please, don't let it be true that you've stolen this,* she begged him.

"I'll wear it to my first day of work," she told him.

Then she turned away, fighting back tears.

CHAPTER SIXTEEN

Chloe was seated at her computer in the *Torch* office when Clark popped his head in. She glanced over at him and finished her sentence, hit SAVE, and smiled cheerlessly at him.

"Hey," he said. "Mind if I come in?"

She waved him in. "Of course not, Clark. What's up?"

He put his hands in his pockets, took them out again, and finally perched on the edge of her desk, peering at her monitor. "What are you writing about?"

She pursed her lips. "A thoroughly uninteresting story about the upcoming pep rally. Rah," she said flatly. She looked at him expectantly.

Clark regarded his friend. There were circles under her eyes, and her hair didn't have that usual flare. She wasn't putting on much makeup—not that she didn't look great without it. And she was often distracted and listless.

"You're . . . okay?" he asked her.

"Sure. I'm fine." Her eyes wide, she looked confused. "What do you mean?"

He hesitated. "You don't seem fine."

"Well . . ." And then she deflated like a balloon. "I can't stop thinking about the Hacketts," she confessed. "I can't believe Marshall's still locked up. It's not fair, Clark. They didn't have any proof that he robbed that store. Now he's in custody, and Principal Reynolds has asked the school board for permission to suspend him."

"Been talking to eye witnesses?" he asked her.

"No." She crossed her arms in a defensive posture. "I heard about it in gym class. Clark, I don't mean to be rude, but I've got, like, twenty minutes to finish this thing."

"Sure." He rose. "Call you tonight?"

"Sure." She flashed him a smile . . . which slipped a little as he walked past her.

"Take care," he said softly.

By the time he had left the office, Chloe was crying.

About an hour later, she left the school grounds. Now she stood before Smallville Juvenile Hall, a place she had never been before, and would never have imagined she would ever visit. It was a cheerless place, everything decorated in industrial gray and pale green.

She didn't know what she would say to Marshall. She wasn't sure she should even be there. But she had given her name at the desk with the full understanding that if Marshall didn't want to talk to her, he didn't have to.

The guard walking beside her was stern and unsmiling, and Chloe swallowed nervously as they came to a fork in the hallway, and he said, "He'll come through there. You'll sit in there."

He pointed to a door at right angles with another door. Both looked thick, and both featured a small square of glass in the center with chicken-wire-like mesh embedded in it. Chloe peered through the square to her right but saw nothing beyond it but another door.

Then the guard unlocked the door in front of her, and she went into a small room, dimly lit with fluorescent lights and featuring a single metal table and two folding chairs, one on either side.

At the guard's nod, she sat in the chair on the other side of the table, facing the door, and folded her hands in front of her. She had not been allowed to bring her purse with her—it had been checked into a locker—and the withdrawal of even that little bit of freedom hit home. Marshall was in a detention facility, and he was in trouble.

So she had come to see him. She just didn't know if it was to make herself feel better or to actually help.

The guard said nothing more to her, only walked to the door they had come through and opened it. He spoke to someone in the hall, then he came back into the room and stood against the wall. He looked a little tired, and when he saw her glancing at him, he smiled.

"You'll be safe," he assured her.

She shifted in her chair, "thank you" not quite managing to make it past her lips.

Then the door opened again, and Marshall came in.

He was escorted by another unsmiling man, and he was wearing handcuffs.

Chloe was shocked. She half rose, holding out a hand, but Marshall either ignored it or didn't see it. His eyes were blank. There was no life there, no emotion.

No anger, no hope.

He shuffled to his chair and sat down. He stared blankly at her, as if he had no idea who she was.

"Hey," she said, leaning forward on the table. "Marshall, I . . . how are you?"

He made no response, had no reaction. She might as well have been speaking to him in a foreign language.

"Is there anything I can do?" she asked.

He stared at her. The silence between them was unnerving.

After about a minute, she rose to go.

"My mom," he blurted. "The only reason I'm hanging on . . ." The despair on his face cut her into pieces. "I'm not mad at you anymore, Chloe. I'm . . . nothing."

Her eyes welled. "Marshall," she said, "I can't pretend that I know how you feel because nothing this terrible has ever happened to me. I don't want your forgiveness because . . . because I don't deserve it." She started crying. "I'm so sorry."

He sighed and inclined his head. "It's not your fault. It was nobody's fault. Just a bunch of bad dominoes." He laughed miserably. "That's what's happened to my family."

"Oh, God."

He said nothing more. After a few minutes, the guard crossed to her side, and said, "It's time to go, miss."

Nodding, she rose, glancing up at Marshall through her lashes, hoping he would say something, anything.

But he didn't.

The guard walked her back to the main desk, where the intake clerk had her sign for her purse.

"It's post-traumatic stress disorder," the guard said to her, as she started to leave. "It could go away, or it could haunt him for a long time. He's gotta talk about it, not keep it bottled up the way he's doing." He sighed and scratched the back of his neck. "I've seen kids come in with bad situations. But this . . . this is *bad* bad."

"It's my fault," she said under her breath. He didn't hear her.

"But the doc says he's gotta let it out, or else he's gonna be stuck with it for the rest of his life." He tapped his head. "He'll just relive it over and over. He'll be in hell."

"He needs to bear witness," Chloe murmured. "Maybe he just needs someone who's listening."

She walked back out into her life. She had no idea what she had hoped to accomplish, but she hadn't managed it.

After school, Rebecca Morhaim came to Chloe, and said, "I think it's time for you to show me the Wall of Weird like you were talking about on my first day here. Because weird things are going on in my life, and I don't know what's really happening and what's not anymore."

"Hey, that's *my* life you're talking about," Chloe said wryly. "Sure. I'll show you."

She moved from her computer desk to the wall where she kept a running clipping service on all the many — many, many — strange things that had happened in Smallville since the meteor shower thirteen years before. As Rebecca gaped, Chloe showed her the guy who had turned into a giant insect, and the plants that grew too fast, and the guy who had killed girls by draining the warmth right out of their bodies. There were hundreds of articles, some with red circles on them, others with penciled notes such as, "For Chloe."

Rebecca stared at it all in total disbelief. Then she said, "So, a lot of things happen here that . . . might not happen anywhere else."

"Nicely put," Chloe drawled.

"Okay." Rebecca's voice sounded small and confused. "Okay."

The new girl turned and left, leaving Chloe speechless.

The thief liked the coffeehouse called the Talon. He liked sitting among the young people; they were all shiny and eager to savor life; they hadn't yet made their big mistakes. Youth truly was wasted on the young.

Mine was wasted in prison.

He did not hold with what his father had liked to say before he'd died three years ago, and that was that getting put away for a decade was probably the only thing that had saved his son's life.

"You were doomed," the old man liked to say. "Born bad. Don't know how, don't know why, but I know it."

When the old man died, the thief did not even shed a tear.

On the table sat a paper bag, and in the bag, what remained of the formula in the vial.

As soon as his business in Smallville was concluded, the thief planned to move to New York, hook up with a chemist he knew, and have some more mixed up. He wasn't sure what he would do after that. Making plans wouldn't be as crucial as they had been up till now.

I'm almost finished here. I've confirmed that my old friend has moved here, and I'm positive it's because the jewels are here. I'm not leaving here without the spoils of war—the bounty we plucked from that jewelry store could set me up for life.

Eleven and a half years, and the bastard's going to pay, that's for sure. With interest.

The thief's name was Jason Littleton, and he had been a member of the gang that had been found guilty of robbing Le Trésor back in Metropolis. Tom Morhaim, now newly relocated in Smallville, had been part of that same gang. However, Jason had also been found guilty of shooting Lee Hinchberger, the security guard who was now poppin' wheelies in a wheelchair.

And that Jason had not done. *I never so much as touched Hinchberger.*

Ol' Tom had pinned that on him, turned witness for the prosecution in return for a lighter sentence, and his accusations had stuck.

Jason had been sentenced to twenty-five years, and the only reason he was out now was exemplary behavior and an excellent lawyer, who managed to get one of his many appeals to go through. With some doubt cast on the legal niceties of various aspects of his case, the courts had decided to cut him loose after eleven and a half years.

Tom had done his full ten, big deal, and now he was here in this tiny town, trying to make a go of it as a decent citizen.

Jason had initially come to Smallville to confront Tom and make him spill his guts about where he had stashed the jewels. He'd gotten a little distracted when he'd learned that Lex Luthor lived here and had decided to try to rob him just for yucks. That was the night the girl had told Luthor about the doctored fertilizer.

It had been so easy to sneak into her room, lift the package, and take it to Shaky. Frighteningly so. Crime paid, that was for sure. All you had to do was be willing to take a few risks. It was like pitching baseball: one over, one under, one on. Try enough things for a long enough time, and something was bound to pay off.

But now, all he had to do was feed Tom some zombie potion, get him to show him where the jewels were, and take them.

Then Tom will never see me again. Of course, he'll never see anybody again. Cuz I'm gonna tell him to walk in front of a bus, same as I told Willie Thorpe.

Jason smiled at the prospect. Then he returned to reading a science fiction novel. He loved science fiction. It was like his own life.

He sat there reading for another ten or fifteen minutes, when a nice-looking kid about sixteen or so came over and said, "Mind if I grab some sugar packets?"

"Help yourself," Jason said easily.

The kid did so, smiling his thanks. Then he went back to a table a few feet away and dumped them into a large cup of coffee.

Jason's pretty brunette waitress came over to the kid's table with a coffeepot in hand, and said, "Pete, is your Uncle Howard still at your house?"

The kid—Pete—laughed ruefully, and said, "Oh, yeah. He's made some friends at the Pizza Palace. They're going to start playing poker together on Tuesdays. This not being Tuesday, he's home at my house for dinner." Pete sighed. "It's hard to concentrate on my homework with all his talking."

"And so you're staying with us for a while tonight," the girl said.

"Hope you don't mind, Lana," Pete replied. "I'm taking up a table."

"Of course not. And there are plenty of tables," she said generously. "Here, let me freshen that." She poured Pete some more coffee. He took an appreciative sip.

Jason went back to his novel.

Then Pete got up and moved toward the bathroom, and Jason realized that he had been at the Talon almost as long as the kid. That sharp little waitress—Lana—was bound to have noticed him. She would be able to describe him to the police if it ever came to that.

Tall guy, dark, hair with gray in it, just sat in here forever, reading . . .

He closed the book and picked up the sack. Then he headed out the door, not a care in the world.

I don't feel so good . . .

Pete staggered into the men's room, which was deserted. Sweat was pouring off his forehead; his stomach was a churning sea of acid. Then he started to shake. Hard. Harder.

He fell onto the floor and hit his head on the tile.

Again, and again, and again.

The world turned inside out, and Pete with it; he was having convulsions. Every bit of him was contracting, releasing; he was slamming his head, slamming it, slamming it.

Harder.

Then he went somewhere else very far away; somewhere deep inside himself.

CHAPTER SEVENTEEN

From his office in Metropolis at the very apex of his building, his view a sprawling vista of the city, Lionel Luthor connected to his call via the secure line, and said, "Yes, General?"

"We have a situation," the man said without preamble. Lionel appreciated the fact that General Montgomery was not using names on the phone. As sure as he was of his own security measures, it never hurt to be careful.

Something his son, Lex, had yet to learn.

"Our operative at the plant feels that it's time to remove the *item* from its present location and take it to another holding facility," the general went on. "Do we have your consent to do so?"

Lionel frowned. He was being cut out of the loop. "Have you figured out who took the sample from the girl?"

There was a pause. Then the military man said, "That's a negative, sir."

"Which is why you want to relocate the *item*," Lionel drawled, not without some sarcasm in his voice. He was furious: the future of the Project was at stake, and all because the government had been unable to stop this Marica Lopez from seeking refuge at Lex's Smallville home. Lionel and his military partners concurred that Lex had probably heard all about the Project from her by now. The question now was, did he believe her?

He probably does. He's probably fallen in love with her. Men in love will believe anything. He grinned wolfishly as he flipped open Maria del Carmen Maldonaldo Lopez's dossier from a stack of documents on his desk and admired her photograph. She *was* stunning.

The *item* General Montgomery was referring to was the rest of the specially processed fertilizer destined for the secret facility in Haiti, where the government was testing its effectiveness for combat. It was being stored in Lex's warehouse, right under his ignorant and intolerably lax nose. Originally, Lionel had considered letting Lex in on the Project, but decided against it. Lex had a strange moral streak. Sometimes it operated, and sometimes it didn't.

He usually manages to ignore it if my life is in jeopardy, he thought dryly.

But Lex had no particular need to know about the Project, so Lionel had decided to keep it to himself.

"Sir?" The general asked impatiently. "Your permission to extract the item?"

"Covertly," Lionel said. "No fuss."

"Of course not. Thank you, sir."

The general disconnected. Lionel did the same.

Back to work, he thought, moving from the Lopez dossier to a medical report, paging through to the conclusions section. It concerned a drug trial that was being held with two of the subjects having been recruited in Smallville. *Ah, our experimental MS drug looks promising. That's good.* He gazed off in the distance and smiled. *That might eventually give our stock a bump.*

I'll let the governor know we've had some good news. He might want a chance to get in on the action.

Appreciative politicians are a great corporate asset.

Humming to himself, he picked up the phone.

T. T. Van De Ven had been put back into play. Now he crouched outside the LuthorCorp fertilizer warehouse on the grounds of the Luthor mansion with his team of agents, waiting. He was frustrated, though not surprised, to discover that Lex Luthor had posted extra guards at the warehouse, making a quiet extraction far more difficult.

It was one of several frustrations. He'd located the Lopez girl, but she was sticking close to Lex Luthor, and Van De Ven had been ordered to keep out of the younger Luthor's crosshairs. Since she'd lost possession of the fertilizer that he'd originally been sent to retrieve, she was less of a priority target, but he figured that eventually she would have to be eliminated. She had seen too much back in Haiti to be left alive.

There was one more shipment of doped fertilizer destined for Haiti. Ten crates had already been misaddressed for shipment to a US naval base in Japan by Norman Wilcox, a Project field operative working undercover at the plant. Without the crates, there would be no more tangible evidence, nothing to link LuthorCorp with the Project. If that was what Van De Ven's superiors wanted, that's what he would deliver.

Since it had to be done, it was going to be done by the best.

Van De Ven grinned in the darkness and commed a line-of-site infrared message to the next commando over.

"Five."

He loved this kind of work. It was the mission that made it exciting, the obstacles to overcome. The end result didn't matter to him—he wasn't a big-picture guy. Action was what kept him loving life.

Wilcox had fed him the pertinent data, and Van De Ven was pleased to see that the field operative had been thorough and correct. As he had reported to their superiors, Lex Luthor had gone for redundant systems in a big way. Rather than simply relying on a high-tech sensor net, Lex had employed dozens of guards walking the perimeter, interior, and hallways of his building, which was smart—there were very few devices that would fool a human's senses, but plenty that would confound a machine's.

The strength of all that human security of course, was also its weakness. People got tired and bored, and didn't pay attention all the time. So Lex had compromised, maybe while he waited for even more security personnel to arrive: Each of the guards carried a transmitter which acted like a mini GPS, mapping him into a grid. A team of three watchers kept track of the grid in a small anteroom near the warehouse rest rooms. Wilcox had provided a secretly taken photograph of the room, showing the three men seated at their monitors, making sure that too many of the guards didn't congregate in one place at one time, and that they all kept walking their territory.

If one person stopped moving, or moved out of their established pattern, the guys in the anteroom had been trained to assume that the system had been compromised.

The key to the mission was unobserved infiltration. He and his men would have to get inside and reach the anteroom without being detected.

In an ideal world they'd then take the fertilizer without ever being seen.

But in this one, they had to move ten huge crates of fertilizer. This was not something he or his men could tuck under their arms. So once the trio in the tower was out, they'd have to knock out the roving guards and load up a truck.

Bigger challenge equals more excitement.

The IR receiver in his ear clicked twice, and he commed a reply of a single click. Time to go.

He and his men moved like black shadows across the LuthorCorp landscaping. A drainpipe on the east wall that was well out of the range of the huge floodlights illuminating the lawn provided easy access for Van De Ven to scale the wall.

Just like having a ladder.

He scaled the pipe quickly, and was soon on the roof.

A series of magnetic alarm sensors ringed one of the air vents; in seconds Van De Ven disarmed them, had the vent off, and was sliding down a rope onto a crossbeam.

He took a long moment to examine the room he was in; night-vision goggles gave him an edge than he might not have otherwise had.

He could see two guards from where he was, and in the far corner of the warehouse he could see the upstairs room that the security team used for tracking everyone.

He couldn't see all of the guards, of course—the warehouse was too big.

But the number he did spot was enough.

The rest of his team were each set to locate a guard and track him. Once he'd taken out the three watchers, they had been ordered to put the guards out.

Van De Ven took a small device from his equipment belt and aimed it at the ceiling between where he was and where the office was.

Pop! There was the sound of a compressed air charge, and the camera was on its way.

A buddy of his had designed the thing after seeing it in a *video game* of all things. The brass had checked it out, loved it, and "appropriated" it.

The tiny solid-state camera he'd fired thumped into the ceiling and stuck, the quickset putty surrounding it activated by the impact.

Van De Ven tapped a switch on the side of his night-vision goggles and his left eye screen displayed what the camera was seeing—a fish-eye view of the entire area between himself and the control room.

Perfect.

Now he could choose his route to the control room. It was like having his own personal satellite.

Van De Ven worked his way across the rafters carefully. The problem at this height wasn't so much the noise, but the dust. He had to work carefully, trying to keep himself away from intersecting paths with the security guards, lest a dust bunny and a sneeze give the game away.

But the camera made it easy.

He slid along the rafters like a black panther in the trees, stealthy, quiet. Within a few minutes he was over the control room. He lowered himself into position, ready to go in.

He checked his watch. *Excellent. Right on time.* The rest of the team should be in place. He toggled the microphone on his regular radio, letting the rest of them know he was going in, and opened the door quickly, stepping inside.

Phat-phat-phat.

The tranquilizer gun he was carrying was a repeater, holding five shots. Fortunately he only needed the three. The curare-based knockout drug was fast and efficient, and the three men dropped like felled apes. He tapped his mic three times; the signal to take out the rest of the guards.

It had gone well. Only one of them, the one who had been walking between the two monitors, had a chance to react before he fell over.

Walking? Why is he walking?

Too late, Van De Ven thought about what having only two monitors meant. He rushed over to the fallen guard and opened his shirt.

Damn. The homing devices worn by the guards on the floor were also worn by the ones up top. Which meant that one of the guards below had probably triggered an alarm before he was taken.

Van De Ven reached up on his equipment belt and uncovered a transmitter secured with Velcro.

In his research for the mission, he'd learned that all the alarm wires going from the plant ran to the local sheriff's office—not too unusual. But what *was* unusual was that before running to the sheriff's, they all ran through Lex Luthor's mansion. There, the billionaire's son could decide what calls the sheriff took, and which ones he might have taken care of . . . by other means.

Van De Ven had planned appropriately. Now he toggled the mic on his radio again.

"Look sharp. Secondary alarm got sent, but I'm taking steps to slow a response. We've got at least ten or fifteen."

He activated the transmitter's power, then pressed a red button. Miles away, the coded radio signature activated two thermite bombs he'd laid near the comms box for the mansion. Things were going to get hot for old Lex for a while.

That ought to keep him busy.

◆◆◆

Unable to sleep, Clark was looking at the stars, which were sparkling and shimmering in the sky like fireflies. He'd read that in space, stars and nebula clusters had colors; he could almost see pinks and turquoises, purples and greens.

He'd always been fascinated by the stars, even before he knew of his own origins. They were incredible glimmering fires high in the sky, on a tapestry of black velvet, so rich you wanted to touch it.

Smallville skies were broad and clear, and the night air was fresh. The world smelled good and hopeful. He couldn't say the same about Metropolis, where the lights on the skyscrapers and streetlamps competed with the stars for brilliance. Exhaust lingered in the big-city air, and there was never a sense of peace there. Busy town, busy people. Same sky, different perspective.

Clark wondered sometimes—like now—what the night sky might be like where he came from. How many moons were there? Was Earth among the pinpoints of light piercing an indigo sky? Did meteor showers pummel the landscape? Did people there stare through their equivalent of telescopes and stargaze, as he did?

Did anyone watch his adopted planet at nighttime, and wonder how he was? And miss him?

He asked these questions in his heart, not speaking them aloud. If there were answers to be found among the stars, they kept them to themselves in utter, serene silence.

He sighed. Silence was not golden. It was frustrating. He felt isolated by the silence of the stars; it punctuated the fact that he was alone on this world, not in the sense of not being welcome, but because he was the only one of his kind. At least that he knew of. If there were other people who had arrived on Earth in spaceships, they, like he, were concealing their identities.

Keeping silent.

He sighed and stretched, moving away from the telescope as he mulled over the events of the past few days. So much had happened . . . and a lot of it was centered around silence. Chloe, accidentally telling the Marshall family's secret. Lex, essentially wanting Pete to suppress the information in his report. And the new girl, Rebecca . . . he was sure she had stories she wasn't telling.

Sometimes it felt as if a secret were nearly the same thing as a lie. He often watched Chloe and Lana exchanging information as if it were some kind of currency, or a present. As far as he could tell, the way girls bonded was through sharing secrets. There were code words: "Don't tell anyone, but . . ." and "This is just between us, okay?" The surest way for one girl to lose a friendship was to violate that trust by sharing a confidence with someone who was not authorized to know.

Breaking silence.

Then he heard a muffled *crump*. Instantly, he knew it wasn't a farm sound or anything that he'd heard before, for that matter. He strained his ears, and listened, directing his focus in the direction from which he'd heard the sound come.

Boom!

Louder this time. And now it sounded more familiar—like that time the gas tank blew up in Pete's car . . .

It was coming from the direction of the Luthor Mansion.

Trouble. I wonder what Lex is up to now?

But even as he thought the words, he was in motion, zooming down the stairs, across the fields, and running to make sure his friend was all right.

As he raced in a blur, Clark tried to think how he could explain his presence to Lex. It was late—past midnight—and a school night as well. What could he say?

Ah, I was just driving by . . .

Why would he be out driving? Getting feed for the animals?

Yeah, Clark, from all the midnight feed stores.

Maybe he could say he was taking a walk.

Sure. Past midnight, on my way to spy on Lex at the mansion.

As he neared the mansion, he could see flames running up the side of the north wall. A window exploded, and a shower of sparks danced along where the sill would have been. One of the gutters broke loose and crashed into a row of bushes beneath it. Smoke boiled up like steam; the sky was blanketed with haze. Crackling bushes shivered as they burned, the energy from the heat making them tremble. The smell of smoke permeated every pore of Clark's body.

Picking up speed, Clark looked hard at the mansion, using his X-ray vision to find people inside.

There.

Two people—Lex and a female—were flailing their arms near the top of the second floor. It was clear they were in distress, shambling through the room, then finding one another and clinging together. The female started to fall, and Lex grabbed her up in his arms and tried to carry her. But he staggered forward, then fell to his knees. Weakening, he lowered the woman to the floor and sagged over her inert form.

Without another thought, Clark dived into the smoke. He worked his way up the stairs, using his X-ray vision to check each step before putting his feet down. He had to go slow or risk missing a hazard.

It was *hot*. His clothes grew singed at the edges, and the air in his lungs grew warm and uncomfortable. Yet he didn't get hurt.

His X-ray vision guided him as he dodged a falling piece of banister. A mirror on the wall shattered, the shards bouncing off him. A wall sconce followed suit.

Nothing slowed him down.

Hold on, Lex, he thought. *I'm on my way.*

Pushing a large chunk of burning wood from his path, he bounded up to the last stair and stepped up to the landing. Flames leaped around him on all sides, orange and red and reddish black, and the air was choked with smoke. He tried to buffet it out of his way, but there was too much of it; it was like pushing at row upon row of blankets strung out across clotheslines.

As he'd been instructed in school years before, Clark knelt on the ground and breathed, unsure if there was a point at which the smoke would be too much for even him. If he had properly surveyed the mansion—and properly visualized the layout in his mind— Lex should be ahead in the next room. Clark moved forward, waving his arms at superspeed, trying again to disperse the smoke out of the narrow corridor area.

Instead his actions fanned the flames, making them burn brighter. The roar around him was startling, but he remained focused.

What if it's too late? he thought. *Bad things are happening everywhere. What if this is one more horrible tragedy?*

He couldn't imagine it.

Scanning once more, he managed to locate Lex behind the next door to his right. He made a fist and slammed it hard on the burning wood. The door fell inward, sending fire and sparks upward.

Clark crawled over the fallen door, ignoring the fact that his clothes were burning. He ignored everything except the fact that his friend was in this room, and he had to save him.

Then he found them. Like two people in a sinking rowboat, they were sprawled on what was just about the only piece of flooring in the room that was not on fire. Lex was curled protectively around an attractive woman with short, dark hair, and both of them were unconscious. Lex looked flushed, and his breathing was shallow. Clark looked deeper, and saw his friend's heartbeat. It was slow, but still regular.

Clark tried to decide what to do. He used his X-ray vision to examine the rest of the mansion, and found, to his surprise, that the room beneath this one was undamaged. He had no idea why, but he could use that to his advantage.

Clark stepped back and used his heat vision to blast an irregular hole in the center of the room, far enough from Lex so that if the wood cracked, it would not weaken the surface beneath Lex and the woman. Then Clark stomped on the floor, driving his leg into it like an axe into a melon. Wood splintered all around him, and he drove the flat of his hand down on it, ripping crossbeams into pieces and shattering subflooring.

There was a cracking and splintering like a hundred branches simultaneously; pieces of wood flew through the air, some catching on fire immediately.

But there was a hole now, a cool, beckoning escape hatch. But pieces of the wood he'd driven through the floor had started to catch fire downstairs. He'd have to move fast.

Clark scooped his friend and the woman up and jumped through, his muscles absorbing the impact easily. He hoped they would be all right as well.

Then he realized he had landed in some kind of tile-enclosed room, something like a bunker, and figured it for one of the many secret places he did not know about in Lex's house. Then he realized that it was really a workout room, which was equipped with a sink, and a pile of fresh white towels; using his superspeed, he soaked them and raced them over to Lex and the woman. He covered them completely, squeezing water from the towels over their hot skin. Then he hoisted them both over his shoulders.

He kicked open the door; the fire raged outside. The only thing he could think to do was to use his superspeed, dashing as fast as he could so that the wet towels would protect Lex and the woman.

Once outside, he laid them on the grass well outside Lex's

mansion. Then he looked down at himself and saw that his clothes had burned so badly that it would be difficult to explain why he himself wasn't injured at all. He thought for a moment, then dashed back through the house and into the tiled room, where, searching through the cabinets in seconds, he located a nondescript pair of gray sweats and a gray sweatshirt. He contracted around them like a quarterback carrying the ball, then dressed in a flash on the lawn, dumping his clothes in the burning bushes.

Then he saw Drew, Lex's assistant, who had not seen him. The man sat on the ground with his head between his legs, coughing hard.

"Hey." Clark crouched down beside him. "You okay?"

"Is Lex all right?" the man asked anxiously.

"Yes. And his . . . friend, too," Clark told him.

Drew closed his eyes. "Thank God. I've called for help," Drew announced, holding up a cell phone. "Did everyone get out? Have you seen any other staff? We have a new security team. There should be six more people inside the house, four security men, my assistant, and the cook."

Clark looked around. In the glow of the house, he saw a huddle of four men in black suits helping a fifth walk among them across the grass. A woman in a bathrobe stumbled along beside them, looking shell-shocked.

"There," he said, pointing to them. "All accounted for."

"Good." Drew slowly got to his feet. "I'll see how everyone's doing."

Forcing himself to move at normal speed, Clark raced back to Lex's side. After a few seconds a bedraggled-looking Lex flicked open his eyes and stared up at him.

"What happened?" Clark asked him.

Lex squinted. "Clark?"

"Hey." He put his hands in the pockets of the sweatpants. "I happened to be in the neighborhood . . ."

His friend grinned weakly. "Uh-huh."

"Seriously," Clark said. "There was this . . . school event, and . . ."

The woman was slowly stirring; that drew Lex's attention away from his feeble explanation.

Then the pretty woman rolled over onto her side and stared at the fire.

"They did it," she said. "Oh, merciful Mother of Heaven, they did it."

"They . . . ?" Clark asked leadingly.

Lex sighed heavily. "Clark, I think there's something you should know."

◆◆◆

Lionel Luthor had been rereading *The Art of War* with a nice glass of burgundy at his bedside in his Metropolis penthouse apartment when the phone rang.

"Sir," a voice said, "there's been a . . . development."

It was General Montgomery again. Lionel listened in stunned silence as the man on the other end described how the "covert" mission to steal a few crates of fertilizer from Lex's warehouse had resulted in half the mansion being destroyed. Though he was relieved to hear that his son was all right, he was outraged by the clumsiness of Project personnel.

"You know this isn't good," Lionel bit off.

"We're aware of that, sir. We're taking steps."

"Roll some heads," Lionel cut in. "Especially the moron who conducted this 'operation.' And get me out of this mess."

He slammed down the phone.

◆◆◆

Surrounded by his own security team, Lex and his guest, Marica Lopez, were treated at the hospital. Unlike anyone else in the ER, the two were escorted to a private room, where doctors and nurses hurried in and out, running tests no one else would have received.

Clark called his father, who drove over; there was some fumbling between father and son about how each of them had managed to have the truck at the same time—Clark had originally told Lex he'd left his truck on the grounds of the mansion when he'd accompanied him and Marica to the hospital in one of the ambulances dispatched to the Luthor compound, but now here was Jonathan saying he had the truck.

". . . because I borrowed it from the Rosses, so we'd have two cars while Martha was here in the hospital," Jonathan finished smoothly, and Clark was taken aback by how smoothly the lie rolled off his father's lips.

After Lex and his friend Marica told Clark and his father everything they could about the fertilizer, they discussed the zombie sightings around town.

Marica had looked at Jonathan Kent, and said, "Whoever stole the sample knew what to do with it. How banal, to create zombies to commit more burglaries."

"It does speak of an unimaginative mind," Lex agreed.

The two smiled at each other, and Clark saw that they were very attracted to each other. Despite the situation they all found themselves in, Clark was touched.

There's all this weirdness and death in the air, but love, too.

Then the two Kent men left together.

"This is all getting very strange," Jonathan said, and Clark found himself bursting out laughing. Sometimes his father had quite the gift for understatement . . .

His father looked at him, then started laughing, too.

It had been a long—*very long*—night.

As Lex and Marica discussed what to do—and where to go— Lex's cell phone rang. It was his father.

"Dad. Yes, hello," Lex said sarcastically. "I'm alive. Is that good news or bad news?"

"Heard you had some trouble down there," Lionel said. "I'm on my way."

"Oh, gee, Dad, want to finish the job they bungled?"

"Don't be an idiot."

Lionel Luthor hung up.

The next day after school, Rebecca went to see Chloe in the *Torch* office, determined to tell her about her father. She was more and more troubled about what was happening. But just as Chloe looked up from her computer screen and smiled at her, Clark Kent strode in.

He saw Rebecca and smiled, then turned to Chloe and said, "If this is a bad time . . ."

"Oh, I was just going," Rebecca murmured.

"No, that's okay," Clark cut in. "I didn't mean that I didn't want to talk in front of you." He came into the office. "Chloe, Lex told me there's some kind of weird fertilizer out there that turns people . . ." He glanced at Rebecca again.

"Go ahead, Clark," Chloe said. "It's all right. Rebecca has been fully initiated into the fact that Smallville is the Twilight Zone." Rebecca nodded.

Clark got down to it. "There's a woman staying with Lex who used to work for a relief project in Haiti. She says LuthorCorp fertilizer turned people into zombies."

The two girls stared at him.

"Her name is Maria del Carmen, but Lex calls her Marica," he continued. "She's terrified. She came to Lex to make him stop the project. They think Lex's mansion was set on fire to kill her."

"What?" Chloe asked, shocked. "Fire? I didn't hear about a fire!" Then, perhaps realizing that she sounded a little callous, she added, "Are they all right?"

"Yes. They had to be treated for smoke inhalation, but they were really lucky," Clark said.

"Zombies from fertilizer?" Rebecca said slowly.

Chloe raised her brows. "There's a new one. And I thought only homework could turn you into a zombie." When neither Rebecca nor Clark responded, she added, "Well, that's certainly Wall of Weird material. And so ripe for sophomoric jokes. Did Lex get a sample analyzed?"

Clark shrugged. "That's the thing. Maria del Carmen—Marica—brought a sample with her for him to look at, but someone stole it."

"Stole it?" Rebecca asked shrilly. Chloe looked at her, and she, in turn, stared back at Chloe.

"In addition to weird people, Smallville does have plain old vanilla bad people," Chloe said to Rebecca. "Lex is rich, so he's a target." She cocked her head, thinking. "And I'll bet someone on his security staff just lost his job, if one of his guests got ripped off."

"Do you think her story's true?" Rebecca asked Clark.

"People have been seeing strangers around town who seem . . . wrong," Clark said. "I saw one."

Chloe nodded. "Could be zombies," she said. "Why not?"

"That's crazy," Rebecca blurted.

"That's Smallville," Chloe retorted, gesturing to the wall of clippings and photographs. "Okay," Chloe said, taking a seat behind her computer. "Let's do a little digging. What did you say her name was?"

"Maria del Carmen. Something and then Lopez."

"Clark," she said impatiently, looking up from her keyboard. "Lopez is as common in Spanish as Smith is in English."

"Sorry." He thought a minute. "I can't remember the rest of her name."

"I'll run it by Lex," Chloe said, then paused, and added, "if it's all right that I know?"

"I think so. I mean, it's pretty wide-open now," Clark replied.

"Well, I have to go to work," Rebecca said. She looked at Chloe. "See you there later, maybe?"

Chloe narrowed her eyes and cocked her head, studying the other girl with frank appraisal. "Everything all right, Rebecca?"

"Sure," she said quickly. "Fine."

Clark turned to Rebecca. "If you see Pete, please let him know I'm working on the implements report." He sighed. "He wrote a pretty harsh paper on the history of pesticides and fertilizers. Lex saw it. Not too happy about it."

"You should show it to your mom," Chloe said pointedly, "especially if it's true that she's in the hospital because of something she ate at his mansion. She'll enjoy a little light reading about the dangers of farming with chemicals."

"There's no proof of that," Clark said loyally.

"Well, I'm really glad that she's okay and that she's going home," Rebecca told him. Her heart leaped a little as he smiled at her.

He is so cute.

Rebecca and Clark both left, and Chloe started researching Maria del Carmen Lopez. Even as she typed in the name, she rolled her eyes, knowing that it was like looking for "Mary Smith" in the Anglo databases of the world.

Sure enough, there were one hundred GoogolPlex matches.

I should have asked for the name of the relief project. I'll make a note of that.

Then she decided to update her files on the Smallville burglaries. She typed in her favorite police files website . . . and sat back to wait for the information to start scrolling.

Then she frowned as a different window popped up . . . and she realized she had typed in the URL incorrectly. She began to hit DELETE, until she began to read the information that was scrolling down her screen: It was a list of people with convictions who lived in and around Smallville . . . and the name MORHAIM, TOM was prominent among them.

Huh?

Chloe didn't know if that was Rebecca's father's name, but she clicked on it and waited to see what popped up.

There were dozens of links, many to front-page stories in the Metropolis papers.

Astonished, Chloe kept clicking.

After only a few minutes, her eyes were bugging out.

Rebecca's father was a convicted felon. He had participated in the robbery of a Metropolis jewelry store, Le Trésor. A security guard had attempted to stop the heist, and he had been shot and wounded by one of Thomas Morhaim's partners—a man named Jason Littleton.

Chloe couldn't believe it. So she clicked on some of the accompanying photographs and studied them, linking up the names with the faces. The first one was of Thomas Morhaim and had been taken shortly after he'd been placed in custody. Then another one, after his trial and conviction. Then his sentencing . . .

. . . and there was a much younger Rebecca in the shot, waving plaintively to her father as he was taken away. The little girl was holding out her arms and crying.

"Oh, my God," Chloe murmured. "Poor Rebecca."

She kept reading the articles. There were pictures of Jason Littleton, a dark-haired man with spinning eyes. He looked mean. She could easily see him putting another man in a wheelchair for life.

Then she moved to more current articles, discovering that Thomas Morhaim had been released from prison about fifteen months ago. That was the end of the stories about him. He had been allowed to sink into relative obscurity.

And they moved here, and I know Rebecca does not want anyone to know this. In fact, I'm sorry I snooped. Too much information has plagued me lately.

She ran her fingers through her hair, not clear on her next move. There didn't seem to be any reason to tell anyone about this . . . not even Rebecca. If she didn't want anyone to know about her dad's past, far be it for Chloe to bring it up.

Or to let her know that I know. Poor girl . . . no wonder she's been acting kind of squirrelly. She wants friends. She's afraid that if we find this out, we won't want to hang out with her.

That's not true, at least not in my case.

So . . .

Chloe closed all the windows and deleted all the links. She powered down and pushed away the keyboard.

. . . My lips are sealed.

She rose and walked to the doorway of the *Torch* office, paused for a moment, then left for the Talon.

◆◆◆

Pete couldn't think, couldn't process. But deep inside him, his consciousness screamed in a constant state of terror, fully aware that something horrible had happened to him.

And so he ran; the adrenaline pumping through his body did horrible things, breaking down the zombie formula and sending it shooting through his body like dumdum bullets. Leaving wounds—by taking away, bit by bit, all the self-awareness that was Pete and leaving . . . something that very badly needed some direction.

He ran screaming, arms windmilling . . . and then he felt an all-consuming, ravening hunger.

He smelled meat and blood all around him.

He dove to the right, and then the left, hands grabbing at the fog in search of something to eat. He ran on, crazed, with no idea that he *was* running.

Part of his brain registered that he was on familiar ground; somewhere the word "friend" registered, but he couldn't put it into context.

Then he saw a figure in the distance.

Food, food, food, came the thought.

He ran toward it, mouth clacking.

When he heard the figure shout, "Pete!" he didn't even recognize his own name.

Clark had to pretend that he had struggled to get Pete bound and into his parents' truck, but he did not have to pretend he was beyond himself with worry as he delivered him to the grounds of Lex's mansion.

Lex and Marica had moved to a small outbuilding pending an investigation of the explosions and the fire. The authorities had asked Lex to leave the property, but he had refused. The compromise was the outbuilding, which he sometimes used to house out-of-town clients or business associates.

They put Pete in a sparsely furnished room. He was still bound, and there was nothing in his dead eyes but fury.

Marica was terrified of him, and Clark didn't blame her. She kept her distance, even from Clark, as if by association he was dangerous, too.

Lex escorted her into one of the two rooms he had had converted into bedrooms for himself and Marica. Drew had accomplished it in record time, and the bedrooms were actually more luxurious than the ones in the mansion, with elaborate wrought-iron headboards, Louis XIV armoires, and, for Marica, an exquisite dressing table.

"You see?" she demanded, as she whirled on Lex in her bedroom. "That guy is a bona fide zombie!"

"Yes, he is," Lex said slowly.

"Do you finally believe me?" she asked shrilly, her eyes brimming with tears.

He nodded. "I believed you before."

"Not entirely." She gave him a penetrating look. "You wanted to, but you weren't positive."

"No," he began, then chuckled softly. "You're right. But now I completely accept that it's real. And that guy is a good friend of Clark's." He sighed. "I apologize for doubting you."

Stymied, she shook her head. "If I had some of that sample left, perhaps we could try to figure out how to counteract it. But without any . . ." She ran her hands through her hair, then dropped them to her sides with a heavy sigh. "There may be more somewhere back in Cap du Roi. We had a lot of it. Dr. Ribero put only that small bit in the pack for me, so that I could carry it easily."

Clark, who had approached the threshold, made a note of that.

He said casually, "Cap du Roi. How do you spell that?"

She told him. Then she said, "What are we going to do? Perhaps we can analyze his blood chemistry."

"I have access to all kinds of experts," Lex offered. "And good lab facilities on-site in our production facility."

"*Bueno. Perfecto,*" she murmured. Clark could practically see her mind racing. "I'll extract some blood, start running panels . . ."

As she planned her strategy, Clark said to Lex, "I'll be in there with Pete," and turned around to go back to his friend.

But Pete was not in the room.

The front door of the outbuilding hung open.

"Pete!" Clark shouted.

He ran out of the building; on either side of a gravel path, four of Lex's security staff lay crumpled on the ground.

"Lex, stay inside!" Clark called to his friend. "Stay there!"

"What's happening?" Marica cried.

Clark bent over one of the guards. The man was still breathing.

Returning his vision to normal, he spied a clump of what looked like small feathers extending from the guard's suit jacket. Clark tugged at it, extracting a small dart.

Clark raced back inside, and said, "Pete's gone. The guards have been knocked out. Call for more help!"

And then he raced off in search of his friend.

With his X-ray vision, he scanned the area. He saw no other people around. No one hustling Pete into a car, no trucks, nothing. He was perplexed.

Then he looked up.

Against a black sky, a blacker shape moved in total silence. It was a helicopter, its blades whirring but making no noise. Focusing his X-ray vision, Clark saw four figures inside. One looked to be Pete, who was bound and gagged.

"Pete!" Clark shouted. "Stop!"

The helicopter rose higher into the sky, and whirred silently away.

Clark was still with Lex and Marica on the mansion grounds when Lionel Luthor appeared in the doorway. The billionaire was surrounded by drama, looming larger than life as he strode into the small building Lex had planned to stay in.

"Son," he said, by way of greeting, "don't you have fire sprinklers installed in the mansion? I specifically order—"

"Yes, I'm fine, Dad," Lex said coldly. He put a protective arm around Marica as she drew closer to him.

The movement drew Lionel's attention to her. "Hello. We haven't met."

She regarded him stonily.

"Don't play games, Dad," Lex said. "You know who she is. Did you come to see if she was still alive?"

Lionel's brows shot up. "Lex, I'm shocked. What are you trying to get at?"

Lex angrily held up his hand. "Pete Ross was just taken away in a stealth copter," Lex continued, "after the poison you helped create turned him into a zombie."

Lionel blinked at him. "Did you have this delusion awake or asleep?"

"Mr. Luthor, Pete is my friend," Clark said, stepping forward. "If anything has happened to him . . ."

Lionel tapped his chin. "One might argue that he will be returned to you good as new. If one knew anything about what was going on here."

"I don't believe you," Marica spat at him. Her dark eyes flashed with fury. "You're a liar and a murderer."

"Hmm. Ouch," Lionel said. He shrugged. "I've booked you into the Smallville Hotel, son. We'll both be in the Presidential Suite. You're welcome, too, of course," he said to Marica. "I believe your home is still intact, Clark?"

"We're staying here," Lex said, raising his chin.

"Here is not safe, son. Here blows up," Lionel replied. "Now, for the lady's sake at the very least . . ."

Lex scowled at his father. Then he smirked. "You've been reading *The Art of War* again, haven't you? I'm supposed to feel safer because you're with me. No one will try to hurt me because you'll be my human shield."

Lionel smiled pleasantly.

Lex glanced at Marica. He said, "He's right. We'll be safer with him."

She stared at him in utter astonishment and opened her mouth to protest. But Clark could see that she was at a loss to come up with an alternative plan.

"All right, then." Lex's voice was icy. "I want Pete Ross back, Dad. The way he was."

"Lex, I know you think I'm all-powerful. It's flattering, really. But if I were involved in such an all-encompassing government conspiracy, do you really think that I could snap my fingers and the entire Department of Defense would do my bidding?" Lionel intoned. He stepped aside, holding out his arm to indicate that Lex and Marica should leave the outbuilding. "We'll talk more in the limo."

As Marica walked past Clark, she turned to him, and whispered, "All the proof is disappearing. Soon I will, too. Help me."

◆◆◆

High above Smallville, T. T. Van De Ven spoke to his superior, General Montgomery, who said, "You have been ordered to stand down. Why are you still in the target location?"

"Sir, I located more . . . proof," Van De Ven said excitedly. "I have . . . living proof, sir. Someone has used the *item* to create that living proof. I captured that proof and it is with me now."

He looked over his shoulder at the young man who was straining at his restraints. He was completely wild. There was nothing human in his actions, no thought, nothing. "My God," the general murmured. "Someone has used the *item*."

"My thinking as well, sir." He paused. "Sir, permission to search the target location for more of the same." Before the general could refuse, he added, "Sir, I am on location and already familiar with the situation. I humbly suggest that I am the best man for the job."

The general sighed. "Permission granted."

Van De Ven nearly whooped with pleasure. He turned to the chopper pilot, and said, "We're going zombie hunting, Johnson."

The pilot smiled back at him. "Aces, sir."

◆◆◆

On the ground, Lionel Luthor seethed with fury. He would not tell his son that he had already demanded that he be given the antidote to the zombie-producing formula, and his request had been denied. He was outraged that he was being treated as a lesser player, and there was no reason Lex needed to know that. Not in a million lifetimes.

The best he could do to prevent that revelation was to hold his cards close to his chest and remain detached. Let Lex stew.

And let him and his beautiful new ally find the antidote themselves.

Then Lionel wouldn't *need* to go hat in hand—if ever he needed the antidote. He'd just get it from his son.

In an atlas in the smoky library of Lex's mansion, Clark found "Cap du Roi" on a map of Haiti.

Then he put on a burst of superspeed that bordered on supersonic, crossing the vast breadbasket of the Midwest, slogging through the swamps of Florida, and racing into the ocean. He swam, too, churning up so much water that he wondered if he looked like some kind of sea monster shooting through the ocean trenches.

The world all blurred past as he raced for the cure in Cap du Roi.

And then he was there.

Clark slowed himself down to what felt like less than a crawl and hunkered low in the darkness of a pale slivered moon, surrounded by the reedy stalks of a sugarcane field in Cap du Roi, opening his senses to the sights, sounds, and smells of this foreign place in an effort to get his bearings. The air felt hot and clammy on his skin, as if a giant, invisible velvet hand held him in its phantom grasp. He shivered in spite of the heat.

A gentle breeze blew, bringing with it the exotic scents of mango and bananas mingled with farm smells that he recognized from his father's and other farms around Smallville; only the dung of these cows, chickens, and other livestock had a more pungent odor than what he was used to. He also detected traces of exotic spices from recent meals and the ash-laden scent of smoldering cooking fires, underlain by the distinctive reek of burned wood, long since extinguished. He could tell by the depth and breadth of this last smell that it covered a large area. A cow bellowed in the distance, followed by the insistent bark of a dog.

Instinctively, he moved quickly through the fields toward the carbon smell of the old fire, skirting ramshackle shanty houses with tin roofs and dilapidated corrals. The bitter scent grew stronger until it overpowered everything else, then he emerged at the edge of a blackened clearing. He stepped gingerly over the charred, skeletal remains of a fence strung with the remnants of broken lights on melted wire just inside the perimeter and followed the fence line, finding sections of it untouched by the fire, all the while watching and listening for signs of activity within. He heard only the rustle, squeaks, and slithering of small animals.

Clark found a battered wooden sign in the bushes beside a dirt road and broken-down gate with the words *"Bien-venue AYUDO"* painted on it and decided to follow the dirt road into the center of the compound. Part of him felt an impatient urgency to rush in and move at high speed, but he made himself go slowly, taking in every detail he could; otherwise, he might miss some small detail that could lead him to the answers he had come here to find.

Dark piles that had been huts with broken frames lined the roads. Collapsed roof supports jutted from them at sharp angles, sticking out like jagged teeth. Many had broken, half-melted metal cot frames. Everything had been burned. No question, this had been intentional—and thorough. *More than burned wood stinks around here,* Clark thought.

The bigger buildings looked flattened under tin roofs. Clark nudged a pile of debris with his toe and turned over a piece of tin from the biggest building, but found nothing except pieces of scorched and partially liquefied metal lab benches and a couple of black, twisted instruments he recognized as microscopes. As Clark pushed aside a piece of tin at one of the smaller main buildings, a large lizard skittered out from under it, startling him. He spotted part of a melted plastic sack with the familiar LuthorCorp logo on it, but it was only a remnant.

No fertilizer.

That's it, he thought. *I've struck out. Dead end. No trace of anything. It's all been wiped out.* He closed his eyes and rubbed his temples, wondering what to do next, thinking that he had no choice but to go back to Smallville. Maybe there was something he had overlooked there. *Maybe I should talk to Lex . . .*

A plaintive, human-sounding screech pierced the air, followed by a chorus of others. Clark's breath caught, then he realized that the eerie sound came from the wild dogs that yipped at the moon. The tropical breeze picked up as if in answer, palm leaves rasped, and tree trunks swayed and moaned. The effect seemed to ripple outward, causing snakes to slither in the underbrush and other animals to scurry in all directions. Clark felt cool sweat trickling down his armpits.

Then the drums began.

He focused all his attention on his hearing, listening to the low, insistent, complex rhythms that beat in his ears in synch to his own heartbeat. The pounding grew in volume, sounding both longer and stronger. The combined effect of hearing and feeling the hypnotic rhythms filled him with a sense of foreboding, yet he felt drawn to investigate. Pinpointing the location of the drumbeats, he moved cautiously through the fields amidst a low, whispering wind that rattled cane stalks everywhere until he saw a glimmer of firelight coming from another clearing located a mile or so from the abandoned AYUDO compound.

Stopping to take it all in, he scanned the remaining distance between himself and the fire with the full sensitivity of his eyes and ears, checking every inch of the area before him to ensure that no one knew of his presence. He glanced up at the crescent moon looming high above, then, in a momentary flash, he sprinted to the base of a large palm that gave him a clear view of everything that went on in the clearing.

The air hung thick and still. A bonfire burned in the midst of a circle of palms that stood like sentinels, guarding the activity between them. Firelight flickered at the edges of the clearing, darkened from time to time by the formless shadows of the dancers moving around the fire in long, undulating movements. Rattles shook in unison with the drums, adding to the strange hypnotic feeling of hearing and seeing the drums as one.

Two men tossed a log on the fire, showering the night sky with a flurry of shimmering sparks while the tempo of the drums increased and the dancers quickened their pace. The flames jumped higher. A tall, muscular, dark-skinned, bare-chested man wearing a huge feathered headdress, flashing a multicolored

robe and a staff with a skull on it, danced wildly in erotic counterpoint to two women who ebbed and flowed with his motion
as if all were attached by an invisible cord. Sweat slicked their
bodies.

Both women wore nothing but long, flowing, brightly colored
scarves. One of them swayed in unison with the other, eyes
closed, a huge snake draped over her shoulders, around her
waist, and down one leg. Her eyelids fluttered open, revealing
white eyes rolled up in their sockets. Her mouth hung open, a
sensuous moan oozing from her lips. She seemed to drop lower
with each beat, her body shuddering as if physically struck with
each thump of the drum.

The second woman moved around her in stagger step, hopping
wildly, first on one foot, then the other, all the while holding a
chicken aloft by its feet, its wings frantically beating the air.
She danced and twirled around her partner like a mad dervish,
eyes closed, seemingly oblivious to anyone and everything
around her, except the constant pounding of the drums.

A ragged assemblage stood around them, it, too, appearing
polarized by opposing forces. On one side, behind the women,
a handful of spindly, bedraggled men and women swayed to the
music, their eyes wide with fear and amazement, and across
from them, behind the man, stood a group that looked even
more bedraggled than the first, only this group stood immobile,
their eyes fixed, staring straight ahead, glassy and emotionless.
Not everyone in this group was dark-skinned like the first. This
one had a few lighter-skinned foreigners, either Americans or
Europeans. Probably AYUDO workers.

The music, dancing, and drumming rose to a frenzied peak
that ratcheted the tension in the air to an almost painful crescendo,
then the woman with the chicken gave a sweeping, low dramatic
twirl that brought her close to the ground. A knife appeared in
her hand as if out of nowhere and in one graceful motion she
gathered the chicken to her breast and cut its throat, sending
blood spurting everywhere.

She let out a chilling cry that touched something deep inside
of Clark, making him feel cold at the core of his being, then
she held the chicken aloft again, showering herself and those

around her with its glistening blood while the bird beat its wings with renewed vigor and agitation.

The whole scene moved with the life of the bird, keeping the frenzied crescendo vital for a few short moments, then it ebbed with the chicken's life, dance and drum fading with each jerk of the fowl's death throes, until all fell silent. Without a word, the animated people behind the women departed to the left, leaving behind the dancers and their zombie charges.

Once they departed, a lone drummer beat a simple beat that galvanized the zombies. The male priest started down a path off to the right, and the zombies fell into single file, shuffling behind him in a swaying gait, followed by the two priestesses who took up the rear, leaving the bonfire unattended behind them.

Clark waited a few moments before following them, checking in front and behind with his heightened senses to make sure no one detected his presence, then he crept down the trail, keeping the sound of the single beating drum as his guide. They went a few hundred yards before he sensed the sound of the drum shifting. He paused, listening until it quickly faded into muffled silence.

Strange, he thought. *It never stopped. Just faded.* He went a few more steps, seeing nothing but a pile of rocks looming in the semidarkness ahead of him. He climbed on top of them and scanned his surroundings. Seeing nothing, he instinctively looked down through the rocks with his X-ray vision and saw a tunnel leading underground beneath him. Pressing an ear to the rocks, he heard the faint sound of the drum continue on for a few more beats before coming to a halt.

His first instinct was to push the rock aside, but he knew that if they had gone underground and disappeared that quickly, then it had to be mechanical, and if it was mechanical, it had to have some kind of alarm or monitoring system on it. If this was some kind of underground compound, it had to have ventilation. Once more, using his X-ray vision, he checked the ground up and down the path and to the sides, searching for another opening. Sure enough, a few dozen yards behind the rock and another ten or twenty off to the right of the path, he spotted a shaft that came up beneath a jagged palm stump. Clark went to it and discovered that it was in fact hollowed out with a vent grate riveted to its base. He heard voices, the crackle of walkie-talkies, the hum of electronics and other activity coming from the vent.

Gripping the grate with his fingers, he pulled up, slowly peeling it back from its frame. After setting it aside, he eased himself feetfirst into the shaft and worked his way down into the darkness below, controlling his descent by pressing his hands and feet against the sides of the vent shaft. About twenty feet down, he came to a T-section. He eased himself down into it and looked both ways. To his right it looked dark, and to his left he saw light. Dropping onto his chest, he crawled along its length on his belly until he came to another grate. He saw a string of lights running the length of a tunnel on the other side of it.

Working the fingers of one hand into the grate, he pushed out on its edges one corner at a time, wincing at the pop of each rivet. Once it came loose, he remained motionless for a few minutes, listening for any sign that he might have been discovered. When he felt confident that no one had heard him, he lowered himself from the vent into the tunnel and set the grate back in place.

He crept down the hall listening to the voices echoing up the corridor toward him.

"That show they put on is good enough for Vegas," a deep voice said.

"Hollywood," another said. "They definitely have these superstitious locals scared out of their gourds."

"They'll never come anywhere near here, that's for sure."

They both chuckled.

Clark pressed himself close to the wall at the end of the tunnel and peered into a big room. Two men in short-sleeved olive green T-shirts and cammo pants, each cradling a semiautomatic rifle, came walking right toward him, heading for the tunnel. He moved past them at high speed, flashing across the room to a spot behind a desk.

"Breeze coming down the tunnel," the deep-voiced one said after Clark had passed.

"We'd better get up there and check the perimeter," his partner answered. "After that security breach with that bleeding-heart

AYUDO woman, we need to keep a close eye on things. We're supposed to shift into phase three any day now."

Clark listened to their footsteps echoing up the tunnel, followed by the sound of hydraulics that he guessed to be the rock doorway sliding open and shut. Looking around, he saw that two airlock-type doorways led off from the room in two different directions. He went toward the one to his left, put his face to the door, and looked through it with his X-ray vision. He saw a wall full of electronic monitors, communication consoles, and computers. Two men manned workstations there. No sign of zombies or the priests and priestesses. They must have gone through the other doorway. Moving to it, he looked through and saw that it led to another corridor. He thought about forcing it open to get in, but feared he might set off some kind of alarm. How could he get in?

While he pondered his next move he heard more footsteps. Looking through the door, he saw another cammo-clad man approach. Clark stepped to the far side of the door and waited for it to open. As soon as the man stepped through, Clark slipped behind him at high speed and made his way down this second corridor, which brought him deeper underground, leading to a complex of rooms that made him think of the ant farms he had played with as a boy, only these ants had a darker purpose.

A horrid stench from one of the rooms assailed his nostrils. Turning his attention toward it, he heard shuffling feet and a strange chorus of wet sounds that went *click clack click clack*. Repelled by the stink and the sounds, yet drawn by curiosity, Clark went toward the room and peered in to see bars like a jail cell enclosing a roomful of zombies. The tall figure of a dark-skinned man, his face half-eaten away, with bulging eyes that looked glassy and empty clutched at the bars, as did others in various states of decomposition. Still others of different races and colors in better shape than the ones at the bars filled the room behind them.

As if sensing him by scent, they looked toward him with unseeing eyes. Arms and legs flopped and shuffled, as a host of drooling jagged toothed jaws moved with increasing frenzy.

Click clack click clack . . .

Followed by animal grunts, agonized moans, and gurgles that sounded far from human. Clark staggered backward in horror. *That's it,* he thought. *I've seen enough. No way I want any of those disgusting things even touching me!*

He backed away from the zombies and scanned the rest of the rooms with his X-ray vision. He saw men everywhere throughout the complex, all armed, carrying walkie-talkies, all dressed in the same military cammo uniforms. Computers had been networked throughout the tunnels and rooms housing command and control centers, and a stockpile of weapons, including semiautomatic rifles and handguns, mortars, grenades, and flamethrowers. Behind one of the doors just off of the room he stood in, he saw a storeroom piled with plastic sacks that had the familiar LuthorCorp logo on them.

Bingo.

He went to the closet, opened the door, and stepped in, closing the door behind him. A wave of nausea swept through him as soon as he entered.

What's happening to me? he thought. *Dizzy. My stomach. I didn't think those zombies spooked me that much.* He took a few deep breaths, but it didn't help. *Better get out of here, quick.*

Fighting the sudden impulse to vomit, he found one of the bags about an eighth full. Tying it into a knot, he wrapped his hand around it and backed out of the room, closing the door behind him. The nausea stayed with him, but the intensity of his sickness lessened some. He leaned against the wall outside the door and, with great effort, tried breathing deep again.

Don't know what's going on here, but I'd better get a move on and get as far away from here as I can.

He turned to run back up the tunnel at high speed. He still moved quicker than any normal man, but his arms and legs felt as though someone had wrapped them in soggy blankets. Every effort took extra willpower, and instead of gaining speed, he found himself slowing. Luckily, no one occupied the room between this tunnel and the last one. By the time he got to the loosened vent he felt winded and ready to vomit again, but this was not the place to slow down or be sick.

Easing the grate out, he tossed the bag ahead of him into the duct and took a moment to try and get his wind again. Sweat poured from him. He wiped it from his face with his sleeve and kept breathing deeply. This time it seemed to work, so he took a little extra time to let his strength return until his nausea diminished.

Whatever it was that made me sick down there, at least it's passing.

When he felt strong enough, he slid the vent grate sideways into the duct, hoisted himself up behind it, and slid into the duct feetfirst, working his way backward past the grate. Once past, he slid it toward the end of the vent until he could fit it back into its original spot, then he inched his way on his hands and knees, moving back toward the vertical shaft down which he had come.

Clark felt more nausea when he slid over the fertilizer bag, but it didn't come as strongly as it had the first time. Dragging the bag behind him, he reached the shaft that led up and out. Not wanting to waste any more time, he tied the bag to the front of his belt and started up the duct, pressing his hands and feet against the sides of the shaft the way he had coming down. He felt his strength diminishing the more he exerted himself with each bit of upward movement, followed by a second, slowly increasing attack of nausea. He barely made it out of the top of the shaft, where he tumbled to the ground in a cold sweat and shivers. Spots danced before his eyes, and he could barely move his arms and legs. Breathing shallowly, he fought to think clearly, trying to understand what was making him so sick.

I don't understand it, he thought, fighting back the darkness that threatened to swallow him. *I can barely move . . . barely breathe . . . no strength. The only things that ever made me sick like this were the meteorites! How in the world?* Blackness washed over him, but he battled it back. *How could it?* Another wave threatened to take him, then it hit him . . .

The fertilizer!

He fumbled with the bag at his belt, trying to untie it while strength ebbed from his whole body, especially his fingers. The more he willed them to move, the less they responded, and his vision blurred at the edges, compressing into a diminishing circle, as if he were being thrust into a narrowing tunnel.

Barely conscious, he loosened his belt, sliding the bag off of it until it fell beside him. He tried pushing it away, but didn't have the strength or the coordination to move any more. In his last moments of awareness, he managed to poke a hole in the side of the bag with the part of his belt buckle that went through the loop.

Green-tinged fertilizer spilled out.

Through a dreamlike reverie, Clark saw a Haitian woman wearing a long, flowing dress and a kerchief around her head appear as if from out of nowhere. She seemed to float toward him, making the sign of the cross over him when she drew close, then she smiled, flashing brilliant white teeth that stood out from the light brown skin of her face and took the bag of fertilizer from beside him, before rolling him over onto his back.

She made a gesture and two dark-skinned men hurried toward them. One took Clark under the shoulders and the other grabbed his feet, then they swiftly followed the brown-skinned woman through a grove of trees and across a few fields to an old shack where they laid Clark down.

"I am known as Mama Loa," she said with a Haitian-French accent.

Clark struggled to respond, but couldn't muster the strength to speak. She put a finger to his lips and her face grew serious.

"Don't try to move or speak right now. You need to get your strength back."

She made him sip a bitter liquid, then lit a cigar and blew smoke over him from head to foot. After shaking a rattle and stroking his head, arms and chest with a feather, she leaned in close.

"I was the head of the village until they came and changed everything," Mama Loa said. "They turned all of my people into zombies. I alone have escaped the Voodoo curse."

The drink jolted Clark wider awake. This wasn't a dream. The Haitian Voodoo woman with the bright dress was real, but she was helping him. She wasn't one of them.

"How did you find me?" he whispered.

"My guides told me you would come. They told me where to find you."

"Guides?"

She made the sign of the cross. "My spirit guides. My *loa*."

He gaped at her. "Um, ma'am . . . I'm not sure I believe in spirit guides."

She held her arms wide and smiled beatifically. "Magical beings are everywhere. Just because we cannot see them does not mean that they do not exist."

His strength and clarity were coming back more strongly by the moment, and, he had to admit, the drink she had given him seemed to help. "No disrespect intended, but I'm not sure I believe that magical beings told you where to find me."

She arched her eyebrows. "You are magical, are you not?"

Instantly on guard, Clark was at a loss for how to answer her.

She smiled. "What is magic but a result for which there is no discernible cause? Is it magic if I call upon my guides for help, but science if you are sent to Earth to help?"

He swallowed.

And she burst into delighted laughter.

Clark sat up under his own power, propped up against an angled plank that leaned against a wall inside the dilapidated shack. A brightly colored woven blanket covered him. Mama Loa's bitter tea had worked wonders, making his recovery swift. He still felt weakened, but the chills and fever had passed, and all of his faculties had returned. He no longer felt sick to his stomach. Now he sipped another tea that tasted like sweet berries.

Clark glanced around the shack, taking in his surroundings. A kerosene lamp burned in the corner. Bundles of herbs of different shapes and sizes hung from the rafters beneath a tin roof. A makeshift series of shelves constructed from warped boards covered one wall. Rows of glass jars with different-colored herbs and powders lined each one. A cot like the ones he'd seen at the AYUDO compound sat against another wall.

Outside, a rooster crowed. Clark looked out the open window

behind the shadowy form of Mama Loa, who worked over a stove that had been fashioned out of a fifty-five-gallon drum. The first indigo tinge of dawn glowed on the horizon below a scattering of stars. Mama Loa turned from a pot she had been stirring and grabbed a small three-legged stool before coming to where Clark sat. After putting a cool hand to his head to check his temperature, she nodded to herself, apparently satisfied, then placed the stool beside him and sat down.

"Your sickness has passed," she said. "Soon you will be all the way back to your old self. I have never seen the zombie powder affect anyone the way it sickened you. Its magic weakens your magic, which tells me just how much you are aligned with the beings of the light who watch over us. It is no wonder my guides told me of you. I know why you are here."

"I can't thank you enough for saving me," Clark said, feeling that his words fell far short of the gratitude he felt toward this enigmatic woman whose power and charisma extended far beyond her appearance. "I would have died there."

Mama Loa waved dismissively. Clark sensed a bit of self-deprecation in her demeanor.

"You would have done the same and more," she said. "The white light of the magic that guides you is an extension of the purity of your heart."

Clark felt embarrassed. He said, "I'm here to find out how to cure someone who's become a zombie."

Mama Loa made the sign of the cross and her eyes took on a faraway look. "Zombies have always been a way of life here. For generation after generation they have come in the night like ravenous dogs, preying on those who are caught unprepared and defenseless. I have tried all my life to stop their creation, but I have no idea how to do that." She put her face in her hands. "And now they have taken my Baby Loa," she whispered.

"There has to be a way to stop them," Clark insisted.

"They grow bolder with each passing day, and, with the distilled potion that this American technology brings, their numbers have grown and the plague that they are has become worse—and now these soldiers."

Clark heard himself say, "Between your magic and my magic we have to end this."

Mama Loa sat up straight, her features set in firm resolution. "The girl, Marie-Claire. She escaped, yes?"

Clark nodded. "Yes. She's in my hometown right now. These guys have been after her. She took a sample with her, but they stole it." *I would have known right away that one of the components was meteor-rock if I'd had a chance to see it.*

"Among other things, she knows a lot of chemistry. She has a university education. She may be able to prepare the antidote. I can help her. Can you put me in touch with her?"

"I don't know . . ."

"You have the magic," Mama Loa said quickly. "It is within your power."

"I don't know how I can do that. If I went to her, she'd know I've been here to Haiti," he told her. "Back where I live my powers are secret. I have to keep it that way to protect my family and those I love."

"I know that, young warrior," she assured him. "I will never tell anyone about you. You have my silence."

"Thank you," he said, relieved.

"Your carry your gift with reluctance," she observed, cocking her head as she studied him. "You will never be like other men. There is no antidote for that which has touched you. The breath of the gods lives in your lungs. Your life will go more smoothly if you look upon your special attributes with more warmth."

"I'll try," he promised her.

"And so, to work," she said. "I may have already lost those that I love," Mama Loa said forlornly. "The zombie plague has an evolution to it. As time passes the zombies get worse and worse until they thrash and moan and gnash their teeth in fevered madness, then they die."

Clark flashed back to the sound they had made with their teeth . . .

Click clack click clack . . .

"What she needs is the fertilizer," Clark said. "That's what I came for."

She looked puzzled. "But you cannot carry it. It brings you sickness."

"If we shield it with lead, I'll be all right," he told her. "It stops the sickness. What about the AYUDO compound? They must have had lead of some type there."

Mama Loa brightened. "Yes. Maybe so."

She rose from the stool and grabbed a brightly colored shawl that hung from a nail on the wall. "Are you strong enough to walk?"

Clark pulled himself to his feet and took a few steps. "Good as new," he said.

She led him through a few cane fields, past a couple of farms, until they came to the remains of the AYUDO compound. Together they walked the ruins while Clark scanned the debris with his enhanced vision. Deep within the charred framework of the gutted infirmary he found the melted remnants of a lead blanket that had been used for medical X rays. Dragging it back to Mama Loa's shack, he stripped all the extraneous material from it.

Using his hands to work the remaining lead like clay, he molded it into a bowl and lid that fit tightly together, then he asked one of Mama Loa's helpers to fill it with the fertilizer, finishing it off by pressing the lid tightly into place over the top. Satisfied that it was safe, Clark pinched the edges with thumb and forefinger to complete the seal.

"The forces of light are with us," Mama Loa said, admiring the finished product.

"*You* are the forces of light," Clark said, turning from his work to hug her, then he picked up the sealed bowl. "Thank you, Mama Loa. If this works, I'll be back as soon as I can with enough antidote for everyone who's been changed."

She smiled, obviously embarrassed. "You are the light that came in answer to my prayers. One small flame that can push back the darkness of a whole room. Now go," she said, patting his cheek. "Get this vile poison to Marie-Claire so the flame can burn higher."

◆◆◆

When Clark got the sample back to Smallville, he left it at the hotel desk for Marica. That was all, just the sample: no note, no explanation, and nothing to indicate that it was from him. He didn't even make sure the desk clerk took it; he simply left it at the reception area and moved away.

Maybe she'll think Lionel gave it to her secretly, he thought. It was the best he could do . . . for now.

Then he went to the hospital to check on his mother.

Chloe had let the requisite twenty-four hours pass while she decided what to do about Rebecca's secret . . . and then another twenty-four.

She finally decided that the best thing to do was to let Rebecca know she knew, and promise her that she would never tell anyone about it.

A sharp undertow of anxiety flowed through her stomach as she strolled casually past the decorative acanthus columns of the Talon toward the bar. Rebecca and Lana were working together; Rebecca was smiling shyly, and Lana was laughing.

She reminded herself that it wasn't all about secrets. It was about motivations. She couldn't help but dig into the former, and the latter was the tiller that she needed to examine—to be sure her ship of truth stayed on course.

She didn't want a repeat of the Hacketts. But now she'd found out why Rebecca seemed so worried.

Duh. Burglaries in town and a convicted felon has just arrived in the neighborhood. It does look bad.

But she wasn't putting any of it in the *Torch,* no way.

Her motivation was to help here— and that was the key. The reason she felt so bad about Marshall was just that— motivation. It was, she'd decided, the difference between good and evil. The same actions, when taken from the standpoint of motivation could be either. Had she been trying to *help*—trying to bring a story to life that needed to be out— like if no one had *known* about the exchange and she'd been trying to help, it might have at least been a worthy action.

But it wasn't. She'd been airing out the dirty laundry after the fact, muckraking in high yellow-journalism style. Dragging it out to show how *clever* she was.

And while it was true that she'd seen that before she'd published the story—it had been too late for Marshall.

But not *this* time. This time it was just going to be a show of support, no *Torch,* no public broadcast.

Lana had just left the bar with a tray of coffee cups and pastries, giving Chloe a wave as she crossed to the other side of the room. That left Chloe and Rebecca alone, and Chloe felt even more nervous.

"So, here I am, intrepid reporter hat placed on the shelf for the remainder of the day." She smiled pleasantly. "Now, what was it you wanted to talk to me about?"

Rebecca looked back at her. Then she caught her breath. She turned pale and bit her lower lip; and Chloe knew that Rebecca had just guessed that her terrible secret was a secret no longer.

"You know about my dad," she said.

A beat, and then, "Yes. I do," Chloe said firmly. "And I just want you to know that I'm here for you." Chloe's voice trailed off.

Tears welled in Rebecca's eyes. Chloe hurried on. "It's okay. I'm not going to tell anyone. No one needs to know. Okay?"

Rebecca said slowly, "You *know*. And you still want to be my friend?"

"Well, yeah," Chloe replied, confused. She tilted her head and put her hand on her hip. "*You* didn't rob a jewelry store."

A tear slid down Rebecca's cheek. At first Chloe thought she was upset, but then she murmured, "Thank you, Chloe. You don't know what this means to me. I've hated keeping this all to myself. I feel like I'm about to burst."

"Do you want to talk about it?" Chloe asked.

"I . . . I don't know," Rebecca said. "There's talk about these zombies, but the burglaries . . . my dad . . ."

"Wow, you've had a lot to worry about," Chloe said.

Rebecca began to cry. "Yes. I have. And I am worried. Really worried." She gazed at Chloe. "I love my dad, Chloe. But it's hard. He was in prison, do you understand that?"

"Yes," Chloe said firmly. "He's a convicted felon."

"Oh, God." Rebecca swayed. "It's . . . I'm so scared. Every time someone finds out, they dump me. And he . . . he keeps going out, Chloe. I don't know where, and yes, okay, weird things happen around here, but the crime rate has soared since we showed up, right?"

"Um, well, 'soared.' That's a relative term," Chloe said.

Rebecca pinched the bridge of her nose, looking unutterably weary. "If I had to go to a foster family again . . ." She buried her face in her hands.

"Oh." Chloe put her arms around her and leaned her against her shoulder.

"Oh, God. Oh, my God," Rebecca murmured.

"What's going on?" Lana called out to the girls as she hurried over. "Rebecca, are you all right?"

There was a moment of silence. Then Rebecca said, "Thank you, Chloe. I'm going to tell Lana, too."

"You can trust her, same as you can me," Chloe told her.

Rebecca turned back around. Smoothing back her hair, she lifted her chin and took a deep breath.

"Lana, my father . . ."

"I know." Her face was soft and kind. "I've known for a while."

At Chloe's surprised look, she said, "A friend of Nell's was an alternate juror on your dad's trial. I was talking to Nell on the phone and it came up somehow."

"And you . . . you still want me to work here?" Rebecca asked uncertainly.

And you didn't tell me? Chloe thought archly, then realized there was still a bit of the muckraker lurking inside her . . . or was it the fact that she and Lana had agreed not to have any secrets, ever since that weird clone-guy had tried to date both of them at the same time?

Lana asked the obvious question. "Is there anything we can do?"

Rebecca shook her head. "Not unless you've got a crystal ball and can tell me where my dad goes at night." She looked at them with misery on her face. "You know what I'm thinking. You can see why I'm scared. These robberies . . . it might be . . ."

"We'll do what we can to help," Lana said. "Clark and Pete—"

"No. Please don't tell them," Rebecca pleaded. She swallowed hard. "Back home . . . back in Metropolis . . . once everyone knew . . ."

"It was hard, wasn't it," Lana said gently. "I so get that, Rebecca. I had my face on the cover of *Time* magazine when I was three years old, and some people still think of me that way. 'That poor girl on the cover of *Time*.'"

"I haven't been able to talk to people about my life." Rebecca's laugh was very sad. "When your father is a convicted felon . . ."

More tears streamed down her face as she searched Lana's face. "You can't know what it's like. He can't even vote. He can never vote again. He has a parole officer. We had to get permission to move."

"It's okay, Rebecca," Lana said warmly. "None of us would ever judge you because of your father."

"She's right," Chloe added. "Clark and Pete are good guys. If something's going on with your dad, you should come to your friends for help. And we are your friends. All of us—Lana, Clark, Pete, and I. We want to help you."

Looping her dark hair around her ears, Rebecca firmly shook her head. "It's bad enough that you two know. I—I'd hate it if they knew, too."

"It'll be between us, then," Lana assured her. "Right, Chloe?"

"Absolutely." Chloe gave Rebecca a hug. "Don't worry. Our lips are sealed."

"So. Let's get back to work," Rebecca said, soldiering on.

Lana smiled. "We're about three mocha lattés and four espressos behind."

"At least business is good," Rebecca ventured, and Lana laughed.

"That's true." She gave Rebecca another quick hug.

Chloe hunkered down on her stool. "I'll sit here and do my work," she said. "I've got an issue of the *Torch* to proof. As usual."

"Thank you, both of you," Rebecca said. "This is . . . this is amazing. You're amazing."

"We're really not," Lana said.

She went off to make a slew of espresso drinks, while Rebecca set cups on trays and filled the orders for pastries. Then she picked up her tray and walked through the crowded coffeehouse.

All around her, people her age were laughing and gossiping. A guy from her math class was holding hands and leaning forward over the table, hanging on every word the cute blonde across from him was saying. It was such a different world from hers — more innocent, kinder.

She watched as a man slid into a booth at the back. He was about her father's age, but not as handsome. He gave her the strangest look as he glanced at her name tag.

"Rebecca," he read. "Thank you, Rebecca."

"Sure." She didn't like him, didn't care for the vibes he was throwing off.

"Actually, I just glanced at my watch," he told her. "I didn't realize what time it is. I have to leave."

"Okay." She flashed him a smile. "Please come back sometime."

"I certainly will." He hesitated. "What time do you close tonight?"

"Eleven," she told him.

"Late for a school night," he observed.

"Well, not all our customers go to school," she replied, shifting her weight.

"I meant . . . for you."

"Yeah, well, as long as I keep up my studies," she said. Then she realized she didn't even want to be having this conversation, so she said, "Have a nice evening," and walked quickly away.

"Are you okay?" Lana asked, as the two met up en route to the bar.

"That guy," Rebecca murmured under her breath, as they stood beside Chloe, who was busily proofing her mock-up of the *Torch*. "There's something weird about him."

They both turned to see him making his way casually toward the Talon's doors.

Lana raised her brows, and said, "Well, if he comes back in, let me know, and I'll wait on him, okay? House rules: Any guy makes you nervous, someone else takes over his table."

"Thank you," Rebecca said in a rush.

Looking up from her mock-up of the *Torch,* Chloe drawled, "He's probably had too much caffeine. Then her gaze trailed past them to the man, who had just turned his head to the left as he pushed open the door.

Her eyes widened. She whispered, "Oh, my God."

"What?" Lana asked.

Chloe blinked, dumbfounded.

"What?" Rebecca demanded.

"Rebecca. I think . . . I'm fairly certain that's Jason Littleton," Chloe blurted. "One of the men who was . . . involved with your father."

Rebecca's knees buckled.

"Oh, God, I knew it," she said miserably. "All the late nights. My dad . . . my dad and Jason Littleton are robbing stores." She pressed her hand against her mouth and began to cry.

Chloe got off her stool, took Rebecca by the shoulders, and marched her toward the staff lounge.

Lana announced, "I'll call the sheriff."

"No. No, please don't," Rebecca pleaded, whirling around. "That man and my father aren't supposed to make contact with each other. It's a condition of Daddy's parole. If the police find out, they'll throw my father back in jail with no questions asked. Even if it's . . . nothing."

Lana and Chloe regarded each other. Chloe's features hardened, and she said, "I'm going to do as Rebecca asks, Lana. Keeping my mouth shut. For now."

"I don't know," Lana said.

"Please, Lana, *please,*" Rebecca murmured.

"All right." Lana nodded. "But we have to find out what he's doing here, all right? Rebecca, I think you need to talk to your father about this."

Rebecca quavered inside. She and her father had never fully discussed the robbery. They had only skirted around it.

But she sensed that doing so was a condition of Lana's not calling the police.

"All right," she said, sagging.

Lana put her arm around her and gave her a hug. "We're here for you," she reminded her.

Then Chloe walked her to the bathroom, and Rebecca broke down again and cried.

While they were gone, Lana paced behind the bar, trying to decide what to do. Finally, she picked up the phone and dialed the Kent farmhouse.

"Clark?" she asked breathlessly, but their answering machine clicked on. She had no idea where Clark was, and she realized that Jonathan Kent was probably at the hospital with Martha.

Then she remembered what Rebecca had said—that her father would be in violation of his parole if he was seen with Jason Littleton, and decided not to leave a message like that on the Kents' phone. It was too public.

She hung up.

A few minutes later, Chloe and Rebecca returned from the ladies' room. Rebecca had been crying so hard it looked as if her eyes were welded shut. Lana took one look at her, and said, "What can we do?"

"She wants to go home," Chloe informed Lana. "I'm going with her."

Lana's eyes widened. "You guys, that man is a criminal." Then she flushed as Rebecca jerked, and said, "I'm sorry, Rebecca, but . . ."

"I want to be with my dad," Rebecca insisted.

"Have you called him? Do you even know he's there?" Lana pressed. "And what if this guy comes looking for him? I really think we should call your father and ask him to pick you up here."

Rebecca hung her head. "This is awful," she croaked.

"It's going to be okay," Chloe assured her. "We'll let your dad know what's going on. He'll take care of it." She smiled at Rebecca, but her expression didn't reach her eyes. "Right?"

Holding back sobs, Rebecca nodded dejectedly. *I'm going to lose their friendship,* she thought. *Who would want to be my friend after this?*

Chloe pulled out her cell phone, and said, "Let's go outside so you can get decent reception."

"Be careful. He might still be around," Lana told them.

Rebecca felt a chill as she glanced toward the door; then

Chloe said, "We'll go out the back way." She smiled at Rebecca. "Good?"

"Good," she murmured.

They turned to go, Rebecca in the lead. She headed for the exit, punching in her home number as she walked.

Then she heard Lana call Chloe in an urgent tone of voice. Chloe said, "Hold on, Rebecca. I'll see what she wants."

"Okay."

Rebecca loitered near the exit. Then the men's room door opened and someone came out.

Idly she looked up. She opened her mouth to scream just as Jason Littleton clamped his hand across it. Something hard jabbed into her ribs.

"It's a gun," he said calmly. "Let's go."

Tom Morhaim returned home from a late shift tired and eager for a beer and some TV. For a moment he was surprised that Rebecca wasn't home, but then he remembered her job at the coffeehouse.

Maybe I should take a walk to the cemetery.

He knew she'd been wondering where he went all the time. His excuse about needing to go on walks was wearing pretty thin.

If she only knew . . . but how am I going to tell her? I've got millions of dollars' worth of jewels buried in Michelle Madison's grave. They've been sitting there for over a decade, and I'm dying to dig them up. We'll be set for life.

But the more he thought about retrieving them, the more he wondered what Rebecca would think . . . and more importantly, how she would react. Back in prison, all those years that he had dreamed about his fortune, she had been little more than an abstraction. He had spun fantasies about how ecstatic she would be—no more scrimping, no more humiliation over wearing hand-me-downs. She was going to live like a princess.

The phone rang, and he expected it to be Rebecca. He hadn't

made any friends yet, and he figured she was among friends down at the coffeehouse.

"Hey, Becs," he said pleasantly.

"Hey yourself, Tom."

His blood froze. It was Jason Littleton. Jason, from the robbery. Jason, who took the rap for shooting the security guard.

"Oh, God," Tom croaked.

"I've got your girl. Rebecca, say hi to your father."

"Daddy!" It was Rebecca's voice. "Daddy, help!"

"It's okay, honey," he said soothingly, but his voice was shaking.

Then Littleton was back on the line. "Guess what, Tom, old friend. You've heard about those burglaries? Me. And the weird white people? Me again. They're zombies, buddy. Just like the papers have been saying. And I have a little vial that turns sweet little girls into zombies. And I'm going to use it in, oh, about twenty minutes unless you get the jewels and bring them to me."

"I don't have them," Tom lied.

"Rebecca, open your mouth," Littleton said off the line.

"No! Don't!" Tom shouted. "All right! Just don't hurt her, okay? Don't hurt her."

Jason chuckled to himself. He was sorry that he hadn't realized the vial was leaking last night when he'd set it on the table at the Talon. It had soaked through the bag, and all he could figure was that the sugar packets in the basket on the table had absorbed the remainder of the liquid. It was all gone—although he knew any decent chemist could extract the molecules off the inside of the vial to re-create the formula for him. But that would take time. His imminent plan to change Tom Morhaim into a zombie would not come to fruition. It didn't matter too much; he'd planned to do so in order to get Tom to tell him where the jewels were. Threatening his little girl was proving to be just as effective.

"So you'll have them to me in twenty minutes, right?"

"No. I mean, they're buried. I have to dig them up." He hesitated, then sighed, sounding defeated. "They're in the graveyard."

"You're kidding." Littleton started laughing.

*After he digs them up, I'll have the zombies kill him. No. I'll
have them bury him alive. Turnabout's fair play. After all, he
buried me alive, in prison.*

◆◆◆

So, we meet in the graveyard. Just like in the movies.

He'd handcuffed and gagged Rebecca and got her in his van.
They drove to the cemetery through the fog, and Littleton parked
off the road.

"This won't take long," he told her.

Dragging Rebecca along, Jason Littleton headed for the graveyard entrance.

You are gonna pay, Morhaim, he thought. He felt in his jacket
for his Anschütz .22. *Pay and pay and pay. And then, you are
gonna die, one way or another.*

He walked on, turning around occasionally to make sure no
one was following them.

The fog gathered in layers, grayish white upon gray upon a
milky, sickly sheen of moonbeams and mist. Streetlamps overhead became dull, clumpy orbs of watery light. A dog barked
hysterically, as if protesting.

A bird cawed, and Littleton murmured, *"'Quoth the raven,
nevermore.'"* That poem had been written by Edgar Allan Poe,
about some guy's dead girlfriend. Poe was twisted and gifted.

*Kind of like Shaky . . . speaking of whom . . . I wonder if he's
just sitting in the crypt, waiting for orders from headquarters.
Maybe with the others. Maybe they ate him before he changed.
Bet they're hungry . . .*

Ahead, the arched wrought-iron sign rising above double
towers of bricks announced that he had reached his destination.
The Smallville cemetery lay dead ahead.

So to speak.

He pushed open the gate, which squealed on its hinges. It
sent a delicious frisson up his spine. Reaching into his pocket
with his free hand, he pulled out his flashlight and held it above
his head, pointing it downward, the way police officers do.

The fog lapped at his kneecaps as he walked forward, moving

solely on instinct. He and Rebecca walked into the thick soup; no matter how he tried to push it away, there was more, and yet more. It was like swimming in a pool of semifrozen ice.

Then—

What the . . . ?

He fell forward, letting go of Rebecca as he tumbled, then landed on his hands and knees on something hard that collapsed beneath his weight.

As he flailed in the wreckage, he understood what had happened: *I fell into an open grave! I landed on a coffin!*

He swallowed. *Did I read any obituaries? Who died recently? More to the point, where's the body?*

Finding the flashlight courtesy of the dulled beam, he grabbed it and scrambled up and out. Rebecca was nowhere to be seen. He got to his feet and gingerly walked forward, feeling with his boot tip as he went, scanning the fog in search of her.

His foot hovered in midair, and he realized he had almost fallen into another open grave.

What is going on?

Perplexed, he scanned his flashlight in a half circle. The light simply bounced off the fog, diffused into a hazy glow. He moved on, feeling as he went.

He didn't encounter another hole as he made his way down rows of headstones, which he kept track of by placing his palm on the top of each one, trying to keep count. He figured he was getting near the crypt where he'd stashed Shaky.

"Rebecca? Honey?" he called out. "Come on, sweetie, make it easy on yourself. Come on out, now."

Then, reaching out with his hand to make a sweep, he made contact with the door of the crypt. It was wide open.

But I locked it.

He froze, listening. Heard nothing.

"Shaky?" he whispered. "Guys?"

Then all hell broke loose.

Skeletal fingers grabbed him; voices rose, howling and screaming and shrieking as several zombies converged on Jason Littleton. Some of their fingers broke off like breadsticks as he extricated himself, using karate moves he had learned in prison.

He swept his leg forward, then executed a roundhouse kick, slamming his foot into ribs that detached, apparently, springing from a sternum and clattering to the stone floor.

The zombies screamed and grabbed for him.

Jason ran. Through the blinding fog and his blinding fear, he ran so fast that he overran, losing his balance and falling hard. His left hand made contact with a headstone, and his flashlight arced out of his grasp.

As he fought to get up, something burst from the ground beside his hand and grabbed him. He shook it off; feeling the sharp fingernails slicing into the topmost layers of his skin.

The dead are rising from their graves!

How . . . how?

It didn't matter how. What mattered was getting the hell out of there in one piece.

He brought his gun down on the searching hand. Bones cracked, and disjointed fingers flailed at him.

This is a nightmare. A living nightmare.

He fought down giddy fear as he flung himself away from the place where the hand had pushed through the earth, fully expecting a wrist to protrude next.

Then he lay as still as death on the ground, panting. He was in shock. Perspiration beaded from his forehead, stinging his eyes.

He tried to formulate a strategy for self-preservation. If there was one thing he was good at, it was saving his own skin.

It occurred to him then that if the fog was hiding the zombies from him, it was hiding him from the zombies. Unless they could somehow bring their other senses to bear—sound . . . smell.

Do they smell me?

He fought down his panic, trying to bring the layout of the cemetery to mind; there were gravestones in rows, then brass memorial squares set into the ground farther out, then trees and bushes. Just beyond the crypt—which was now behind him— there were plenty of trees.

Could hide me, could slow me down.

Shaky was missing; he had escaped from the crypt. No single

zombie would have been strong enough to force the thick door open alone. It would have taken cooperation.

Or a lucky accident of combined brute strength.

He prayed it was the latter.

He sensed movement all around him in the fog. He heard wild shrieks.

Maybe if I get to the cemetery entrance . . . and shut the gate . . . maybe that will contain them.

It was his only plan; therefore, his only shot.

He rose, and began to run.

For a second, he heard only his own footsteps, and he smiled grimly. Wherever they were, they weren't around him.

And then the screams grew thicker and more concentrated; something swiped at the back of his head, and he gave a bellow of fear.

They were behind him, and they were running him to ground like a dog.

The cemetery gate was a lifetime away . . .

As soon as Chloe and Lana had realized that Rebecca was missing, they searched the Talon and the surrounding area; then Lana told the head waitress to take over, and they raced out the door to Chloe's car. Leaping behind the wheel, Chloe nodded as Lana said, "Okay, I'm calling the sheriff."

"With you all the way," Chloe said.

Lana punched in the number, and said, "Hello? It's Lana Lang. A girl's been kidnapped." She gave all the details, including the identity of Jason Littleton. The deputy assured her they would check it out, and she disconnected.

"Let's go to her apartment," Lana suggested. "Maybe he'll take her there." Then she looked at Chloe. "Except I don't know where she lives."

"I don't either."

They looked at each other in frustration. "We'll have to start searching," Chloe said. "Just drive around until we see or hear something unusual."

"Like, um this?" Chloe asked, pointing through the windshield.

A man in a pair of jeans and windbreaker was racing toward them, his arms windmilling wildly. And behind him . . .

Chloe couldn't believe what she was seeing.

A dozen zombies, maybe more; some were half-decomposed and some looked pretty okay and some . . . some were rotting skeletons that straggled after the others.

"Oh my God," Lana gasped.

Chloe tried to drive up to Littleton, rolling down the window, and shouting, "Get in the car!"

He ignored her, or couldn't hear her, and then he was weaving into the brush at the side of the road.

The zombies howled after him.

Chloe gave chase.

Lana said, "I'm trying Clark again."

Clark had just gotten home from the hospital. His mom was having a bad night, and his father was going to sleep at the hospital.

The phone rang, and he frowned; it was late.

It was Lana.

"Clark? Rebecca's been kidnapped by this man who knew her father. We're at the cemetery. It's . . . there are zombies!"

"Get out of there," he said. "I'll wait there for the sheriff."

"But Rebecca—"

"Get out of there!" he insisted.

He got in the truck and drove as fast as he could, realizing that he could make far better progress on foot. But as usual, there would be questions.

Then he saw a man—*must be Littleton*—and the man was not alone.

Five or six white-faced figures were converging on him in the fog.

Zombies.

Clark raced toward them, shouting, "Hey!" to the man.

In the clearing mist, Clark could see the man's face. He was terrified. Clark rushed toward him, remembering too late that the zombies had ingested something that included traces of meteor-rock.

Pain. Intense. Debilitating.

He fell to his knees. One of the zombies rushed up to him, snarling, and bent over him, trying to sink his teeth into Clark's face. Clark easily pushed him away, but another came to take his place. The zombies were on him, dogpiling him. The pain seeped into him, through skin, bones, and muscle; his head began to throb. The veins on the backs of his hands rose and burned.

The zombies were all over him, slashing at him, trying to get a grip on an arm, a leg, seeking purchase anywhere so they could have a nice meal of raw human flesh. It was not their frenzied attack that debilitated him; it was the meteor fragments carried inside each of them, and the combined effect was sapping Clark quickly. Gasping and in intense pain, his ability to fend them off was evaporating.

He moaned, trying to at least roll away from the zombies, but they stuck with him, not giving him an inch as their teeth *clacked-clacked-clacked* in their heads.

A terrible stench rose from one of the zombies as Clark grabbed its arm, and the entire thing broke off in his grasp.

Then he heard footsteps, and Chloe saying, "Clark, it's us! Hang in there!"

Lana and Chloe ran toward him.

I told you to go away, he thought dully.

He heard punches and whacks; felt hands loosen their grip on him when the fog was split in two as he caught sight of his friends battling the zombies. He couldn't keep track of the action—he was fading fast—but he could tell that the girls were winning.

Then the pain and the poisonous effects took hold, and he was immobile, and nearly unconscious. Everything was a jumble of sound and sight, nothing clear. He heard breaking bones and growls and the occasional, "You guys okay?" as Chloe and Lana pushed back the zombie assault.

He had no idea how long they fought; then someone was grabbing his arms and someone else his ankles. They were hurrying him out of there, and he was grateful for that. Lana had her arm around him, and she was half-dragging him, half–being dragged by him.

CHAPTER TWENTY-ONE

The fog pressed in, feeling cold and clammy on Rebecca's cheeks and hands, muffling everything. She shivered, pulling her jacket tighter. She had gotten away from Jason Littleton, then had been surrounded by monsters. Running away, she had fallen, smacked her head on a gravestone, and passed out. Now, as she came to, she was eerily alone. The wind soughed through the shadowed branches of a huge elm that loomed over them, and the dim gray glow of the moon faded in and out from above.

Then she heard the distinctive sound of shoveling. She peered around the side of the gravestone.

It was her father, digging up a grave.

"Daddy?" she managed, but her voice came out a dry rasp.

Then a shot rang out. She screamed, and her father shouted, "Keep your head down, Becs!"

She started to lower her head, then saw Jason Littleton racing toward her father, who stopped shoveling and stared at him.

"Tom, long time," Littleton said. "Don't stop digging. Those kids slowed the zombies down, but you can bet they'll be back. We've got minutes at best."

He continued, "Thought you were slick, hiding *our* jewels here in someone's grave, making everybody think you're some poor slob, whining and sniveling over your poor dead wifey." His voice hardened. "If you had whacked that guard the right way in the first place, he wouldn't have lived to testify against us. You couldn't even do *that* right." He shook his head.

"Then you go and pop *me* for the deed," he added.

Rebecca gasped. Her *father* had shot the guard? Her *father*? Rebecca bit her lip to keep herself from screaming.

"Listen, Jason, I was hiding the stuff here for the both of us. As soon as I got things in line with my kid here in Smallville, I was going to come get them, fence 'em off, and send you your half of the green. Really."

Littleton motioned toward the gravestone with his head.

"Michelle Madison know you were gonna take them jewels back from her after all these years?" He smiled. "Were you gonna stiff her, too?" He chuckled at his own sick joke.

"Real funny, Jason."

"Well, I'm going to let you prove to me that you were gonna do me right." Still training his gun on Rebecca's father, Littleton knelt down, picked up a spade, and tossed it to Tom. "Dig 'em up. And make damn sure the hole is deep and wide enough for a man."

Tom held the shovel without moving.

"Now!" Littleton said, stepping toward him. He cocked the gun and pressed it hard to Tom's forehead.

Tom did as he was told, shoving the spade into the soil and pressing down with his foot until he worked up a chunk of turf, then he shoveled again, digging deeper. "We can work this all out . . ."

Littleton kicked him in the side, making Tom double over.

"Shut up and dig it up quick so we can get this over with. I've waited too long for this." He looked over his shoulder. "If those damn freaks come back . . ."

Tom started digging again.

"Faster!" Littleton said, slapping Tom in the back of the head.

Only the sound of the spade biting into the ground followed by the thump of tossed dirt filled the fog-shrouded night.

Then Rebecca heard strange scratching noises and a faint *click-clacking* sound from somewhere behind them.

"Hey, shut up a minute," Littleton hissed, cocking his head.

Tom stopped digging.

Other noises came from behind and around them from all directions.

A chill tickled Rebecca's spine, and her mouth went dry.

Click clack click clack . . .

Then a loud *click* came from in front of them, from the shovel hitting something hard.

Tom dug and scraped more with the shovel. Then he ducked into the hole on his hands and knees, making more scraping and grunting noises until he pulled a plastic-wrapped metal briefcase free from the hole and tossed it up on the ground at the grave's edge.

Click clack click clack . . .

"Open it," Littleton said, with an edge to his voice.

Tom hoisted himself from the hole, crouched low, and looked around, eyes narrowed, listening. Both he and Littleton remained still for a long time, as if the whole scene had been frozen in video freeze-frame.

While they looked down, Rebecca saw the zombies—hulking, broken-down, half-human-looking shadows shuffled through the billowing mists. Arms stuck out at odd angles, fingers splayed stiffly. Rebecca heard low moans, wheezing, and the ever-present, wet-sounding *click clack click clack* . . .

Coming from in front *and* behind her.

"Daddy!" she cried.

Then she saw Clark, Chloe, and Lana, too, hurrying toward her. Clark was hurt!

Jason Littleton grabbed the half-rotted briefcase and turned to run. But the zombies formed a semicircle that extended behind Rebecca and Chloe, and around to where Clark and Lana stood. Clark looked terrible.

Littleton pointed the gun in the air and fired a shot that made Rebecca's heart jump into her throat. A row of vacant stares turned toward them and the zombies stopped their advance. Together they swayed as one, jagged teeth clicking, their drooling mouths gnashing, as if attending some ghoulish undead rock concert.

Rebecca got to her feet, shouting, "Daddy!"

"Honey!" Tom's voice was anguished. "Get the hell out of here!"

"Run!" Clark yelled.

Without a trace of fear, he turned to face the onslaught of zombies. But they scrambled all over Clark, pushing him down on his knees, as Lana hit and kicked at them.

Chloe shouted, "Clark!" and ran to join the battle.

"Daddy!" Rebecca cried. "Daddy, say you didn't shoot that guard!" If they were going to die tonight, she was going to die knowing the truth about her father.

"I didn't! I didn't!" he shouted back at her. "I didn't mean to!"

"You liar!" Littleton shrieked at him. Then he shot Tom Morhaim at point-blank range.

Rebecca screamed, collapsing to the ground. She crab-walked toward her father, shrieking, "Daddy! Daddy!" She smelled something disgusting behind her as a zombie lunged for her arm. She screamed again.

And then, without warning, Jason Littleton dropped to the ground, blood spurting from his chest.

"Stand back!" someone yelled—a male voice Rebecca had never heard before.

She paid no attention, intent only upon reaching her father.

A thick stream of diesel-smelling flame spewed out from between two monuments, spreading in a steady line across the zombies, who screeched inhuman shrieks that made Rebecca sick to her stomach.

As if connected by invisible cords, the zombies who had been clambering over Clark fell back and retreated into the chaos with all the others, as they ran helter-skelter in blind panic.

A man dressed all in black, wearing a hood, advanced with the flamethrower, methodically incinerating the zombies like some dark, postapocalyptic exterminator.

Rebecca ran to her father's side. He was lying on the ground, still gagging. His eyes had a faraway, glassy look. She looked back to see Lana, Chloe, and Clark, giving as good as they got, although Clark seemed half-dead himself.

The zombies burned.

They screamed.

Rebecca's father lay silent on the grass, blood gushing from the wound in his chest.

Then Pete Ross walked from behind the man who was dressed in black, saw Clark, said, "Hey," and collapsed.

◆◆◆

Shortly after the mop-up operation was complete, T. T. Van De Ven was summoned to HQ in Metropolis. He stood at attention before the Project's board of directors—a committee made up of high-ranking military personnel and one civilian, Lionel Luthor, the industrialist who had made it all possible.

Luthor glared at him. "You imbecile. Who gave you orders to set my house on fire?"

"Before you go on, sir," General Montgomery said, "I'd like to point out that Field Operative Van De Ven successfully eliminated all evidence of the Project from Smallville and returned your son's friend to him fully restored to health."

"Then I would postulate that not all the evidence was eliminated," Lionel snapped.

The colonel looked confused. "We assumed that the return of this young man, this . . . Pete Ross . . . was imperative."

Lionel Luthor said nothing. But he turned and pointed at Van De Ven, and said, "I want that man court-martialed."

"Agreed," the general said.

Van De Ven's mouth dropped open.

"Sir," he began.

"Shut up," the general ordered him. Then he said, "Gentlemen, I move that we shelve the Project."

No one dissented.

Clark's mother leaned heavily on his arm as he and his father escorted her into the house. She was pale, but she looked better than she had in a long time.

Best of all, she was home.

Chloe, Lana, Pete, and Rebecca greeted the three Kents, jumping up and yelling "surprise!" as Jonathan opened the door, and Clark walked his mother over the threshold.

"We made you guys some lunch," Rebecca said. She smiled shyly at Chloe and Lana, who both smiled warmly back. "Sandwiches and fruit."

Tom Morhaim had survived, but barely. He had been taken back to jail in Metropolis in a prison ambulance, and was awaiting a new trial in the infirmary, as he had confessed that he, not Jason Littleton, had shot Lee Hinchberger.

Rebecca had no idea if she would ever be able to forgive him for that. His confession was much too little, much too late.

With the Kents' help, Rebecca was placed with a very loving older couple who had longed to become foster parents for a number of years. She would remain with them until she turned eighteen . . . but Clark agreed with his mother's assessment that this new relationship was something that would last much longer than that: The Kendalls doted on Rebecca, and she on them.

The best thing was, no one had turned their backs on her in her time of need. Rather, they had rallied around her.

Rebecca Morhaim was finally among friends.

"What a nice thing to do. Thank you," Martha said warmly to the group.

"*Organic* fruit," Lana added. "No pesticides. We don't want you ending up back in the hospital!"

"Nothing to make you sick," Chloe elaborated. "Everything is yuck-factor free."

"Funny thing about that," Martha said, giving them all a look. "It wasn't anything on the fruit at Lex's house that landed me in the hospital. It was mold, growing on the peanuts we also ate that day. If there had been some kind of agent on the nuts to destroy the mold, I wouldn't have gotten sick.

"I got sick precisely because the peanuts were untreated."

"And I'm putting that in our report," Clark said to Pete, who smiled wryly at him.

"In a footnote," Pete shot back.

"A really big footnote," Clark said. "It's worth mentioning."

"Let's eat," Martha suggested. "I'm hungry. The only decent food I had in the hospital was the sandwich Jonathan smuggled in from the cafeteria."

Clark looked questioningly at his dad, who held up his hands, all innocence, and settled Martha in at the dining room table.

Soon the Kent family farmhouse was noisy with the laughter of a large family, celebrating life and health together, as families should.

Maria del Carmen Maldonaldo Lopez accepted a glass of champagne from the flight attendant and sipped it appreciatively. "Very nice," she told the woman.

"Thank you," the flight attendant replied. Then she turned to the only other occupant of the private Learjet and asked, "When would you like me to serve the filet mignon, Mr. Luthor?"

"You hungry?" Lex asked Marica.

"Not quite yet."

The jet waggled its wings as it crossed the fertile fields surrounding Smallville, each one a bright green or golden postage stamp as the aircraft gained altitude. Marica, wearing one of the many other outfits Lex had just happened to have in her size, leaned against the seat and sighed heavily.

"*Adios,* Kansas," she said softly. She glanced at Lex. "Do you still believe your father was involved with the creation of the zombies?"

"Oh, yes," Lex told her. "But he'll never admit it out loud. My father is all about discretion and subtlety." He shifted, facing her more fully while he sipped his champagne. "Maybe he couldn't give us the antidote. He wouldn't want me to know that. I think he was trying to make amends by leaving that sample for you at the reception desk."

She smiled to herself. With that sample, and Lex's lab, she was fairly certain she had an antidote of her own. Friends of hers were taking it to Haiti, and would be informing her about its success.

"And in the bargain," he added, "the research you did on datura's effects on the brain have yielded some interesting data on other neurological contaminants. It might even help with MS. And, of course, LuthorCorp plans to be on the cutting edge of that data curve."

"So your investors will be happy," she pointed out.

"Everybody wins," he concurred. Then he shifted, sipping his champagne. "Have you decided what you're going to do when you get home?"

She nodded. "Well, I do agree that it's no use trying to expose what went on back there. No one will believe me. I have to assume that the government realizes that, and will leave me alone. In return, I will work to improve a lot of developing nations as 'a lady,' as my parents would say."

She looked a little sad, as if the exciting part of her life had just ended.

"I have an education, and I have privilege. I'll set up a foundation and get all my parents' rich friends to contribute."

Smiling, Lex reached into the pocket of his Italian sports coat and brought out a leather checkbook. As he flipped it open, he retrieved a pen from his pocket as well.

"Will a million be a satisfactory first contribution?" he asked.

She momentarily looked dazed. Then she grinned at him and said, "Two million."

Without a moment's hesitation, Lex wrote the check.

After the party was over, and Martha Kent was resting, Clark took off, moving at a blur. He had a rendezvous to keep in Cap du Roi.

He was certain Mama Loa knew he was coming, and she would be waiting for him.

It was very late at Smallville Juvenile Hall. Most of the inmates were asleep.

But in a small office, in a soft, comfortable chair, a psychologist named Dr. Miranda Nierman sat, holding back.

Across from her, words spilled out of Marshall Hackett's mouth.

"I hate him! I miss him! How could he do this to us? How can I ever forgive him?" he demanded without taking a breath.

She listened, not speaking, aware that she was witnessing the breaking of a heart. It was a wound that was necessary, if Marshall was ever going to heal.

"How am I ever going to stop hurting?" he shouted at her. "How do I make this stop?" He burst into heavy sobs, another horrible aftermath of his family's tragedy.

"It's not fair. I can't believe how unfair it all is," he told her. "I hate this. I hate it!"

You should, she thought. Her heart was breaking, too—for him. It was a struggle not to interrupt, to ease the tension she herself felt by giving him bromides—*It's always darkest before the dawn; time heals all wounds . . .*

It would be so easy for her to do that to him.

And so unfair.

Make me a witness, she thought, hearing an old song in her head.

And so Dr. Nierman kept vigil over Marshall's pain.

Kept silence.

Rebecca, Lana, and Chloe stayed up watching old movies and eating popcorn at the Sullivan home the night Martha Kent came home from the hospital. They sat in the living room, and didn't speak.

After a while, a tear slid down Rebecca's cheek. Lana gave her hand a pat. Rebecca leaned her head against Lana's shoulder and let the tears come.

No one spoke.

No one had to.

In Haiti, Clark learned that someone else had already prepared an antidote and administered it to all the victims in Cap du Roi. In addition, the secret government facility had been sealed up. Clark could see parts of it with his X-ray vision; it looked as if it had been bombed underground. Huge piles of rubble filled the tunnel and the elevator shaft.

Lionel's doing? he wondered.

Mama Loa held a party to celebrate the liberation of her people and an end to the torment and fear. At her urging, Clark stayed for it, dining on roast chicken and mangoes, watching the dancers swirl in colorful clothes. The drumbeats sang in his blood.

She walked up beside him as he gazed up at the stars. He studied them, then turned to her, and asked sadly, "Why didn't they give me a message? Why didn't my parents tell me who I am, and why I'm here?"

The firelight crackled, casting her face in soft light. Beyond them, her son Baby Loa, who had fully recovered, strummed a guitar and began to sing.

"You know," Mama Loa said wisely. "You know who you are. And why you're here. Every day, your heart tells you, does it not?"

Clark gazed up longingly, silently, at the stars.

Listening to the sound of silence.

SMALLVILLE

SHADOWS

Diana G. Gallagher

For Kyle William Streb,
super grandson #4,
with all my love.

PROLOGUE

October 1989

Master Sergeant Adam Reisler replaced the last panel on the environmental control console, but his mind was not on missile support systems. His son, a junior at Middleton, was playing defense in today's big homecoming game against Smallville High. Steve Bacic, one of the Crows' best offensive players, wouldn't be easy to cover, but Joe was confident and determined.

Just like his dad, Adam thought, smiling. He had worked hard to rise through the enlisted ranks, and he never shirked his duty or questioned the responsibilities associated with his job. Every maintenance detail was as vital to national security as the two-man teams in charge of the launch protocols for the Minuteman II missiles deployed throughout the Midwest.

But today I'd much rather be in the bleachers cheering on my kid than running another routine inspection of R-141. Adam glanced toward the Power Control Center on the far side of the huge steel-reinforced concrete structure known as the Launch Facility Equipment Building or LFEB.

Staff Sergeant Jonah Wallace ducked out of the cramped room that housed the diesel engine. Fueled from a fourteen-thousand-gallon tank buried in concrete beside the LFEB, the generator powered the installation when commercial energy sources failed.

Wallace gave Adam a thumbs-up, flipped off the light, and secured the engine room door. The loud mechanical noise that overwhelmed the equipment complex made talking a useless exercise. They both wore protective covers over their ears to lessen the deafening effects.

Rising, Adam waved Wallace to follow him back to the massive entry door. The distance from the back wall of the LFEB to the far side of the Launch Control Center located across the tunnel junction was 120 feet. Another access tunnel forming the stem of a T behind the elevator shaft ran outward 100 feet and connected the operations complex to the silo. The missile shaft extended 80 feet below the level of the main facility, which was 60 feet underground.

Adam was not just anxious to find out who had won the big game between archrivals Middleton and Smallville. The missile had been taken off-line, so it couldn't be launched while his men were working in the silo. The sooner they were done so that the bird was free to fly again, the better. Although the Russians had left Afghanistan in defeat last February, and several Eastern European countries had broken their ties to the Soviet Union, the USA couldn't let down its guard.

Adam paused by the chemical, biological, and radiological filter he had inspected when he first arrived. The equipment had checked out, but as usual, he hoped the device would never be tested under fire. Washington insiders believed the Cold War was winding down, but until one of the superpowers blinked or surrendered, the termination of the mutual annihilation threat was nothing but academic wishful thinking.

When Wallace caught up, Adam stepped onto the hinged drawbridge that spanned the space between the lime green concrete walls and the steel floor.

Provided an enemy bomb didn't score a direct hit, the Launch Facility was safe, designed to withstand the shock of a near miss. The floors in the Equipment Building and the Launch Control Center were suspended from the ceiling and rested on hydraulic shock isolators measuring a foot across and twenty feet tall. Everything, including the twenty-ton air conditioner, was bolted to the steel platform. Under attack, the floor would shake and bang into the walls, but damage would be minimal.

Theoretically, Adam thought, shouldering his tool bag to push open the thirteen-ton LFEB door. It was balanced so one man could open it from the inside, but since the air pressure was lower in the tunnel junction, the combined weight of two men was needed to push it closed.

Adam led the way into the access tunnel, and Wallace turned off the lights as he passed through. After the door was pushed back in place, Adam spun the wheel to lock it and stowed his earmuffs.

"Think the game is over, yet?" Wallace's son was still in grade school, but he followed the local high school teams.

Adam glanced at his watch. "Probably, but we'll have to wait until we get topside to find out the score."

"Yeah, but we might not have to wait for the KTOW radio report." Wallace chuckled as Adam lifted a headset off a holder in the curved wall. "If the Crows won, they'll post the final score on the water tower as soon as they can get someone up there with a bucket of paint and a brush."

Nodding, Adam fitted the headset over his ears and pressed the call button. Although the sound of machinery rumbled through the tubular corridor, it was quiet compared to the din in the LFEB.

"B Team," Technical Sergeant Ron Jackson answered from the silo. "We just finished over here, Sergeant. We can hand this baby back to Control anytime."

"Pull the SCS and get back here, then," Adam said. The Safety Control Switch in the Launcher Equipment Room was used to safe the missile manually. Once work in the silo was completed, the switch was thrown back to return command of the bird to Launch Control. "As soon as LCC confirms they've got the power, we'll get out of here."

Adam replaced the headset and reached for the phone. Every silo was hardwired to the commander's console at the Launch Control Center. Fifteen Launch Control Facilities in the Missouri-Kansas region were responsible for 150 missiles. R-141 was mated with Romeo Eight.

Romeo Fourteen, the installation Adam's environmental systems team had just finished inspecting, had been built as a Launch Control Facility for ten additional missiles in the central Midwest. Budget cuts had prevented it from becoming operational. Although the underground complex had been completed, the remote silos and on-site support structures for the LCF had not progressed past the blueprint stage.

The installation was located on land the government leased from the Creamed Corn Factory, a local business that was owned and operated by the Ross family. Surrounded by fallow fields, the one-hundred-ton concrete silo lid, entry hatch into the operations complex, ventilation shafts, and a locked chain-link and barbed-wire security fence were the only evidence of technology in the rustic landscape. Since the environmental, security, communication, and monitoring systems were functional, Romeo Fourteen was maintained as an emergency backup site, but the commander and deputy's safes in the Launch Control Center had never contained Sealed Authenticators or launch keys.

When Adam picked up the handset, the Maintenance Control Network was activated and a light flashed on the commander's console in Romeo Eight many miles away.

"Capsule," Captain Timothy answered. "How's it going out there?"

"Jackson is throwing the SCS now, sir," Adam said. "Your board should be lighting up."

"Got it," Timothy said over the sound of a routine alarm. The alarm went silent when he hit the reset button. "The printout confirms. R-141 is ours."

"We'll radio back in when we're packed up and outside the perimeter, sir." Adam glanced back as Jackson, John Harris, and their security escort, Everett Corey, emerged from the connecting tunnel hatch.

After signing off, Adam joined the other four men in the elevator. A staircase spiraled up around the elevator shaft, but no one climbed seven stories to the surface unless an emergency threatened to take out the power.

"I hope Joe stopped the Smallville offense cold today," Corey said.

"Me too." Adam pulled the outer wire cage doors closed. The interior elevator doors closed when he punched the UP button. An athletic scholarship was Joe's best chance to get into a good university, an essential step to being signed by the pros. If Joe's higher education depended on Adam's military pay, the boy would be commuting to East Hennessey Community College in Metropolis, where his dreams of goalpost glory would die.

"Yeah." Jackson shifted his tool bag. "The Crows' winning streak is getting really old."

"Unless you're from Smallville," Harris said. His poker face dissolved into a boyish grin.

"I forgot you were from around here." Jackson arched an eyebrow. "Do the Smallville jocks really turn some poor sap into a human scarecrow for luck in the Homecoming game?"

Harris shrugged. "If they do, they don't talk about it."

The elevator lurched to a stop. Since there wasn't a ranch house—an aboveground equipment and supply building that housed security personnel, maintenance teams en route between LFs, and others who supported the launch teams—the lift opened onto a platform eight feet below ground.

Wallace headed up the ladder first and opened the hatch. He climbed out and paused to take in the crisp October air.

"Man, what a perfect day."

Adam nodded in agreement as he stepped outside. White cumulous clouds dotted the azure sky, and the woods between the Stoner farm and the factory's expansive cornfields were vibrant with crimson and gold leaves. The top of the water tower was visible on the horizon, but they were too far away to read anything written on the tank.

"Do you think Howard is watching us?" Corey asked as he gave Harris a hand up.

"Wouldn't surprise me," Adam said.

Howard Stoner owned the neighboring farm, and the government paid him not to plant the fields near the Launch Facility. A Vietnam vet in his midforties, Stoner kept watch over the sensitive missile site. Although the installation was secure, the farmer considered it his patriotic duty to make sure no unauthorized personnel tried to break through the fence or into the silo.

"What the hell is that?" Wallace frowned.

Adam followed his gaze, tracking a glowing orb that trailed plumes of black smoke across the sky. "Get back down that ladder! Now!"

A split second after Adam spoke, the unidentified object struck a nearby cornfield. The impact set off the Preliminary Alert System sirens in Romeo Fourteen, which triggered the PAS in the distant, Romeo Eight Launch Control Facility. Smoke and debris spewed skyward as the unidentified burning object carved a scorched path through the corn.

Corey and Harris had joined Jackson on the elevator platform when the second orb hit the town.

"I thought the Soviet Union was on the brink of falling apart!" Wallace yelled as he threw his tool bag through the hatch and dropped. "Why would they want to start World War III now? In Kansas?"

"Let's not jump to conclusions," Adam advised as he moved down the ladder. Judging from the explosions, he didn't think the incoming objects were nuclear warheads.

"Who else but the Russians?" Jackson demanded as he started down the spiral staircase.

"We'll find out when I call Command," Adam muttered to himself, wincing when the water tower exploded. Steam, twisted metal, and splintered wood fell from a billowing fireball as he closed and sealed the hatch.

"This doesn't feel like a nuclear attack." Corey called out as he raced downward behind Jackson and Harris.

"No, but whatever it is"—Adam raised his voice to be heard over the blare of the PAS siren—"the safest place for us is sixty feet down in the LCC."

"I won't argue with that." Wallace hit the bottom of the shaft within a second of the three men ahead of him.

Turning left toward the Launch Control Center, they waited for Adam outside a curved yellow line painted on the floor. The line marked the swing arc of the six-ton door into the LCC. In an operational Launch Control Facility, the door could only be opened from the inside. They would also need to coordinate their entry with Romeo Eight because only one LCC door in the entire network was allowed to be open at any one time. However, since Romeo Fourteen was nothing but an expensive missile silo, the NCO in charge of the maintenance detail had the lock codes to access the restricted area, and he didn't need permission.

No one said a word as Adam checked his crew log for the second time that day and punched the lock code into an electronic panel. He and Wallace had inspected the LCC before they had gone into the Equipment Building. At least, they knew all the environmental systems were working.

Adam glanced at the red-stenciled warning on the massive door as it swung open.

NO LONE ZONE. SAC TWO-MAN POLICY MANDATORY.

If Romeo Fourteen had been utilized for its original purpose, no solitary individual would ever have access to the Sealed Authenticators and launch keys stored inside. But there were no launch protocols in this LCC, so the rule did not apply.

The entry through the thick wall was a narrow tunnel. The men followed Adam single file, stooping slightly to avoid the low ceiling. Wallace, the last man in, triggered the door to close, spun the wheel to lock it, and slipped the dead bolt into place.

The steel drawbridge between the walls and the floor of the outer room clanked as Adam jogged across. The rush of temperature-controlled air that protected the electronics added to the noise levels. Earplugs were usually worn in this section, but he couldn't spare the time to find them.

Adam tried not to assume the worst as he kept moving past a galley kitchen on the left and a latrine and storage locker on the right. Still, his wife and son were on his mind as he ducked through a doorway into the acoustical enclosure of the Launch Control Center proper, where rubbery floors and walls absorbed excessive noise.

Adam tried to force the thoughts of his family to the back of his mind as he dropped his tool bag and slid into the commander's chair. He silenced the PAS alarm, picked up the handset, and punched the call button for the LCC commander at Romeo Eight.

"Capsule. Identify yourself, please."

"This is Master Sergeant Adam Reisler on routine maintenance duty at R-141." Adam checked his crew log again and gave Timothy the team's assigned Maintenance Control Number.

"Roger, Sergeant," the captain said. "That checks."

Even though Captain Timothy sounded cool and collected, Adam didn't dare breathe easy. Every man and woman assigned to the Strategic Air Command missile defense system had nerves of steel. They didn't crack under pressure.

"Guess you're wondering what's going on out there." The tone of Timothy's voice remained matter-of-fact.

"Yes, sir," Adam responded evenly, sensing the tension in the men standing behind him. "We're a little curious. The Smallville water tower just blew up, and—"

The floor under Adam's feet shuddered, a sure sign that one of the objects falling from the sky had landed way too close for comfort.

"It's a meteor shower," the captain explained. "Sorry we didn't warn you, but nothing registered with the Twenty-fifth SW until they entered the atmosphere and started heating up. NORAD was notified immediately, and they've confirmed. It's meteors."

Adam nodded, letting out a long sigh. The Twenty-fifth Space Wing was a global network of missile warning sensors that also tracked every man-made object in space. A swarm of cold boulders the size of trucks or smaller wouldn't be easy to spot if no one was looking for them.

"Thanks, Captain," Adam said. "Give us a heads up when it's over, okay?"

"Will do." The line went dead.

"Rocks?" Jackson exclaimed with an incredulous lilt.

"From outer space." Harris wiggled his fingers in the gesture people often used to indicate something bizarre and creepy.

"What's that supposed to mean?" Jackson frowned.

"Well," Corey drawled, "if this was a science fiction movie, it might mean an alien invasion."

"Yeah, right." Jackson laughed.

"Except this isn't a movie. This is real life—" Wallace cringed when the floor underneath them shook again, and the power went out.

When the diesel kicked in a second later and the lights sputtered back on, Adam's pulse was racing. "Real life with a megaton punch."

CHAPTER 1

Present Day

Heading home from school, Clark followed a route through the woods and fields that he didn't use very often. It passed too close to a neighboring farm and skirted the far side of the LexCorp Fertilizer Plant property. He just didn't want to risk running into the surveyor he had spotted along his regular path yesterday. Sometimes he was late and missed the bus. Today he wasn't riding it because he had stopped by the Talon to unwind over a cappuccino with Pete Ross, his best friend since first grade.

As luck would have it, one of the waitresses had called in sick, and Lana Lang, the manager and unrequited love of his life, had been too busy to talk. He wanted to be more than friends, but the secrets he couldn't discuss always stood between them, a barrier to the total honesty Lana needed, but he still enjoyed her company.

Clark continued home, staying well out of sight of the two-lane state highway that intercepted Hickory Lane, the country road that ran past the Kent farm. Route 19 was too heavily traveled to be safe. Though a casual observer probably wouldn't realize that blur speeding through the corn at Mach 2 was a teenager, he had learned it was best not to take any chances.

Curiosity once aroused was impossible to suppress, an aspect of human nature Chloe Sullivan, aspiring investigative reporter, editor of the *Torch*, and another of his closest friends, demonstrated with maddening regularity. Chloe's insatiable desire to know had given him more than a few uncomfortable moments over the past couple years, since moving out of adolescence toward adulthood had caused his latent powers to emerge.

This afternoon was no exception. Knowing Lana was short-handed, Chloe had volunteered to dump the Talon trash. She had come through the back door just as a car screamed out of the alley, a moment after Clark saved a cat from being flattened under the tires. The startled animal had dulled its claws digging into his arm before it sprang free and ran away. Although Clark was adept at inventing lame explanations for the inexplicable, Chloe's inquiring mind never took anything at face value.

Chloe was probably in the Smallville High classroom that served as the *Torch* office right now. Clark envisioned her sitting at her desk, absently twirling a lock of blond hair as she mulled over the improbable facts: that the car had seemed to pause with wheels spinning a foot off the pavement an instant before Clark appeared holding a yellow tabby cat. Hopefully, she'd conclude that the glint of afternoon sun off polished metal had created an illusion.

If I'm lucky. Frustrated by the constant need to be on guard, Clark whacked a dangling limb off a maple tree. The branch disintegrated into splinters and sawdust with the force of the blow.

Other teenagers' raging hormones give them acne or fits of moody rebellion, Clark thought, peeling a strip of loose bark off a dead tree as he zoomed by. He had suffered a personality melt-down into dangerous delinquency because of red meteor-rocks, which a jewelry company had substituted for rubies in the Smallville class rings. *On top of X-ray vision and a heat ray that almost burned down the school and the Talon.*

Clark had learned to control his fiery gaze, but being able to cook an egg at thirty paces just by looking at it was not the most useful of his incredible gifts. The bus left without him more often than not, so his ability to navigate the dense woods at high speed without running into anything came in handy almost daily.

Clark made a sharp right to avoid a dense thicket and jumped a tree lying across the path. His reflexes were instantaneous, too fast to clock by any conventional means.

Not that anyone will ever get the chance to time me, Clark thought, smiling as he ducked under a low-hanging branch. A flurry of dislodged leaves swirled in his wake.

Pete was the only person besides his adoptive parents, Jonathan and Martha Kent, who knew about his extraordinary abilities. Clark hated lying to Lana and Chloe, but he had no choice. As his father had drummed into him over the years, the truth was too dangerous and the responsibility too great.

Pete had almost died learning that some people would stop at nothing to find out Clark's secret. Pete was threatened by a doctor who planned to inject him with a lethal meteor-rock formula in order to find out who the ship belonged to. Imminent death had not broken Pete's silence, but there were too many vicious people like that doctor in the world.

When Sam Fallon had tried to blackmail Clark into stealing an incriminating police file, Clark had double-crossed him. In retaliation, the dirty Metropolis cop had framed his father for murder. Jonathan wouldn't be intimidated by Fallon's threat to reveal the family secret, either. That was the only time Clark had been so angry he wanted to kill. He had outsmarted Fallon instead, but the memory of his destructive rage still gave him nightmares.

Clark deliberately avoided speculation about how Lex Luthor would react if he knew. Deep down, he suspected that the son of Lionel Luthor, a corporate tycoon whose wealth had been accumulated with unwavering ruthless resolve, wouldn't be able to resist exploiting the boy he called friend.

That was a test of character Lex would never have to pass. There was no way Clark would ever tell him or Lana or anyone else he cared about that he had arrived on Earth in the midst of the 1989 meteor shower.

I wouldn't have told Pete, either, except that keeping the secret wasn't worth losing his friendship. Besides, the truth had been the only way to explain why the Kents had a legitimate claim on the spaceship Pete had found in a cornfield after the Spring Formal twister.

Clark came to an abrupt halt in the trees lining the old government access road behind Howard Stoner's farm. The stench of fertilizer chemicals and the damp musk of forest decay drifted on a light breeze. Irritated by the combined odors, he wrinkled his nose as he scanned the large field that bordered the LexCorp plant property.

In keeping with the Arms Reduction Treaty George H. W. Bush and Mikhail Gorbachev had signed in 1991, the military had stripped and vacated the local Minuteman II missile silo in 1994. When the government left and the lease on the land expired, ownership had reverted to LuthorCorp. Mr. Stoner had maintained surveillance when the Launch Facility was active and, even though LexCorp owned the site now, he still felt duty-bound to protect the empty installation from vandals.

Most people had either never known or had forgotten that Smallville was once on the front lines of the country's missile defense system. Clark had researched the Launch Facility after he stumbled across it a few years back, when Mr. Stoner had tried to chase him away. On the rare occasions when he came this way, he always slowed to a normal pace in case the farmer was playing sentry.

Spotting Mr. Stoner heading toward his barn, Clark kept walking. The weeds that had overgrown the rutted dirt track from lack of use had been flattened. Someone had driven this way recently, probably by mistake since the road dead-ended. He hoped so. If people started using it, he'd have to find another alternate route.

Clark had no reason to hurry and didn't mind the leisurely pace. Except for a biology paper that was due the end of next week, he had finished his homework in study hall, and no practices had been scheduled for track or the swim team.

Like I need to practice, Clark scoffed with a disgruntled sigh. His remarkable memory and high IQ were much easier to hide — or explain when he slipped — than his exceptional speed, strength, and coordination. However, the physical attributes that made training unnecessary also gave him an unfair advantage in competition. After his father convinced him that football was too dangerous for everyone else if he played, he had begun participating in individual sports. He always performed at a level he thought he could have achieved with normal abilities. Only Pete knew he was holding back.

The farm chores his father gave him as a matter of principle, since he could do them without breaking a sweat, wouldn't take more than a few minutes. And he had no casual or pressing social engagements to round out his pathetically boring schedule.

Clark sighed again, recalling the conversation he had just had with Pete at the Talon. *Maybe it is time I started dating.*

Now that Lana was living at Chloe's house, having a romantic relationship with either one had gotten way too complicated. Clark, Lana, and Chloe had decided to just be friends after Ian Randall and his instant clone had almost killed both girls. It wasn't an ideal situation, but neither was constant emotional turmoil. He had warned Chloe and Lana that Ian was using them to secure the Luthor Foundation College Scholarship. They had both misread his intentions and dismissed his concern to side with Ian, a boy they hardly knew. He had finally come to terms with some undeniable truths. Lana couldn't deal with his secretive nature, and Chloe couldn't deal with being second to Lana. He was just tired of worrying about everyone else's feelings while his own were being shredded by misunderstanding, circumstance, and bad timing. Letting go had been sad, but liberating, too.

Deciding to date is one thing, Clark thought with a glance back at Mr. Stoner. *Going out on one requires a hot prospect I don't happen to have.*

Clark tensed as the farmer turned toward him, but Mr. Stoner wasn't going to run him off. The man clutched his throat as though he was choking.

"Mr. Stoner?" Clark called out.

The farmer sank to his knees and fell over, unaware of the boy streaking toward him. He wasn't breathing when Clark reached him.

"Hang on, Mr. Stoner." Clark dropped his books and tilted the man's head back to begin mouth-to-mouth. As he leaned over, he was stricken with a wave of familiar nausea.

Meteor sickness!

The effects diminished when Clark sat back on his heels, which meant the offensive alien material was near or on the man's body.

Bracing himself, Clark shoved his hand into the overall bib pocket on the man's chest. He bore the pain of muscle and tendon being twisted off bone and gritted his teeth while he patted down the man's sides. All the pockets were empty.

Did Mr. Stoner eat meteor particles? Clark wondered as he moved back out of range. Since he couldn't resuscitate the man without passing out, his ability to help was severely limited.

Unwilling to do nothing, Clark scrambled to his feet and sped to Stoner's small farmhouse. When he returned from Vietnam, the farmer had become a recluse, never marrying and living alone. Clark leaped over four steps onto the porch and pulled the screen door off its hinges in his frantic haste. Flinging the door aside, he burst into the small kitchen and dialed 911 on the wall phone.

"I was just walking by on my way home from school," Clark told the dispatcher after he identified himself and gave the address. "He looked like he was choking, but I suppose it could have been a heart attack."

"The rescue units are on the way, Mr. Kent." The woman's voice was void of emotion. "You will stay there, won't you? The police will want to get a statement."

"Yeah, I'll be here." Hanging up, Clark took a deep breath and glanced out the open doorway. He didn't want to leave Mr. Stoner lying in the field alone, but he had a bad feeling.

"Maybe because I've got a thicker police file than most of the petty crooks in Smallville," Clark muttered, dialing his home number.

His mother was working as Lionel Luthor's executive assistant at the Luthor mansion, and his father was setting fence posts. Except for the back pasture, they had replaced the fence the tornado had torn out the previous summer. Clark hoped to catch Jonathan on a break, but the answering machine picked up. He left a message.

"Dad, I'm at the Stoner farm waiting for the police so I'll probably be late. Mr. Stoner just collapsed in his field. He's— he's dead."

Clark replaced the receiver. His heart was heavy. This wasn't the first time he hadn't been able to save someone, but that didn't make the failure easier to bear. He would never get over losing Ryan James. He had been the young mind reader's Warrior

Angel, the boy's comic book hero come to life, except that all his powers couldn't cure a brain tumor.

Clark raced back to the farmer's body, unable to shake a persistent sense of dread. What if the next person he couldn't save was someone else he loved?

Clark glanced over his shoulder as a silver Porsche turned into Howard Stoner's driveway and stopped by the sheriff's patrol car. The roadster was the classic silver with black interior Lex Luthor seemed to prefer. The red Ferrari Clark had once borrowed was a holdover from the young entrepreneur's earlier life as a wild playboy in Metropolis.

"Nice car," Clark said, as Lex Luthor eased out.

"The GT2," Lex explained. "I'm test driving it for a few days." Impeccably dressed in a camel blazer, white shirt open at the neck, and dark brown slacks, Lex closed the door without a glance at the dust clinging to the perfect paint. "I like the Lamborghini Diablo VT better."

"Tough choice," Clark quipped.

"I don't have to choose, Clark," Lex said evenly. "Just decide whether I want to buy."

"Right." Clark shook his head with a sardonic grin. The combined price of both cars was probably close to $450,000, more than most people in Smallville made in ten years.

The heir to the Luthor fortune was not as indifferent as his father to the financial hardships borne by the working class. Blindness and a limp, the result of injuries incurred during a recent tornado, had not softened Lionel's heart or changed his perspective. Lex, on the other hand, often opened doors that might otherwise be closed to those who were willing to work and take risks.

The managers who mortgaged their homes to help buy the fertilizer plant from LuthorCorp had not just demonstrated faith in Lex, but also in themselves. Lex expected them to produce, but he also appreciated their courage and ambition. When anyone impressed him, as Lana had with her plan to turn the old Talon movie theater into a chic bookstore coffeehouse instead of a parking lot, Lex was generous with his praise and support.

The only exceptions to the Lex Luthor rule of personal engagement seemed to be Clark and his dad.

Clark knew that Lex's relationship with Lionel was more a war of wills than a bond of affection. For whatever reason, the young Luthor missed no opportunity to try to win Jonathan Kent's respect and approval. All his efforts had been futile, and that was before they found out Lex had hired the *Inquisitor* reporter, Roger Nixon, to investigate the car accident that had brought Clark and Lex together. Even though Lex had shot and killed Nixon to save Jonathan's life, he had little hope of getting into the elder Kent's good graces. Some burned bridges simply couldn't be re-built.

But it can't hurt to try. Clark wasn't thrilled with Lex's compulsive curiosity, either, but unlike his dad, he sensed there was a decent man beneath the hard exterior. For one thing, Lex had promised him the accident case was closed.

Lex's bald head gleamed in the late-afternoon sun. Lex had lost his hair in the meteor shower when he was nine, and growing up bald had been as influential in his development as his demanding father. The entire Luthor fortune could not have bought the inner strength and self-control the poised young man possessed.

As they strode into the field, Lex gestured toward the sheriff's deputies and paramedics gathered around Howard Stoner's still form. "I heard you were a witness to this."

"Where'd you hear that?" Clark asked, but only to tease his unlikely friend. Nothing happened in Smallville or Metropolis that Lex didn't know about. If by chance he didn't know, he had the resources to find out.

"Your use of barbed nuance is improving, Clark." Lex rarely smiled, but his inflection betrayed amused approval. He moved on without addressing the question. "What happened?"

Exhaling, Clark shoved his hands in his pockets and related the basic details. There wasn't much to tell, but his remorse was evident when he finished.

"It wasn't your fault." Lex fixed Clark with his steady gaze. "It sounds like Mr. Stoner died of cardiac arrest or respiratory failure. In either case, there wasn't anything anyone could have done to prevent the inevitable."

"On one level I know that, but on another . . ." Clark let his voice trail off as the paramedics picked up the stretcher with the farmer's body.

The men moved past Lex at a discreet distance. Out of fear or respect, Clark couldn't tell. In one way or another everyone in town depended on LexCorp and the fertilizer plant.

"What are you doing here, Lex?" Clark asked.

"I came to see if I could help a fallen neighbor—" The end of Lex's sentence was lost in the whupping sound of a helicopter flying in from the east.

Clark shielded his eyes with his hand as he looked up. "Your Dad?"

"Not a chance," Lex said. "My father doesn't pay his respects to anyone unless it represents a profit. Besides, he's getting ready for a business trip to New York."

"New York?" Clark's gaze snapped back to Lex. "Is my mother going with him?"

"No. Starting tomorrow, Mrs. Kent will have a week off with pay." Lex shook his head slightly, a rare demonstration of amazement. "My father is obviously pleased with her work."

"I know she likes her job, but it'll be nice having her home for a few days." Clark waited until the chopper was close enough for people with normal vision to read the printed words on the door. "It's from the Center for Environmental Protection. Who called in the CEP?"

"Your father, perhaps." Lex yelled to be heard over the sound of the descending helicopter.

Clark looked toward the drive as his father stepped out of the used red pickup they had bought after Roger Nixon blew up the old blue Chevy. The insurance money had been just enough to cover the purchase price, taxes, and licensing fees.

Jonathan stuffed a pair of leather work gloves into the back pocket of his worn jeans and slammed the door. His total disregard for appearances—scuffed boots, a denim shirt with frayed cuffs, and the shadow of a beard on his lean, weathered face— spoke of his confident, independent nature.

The air churned up by the chopper setting down several yards away whipped through Clark's dark hair. A dozen questions swirled through his head as his father drew closer. Had he come to offer support, or did he have another motive? Lex seemed to think the latter, but except for being causally acquainted neighbors and members of the Grange, the Kents had no connection to Howard Stoner or his farm.

A young man wearing a navy blue CEP jacket and cap got out of the chopper before the rotor blade stopped turning and jogged across the field. He and Jonathan reached Lex and Clark at the same time.

"Mr. Kent?" The CEP agent's glance flicked from Lex to Clark's father.

"That's me." Jonathan extended his hand, his expression grim. He put his other hand on Clark's shoulder. "This is my son, Clark. He saw Howard collapse."

"Gary Mundy," the young man said. "The field agent assigned to the case."

Guess that answers that. Clark's jaw tightened with the realization that his dad had called in the local environmental watchdog organization. Since Jonathan hadn't even given Lex a nod of acknowledgment, it wasn't hard to figure out why.

"Isn't it premature for the Center of Environmental Protection to be involved?" Lex asked. He handled Jonathan's snub with quiet diplomacy, by not recognizing that the slight had occurred.

Jonathan anticipated Mundy's next question. "Lex Luthor, CEO and controlling owner of the Smallville Fertilizer Plant."

"Mr. Luthor." Mundy nodded curtly, but he didn't offer his hand. "My field tests may take several days."

"What exactly are you testing for?" Lex pressed.

Clark grew increasingly dismayed as he followed the exchange. The CEP and the Luthors' corporate interests were almost always opposed, but Lionel and Lex usually prevailed. No one could prove that the preferential treatment and legislative cover their business enterprises enjoyed were secured with political contributions or intimidating practices.

"Chemical contamination from your plant, Lex," Jonathan said.

Clark sagged. "Dad—"

Jonathan silenced him with a sharp look. "If Howard didn't die of natural causes, the town has to know what did kill him."

Lex was unperturbed. "Wouldn't it be easier and less costly to wait for the medical examiner's autopsy report tomorrow?"

"Maybe, but the data from my initial tests won't go to waste." Mundy shrugged as he surveyed the unplanted field. "I'll just add the results to the database we keep on this whole area."

"I see." Lex's calm tone and demeanor didn't fluctuate as he continued. "It would be wise, Mr. Mundy, to be absolutely certain you have irrefutable evidence that my company is responsible for Mr. Stoner's death before CEP or anyone else files an official complaint."

"Is that a threat?" Jonathan's blue eyes narrowed.

Clark winced. His dad blamed himself for bringing the fertilizer plant with its smokestacks and toxins to Smallville. Lionel had formed Metropolis United Charities for the sole purpose of arranging Clark's no-questions-asked adoption. Jonathan had not known the process was a sham until after the fact. In return for Lionel's silence, he had reluctantly agreed to convince the Ross family to sell the Creamed Corn Factory to LuthorCorp. He had done it to protect Clark and his mother, but Jonathan had never forgiven himself for giving in to Lionel's extortion. His guilt fueled the belief that Lex was as unprincipled as his father.

"It's good business, Mr. Kent," Lex said calmly. "I really don't want to see you in court."

And Lex was always giving Jonathan reasons to think he was right.

CHAPTER 2

Pete hustled to keep pace with Clark's long stride as he marched into the *Torch* office. Chloe was seated at her desk, surrounded by files and notes, staring intently at her green computer.

"Why weren't you on the bus, Chloe?" Clark asked.

"What?" Chloe blinked with surprise as she looked up from the screen at Clark. "You were?"

"Clark was *waiting* at the end of his driveway," Pete said with a grin. "That's got to rate a couple inches on the front page of the next edition."

Ordinarily, Clark was immune to the teasing about his proclivity for being tardy, but he resented it today. Mr. Stoner's death was weighing on his mind, but his unease was lost on his friends. Pete knew he didn't have to rely on ordinary modes of transportation and was needling him in fun. Although Chloe was intrigued by how often Clark beat the bus, she was enjoying the friendly banter at his expense too much to mention it. Rather than make them uncomfortable, Clark let the humor run its course.

"Below the fold, maybe." Chloe squinted, pretending to consider the suggestion. "If it's a slow news cycle."

"Around here 'slow news cycle' stretches the bounds of the probable, doesn't it?" Pete walked past her and dropped into a straight-backed chair at another desk under the windows. "This is Smallville after all."

"Good point, Pete!" Chloe's smile faded into a feigned look of regret. "You're going to have to do better than making the bus to meet my editorial criteria, Clark."

"Doesn't seeing somebody die qualify?" Pete asked, pained expression flashing across his face the moment after the words were spoken. "Sorry, Clark. I didn't mean to sound so—"

"Insensitive?" Clark perched on the corner of the desk that stood back-to-back with Chloe's in the center of the room. He held Pete's dark gaze for a moment before letting him off the hook. "Not a problem, Pete. You were just stating the facts. I did see Howard Stoner die."

"At the risk of sounding even more insensitive," Chloe said, "people die in Smallville all the time. What's the hook with Mr. Stoner?"

"You mean a startling and/or strange angle?" Pete shrugged. "There isn't one, is there, Clark?"

"I don't know about 'strange,'" Clark said, "but it's pretty startling to watch someone drop dead."

"On a scale of what to what?" Pete asked, clasping his hands on his knees. "I mean compared to killer posies, girls that suction body fat, and tormented teenage poets who turn into sunlight monsters and toss people through windshields?"

Pete's yardstick for measuring the bizarre was based on numerous odd and ghastly experiences that were routine by Smallville standards. The country's most prestigious academic, scientific, and government institutions gave no credence, at least publicly, to the idea that meteor-rocks caused molecular changes in some individuals under undetermined, and perhaps myriad, conditions. Chloe had independently arrived at that theory after she moved to the farming area from Metropolis in the eighth grade. Although the evidence, by chance or design, never survived long enough to prove or refute the meteor hypothesis, Clark, Lana, Pete, and Clark's parents all had reasons to believe it.

"On a scale of one to ten?" Clark hesitated.

"Mr. Stoner gets a spooky factor of zero," Chloe answered. "His death isn't relevant to life at Smallville High, either. Sad, yes, but not exciting enough to risk testing Mr. Reynolds's idea of acceptable topic parameters."

Clark understood Chloe's concern. She had been fired as *Torch* editor once for writing inappropriate articles based on conjecture. Now, rather than tempt the wrath of authority, she censored her more outrageous inclinations before the school newspaper went to press.

The new principal was more willing to give Chloe creative latitude than the old one, who had been crushed between his car and the back wall of his garage. Although Chloe knew more about that incident than the professionals reporting in the *Smallville Ledger*, she had curbed her investigative instincts to write a noncontroversial, tasteful obituary for the deceased principal.

If Chloe had to go to the mat for a story, the story would have to be worth putting everything on the line. Clark, however, wasn't interested in a headline.

"This isn't about a story, Chloe," Clark said. "I had another reason for wanting to talk to you on the bus."

"Which brings us back to Clark's original question," Pete said. "Why weren't you on the bus, Chloe?"

"Lana wanted to do some research in the library before class, so I rode in with her and Dad." Chloe sat back with a sigh. "This paper doesn't write or publish itself, you know. I've already drafted a scathing critique of the cafeteria's most recent assault on student stomachs—"

"You mean that ground beef in white gravy stuff they served on burned toast last Wednesday?" Pete asked.

"That tasted like paste?" Clark grimaced.

"Exactly," Chloe said. "And I've exchanged two e-mails with Chad."

"Who's Chad?" Pete asked.

The answer popped up from the reams of trivia stored in Clark's memory. "Isn't Chad your Goth friend at the Medical Examiner's Office?"

"The dark and brooding one and only." Chloe laughed. "Do you know how many shades of gray there are?"

"I don't care." Pete held up a hand to end further discussion.

"Can you find out Mr. Stoner's cause of death?" Clark asked.

"Asphyxiation." Chloe tapped a command on her keyboard, starting the printer. "Like I said before, unless something unusual turns up in the lab work, Mr. Stoner's demise is strictly obit material."

Clark took the e-mail Chloe pulled from the printer tray. Chad's memo style was short and to the point. The one word answer, "asphyxiation," was apparently in response to a question Chloe had e-mailed him about the farmer's death. *So she was curious*, Clark realized. *Until Goth Guy's message killed her hopes for a scoop she could peddle to the* Ledger.

"He choked to death?" Clark asked.

"Not necessarily," Chloe said. "A lot of things could have made him stop breathing."

"I saw him grab his throat before he collapsed." Clark stared at the floor, frowning as he replayed the events of the previous afternoon in his mind. Whatever had stricken the farmer had been sudden. "Will Chad give you the lab results?"

"Sure." Chloe nodded. "Do you think something funny might turn up?"

"No, just curious." Smiling to mask his distress, Clark handed the e-mail back. Something in his tone or manner had registered on Chloe's reporter radar, but there was no hot story to pursue. He just wanted to know, beyond any doubt, that there was nothing he could have done to save the dying man.

Max Cutler glanced over the unoccupied round stools at the lunch counter in the Uptown Diner. All the red vinyl seats were torn and patched with gray duct tape. He chose the stool with the fewest repairs to prevent snagging his trousers.

Dressed in a blue suit and red tie, Max stood out like a solitary red barn on the vast prairie among the truckers and farmers. However, his current circumstances didn't require a cover that blended in. He had spent the morning posing as a real estate developer from Metropolis looking to buy large tracts of land. Economically depressed people who were anxious to sell large tracts of land were always eager to talk to a prospective buyer.

So far, he hadn't learned much, but it was too early to say if that was good or bad.

"Coffee?" A heavyset, middle-aged woman wearing a pale green-and-white waitress uniform asked without smiling.

"Please. And a Danish." Max set the overturned cup on his saucer upright and glanced at the name tag pinned to her apron. CARLA SUE.

"Heated with butter?" Carla's dour expression didn't change as she finished pouring. She reached into a tub of ice under the counter and set a chilled dish of creamer packets in front of him. "Apple or cheese?"

"Apple, heated, no butter." Max answered with a strained smile. Standing just under six feet tall, with a muscular physique, he had a classic chiseled profile and straight teeth. Lacking the patience to fuss with his unruly, thick brown hair, he kept it clipped short. He was not Hollywood handsome, but most women found him attractive and charming. Carla Sue obviously did not.

Annoyed, Max unfolded the local newspaper he had purchased from a coin box outside. Making idle conversation with the brusque waitress might not be necessary. The Smallville *Ledger* was a journalistic joke compared to Metropolis's *Daily Planet*, but it might have the answers he was looking for. He took a careful sip of black coffee and scanned the front page.

The elderly man sitting two stools down leaned closer. "You that fella looking to buy some land for a housing project?"

"Yes, sir, I am." Max set down his cup to shake the old man's hand. "Max Cutler."

"Hank Sidney." Hank dropped a spoon on his saucer and picked up his cup. "You can probably get the Stoner farm pretty cheap if Lionel Luthor wants to sell."

"Stoner farm?" Max adopted a studied look of puzzled ignorance.

"Top of page two," Hank said. "Poor Howard just keeled over dead yesterday. Didn't leave any family that I know of."

"Really?" Max lifted the paper out of the way as Carla Sue returned with the Danish. "Just up and died, huh? For no reason?"

"Nothing weird, if that's what you're getting at." Hank sighed and rubbed the stubble on his chin. "Of course, there's probably a bunch of legal stuff to be cleared up. Before the land can go on the market, I mean."

"Probably, but thanks for the tip." With a curt nod, Max turned his attention back to his breakfast and the news story about Howard Stoner's death on page two. The only information of any interest in the short article was the undisclosed identity of the teenager who had found the body.

Ten seconds after Hank drained his coffee cup and left, Carla

Sue was back. "Believe me, mister, you don't want to build houses on the Stoner property."

Max swallowed a bite of his warm pastry. "Because that guy died?"

"Maybe," Carla Sue answered cautiously.

"Hard thing for a kid to see," Max said, fishing for a name. "I hope the experience doesn't traumatize him."

"It won't." Carla Sue sounded certain. "Clark Kent was raised on a family farm. Got loving parents. He's one of the most down-to-earth kids in town."

Max pressed on without a hint that he had learned something he needed to know. "So why wouldn't I want to build houses on the Stoner farm?"

Still holding a coffeepot, Carla Sue cast a wary glance at the door. "Because it's right next to the LexCorp fertilizer plant."

After he retired as a CIA field agent to seek more lucrative employment, Max had put many of his acquired intelligence-gathering techniques to use in the private sector. All his professional methods were effective, but none had proved as informative dollar for dollar as the waitresses in the coffee shops throughout America.

"Hmmm." Max arched an eyebrow. "A fertilizer plant could present some difficulties. The plant must really stink up the neighborhood."

"Much worse than that, pal." Carla Sue lowered her voice. "People around here suffer from all kinds of odd sicknesses. A lot of them die suddenly, just like Howard Stoner, and there's only one explanation that makes any sense at all."

Max blinked. "Which is—"

Carla Sue rolled her eyes and hissed. "They've been exposed to some kind of poison runoff from that plant! Not that anyone will say so—except me, of course."

Max didn't have to ask for clarification. In a town the size of Smallville, at a time when small family farms were increasingly unable to compete with more efficient agribusiness corporations, an enterprise such as the fertilizer plant would be the main support of the community.

"Don't the police get suspicious?" Max asked softly.

"Ever hear the saying, 'You can't fight City Hall'?" The large woman shook her head, sadly. "Around here nobody tangles with Lionel or Lex Luthor. Nobody. Not even the sheriff, if he can help it."

"I will keep all that in mind, Carla Sue. Thank you." Max pulled a ten from his wallet to pay for his three-dollar meal. "Keep the change."

"Come back anytime." Carla Sue's expression remained stony as she put the money in her apron pocket. "But if anybody asks, you didn't hear nothin' about nothin' from me."

"About what?" Max asked.

He drank another leisurely cup of coffee and finished browsing through the paper to dispel any speculation about his conversations with Hank and the waitress. He left the diner without another word to anyone, stopped by the drugstore to buy two paperback spy novels, then drove his rental car out of town at exactly two miles over the limit. The speed was calculated to reflect the driving habits of most people. As expected, the cop in the patrol car he passed paid no attention to him.

Max didn't reach into his inside jacket pocket for the cell phone until he hit Route 19.

The phone wasn't there.

"What the hell?" Slamming on the brakes, Max swerved onto the shoulder and threw the gearshift into park. His throat went dry, and he tightened his grip on the steering wheel to stop his hands from shaking. He filled his lungs with air and exhaled slowly, forcing himself to calm down.

As part of his cover, Max had stayed at a motel the night before. He remembered using the cell phone to call Dr. Farley that morning from the car after he had checked out.

Remembering that cleared Max's muddled mind. He had been annoyed last night when he realized he hadn't packed the cell phone charger. This morning, to boost the drained battery, he had plugged the phone into the cigarette lighter adapter, which he *had* remembered to bring.

Max glanced at the ashtray in the console below the radio. The cell phone was lying inside the plastic insert where he had left it. Taking another deep breath, he picked up the phone and speed-dialed.

"Yes?" Dr. Lawrence Farley answered abruptly. Caller ID had informed the scientist that his operative was checking in.

"Nothing," Max said, and disconnected.

Considering Dr. Farley's less-than-stellar scientific reputation, it wasn't likely anyone would go to the expense or trouble to listen in. Even so, maintaining meticulous security was a habit Max's covert ops training would not allow him to break.

Dr. Farley was just one of many oddball researchers funded by Continental Sciences, a consortium of banks and businesses headquartered in France. Since the geneticist had been dismissed from the university after losing a government grant, his project proposal had been met with little enthusiasm. However, the men on the consortium's board had accrued great wealth by gambling that an unorthodox or seemingly preposterous area of study would eventually pay off.

Dr. Farley had sold Max on the financial potential of his idea with a single key point. Development of a technology often occurred before all the possible applications were understood. The unique and specific technological requirements of the space environment and program had resulted in thousands of product spinoffs, particularly in the fields of medicine, miniaturization, and computers. While the government was mandated by law to make any discoveries freely available, he and Dr. Farley were motivated by the promise of profit.

There's no such thing as being too careful, Max thought as he drove back onto the highway. Scientific and industrial espionage was as cutthroat and dangerous as the political game, especially when billions of dollars were at stake. He would brief his partner in person, which would take all of five minutes.

Max couldn't believe their accidental luck. Isolation wasn't the only benefit of setting up shop in Smallville. Not a single person he had contacted suspected that Howard Stoner had been murdered. Even better, since everyone assumed the fertilizer plant was responsible for any unexplained deaths in the area, the Sheriff's Office probably wouldn't open an investigation. It made sense that nobody, including the authorities, would want to rock the boat that paid the bills.

It was also imperative to confirm that his assumptions were correct and no loose ends remained to trouble them later.

Dr. Farley would be greatly relieved by his report, which would settle Max's jangled nerves. When the scientist worried too much, he had trouble concentrating on his work, and the work was vital to his future.

Max sighed as he put the cell phone back in the ashtray. He could no longer delude himself that his memory lapses were temporary aberrations. The mental blanks and spasmodic shakes were symptoms of something much more serious.

"Mrs. Kent to the rescue!" Lana rushed forward to greet Clark and his mother, but her gushing gratitude was aimed directly at Martha. "You're a lifesaver."

"You're lucky Lionel went to New York, and I had today off." Martha held the Talon door open for Clark.

"Thanks." Clark exchanged a knowing glance with his mom. The tray laden with freshly baked pies wasn't heavy for an alien with super-human strength. He could have easily balanced it on one hand to open the door, but he was supposed to be human. His mother had been acting out the charade of the Kent kid's normalcy for so long her responses were automatic.

"I know." Lana's bright smile lit up the entryway. "I couldn't believe the bakery shorted my order! I was in a panic this morning until Clark told me you were home."

"Where do you want these, Lana?" Clark asked.

"On the back counter by the pie case." Lana waved toward the far side of the room, then inhaled, closing her eyes to savor the scents rising off the warm pies. "These smell heavenly."

"Tell me about it," Clark said. The aroma of apples and custard spiced with cinnamon and nutmeg had driven him crazy since they had left the farm. "Tortured by tantalizing temptation all the way into town, and no way to sneak a taste."

"Not if you want to keep your fingers." Martha smiled. "I set aside two pies for you and your father."

"Two pies each?" Clark asked, sagging when his mom shook her head.

Lana laughed at the affectionate repartee.

Clark's heart seemed to swell as he looked into Lana's gentle brown eyes. Everything outside the frame of her flawless face and long, dark hair lost focus. The effect she had on him was as disconcerting now as it had been the first time he had noticed she was a *girl*, back in middle school. *Just friends*, he reminded himself, ignoring the warm flush that crept up his neck as he edged past her.

Lana walked behind Clark with Martha. "I really can't thank you enough, Mrs. Kent. I was dreading having to spend all night explaining why we didn't have any pie. Now we've got the best pie in Kansas."

"I was happy to do it." Martha's blue eyes sparkled above a beaming smile as she handed Lana the bill.

"I'll vouch for that." Clark set down the tray. "To watch her in the kitchen, you'd think she gets up at five every morning to bake muffins for fun."

His mother had started a home baking business to earn extra money before Lionel Luthor had hired her. Except for the occasional special order, such as the wedding cake for Lex's disastrous wedding to Desiree Atkins and Lana's emergency pies, she sold muffins to convenience stores, the retirement center cafeteria, Denehey's Pitstop, the Talon, and the Uptown Diner. She worked too hard, but she wouldn't give up either endeavor. Being perpetually broke was not the only reason. She loved the challenge of dealing with the headstrong corporate mogul and the personal sense of accomplishment represented by the long list of muffin clients. His dad complained now and then, but didn't interfere.

"You mean she doesn't slave over a hot oven for fun?" Lana pretended to be shocked as she opened the cash register and handed an envelope to Martha.

"Actually, she does," Clark admitted.

"How about a mocha cream cappuccino?" Lana shoved the

cash drawer closed. "My treat for service above and beyond, Mrs. Kent. You, too, Clark."

"I'd love one, Lana, but I've got a date with a pair of scissors at Charlene's. I am weeks overdue for a trim," Martha replied, patting her shoulder-length, auburn hair as she slipped the envelope into her purse. "But Clark doesn't have any plans."

"No, I'm free." Nodding, Clark folded his arms and looked at Lana. "If the offer's still open, and you can sit down for a few minutes."

The hesitation before Lana accepted the invitation was almost imperceptible. "We're kind of busy, but—since everyone showed up for work today, a cappuccino break sounds great."

Martha called back over her shoulder as she walked away. "I'll be done in an hour if you want a ride home, Clark."

"I'll be here." Clark's eyes filled with admiration as he followed his mom out the door. He was certain that no one but Martha Kent could have coped with raising a willful child who used hay bales as building blocks and won tug-of-wars with stubborn cows. He was also positive that no one could have taken better care or loved him more.

"You might as well sit down and relax while I make these, Clark." Lana pulled two large cups off a shelf.

As Clark scanned the crowded room, he caught Sharon Farley watching him. She sat by herself near one of the supporting pillars decorated with Egyptian graphics. Pretty, with gray-green eyes, short blond hair, and freckles, she nervously averted her gaze. The girl hadn't been very sociable since transferring to Smallville High three months before. Some kids thought she was conceited, others assumed she was shy.

Maybe nobody's tried to make her feel welcome.

Although it wasn't deliberate, Clark felt badly for making her feel self-conscious. There was a free table next to Sharon, which gave him an ideal opening. He ambled over and spoke as he sat down.

"Hey, Sharon. How's it going?"

Sharon sat with her back to the pillar and her feet propped on the opposite chair. She looked up from a paperback book with a start. "Uh, fine."

"Clark Kent." Clark folded his arms on the small, round tabletop and smiled. "We're in the same biology lab, but I don't think we've actually met."

"Yes, I know. I mean, no, we haven't—" Sharon winced. A stressed smile emphasized an expression of aghast disbelief, as though she had just committed the social gaffe of the year.

"Until now," Clark added, to put her at ease.

"Until now." Sharon sighed with an apologetic shrug. "So— have you picked a subject for your biology paper, yet?"

"No, but I've got a couple ideas." Clark had the distinct impression Sharon was surprised and pleased that he knew her from class and had made the effort to engage her in conversation. "To be honest, the 'lifestyles of primordial single-celled organisms' isn't particularly inspiring or exciting."

"Maybe not"—an impish twinkle brightened Sharon's eyes— "unless you're the first single-cell to get the bright idea of combining with another single-cell to reproduce, thus changing the pace and character of evolution forever."

Was that a serious attempt at conversation, or is she flirting? Either way, Clark was momentarily speechless. He recovered quickly. "I don't think conscious thought was a factor."

"For what?" Lana set down two cups of cappuccino laced with chocolate and topped with whipped cream.

"Topics for our biology papers." Clark nodded at Sharon. "We're in the same class."

"Hi. I'm Lana." Lana smiled and slipped into the chair opposite Clark. "And you're Sharon, right? Am I interrupting?"

"No, not at all. I've got a lot of homework anyway." Sharon held up the paperback.

"Are you sure?" Lana twisted to look behind her.

"Thanks, Lana, but I can't today." Sharon pulled a small notebook out of her backpack and began to write, leaving no doubt that the conversation was over.

"Okay." Lana turned back to Clark with a confused frown.

She shrugged, sighed, and picked up her cup.

"Busy place," Clark said. Although sitting so close to Lana incited his hormones to riot, he was determined to make the "just friends" pact work for real and not merely as a pretense. "Almost every table is taken."

"Yeah." Lana gave the crowd a sweeping glance. "Thank goodness. I think Lex will be pleased with this month's financial report."

"I'm sure he will." Clark lifted his cappuccino cup and sipped, pretending to be afraid he'd burn his mouth.

"So you had quite a day yesterday," Lana said. "It must have been terrible, seeing Mr. Stoner die like that."

Clark nodded. "Not my idea of a fun afternoon. He was walking across his field one minute and then—wham. His air is cut off, and that's it."

"He choked on something?" Lana frowned. "The newspaper didn't say anything about that."

"I'm just guessing, based on what I saw." Clark sighed. Behind Lana, Sharon was still scribbling in her notebook.

"Well, the *Ledger* got the time wrong, too." Lana shook her head. "You left here at four-twenty-five, so you couldn't possibly have called 911 from Mr. Stoner's house at four-forty."

Clark swallowed hard. He hated being in a position where a lie was his only option. For someone who could run faster than a jet could fly, it was entirely possible to have made a phone call from the Stoner farm fifteen minutes after leaving the Talon. He wished he could tell Lana everything, but he couldn't ask her to bear the burden of knowing. Pete was still constantly stressed out by the fear that he might let Clark's secret slip. Clark regretted that, but he couldn't take the truth back after it was known. So he felt it was best to keep Lana from knowing.

"It's the Smallville *Ledger*, Lana," Clark said. "Not the *Daily Planet*."

Lana shrugged. "Yes, but they usually don't make such sloppy mistakes."

Clark decided to let the subject drop.

At the next table, Sharon shoved the notebook and pen into her backpack and zipped it up.

Preoccupied with the disturbing necessity of deceiving Lana,

Clark didn't register that Sharon's fleeting glance and smile had been meant for him until the girl was gone.

Lie to one girl and brush off another. Way to go, Clark, he berated himself. For a supersmart guy, sometimes he was really dense.

Clark paused at the top of the stairs. Judging from the intense discussion going on in the kitchen, his parents weren't expecting him to come down early. Even he was a little surprised that the new morning routine was working so well.

His mom had suggested putting his new alarm clock on the chest across the room so he had to get up to turn it off. Before, crushing clocks had been an unavoidable consequence of hitting the snooze alarm when he was awakened suddenly from a sound sleep.

"But Lex wasn't responsible for poisoning the herd, Jonathan," Martha said evenly. "A man pretending to be that girl's dead fiancé did."

"You're missing the point, Martha." Jonathan sounded annoyed. "If someone doesn't take a stand soon, the Luthors will just keep poisoning this county until nothing can live here."

"I know, but that's not *my* point," Martha countered.

Clark felt uncomfortable eavesdropping. His parents often disagreed, but they rarely had a heated argument. He wasn't sure what to do. He just knew that he didn't want to walk into the middle of verbal parental combat.

"You're not defending *them*, are you?" The edge of irritation in Jonathan's tone sharpened.

Sighing, Clark focused his X-ray vision on the floor. Wood and air ducts vanished to reveal the solid objects in the kitchen. His father's skeletal form was seated at the table. His mother bent over to pull a muffin tin out of the oven.

"No, but some hotshot attorney will, and *that's* my point." She kicked the oven door closed with her foot. "You can't sue LexCorp for illegal polluting without proof."

Dad wants to sue Lex? Stunned, Clark blinked. His vision flickered back to normal for a second before he readjusted.

"If the CEP tests prove that chemical seepage from the plant

caused Howard Stoner's death, I'll have all the proof I need."
Jonathan drained his coffee mug and set it down.

"Maybe." Martha gingerly transferred the hot muffins to
delivery boxes. "Here's something to think about, though. The
main reason my father's law practice was so successful is that
he never took a case he wasn't sure of winning."

"Let's leave your father out of this, okay?" Jonathan snapped.
"There's a principle involved, Martha," he continued, softening
his tone. "This has nothing to do with money."

"It has everything to do with money, Jonathan." Martha untied
her apron and draped it over a chair as she sat down. If she felt
stung by her husband's remarks, she didn't let it show.

"Maybe you're right," Jonathan said. "Since money is all the
Luthors care about, losing a few million will hit them where it
really hurts—in their bank accounts. It's their Achilles' heel."

"If we win, yes," Martha agreed. "But there are some hard
facts about how the judicial system works we can't afford to
ignore. All the new laws tend to favor big business over us little
people."

Jonathan nodded, but he wasn't deterred. "I was thinking
about a class action lawsuit. The united-we-stand approach would
give us a fighting chance."

"Don't get me wrong, Jonathan." Martha placed her hand over
his. "I'll be right there fighting with you, if you decide this is
something you have to do. I just want to be sure you understand that if we lose in court, we'll have to sell the farm to pay
for it."

"Some fights are worth the risk." Jonathan clasped Martha's
smaller hand in both of his.

Taking that as an all clear, Clark zipped down the stairs.

"What's the rush, son?" Jonathan glanced at the clock on the
stove. "The bus won't be here for another half hour."

"Breakfast." Clark dropped into a chair beside his dad. "I was
hoping Mom made an extra tin of muffins."

"Blueberry or bran?" Grinning, Martha pushed a basket across
the table.

"Both." Before his mother finished removing the cloth napkin
that had kept the muffins warm, Clark jumped up, pulled a glass

from the cabinet, opened the refrigerator, poured himself some OJ, grabbed the butter dish, and returned to his chair. "Do we have any more of Martha's Wild Strawberry Jubilee?"

"I'll get it." Jonathan stood up to refill his coffee mug and brought a jar of homemade jam back to the table.

Clark unscrewed the lid and pried the paraffin seal out with the tip of his knife. Every batch of his mom's jams and jellies was dubbed with a fanciful Martha name. His favorite was still Martha's Moose Morsels, a blackberry and red currant concoction she had created and he had named when he was eight.

Rising, Martha set the empty muffin tins in the sink. "I've got to change and make my deliveries. There're so many things I need to catch up on around here, I don't want to waste a minute of my week off."

After his mother went upstairs, Clark bit into a blueberry muffin. He chewed slowly, enjoying the taste of tart berries and warm, buttery bread while he put off asking his dad about the lawsuit for a few more seconds.

"It might be a good idea to take the bus or ride into town with your mother today." Jonathan blew on the hot coffee to cool it. "We wouldn't want Mr. Mundy to catch a glance of you whizzing by while he's collecting soil samples from Howard's field."

"No, that wouldn't be good." Clark brushed the crumbs off his jeans. The CEP agent had seemed pretty sharp, and probably wouldn't miss a disturbance that cut through the woods like a horizontal twister. "I probably shouldn't say this, Dad, but—"

"But what?" Jonathan lowered his cup.

"You don't have to sue Lex." Clark took a breath and plunged ahead. "Anytime there's damage linked to the fertilizer plant, Lex pays for it—even when it's not his fault, like when we lost the herd."

"That's the problem, though, Clark." Jonathan didn't raise his voice or get defensive. "LuthorCorp leaves environmental destruction, death, and ruined lives in their wake with impunity."

"LuthorCorp maybe, but Lex always tries to make things right," Clark argued. "What about Earl Jenkins? Lex wasn't even in charge of the plant when that explosion happened. He didn't even know there *was* a level three, but he's paying for Earl's treatment's anyway."

"Ask yourself why, Clark," Jonathan suggested. "What's the real reason Lionel is paying to find a cure for Byron's problem with sunlight?"

The teenager Clark and Lana had befriended suffered from side effects as a result of being in a Metron Pharmaceuticals' medical study when he was eight. Clark wasn't surprised when Chloe found out that Metron was a subsidiary of LuthorCorp.

Clark sighed, but he didn't interrupt his father.

"Because he feels remorse and responsibility for his actions? No." Sitting back, Jonathan rubbed his chin and looked past Clark at the wall.

"Okay," Clark said. "Then why?"

"Because your mother convinced him that a generous and genuine attempt to help was more cost-effective than trying to recover from a drop in the LuthorCorp stock price."

"At least, he's doing something." Clark had a habit of looking for the best in people, even those with few redeeming qualities. His father usually admired that particular character trait, except when Clark applied it to anyone surnamed Luthor.

"You and your mother both have a blind spot when it comes to Lex and his father." Jonathan was more perplexed than angry, and he couldn't hide his frustration.

"Maybe your *prejudice* is what's off. Not our *judgment*." Clark felt frustrated, too.

Jonathan stood to get another cup of coffee. The pot was empty, and he set it down harder than he had intended to. "Someone has to stop them from buying people off to avoid embarrassing court appearances and bad press. The Luthors use their money to make sure that no costly precedents are set."

"But if you push this lawsuit, and we don't win—" Clark looked away.

The thought of losing the farm was something the Kents lived with every day. Defaulting on their loan because they couldn't make a financial go of it was one thing. Clark just couldn't accept selling to pay for losing a misguided lawsuit they shouldn't have filed in the first place.

"I haven't made a decision, Clark. Consider me an exploratory committee of one." Jonathan smiled to reassure him. "I'm just looking into the possibilities, getting some advice. That's all."

Clark nodded and reached for another muffin. There was no point in pressing the argument. Once his father set his mind on something, he had to follow through. With luck, the medical examiner's lab report would show, beyond doubt, that contamination from the fertilizer plant was not a factor in Howard Stoner's death.

Nothing less than absolute proof of Lex's innocence would convince Jonathan Kent to back down.

Pete leaned against the wall, watching Clark shove books into his locker. Carrying the extra weight wouldn't bother his powerful friend, but nobody hauled afternoon work to morning classes.

"Did Chloe hear back from Chad, yet?" Clark asked.

"She didn't say anything on the bus, so I guess not." Pete shrugged. Clark had ridden into town with his mother. He didn't know Chloe had adopted a wait-and-see attitude regarding Howard Stoner's sudden death. "Our intrepid *Torch* editor doesn't seem to think anything weird is going on."

"Or maybe she's just keeping a lid on because she doesn't want to give Reynolds any ammunition." Clark slammed his locker closed. "Why buy trouble for nothing?"

"Excellent point," Pete said. Chloe's investigative instincts often overrode her better judgment. However, she had no problem subverting her inner reporter if the survival of the school newspaper and her job as editor were threatened.

"Believe me," Clark continued, "if something even a little unusual turns up in Mr. Stoner's lab report, Chloe will be all over this story for the *Torch*."

"Or the *Smallville Ledger*," Pete added. He turned, surprised by a muffled gasp behind him. He didn't know how long Sharon Farley had been standing there. A stricken look faded from her face.

Upset because we ignored her or embarrassed because we caught her eavesdropping? Pete wondered.

"Hi, Sharon." Clark smoothed over the awkward moment with a friendly smile. "Do you know Pete Ross?"

"From English class." Sharon nodded, her mouth pressed in a tight smile. She clutched a notebook to her chest as though it was the only thing keeping her afloat in a stormy sea.

"Going through *A Tale of Two Cities* line by line," Pete joked. "Kind of takes the fun out of reading the story, though, doesn't it?"

"Uh-huh." Sharon cleared her throat and handed Clark paper-clipped pages that had been torn from magazines. "I, uh—thought these might give you some ideas, Clark—for your biology paper."

So she was working up her courage to interrupt, Pete realized. He couldn't imagine being so shy that just talking to someone was traumatic. It seemed especially sad for a girl as pretty as Sharon Farley. Apparently, Clark had breached the introduction barrier in the not-too-distant past and just hadn't thought it was worth mentioning.

"'The Absence of a Fossil Record' and 'Single to Multi-cellular Organisms: The Missing Leap.'" Clark read the titles and scanned the top pages of both articles. "An interesting concept."

"I thought so. Maybe it will help." Sharon's hesitant manner eased as she began to relax.

That wholesome Clark Kent appeal is certainly working like a charm. Considering Sharon's obvious infatuation, Pete had to wonder if all females were born with some instinctive mechanism that sensed a superior male, the primal prerequisite for the perpetuation of the species. *For all the good it will do her. Clark doesn't have a clue that she's interested in him!*

"It might." Clark glanced at the torn edges of the pages. "Where did you find the magazines?"

"My dad never throws away anything related to science." An unexpected smile brightened Sharon's face. "But he keeps all of it hoping that I *will* get interested enough to rip out the articles."

"Is your father a scientist?" Pete asked.

"He was. He worked for a university back East." Sharon sighed. "But he lost his research grant and decided on a midlife career change."

That explained the magazines, Pete realized, but his question had also struck a nerve. He hated having to explain why his father and uncle had sold the Creamed Corn Factory to Lionel Luthor shortly after the 1989 meteor shower. He didn't put Sharon on the spot by asking what her dad was doing now.

She volunteered the information with a sheepish grin. "My dad has a wild imagination so maybe he'll make a great science fiction writer."

Pete started. "He's writing a book?"

Sharon nodded. "A novel. We moved to Smallville so he could work without distractions. Nobody knows us so nobody bothers him."

"Isn't that a little hard on you?" Clark asked.

"A little, but it's getting better." Sharon blushed.

"Well, thanks for these." Clark slid the magazine pages into his backpack.

"It's the least I could do," Sharon said. "I know I wouldn't be able to keep my mind on school stuff if I saw someone die."

Clark shrugged, his expression troubled. "I was just sorry I couldn't do something to save Mr. Stoner."

"Maybe it was hopeless," Sharon offered as consolation. "Does anyone know what killed him?"

"Asphyxiation," Pete said, "but we won't know what caused that until Chloe gets the autopsy lab report."

Sharon blinked. "Chloe has an in with the medical examiner?"

"Chloe has sources everywhere," Pete said, then suddenly realized he might have said too much. He relaxed when he realized that Sharon's attention was locked on Clark.

When Pete first learned about Clark's gifts, he had been a little envious and a lot intimidated. Even though Clark didn't flaunt his abilities, how could he or any other red-blooded boy from this planet compete? Then Pete had realized that Clark was light-years behind him when it came to dealing with the opposite sex. He had made it his personal mission to improve Clark's love life—whether Clark approved or not.

And the immediate circumstances demand an instant intercession, Pete decided.

Clark wasn't picking up on Sharon's inept cues, but they both had a biology paper to write. Not much, but it was a starting point. More importantly, Clark didn't have a history of friendship to overcome with the new girl. There was no telling how long the "friends only" policy with Lana and Chloe would last, but for now, the pledge was in effect.

Still, swimming the Atlantic might be easier than playing Cupid for Clark. Pete sagged with dismay when Clark suddenly ended the conversation.

"Speaking of the *Torch*, I have to go explain to Chloe why I'm not done with the overdue library book list for the next issue." As Clark started to leave, the first bell rang. "Guess I'll have to catch her later."

Pete sighed as Clark shouldered his backpack and took off down the hall. His first class was in the opposite direction.

"Don't mind Clark, Sharon. He can be a little—" Pete's explanation hung in the air as he turned. "—manic."

Sharon was already walking away.

Chloe Sullivan sat back in her desk chair. She eyed Sharon Farley's earnest face with the suspicious mind of a reporter trying to peel layers of spin off the facts. "You seriously won't mind doing cafeteria polls?"

"Actually, I can't think of a better way to get to know some of the kids here." Sharon's gaze drifted around the *Torch* office, then snapped back to Chloe. "Because if I'm doing a poll, I'll have a *reason* to talk to people, you know?"

"Well, there is a certain logic to that." Chloe smiled, appearing more at ease than she was. She had been completely unprepared when the new girl walked in, practically begging to be on the school newspaper staff.

Chloe's only impressions of Sharon Farley were vague at best. She was cute in an all-American way, with a trim figure, short blond hair, and freckles, but she had stayed removed from Smallville's teen set during her three months at the high school. Since Clark typed up the lunch menu, sport schedules, club activity notices, and other miscellaneous filler pieces, almost every cub reporter assignment on the *Torch* required face time with people—students and teachers. A timid new kid wasn't really a good fit.

As though sensing her uncertainty, Sharon edged her chair closer to the desk. She leaned forward with a white-knuckled grip on the notebook in her lap. "What about a trial period?"

"Like probation?" The idea hadn't occurred to Chloe, but she liked it. She also admired Sharon's tenacity, even though the go-get-it personality was incongruous with the rabbit rep Sharon had acquired.

"Yes, for a week? Maybe, two?" Sharon asked hopefully. "Then, if I don't meet your high standards for the *Torch*, I'll bow out without a fuss. Promise." She crossed her heart.

Chloe's baloney detector red-lined. She didn't mind being known as a hard taskmaster, but performance and attitude were what counted, not suck-up compliments. Still, a trial week seemed fair. Besides, if Sharon spent her lunch periods asking students how they really felt about the new principal's closed campus policy, she wouldn't have to.

"All right, we'll give it a try." Chloe held out her hand to shake on it. "I've got a student survey I want to start during lunch on Monday, so rest up over the weekend."

"Great!" Sharon beamed. "This is so exciting. I've never told anyone this, but I love solving mysteries, getting down to the bare bones of what's what."

"Really?" Chloe tried to look interested.

"But I'm thinking about going into journalism, as a career," Sharon went on, "instead of law enforcement. Being a cop would be way too dangerous."

Journalism in Smallville is way too dangerous. Chloe nodded to cover her dismay. After months of isolation, Sharon obviously had reams of pent-up conversation ready and waiting to roll off her tongue. *And, apparently, I just opened the floodgate.*

"Like that dead farmer Clark Kent found." Sharon shuddered and lowered her voice. "How come nobody thinks it might have been foul play? How often do people die in the middle of fields around here?"

More often than we like to admit.

Chloe sighed. The *Smallville Ledger* hadn't published Clark's name because he was a minor, but everyone in town had known he found Mr. Stoner before that edition hit the streets. The truth was, Chloe hadn't dismissed the possibility of foul play. She was just waiting for hard evidence.

A good reporter doesn't jump to conclusions, Chloe reminded herself. *She just explores all the angles on the QT. Then, if it turns out that Mr. Stoner had a heart attack, I won't have to grovel or apologize or print a retraction.*

Chloe repeated the new mantra frequently to keep from stepping over the line with Mr. Reynolds. In Smallville, foul play was always a possibility until something disproved it, but most people blamed the fertilizer plant for inexplicable illness and death. Very few thought the meteor-rocks caused the strange things that happened in the area, but that didn't make the theory untrue.

Sensing a potential ally, but wary out of habit, Chloe chose her words carefully. "I haven't dismissed the idea that Mr. Stoner might have died from something other than natural causes, Sharon. It's just that the school authorities tend to freak if the *Torch* speculates. We have to be able to prove what we print."

"See?" Clark elbowed Pete as they came through the door. "I told you Chloe was just being careful."

"Hi, Clark!" Sharon grinned.

Chloe noted the sparkle in the girl's green eyes as they followed Clark into the room. A hint of crimson bloomed on Sharon's cheeks, and her breath caught in her throat when he smiled.

All the symptoms of a Clark crush, Chloe observed.

Suddenly caught in the grip of conflicting emotions, Chloe rejected jealousy in favor of empathy. Sharon didn't yet know she had competition she couldn't beat.

Although she, Lana, and Clark had agreed to avoid complications that could ruin their friendships, Lana also needed time to grieve for her fallen ex-boyfriend. Clark was honoring that, but keeping his emotional distance didn't alter how he felt. He loved Lana.

And Chloe loved him. She had been overjoyed when Clark asked her to the Spring Formal. Then, after promising not to, he had abandoned her on the dance floor to check on Lana. Chloe was strong and resilient, but her self-respect wouldn't survive another botched attempt at romance with Clark Kent. In the end, it was easier to accept Lana's hold on his heart.

Eventually, Sharon would figure out that Clark wasn't tied down *or* available. In the meantime, Chloe would try to cushion the girl's inevitable appointment with heartbreak.

"Hey, Sharon." Clark sat down at the desk opposite Chloe. "I'm surprised to see you here."

"I'm not," Pete muttered as he pulled up an empty chair.

"Starting Monday, I'll be part of the *Torch* team," Sharon explained.

"Really?" Clark cocked an eyebrow at Chloe.

"You know those student polls you and Pete won't do?" Chloe asked. "Sharon will."

"I'll give it a shot, anyway." Sharon glanced at the large clock on the wall above the black filing cabinets. "I'd love to hang out, but I've got math this period."

"Take it easy." Clark turned back to Chloe before Sharon reached the door. "Any word from your man in the Medical Examiner's Office?"

"Not yet." Chloe frowned when she realized Sharon had paused in the doorway. "Was there something else, Sharon?"

"Uh—no, I was just wondering . . ." Sharon shook her head. "Nothing."

No one said anything until the girl was gone.

"Why would someone who quakes at the thought of talking to strangers *want* a job talking to strangers?" Pete asked.

"So they won't be strangers," Chloe said. "Or so she said."

"You don't believe that, either, do you?" Pete looked at Chloe.

"Nope. Not for a minute," Chloe said with a smug smile.

"Why not?" Clark frowned, puzzled. "Asking a survey question seems like a great way to start a conversation with someone you don't know."

"Yeah, but getting to know the student body is not why Sharon Farley wants to work on the *Torch*." Chloe threw up her hands when Clark just looked at her. "She wants to get to know *you*, Clark. Specifically."

"You're kidding, right?" Clark's surprised glance flicked between his two friends.

"Not kidding." Pete slid off the table. "If you're seriously thinking about dating, Sharon Farley is primed to say yes when you call."

Dating? Stunned, Chloe stared as Pete handed Clark a folded paper.

"Sharon's phone number," Pete explained. "I took the liberty of calling information."

Chloe's heart sank when Clark put the paper in his shirt pocket and glanced toward the door. The curious interest in his eyes conveyed the gist of his thoughts.

Clark was going to make that call.

"Don't forget to turn out the lights when you come up, Clark." Martha paused halfway up the stairs.

"I won't." Clark smiled. "Goodnight, Mom."

"See you in the morning." Yawning, Martha hurried up to the second floor.

When he heard the bedroom door close, Clark got up from the kitchen table. His father had been asleep for an hour, and his mother had just finished her ironing. He had changed his mind about calling Sharon Farley three times while he waited for his mom to go to bed. If he decided to ask Sharon out, he didn't want anyone listening to his side of the conversation.

Clark sighed as he put the cordless handset on the table and sat back down. Pete and Chloe had tried to act as though going to the movies with someone was no big deal. He knew better. They really thought that spending a Saturday night with Sharon would be a breakthrough event. His parents would probably have a similar reaction.

It's like I'm finally putting Lana behind me.

Exhaling again, Clark rested his chin on his folded arms. He loved Lana, in the truest sense of the word, but also in a way that transcended the mundane. She would always be a part of his life, as important to his existence as breathing. But destiny, for reasons real or imagined, seemed bent on making sure they never became a couple.

Whitney's death had put Lana's obsession with Clark's secrets into a more realistic perspective, but the lack of trust remained an obstacle. A close relationship couldn't survive without honesty. Intuitively, they both seemed to know that any mutual romantic interest was best left alone, at least for now. Instead, they clung to the long friendship, which would survive time and circumstance.

Including taking Sharon Farley to see the latest Jackie Chan film.

Taking a deep breath, Clark unfolded the paper Pete had given him with Sharon's number, picked up the phone, and dialed her house.

Sharon answered on the third ring. "Hello?"

"Hi, Sharon. This is Clark Kent."

After Clark hung up, Sharon sat back with a smile. This was the first social telephone call she had gotten since moving into the rented house on the outskirts of Smallville.

"Who was that?" Her father peered over the top of his newspaper.

The headline of the *Smallville Ledger* read: Farmer Suffocates in Field. Sharon had read the story earlier. The reporter who wrote it didn't know anything more than Chloe and probably didn't have the junior journalist's connections. As Lana had pointed out yesterday, the local paper had mistakenly reported the time Clark made his startling discovery.

"Clark Kent," Sharon answered. Setting the cordless back in its cradle, she drew her knees up to her chest.

The corner of her father's left eye twitched, a sign that he was struggling with a "daughter dilemma," his code for her perplexing teenage problems. "The boy who found Howard Stoner?"

"That's the one." Sharon smiled. Fifty-three and graying at the temples, Dr. Lawrence Farley looked like a stiff, out-of-touch scientist in his starched white shirt and blue, herringbone tie. He *was* totally uptight, and she couldn't help teasing him. "We're going to the movies tomorrow night."

Dr. Farley flinched. "On a date?"

"Yes, on a date." Noting the tension in his neck, Sharon hastened to reassure him before he had a stroke. "Can you think of a better way to get a teenage boy talking about his exciting adventures?"

"Perhaps, not." Dr. Farley's perpetual frown deepened. "Assuming boys are still prone to bragging about their exploits to girls."

"They are." Sharon decided not to mention that Clark Kent was not like other guys his age. Talking to her at the Talon had been a genuine gesture of friendship, not a put-down or a come-on. Clark had been honestly concerned that she had torn the evolution articles from someone else's magazines and might get into trouble, and he regretted not being able to save the dead farmer.

"Just be careful." Dr. Farley carefully folded the paper and placed it on the end table. "I could face criminal charges if anyone finds out what I'm doing here—"

"They won't," Sharon interrupted, recalling a snippet of conversation she had overheard between Clark and Lana at the Talon.

"I'm just guessing, based on what I saw," Clark had said.

Which was what exactly? Sharon wondered. Since Clark wasn't upset or spooked, it was probably nothing they had to worry about.

"I don't think there's a problem, Dad," Sharon said.

"I hope you're right." Dr. Farley glanced at his watch and sighed.

When he stood up, Sharon was once again grateful that she had inherited her mother's looks and physique. Her slender frame gave the illusion that she was taller than five-foot-five. Her father was only three inches taller and losing his fight with a steadily thickening middle. He had been tennis fit with a charming grin before her mom died of pneumonia eight years before. He rarely smiled now.

"Dinner in fifteen minutes." Dr. Farley removed his glasses and slipped them into his shirt pocket. "Then I have to go back to work."

"Please, take the box back with you." Sharon glanced at the lead-lined container on the side table in the front foyer. Her father's fear of legal complications was nothing compared to her dread of having meteor-rocks in the house.

Max Cutler paused on the edge of the woods to study the soft ground. It had rained recently, but Layton Crouse's tracks were not easy to spot, even though he knew what to look for. Knowing that the mutant hunted in a circular pattern helped.

Moving out slowly, Max swept his gaze back and forth across the terrain to both sides and straight ahead until he spotted a clump of feathers. He squatted to examine the dead bird and noticed the palm-sized depression nearby. The three other imprints that marked the expansive, lumbering stride were positioned right where he expected. Layton's reach measured just short of twelve feet at its extreme limits. By digging in with his hands, he could pull his body and legs forward in a fluid motion that resembled a running ape.

More efficient and elegant, but apelike nonetheless, Max thought. The leisurely four-beat gait was only one of Layton's exotic modes of movement.

Rising, Max sighed with annoyed exasperation. Given his contributions to the project, being left alone to watch golf on Saturday afternoons didn't seem like too much to ask. However, Dr. Farley could neither find nor control the escapee.

Max did not negate his partner's value. There wouldn't be a project without Lawrence Farley's theories and scientific expertise. Still, acting on connections he had established while working for the CIA, Max had contacted Continental Sciences and arranged the financing. He had also supplied the required function data for the prototypes, recruited the volunteers, found the ideal location to conduct the experimental phase, then designed and supervised the installation of a high-tech security system worthy of a black ops facility.

But Farley was anxious about his daughter's impending date with the Kent kid and had forgotten to secure the entry hatch before he entered the elevator. While the scientist could contain and sedate the other failed experiments, Layton was unaffected by drugs and had a predator's need to prowl. Plus, Layton's control was improving, and he was learning to squeeze through smaller and smaller openings. So instead of watching the final holes in today's PGA tournament round, Max was chasing down a psychotic killer.

Max kicked the limp body of the bird aside with a snort of disgust. Espionage professionals wouldn't have hesitated to terminate a liability such as Layton had become. But, even though Farley was responsible for turning him and four others into genetic monstrosities, his warped ethics wouldn't tolerate permanent disposal.

"These are men, not lab rats!"

That was true. The men Farley had modified in the early human experimental phase passed the time cowering in corners, staring at the walls, pacing, weeping, or making as much noise as possible. Their bizarre behaviors were in constant flux and too numerous for anyone but the scientist to catalog.

When the rats went insane, they ate their own tails before they tore each other apart. Prior to that, they were perfect little subjects with a variety of engineered abilities. At least the latest batch of his precursors had been.

But the missing Layton and fate of his sanity weren't his only problems at the moment.

A shiver traced the curve of Max's spine as the sun dipped behind the LexCorp fertilizer plant on the far side of the cornfield. He had an hour at most before sunset, and judging by the pattern of prints, Layton had cut back into the woods instead of completing the circle.

Something had caught his attention and lured him off course.

Layton's senses had been enhanced as an unintended side effect of the molecular transformation process. Any living thing within range of the madman's ability to smell, see, or hear would satisfy his crazed desire to kill something. Layton seemed to achieve the same bloodthirsty high from ripping rosebushes out by the roots as he did from strangling cows.

Cursing, Max moved into the trees. Since Max's own alter-form wasn't appropriate for a capture mission, Layton had the advantage. The fugitive's ability to shift bone and muscle into an elastic rubbery state made him harder, if not impossible, to track. He could stretch or swing from tree to tree without touching down. As the project progressed, Farley hoped to re-create Layton's physical properties without the mental deviations.

A chorus of animal squeals shattered the twilight stillness.

Homing in on the high-pitched screams, Max raced through the dense woods. The urgency that empowered his legs had nothing to do with the senseless slaughter of wild woodland creatures, however. The killing spree was a reminder of what terrified him most: Farley had not isolated the cause for the loss of mental acuity in Layton and the others.

They had all been derelicts scrounging out an existence in the alleys of the Metropolis warehouse district. Feeble-minded, drunks, and addicts, they had signed their lives away in exchange for an unending supply of their chosen poison. Farley was convinced their moronic mentalities and damaged brains simply couldn't adapt to the stresses of transformation. The doctor had made some adjustments to the process, and the altered rats had thrived.

Consequently, when Layton first escaped three weeks ago, they had accelerated the schedule for Max's procedure. That he would undergo the process had always been part of the plan. Max had to be an alter-form to command them. Layton had proven that necessity repeatedly. Even in the delirium of a feeding frenzy, the elastic mutant obeyed him.

Since Max was strong in body with a disciplined mind, and the rats appeared stable, Farley had been confident that he wouldn't suffer any mental deterioration. Then a week ago the rodents had gone berserk, and Max had forgotten the password to access his computer files.

Max stopped abruptly, stricken with the shakes as the memory of that traumatic moment rushed back. The trees seemed to close in around him, and he closed his eyes to shut out the claustrophobic illusion. He concentrated on breathing, trying to still his racing pulse as the horror of that fatal instant battered him again.

Max still didn't know how long he had stared at the blank rectangular box in the password access window on the computer screen before he stood up to get a cup of coffee. He had glanced at the lone rat left in the laboratory cage as he picked up the pot. The pitiful animal was running in circles, chasing its tail, and slamming its head into the glass.

Glass had always formed the boundaries of the rat's world, and yet, it had forgotten the glass was there.

Just as he had forgotten the password he had been using since they had set up shop in the old missile silo.

Max didn't forget things—ever. In that flash of insight seven days ago, he had realized that his mind was failing, too.

Layton was the key to whether or not the process of his mental deterioration could be slowed, stopped, and perhaps reversed. The elastic mutant's mental and physical condition was stable, which Farley insisted made him important to finding a fix. That, not the scientist's sensibilities, was the only reason the lunatic Layton was still alive.

"What's going on here?"

The sound of a man's voice brought Max to a halt just before he broke from the trees. Hanging back, he peered through a natural mesh of twig and leaf. A young man wearing a CEP cap and jacket hurried across the field. Max identified him as Gary Mundy, the environmental agent mentioned in the newspaper article about Stoner's death. Mundy must have been conducting tests in the fallen farmer's field when he heard the animal squeals. Max was too late to intercept the agent before he saw the pile of mutilated rabbits.

Shocked into mute paralysis by the carnage, Mundy didn't see Layton emerge from a hole in the ground behind him. The mutant had apparently slithered right into the rabbits' burrows to grab them from their nests. Elongated from head to toe and streaked with dirt, he still looked vaguely human as he shot across the furrowed ground.

Mundy yelped and dropped his soil sample tube as one of Layton's spaghetti-thin arms wrapped around his ankles. The agent toppled like a felled tree, and Layton's other arm snaked into his mouth, cutting off his air. The young man struggled for an agonizing moment before Layton crushed his ribs and tore into his flesh with his teeth.

As a precaution, Max waited until the mutant's murderous impulses had completely abated. He stepped out of the trees as

Layton tossed Mundy's lacerated body onto the heap of dead rabbits.

Layton's stretched limbs and torso snapped back to normal when he saw Max. Knobby-kneed and gaunt, with stooped shoulders and a sunken stomach, the man's naked body was almost as grotesque as his misshapen alter-form.

"Come on, Layton. Time to get back inside." Max considered hiding Mundy's corpse but thought better of it. If the agent vanished, the authorities would mount a search of the area as soon as someone reported him missing. A broken body might prompt an investigation, but he could easily misdirect the search for evidence. With luck, the death would ultimately be classified as another unsolved, Smallville mystery.

"Hi, Max." Layton's words were slightly garbled, an effect of the mutation's diminished intelligence. "You mad?"

"No, I'm not mad." Max shook his head. Since Mundy had seen too much, Layton had saved him the trouble of killing the agent himself. "But I need you to do me a favor."

"Okay, Max." Dirty and docile, Layton patiently waited for instructions.

Instead of heading straight toward the chain-link fence that enclosed the old missile launch facility, Max retraced his path. He instructed Layton to slither behind and erase his footprints. With the sun sinking in the western sky, Max hurried on a circuitous route through the woods to Stoner's gravel driveway. Once there, he had Layton re-form. As they headed across the field to the dirt access road, he walked in the naked man's tracks to obscure the impressions made by bare feet. His own boot prints were lost in the dozens left by the sheriff's deputies and paramedics the afternoon Stoner died.

Not all his bases had been covered yet, however. They still didn't know how much Clark Kent had actually seen that day that Stoner died.

◆◆◆

"I didn't realize Jackie Chan was so funny." With both hands on the steering wheel and her attention on the road, Sharon laughed softly. "I thought his movies were just kung fu fights and stuff."

"You haven't seen a Jackie Chan film before?" Clark asked. He had suggested going to the martial arts comedy because it would be simple, entertaining fun. No depth, sap, or gory mayhem that would make either of them uncomfortable. He was uncomfortable enough without any external help.

"No, but I guess I should have," Sharon said. "Does he really do all his own stunts?"

"That's what they say." Clark shrugged. "I'm not sure."

For the first time since he had asked Sharon out, Clark started to relax. His parents' attempts to pry, without seeming to pry, had just added to his misgivings. He had been blunt, limiting his responses to Sharon's name, their destination, and estimated time of return. To avoid a full-scale interrogation, he had let Sharon drive instead of asking to borrow the family pickup. He had dashed outside the instant she pulled into the driveway, but his mom had not been able to resist peeking through the curtains. As they drove off in Sharon's 1987 Audi sedan, Martha Kent's curious gaze had burned into his neck with the intensity of an alien heat ray.

Clark couldn't tell if his mother and father were glad or sorry that he was making an effort to move beyond Lana. He hadn't known the answer to that himself—until now, after he had gone on an actual date with someone else.

Once Sharon Farley got over being shy, she was intelligent and pleasant with a witty sense of humor. He had enjoyed her company, but . . . she wasn't Lana.

Everyone close to him thought his infatuation with Lana was futile. Maybe it was, but he couldn't help how he felt. Eventually, he would resolve the emotional dilemma one way or another. He might even fall in love with someone else, but Sharon wasn't that someone.

Sharon sighed, as though she had just made a tough decision. "I'm not sure how to say this, Clark, but I was wondering—"

"About what?" Clark asked, anticipating an awkward scene. He didn't want to hurt Sharon's feelings, but if she hinted about "doing this again," he'd have to be honest. It wouldn't be fair to lead her on.

Sharon sighed again, heavily. "Chloe's Wall of Weird."

Surprised, Clark hesitated. "Yeah?" He started. "What about it?"

"It's just so—creepy!" Sharon shivered with dread. "Don't you worry that something awful might happen to you?"

"Like growing an extra thumb or waking up covered with green spots?" Clark smiled, with relief, to put Sharon at ease, and to cover his unspoken lie. Unless fate was sitting on some additional surprises, being an alien who got sick around green meteor-rocks and mean around red ones seemed to be the extent of his Smallville maladies. "Not really."

"I wish I was that sure." Troubled, Sharon caught her lower lip in her teeth. "There're too many instances of strange things in this town to be coincidence. There must be a reason, some common denominator."

"Most people blame the fertilizer plant," Clark said. He didn't mention that his father was one of them.

Sharon frowned. "If chemicals got into the groundwater or something, that might account for some of the sicknesses."

"Except the county tests the water regularly, and no one's ever found proof of seepage from the plant," Clark explained. It wasn't right to give Sharon the impression that LexCorp was responsible for the strange things documented on Chloe's Wall of Weird.

"That doesn't exactly make me feel safer," Sharon said.

Clark understood her fear, but it was probably groundless. "You live in town, Sharon, a long way from the fertilizer plant."

Since Sharon had just moved into Lowell County, her suscep- tibility to the mutating effects of the meteor-rocks was minimal, too. The more severe molecular anomalies occurred in people who had lived through the meteor shower, particularly as young children. As long as she wasn't exposed to meteor-rocks for any length of time, Sharon should be okay. Unfortunately, he couldn't explain that without explaining Chloe's meteor theory, which might be more upsetting than reassuring.

"The Sheriff's Office here doesn't exactly instill confidence, either." Sharon's gaze flicked to Clark's face for an instant. "I did some checking. There have been dozens of unexplained deaths in Lowell County over the past several years, but it's like the local cops don't care."

"They care," Clark said. "It's just that this is a small farming community with limited resources. Unless it's an obvious murder, the sheriff can't afford to investigate."

"Well, Chloe hasn't ruled out foul play." Sharon's tone was casual, but she flashed him an impish smile. "And apparently, neither have you."

"What gave you that idea?" Clark was completely taken aback. He hadn't even considered murder as a possibility. He definitely hadn't said anything to suggest it.

"Mr. Stoner's autopsy lab report!" Sharon rolled her eyes. "You're obviously anxious to get the results."

"I'm curious," Clark admitted, with a shrug to mask his anxiety.

"Right." Sharon scoffed. "Chloe told me she has to be able to back up all her *Torch* stories with proof. I'm sure the high school newspaper doesn't have an eyewitness exclusive for very many dead guy articles."

More than you could possibly know.

"We've actually solved a couple cases at the *Torch*," Clark said with a touch of bravado. Sharon didn't seem to have a motive beyond idle curiosity, but he couldn't be sure. Instead of denying his interest, he tried to dilute the significance with mild bragging and truth that sounded like a lame excuse. "We just can't always print what we know or take credit."

"So you *do* think someone killed Mr. Stoner," Sharon said.

"I didn't say that," Clark hedged.

Sharon, however, was fixated on the idea of murder. She frowned as she mulled over the possibilities. "If someone slipped him poison, it would show up in the lab work."

"Yeah, but if the medical examiner suspected that, he would have asked the lab to do the work stat," Clark said. "Besides, if Chloe honestly thought Mr. Stoner had been murdered, she wouldn't care if Mr. Reynolds disapproved. She'd be hounding her friend for the lab results every hour on the hour."

"Chloe's interested," Sharon insisted. "I could tell."

Clark gave up trying to dissuade Sharon from her line of

thought. However, she wasn't even warm about his interest in the case. Wondering if he could have saved Mr. Stoner was part of it, but that also served as a feasible cover story for Chloe. He couldn't tell Chloe he thought meteor material would turn up in Mr. Stoner's stomach because he couldn't explain why. Chloe didn't know meteor-rocks made him sick. The nausea he had felt near the farmer's body couldn't have been anything else, but he hadn't found any meteor fragments in Mr. Stoner's clothing. After the body was loaded into the ambulance, he had gone back to check the spot where the farmer had fallen. He had not gotten ill.

If Howard Stoner had died of natural causes or meteor-rock ingestion, then his father wouldn't have grounds to sue Lex. Clark hadn't mentioned that to Chloe or Pete, either. He was hoping his dad would give up the idea of a lawsuit before Lex found out about it through the local grapevine.

"I've never had a chance to work on something this important before, Clark." Sharon slowed the car as they approached the turn off onto Hickory Lane. "Chloe won't have a problem with that, will she?"

Since he wasn't sure how Chloe would feel, Clark glossed over the question. "Provided there *is* a story, it's hard to say. I know Chloe will be grateful if you do a good job on that cafeteria poll."

Sharon turned left onto Hickory Lane without asking if he wanted a coffee nightcap at the Talon. Clark's ego wasn't bruised because she didn't want to prolong the date. That was actually a relief. But it was marred by the suspicion that Sharon had ulterior motives for going on this date.

Monday after school, Clark ran home by an alternate route to avoid the being seen by the CEP agent working at Stoner's farm. He wanted to get his chores out of the way before he met Chloe back at the *Torch*, and riding the bus took too long. Chad had promised to call her by five with an update on Howard Stoner's lab work.

Since the pickup wasn't parked in the driveway, Clark was surprised to see his father sitting at the kitchen table.

"Did Mom go somewhere?" Clark dropped his books on the stairs on his way to the refrigerator.

Jonathan frowned. "She's at Mrs. Bronson's having her secondhand clothes altered."

"Oh." Clark winced as he searched the open fridge for a quick snack.

Since they needed his mother's paycheck from Lionel to keep the farm going, she had refused to invest in a new business wardrobe. She was a capable seamstress, but she no longer had time to make her own clothes. Instead, she spent an occasional Saturday shopping at thrift stores and outlet malls in the Metropolis suburbs. On her last outing, she had been thrilled to find three outfits that were practically new and only needed minimal alterations.

Martha Kent viewed the bargain-hunting expeditions as a challenging game. His dad felt humiliated by the necessity but tried not to show it. He didn't always succeed.

Jonathan answered the phone as Clark emptied the milk carton into a glass.

"Mr. Small! Thanks for returning my call." Jonathan sat back. "Henry, then."

Clark listened as he made himself a cheese and peanut butter sandwich, a flavor combination no one else on Earth seemed to enjoy as much as he did.

Henry Small, a direct descendant of the town's founding

family, was an attorney, environmental activist, and outspoken opponent of the Luthor corporations' unchecked polluting practices. He was also Lana's biological father. According to her, Mr. Small had forsaken the prestige of editing a law journal to handle hopeless cause cases from his home.

Clark sat down with his milk and sandwich as his dad finished outlining the situation.

"I've talked to every lawyer in Smallville and Metropolis who isn't on a Luthor payroll, Henry," Jonathan explained. "Most of them don't want to be on the Luthors' black list for any price. The rest want more money than I make in a year as a retainer."

Chewing slowly, Clark felt a ray of hope. Maybe he was worried for no reason. His father *couldn't* sue LexCorp if he couldn't find a lawyer to take the case.

Jonathan wouldn't be much better off if Mr. Small agreed to represent him. According to Mrs. Small, the lost cause advocate had the attention span of a gnat. His interest in anything was subject to abrupt shifts that left his clients and cases hanging. Lana wasn't convinced his wife's assessment was accurate, but the jury on that one was still out.

Clark fine-tuned his hearing to pick up the lawyer's voice.

"Have you thought about mounting a class action suit?" Mr. Small asked. "That would reduce the amount each individual has to pay."

"I thought of that and made some calls." Jonathan picked up his pen and tapped the pad in front of him. The repetitive motion helped defuse his anger. "Nobody will join a case against the town's main employer."

"I know." Mr. Small sighed. "I have a hard time getting anyone to sign a petition that involves the plant. Can't say that I blame them."

Clark couldn't, either. With the possible exception of the weather, the LexCorp fertilizer plant was the single most important factor in Smallville's economy.

"Except that people are dying." Jonathan's expression had shifted from hopeful to discouraged to grave during the course of the discussion. Now his jaw flexed with determination.

Clark washed down the sandwich with the last swallow of

milk. The look on his father's face did not bode well for the Kents's meager fortunes. In spite of the obstacles, his dad wasn't even close to giving up.

It isn't just the possibility of losing the farm that bothers me, either, Clark realized. He hated being torn between Lex and his father, and a legal dispute was too important to avoid choosing sides. And this time, unless irrefutable proof of Lex's guilt turned up, he was afraid his father was on the wrong side.

"Something killed Howard Stoner, Henry," Jonathan continued, "and that farm is a little too close to mine not to be concerned."

"Did the medical examiner find anything that supports chemical poisoning as the cause of death?" Mr. Small asked.

"The lab reports won't be in until later today or tomorrow," Jonathan said.

And with any luck they'll get Lex and me off the hook, Clark thought. He sped to put his glass and plate in the sink and returned to his seat without missing a word.

Mr. Small hesitated before suggesting, "You could give Joe Reisler a call."

"Reisler? That name sounds familiar." Jonathan wedged the phone between his shoulder and chin as he jotted it on the pad.

"Football." Mr. Small laughed. "Joe played defense for Middleton back in the late eighties. He blew out a knee his senior year at Kansas State and couldn't go pro."

"I'm sorry," Jonathan said, his expression puzzled.

"So was he, but he got student loans to finance the rest of his education," Mr. Small said. "His dad was a military man. Worked on missile maintenance as I recall."

"And why should I call Mr. Reisler?" Jonathan asked.

"Joe just passed the bar and opened a one-man law office on Bison Boulevard in Middleton," Mr. Small said. "I know he could use the work. I just don't know if he wants to kick off his career by taking on the Luthors."

Clark wasn't sure how to view being referred to another attorney by Mr. Small. It was possible he recognized his own limitations and honestly wanted Jonathan Kent to have decent legal representation in a fight against Lex Luthor. Or maybe he already knew the case was a lost cause.

"Nothing ventured." Jonathan smiled. "Thanks, Henry. I'll get in touch with him this afternoon."

"So you're really serious about suing Lex, huh?" Clark asked after his dad disconnected.

"Yes, Clark, I am," Jonathan said.

"Why now?" Clark was honestly perplexed. Other opportunities to file lawsuits against the Luthor corporations had come and gone for various reasons, usually lack of evidence. The difference this time eluded him.

"Because I'm tired of being a helpless bystander when disaster strikes." Weariness and stress accented the lines farm life had prematurely etched in Jonathan's face. "I can't fight tornadoes or a rotten economy or a political juggernaut that pays back agribusiness contributors at the expense of family farmers."

"What does that have to do with Lex?"

"Nothing and everything." Jonathan exhaled, as though struggling to find the right words. "Lionel didn't escape the tornado unscathed, but going blind didn't ruin his life. It's inconvenient, but not totally debilitating because he can afford every technological advance science develops. If money is the only thing standing between Lionel Luthor and a cure, he'll get the cure. How many other people do you know who could say the same thing?"

"None, but—"

Jonathan cut off Clark's argument. "The point is that they *are* responsible for some of the disasters that strike this town, Clark. And they'll just go on buying their way out of problems that ruin other people's lives unless someone takes a stand to stop them."

"'Someone' meaning you."

"Apparently if I don't do it, no one will." Jonathan's bitter disappointment at the lack of community interest in joining a class action suit was evident in his clipped tone. "And working through the courts is the only way to beat them."

"If Lex is guilty," Clark added. He couldn't betray truth and justice just to make a point, and neither could his father.

"That's up to a judge and jury to decide, isn't it?" Jonathan keyed the number for information into the phone. "Middleton, Kansas. New listing for Joe Reisler, Attorney-at-Law."

After his father finished writing down the telephone number, Clark gripped his arm to stop him from dialing. "Shouldn't we wait until the lab report comes back? Just in case Mr. Stoner died of some natural cause?"

"I might have to wait a couple days for an appointment, Clark. I can always cancel."

"Do we really want to pay for a cancellation?" Clark didn't know if Joe Reisler charged for consultations or broken appointments. He just wanted his dad to stop and think before he did something he couldn't undo. One thing wasn't in doubt. Within a few hours of making an appointment to see Joe Reisler, Lex would know that Jonathan Kent intended to sue him.

"All right. One more day can't hurt." Jonathan stood up and put the phone back on the base to recharge. "If you need me for anything, I'll be mending the fence in the back pasture."

Clark finished his chores before his father's tractor reached the crest of the hill. He was halfway to Smallville before Jonathan drove into the north pasture.

CHAPTER 7

"Hey, Chloe!" Sharon breezed into the *Torch* office. "Got a minute?"

Chloe noted the girl's perky attitude and forced a tight smile. In snug designer jeans with a T-top and matching bell-sleeved cover-up, Sharon defined casual style. If she knew she was knockout gorgeous, she didn't show it, which made it really hard to dislike her.

"Sure, Sharon," Chloe said. "What's up?"

"Nothing in particular." Sharon paused to read a flyer for the Public Library Book Fair tacked on the wall by the door. "Just thought I'd drop by, in case you needed help with anything."

"Oh, well—" Chloe shrugged. "Nothing comes to mind right now."

"Oh." Sharon sank into the chair where Clark usually sat. "Well, uh—maybe I could write a review of the movie Clark and I saw Saturday."

"There's an idea." Chloe nodded, her smile frozen. Sharon's sunny demeanor suggested to Chloe that the evening had not been a disaster. For a moment, Chloe was sorry she had given Sharon a trial week at the *Torch*, but she was a woman of her word, and that was that. Besides, Clark's love life was none of her business.

Not anymore, Chloe thought, trying not to glare at the girl with the telltale, bright-eyed glow. Sharon looked just as Chloe had felt while dancing with Clark at the Spring Formal.

A back issue I am not going to open—ever again. She meant it. Clark Kent was old news in the Chloe Sullivan archives. *End of story, exclamation point.*

"Maybe it could be a regular thing," Sharon suggested in earnest. "A girl's take on guy flicks or something."

Chloe loved the idea, but she blurted out the other thought that popped into her mind. "Clark asked you out to the movies again next weekend?"

"No." Sharon shook her head, but she didn't seem upset.

Did that mean Sharon expected Clark to ask or that she didn't care if he didn't? Chloe didn't want to admit it, but she really hoped the Sharon/Clark thing fizzled quickly. Wondering about it was way too distracting.

"I was also wondering—" Sharon hesitated, as though she didn't know how to phrase what she wanted to say.

"What?" Chloe inhaled sharply, expecting a bombshell. "Please, don't tell me you hate doing the cafeteria poll."

"The poll?" Sharon waved away Chloe's concern. "No, that went great. I must have asked over fifty kids about the closed campus thing today."

Not bad for a shy, retiring type, Chloe thought. For someone who had tried to fade into the walls for three months, Sharon was demonstrating a remarkable gift for gab.

"The results aren't exactly a surprise," Sharon added.

"Everyone hates it, right?" Chloe hadn't chosen the topic to find out what the student body thought. She had picked it to test how open-minded Principal Reynolds really was about *Torch* content. The lockdown policy had been his first official act when he had replaced Mr. Kwan as principal.

"Ninety percent opposed," Sharon said.

Chloe blinked. "Actually, that is a little surprising. What did the other ten percent say?"

"No comment." Sharon grinned. "I told everyone the poll was anonymous, but some people just didn't want to take a chance. I bet Mr. Reynolds isn't as tough as he looks, but—"

A tone on the computer cut Sharon off and alerted Chloe to incoming mail. As she was about to click the new mail icon, Sharon abruptly changed the subject.

"Do you know what time Clark called 911 when he found Mr. Stoner?"

"Around four-thirty, wasn't it?" Curious, Chloe minimized the Internet program and opened her Howard Stoner file. She had saved every reference she had collected on the incident. "According to the dispatcher's report, he called at four-forty. Why?"

"Wow. You really do have sources everywhere." When Chloe

arched a questioning eyebrow, Sharon added, "Pete mentioned it." She suddenly glanced at the clock and gasped. "Uh-oh. I didn't realize it was so late. I've got to get home."

"But—" Chloe rose as Sharon dashed for the door. The girl hadn't explained why she was interested in Clark's 911 call. "Clark will be here any minute if there's something else you want to know."

"Can't." Sharon paused in the doorway. "I promised Dad I'd stop at the store. Tell Clark I'll see him tomorrow!" She vanished from view, then ducked back. "He can call me tonight—or I'll call him. Either way."

"Uh-huh." Chloe settled into her chair again with the uneasy feeling that something about Sharon was off. The girl seemed to switch personalities as often as other people changed clothes. The once shy, overly curious, and suddenly ditzy shtick reeked of phony. Chloe was so deep in thought she didn't hear Clark come in.

"Clark to Chloe. Come in, Chloe."

"Huh?" Chloe looked up to see Clark waving at her. She did not mince words or beat around the bush. "Why would Sharon Farley want to know what time you called 911 about Mr. Stoner?"

"She probably thinks it works into her murder theory somehow." Clark shrugged with a tolerant smile. "She's got investigative reporter-itis as bad as you do."

"What makes you say that?" Chloe asked, curious.

Clark sat in the chair Sharon had just vacated. "I think she went out with me to get close to you. Because you call the shots at the *Torch*."

"No way." Chloe kept her expression neutral. Clark didn't need to know she was glad that Sharon's motives might not be romantic.

"I swear." Clark held up his right hand. "She wants to work on the story with your blessing."

Chloe was flattered, relieved, and annoyed. Wanting into the inner circles of the *Torch* explained Sharon's incongruous personality shifts and why she had become so friendly so fast. Chloe didn't necessarily approve of Sharon's using Clark to advance her journalism career at Smallville High, but she understood it.

"Does Sharon know something we don't?" Chloe asked.

Clark shook his head. "Don't think so. She wants to be a reporter, and she hasn't lived here long enough to know that Mr. Stoner's death is probably just a—death."

"Maybe, maybe not." Chloe had lived in Smallville long enough to know that most things weren't as obvious as they seemed on the surface.

"Any word from Chad?" Clark asked.

"Oh!" Chloe's head snapped up. "I just got an e-mail from someone. One sec."

Chloe brought the Internet screen back up and clicked for her e-mail listings. The new message wasn't from her friend at the Medical Examiner's Office, however. It was a Breaking News memo from Paul Treadwell, the morning news guy at KTOW. The local AM station sent bulletins to subscribers when news-worthy events happened in Lowell County.

"Oh, my God." Chloe stared at the screen. "That CEP agent was found dead in Stoner's field this afternoon."

"Gary Mundy?" Jumping up, Clark rounded the desk. He rested his arm on the back of her chair and read over her shoulder.

Chloe's detective synapses fired up as she skimmed the text. The sheriff had gone out to the farm after the Center for Environmental Protection in Metropolis had notified him that Gary Mundy was missing. The agent hadn't checked in since Saturday noon, right before he left for the field.

Chloe read the last sentence aloud. "'The badly bruised and lacerated body was lying on a mound of dead rabbits.'"

"That doesn't happen every day," Clark said.

"No, it doesn't." Frowning, Chloe minimized the e-mail window and opened another bookmarked file. "And neither do a couple of other weird things that have happened around here in the past three weeks."

"Like what?" Clark asked.

"Like all of Wilma Roman's rosebushes were pulled up by the roots and torn apart." Chloe clicked links to the relevant *Smallville Ledger* articles as she talked. "Bob Gunderson found two cows dead one morning. Their windpipes were crushed.

Donna Bell's apple tree was stripped of fruit, and Marvin Cates found dead snakes in his shed."

Clark whistled. "Not a typical crime spree."

"Nope." Chloe blew a lock of hair off her forehead. "And now we've got *two* guys who died in the same field."

Clark glanced at the time. "It's almost 5:00 P.M. Can you get in touch with Chad?"

"If I don't hear from him before he leaves work, I can call him at home later," Chloe said as she leaned back. She had been speaking in generalities when she had told Sharon she hadn't ruled out foul play in Mr. Stoner's death. For one thing, there hadn't been an apparent motive. However, if the rabbits were a hint, maybe motive didn't apply. Maybe the killer just liked to kill stuff.

"Do you have to go anywhere right now?" Chloe asked.

"No, I've got some free time," Clark said. "Why?"

"Two computers doing an Internet search are faster than one," Chloe explained. Although the recent wave of destruction had the stamp of Smallville strange all over it, it would help to know if a similar pattern of crimes had happened anywhere else.

Clark sat back down at the other desk and stretched to limber up. "What do you want to know?"

Are you going to ask Sharon out again?

"Start with these and see what turns up." Chloe scribbled several search reference phrases on a piece of paper and handed it to him.

"Hi, Lana."

Lana didn't recognize the voice until she turned and saw the new girl sitting at a table near the cash register. "Hi, Sharon."

"You remembered my name!" Sharon grinned, pleased. "Are you busy?"

"Well, I, uh—" Lana faltered.

She hadn't seen Clark all weekend, but Chloe had filled her in on the latest, disturbing developments. Sharon had a crush on Clark, and Pete had convinced him to ask her out. Lana knew she couldn't complain because Clark had taken someone to the movies. Since she hadn't come to terms with Whitney's death or sorted out her feelings for Clark, their relationship had been stuck in friendship limbo. She had no right to interfere with his personal life. *And I have nothing to say to his new girlfriend.*

"I just wanted to apologize," Sharon said.

"What for?" Lana frowned, puzzled.

"For seeming like a totally conceited snob." Sharon glanced around the nearly empty restaurant. "Can you sit a minute?"

"Sure." Lana couldn't bring herself to be rude. As Chloe had pointed out, Sharon didn't know about her long, sometimes tense, never boring, often awkward friendship with Clark Kent. Besides, the Talon was in an obvious lull between the after-school rush and the after-dinner coffee-and-dessert crowd. She couldn't use being busy as an excuse. "For a minute."

"Thanks." Sharon took a deep breath. "I didn't mean to ignore everyone. It just takes me a while to get to know people. Like my father, I guess. We moved to Smallville because he wanted to write in 'quiet obscurity.'"

"Being the new kid in town must be hard," Lana said, smiling. "I should be the one apologizing—for not trying to get to know you."

"I miss my old friends, but—" Sharon shrugged. "I'm just glad we're getting acquainted now. I know you and Chloe and Clark and Pete have all been friends like forever."

"Seems that way sometimes." Lana started to rise. "We'll have to talk again soon, but right now, I really should—"

"I'm working on a story for the *Torch*," Sharon announced. "I never expected to find anyone in Smallville that wants to be a reporter as much as I do."

"Clark?" Lana knew he was thinking about studying journalism in college. She just hadn't realized he had made up his mind.

"No, Chloe." Sharon exhaled. "I'm really going to have to hustle to keep up with her."

"Oh, right." Nodding, Lana settled back. Sharon wanted to talk, and since she hadn't made an effort to be friendly before, the least Lana could do was listen for a few minutes.

"Clark is nice," Sharon said. "A little closed off, though."

"You noticed?" Lana quipped.

"Hard not to." Sharon shook her head slightly. "I tried getting him to talk about finding Mr. Stoner for my article, but he didn't have a lot to say."

"Maybe there isn't much to tell," Lana suggested.

"That's probably it, but you just never know where you're going to end up once you start stringing the facts together." Sharon sipped her soda. "Are you sure he left here at four-twenty-five that day?"

"Yes, positive—" Lana hesitated. She didn't appreciate being pumped for information on the pretense of friendship. However, before she could get up to leave, Sharon suddenly remembered that she was in a hurry to get home.

"When my dad gets into his writing, he forgets to eat." Sharon grabbed her books and stood up. "Seriously. I've got to go. Thanks, Lana."

Lana watched the girl leave feeling slightly stunned. Except for the fact that she hadn't given away any deep dark secrets, the encounter left her with a sense of having been scammed.

Or maybe jealousy was clouding her judgment. *That* was a secret she had no intention of sharing with anyone.

Pete grimaced at his plate. "I am so tired of eating hamburgers that could pass as hockey pucks."

"It's Tuesday, Pete." Clark pulled two tuna sandwiches out of the brown bag lunch his mom had prepared that morning.

"Exactly." Pete threw up his hands. "Every other Tuesday it's the same thing: hamburgers on stale buns with beans and fries. How come they never change the menu?"

"So I won't have to retype it every other week," Clark replied, grinning as he handed Pete one of his mother's homemade chocolate chip cookies. "Whenever you get tired of Tuesday hamburgers just remember that white-paste glop they gave us last Wednesday."

"Actually, except for the burned toast, I didn't think it was that bad." Pete took the cookie and set it aside. "My great-uncle Willie used to make something just like it."

Clark shuddered. "Must be an acquired taste, then."

"Must be." Pete took a bite of hamburger and scanned the cafeteria as he chewed. "I see Sharon's still conducting Chloe's closed campus policy poll."

Clark nodded as he followed Pete's gaze. Sharon was moving from person to person with a smile and a clipboard. He wondered how she remembered the people she had already asked and how much Chloe cared about accuracy.

"I told her the way to Chloe's editorial heart was through the student survey," Clark said.

"I don't think it's *Chloe's* heart she cares about." Pete grinned and picked up a fry.

Anticipating another interrogation about past or future dates, Clark tried to cap Pete's curiosity with the same ploy he had used on Chloe. "Sharon's an aspiring news hound. She's more interested in getting in good with Chloe than going out with me."

"Oh, yeah, right." Pete rolled his eyes, then nodded toward

the door. "Looks like something lit a fire under our fearless *Torch* editor."

Clark turned to look as Chloe rushed into the cafeteria. Sharon noticed her, too, and followed.

"News conference. Right now." Chloe stopped at the head of the table, unaware that the other girl was behind her. It was too late to retract.

"Is this about Mr. Stoner?" Sharon's eyes shone with excitement as she sat in the chair beside Clark.

"Uh—yeah, but it's not for public consumption." Chloe shot Clark a helpless look.

"Oh, right." Sharon snapped a clean piece of paper over the poll on her clipboard and whispered. "Is it okay if I take notes?"

Clark shrugged. He didn't see any gracious way to cut Sharon out of the discussion. However, it was Chloe's call to hold back whatever she had learned until later or bring Sharon in now. She opted to bring Sharon in.

"I got the lab results back from Chad," Chloe said.

"And?" Sharon leaned forward.

Chloe lowered her voice. "They found meteor dust in Howard Stoner's lungs."

Sharon inhaled softly.

"Really?" Clark acted mildly surprised, but that's what he had expected. The presence of meteor particles in Mr. Stoner's lungs explained why he had felt sick when he tried to resuscitate the dead farmer.

"How does someone get meteor dust in his lungs?" Pete asked.

"The dust must be in the field," Sharon said. "Those clippings on Chloe's Wall of Weird said the meteors hit all around Smallville."

Although Clark hadn't felt sick anywhere except near the body, he also hadn't walked every square inch of the field. So Sharon's theory was not outside the realm of possibility. Mr. Stoner hadn't grown anything in that particular field as far back as he could remember. Given the varied effects meteor material could have on living things, the farmer might have given up planting the field if his crops repeatedly died or rotted.

Pete squinted. "I suppose he could have kicked up a cloud of the stuff and inhaled it. Is that what killed him?"

"They don't know why he stopped breathing, but that's one theory." Chloe paused to look at each one in turn. "That's not all, though."

"What else?" Clark asked.

"They put a rush on the CEP agent's lab work because his death was so violent," Chloe continued. "They found meteor dust and traces of human saliva in Mr. Mundy's wounds. Someone used teeth to rip his body open after he choked to death."

"Oh, gross!" Sharon gagged and clutched her stomach as though she was going to be sick.

Clark sympathized, but he didn't try to temper Sharon's horrifying introduction to Smallville reality. Dealing with gruesome facts was common in the *Torch* regulars' experience. The newcomer would either drop out or learn to cope.

"Was there dust in his lungs, too?" Pete asked. The last bite of his hamburger vanished into his mouth.

"His throat, but that's not all." Chloe was bursting with her news. "There's an old missile silo just beyond Mr. Stoner's field, and guess who owns it?"

"Lex Luthor," Clark said. "It was actually a missile launch facility, but they never equipped it with launch keys. There was an armed Minuteman II in the silo for years, though, until 1994."

"Armageddon on our doorstep, and no one ever knew!" Pete quipped. "How come *you* know so much, Clark?"

"Yeah." Chloe was obviously annoyed that he had stolen her thunder about the military installation in Lex Luthor's corporate inventory. "Show off."

Sharon appeared to be in shock. Her face was ashen, and she swallowed hard. Apparently, the luster had suddenly worn off her romantic notions about reporting on murder and malice. Still, considering the serious, bizarre twists the situation had taken, Clark thought she was holding up fairly well.

"I checked it out a long time ago," Clark explained. "The land and the installation reverted to LuthorCorp when the government stripped the facility and moved out. Lex took possession when he bought the plant."

"Which doesn't explain how Chloe's nose for news caught the scent and tracked it down," Pete observed. "I mean, how do you make the leap from meteor dust in a dead farmer's lungs to a missile silo?"

Chloe's deflated ego was forgotten as she briefed Pete and Sharon on the unusual vandalism occurring around Smallville the past couple weeks. "When Clark and I didn't turn up any other flora and fauna crime clusters, I started a random search for meteor references using some new key words, like 'military response.'"

"Those results must have been interesting." Pete pushed his plate aside and folded his arms on the table.

"Actually, not very." Chloe sighed. "NORAD knew the meteors were meteors, so they didn't even scramble jets to investigate."

Good thing. Clark shuddered to think what might have happened if the Air Force had found him and his spaceship instead of Martha and Jonathan Kent.

"There wouldn't have been much point to shooting rocks out of the sky," Chloe added.

"Probably not." Pete exchanged a quick glance with Clark before turning back to Chloe. "But I still don't get the interest in an old abandoned missile site."

"Lex owns it," Chloe said. "What if LexCorp is using the old launch facility for some dangerous new project?"

"Wait a minute." Sharon sat back, raising her hands in a braking gesture. "Isn't that jumping to conclusions? You're talking about a corporation with a whole lot to lose and tons of resources, Chloe. We're just high school kids! Even if you're right, how could we possibly prove it?"

"I agree," Clark said. He held Chloe's gaze, hoping she got the message to tone it down. The preconceived notions of Luthor guilt that dominated much of Smallville's thinking hadn't influenced Sharon's perspective.

Chloe glared at Clark, bristling. "Tackling the tough stories separates the pros from the amateurs."

Chloe's reaction took Clark by surprise. He hadn't meant to insult her. He was just tired of the knee-jerk accusations against Lex every time something weird happened.

"Maybe," Sharon countered defensively, not realizing that Chloe's barbed comment had been aimed at him, not her. "But if people get sick and die around meteor-rocks, I don't want to go anywhere near them."

So much for protecting Sharon from Chloe's theory. Clark hadn't said a word about it, but the girl was sharp. She had connected the dots between the Wall of Weird and the dual meteor dust references in the autopsy lab reports to make a logical—albeit flawed—assumption.

"Unless you drink meteor-grown vegetable shakes like someone we used to know," Pete explained, "you don't have to worry, Sharon."

"Right." Chloe made an effort to sound positive. "The meteor-rocks are safe unless you're mega-exposed somehow."

"Like a lot of kids who grew up here, who were little kids when the meteors struck in 1989," Pete added.

"But even *that's* just a theory," Clark said. Although the growing body of evidence supported Chloe's conclusions, Sharon was already worried about chemical contamination from the plant. Since she had to live in Smallville, it seemed cruel to scare her without cause. Her dad's rented house was located in a neighborhood that hadn't sustained a direct meteor hit.

"If it'll make everyone feel better," Clark said, "I'll ask Lex if anything's happening at the old silo."

"Would he tell you?" Sharon asked.

"No way!" Pete scoffed. "If something's going on nobody knows about, it's probably illegal. Believe me, Lex Luthor won't say or do anything that might hurt Lex Luthor."

"But it can't hurt to try, Clark," Chloe said. "I wouldn't bet money, but you're probably the only one Lex would tell."

Clark didn't bother arguing, but he was plagued by some troubling thoughts as he headed to class.

He didn't take the route past Stoner's farm home very often, not unless he had to avoid being seen by someone like the surveyor. Lex could have moved half the plant into the launch facility without his knowing it. Last Thursday he hadn't seen anything that indicated the silo was being used—except the flattened weeds in the dirt access road. That was probably worth checking out, regardless of what Lex had to say.

Although Clark didn't dwell on it, neither he nor Lex had perfect records when it came to honesty. The difference was that Lex's personal survival didn't depend on his lies. Lex knew he had come close to losing Clark's trust and friendship when he had hired Roger Nixon to investigate the Old Mill Bridge accident and the Kents' family history. Clark wanted to believe that Lex wouldn't risk lying to him again.

Asking about the silo wasn't the only reason Clark wanted to visit the Luthor mansion. If Lex hadn't yet heard about Jonathan Kent's plan to sue, Clark had to decide whether or not to tell him. As the discussion with Chloe had just shown, the presence of meteor dust in the bodies cast doubt, but did not eliminate Lex as a suspect. However, since the lab reports hadn't provided absolute proof, he hoped to talk his father out of filing the lawsuit.

And if he couldn't?

Clark wondered how he'd feel.

He was certain that if the roles were reversed, he'd rather find out he was being sued from the friend who was suing him than from a stranger.

Wouldn't he?

Martha Kent kept the heavy roll of fencing wire standing upright while her husband stretched an unwound portion between posts. The spring tornado had torn out miles of fence on the Kent farm. Insurance had covered the cost of new materials and labor, but they had elected to do the work themselves rather than hire a contractor. Although it had taken months longer, replacement would be complete within a week or two. The money they saved had gone into Clark's college fund.

"Such as it is," Martha muttered. Every night she prayed that Clark would earn an academic scholarship. He could not accept one for athletics because of his unearthly, natural advantage.

"Did you say something, Martha?" Jonathan wiped his forehead with the back of his leather-gloved hand as he glanced back.

"Just muttering to myself, Jonathan." Beyond him, Martha saw a hyperwind cut a path through the corn. "There's Clark!"

Jonathan and Martha both held on to their hats as Clark braked between them.

"Hey, son." Jonathan waved at the wire. "Give me a hand with this, will you?"

"Sure." Clark grabbed the wire in his bare hands and pulled it taut between posts. He held it in place while his father secured it with U-shaped brads. "The lab report on Mr. Stoner came back today."

Jonathan nodded. "I heard. Mr. Mundy, too. Both bodies contained meteor particles."

"Right." Clark took a breath. "So it probably isn't Lex's fault."

"Clark—" Martha smiled tightly. Things were tense enough without having additional strain between father and son. "We've already discussed it."

The look of hopeful relief on Clark's face became worried frustration when he caught her meaning. Martha understood. Nothing she had said all afternoon had made a dent in Jonathan's stubborn determination to proceed with the lawsuit.

"I'm calling Joe Reisler tomorrow." Jonathan gave the first brad a final whack with the hammer.

Martha saw Clark's jaw flex and sighed. Jonathan and his adopted child did not have a single drop of blood in common, yet they were so much alike in so many ways. Jonathan always tightened his jaw when he had made up his mind to do something he knew he shouldn't.

Like sue Lex Luthor.

Clark had decided to dig in his heels on the other side of the argument.

"Lex didn't drop the meteor-rocks on Smallville, Dad," Clark said with commendable calm. "So I don't understand how you expect to connect him to Mr. Stoner's death."

"Two words, Clark." Jonathan held another brad in place and swung the hammer with a steady hand. Whack! A second swing embedded the curved top of the brad in the wooden post. He reached into his pocket, pulled out another brad, and held the prongs against the post. "Level Three." Whack!

The hammer hit the brad with such force, Martha could almost feel her teeth rattle in her head. Clark didn't flinch, but his frown indicated his dad had scored a point.

When Lionel Luthor was running the fertilizer plant, he had authorized experiments on corn in a secret, underground level of the plant. Earl Jenkins, a family friend who had once worked on the Kent farm, had been working in the area when an explosion occurred. The blast left Earl with thousands of meteor particles embedded in his skin. He still suffered from violent shaking episodes as his body attempted to purge the foreign substance.

"It's not out of the question, Clark," Martha said gently.

She knew how much her son valued his friendship with Lex. While she didn't trust the young Luthor as implicitly as Clark, she respected the bond. However, now that she knew firsthand how Lionel operated, she couldn't deny that both men were probably capable of despicable things.

"What if it isn't Lex?" Clark looked up, his expression hopeful. "What if the dust is in the field? Some of the meteors were pulverized when they hit."

Martha suspected he was grasping at straws in a desperate attempt to put his father's intentions on hold. She didn't interfere.

Jonathan nodded. "I suppose that's possible."

Clark jumped through the verbal opening. "Just give me one more day to find proof—one way or another."

Martha saw a fleeting, uncertain frown cross Jonathan's face and crossed her fingers behind her back.

"How are you going to do that?" Jonathan's voice oozed skepticism, but Clark was undeterred.

"For starters, I'll ask Lex." Clark hastened to add, "I was going over there anyway, to ask about that old missile installation for Chloe."

"I'd forgotten all about the missile silo," Martha said. The launch facility was a chilling reminder of her terror the day of the meteor shower.

She and Jonathan had been driving along Route 19 when the first meteor hit. For a few seconds, she had thought the United States was under attack, that the disintegrating Soviet Union had decided to collapse with a nuclear bang. She had cast a split-second glance across acres of corn toward the underground military installation, fully expecting to see the Minuteman II roar out of the ground on its unthinkable mission of mutual annihilation. The destruction wrought by the flaming rocks had been devastating, but the community had recovered.

Nothing would have survived the horror of the other scenario.

Jonathan walked to the tractor to refill his pocket with brads. He paused to stare across the pasture for a moment then looked back at Clark. "Howard Stoner had a thing about protecting that missile silo."

"Yeah, I know. He used to chase me away. I always thought it was funny because Mr. Stoner didn't know I could rip the entry hatch off its hinges." Clark laughed warmly at the memory of the farmer. "I guess he took his patriotic duty very seriously."

"He did." Martha agreed with a smile. "Although I think he may have missed getting a monthly check from the government more."

"Check for what?" Clark asked.

Jonathan shook his head as he trudged back to the fence. "The government paid LuthorCorp and Howard Stoner *not* to use the fields that bordered the missile site. The money was just pocket change to Lionel, but it probably accounted for half of Howard's annual income."

"Losing it must have hurt," Clark said.

Martha nodded. "Yes, but it didn't stop Howard from making sure that local kids didn't break in and tear the place apart."

"So you'll give me another day?" Clark's dark eyes twinkled as he suddenly shifted course.

"He's just going to keep pestering you if you don't agree, Jonathan," Martha said.

Jonathan raised his eyes and hands to the sky in surrender. "All right! One more day." He pointed the hammer at Clark. "One!"

CHAPTER 9

Standing outside the closed door into Lex Luthor's office, Clark paused to cement his resolve. He could think of fifty other places he'd rather be than the mahogany halls of his friend's home. The interior of the Scottish castle, which Lionel had transported across the Atlantic and half the North American continent in crates, was as imposing as the illusion of regal impregnability the structure's turreted design, stone façade, and sheer mass created.

Ordinarily, Clark enjoyed walking through the spacious rooms and down the long halls. He was always spotting some antique knickknack or carved design in the woodwork that he hadn't noticed before. Most days, however, he wasn't trying to find out if Lex was guilty of some horrendous misdeed. He needed a moment to compose the least offensive way to say what he had come to say.

Since he couldn't see through the decorative cut glass in the door with normal sight, Clark focused his X-ray vision.

Lex Luthor was seated at his desk with his feet propped up. He raised a glass to his mouth without turning his head from the laptop computer in front of him. Since alcohol dulled his mental edge, Lex didn't drink while he was working. At least Clark wouldn't be interrupting anything important.

"Come on in, Clark!" Lex called, his voice muted by the door.

Clark sighed. The current butler wasn't as lax as some Lex had employed and had used the intercom to announce Clark's arrival. As he opened the door, Lex swung his feet to the floor.

"Did you get lost?" Lex arched an eyebrow. Beneath an expanse of scalp unadorned by hair, the subtle gesture seemed amplified.

"No. Just not in a hurry," Clark said.

"Because your father is thinking about suing me?" The calm timbre of Lex's voice held steady, but Clark did not mistake that for a clue regarding his mood. At their most vicious, both Luthors were portraits of quiet control.

Clark dropped into a chair and clasped his hands between his knees. "I was hoping you hadn't heard, yet."

"Jeff Carter of Carter and Swain in Metropolis called me yesterday." Lex swirled the ice in his glass. "Probably the instant your dad hung up. For the record, they'll have points deducted for betraying a prospective client's confidence."

"You don't seem upset." Clark sat back and rested his arms on the sides of the upholstered chair.

"I'm not." Lex pushed the laptop aside, clearing his view of Clark.

"Why not?" Clark knew better than to second-guess Lex Luthor's motives.

"For one thing, your father is an idealist, who believes that everyone is innocent until proven guilty," Lex said. "And while he may have an irrational dedication to principles that conflict with his own best interests at times, he is not a foolish man. Jonathan Kent won't sue me or anyone else without proof, and there isn't any."

"You saw the lab reports, too?" Clark asked.

"On advice of my attorneys, I can't discuss it." Lex rose to top off his drink. "The CEP inquiry is still open, and LexCorp has other, unsettled complaints. My PR Department is already over budget for the year."

Clark just nodded. Trying to understand the complexities of Lex's financial empire would give him a headache, if he could get headaches.

"Would you like something?" Lex replaced the stopper in the decanter of Scotch. "Soft drink? Water?"

"No, thanks." Clark shook his head. "I have another question, though."

"What's on your mind?" Lex took a healthy swallow of the amber liquor, undaunted by the fiery bite.

Clark opted for blunt candor. "Have you expanded the plant's research and development operations into that old missile installation?"

"No."

Clark watched Lex's face, but there was no hesitation, no shift of the eyes or other sign that he was lying.

Lex's brows knit. "Why?"

"Just heard some casual speculation," Clark said. That was a partial truth, but he would be more specific if Lex asked.

Apparently satisfied, Lex didn't follow up. He walked back to his desk and turned the laptop toward Clark. A detailed graphic of a woodland scene complete with a mounted knight, horse-drawn coach, and wildlife was displayed on the screen.

"Have you ever tried one of these on-line role-playing games?" Lex asked.

"The monthly fee isn't in *our* budget." Clark stood up as Lex sat back down. "I thought you didn't like to play games, Lex. Of any kind."

"I don't, but millions of people *are* willing to pay for the privilege." A slow smile tugged at Lex's mouth as he sipped Scotch and watched the screen. "I have no doubt that there's an angle or an advance that no one has thought of, developed, or cashed in on, yet."

Clark had no doubt that he was right.

◆◆◆

"Mrs. Kent?" Sharon paused at the white picket railing on the Kent porch when Clark's mother stopped a red pickup by the barn and turned off the engine. She had hoped to intercept Clark before he went to see Lex Luthor.

"Can I help you?" With auburn hair, blue eyes, freckles and a warm smile, Martha Kent was not at all what Sharon had pictured. Blue jeans, a short-sleeved tailored shirt, and a straw hat seemed like fashionable country wear on her trim figure.

"I'm Sharon Farley." Sharon extended her hand as she descended the porch steps.

Martha hesitated. "Oh, Sharon." She nodded, her smile widening when she realized her visitor was Clark's Saturday night movie date. Her handshake was firm and sincere. "How nice to meet you."

"You, too." Sharon smiled back. "I was looking for Clark. Is he here?"

"No, I'm sorry, he's not," Martha said.

"Oh." Sharon sighed with disappointment. There was a hint of regret in Martha's tone, but she didn't volunteer any information. Her brief answer made it clear she wouldn't divulge any details about her son's whereabouts.

Sharon, however, already had a good idea where Clark had gone. She just needed to know when.

"Long ago?" Sharon asked. Since Martha had the pickup, the Kent's only road vehicle, she also knew Clark was on foot. "If I catch him, I'll give him a ride back into town."

"It's been twenty minutes or so, but I don't know if he went back to town." Martha shrugged. "Sorry I can't be more help."

Sure you are, Sharon thought as she waved a polite good-bye and got back into her car. She turned right out of the driveway and headed toward the highway.

There wasn't anything in particular Sharon could put her finger on, but a subtle aura of mystery seemed to surround Clark Kent. Saturday night, she had had the distinct feeling that he knew more than he wanted to say about meteor-rocks and Smallville's suspicious mortality rate. Martha and Lana were almost as reticent, as though they feared letting some awful secret or damaging piece of information slip.

Sharon turned onto Beresford Lane and slowed the Audi. Since Clark had promised Chloe to ask Lex Luthor about the status of the old missile installation, she was sure he had gone to the mansion. *She* wasn't going to ring the doorbell, but if she could connect with Clark when he left the estate, she might be able to find out what *he* had found out.

"That's what good reporters do, right?"

Sharon cruised the two-lane road, looking for a likely spot to park and wait. Even if Clark was running cross-country, he hadn't had nearly enough time to reach Lex's formidable home.

Unless, of course, the amount of time between when he left the Talon and called 911 last Thursday had really been fifteen minutes and not twenty-five or thirty as everyone assumed.

Two dirt drives cut into the woods and farm fields across from the Luthor property. Sharon pulled into the second drive a short distance down the road from the Luthor gate and turned the car so it was facing the road. While the trees weren't perfect cover, the silver Audi wouldn't be immediately apparent to anyone coming down the Luthor's winding drive.

The front entrance of the mansion was obscured by landscaping and stonework, but Sharon had a clear view of the grounds. She watched in amazement when Clark emerged from the house a few minutes later and ran across the manicured lawn into an expanse of dense woods.

Leaving Lex to figure out how to capitalize on virtual empires, Clark left the mansion grounds at an easy loping pace. He didn't head home when he ducked into the woods, but turned toward Stoner's farm. Although he hoped Lex hadn't lied, there were things he felt compelled to check out. After all, the dirt access road had been used recently, two men had died in the field near the silo within days of each other, and both bodies had contained traces of meteor dust.

Because Lex had previously financed Dr. Hamilton's research before the mineralogist died from a lethal dose of meteor formula, Clark's suspicions weren't unfounded. He wasn't sure how much Lex knew about the potent properties of meteor-rocks, but the young entrepreneur knew enough to be dangerously curious about the untapped potential.

That was definitely true of Lionel. Clark and his parents would never have known that the senior Luthor was assembling a dossier on him if thieves hadn't broken into Lionel's vault and taken his mom hostage. Clark had burned the files with his heated gaze, but Lionel was a threat they could only guard against, not eliminate.

It wasn't outrageous to think that Lionel might be up to something that Lex knew nothing about. Lionel hadn't disclosed the existence of Level Three or the experiments he had authorized when Lex had taken over management of the Smallville plant. Considering the ongoing power struggle between father and son, Lionel was not above trying to humiliate and demoralize Lex by operating a clandestine project in the missile silo on LexCorp property.

Certainly no one else was capable of keeping Lex in the dark, Clark realized.

Since new, innovative technologies and scientific advances were vital to the future of both Luthor corporations, continued research and development was imperative. However, to avoid a repeat of the Level Three fiasco, the more dangerous research projects would be moved to remote locations.

The abandoned missile installation was ideal for that purpose, too.

Clark ran at a normal pace until he was well beyond sight of the road. At superspeed, he covered the remaining distance to Howard Stoner's farm in less than thirty seconds.

Clark came to a halt in the trees by the gravel driveway and cautiously stepped into the open. No one else was in sight or within range of his acute hearing. Yellow crime scene tape was the only sign that the sheriff's deputies and forensic teams had been at work. The tape was strung from the driveway through the woods to a spot that probably marked where Gary Mundy had fallen.

Starting to the left of Stoner's small farmhouse, Clark panned the entire area. His gaze moved right across the field, past the access road and woods, to the chain-link fence that enclosed the entrances into the launch facility and silo. He shifted to X-ray vision, which identified animal bones, a broken plow blade, other tools, and nonglowing rocks buried in the field. The large fenced-in yard had been cleared of all metal objects except for scattered nails and the hatch entrances into the silo shaft and launch center. From Clark's vantage point, the site looked undisturbed.

Finding the source of meteor dust was his first priority. He began jogging the field, postponing a closer inspection of the underground military installation, which had been built several years prior to 1989. That meant the government had been paying Stoner to let the field lie fallow long before the meteors hit. If meteor dust had rendered the land arid, the farmer wouldn't have known it until he tried to grow a crop—after the facility was decommissioned and the missile removed.

Maintaining a steady pace, Clark moved in a systematic pattern back and forth between the access road and the dense woods on the field's western edge. At high speed, he could have covered the rutted acreage in a few minutes rather than thirty, but he couldn't take the chance that someone on the official investigative team might show up.

When Clark completed the final leg, he knew the field was clean. Small pockets of meteor dust might be hidden beneath the surface, but Stoner's field had obviously not been a primary landing zone for a meteor that blew itself to smithereens on impact.

Clark glanced toward the LexCorp property to the south and west. A wide strip of woods hid the plant building and most of the intervening cornfield from view. The cornfield was the favored location for the ritual the Smallville football team enacted every fall for good luck in the Homecoming game, turning a freshman into a human scarecrow. When Clark was a freshman, they had picked him. Lana's meteor necklace had made him too weak to help himself, and Lex had freed him.

In 1989, a large, blazing meteor had landed in that same cornfield. The impact had robbed Lex of his hair, flattened every cornstalk, and probably strewn meteor residue over the entire field.

Clark had assumed Mr. Stoner was walking back to his house after checking the missile silo when he collapsed. Perhaps he had been coming back from the LexCorp field. Clark made a mental note to check there, too, after he explored the crime scene and the fenced enclosure.

Being careful not to disturb anything, Clark followed the yellow tape from the chalked outline of Gary Mundy's body into the woods. The tape paralleled a wide, shallow furrow. The snakelike trail looked as though something heavy had been dragged from the death scene to the gravel drive. *Like what?* Clark wondered. The body would have been taken out on a stretcher. *A bag of dead rabbits, maybe?*

Since he hadn't experienced any meteor sickness near the yellow tape or the drag depression, Clark pushed those speculations to the back of his mind and headed for the chain-link fence.

The enclosed area was roughly the size of a football field, and Clark took his time walking around it. While he hadn't paid close attention to the site since his initial discovery years before, his mind retained almost everything he saw in passing. If anything was different, he would notice.

Clark peered through the wire mesh at the huge, six-sided lid over the actual silo. The massive concrete cover measured ten feet across and three feet deep and weighed one hundred tons. It was mounted on rails and automatically slid away from the shaft opening during a launch countdown or when properly keyed during certain maintenance procedures. Sections of the metal railing that circled the lid were missing or broken. The shaft that housed the nuclear warhead and delivery system ran 140 feet straight down, 80 feet below the level of the launch control and equipment areas. A smaller, emergency exit hatch was positioned 10 feet from the lid.

Another personnel access hatch measuring 3 feet across was located 100 feet east of the silo lid. A four-foot-by-six-foot concrete slab and two ventilation openings, which were flush to the ground and covered with wire mesh, were the only other exterior signs of the subterranean military facility.

However, the weeds inside the fenced area had been mowed recently. *By Howard Stoner or someone else?*

As Clark's gaze swept the compound, everything he had learned about the installation when he was a kid instantly came back to him. The text, photos, and diagrams he had found in the public library so long ago were just as clear in his mind now as they had been when he first saw them.

A metal staircase spiraled downward around a central elevator to the facility 60 feet underground. The elevator opened into a spacious junction where the hundred-foot silo tunnel connected to form the stem of a T. The Launch Facility Equipment Building on the right and the Launch Control Center on the left of the elevator formed the top of the T and measured 120 feet from outer wall to outer wall.

Clark was glad he had memorized the layout. His X-ray vision couldn't penetrate the lead-lined silo lid and smaller access hatches or 60 feet of dirt, rock and concrete.

The Launch Control Facility had been a completely self-contained environment when it was operational. Buried cables had supplied electrical power, but in the event the commercial source was cut off, the Launch Facility Equipment Building had been equipped with a diesel generator as backup. The emergency engine was fueled from a fourteen-thousand-gallon storage tank buried outside the steel and concrete walls of the LFEB.

Clark jogged to the gate on the southern side of the fence. The dirt drive that connected the installation to the access road ran through another densely wooded area. The wheel ruts in the drive were overgrown with grass and weeds that had not been driven over lately. However, the chain that held the two gate panels together had been outfitted with a new padlock.

Clark stared at the lock and considered his options. Only two scenarios made any sense: Howard Stoner had been maintaining the grounds and buying new locks as needed or someone else had access.

Either way, Clark had to know. If Lex was lying or being lied to and the missile site was in use, it was probably being used for illegal and dangerous purposes.

Clark knew that Lionel equipped himself and his surroundings with state-of-the-art security technology. His X-ray vision hadn't located any cameras, and he didn't see any sensor wires attached to the fence, which was designed to keep trespassers out. The chain-link portion was ten feet high and topped with three strands of razor wire angled to the outside.

Though Clark could easily jump the fence, he wouldn't be able to explain how he had gotten inside without breaking the lock if someone found him. He pulled the body of the lock down hard, breaking the inner lock mechanism. After slipping through the gate, he put the chain back in place so the panels wouldn't swing open and looped the lock's U through the links.

Once inside the fence, Clark still didn't see anything that struck him as unusual. Mr. Stoner could have kept the path between the gate and the personnel hatch worn down, especially if he had been adhering to a regular maintenance schedule since 1994. Except for the tire marks made by a riding mower, there were no vehicle tracks.

Clark walked around the large silo lid, which appeared to be firmly in place. Like the lid and the primary personnel hatch, the bulk of the secondary exit hatch was above ground. He wondered if Lex was still paying for power, if only to lock and open the automatic entry mechanisms. Then he noticed that the heavy, raised gasket between the above- and below-ground segments of the thick cover was not properly aligned. The hatch was not completely closed.

Curious, Clark grabbed the edge. The balance mechanisms, which allowed a normal man to open the hatch, were broken, but he lifted it with ease. The steel-and-concrete cover swung up against and rested on a metal brace, which supported its weight. Clark braced himself to look down into the pitch-black darkness of a narrow, sixty-foot tube. Instead, he was surprised to discover that the tube had been filled with cement.

"Nobody's getting in or out that way," he muttered as he lowered the circular cover.

The blocked hatch just raised more questions. Had Lex filled in all the hatches to eliminate the risk of liability? Other abandoned launch facilities, some dating back to the era of Atlas and Titan missiles in the 1960s, had been used for unauthorized parties and campsites or had been vandalized. One silo he had read about was half-filled with water. By their nature and design, the abandoned missile complexes held many dangerous traps for unsuspecting teenagers. In the interest of lower insurance premiums, preventing anyone from getting in—ever—made sense.

Except that Howard Stoner would never have let such desecration occur without a fight, and the *Smallville Ledger* would never have passed on a dispute between a local and a Luthor.

There was only one way to be certain. Clark had to check if the elevator shaft and platform area had also been filled in with concrete.

As Clark approached the main personnel hatch, he thought he heard a faint, almost imperceptible hum. It reminded him of the vibration in the wire fence when his father had hit the brads with his hammer, just smoother and quieter.

Working machinery 60 feet down could send a vibration

through pipes and other conduits to the ground. He alone on Earth would be able to detect it.

With his senses focused on the ground and the hatch, everything else became perceptual white noise. Something was humming below. Clark slipped his hand under the handle and prepared to break the electronic lock. Was Lex paying for power to keep the interior equipment functional and the installation locked? Or was someone else?

"Hi, Clark," a girl said. "What are you doing?"

Clark's head snapped around as he straightened. "Sharon! What are you doing here?"

"Looking for you." Sharon smiled with a sheepish shrug and adjusted the bag slung over her shoulder. "And I asked you first. What are you doing?"

Clark quickly devised a reasonable cover for his shocked reaction. Since truth often camouflaged itself, he was honest with an embarrassed grin. "Getting caught trying to break into Lex Luthor's missile silo."

"Any luck?" Sharon smiled, folding her arms tightly over her chest. She clutched a bulky cell phone and seemed nervous. Clark wasn't sure why.

"Nope. It's locked." Clark shrugged and mentally retraced his actions.

He could only guess how long Sharon had been watching him. He glanced across the field, but the silver Audi wasn't parked in the gravel drive by Stoner's house. Since she hadn't walked to the farm from town, she must have driven up and parked on the access road when he was focused on the vibration by the primary hatch. There was no other window of opportunity in which she could have sneaked up on him. He was certain she had not seen him lift the broken hatch cover.

"Caught, huh? I guess that means Lex didn't give you permission to poke around," Sharon stated flatly.

"I didn't ask," Clark said, still puzzling over her obvious distress. Was she nervous because they were both trespassing?

"Oh." Sharon glanced around the yard.

"You said you were looking for me," Clark said to distract her. He'd have to come back another time to continue his investigation. Until he determined the nature of the threat, if there was a threat, he couldn't involve anyone else. Not directly.

"Oh! Duh." Sharon laughed. "It's just that, well—all that talk about meteor dust with magic powers and stuff is, well—"

"I don't think anyone said 'magic,'" Clark corrected when she paused.

"Not exactly, no." Sharon sighed. "The thing is, Chloe's meteor theory is way too out there to be believed."

Clark didn't comment. The idea that meteor-rocks were dangerous had upset Sharon at lunch. Her denial might be a subconscious defense to alleviate her fear, but it was better to say nothing until he knew for certain.

"I don't want to pull the permit on anyone's parade, but I just can't buy the idea that a bunch of rocks from outer space are killing people." With a tight grip on the cell phone and her arms still folded, Sharon stared at the ground. When she looked up, she spoke hurriedly, as though trying to convince herself. "Even you said it was just a theory."

"It is," Clark agreed. His family and the *Torch* team knew from experience that the theory had proven out, but no hard evidence existed. It seemed pointless for Sharon to lose sleep over something that probably wouldn't affect her.

"So then the problem *is* chemical contamination from Lex's plant," Sharon said.

"Not necessarily," Clark countered.

Sharon's eyes narrowed and her arms tightened. "Chemical pollution makes more sense to me."

It would make more sense anywhere but Smallville, but to say so would just drive the discussion in an endless circle.

Clark's attention zeroed in on her fear instead. If she was so worried about chemical seepage or meteor dust, why was she on the site of two suspicious deaths? And why had she decided to look for him there? In fact, she still hadn't explained why she wanted to see him.

"So why were you looking for me again?" Clark asked as he started walking toward the gate.

"Uh—" With a glance over her shoulder, Sharon turned to walk beside him. "Actually, I went looking for you at your house, Clark. I didn't expect to find you here, beating me to the scoop."

Clark looked at her askance. "What scoop is that?"

Sharon rolled her eyes in disbelief. "That chemicals from the plant killed Mr. Stoner and that environmental agent."

Clark felt as though he was stuck in an endless loop. "There isn't any evidence."

"Not yet." Sharon looked annoyed. "I came here to find some."

With what? Clark wondered if she had left her specimen collection equipment in her car. A science kit wouldn't fit in her shoulder bag. He began to doubt the rest of her story, but rather than challenge her, he let her talk.

"Chloe was right," Sharon said. After they slipped out the gate, she stared past Clark into the yard as he pulled the swinging panels closed.

"About what?" Clark secured the panels with the chain and broken lock.

"What separates the amateurs from the pros in the newspaper business." Sharon dropped the phone in her bag and flipped it back over her shoulder. "The pros don't let their fears stop them from getting the story."

"That comment was directed at me, not you." Smiling, Clark's gaze scanned the woods between the enclosure and the access road. "Where are you parked?"

"Over there." Sharon pointed down the drive, but she had walked through a cleared area between the trees and the boundary of Stoner's field.

"You probably think I take this whole reporter thing too seriously." Sharon carefully stepped around a tall, prickly thistle. The purple flowers were beautiful, but difficult to remove when they snagged in animal fur or fabric.

"No, I'm thinking about going into journalism, too." Clark spotted a small cloud shadow ahead. He hadn't noticed any clouds in the sky and started to look up. A twinge of meteor nausea suddenly gripped his stomach. Assuming a rock or pocket of meteor fragments was buried in the dirt, he moved to the side. The symptoms began to subside.

"Do you have your professional sights set on the *Daily Planet* like Chloe?" Sharon asked.

"I'd probably be happy at the *Ledger*—" Clark faltered as his temples began to throb with a dull ache. The veins in his hands twisted, and he stumbled. Through blurring vision, he saw the shadow flow toward him and over the toes of his boots.

His last coherent thought before the agony overwhelmed him was that the air around him was still and the cloud was riding currents high above.

"Clark?" Sharon put her hand on his arm. "What's wrong? Are you sick?"

Clark doubled over in pain, unable to answer. For an instant before he collapsed and faded out, he saw the darkness creep up his jeans and envelop his legs.

Time slowed as he hovered in an undulating nexus between the torment of awareness and merciful unconsciousness. Sharp pains erupted in his chest and sent burning spasms of pain through his body. Waves of nausea roiled in his stomach and every muscle screamed. When the agony began to recede, Sharon's hysterical voice penetrated the pounding in his ears.

"Clark! What's happening?"

The pain faded, yet lingered.

Clark groaned as frantic hands closed on his arm and rolled him on his back off the meteor material in the ground. The debilitating symptoms of his sickness abated quickly, but not completely.

"Clark?" Relief flooded Sharon's frightened green eyes when he opened his. "What the hell just happened?"

Still groggy, Clark dragged himself farther from the infested spot. He didn't see any green rocks or flakes, but dirt couldn't protect him from meteor fragments buried just beneath the surface. When the fuzzy feeling in his head didn't go away, he wondered if he had just found what he had been looking for: an area near Mr. Stoner's field that was permeated with meteor dust.

"Sorry about that." Clark struggled to his feet, but the effects didn't dissipate when he was standing up. He swayed slightly as he brushed dirt and dried grass off his clothes. That helped, but he was still not back to Clark Kent normal.

Except for a brief period when a lightning strike had transferred his gifts to Eric Summers, Clark's only experiences with physical vulnerability were his violent reactions to meteor-rocks. The magnitude of the effects and how much he suffered depended on the amount of meteor he was exposed to, at what distance, and for how long. The symptoms usually passed as soon as he was out of range of the alien radiation. At the moment, he was still suffering from low-level exposure.

"Can we get out of here?" Clark asked.

"Sure, but—are you sure you're okay?" The smattering of freckles across Sharon's nose and cheeks stood out in stark relief against her pale skin. She tightened her grip on his arm to keep her hand from shaking.

Clark nodded and offered the first plausible explanation that came to mind. "Maybe I just got a whiff of whatever killed Mr. Stoner."

Sharon gasped and pulled him toward the road. "Come on, Clark! Move!"

Clark was not proud of misleading the girl, but he couldn't explain that he was allergic to meteors in any form. For now, it wouldn't hurt to let her believe that something unknown was to blame. It seemed unlikely that the green particles had shown up in both bodies by coincidence. That didn't mean the alien material had killed Howard Stoner and Gary Mundy, but the dust had to be related.

Sharon had turned the Audi around before she parked on the road near the rutted drive into the missile compound. As soon as they were inside and buckled up, she fired up the engine, jammed the gearshift into drive, and took off in a spray of gravel and dirt.

Still feeling dizzy, Clark fumbled with the doorknob. The door banged open as he stumbled into the Kent kitchen.

"Clark?" Martha set aside the shirt she was mending.

Clark didn't want to upset his mom, but he had used up his reserve energies on the drive home with Sharon. He had briefly considered refusing a ride, but that had two major drawbacks. There wasn't a reason to walk rather than ride that would make sense to Sharon, and superspeeding cross-country would have required him to run naked through the woods. He couldn't speed wearing clothes that were contaminated with meteor dust.

Having to act as though he was fine all the way home had been hard, but not impossible. Sharon was so freaked by the idea that she had been exposed to some unknown poison, he had struggled to maintain the pretense. Short of confessing that he was a superhuman being with a deadly response to meteor-rocks, he had tried to convince her that the danger was minimal. She had finally agreed that Mr. Stoner might have died because of prolonged exposure to the mysterious toxin.

If they finally determined that meteor dust was the lethal substance, he could argue that he was more susceptible to the radiation than she was. The people who were allergic to bee stings and thousands of ordinary foods or substances were the exception, not the rule. It was the best he could do under the circumstances.

Unaware that anything was amiss, Martha rose from the rocker. She glanced out the window as Sharon peeled out of the driveway. "Was that Sharon?"

"Yeah." Clark pulled his shirt over his head, dropped it on the floor, unbuckled his belt, and kicked off his shoes.

"She came by earlier," Martha said.

"She told me." Clark shed his jeans, pulled off his socks and tossed them on the shirt. The instant he kicked the pile of clothes across the floor, he felt better.

His mother paused in the opening between the kitchen and the living room. Her expression was casually curious. "Is this a hormonal thing?"

"No." Clark sped halfway up the stairs and stopped.

There had been many moments in Clark's life when he was especially grateful that Martha Kent was his mom. A few stood out, such as the day he had hit a baseball clear across the front pasture, through the kitchen window, and into a freshly baked pie cooling on the table.

He had been seven and terrified that the woman he loved so much would finally decide she just couldn't deal with a one-boy wrecking crew. He had already broken a milking machine that week. His father had gently admonished him to be more careful. His mother had calmly observed that at least the cow's udder hadn't been in the suction tube when he accidentally squeezed it closed. That afternoon, she had washed the apple filling off his baseball and handed it back with a smile. Not a word about the ruined pie—ever.

Now was a moment like that. Martha Kent took it for granted that her son had a good reason for stripping to his shorts in the kitchen.

"Would you do me a favor, Mom?"

"Sure." She waited, unperturbed, to hear what he had to say.

"I think there's meteor dust in my clothes," Clark explained. "Would you mind shaking them out to check?"

"No, of course not." Martha gathered up the pile to take it outside. "Are you all right?"

"I was a little light-headed on the way home, but that's mostly gone now," Clark said. "I'm sure a shower will wash away anything that's still clinging to my skin."

Martha glanced at Clark's clothes with distaste. "Maybe I should just burn these and bury the ashes."

"No, don't do that!" Clark hadn't meant to snap and softened his tone to explain. "I need a sample of the dust for Chloe's forensic friend to analyze. I picked it up near the field where Mr. Stoner died."

"Where exactly?" Martha's brow furrowed.

"Between the access road and the missile silo," Clark said. "If a meteor hit hard enough, it might have exploded into dust and powder that filtered deep down into the soil—except for a few pockets of concentrated particles."

Nodding, Martha moved to the counter and reached for a grocery bag in the cabinet under the sink.

Clark continued. "If the dust in my clothes is a match for the dust they found in Mr. Stoner and Mr. Mundy, then Dad's Level Three theory will be a no-go."

"Because the dust is in the ground and not part of a LexCorp research project," Martha added for clarification. She carefully put Clark's clothes in the brown paper bag.

Or a LuthorCorp project, Clark thought. "Right."

"That's an interesting theory, Clark," Martha said. "Except for one thing."

Clark frowned, hoping he wasn't going to get a lecture about sticking together as a family. He didn't like working at cross-purposes with his dad, but he couldn't shake the feeling that his father was making a huge mistake. Jonathan had been wrong about Lex's business activities and motives before. He was just too stubborn to admit it.

"After you left, I came back here and did some checking." Martha sighed. "Immediately after the meteor shower, NASA and several universities used radar tracking records and on-site inspections to map every impact they could identify."

"And?" Clark prompted.

"The meteor hit on the plant property was the only one close to the Stoner Farm," Martha said. "The debris radius was measured and confirmed with accurate and extensive tests. If there's meteor dust on the Stoner side of that old missile launch facility, it didn't come from an original impact."

"Clark?" Jonathan stuffed his gloves in his back pocket as he called up to the loft in the old barn. The porous wood had absorbed the pungent odors of old hay, horse, and harness over the decades, and the familiar scent soothed him as no manufactured tranquilizer could.

"Up here, Dad!" Clark called back.

Jonathan paused, hesitant to disturb the dust motes suspended in the morning sunlight streaming down the stairs. The sight reminded him of the many hours he had spent sitting and staring out the upper-level door when he was a kid. In spite of Hiram Kent's no-nonsense personality, he had honored his son's need for personal space. As long as his chores were done, his father had left him alone.

When Clark was old enough, Jonathan had blocked off the lower section of the door to form a window. He had added railings and shelves, moved in an old desk and sofa, scrounged a radio and bought a telescope so his adopted boy would have a special place to call his own. Clark spent so much time in the loft at first he had started calling the hideaway his son's Fortress of Solitude. The designation had stuck even though Clark entertained more company in a month than Jonathan had in a lifetime.

"You're up early, son."

"Just trying to get ahead on my homework." Clark shuffled magazine articles and printed Internet reference pages into a neat pile and slid them into his binder notebook. The notebook went into his backpack, which he zipped with lightning speed.

"If you don't get moving, you're going to miss the bus," Jonathan said.

"Chloe's picking me up." Clark glanced at his watch. "Any minute."

"I thought only seniors were allowed to drive to school under the Reynolds regime," Jonathan said.

"Those are the rules," Clark muttered, "until he decides to change them."

Clark's sour expression revealed a normal objection to authority that Jonathan found oddly reassuring. Although Clark had never mentioned it, he suspected his unbelievably well behaved son had had some kind of run-in with the new principal. But, until the school started calling to complain or sending home notes, he wasn't going to worry about it.

"Lana said she could park at the Talon," Clark went on. "We're dropping that meteor dust sample off at the medical examiner's on our way in."

Jonathan frowned. They didn't know whether or not prolonged or repeated exposure to the alien radiation was having a cumulative effect on Clark. The less time he spent around the green poison the better. Although the thimbleful of meteor dust Martha had shaken out of his clothes yesterday had made him more uncomfortable than sick, a word of caution seemed advised.

"Did you put a lead lining in your backpack?" Jonathan quipped.

"No." Clark grinned. "The dust is in a plastic bag on the porch. Don't worry, Dad. I can handle being a little dizzy on the ride into town."

Jonathan nodded, but the lab test was probably irrelevant. "I thought your mother explained that meteor dust couldn't have gotten that close to Stoner's field when the meteors hit."

"She did, but I'm working on another theory." Clark slung his backpack over his shoulder. "I know you only promised to wait one more day before calling the lawyer, Dad, but—"

"Joe Reisler called me last night," Jonathan said. "Henry Small gave him my number."

"Dad!" Clark's face darkened with disappointment and frustration.

Jonathan had lain awake past midnight thinking about what to do. As certain as he was that Lex and Lionel Luthor had caused more health and environmental harm in Lowell County than anyone realized, he couldn't avoid another, more disturbing truth—not if he was being totally honest with himself.

He *did* resent Clark's friendship with Lex, but it wasn't a matter of jealousy. It was knowing that no matter how hard Lex tried to reject or deny it, he was his father's son. Sooner or later the bond between the two young lions would be ripped apart because they were who they were—one the product of Lionel's relentless challenge and calculated cunning and the other molded by Martha's trust and unconditional love. The only uncertainties were what would cause the rift and when.

When he rose at dawn, Jonathan knew the catalyst wouldn't be him and the breakup wouldn't be now.

Before he could make his position clear, Clark's feelings boiled over.

"Look, Dad, I know you don't trust Lex and you don't think I should, either, but I'm not against this lawsuit because I'm blind to the facts. It's because I think you are!"

"Clark—" When Clark's rant continued uninterrupted, Jonathan let it run its course.

"I felt this weird vibration at the old missile silo yesterday so I *do* think there's something going on. I'm just not sure what, or that Lex is behind it." Clark's stare was hard and unflinching. "So do what you want about getting a lawyer and filing a lawsuit, Dad, but I really wish you trusted me enough to wait."

"I do trust you, Clark," Jonathan said. "That's why I told Mr. Reisler I'd call back when and *if* I need a lawyer."

Jonathan rarely stunned his son into speechless amazement. Having *that* role reversed was a rush. Now Clark knew how his father must have felt the first time he saw his five-year-old son using metal pipes and tractor tires as Tinkertoys.

"Chad said he'd take the sample over to the lab right away." Chloe braked the car at the four-way stop and checked for oncoming traffic. "He's pretty sure we'll have an answer this afternoon."

"Great." Clark tried to sound enthusiastic, but it wasn't easy. His head buzzed with a thousand pinpricks, as though his brain had fallen asleep from lack of circulation. Sitting in the back seat wasn't much protection from the plastic bag of meteor dust in Chloe's shoulder bag. The only advantage was that the two girls up front seemed unaware of his sickly state.

"Is Chad always this cooperative?" Lana sat in the passenger seat.

"I promised to do his makeup shopping at Arlene's the next time I'm in Metropolis." Chloe turned left onto the county highway that cut through the north side of town.

"Why?" Lana asked, amused. "Chad goes Goth day and night in Smallville so he can't be too embarrassed to buy makeup."

"No, but it's a huge hassle getting anyone to wait on him," Chloe said in disgust. "Wearing basic black in broad daylight may be out for the fashion sensitive set, but the dark side of style isn't contagious."

"I think most people can accept basic black. It's the pierced tongue they can't deal with," Lana said.

"Probably," Chloe agreed. "You don't want to stare, but you just can't help it."

Lana glanced back with a concerned frown. "You're awfully quiet, Clark."

"Just thinking about my biology paper," Clark said.

"What did you settle on for a topic?" Chloe flipped the signal lever on and turned right.

"Whether or not multicellular organisms evolved from single-celled organisms or arose independently." Clark closed his eyes for a second, but that just made the chaos inside his skull worse.

"Really?" Lana sat back with a nod. "Where'd you get that idea?"

"From Sharon." Clark wished Chloe would get to the county medical building soon. Once the meteor dust was out of the car, he wouldn't sound like he was gargling nails.

"Sharon came into the Talon the other day." Lana hesitated then smiled. "She seems—nice. A little curious."

"She's new," Clark said, economizing on words until the spinning stopped.

"Just beware of getting too bosom buddy with her," Chloe said. "Once Sharon gets over being shy, she doesn't stop talking."

"She's trying to impress you, Chloe," Lana said.

"Impress me?" Chloe was genuinely surprised. "Why?"

"Because you edit the *Torch*." Clark's voice cracked with the strain of covering the slight but steady draining effects of the meteor dust. "She told me the same thing yesterday at the missile silo."

Lana frowned and faced forward as Chloe drove into the business complex where Lowell County had annex offices.

"You took Sharon to the missile silo?" Chloe pulled into a spot, shifted into park, and turned to glare at him.

"I didn't *take* her," Clark said, suddenly irritated. "She just showed up. You pretty much dared her to prove herself with that remark about pros and amateurs."

"How much of a pro does she want to be?" Chloe asked, alarmed. "And how much does she *know*? Enough to beat me to the *Smallville Ledger* with a story?"

"Sharon wants to be the new star reporter at the *Torch*, Chloe." Talking was an effort, but the sooner Clark said what needed saying, the sooner Chloe would take the dust sample inside. "And she thinks chemical contamination from the plant makes more sense than killer rocks, so you don't have to worry about being scooped."

Chloe scowled. "Only because the *Ledger* doesn't buy plant conspiracy articles."

Not unless the evidence to back them up is ironclad and libel-proof, Clark thought wearily. *Which is never.*

"I don't know why you told Sharon about my meteor theory in the first place." Chloe pushed open the door and grabbed her bag.

"I didn't," Clark objected.

"Well, neither did I." Chloe slid out, closed the door, and pulled the plastic specimen bag from her bag as she stalked toward the front door.

Lana winced. "I think you touched a nerve."

Clark began feeling better the instant the meteor dust was out of the car. He nodded as his head cleared. "Apparently, but I don't think Sharon is trying to unseat Chloe as the intrepid defender of truth at Smallville High."

"I'm not so sure," Lana said softly. When she caught Clark's quizzical look, she started to explain. "It's just a feeling, but—" Her smile tightened. "It's probably nothing."

Clark's clarity of mind sharpened as his body recovered from the meteor sickness. He slipped into pensive thought as he settled back. Lana seemed unsure about Sharon, and Chloe felt threatened. He didn't know why they had formed their opinions, but something about Sharon bothered him, too. He just couldn't figure out what. She had an explanation for everything she did, assuming she really wanted to be a reporter. What if she was just using the *Torch* as an excuse to gather information? About the people she wanted as friends, the Stoner story, or both?

Clark gave everyone the benefit of the doubt—until they gave him reason to doubt.

He had noticed inconsistencies with Sharon's story yesterday, particularly the absence of specimen collection equipment in her car. In spite of being groggy from the meteor dust clinging to his clothes, he had mustered enough energy to focus his X-ray vision on the Audi's trunk. The contents had been easy to identify: books, a jacket, a flashlight, a boom box, and a case of CDs.

Unless Sharon had planned to collect soil samples in CD jewel cases, she had nothing suitable in the car.

Clark cupped his chin as his thoughts flowed in logical progression. If Sharon hadn't gone to the silo to look for evidence, what was she doing there? Even if his mom had known his plans, she wouldn't have told a girl he had just met where he had gone. Sharon knew from the conversation at lunch that he intended to see Lex, but he hadn't said a word about going to the missile launch facility.

Stumped, Clark leaned forward. "What is it about Sharon that doesn't feel right, Lana?"

"Nothing." Lana shrugged. "Really." She seemed relieved when Chloe rushed out of the building and down the walk.

Chloe jumped back in the car and slammed the door. "According to county time, my watch is five minutes slow. If you guys want to get to school in one piece before lockdown, sit back, hang on, and let me drive."

"I am *so* glad Mr. Reynolds gave me an exemption because I work." Lana braced with a hand on the dash as the car shot backward.

Clark knew Mr. Reynolds wasn't dispensing special favors. Lana used her free periods to keep up with Talon business, a responsibility the principal supported.

"Right." Chloe yanked the steering wheel hard to the left. "You'd think being the editor of the *Torch* would qualify me for the prisoner work release program, too, but no."

Clark sighed as Chloe gunned the engine, and the car sped down the drive. Lana had obviously wanted to say something about Sharon and had thought better of it. He didn't know what or why, but he didn't have the patience for guessing games or the emotional fortitude to press. If it was important, she'd tell him when she was ready.

"I assure you, Dr. Farley, I haven't said a word to anyone." Lex swiveled his desk chair toward the window, away from the medieval virtual world displayed on the computer screen. He did not appreciate having his train of thought interrupted for trivial matters. "I honor my agreements, including the privacy clause in our contract."

"Then explain why that Kent boy was trying to break into this installation after leaving your mansion?" The geneticist was furious, but with the wrong person.

"I don't know," Lex said with steely calm. He was incensed by the insinuation, intrigued by Clark's interest, and annoyed by the man's bluster. Farley's security measures had made teenage breaking and entering difficult to the point of impossible. "Perhaps, you should ask your daughter."

The irate father sputtered. "Sharon has nothing to do with this, Mr. Luthor."

"Quite the contrary, Dr. Farley." Lex's modulated voice did not betray the depth of his displeasure. When he wasn't busy adding to his wealth, he enjoyed toying with people. He always held the winning hand—except with his father. That would change, sooner rather than later if his assumptions about Farley's work were correct.

Although Max Cutler, Lawrence Farley's partner, was ex-CIA and an expert in matters of surveillance and security, Lex was confident the mansion system was superior. Another clause in the lease agreement gave Farley the right to refurbish the underground facility to suit his needs, including the installation of security equipment at his own expense. However, while Lex knew exactly when and where Sharon Farley had parked to watch his estate yesterday afternoon, the doctor could not have known Clark was on the missile silo site unless his daughter had told him.

Lex prided himself on his powers of deduction, which the

scientist was grossly underestimating. The lease had been written to give him final approval of Cutler's plans and a LexCorp security team inspection after the modifications were completed. The lack of surveillance equipment above ground was deliberate. There were no cameras or sensors that would alert the casually curious or the educated professional that the underground installation was occupied. Even Howard Stoner, a potential problem, had been utilized to Farley's advantage.

Since everyone in Smallville knew that Stoner was the missile site's self-appointed sentinel, Cutler doubled what Lex had been paying the farmer to keep watching and to keep quiet. To all outward appearances, nothing had changed. In the two months since Farley and Cutler had finished moving in, all evidence of their activities had been removed. Even the weeds on the road, drive, and yard had grown back. For an extra twenty dollars a week, Stoner had mowed the enclosure to hide the footprints and trampled vegetation that marked Farley's and Cutler's comings and goings.

If either man had emerged from the facility to apprehend a trespasser, Clark would have returned to the mansion to report that someone *was* using the old missile silo—with or without Lex's knowledge.

The only way Farley could possibly have found out that Clark was in the enclosure was if someone Clark knew, but didn't associate with the facility, had told him.

"If Sharon hadn't been spying on me, she wouldn't have known Clark was here," Lex said. "She obviously followed him."

"No, she didn't," Farley huffed. "He was here when Sharon arrived to warn me that some of the local kids were getting too curious about this place."

Exactly, Lex thought. Seeing Howard Stoner drop dead must have aroused Clark's interest in the old missile site nearby. Clark had an uncanny knack of finding trouble that didn't find him first.

An accusatory edge crept into Farley's tone. "Apparently, you and the Kent boy are friends."

"My friendship with Clark is irrelevant," Lex said coldly. "The local kids, who know that old military installation is there, have *always* been curious about it. That's why *I* paid Howard Stoner to watch the place. Now, he's dead. Why is that, Dr. Farley?"

"I have no idea." Farley matched Lex's icy calm.

Lex didn't know if Farley was implicated in the deaths of Howard Stoner and Gary Mundy or not. The presence of meteor dust in both bodies was odd since Stoner's field hadn't sustained a direct meteor hit in 1989. Perhaps the burrowing rabbit population had unearthed an undiscovered impact pocket of pulverized dust. That would explain the presence of the green particles in the dead rabbits, but not why they had been battered and left in a pile. And meteor dust couldn't account for Mundy's death, either.

Stranger things had happened in Smallville, especially since the meteor shower. Before Dr. Hamilton died, he had proposed an interesting theory about the ability of meteor material to change some organisms at the molecular level. Lex's and many other original victims' blood had extraordinarily high white cell counts. Although Lex had gone bald, his asthma had been cured, and he hadn't been sick since that October day. Not even a sniffle.

But the meteor-rocks didn't have an effect on everyone, and those who were susceptible reacted in different ways and to varying degrees. His experience with the extraterrestrial rocks was limited, but he was sure of one thing. The mutating properties couldn't be harnessed to produce a controlled, calculated result—except death.

None of that was his concern, however. He had legally insulated himself and LexCorp from any liability resulting from the rental lease.

"Is there anything else I can do for you, Dr. Farley?" Lex asked as a courtesy. There was only so much he was willing to do to pacify his outraged tenant.

"I told you I needed peace and quiet before I signed the lease, Mr. Luthor. You assured me I would have it."

Lex chose not to argue. Keeping the young and curious away from the property was a reasonable request under the circumstances.

"I'll have a word with Clark," Lex said. "Now if you'll excuse me—"

Lex glanced at the precise Swiss clock on his desk as he hung up. Classes at Smallville High wouldn't be over for a few hours.

Since time was money, he turned his attention back to the computer adventure game.

It was necessary to understand how something worked before making a significant investment. He had recognized the relaxing escape qualities of the ongoing scenarios immediately. However, he wasn't playing to relieve the stress of an everyday life. He was playing for real, for keeps, and for much higher stakes. He was focused on conquering the real-world masters who were making fortunes providing realistic role-playing games for paying adults. He had already ascertained that the gaming community could be induced to abandon current realms for a more intricate and exciting virtual world. He just had to identify and incorporate that elusive, missing element they all wanted and couldn't find—yet.

Which involved spending a few dollars and some time talking to people within the context of their alternate, cyberlives.

Lex fitted a headset over his ears and adjusted the mike. "Kilya? Are you there?"

"Hi, Dome. Thought I lost you."

"You did. I had to leave for a few minutes, and someone killed me." Lex knew nothing about the real woman who had befriended his pathetic character, but he had grown rather fond of Kilya Warcrest, the brazen lady barbarian who had taken pity on a new player. "I still have five gold pieces hidden away, though."

"Good. You'll need them to buy a Lazarus ritual." Kilya laughed.

"So I'm not really dead?" Lex asked.

"Only temporarily," Kilya said, then added, "Unless we can't find a priest before your window of renewal expires."

Lex made a note to push his accountants. If the numbers added up, a new subsidiary of LexCorp would be in the works before he finished breakfast tomorrow. He'd have the best graphic artists, programmers, and fantasy writers in the country on the payroll by noon.

◆◆◆

Chloe breezed into the *Torch* offices and keyed the computer to sign on to the Internet before she even sat down. Although

Mr. Reynolds wouldn't give her a campus exemption like Lana's, he had given her permission to work on the newspaper before and after school and during study halls. She had spent most of the last period in the library getting the research for her biology paper out of the way so she could concentrate on the important stuff.

"Like finding out what the hell Sharon Farley is really up to." Chloe dropped her books on the side desk and popped the top on a cold soda she had just gotten from the machine outside the cafeteria.

Something Clark said that morning had jump-started her investigative instincts.

Chloe hadn't told Sharon that meteor-rocks might be responsible for many of the strange ailments and deaths in Smallville, and neither had Clark. Although Sharon had spent quite a long time perusing the Wall of Weird, was she smart enough to make a connection that the best EPA and NASA scientists rejected? Were the new girl's powers of observation and deduction good enough to make the leap from meteor dust in two bodies to "killer rocks"?

Clark seemed certain that Sharon didn't buy the meteor theory. Chloe wasn't so sure, but that wasn't the only thing that disturbed her. Since Sharon had argued against investigating Lex Luthor's missile silo site, why had she gone there? Although Chloe couldn't discount the possibility that Sharon was just going after a story, she couldn't ignore the gut feeling that something wasn't right, either.

Clark and Pete came in as Chloe sat down and pulled up her incoming e-mail menu. They took their usual positions at the desks behind and in front of her.

"Heard back from Chad, yet?" Clark asked.

Chloe scanned the e-mail list and shook her head. "Not yet, but it's only three. I've got something else that's pretty darn interesting, though."

"The cafeteria hired a new cook?" Pete asked hopefully.

"No, but this came up at dinner last night, when I mentioned the missile silo to my dad." Chloe shifted her gaze from Pete to Clark. "I was just making conversation. I didn't expect to find out that one of his best friends wrote an insurance policy on the site three months ago."

Clark sat up. "What kind of policy?"

Chloe loved it when she got Clark's attention with an information coup. Her father only knew about the policy because Wayne Baum had called to crow about scoring a LexCorp account. For a small insurance agency trying to compete in Metropolis, doing any business with a Luthor was a professional and financial boon.

"All the usual damage coverage for a property," Chloe explained. "But the main thing is that it protects Lex and LexCorp from any liability resulting from renter activity."

"So someone is definitely using the place." Clark frowned.

"We don't know that," Chloe cautioned. Sometimes she had to play devil's advocate to keep people on track with the facts. "Maybe Lex is just covering all his bases before he tries to rent it."

Clark didn't argue with her logic.

"Who would want it?" Pete pegged the obvious question.

Chloe voiced the obvious answer. "Someone who's doing something they don't want anyone to know about?"

"Something they'd kill to protect?" Pete scowled. "We've got two dead guys and a pile of broken rabbits, remember."

"Slaughtered snakes and two strangled cows," Clark added.

"Don't forget the rosebush massacre," Chloe said. "All incidents that probably qualify for Wall of Weird status."

"Is the sheriff making any progress on the case?" Clark leaned back with his hands clasped behind his neck.

"They don't have a suspect," Chloe said. "I called my friend at the department this morning. The only thing they know is that the CEP agent was dead before someone took a few chunks out of him."

"But we still don't have a likely candidate for who," Pete said.

"What do we know about Sharon's father?" Clark asked.

"You don't think Sharon's dad munched a bunch of Mr. Mundy, do you?" Pete was aghast.

Clark laughed. "No, but he might have rented Lex's missile silo."

"You think?" Chloe raised an eyebrow. Their thoughts were obviously running in similar circles. Sharon's insufficiently explained trip to the missile silo yesterday was apparently bugging Clark, too.

"A missile silo instead of a cabin in the woods." Pete shrugged. "I suppose if someone wanted to be left alone to write a novel, that would work."

"Maybe," Clark said, "but before he decided to write science fiction, Dr. Farley did some kind of scientific research at a university."

Pete pointed as his memory sparked. "Until he lost his grant!"

"I'm on it." Chloe turned to the computer to begin an Internet search for anything she could find on Dr. Lawrence Farley. When her cell phone rang, she answered absently, "Chloe."

"Sorry to bother you, Chloe," Lex Luthor said, "but I need to get in touch with Clark. Will you give him a message?"

"Uh—he's right here. Hang on." Mouthing Lex's name, Chloe thrust the phone at Clark.

"Hey, Lex. What's up?" Clark nodded as he listened, then glanced at the time. "The last bell rings in five minutes. As soon as the gate's unlocked, I'll go right over."

"Right over where?" Chloe asked when Clark handed the phone back.

"The Talon to meet Lex. He didn't say why, but I wanted to see Lana anyway." Clark stood up with a pensive frown. "Do you know if something happened between her and Sharon, Chloe? Something she wouldn't want to talk about?"

"She hasn't said anything to me." Chloe looked up from the keyboard. "But you'll have to wait to ask her. One of the other waitresses needed tonight off, so Lana changed shifts."

"What time will she be in?" Clark picked up his books.

"Five?" Chloe shrugged. "I didn't ask. I wasn't worried about getting my car back because I have so much to do here. And now that I'm researching Sharon's dad, I've got even more."

"I'll help." Pete slid into Clark's chair and turned on the computer.

"I'll check back later." Clark paused at the door. "Can you

find out if the missile silo is plugged into Kansas State Water and Power, and who's paying the bill?"

"Probably." Chloe waved without taking her gaze off the monitor. Every journalistic synapse fired up as she clicked on the first link. The Stoner story had finally gotten hot.

Clark sorted through everything he knew as he walked to the Talon. Lex had called from the road and wouldn't arrive for a few minutes, yet.

From what he heard at the site, he was certain that machinery of some sort was being used in the underground installation. He couldn't tell Chloe and Pete how he knew, but he had more than a slight vibration to support that someone was down there. Lex was extravagant, but he never wasted a dollar. He would not have bought insurance against renter damage unless he had rented the property.

Clark made a snap decision not to tell Lex that he knew about the policy. Wayne Baum shouldn't have disclosed his business dealings with LexCorp, but he had told Mr. Sullivan in confidence. Chloe's dad had told her without knowing the information might be relevant to a crime. Lex would have a legitimate complaint if he knew, but he might also retaliate in a manner more harsh than the indiscretion warranted. The leak was an unfortunate fluke. Clark wouldn't be indirectly responsible for ruining Mr. Baum's business.

As he approached the Talon, Clark slowed down again. He hadn't decided whether to confront Lex or not. Technically, Lex hadn't lied about using the missile silo, but he had deliberately misled him.

Based on the body of circumstantial evidence, Lawrence Farley was almost certainly Lex's tenant. Dr. Farley and his daughter had moved to Smallville three months ago, around the time Lex was having the insurance policy on the property drawn up. If Sharon's father had rented the silo, that would explain why she didn't have any soil sample gear with her yesterday. She hadn't gone to the site looking for evidence against LexCorp. She had gone to warn her father that the *Torch* staff was getting too curious about the place.

When he had asked Lex if the plant's research and development operations had expanded into the missile facility, Lex's answer in the negative had been correct. *Renting* the property wasn't the same thing. Since Lex wouldn't disclose anything if he was on the defensive, Clark had nothing to gain by bringing up the clever spin. Letting it slide, on the other hand, might be beneficial.

As usual right after school, the Talon was packed. Teenagers and shoppers had staked claims to every chair around every table. Laughter and shouted greetings rose above the steady drone of conversation and the clink of glasses, coffee cups, and plates.

Lex almost hit his head on a hanging plant when he stood and waved from a corner table.

Clark ducked under another plant to drop into the opposite chair. "I think Lana forgot that most people are taller than she is when she put these up."

"The dangling danger adds a certain charm." Lex flipped a trailing vine into the hanging basket, then raised his demitasse cup and nodded toward a frosty glass. "I ordered you a root beer, but feel free to get something else."

"Root beer's great. Thanks." Clark took a swallow, hoping Lex wouldn't waste time with small talk. He had called him here with a purpose, and Clark didn't want to sit for too long wondering why.

"This is rather awkward, but necessary." Lex stared into his dark espresso for a moment before meeting Clark's gaze. "I wouldn't even bring this up except that it involves a promise."

"What's going on?" Clark prodded.

"I know you were at the missile silo site yesterday," Lex said, "and I have to ask you to stay away."

"Okay." Clark nodded. "Why?"

A flicker of surprise registered in Lex's eyes, as though he hadn't expected Clark to agree so readily. "I've rented the property and privacy was part of the lease agreement."

"To Dr. Farley," Clark said matter-of-factly. Lex's stony expression didn't provide the confirmation he was hoping for, however.

"What makes you think that?" Lex asked after a prolonged pause.

"A couple of things," Clark said, "but mainly because I ran into his daughter out there yesterday. Either Sharon told you I was at the missile silo or her father did. There's no other way you could have known." The logic wasn't perfect, but it had the desired effect.

"You didn't hear that from me," Lex said pointedly.

Clark realized that the agreement must have a secrecy clause, too. Lex wasn't free to divulge his tenant's name, but he couldn't stop someone from guessing.

Clark took another swallow of soda and nodded to convey that he understood. However, he couldn't ignore the fact that people had died. An insurance policy might protect LexCorp from some liability, but it wouldn't stop his father from holding Lex responsible. If Dr. Farley was engaged in something criminal and Lex knew, he was an accomplice.

"Do you know what Dr. Farley is doing, Lex?" Clark tackled the situation head on. "Because if whatever it is had something to do with Mr. Stoner's death, and the sheriff finds out someone's there—"

Lex cut him off. "I don't know, Clark, but I have arrived at some educated guesses."

Clark's throat tightened, but he choked back his questions. Lex Luthor couldn't be pushed, but he might give. *Especially if he thinks it might discourage Dad's quest for legal satisfaction.*

Lex took a sip of espresso. "Dr. Lawrence Farley is a geneticist. He was researching stem cell manipulation in conjunction with engineered evolution potential during his tenure as a professor—until the government pulled his grant last year."

Clark's eyes widened with interest. No wonder Sharon knew so much about fringe theories of evolution. Since Lex had no qualms about discussing Dr. Farley's work, he didn't interrupt.

"His career should have been over," Lex continued, "but Europeans aren't nearly as squeamish as Americans regarding certain areas of medical curiosity and endeavor. Dr. Farley found a partner with a background in security and acquired private funding."

"From where?" Clark blurted out the question without thinking.

"There are financial consortia overseas that gamble on risky orphan projects," Lex explained.

Clark wasn't sure what Lex was trying to tell him. LuthorCorp, Lionel's umbrella corporation, had subsidiary medical companies that did not believe "do no harm" was a priority. Studies using human test subjects at Metron Pharmaceuticals had resulted in several deaths and complications for which there was no cure.

"Unfortunately for my father, the federal government has restricted stem cell research and therapeutic cloning in this country." Lex's brow furrowed slightly. "And, of course, both therapies show promise for repairing optic nerves, which would cure his blindness."

"That would be fantastic." Clark wanted to believe Lex's interest in Dr. Farley's research was motivated by altruism rather than profit.

Lex's enthusiasm was less than exuberant. "I'm responsible for my father's condition. Erasing that would be worth something to me."

The rare glimpse into Lex's emotional psyche surprised Clark. Lex was more concerned with being free of the guilt than whether or not his father's sight was restored. Apparently, he had agreed to the secrecy clause because he thought Dr. Farley was continuing his stem cell research. Lex could plead ignorance if the geneticist's illicit scientific work was discovered.

Does that work involve meteor dust? Clark wondered.

"Sharon said her father's writing a book," Clark said.

"I'm certain Dr. Farley is writing something he wants to protect until he can publish," Lex said.

Since Dr. Farley couldn't publish findings on illegal medical research, Clark realized Lex was sending him another guarded message.

"No doubt that's one reason why he asked permission to install a sophisticated security system and wishes to be left alone." Lex drained the small cup and set it down.

Warning noted, Clark thought, but filling an access tube with cement was not exactly state-of-the-art technology.

◆◆◆

Dr. Lawrence Farley finished loading the wheeled utility cart and locked the cabinet door. The stock of chocolate, cheap wine, and cigarettes would last another week. Layton preferred fresh kill, but they could no longer trust him to hunt in the silo, tunnels, and equipment area of the facility. He had developed a taste for beef jerky, but Sharon had forgotten to buy more when she had done the grocery shopping. Today, Layton would have to settle for chocolate. There was no suitable substitute for morphine, but Hoover's time would run out before his supply of the drug.

Hoover had been Farley's first experimental human subject. Reduced to a mass of pulsating tumors that left him barely recognizable as a man, he would have died two months ago if not for his amazing immunity to toxins. The cancers adapted to and absorbed every poison Farley had tried except morphine. The drug's lethal effects were taking longer than he liked, but at least Hoover was in a constant stupor, removed from mental and physical pain.

Farley was beginning to agree with Max. Mercy killing would be humane for the four others who had preceded Layton Crouse.

Sighing, Farley left the lab complex. The sphere once called the Launch Control Center, Max had divided into a lounge, office, and combination laboratory and infirmary. He had also soundproofed the galley, latrine, and large storeroom outside the lab and muffled the forced-air conductors. Earplugs were no longer a necessity, saving time and trouble. The metal bridge that linked the habitation area to the six-ton door into the junction tunnel still clanked dreadfully, however.

When the Missile Launch Facility was operational, the massive door had been locked at all times. Strict procedures had been followed to prevent the authenticators and launch keys from being accessed by the wrong people. Only one LCC door in the Midwest network of ten Launch Control Facilities had been allowed to be open at any one time, and no individual could enter a sensitive LCC area alone. Once the two-man teams had been cleared and admitted to the Launch Control Center, they had been locked in until their relief arrived.

Farley left the massive door open. He and Max, and Sharon on her rare visits to the underground compound, ran in and out of the lab complex too often to deal with the locking mechanism.

The floor of the Launch Control Center, and the even larger Launch Facility Equipment Building across the tunnel, which housed the diesel generator and climate control systems, rested on huge shock absorbers. Metal ramps bridged the gap between the floor and the walls, which had been designed with flexibility to withstand a close nuclear hit.

Edgar began calling and banging on his cell door when he heard Farley's footsteps on the metal bridge.

"Max!" Farley called out as he exited the narrow passage through the thick wall into the spacious tunnel hub. The LCC, LFEB, and elevator all opened into the central area. Six cells had been built into the original space: three along the blank wall opposite the elevator doors and three on the wall between the equipment room door and the silo tunnel. Five of the six-foot-by-eight-foot cubicles were occupied. The sound of Farley's voice was drowned out by Edgar's thumps and demanding cries.

"Shhhmok! Now, Faley!"

"Settle down, Edgar, or you'll have to wait until last," Farley snapped.

The mutant-man shut up.

Farley glanced toward the open hatch behind the elevator. The extension tunnel ran one hundred feet west to the missile silo. The silo floor was eighty feet below the complex level, which was sixty feet underground. Until it had been removed in 1994, a Minuteman II had stood tall and proud in the shaft, ready to fly in defense of the country.

Now the deep, empty shaft was a hazard, and the connecting tunnel served as a jogging trail and exercise room for Max Cutler. The ex-CIA agent had been a dangerous man before he had submitted to the molecular enhancement procedure. Farley was now working to arrest the progress of the problematic side effects. If he could stop Max's decline into insanity, the result of accelerated deterioration of nonregenerating neurons in the brain, Max would be a spy unlike any ever known.

In his dark alter-form, Max was impervious to all toxic substances and conventional weapons. He could easily invade any lit place anywhere without being noticed, an ability that gave him unprecedented information-gathering potential. His ability to infiltrate and memorize data he heard or saw would command a high price from government, corporate, and industrial sources. Some would pay for the intelligence itself. In other cases, a force of engineered spies-for-hire would use what Max learned to complete other difficult missions. There was no limit to the possibilities or the wealth they would both acquire.

If the unsolved mental problem doesn't doom Max and the project first, Farley thought with a sigh. He wiped nervous sweat off his forehead as he unclipped his walkie-talkie and pressed the call button. The installation was too far below ground for cell phones to work.

"This is Max." The agent was breathing heavily.

"Time to pacify the patients."

"They're freaks, not patients," Max snapped.

"They still need their rations." Farley winced, anticipating Max's next response. The agent despised his euphemistic code word, but that was too damn bad.

"Whatever," Max scoffed. "I'll be there as soon as I finish my run."

Ignoring the distressed noises emanating from the cells, Farley pocketed the comm-device and began portioning the tranquilizing substances. Like the euphemism, his carefree tone was a cover for a deep revulsion, not just for the victims of his initial botched experiments, but with himself for abandoning all sense of decency and principle.

When the government canceled his research grant, he had thought his future, and by extension Sharon's, had been canceled, too. Others in his field had found legal, lucrative outlets for their uninspired expertise without too much delay. He had been ostracized. His premise that evolution could be engineered to specification and advanced on a molecular level was too preposterous to be taken seriously. No one had understood the potential of the green meteor material he had found in Dr. Hamilton's old university lab. He had applied the unknown substance in his genetic manipulation of rats with erratic but fascinating results.

Outraged, indignant, and desperate after his dismissal, he had been anxious to talk when Max Cutler approached him with his super-spy project proposal. With Continental Sciences of Europe providing the funds, it was a once-in-a-lifetime chance to continue his work unhampered by academic ridicule or government oversight.

Now, everything depended on whether or not he could stabilize the cellular erosion in Max's brain.

Farley tried not to think about what would happen if he failed. Without Max Cutler to control and operate a fleet of specialized agents, there wouldn't be a financial empire. His work would be worthless and a threat. He would have no choice but to destroy all evidence of the project, including the bodies of his hapless volunteers.

All he had to do was turn a key and push a button.

But Farley wasn't the only person wondering, What if?

Trained to think of every possible contingency, Max had extrapolated and planned for several emergency scenarios.

If the power failed and the electronic locks on the cells opened before the generator came on-line, gas would be released from canisters to subdue the patients—except for Hoover, who was immune, but harmless. Gas masks were stored throughout the installation for his and Max's protection.

The self-destruct mechanism had been installed in a case by the elevator. If the mutant-men couldn't be controlled or he and Max had to abandon the project to escape apprehension, the simple, two-step activation process would initiate a five-minute countdown. The agent had rigged the underground missile facility to implode, making a search of the rubble impossible. If anything bad happened to Max, the explosive charges would obliterate his existence, too.

They had thought of everything, except the insidious madness.

"Damn!" Max rushed out of the silo tunnel and came to a

sudden stop. Breathless, he bent over with his hands on his knees, his sweat towel dragging on the floor.

"What?" Farley's voice cracked, and his left eye began to twitch. Max had always made him nervous, but his anxiety response had gotten worse since the agent had begun showing signs of mental deterioration. The slight memory lapses and minor tantrums were not as worrisome as Max's irrational fear of the dark.

"Lightbulb burned out." Flipping a towel over his shoulder, Max joined Farley at the cart. "You'll take care of that, right?"

"As soon as we're done here," Farley promised. He loathed making the afternoon rounds to check the patients, but Max could not properly assess their conditions. The agent's untrained eye might miss a subtle, yet critical physiological change. It was enough that Max was willing to distribute the morning and evening meals without his help.

"Shhhmok." Edgar's gnarled, hairy hand slipped through the window bars of the first cell. "Pease, Faley."

"You can smoke after we see how you're doing, Edgar." Farley waved the reluctant man back.

All Farley's modifications had been intended to enhance an espionage agent's performance: strength, immunities, reflexes, camouflage, and retention. When he and Max had first conceived the idea of designer spies, Farley thought he could create specific alterations in the first few volunteers. He had hoped to isolate the various genetic patterns so more than one attribute could be incorporated into future models.

Edgar had grown barbed hairs on his hands and feet that allowed him to scale walls and hang upside down from the ceiling. That was the intended result of Farley's engineering, except that the wiry hair had grown over the small man's entire body and face and was too tough to shave. Even if he hadn't degenerated mentally overnight, Edgar couldn't blend in with the general population.

When Edgar didn't obey, Max barked, "If you want your cigarette, you'd better move. Now!"

Pouting, Edgar sprang backward and stuck to the far wall.

"Excellent, Edgar." Farley smiled with an approving nod as

he entered. With everyone except Hoover, who was always spaced on morphine, praise seemed to soothe the mutants' violent tendencies.

Max shook a cigarette from an open pack and held it up for Edgar to see.

Edgar hissed through rotted teeth, his version of a laugh.

Farley picked up the dirty bucket commode, set it outside the door, and moved a clean one in. He and Max made the exchange in every cell twice a day. Blankets, pillows, and air mattresses were cleaned or replaced as needed.

When the basic sanitary chores were done, Farley ran Edgar through his rudimentary paces. Except for the worsening speech impediment, he didn't detect any changes. Unlike the mental aberrations, the physical effects of the procedure manifested quickly and became permanent within a couple of weeks. Max's condition was following an identical physical pattern, but with a much slower rate of mental deterioration.

"Okay, Edgar." Farley backed out of the cell, smiling up at the bright eyes looking down. "Very good."

The instant Farley closed the door, Edgar dropped to the floor. He thrust his hand through the bars of the small, rectangular window set in the solid, steel door. "Shhhmok!"

"Here you go, pal." Max lit the cigarette and handed it to the addicted mutant.

Farley moved on to the next cell. The only humanity the volunteers had left was their habits and addictions. Out of pity at first, Farley had positioned a TV in the tunnel junction where all the subjects could see it. Max had taken it down when they realized no one was watching. The men's minds had become so primitive, they were content to rock, pace, whine, shout, or sit.

When Edgar wasn't smoking the cigarettes they rationed to keep him calm, he flitted from one wall to another—all day and most of the night.

"Hoover's not looking very good, Doc." Max peered through the bars of the next cell.

Farley nodded with a cursory glance at the human tumor. Hoover rested on a pile of blankets with his back braced in the corner. His empty eyes appeared sunken in the cauliflower growths that sprouted from his forehead and cheeks. The lumps, bulges, and festering sores that covered his grotesque body didn't exist in his drugged oblivion.

Farley eyeballed the IV bag hanging from a ceiling hook. The tubes were in place and the needle secured in the back of Hoover's enlarged hand. Farley decided to increase the drip rate when he replaced the morphine. If Hoover was lucky, his body would relinquish its tenacious hold on life by morning.

"Let's move on, Max." Farley stepped up to the third cell on the back wall. He took a plastic sipper filled with red wine off the cart and stood back while Max unlocked the door.

Cooper stood in the middle of the padded cell, swatting at the splotches of color that faded and blossomed on his skin. Pinks, greens, and yellows mingled with and overlapped shades of brown, tan, and gray. The camouflage shifted at random, completely beyond the madman's control. His appetite had dwindled along with his mental capacity, which had turned him into a kaleidoscopic, skin-and-bones caricature of a man. Wine was the only thing that diverted Cooper's attention from his futile attempts to catch the fleeting patterns.

"Get back, Cooper," Max ordered. When the Harlequin flailed his arms, Max shoved the wine sipper into his hands. The commode bucket sloshed when he yanked it away from the wall.

Max muttered something unintelligible.

Farley exchanged buckets without a word. Whenever Max complained about the unpleasant duty, he offered to bring someone else in for a third of the cut. Once the agent had dared to suggest that Sharon help out. Farley had threatened to walk. It was bad enough his daughter knew about the "Frankenstein project," as she called it, and that Max had used her to find out what the Kent boy knew about Stoner's sudden death. In spite of his assurances, she was convinced that her genetic structure could be damaged by casual exposure to the meteor material. The idea was ridiculous, but the last thing they needed was a hysterical girl in the lab.

Max slammed Cooper's door closed. "You'd better finish with these guys soon, Doc, 'cause my patience is running out."

Farley's eyes flashed. "Your only hope of avoiding the same

fate as these guys is to let me work in peace."

"Yeah, yeah." Sighing, Max pushed the cart past the equipment room door.

Farley didn't mention that he was seriously considering putting the others out of their misery. He was not fond of the tedious chores, either, but the subjects hadn't outlived their usefulness, yet. One or all of them held the clue to Max's mental survival.

Max grabbed a large chocolate bar for the resident of the fourth cell. Nathan could condense and expand his cellular structure, which gave him a stunted ability to morph into crude, basic shapes. At the moment, he looked like a lumpy cube with his facial features squashed into a three-inch oval area. An arm shot out from his side to snatch the candy bar from Max's grasp.

Nathan was a crude version of the elegant elasticity Farley had achieved with Layton.

Farley nervously glanced past the empty fifth cell that had Max's name penciled in. They never acknowledged its presence.

The sixth cell had been elaborately modified for Layton Crouse's comfort and containment. In addition to the bucket, air mattress, pillow, and blanket, Layton had been given hand-held video games, picture books, puzzles, and plastic building blocks to keep himself amused and entertained.

Compared to the other four, Layton was a resounding success. His ability to transform into a fluid, rubbery state showed enormous promise. His form had spontaneous shape memory, and even though he possessed the mental processes of a slow three-year-old, he had learned to fine-tune and control his malleable body, which had caused them more trouble than Max thought Layton was worth.

For a while, Layton had been content to hunt the wild rats that infested the Launch Facility Equipment Room and silo. He had also enjoyed racing back and forth in the long connecting tunnel. Max could control the child-like monster except when Layton's predatory bloodlust took over, as it had the first time he escaped. With his twelve-foot, loping gorilla stride, Layton had easily outrun Max down the connecting tunnel to the maintenance tube by the silo shaft. The hatch was broken and he had flowed to freedom through a wide crack between the ground and the cover. As soon as Max brought him back, they had filled in the access tube with cement.

For all the good that did us, Farley thought. Despite their efforts to contain him, Layton had repeatedly broken out of the installation. The mutant had refined his rubbery form to access smaller and smaller escape routes, which demonstrated Farley's success while endangering the project. However, until Gary Mundy had made the fatal mistake of interrupting his killing frenzy, Layton's victims had been plants and animals. The incidents had no doubt baffled the sheriff, but tracking down a vandal who stripped the apples off a tree hadn't become a priority.

Nobody was looking for a naked human rubber band, either,

They had been fortunate, Farley knew. Except for the kids who worked on the school newspaper, no one seemed inclined to try to figure out what had killed the farmer and the environmental agent or why.

That wouldn't happen again. Max had found every opening larger than half-inch PVC pipe and capped it. All the ventilation grates, ducts, and vents had been fitted with wire mesh. Layton would have to assume the size and shape of a spaghetti strand to escape his sealed cell now, and it was doubtful that he could. If he ever managed that, however, there was no foolproof way to contain him. Rather than go to the trouble and expense of a lockdown, which meant switching to emergency power, maybe they could bribe the mutant into behaving. The only alternative was elimination.

"Do you have jerky for Layton today?" Max locked Nathan's door.

"Chocolate," Farley said.

"Well, it's not rabbits or snakes, but—" Max looked through the shatterproof glass over Layton's window and froze.

Farley's heart lurched as he stepped up to the door.

Layton's cell was empty.

Lana parked Chloe's car in a dirt-and-gravel area off the drive by the pasture fence. She hadn't planned to come to the stable today, but when Margo asked for the night off, she had gladly switched shifts. Cruising the Kansas countryside on horseback was the best way she knew to wrestle with problems. Riding cleared her head and helped her solve them.

Sighing, Lana stuffed her wallet under the driver's seat. She had been troubled all day because she hadn't given Clark an honest answer when he asked about Sharon Farley that morning.

At first, Lana thought she was just being fair to the new girl. Whether Sharon really was shy or just trying to decide what students she wanted as friends, it had taken her three months to open up. It didn't seem right to assume Sharon was up to something devious just because she seemed too curious.

However, as the day wore on, Lana couldn't deny the real reason she had clammed up. *And it wasn't out of consideration for Sharon.*

She had been afraid Clark would think she was jealous if she said Sharon was a phony. In fact, that's exactly what she *had* thought after Sharon left the Talon; that maybe she couldn't trust her judgment where Clark Kent was concerned.

Lana had decided to find Clark and explain before school let out, but then she had realized something else. Just because she and Chloe had mistaken Clark's warning about Ian as jealousy didn't mean that Clark would react to her warning about Sharon the same way. Even hinting that he might would be an insult.

So now the whole day is gone, and my chance to fix this is fading fast. Lana didn't know what to do, except go for a gallop and hope she could figure it out.

Lana locked the car door and slipped Chloe's keys into her jeans pocket. Three other cars were parked in the gravel parking area, but she didn't see anyone—or hear anyone. The black barn cat wasn't curled on the bench by the stable door soaking up the late-afternoon sun, and the stable manager's dog didn't run out to greet her.

Frowning, Lana scanned the carefully tended grounds. The white board fences around the show and practice rings gleamed against the meteor green of the surrounding meadow. A wren flew into the eaves of the raised judges' stand to tend her nest, and squirrels scampered around the permanent hedge-and-board jumps that formed the outside hunter course. The broodmares calmly grazed in the pasture, and the horses inside the barn were quiet.

Everything seemed normal, except that no one was around.

Then she noticed that the large horse van wasn't parked in its usual spot behind the barn.

"Oh, of course!" Lana suddenly remembered that Walter Holtz, the stable manager, had taken the barn's top show riders and their horses to the Equestrian Center in Metropolis.

The semiweekly outings had started last month and would continue until Mr. Holtz found a new hunter-jumper trainer to employ full-time. Rowdy James, the nearly deaf, cranky, aging stable hand, was probably taking a nap in the hayloft. The old man worked as little as possible and complained about everything constantly and loudly. The stable wouldn't be the same without him, but she was glad he wasn't around to talk her ear off now.

The tranquil setting had a soothing effect as Lana walked toward the barn. She noticed a black helmet and leather gloves lying on the stepped mounting block and wondered who had forgotten them. Everyone loved going to the enclosed arena in the city to train, and things often got left behind in the excitement. As soon as she could afford it, Lana intended to get back into serious training and competition, too.

The large double doors on the front of the stable were open, and she could see Coral Roman's gray mare, Fiona's Luck, in the first box stall. With ears perked forward and nostrils flaring, the mare's attention was on something unseen deeper within the barn. When Lana got closer, she understood why the horse was so fascinated. Someone was rummaging around in the feed room.

Lana's smile faded when she paused to glance through the vertical bars of Fiona's stall door. The mare's dappled gray coat glistened with sweat, and every muscle was spring-coiled. The horse wasn't anticipating her next meal. She was frightened and poised to fight or flee.

From something harmless, Lana wondered, or did the animal sense a definite danger?

Every instinct told Lana to run, but she couldn't abandon the horses in the stalls that lined the wide central aisle. The bay gelding on her left nervously paced a circle, and another farther down snorted and pawed the floor. Tension gripped every animal in the barn. If the threat was real and not hyper horse-imagination, she could open the stalls to free them.

If necessary, she thought with an anxious glance toward the feed room halfway down the aisle on the left. She was *not* leaving without her pinto, but he was stabled at the far end of the barn.

Lana considered circling around the outside of the building to avoid being seen by whoever—or whatever—had upset the horses. But she had to open the doors on the far end to get her horse out, and the hinges creaked. Her chances of making a quick, fast getaway would be better if she reached the horse first and opened the noisy doors to leave, rather than enter.

Lana moved to the wall just past the bay gelding's stall. On the right between Fiona's stall and the next stall down, a smaller aisle branched off. She paused to peer down the short, narrow corridor, but the doors into the office and tack room were closed.

Lana's mind raced through possible reasons for the prevalent tension as she inched toward the feed room. Grain and feed mixtures were stored in metal containers, and unopened bags were stacked until needed. The feed room and barn were swept or blown clean twice a day, and hay and straw were kept in the loft. No tinder material was left lying around to combust spontaneously. Fire seemed unlikely unless a wire had shorted out or an intruder had deliberately set one.

That thought gave Lana pause. Anyone despicable enough to risk killing a barnful of horses wouldn't think twice about hurting a teenage girl.

She had left her cell phone home so she wouldn't lose or break it, a decision that seemed foolish now. As other riders had learned, the small phones slipped from pockets or came unhooked and were impossible to find on wooded trails or open meadows. Annie Frame had been kicked with a cell phone in her pocket. Her hip was bruised, and the phone was smashed. The cell phone survival rate after being stepped on by fifteen hundred pounds of horse was also zero. Such accidents were rare, but Lana didn't need the unnecessary expense of replacing a phone. She obviously needed to rethink that—later.

Lana stopped and glanced around for anything she could use to defend herself. Metal hooks, rounded halter and bridle holders, and metal blanket bars were attached to the outside of each stall. Wooden boxes with sloping, hinged lids were spaced at intervals along the walls. Each box was filled with brushes and other grooming tools and products.

As she edged past Artax's empty stall, Lana quietly lifted a leather lead with a chain extension and heavy snap-clip off a hook. She wasn't strong enough to choke anyone with the shank, but she could throw an intruder off stride and buy time if she hit an eye with the snap. She coiled the leather and chain and folded her hand over the snap to muffle any metallic sound.

Next, she carefully sorted through the bristle brushes and rubber currycombs in the grooming box until she found a hoof pick. The hooked metal tool was used to remove collected dirt from the underside of a horse's hoof and could function as a weapon. Lana slipped it into her back pocket and slowly advanced on the feed room.

Thwhap!

The odd sound was followed by a squeal that was abruptly silenced.

Lana halted, swallowing a gasp, her heart pounding wildly in her chest. As much as she loved her horse, she suddenly questioned the wisdom of her actions. Perhaps, a better plan would be to back up and detour into the stable office, where she could use the phone to call for help.

Help with what? Lana took in a deep breath to calm her rattled nerves. She would feel like a complete fool if the sheriff or

Clark raced to her rescue only to discover she had been spooked by—

"Yeow."

—the cat!

Sagging with relief, Lana exhaled slowly. The noise had signaled a bad end for a mouse that had not been quick enough to elude feline fang and claw. Mr. Holtz had let the black stray settle into the barn when he proved to be an adept mouser. The boarders called him Ninja Cat because he yowled as he attacked.

Disconcerting, but effective, Lana thought as she moved into the open doorway.

All the intellectual and emotional defenses Lana had built to insulate herself from shock shattered. She had honestly believed she'd been tempered by her experiences over the past couple of years to cope with anything. She had been cocooned as bug boy Arkin's future mate, turned into a sizzling, heartless vamp by an extinct flower, and forced to witness a bad cop's crimes through his eyes because she had been knocked unconscious in a gas-line explosion.

However, none of those bizarre and inexplicable events had prepared her for the gross scene in the stable feed room.

Time slowed as Lana's gaze swept the room, taking in every significant detail. Ninja Cat crouched on a high shelf between large plastic jars of vitamin supplements, oils, and medicines. The fur on his tail and back bristled, and his fangs were bared in a silent hiss. Thirty or more dead mice were piled on the floor under the shelf.

A tall, attractive man with a muscular build and short, brown hair leaned on a cabinet storage counter, using his cell phone antenna to scratch his back. Lana recognized him from a brief conversation they had had at the Talon last week. Max Cutler had been introducing himself to businesspeople around town, claiming to be a real estate developer.

Mr. Cutler didn't notice her in that first split second because his gaze was fastened on the horrific creature sprawled on the floor. It looked like a human squid with four elongated appendages. One of the tendrils whipped out, stretching as it snapped across the room to snare one of the dead mice in a rubbery hand. The elastic arm snapped back to almost normal size and shape and shoved the furry body into an expanding mouth. It swallowed the animal whole, then giggled.

Lana clutched her stomach and covered her mouth to muffle a sickened gag. She didn't understand Mr. Cutler's connection to the monster, but he was definitely not in Smallville to buy large tracts of land.

"C'mon, Layton," the man muttered under his breath.

As Lana backed up a step, the metal snap slipped from her grasp. In her shock, the arm holding the leather and chain lead shank had gone limp at her side. When the large snap hit the floor, Max Cutler and Layton both turned to stare.

I am so dead. Still clutching the coiled lead shank, Lana turned and ran.

This time, Max didn't stop to think before making the transition to his alter-form. Since the girl hadn't come between Layton and his Mickey Mouse snack, the AWOL mutant had no interest in her.

It was up to Max to neutralize the threat. Lana Lang had seen too much, and she couldn't be allowed to escape.

Max's alter-form was activated an instant before the young manager of the Talon realized that she had inadvertently attracted his attention.

His body went numb. As it crumpled to the floor, his conscious mind was driven downward by processes he could not define and didn't comprehend. One moment he was looking at the girl through human eyes. Then his senses were part of the dark shadow that Max Cutler had become. He did not smell, hear, see, or feel in the traditional sense, but his perceptions were all-encompassing and acute.

Max sensed Lana running toward the door and focused on his target.

"Go, Max!" Layton cheered, laughing as the sentient shadow shot forward.

Max sped across the brick floor, fleeing the gray light in the barn for the brilliance of the late-afternoon sun. Once he was outside, chasing the terrified girl filled him with an ecstatic energy he hadn't felt since he had overwhelmed and killed Howard Stoner.

The farmer had become an expensive annoyance. Farley had doubled Stoner's salary to continue doing what he had been doing for Lex Luthor: keeping the locals away from the silo enclosure and keeping his mouth shut. They had paid extra to have the fenced-in area mowed, but that wasn't enough for the greedy hick. Howard Stoner had threatened to call the cops about Layton, the "creepy thing" he had seen ooze out of a buried cable trench.

Max had found the runaway before Layton started another extermination rampage. He had brought the naked mutant back immediately, but not before the farmer saw them. Continental Sciences had been generous, but Max had no intention of wasting good money on a blackmailing snitch.

As Stoner stomped across the field toward his house, shadow-Max had attacked him. A large segment of his shadow-self had flowed down the man's throat into his lungs, cutting off his air. When he was certain Stoner was dead, he had started to extract and retreat. He had just slipped off the body when the Kent kid had suddenly shown up.

Max hadn't a clue where Clark had come from or how he had gotten there so fast. When the teenager ran into the house to call 911, he had flowed away from the body and back to the underground installation.

The unplanned field test seemed to confirm Dr. Farley's assertion that no one would notice a shadow, not even if it was out of position in relation to the lighting. Max didn't think Clark Kent had seen him on the ground by Stoner's body, but he hadn't been certain. Since being certain was critical to the safety of everyone in the project, he had talked Sharon into finding out.

Lana ran, reaching into her pocket for her keys without breaking stride. Max wrapped around her ankles before she made it to the car.

Crying out in terror, the girl frantically tried to beat him off with a coiled strap, but leather and chain had no effect on the gossamer substance of his shadow-form. Unlike particles of light, he had miniscule mass that was impervious to injury. He could also exert force many times greater than should be possible for his size. As he tightened around Lana's legs, she lost her balance and fell over.

Sharon will be sorry she missed this. Usually, Max took perverse pleasure in thwarting Farley's spoiled brat. She had been a thorn in his side from the moment they had moved their operations to Smallville.

Even now, Sharon's whining complaints played in his mind like a CD caught in a defect loop.

"I hate it here! Everything smells like manure!"

"Why would I want to be friends with a bunch of farmers?"

"Shopping for clothes in this cow town? Not in this lifetime."

Dr. Farley made excuses for Sharon's petulance, but she was old enough to understand the dangers they faced and the rewards they stood to gain. Smallville *was* a cow town, which made it an ideal location for their illegal, clandestine enterprise. The world was full of worthless airheads Sharon could befriend *after* their fortunes and futures were secure.

Sharon had finally earned her keep when she agreed to spy at the high school. Her decision had nothing to do with helping him, however. She had had her own reasons for accepting the mission: to relieve her self-inflicted boredom, because Clark Kent met her teenage standard for cute-enough-to-date, and she wanted to protect her father. As a bonus, she couldn't resist the challenge of snagging Clark away from the Lang girl, who had a secret thing for him. The thrill had only lasted through the movie date, but that was long enough to find out what the boy had seen the day Stoner died.

Sharon was convinced Clark Kent hadn't noticed anything strange. He *was* strange.

Max had thought Sharon was imagining things, until he brought the kid down as he was walking away from the silo site.

Sharon had found Clark snooping around the yard. They still hadn't figured out how he had managed to break the lock on the gate. While she had kept him talking, Sharon had held down

the call button on the walkie-talkie she carried for use underground. That had alerted Farley to the problem above while
preventing the scientists from returning the call, which would
have alerted the boy to their presence. When Sharon had seen
his shadow-form emerge through the wire mesh over a vent, she
steered Clark away from the shaded woods.

Even at full strength in direct sunlight, Max had expected
some resistance from the strapping young man, but he had felled
Clark Kent with almost no effort. When he realized the kid was
reacting to the meteor dust in his alter-form, he had aborted the
mission.

Clark Kent was too valuable to kill.

Lana Lang was not.

She's just unlucky with a rotten sense of timing, Max thought
as he spiraled up and around Lana's legs, tightening his hold.

When Max had begun tracking Layton, he quickly realized
that the mutant was headed for a cluster of farms. The stable
complex with its main barn, outbuildings, and manager's house
had been the first source of abundant rodents in Layton's path.
Max had emerged from a wooded area at the crest of a rise
expecting to find horse and human carnage he could not possibly
cover up. Instead, Layton had hunkered down by a tractor to
wait until the truck loaded with horses and a minivan full of
girls had driven away.

By the time Max reached the barn, the elastic escapee was
merrily catching and crushing mice in a feed storage room.
Because of the late hour and distance from the silo, he had called
Sharon's cell to ask for a ride back to the underground installation. If Lana had arrived fifteen minutes later, Layton would
have been finished feeding, and they would have been long
gone. The pile of uneaten dead mice would have been just another
unexplained Smallville curiosity.

Stunned after her fall, Lana hesitated for a moment before
she tossed the useless leather shank aside and dug into the dirt
with her fingers. Max flowed around her torso as she tried to
drag herself closer to the car. When crawling proved futile, she
clawed at her chest to pull him off, but she couldn't hold on to
a substance that separated and re-formed beyond her grasp. Her

struggle intensified as he contracted to cover her mouth and nostrils, muffling her screams and blocking her air.

The termination was necessary, but he respected the girl's desperate fight for life.

Max didn't want to die, either.

The Audi skidded as Sharon yanked the wheel to turn onto Rolling Hills Road. She had just turned into the Kents' drive when Max had called asking for a ride. She was getting really tired of being ordered around by Max Cutler, especially when he couldn't make up his mind.

"Go get Clark Kent, come get me." Sharon huffed with derision. She didn't care that Max had once been an experienced but underpaid field agent for the CIA. He was just another one of her father's less-than-perfect experiments now. He had probably forgotten he had sent her to find Clark. "Jerk."

Max wasn't the only one who wanted to find out why Clark Kent was totally normal except when he was exposed to meteor material.

Or how he gets from one place to another faster than a speeding car, Sharon thought.

She had become suspicious when she realized that neither Lana nor the *Smallville Ledger* had gotten the times wrong the day Clark had found Mr. Stoner's body. He had left the Talon at four-twenty-five and called 911 fifteen minutes later. Since he could have hitched a ride, which would account for the discrepancy, she had put it out of her mind. Then Clark had left Lex Luthor's mansion on foot and arrived at the missile silo faster than she had been able to drive. Even taking into account the shorter cross-country route, the feat was impossible unless his running ability had been artificially enhanced.

There was no doubt that the green meteor dust her father used to engineer his subjects altered cellular integrity, usually in ways he didn't anticipate. Although her dad could now induce specific physical changes that were stable, he hadn't conquered the problem of neuron deterioration, which would turn Max into a blithering idiot like Layton and the others within a couple of weeks, if not sooner.

Regarding Clark, Max and her father had finally reached the same conclusion she had. Since Smallville was the site of the 1989 meteor shower, Clark's superspeed was probably the result of meteor exposure. That together with all the incidents documented on Chloe's Wall of Weird proved *her* worst fear, which her father had been denying.

Casual exposure to the meteor-rocks could cause erratic, usually horrible, and perhaps fatal physiological changes.

Except in Clark Kent's case.

Clark seemed to have a meteor-induced, stable physical ability, and he was not a mental midget. They had to find out why.

He was Max Cutler's only hope, and maybe hers, too.

Sharon strongly suspected that her father's precautions with the meteor-rocks had been inadequate, and that she had been contaminated. She wasn't exhibiting any effects she could identify, but she was certain the vile radiation was busy scrambling her DNA.

Spotting the stable sign up ahead, Sharon slowed her car and turned down a tree-lined drive. The fences, barns, livestock, open fields, and stands of forest that everyone in Smallville treasured would never feel right to her. She missed the sprawling malls, country clubs, exclusive shops, and exotic restaurants of the East Coast suburbs.

When Sharon reached the circular drive in front of the barn, she slammed on the brakes. There was no sign of Layton, but Lana Lang was lying on the ground with Max's dark shadow wrapped around her face.

Throwing the gearshift into park and leaving the motor running, Sharon jumped out of the car and rushed to the fallen girl. "Get off her, Max!"

The shadow shimmered angrily, but Max didn't obey.

Lana's breathing was getting shallow, but for the moment, she was still alive. A leather strap with an attached chain and halter snap was on the ground beside her. If she had been going to the pasture to get a horse, why had Max attacked her? Was he becoming a mindless predator like Layton ahead of schedule?

Sharon wondered, but Lana's predicament demanded her immediate attention.

"If you kill that girl, Max, you might kill your chances for a cure." Sharon stood back with her hands on her hips and relaxed when shadow-Max flowed off the girl onto the dirt drive.

Max's perceptions were so sensitive he could detect nuances of body language and expression. Although he couldn't speak in his alter-form, he understood everything and found innovative ways of communicating.

Sharon watched as Max's shadow shifted into a ribbon that formed the word, "Why?"

"Because we need Clark Kent, and Lana is one of his closest friends. We can use her as bait to snare him," Sharon snapped. A week ago, Max would have understood that without an explanation. Angry and afraid, she lashed out with snide disdain. "Run along and find your body, Max. Then round up Layton so we can get out of here."

Max's shadow rocketed toward the barn. He was upset, but it wasn't her fault he was less than the man he had been.

Lana moaned as she sat up and rubbed a bump on the bone ridge above her eye. She sprang to her feet, as though suddenly remembering why she was on the ground. Her fearful gaze settled on Sharon as she reached for something behind her back.

"What's going on, Sharon?"

"Nothing." Sharon pulled her fist back and hit Lana in the jaw.

Already weakened from her encounter with Max, Lana crumpled to her knees. A hooked metal tool fell out of her hand as Sharon kicked her in the skull, knocking her out. The girl collapsed as Max came storming out of the barn with Layton trailing behind him.

Sharon had seen Layton in all his glory once before, but that didn't diminish her revulsion.

The scrawny naked man waved with a toothless grin. "Hi, Sharn."

Sharon leveled Max with a piercing stare. "Do *not* let him touch me."

"Get a grip, Sharon." Max picked up Lana's limp body and nodded toward the car. "Open it."

Layton opened the back door and climbed inside.

Sharon smiled as the agent set Lana's unconscious body on the back seat beside Layton. "Why the hurry, Max? The sun won't set for another hour."

"Shut up." Max slid into the driver's seat and slammed the door.

Laughing, Sharon got in the passenger side and speed-dialed Clark. She let it ring, but no one answered.

"You don't have to hang with me, Pete." Chloe glanced at the clock on the wall behind him. Three hours had passed since Clark had left the *Torch* offices. "It's almost six."

Chloe had drafted an article titled "Lockdown or Lockup" as a companion piece for the *Torch* cafeteria poll on the closed campus policy. Pete had patiently searched the Internet for information on Dr. Lawrence Farley. They were both starting to bog down in boredom.

"What?" Pete looked up sharply. "Well, that explains why my stomach is growling. Do you still have emergency rations stashed somewhere?"

"Oatmeal granola bars and a bag of Really Sour Jells." Chloe pointed toward the filing cabinet on the wall behind her. "Top drawer."

"That should take the edge off." Pete stood up and stretched.

Chloe looked back at her computer monitor. After Clark had called to report on his conversation with Lex Luthor, she had narrowed the Internet search parameters. She wasn't sure what Dr. Farley was up to in his missile silo, but she didn't think it involved legal, or even illegal, stem cell research.

"I thought Chad said he'd get back to you before he left work today." Pete paused behind her chair and ripped the wrapper off a granola bar.

"He did, and he will," Chloe said. "Chad never breaks his word. I'm staying until I hear from him."

"I am, too, then." Pete balled the wrapper and tossed it into a wastebasket across the room. "So what's your theory if Clark's dust matches the stuff they found in Mr. Stoner and the environmental guy?"

Chloe hedged. "I'd just be guessing."

"Your guesses are usually right." Pete popped a sour jelly candy into his mouth and pulled a chair up beside her.

"Okay, in a nutshell—" Leaning back, Chloe rattled off her

conclusions. "For starters, Sharon wasn't ever interested in Clark."

"What?" Pete sat back so hard the chair almost tipped over. "No way! She was putting the moves on him, Chloe. I know it."

"She probably was," Chloe agreed, "but not because she liked him."

"And this is based on what?" Pete's skepticism was pointed. "A little residual Clark crush of your own, maybe?"

"Not!" Chloe's hand flew out and smacked him in the chest. "I think she knew that meteor-rocks have bizarre effects on some people before she suddenly decided to talk to us."

Pete frowned. "It was kind of sudden, wasn't it?"

"Very." Chloe picked up a pencil and nibbled the eraser. "Like two days after Clark saw Mr. Stoner die in the field next to the missile silo her scientist father is renting. Much too convenient, don't you think?"

"Yeah." Pete exhaled. "And I practically shoved Clark into Sharon's arms."

"No, you *did* shove Clark into her arms." Chloe shrugged. "But since he wasn't suckered by Sharon's baby blues, you're forgiven."

"That makes my day," Pete quipped.

Rising, Chloe began to pace. "So tell me if you think this is a reach."

"Listening," Pete said.

"We've got a lunatic on the loose who kills snakes, and Mr. Mundy's body was found on a pile of dead rabbits. Sharon's father was a geneticist until the government pulled his research grant, and he rented Lex's missile silo because he doesn't want to be bothered. Plus, the saliva in Mr. Mundy's wounds was human."

Pete waited for the punch line.

"What if Dr. Farley is messing around with the effects of meteor dust on DNA?" Chloe asked.

"Making monsters?" Pete wasn't kidding.

"Maybe." Chloe frowned, tapping the pencil against her cheek. "Clark thought his meteor dust came from the ground, but what if he was in contact with something else and just didn't know it."

"Is that possible?" Pete asked.

"We're dealing with meteor-rocks, Pete. Anything is possible." Chloe dropped back in her chair. "Remember Amy Palmer's brother and the invisible skin cream?"

"Yeah. Smelled like a rose, but wasn't a rose." Pete's gaze flicked to her computer screen when the mail tone chimed. "Incoming."

Chloe was already bringing up the menu. The message was from Chad, and as usual, he didn't waste words.

```
New specimen matches Stoner and Mundy. Chad
```

"Guess that answers that." Pete rested his elbows on his knees. "So what do we do with it?"

"Call Clark for starters," Chloe said. "It's really looking like we've got two meteor murders."

As Chloe reached for her cell phone, it rang. She glanced at the Caller ID readout and hit *send* to connect her father. If his plans hadn't changed, he was working late filling a big order.

"Hi, Dad! Are you still at the plant?"

"Yes, why aren't you home, yet?" Mr. Sullivan asked.

"Homework and the *Torch*." Chloe cringed slightly. "I'll be leaving here soon."

"Is Lana there?" Her father asked abruptly.

"Lana? No," Chloe said. "She's working Margo's shift tonight. Try the Talon."

"The Talon called me," Mr. Sullivan explained. "Lana was supposed to be there at five. She didn't show, and it's after six. I've called the house and left messages on her cell, but she hasn't called me back."

Chloe frowned. Lana was infuriatingly punctual and considerate. She would have called the Talon to say she would be late—unless she went to the stable and left her cell behind again. That, in Chloe's opinion, was worse than not having one like Clark.

"I tried the barn. No answer there, either." Mr. Sullivan sighed.

"We have to get this order out on schedule, Chloe. I can't leave work right now."

Her dad sounded frantic, which was easy to understand. Lana's Aunt Nell hadn't been wild about leaving her niece in Smallville when she moved away. She had only agreed because Chloe's father was a respected member of the community and a wonderful parent. Now he was responsible for Lana.

"Do you want me to go check the barn?" Chloe asked. "It won't be dark for a while yet."

"The Kents are closer," Mr. Sullivan said. "I'll call the farm and see if Clark or Jonathan will go."

"Call me back if you hear from Lana, okay?" Chloe ended the call and frowned.

"That didn't sound good," Pete said.

"No, not good at all." Since Clark didn't have call waiting, Chloe gave her father time to call first. After a couple of minutes she speed-dialed Clark's number, but the line was still busy.

Chloe jumped up again and paced around the two central desks. The line was busy so at least someone was home at the Kent farm. She wanted to tell Clark that the meteor dust he had picked up near the silo matched the samples from the dead men.

With Lana missing and something running around Smallville killing weird stuff on what seemed to be a mindless whim, it was life-and-death important.

Clark also didn't know yet that LexCorp was still paying the bill to Kansas State Water and Power for the missile facility.

Clark sat at the kitchen table, making notes in a spiral note-book. After coming home from meeting Lex at the Talon, he had been helping his dad and mom with the last section of fence in the back pasture. He had returned to the house with his mother ten minutes ago. When she went back to the pasture with coffee and snacks for his dad, he had stayed to finish his biology paper. It was almost done and ready to type into the *Torch* computer for printing, but he was having trouble concentrating.

He couldn't stop thinking about the old missile silo and why Sharon's father had paid for security modifications in a property he didn't own. Maybe he didn't understand because his family had to count every cent. To Lex, the expenditure made sense. If Dr. Farley's potential financial gain was big enough, a throwaway investment to secure the source of future wealth would be worth it.

Dropping his pen, Clark rocked back on the hind legs of his chair. If money was motivating Dr. Farley's activities, how sure of making a fortune was he? Would he kill to protect his secret cash cow until he was ready to cash in?

The theory was sound, but the only signs of a killer were the victims. Rosebushes and rabbits wouldn't threaten anyone's future revenues. Had Mr. Stoner and Mr. Mundy just been in the wrong place at the wrong time or had they stumbled on the valuable secret?

Clark sighed as he mulled over the facts. He had been sickened by meteor dust his clothes picked up from the ground. Sharon was too afraid of meteor-rocks to carry one, and no one else had been around.

But what if Sharon's father found the meteor property that produces invisibility? It had happened before, to Jeff Palmer.

When the phone rang, Clark sped into the living room to answer. He was surprised to hear Mr. Sullivan's voice and dismayed by his reason for calling. Lana had not shown up for work, and she had not called in.

"I don't know if Lana tried calling here, Mr. Sullivan." Clark didn't try to explain that their ancient answering machine had stopped working earlier that day and money was too tight to pay for a new one immediately. "Until ten minutes ago, no one was home to answer the phone."

His mother always carried her LuthorCorp cell phone, but none of his friends had the number.

"Could you or your Dad run over to the stable, Clark?" Mr. Sullivan asked. "Lana's probably there, but I'd feel better if I knew for sure."

"I'll go, Mr. Sullivan," Clark said. Hearing the worry in the older man's voice, he tried to reassure him. "Lana rides whenever she can. If she hasn't come back to the barn, I know some of the places she goes."

The cemetery came to mind. Not everyone knew how often Lana visited her parents' grave.

Clark sped out the door within a split second of hanging up from Mr. Sullivan.

He had been speeding around Smallville for as long as his parents had let him out of their sight. He had memorized less-traveled routes to every corner of the county and all major locations in between. However, in extreme emergencies, he used secondary roads and highways.

Lana was missing, and he knew she would never have ducked her shift without a good reason or calling to explain. He took the road.

Clark sped a mile down Hickory Lane then raced through the Gundersons' back cornfield to Jackson Road. After cutting the corner through Shaver Woods, he took a dirt road that came out on Rolling Hills Road. He crossed a pasture, then sped along the edge of the woods, leaping hunter brush jumps incorporated into fences. When he came into visual range of the stable, he slowed and walked out of the trees behind the tractor shed.

Mr. Holtz, the stable manager, stood in a large horse van in front of the barn. One horse was still waiting on the truck to be unloaded. A dark-haired girl walked another horse into the barn. Two blond girls were pulling riding gear out of a minivan that blocked Clark's view of the cars lined up behind it. His X-ray vision penetrated the minivan and three other cars before he recognized Chloe's. Lana had been here.

Clark seriously doubted Lana would have taken her pinto somewhere by truck without mentioning it, but he had to ask. He approached the horse van as Mr. Holtz snapped a lead shank on the charcoal bay's halter ring.

"What brings you out this way, Clark?" Mr. Holtz unhooked a metal bar in front of the horse and led the animal down the loading ramp. The ramp slid in and out of a floor slot in the side of the van. Safety railings folded up on either side and locked in place.

"I was looking for Lana," Clark said. "Is she here?"

"I haven't seen her." A wiry man of fifty with short, curly hair and twinkling eyes, Mr. Holtz smiled. "But I just got back from a training trip to Metropolis."

"I see that." Clark glanced toward the barn. If Lana was out riding, the pinto wouldn't be in his stall. "Mind if I look around?"

"Not at all." Mr. Holtz handed Clark the lead shank. "Take Domino inside with you. If Katie doesn't get him first, third stall down on the right."

The dark horse with one white sock and a white strip that angled off his nose, nuzzled Clark's chest.

"Let's go, Domino." Walking with the horse on his right, Clark entered the stable.

Micheline Jordan, a senior at Smallville High, was inside the second stall down on the left. A sign over the door read, Artax.

"Have you seen Katie, Micheline?" Clark asked.

"I think she's helping Kelly put the tack away." The girl slipped an unbuckled halter off her horse's nose and gave Artax a pat as she left the stall and secured the closer.

Everything in its proper place, Clark thought as he watched Micheline hang the halter and rope lead on a holder outside the stall. Mr. Holtz ran a tight stable with strict rules. Lana often teased Chloe that the show barn was neater and cleaner than their room. Chloe always retorted that a little clutter was a sign of a free spirit and didn't care.

"I can take Domino now." Katie Picken ducked out of a smaller aisle on the right. Slim and blond, with a warm smile, she took the horse's lead from Clark's hand.

"Thanks." As Clark started toward Lana's stall at the end of the barn, a girl screamed. Checking his impulse to speed, he hurried to the feed room. Jessica collided with him as she ran out the door. "What's the matter?"

"It's so awful!" Pale and shaking, Jessica pulled away and bolted for the office.

Fearing the worst, Clark jumped into the small storeroom. He was both revolted and relieved when he saw the pile of dead mice. A black cat sat nearby.

"Whoa! Ninja buddy!" Mr. Holtz paused in the doorway with

an astonished grin. "There must be over fifty mice in that pile! Is that a great cat or what?"

"Unbelievable," Clark said. No cat could possibly kill that many mice. The mysterious rosebush and rodent killer was clearly the culprit, but it was easier to let the cat take credit. He was now faced with a more serious problem.

Ducking out of the feed room, Clark quickly confirmed that Lana's horse was still in his stall.

Bad news. Clark rushed back outside to check Chloe's car. A pile of dead mice and a pile of dead rabbits couldn't possibly be an unrelated coincidence. His thoughts skipped quickly from one fact to another, drawing ominous conclusions.

Judging by everyone's reactions, Lana had not yet arrived and the dead mice had not been in the feed room when Mr. Holtz and the girls left for Metropolis. Consequently, Lana might have been at the stable, probably alone, when the mouse murders had taken place. Clark's only ray of hope was the absence of a body in the feed room or in Chloe's locked car.

The second wave of relief passed as Clark scanned the parking area for clues and wondered what to do next. A metal hoof pick and a leather lead shank were lying on the ground. It was unlikely one of the other girls had dropped the items so far from the horse van and barn. Everyone associated with the show stable took meticulous care of the expensive equipment, especially Lana. Recent footprints and larger impressions in the dirt suggested that a struggle might have taken place, and that someone might have fallen.

Fearing the worst, Clark jogged up the drive.

The missile silo was the one thing that seemed to connect the various threads. Two men had died nearby, and both bodies had been contaminated with meteor dust. Although the series of vandalism incidents had taken place over a couple of weeks in different locations, the destructive similarities couldn't be ignored. He knew from Lex that Sharon's father was engaged in unknown work he didn't want disclosed. It wasn't outrageous to think Dr. Farley might be using meteor dust, some of which might have dropped on the ground where he had come in contact with it. If that were true, then it was possible the scientist had deliberately or unintentionally created an unpredictable predator.

What if Lana had seen something Dr. Farley didn't want her to see?

Would he kill to protect his secret cash cow until he was ready to cash in? Stoner and Mundy are both dead!

Clark's own thoughts about Dr. Farley's possible motives came back to haunt him as he ran across Rolling Hills Road and down another farm drive. If his hunch about the scientist was wrong, no one would be harmed. As he took off through the corn toward Stoner's farm, he realized that if he was right, it might already be too late to save Lana.

Pete glanced at Chloe as they drove down Hickory Lane toward the Kent farm. The top of his vintage blue convertible was down, but she wasn't fretting about having to push her windblown hair out of her eyes and mouth. Chloe was really worried.

"You'll run the battery down," Pete admonished when Chloe hit her cell phone redial again.

Chloe had been trying to reach Clark since her father had called to report that Lana was missing. She had gotten a little frantic when no one answered the Kents' phone after the initial busy signal. She'd tried calling her father back, but it was after six and she got an automated menu. Since Lana hadn't been found, she didn't leave a message on his voice mail.

They hadn't had much better luck at the stable. After repeated tries, someone named Kelly had answered the office phone. She hadn't seen Lana or Clark, but she made it clear she couldn't talk. The manager and several girls had just returned from Metropolis, and they were swamped with work.

Too upset to sit around doing nothing, Chloe had insisted on driving out to the Kent farm, Clark's last known location.

"Still no answer." Chloe signed off and pulled a charger cord out of her shoulder bag. She plugged it into Pete's cigarette lighter and connected the phone to recharge it. "Thanks for reminding me about the battery, Pete. I don't want to run out of juice if things get rough."

"Which they always do." Pete wasn't a wimp, but he had sustained more than his share of bumps, bruises, and contusions since he had become super Clark's stalwart, but strictly human sidekick.

As they passed under the Kent farm sign, Chloe pointed at a tractor moving slowly across the pasture. "There's somebody."

"Clark's mom," Pete observed. "Mr. Kent doesn't wear straw hats tied on with red scarves."

Rolling her eyes, Chloe stepped out as soon as Pete came to a stop. Pete followed her toward the barn.

Martha parked by the grain silo and turned off the tractor engine. She smiled as she climbed down. "Hi, Pete! Chloe. If you're here to see Clark, I think he's inside working on his biology paper."

"Wouldn't he answer the phone if he was in the house?" Chloe asked. "I've been calling for half an hour."

"Oh." Martha frowned as she pulled an empty basket from under the tractor seat. "Is it important?"

"Uh—well, we're just all have trouble connecting," Chloe said. "Lana, Clark, us—"

"Especially Lana." Pete didn't want to alarm Clark's mother, but people were starting to vanish without a trace. "We thought Clark was going to look for her—

"Maybe he went with Sharon," Martha said.

"Sharon?" Chloe asked, surprised.

"She drives a silver Audi, right?" Martha started walking toward the house. "I'm sure I saw her car pull into the drive on my way out to the pasture. Clark came back to the house right about then."

"Thanks, Mrs. Kent." Before Chloe could start grilling Clark's mom in earnest, Pete pulled her away. If something came up that required parental help or interference, they could call back. "Are you going to be here?"

"Somebody's got to make dinner," Mrs. Kent said.

Pete didn't broach the subject of a plan until he and Chloe were back in the car. "Where to now?"

"The stable," Chloe said without hesitation. "As far as we know, Dad got in touch with Clark and asked him to look for Lana. Maybe he hitched a ride with Sharon."

Pete didn't think so. Clark could have gotten to the horse farm quicker under his own power.

"What was Sharon doing at the Kent farm?" Chloe's eyes narrowed.

"Looking for Clark?" Pete suggested.

"Why?" Chloe's dark scowl deepened.

"I don't know," Pete answered honestly. "But if Clark and Lana aren't goofing off in the horse barn, I think we'd better check the old missile silo site."

The sun was sinking in the western sky when Clark stopped in the trees lining the old access road by Stoner's field. It was hard to believe only a week had passed since he had been here the last time, walking home from school with nothing on his mind but the everyday problems of an alien teenager with amazing abilities he had to keep secret.

Seeing Mr. Stoner die made his complaints seem trivial.

Clark thought back to the sequence of events that day, but with the exception of the farmer's sudden collapse, nothing unusual had happened.

Nothing that he knew of.

Clark scanned the surrounding terrain as he stepped out of hiding. He had thoroughly canvassed the missile site for surveillance equipment the other day and found none. Now, he was wary of human eyes or the unknown predator with a taste for snake. Although he didn't sense anything, staying under cover as long as possible seemed prudent. He jogged across the road and down the shoulder.

A thick stand of trees stood between the road and the missile silo site a hundred yards in. Sharon's silver Audi was parked on the drive to the enclosure gate beside an older model SUV. *Her father's car, perhaps?* Clark paused to inspect both vehicles with his X-ray vision. Nothing inside the trunk of Sharon's car had changed since he had looked the last time. The SUV was littered with fast-food wrappers, magazines and newspapers, a toolbox, jumper cables, and assorted outerwear. He didn't see anything that suggested Lana might have been in either vehicle recently.

As Clark sped through the wooded section to the gate, he reminded himself that he was acting on gut feelings, making assumptions based on Lana's personality and circumstantial evidence that implicated Sharon and her dad. Not a whole lot was clear except that Lana Lang wouldn't flake out on her responsibilities or worry her friends and surrogate family.

Something was wrong.

In the gray twilight before sundown, the visible remains of the installation inside the chain-link and razor-wire fence seemed more sinister than in broad daylight. The broken lock on the gate hadn't been replaced, which surprised Clark—until he remembered that Dr. Farley's partner had a background in security. The broken lock and lack of cameras or sensing devices was probably deliberate. There were no aboveground signs that anyone was inhabiting the installation below.

Clever, Clark thought as he eased through the gate and replaced the chain. Farley's security expert couldn't have known that a local kid had the strength to lift the heavy broken hatch over an access tube that had been filled with cement. And that begged the question: Were they trying to keep the curious out or something terrible in?

Clark spun when a whirring noise sounded behind him. He quickly trashed the idea of jumping the fence and speeding into hiding as the automated primary hatch swung open onto the weight-brace. His X-ray vision couldn't penetrate the lead-lined silo lid or hatch cover to find out if Lana was in the facility below. He would have to break in or be invited.

As Sharon Farley climbed out, he decided to try for the invitation first. Although he wasn't positive, he didn't think she knew that he suspected her father of dangerous, criminal activity involving the dreaded meteor-rocks. If he forced his way inside, there would be no question that was what he thought.

And his suspicions could be wrong, Clark realized as Sharon

palmed one cell phone and dialed another. Her father really *could* be an eccentric who was writing a science fiction novel locked in a missile silo. Or he could also be a paranoid scientist involved in legitimate research.

Clark didn't actually believe that, but he had nothing to lose by acting as though he did. *At least until my suspicions are confirmed and I find Lana.*

Given Sharon's fear, it was reasonable to assume that her father kept his meteor-rock supply locked in lead, if he actually had meteor-rocks. There was a minimal risk, but that was a chance Clark had to take. If Dr. Farley and his security man were responsible for the murders and assorted mayhem, he felt confident he could rescue Lana and escape to tell the authorities.

Sharon didn't realize that someone else was in the compound when her speed-dialed call went through. "Hi! Is Clark there?"

Clark stiffened at the sound of his name. He didn't know whether to be alarmed or not, but the fact that Sharon wanted to talk to him would make his charade easier to pull off.

"I'm right here." Clark walked toward her with an impish smile.

Sharon snapped the compact flip-phone closed as she turned to stare. "What are you doing here, Clark?"

"Just looking around." Clark paused beside her to glance through the hatch. A metal ladder descended to an elevator platform eight feet down.

Sharon deliberately moved between him and the opening. "Looking for what?"

"I thought that was obvious yesterday. I want to get a look inside this old launch facility." Clark took a cue from Pete and told the truth. "I've been fascinated with this place since I was a kid."

Sharon frowned. "That doesn't explain why here and now."

"I didn't believe that you were here to get evidence against LexCorp yesterday." Clark shrugged. "Lex told me to stay away because he had rented the place. It wasn't hard to figure out that your father was the tenant."

"Uh-huh." Sharon eyed him uncertainly.

Clark glanced at the cell phone. "Must be lousy reception down there. No phone line?"

"Yes, and no." Sharon stepped away from the hatch and folded her arms in the same apprehensive manner as she had the day before.

The nervous gesture drew Clark's attention. Sharon had *two* devices: the cell phone and another, slightly larger black case that she had been carrying the day before. "Two phones?"

Sharon held up the larger device. "Walkie-talkie."

Clark realized she was holding down the CALL button, opening the line to someone with a similar device below. He thought he had considered every contingency, but apparently not. Their entire conversation, from the moment he had stepped forward, had been overheard.

The nausea caught Clark off guard just as he made the decision to speed to safety to reconsider his options.

A sickening sensation spread up his legs. Fighting a losing battle against the debilitating effects of meteor material, Clark glanced down as he began to fade out.

A dark shadow twined around his legs as hands attached to deformed, elastic arms wrapped around his torso and pulled him into the hatch.

Clark fell 8 feet down onto the metal floor outside the elevator. The bands circling his chest tightened. It felt as if a thousand cactus spines filled with acid had pierced his shirt. White-hot knives seemed to slice through muscle, tendon, and bone trapped under the dark shadow binding his legs. The pain was excruciating, but it helped him fight the haze that was dragging him into unconsciousness. His captors were infested with meteor dust, and he was helpless to break their grip. Still, he wouldn't be completely lost if he could stay awake and focused.

Information was his only chance and ally.

"Watch it, Max!" Sharon snapped. "I wasn't going to lock you out, so just chill! It's not even dark, yet."

Sharon's comment implied that the shadow was afraid of the dark. However, the elevator platform was too brightly lit for Max's phobia to help Clark now.

Everything suddenly became irrelevant when a tentacle whipped out and flattened over his face. Already breathless from the jolts of electric pain stabbing his heart and lungs, Clark gasped when his oxygen was cut off.

"Stop it, Layton!" Sharon screamed. "Get off!"

The mask of rubbery flesh trembled, but it didn't loosen its smothering hold. Running out of air and blinded, with his X-ray vision rendered useless, Clark could only listen.

"Max! That idiot is supposed to carry Clark, not strangle him! Do something!" Sharon sounded frantic.

Assuming Max was the shadow, Clark had no idea what Sharon expected him to do. Apparently, neither did Max.

"How should I know!" Sharon stamped her foot with an angry, frustrated grunt then paused. "Wait a minute."

I don't have a minute, Clark thought, as a numbing fog settled over his mind. If Sharon's annoyed attitude was a clue, she didn't want him to die. He clung to that dismal hope as he started to black out.

"Listen, Layton. I just bought a whole bunch of beef jerky."
Sharon spoke with the exaggerated sweetness adults used to
coax a child. "I'll give you some as soon as we get down to the
lab, if you let the man go."

The suffocating hand zipped off Clark's face, but he couldn't
breathe until the constricting bands slipped off his chest. Clark's
normal vision cleared as he drank in labored gulps of air. His
legs were still imprisoned by the meteor-shadow, but he had a
reprieve from imminent death.

He could not escape an analysis of his miscalculations.

It was obvious now that this shadow had attacked him when
he left the enclosure yesterday. Sharon had deduced that he
reacted with violent illness to meteor dust. When she saw him
in the enclosure, her nervous concern had been an act. She had
called his house to lure him into a trap. He had saved her the
trouble and walked right into it. Max and Layton, creatures of
Dr. Farley's mad experiments with meteor-rocks, had been lying
in wait to capture him.

Sharon had clearly been confident she could entice him to the
silo site, which meant she had something he couldn't ignore.

Lana.

Rather than dwell on his past mistakes, Clark concentrated
on the problems at hand. He couldn't move with Max wrapped
around his legs, but as long as he was conscious, the meteor-
enhanced entities had no power over his perceptions or wits.

Sighing, Sharon hit a button on a control panel by the ladder.
The heavy hatch whirred as it slowly closed, and the electronic
lock engaged. She stepped up to the elevator and pulled a lever
to open the metal-mesh doors that covered the ordinary elevator
doors. She punched the button to open the lift and turned to the
naked man squatting in a corner.

Except for his immodest "altogethers," Martha Kent's polite
term for nudity, Layton looked like a normal, skinny, old guy.
He would take some getting used to, Clark realized when the
man's arm suddenly snaked toward Sharon's boot.

Sharon jumped back, wagging a stern finger. "Don't do that.
If you want your snack, help me move Clark into the elevator."

"Kay, Sharn." Layton grabbed on to the railing at the top of the metal stairs that curved down around the elevator shaft. He pulled himself across the platform like a monkey swinging from vine to vine.

As Sharon and Layton dragged him into the elevator, Clark pretended to be groggy, but he was memorizing every detail of the layout for reference later. When the lift doors closed, and they started downward, another question popped into his head.

Why had Sharon *wanted* to capture him?

Clark had a sinking feeling that he would find out soon, and he probably wouldn't like it.

When the elevator doors opened 60 feet down, Clark had a floor level view of the tunnel junction. Straight across, the door into a small room stood open. A man of average height and weight with graying hair came out, carrying an empty plastic bag.

Dr. Farley, I presume.

What Clark saw beyond the scientist was an outrage against science and humanity. The monstrosity in the corner of the cell was a bloated mass of tumors, sedentary and spaced out on whatever dripped from an IV.

Dr. Farley closed the cell door and dropped the empty IV bag into a bucket by the wall.

"I thought Hoover died," Sharon said, as her father walked toward them.

"It won't be long." Dr. Farley stopped just outside the open lift doors.

Not even a flicker of interest shone in Clark's eyes as the scientist stared down at him. If they thought the meteor-rocks affected him mentally as well as physically, they might let down their guard at an opportune moment. He had to be prepared to take advantage of any opening. However, he did not underestimate the intelligence and cunning of his adversaries. He could not count on Dr. Farley or his mutated minions to be careless, but survival always trumped greed as a motivator.

Sharon hugged the elevator wall as Layton jumped out. Surprised by the rubber man's unexpected move, shadow-Max slipped down around Clark's ankles. His symptoms abated to a degree, but Clark made no move that betrayed his improved condition.

"What is it, Layton?" A tremor shook Dr. Farley's voice.

"I promised to give him some jerky when we got down here, Dad." Sharon turned a key to keep the elevator doors open and stepped over Clark to exit. "We should probably lock Layton up—while we can. I'll wait."

"Yes, of course." Nodding, the scientist turned and disappeared behind a thick wall.

With Sharon's attention on Layton, Clark studied his surroundings. The basic layout of the interior matched the references he had read: tunnel to the missile silo behind the elevator, Equipment Building on the right, and the Launch Control Center on the left.

The Launch Facility Equipment Building, or LFEB, was a huge room that housed the emergency diesel generator, the power distribution system, and an air conditioner that weighed twenty tons. A fourteen-thousand-gallon fuel tank was buried outside the steel-and-concrete walls.

Clark's gaze jumped to the Launch Control Facility on the left, where Dr. Farley had gone. That section had been home for the two-man missile launch teams on duty when the Minuteman II was in the silo. They had been locked inside for the duration of their watch. A curved yellow line painted on the floor outside the LCC indicated the swing arc of the massive door. Now, the door was standing open.

Six rooms like the one holding Hoover had been added in the tunnel junction: three along the far wall and three on the wall between the Equipment Room door and the silo connection tunnel. The small, rectangular windows in each door were barred. The victims of Dr. Farley's early experiments were apparently confined in the small rooms. Clark was certain the men could not have known what fate awaited them when they had agreed to join the insidious project.

Through the small window, Clark caught a glimpse of the man in the cell to the left of Hoover. Swirls of color faded and shifted on his skin, apparently driving him crazy. *Like a chameleon*, Clark thought.

Despite Max being looped around his feet and ankles, Clark was able to muster enough X-ray vision to see through the fourth metal door. The density of that subject's bones was different than the skeletons he usually saw. As he watched, the man's bones shifted shape and position, changing from a crude cube into an oval.

Max and Layton were obviously more advanced, with relatively stable physiologies by comparison.

Dr. Farley returned with a jar of beef jerky. When Layton lunged for his treat, the scientist barked, "Back in your room first!"

Layton hissed, but he ran through the sixth door. He grabbed the sticks of jerky Dr. Farley offered and squatted on an air mattress covered with a blanket.

Sharon visibly relaxed when her father slammed the door. A green light on the electronic lock turned red.

"Shhhmok!" The man in the cell closest to the LCC door clung to the inside of his door and rattled the window bars. He was covered in stiff, barbed hair and resembled a porcupine. "Now, Faley!"

"No smoke now, Edgar." Dr. Farley pulled a canister from his lab coat pocket. He dashed to the first cell and threatened to spray the man. "Be quiet or no cigarette later, either."

Pepper spray or Mace? Clark wondered.

Edgar smashed his fist against the door and leaped onto the ceiling.

"C'mon, Dad." Sharon rolled her eyes and grabbed Clark under his left arm. Her father lifted him on the right, and together they dragged him through the installation.

Clark let his head loll to one side, but he was aware of everything. He was facing backward and noted the emergency box on the wall by the elevator. It reminded him of the glass boxes that contained fire alarms at school. A key was inserted in a slot beside a single button inside this red-trimmed glass case.

As they moved farther from the elevator, the open, metal stairs that spiraled up around the central shaft became visible. Six feet farther on and Clark could see the entrance to the connecting tunnel. The hatch, which locked from both sides, was open. The tunnel was 100 feet long and connected to a maintenance area attached to the silo shaft. The secondary access tube had opened in the maintenance room—before it had been filled with cement.

The cemented crew exit was impassable, but Clark doubted they had filled in the actual silo. The shaft was 10 feet across by 140 feet deep and the automated concrete, steel, and lead-lined lid weighed one hundred tons. Away from the sickening influence of meteor material, he could easily climb the metal rungs recessed into the silo walls. But even he might break a sweat trying to manually slide the massive lid aside.

"Wait a second, Dad." Sharon paused at the curved yellow line to catch her breath. "He's heavier than I thought."

Clark glanced at the door into the Launch Facility Equipment Room across the wide tunnel junction. He strained to hear, but didn't detect the rumble of the emergency generator. The facility was operating on commercial power. The wheel on the door was probably locked, which wouldn't be a problem if he was functioning at full strength. However, since there wasn't another way out of the room, the equipment room couldn't be used as an escape route, only as a place to hide and evade.

"Let's go, Sharon," Dr. Farley urged. "Max has been separated from his body long enough."

Max changed position to rest on Clark's shins, giving the impression he had heard, understood, and agreed. The shift wasn't a definitive indicator, but his actions supported the theory. Every move the shadow made was calculated.

Clark's arsenal of information about Max had just doubled. Now he knew two of his weaknesses: separation from his actual body and the darkness.

The wall into the LCC was so thick it was more like a short tunnel than a doorway. The heels of Clark's boots clattered over the metal bridge that spanned the gap between the wall and floor, which was mounted on twenty-foot-tall shock absorbers. The doorway at the end of the bridge had not been part of the original design. Soundproofed walls had been added to enclose the kitchen, latrine facilities, and a storeroom positioned outside the actual control center.

When Dr. Farley paused to key the electronic lock on the

storeroom door, Clark risked a glance into the LCC. The section visible through the open door had been converted from a missile launch command post into a laboratory and infirmary.

Being dragged by the arms was not the way Clark had always envisioned taking a tour of the underground military complex, but it had served the purpose. When he broke free and found Lana, he would know how to get out.

And, in spite of the sharp pains shooting up his legs and the steady throbbing in his hands and head, that break was coming soon. Sharon and Dr. Farley knew that meteor-rocks made him sick, but they couldn't know about his gifts. He could act only when Max stopped functioning as manacles and reunited with his human body.

Dr. Farley pushed the door open. As he and Sharon dragged Clark inside, he let his head fall back to get a quick take on the room.

The only illumination came from a single lightbulb in a protective wire cage on the ceiling. The light was turned on. The cage's dimensions were roughly ten by twelve. Locked metal storage cabinets lined the walls on the right, left, and along the back. The body of a tall, muscular man was slumped on the floor to the left of the door.

Lana Lang was unconscious with her hands and feet tied.

Clark's throat constricted at the sight of her petite frame sprawled in the back, right corner. Lana was breathing, but probably drugged. Her jeans and tailored print shirt were rumpled and dusty. Dirt was lodged under broken fingernails, and a red abrasion blazed on her pale cheek. She hadn't been taken prisoner without a fight.

When Sharon and her father dropped Clark in the opposite corner, the shadow grew restless. It flowed upward, as though Max knew his feather-light touch was a torture and was taking out his separation anxiety on Clark.

"One more minute, Max." Dr. Farley left again, leaving Sharon standing in the doorway.

The shadow settled on Clark's stomach.

Despite the agony that twisted his intestines, Clark carefully planned his moves. The meteor dust that powered Max's dark essence would be incorporated into his solid body when the shadow merged. Clark would have to avoid close contact with Max in human form, too. He would also need a few minutes to regain his strength once the meteor dust was removed, especially after the lengthy exposure. His best bet was to wait until he and Lana were alone and locked in.

Dr. Farley had other plans.

The instant the scientist returned carrying a heavy, locked box, Clark knew that escape would not be easy. He cringed when Dr. Farley set the box on the floor by the wall just to his left. The doctor keyed the numbered combination and opened the lid to reveal six meteor-rocks. The smallest was the size of a baseball, the largest a brick.

"Is that absolutely necessary?" Sharon's fear of the alien rocks flared as she backed out the door.

"Yes," her father answered impatiently. "How many times do I have to tell you? Unless the element is injected directly into your system, the stones are perfectly safe."

"Then how come they turn Clark into jelly?" Sharon stubbornly hung back.

"That's what we want to find out, isn't it?" He pulled several lengths of rope from his pocket and shook them at her. "Tie him up, Sharon, as a precaution."

Clark was in so much pain he couldn't fight when Sharon wrapped a rope around his wrists.

At the stable, Chloe tried the driver's side door of her car then threw up her hands. It was locked, and Lana had the keys.

Wherever Lana is.

"So let's see if I've got this straight." Pete leaned on the hood. "We know Lana was here because your car is here, but nobody saw her. She's not here now, but her horse is, so she's not out riding. Clark came here looking for Lana and everybody saw him except Kelly."

"Right," Chloe said. "Because Kelly was in the tack room when Clark was in the barn."

"And nobody saw him leave." Pete braced his chin on his hand. "You'd think they'd be totally freaked about all those dead mice."

"They think the cat did it." Chloe sighed and ran her hand over her tangled hair. They only had one option left. "Next stop, the missile silo."

"Okay." Pete turned and jumped into the convertible without opening the door. "I've got a baseball bat and a can of fly spray in the backseat."

"What for?" Chloe asked as she opened the passenger door and got in.

"Just in case we run into the Big Creepy, and it wants a people or two for dessert." Pete shuddered and started the car.

"I'll take the fly spray." Chloe settled back and held her hair down with both hands.

In close proximity to a concentrated supply of meteor-rocks, Clark's ability to withstand the pain without blacking out was in jeopardy. It was not in his nature to surrender, no matter how hopeless a situation seemed, but he only had one weapon at his disposal now, his ability to think. He had to stay awake and cognizant.

Every nerve felt as though it had been set on fire. Yet, somehow, Clark managed to care when shadow-Max fled his body to return to his own. The pain didn't decrease when the meteor-enhanced darkness was gone, but the reunion diverted Dr. Farley's attention. The scientist hovered over the anxious shadow essence, which darted back and forth by Max's feet.

"Relax, Max. Your mind knows where it belongs," Dr. Farley said.

"It gets worse every time." Sharon watched from the doorway, where she had retreated as soon as Clark's hands and feet were tied. She chewed on her knuckle, her gaze riveted on the confused shadow.

Her father shot her a warning look.

Clark made a note and turned his attention to putting a little distance between himself and the box of meteor-rocks. He usually suffered in silence, but he hoped a few moans would disguise that fact that his agonized writing had a purpose.

Groaning, Clark pulled his knees up, rolled to alter his angle, then straightened in a faked convulsion. He aimed his feet at the box. When he hit it, the box turned so the open lead lid acted as a shield, blocking some of the radiation. He waited a few seconds then tried the maneuver again to position the box for maximum effect.

"Knock it off, Clark!" Sharon hissed with a quick glance in his direction.

Ignoring her, Clark doubled up, moaned softly, and inched toward the center of the room. Adjusting the positions of the box and his body was not a perfect solution, but it made the agony tolerable.

On the plus side, Sharon and her father were oblivious to the enormous benefits of the subtle corrections.

But Lana hadn't moved.

"That's it, Max." Dr. Farley took a step back as the shadow suddenly attached to Max's feet.

A wave of darkness rolled over the body and was absorbed in his head. Max sat up and began to rock, holding his head in his hands. "Empty, empty, nothing there."

Dr. Farley placed a tentative hand on the man's shoulder. "You're fine, Max. Remember who you are."

Max nodded, fighting a panicked disorientation. "Cutler. CIA. Once. Not now."

Max Cutler was not someone he should take lightly, Clark realized. He couldn't fathom why someone with the ex-CIA agent's looks and skills would volunteer for such a dangerous experiment. No amount of money could possibly be worth the threat to sanity and life.

Dr. Farley helped Max to his feet. He turned to Sharon as he ushered the shaken man through the door. "Keep an eye on them. I'll be right back to get the lab samples."

"How long before Max can take over the watch?" Sharon was not worried about Max Cutler's health and welfare, but about her own. Her fear of meteor-rocks could be used against her. Clark just had to figure out how.

"When he feels like it," Dr. Farley retorted sharply. He closed the door as he left. A small green light blinked to red on the locking mechanism.

Sharon leaned against the doorjamb, her stony gaze fastened on the box of meteor-rocks. When Clark chanced another glance at Lana, she caught it.

"She's just heavily sedated, Clark." Sharon's tone was cold and devoid of sympathy. "It's harmless stuff, and it'll wear off."

"Why?" Talking was a struggle, but necessary to verbally manipulate the situation.

"Are you here?" Sharon seemed to welcome the chance to talk. "Because you're a stable meteor-mutation, Clark. It is absolutely imperative that my father finds out why and how to duplicate the effect. In case you hadn't noticed, all his patients are bonkers—or soon will be."

"But I'm not a—"

"Don't even try to lie, Clark." Sharon cut him off. "You have unnatural speed, and you fall apart when you're around meteor-rocks. So don't deny what you are when the evidence is so obvious."

Her knowledge of his ability to speed surprised him. He had taken all the usual precautions since getting to know her. However, he hadn't taken into account that her interest in him had nothing to do with dating.

"You may not believe it," Sharon continued, "but I'm not happy about how this has to end."

"How is that exactly?" Clark had the uncomfortable feeling that the girl was trying to mess with his mind, to terrorize him with a fate she thought he couldn't avert.

Sharon hesitated then shrugged. "After my father has what he needs, Shadow-Max will enter your windpipe. You and Lana will die of asphyxiation with meteor-dust residue in your lungs— just like Howard Stoner. We'll even leave your bodies in Stoner's field to divert the investigation from ourselves."

"Like Gary Mundy?" Clark hated loose ends. He needed all the information he could get.

Sharon shook her head. "Mundy got between Layton and his rabbit food. Bad move. Either way, you and Lana will just be two more mysterious Smallville deaths that no one can explain."

"You may be making a big mistake," Clark said, throwing the first stone of his verbal attack.

"Don't think so. We can't afford to leave any witnesses." Sharon's gaze flicked from Clark to Lana and back. "It's you and Lana or us, so you lose."

Don't count on it, Sharon.

Chloe left her bag in the trunk of Pete's car. She was still dressed in her school clothes, a tan blazer over a stylish blouse, black slacks, and ankle boots. It wasn't ideal attire for sneaking about in the woods, even worse for breaking into an underground missile silo, but at least she wasn't wearing shoes with awkward heels.

"Here." Pete shoved the aerosol can of fly spray into Chloe's hand and shouldered the baseball bat.

Chloe slipped her cell phone into her jacket pocket along with the capless fly spray can. The makeshift weapon would only be as effective as her ability to use it quickly. With her finger on the nozzle button, she whispered, "Ready?"

Pete nodded and tightened his grip on the bat.

Chloe led the way down the drive, through a dense thicket of trees, past an SUV and Sharon's silver Audi. It was darker in the wooded area than in the open, and she stayed on the drive. She had vetoed bringing a flashlight in case someone was watching.

Clark hadn't noticed any surveillance equipment when he had cased the fenced enclosure the day before. That had been enough to convince Pete they wouldn't be seen, but she wasn't so sure. Anyone who was conducting shady research in an old military installation wouldn't rely on luck for security.

"Ow." Chloe winced as she tripped over a tree root. She and Pete both froze at the edge of the woods, twenty feet from the double, chain-link gate.

The gray of twilight deepened into night as the sun slipped below the horizon. Nothing stirred except birds settling into nests and nocturnal animals venturing out to forage.

No alarms blared, and no guards leaped from hiding to surround them.

"See? There's nothing to worry about," Pete said.

Chloe frowned as she scanned the fenced-in yard. It was too

dark to see much. Cameras and sensors could be equipped with night vision, but the technology probably couldn't be easily hidden. Clark hadn't noticed any devices attached to the fence, the ventilation pipes, silo cover, or entry hatch.

Maybe the best security *was* not having any that announced there was something worth guarding.

She had to make a decision. Once they stepped out of the trees, there was nowhere to hide. No trees or brush grew in the area around the outside of the high fence or inside the enclosure, and the weeds had been mowed. Either they risked getting caught or they turned around and left.

"How sure was Clark?" Chloe whispered the question.

"Trust me, Chloe," Pete said. "If Clark said he didn't find any snooper cams, there aren't any."

"Okay." Chloe sighed. Pete was so positive that she dropped her objections and walked quickly toward the gate.

At first glance, it looked as though the chain holding the two panels closed was padlocked. They quickly discovered that the lock was broken and looped through the links to give the appearance of being secure.

"That was easy," Pete said, once they were inside.

"Too easy." Chloe replaced the lock as Pete moved toward the first raised hatch. In spite of the cloaking darkness and his security assurances, she felt exposed and vulnerable. However, they were committed and someone had to find Clark and Lana. No one else knew they were *both* missing.

"Should we call Clark's parents?" Chloe asked as she joined Pete by the entry hatch into the underground facility.

"Probably," Pete said. "But we might want to call Lex first."

"Lex?" Chloe was startled by the suggestion. "Just because Lex told Clark he's not involved with whatever's going on here doesn't mean he's not involved."

"True." Pete nodded. "So if we call and ask him for the combination to unlock this hatch and he doesn't give it to us, we'll know he was lying."

Chloe dialed the Luthor mansion. An assistant answered and politely asked her to wait a moment. Seconds passed before Lex picked up. "Lex, it's Chloe."

"Yes, Chloe." Lex sounded preoccupied. "What can I do for you?"

Like his father, Lex Luthor had no use for hemming and hawing. Chloe was blunt. "I think your tenants may be holding Lana Lang and Clark Kent prisoner in the missile silo. Can I get the lock combination for the entry hatch?"

Clark found little satisfaction in Dr. Farley's failed attempts to draw blood from his impenetrable skin. When the befuddled doctor couldn't even secure a dermal sample with a puncture instrument used to extract biopsy specimens, he settled for a swab from inside Clark's mouth.

Been there, done that, Clark thought with a sigh. The court had ordered a DNA test to prove whether or not he was Rachel Dunleavy's son. A bizarre series of coincidences had made that seem possible to everyone except Pete and his parents. To protect his alien identity, he had broken into the lab, taken the sample, and replaced it with a swab from Pete.

Now Clark not only had to free himself and rescue Lana, he had to destroy Dr. Farley's swab specimen and records.

At the moment, he could barely manage to breathe and talk at the same time. Both basic activities were essential to survival.

Clark glanced at Lana again, looking for changes in her condition. A few minutes ago, she had frowned and shifted position, but she had shown no other signs of waking up.

Sharon sat in the front right corner, as far from the open box of meteor-rocks as she could get in the small room.

"He's lying to you," Clark said.

"Shut up." Scowling, Sharon wrapped her arms around her drawn-up knees. The abrupt response was indicative of intense fear.

Clark had struck a chord, and he had no problem lying to a liar who intended to kill him and one of his best friends. "Suit yourself, Sharon, but I know from experience that those green rocks aren't safe. One day you're fine, and the next—"

"What?" Sharon asked when he didn't continue.

"This stuff doesn't have to be injected to create massive changes," Clark explained. He was surprised at how easily he fabricated fibs, but he didn't have a variety of tactics to choose from. "You don't even have to be exposed over a long period time."

"I want to know what happened to *you*," Sharon pressed.

Clark thought about asking her to close the lead box before he answered but decided against it. She was too sharp not to see through the ploy. She had to decide on her own, with no prompting.

"I went swimming in Crater Lake," Clark said, still lying. "Once."

"Crater Lake as in meteor crater?" Sharon asked. "It has meteors in it?"

"Technically it has meteor*ites* in it," Clark explained. "Meteoroids become meteors when they hit the atmosphere and start burning up. After they hit, they're meteorites. Everyone around here just calls them meteor-rocks, though."

"I don't need a science lesson, Clark!" Sharon's eyes flashed. She made an effort to calm down when Clark managed a weak shrug. "What happened after you went swimming?"

"I was fine when I went to bed that night. When I woke up, I could dodge a speeding bullet. And as you know, I get really weak around meteor-rocks."

"Overnight?" Sharon was skeptical.

"Overnight," Clark insisted. He gambled, and asked, "How long did your father's victims take to mutate?"

"Not very long," Sharon admitted, with a worried glance at the box. "How old were you?"

"Eleven." Clark chose a number at random and went on, combining fact and fiction. "Not everyone reacts to meteor material the same way. Most people who live in Smallville are in denial, like Pete and Chloe. Nobody can live day after day thinking they could wake up one morning with insect mandibles instead of teeth."

Sharon inhaled, her eyes widening.

"Instant mutations," Clark said. "Happens all the time."

"That's it." Jumping to her feet, Sharon punched four numbers into the electronic lock. When the red digital light turned green, she opened the storage room door and shouted toward the lab. "Max! I need you!"

Clark's bolstered spirits deflated. He had missed his chance to bully her into closing the lead box while they were still alone. Now, she was plotting her moves with the same care he had taken. There was no question that Sharon was going to remove the meteor-rocks, just not before Max was there to make sure the prisoner stayed too sick to move.

"What is it?" Max Cutler appeared in the doorway.

The ex-agent had the slightly haunted look of someone who was being stalked by an unspeakable horror. In Max's case, the horror was his own swift decline into madness. He knew that without a medical miracle he was condemned to become a moronic freak locked in one of Dr. Farley's cells. The certainty was wreaking havoc with the shadow-man's emotional equilibrium.

"You have to separate again, Max," Sharon said, "to keep Clark under control."

"Forget it." Max angrily turned to leave.

"No!" Sharon grabbed his arm. "You do what I say, Max, or I swear, I'll convince my father not to give you the cure when he finds it. And he will find it. Just look at Clark. He's the key."

Max cast a questioning glance toward Clark. From his own observations, the agent knew that Clark seemed to be a normal kid—with a velocity anomaly and a meteor allergy.

"Clark's been like this since he was eleven!" Sharon drew Max's gaze back to make her point. "Years, Max, and he's perfectly stable. He gets A's in school because there's no neuron loss in his brain. He's your only hope."

"Unless your shadow-self takes over before Dr. Farley finds the cure," Clark interjected. He might not be able to outwit Sharon, but Max was on the edge and susceptible to suggestion.

"What do you mean?" Max asked, frowning.

Sharon fumed. "One more word, Clark, and I'll feed Lana to Layton."

Clark knew Sharon wasn't bluffing. He had seen fear manifest itself in many ways since he had started investigating local meteor mishaps with Chloe and Pete. Fear could reduce a tough guy to tears and turn a physical weakling into an emotional giant. Some people became stronger and more determined. Sharon Farley was one of those, but with a mean streak.

"Dad is already testing the specimen he took from Clark, Max," Sharon said. "He'll have an answer soon, I'm sure. Then after Clark and his girlfriend are gone, you can stay connected to your body until Dad stabilizes your condition."

Max hesitated, swayed by her arguments.

"In the meantime"—Sharon's voice rose with hysteria— "*nobody* is safe if those rocks are radiating their poison into the whole installation!"

Max looked toward the glowing green rocks in the lead box on the floor and shielded his eyes. The gesture was an unnecessary, but instinctive response to a known danger.

Sharon eased up. "I can't close the box until shadow-Max is making certain that Clark can't go anywhere."

Exhaling, Max nodded. He sat down and closed his eyes. Within a few seconds, a shimmering dark emerged through his facial pores and flowed toward his feet. As the dark essence combined with his actual shadow, Max's body slumped. It fell on its side when shadow-Max separated. The sentient substance did not have to be told to encircle Clark's legs.

"Great, Max. Thanks." Sharon kicked the top of the meteor box closed and picked it up.

Before she reached the door, Clark was feeling a slight lessening of the debilitating effects. Still, the only thing his fast-talk maneuvering had accomplished was to exchange one source of meteor contamination for another. However, since the meteor dust in shadow-Max wasn't as potent as the box of meteor-rocks, the effort hadn't been a complete failure.

Clark was also aware that the switch might have benefits he hadn't had time to explore, yet.

"Don't close the door!" Clark pleaded.

Sharon rolled her eyes and slammed the door behind her. The green lock indicator turned red.

Something had finally gone right, but Clark had only scored

a minor victory. Darkness could be used to neutralize Max, but with the shadow-entity firmly wrapped around his legs, he couldn't use his gifts to find out how.

   Lex got into the silver Porsche GT2, which was parked in front of the mansion. He placed his cell phone in the hands-free device on the dashboard and started the engine. He was waiting to hear back from his lawyers and Chloe Sullivan and needed to talk, steer, and shift simultaneously.

   Lex had been in the final phases of setting up Great Games, Ltd. when the spunky young journalist called. Chloe wanted the lock code to access the primary personnel hatch at the Launch Control Facility, and he had given it to her.

   The lease agreement with Lawrence Farley did not bind him to the secrecy clause if the doctor was engaged in illegal activities. While Lex supported stem cell research and therapeutic cloning for medical purposes, he didn't want to be accused of guilt by association with Farley. Protection against prosecution had been his motivation for the "illegal activity" provision. Fortuitously, by definition, kidnapping was covered.

   Great Games, Ltd. was a tribute to Alexander the Great, the inspiration for Lex's own name. Given the financial triumph he anticipated, the reference was entirely fitting. It would be an annoying reminder to his father that the son was more than capable of building an empire of his own.

   The new subsidiary of LexCorp would be dedicated to all computer entertainment projects, including the development of a virtual visor to provide players with a perceptual sense of actually being in, not just looking at, their make-believe worlds. Current technology was limited to three-dimensional glasses or virtual bodysuits that were too bulky, expensive, and primitive to catch on with individuals. The Lex-Connect visor would be inexpensive, easy to install and operate on any home computer, and programmable for person-to-person interaction and communications with selected players.

   Kilya had come up with the idea when he had asked her to

think outside the box of what was presently possible. Once his technical teams had a concept to work with, they had quickly ascertained the feasibility and projected costs. Since the Lex-Connect would only function with the fantasy worlds created by Great Games, Ltd., the three role-playing scenarios he had approved to launch the visor would quickly gain in popularity.

He had hired Kilya Warcrest to run the on-line PR and promotion department. Her husband, Trenal Bonecaster, had turned out to be a brilliant concept and graphic designer. The LexCorp board members still thought the enterprise and new hires were a joke. They'd be laughing for joy when millions were signing on to play virtual Macedonia, Rio Grande, and Centauri Station at twenty dollars a month per player.

Ancient warriors, Texas, and the wild side of space exploration, Lex thought with a profound sense of satisfaction. He might have to check into his cybercreations every once in a while, just to relax.

The phone rang, snapping Lex back to the second of his immediate concerns. Chloe's cell phone number appeared on the digital readout.

"Yes, Chloe." Anticipating a problem following Chloe and Pete's intrusion, Lex had decided to drive over to the missile silo to pacify Dr. Farley personally.

"The lock code doesn't work, Lex," Chloe said. "We can't get in."

"Are you certain you punched the correct sequence?" Lex asked. He frowned as Chloe read the lock code back to him. It was correct.

"We tried three times, Lex," Chloe said. "Access denied. They must have changed the code."

"Apparently." Lex struggled to maintain the unflustered Luthor timbre in his voice. "Wait there and keep your cell phone on, Chloe. I'll call back shortly."

Lex seethed as he stared out the windshield. Farley and Cutler had not been authorized to change the locks on the entry hatches. In fact, they had been expressly *forbidden* to do so. Secrecy and privacy from outsiders was one thing, but Lex had balked at not being able to access his own property.

Lex had employed one of the best security companies in the country to install a state-of-the-art system the tenants should not have been able to dismantle. However, in spite of their assurances, his expensive "experts" had underestimated Max Cutler's abilities and the extent of his CIA training. The ex-agent had not only overcome the obstacles intended to prevent him from changing the code, he had done it without anyone knowing the system's integrity had been breached.

Impressive, but annoying, Lex thought. There was, however, a positive aspect to the unexpected development. As soon as the immediate situation was settled, he'd have the security and surveillance systems in the mansion and the plant checked and modified by specialized "experts" with government agency training and expertise.

First, he had to help Chloe access the underground installation.

He could not call Dr. Farley to demand that he open the hatch. Cutler had not activated the phone lines for fear of being wire tapped. Cell phones didn't work so far underground. They used ordinary walkie-talkies to communicate within the facility itself.

Lex had thought Cutler and Farley's concessions to paranoia were extreme, even given the mostly financial penalties for conducting illegal medical research. However, he had never confirmed his assumption that they were working with stem cells. It was possible Farley had developed something legal and innovative that other interests might want to steal—or stop.

That might explain the situation, but it didn't solve the problem.

Whether Clark Kent and Lana Lang had been kidnapped or not, he *would* get into his missile silo.

Lex had estimated Farley's power consumption and collected in advance because the Kansas State Water and Power account for the missile installation was still billed to LexCorp.

Lex dialed the phone as he roared down the drive.

Clark's patience was running out. Although the pain wasn't as great now that the box of meteor-rocks was gone, an agonizing misery of one kind or another had seeped into every cell. Max being wrapped around his ankles, combined with the long exposure to meteor material, had drained his energies and depleted his visual powers. He couldn't see though paper or use his vision to even heat water. The frustration was compounded by Lana's muffled cries in her sedated delirium. At least she was starting to revive.

Clark didn't let himself get really angry very often. He didn't want to take the chance that he might destroy something it would take the rest of his life to pay off. The treacherous Dr. Farley might qualify for retribution, but the facility belonged to Lex.

So even if he could, breaking things was out. He had to make his move soon, though, before Sharon or her father came back. However, he hadn't finished tearing down Max's defenses.

"I can't believe you're letting Sharon play you like that, Max," Clark said. "She's a spoiled brat."

As Clark expected, the shadow flexed and tightened. The conversation during the past several minutes had not been one-sided. He talked, and Max reacted. He had learned that the agent despised Dr. Farley's daughter, was terrified of turning into Layton, and was becoming increasingly agitated whenever he said anything.

"What does Sharon know about anything?" Clark scoffed. "I can't even *imagine* what it would be like to have my mind separated from my body."

Max began to twine up Clark's legs. The pain intensified the closer the shadow got to his torso and vital organs, which was obviously the intention. Whether Max was moving to punish him or silence him, Clark knew the agent's confidence was on the verge of breaking.

"I've heard they experience the same fear"—Clark paused for effect—"of not being able to get back into their bodies. How far away do you think they go?"

Max slid back down to Clark's shins, perhaps hoping to convince him to shut up or change subjects.

"I'm tied up, Max," Clark said weakly with a despondent sigh. "I've been exposed to you and those rocks for so long, it'll take me a week to recover. You don't have to stay so far away from your body."

Clark closed his eyes and sighed again. He wasn't sure how shadow-Max did it, but he perceived everything. He wanted the agent to think he was surrendering to the futility of his circumstances.

Max became still.

Clark concentrated on breathing. The solitary lightbulb in the ceiling shone with an unrelenting glare. It blazed against his closed eyelids as he prepared to focus his depleted power on a single desperate act.

The shadow weighed almost nothing, yet Clark was aware of every tremor. Max moved another few inches, paused, then moved over his ankles and stopped on his shoes.

Clark waited, breathing.

When Max hit the floor and bolted for his body, Clark had two seconds at most. His eyes snapped open. The heat ray was weaker than normal, but already aimed at the bulb. Everything Clark had went into the burst of alien energy that shattered the fragile bulb and cast the room into total darkness.

He did not hear Max scream, but he sensed it.

Freed from direct contact with the meteor dust in Max's shadow, Clark began to recover. The pain receded quickly, but his full strength did not return. He strained and was able to break the ropes that bound his hands and untie the ropes around his feet. As he scrambled over to Lana, he wondered how long it would take to recharge.

"Lana?" Clark whispered, and gently shook her shoulder.

"Too early." Lana tried to brush him off, but her hands were still tied.

Clark's vision didn't adjust to the dark right away. Clasping Lana's hands to hold them still, he fumbled the knot untied, then moved on to the ropes binding her feet. When she was free, he stood up and stretched to get his own muscles working again. He wasn't sure how long it had been since Sharon had left with the box of meteor-rocks. Locked in a room with no one to talk to but a frantic shadow had distorted his sense of time.

But not my sense of urgency, Clark thought. *It's time to get out.*

A slight dizziness swam in Clark's head as he leaned over to pull Lana to her feet. She swayed unsteadily and leaned against him. Although she was standing, she was still heavily sedated, and he was too weak to carry her.

With an arm around Lana's shoulders, Clark urged her toward the storeroom door. Her feet moved, but she clung to him to stay upright. Since his eyes hadn't adjusted to the dark, he held his arm out so they wouldn't collide with a wall. They both stumbled over nothing, Lana in a stupor and he from the lingering exhaustion. The prolonged weakness puzzled him, until he saw the glowing green sheen on the floor ahead.

Meteor dust.

He had thought the shadow entity would be disabled in the darkness. Instead, the dark essence had been absorbed, and Max Cutler had died.

Clark did not have time for regrets. He hoped that once he was out of the cramped room and away from the residue, his recuperative powers would speed up.

"I'm tired." Lana slipped from his grasp and slumped to the floor behind him.

Since Lana was fine for the moment, Clark turned his attention to the door. The red light on the electronic lock was a beacon in the dark, guiding his hand. However, as he reached out to grab the handle, he realized that they wouldn't be getting out of the room soon.

Shadow-Max had expired by his body's feet, leaving his meteor-dust remains directly in front of the door.

Clark didn't have the strength to break the electronic lock.

Cursing the slow, but steady pace of the tractor, Jonathan turned into Charley Haskin's cornfield. He cast a wary glance toward his neighbor's distant farmhouse when a dog barked an intruder alert. Charley was a levelheaded man, but he kept a loaded shotgun by the back door. Rather than risk being shot at, Jonathan turned off the headlights, hunched over the steering wheel, and kept going toward the fertilizer plant.

When Chloe had called a short time before, she had delivered her message in an anxious rush. She was waiting for Lex to call back and hurriedly explained that his renters in the old missile installation might have taken Clark and Lana hostage. She didn't say why before she hung up, only that a Dr. Farley was likely experimenting with meteor dust in ways that had probably killed Howard Stoner and Gary Mundy.

Jonathan had almost called her back, but leaving the line open so Lex could get through was more important. As much as he distrusted Lex Luthor, he couldn't deny that Lex cared about Clark. Since LexCorp owned the old military facility, Lex might have information that would help resolve the situation.

Provided Lex wasn't responsible for the crisis in the first place. Jonathan still suspected that Lex had had something to do with the hostage situation that had imperiled his father and Martha at LuthorCorp. He just couldn't prove it.

However, if Chloe's information was correct, Howard Stoner and the CEP agent had not died because of chemical contamination from the fertilizer plant. Clark had been right to stop him from launching a premature lawsuit.

When Jonathan came to the end of Charley's field, he turned onto a dirt access road that skirted the fertilizer plant property. He couldn't risk having the old machine break down, nor did he want to waste time. Keeping the gears set in low for rough terrain, he pushed his speed to twenty on the rutted track.

Martha had taken the pickup to the grocery store for muffin

supplies. The retirement center was having a visitors' reception tomorrow, and they had forgotten to call to double their regular order. While she always had the LuthorCorp cell phone with her during business hours, his wife had walked off leaving it on the kitchen counter, plugged in to recharge.

Jonathan had had no choice but to take the tractor cross-country. He just hoped he got to the old missile site in time to help his son.

◆◆◆

Chloe paced, checking the digital readout on her watch to mark time and her cell phone screen to make sure she hadn't missed any calls. Jonathan Kent was on his way, but it would take him a while by tractor. Lex still hadn't called back.

Pete had taken the broken padlock and chain off the gate and stuffed them in his back pockets. They weren't ideal weapons, but he had to work with what they had.

Know the enemy had been on his mind as he walked the yard in a quick reconnoiter of the enclosure.

The automated lid over the shaft where the Minuteman II had stood rested on a metal frame of ten-inch-wide rails. Pete still didn't know the extent of Clark's abilities, but at three feet high and ten feet across, the concrete-and-steel silo cover might be too heavy for his alien friend to move.

The smaller hatch a few feet away appeared to be broken. The ground seal was out of line and the digital readout on the locking mechanism was dark. Pete tried, but he couldn't budge it. Clark probably could, which wasn't a good sign.

The only way anyone could hold Clark Kent hostage was by exposing him to meteor-rocks. Since Clark was nowhere to be found, that was exactly what Pete thought had happened.

"Did you find anything?" Chloe asked, as Pete walked toward her across a cement slab on the ground. The aluminum baseball bat still rested on his shoulder.

"Nothing that will help us get inside." Pete dropped the bat and knelt by the main hatch. "Although I'm not sure what we'd do if we could."

"Me, neither." Chloe's shoulders sagged. "I was sort of hoping we'd open the hatch, and Clark and Lana would rush out."

"That would be good, but probably too much to hope for." Pete began to punch random numbers into the lock panel. He didn't expect to hit on the right combination, but trying to open the hatch might alert someone inside to their presence. If anyone wanted to get out to get them, they'd have to open the hatch to do it.

"For all we know, there's more than one creepy killer." Chloe scanned the dark enclosure again.

"That's a possibility," Pete agreed. "So bring your trusty fly spray over here. Just in case something besides Clark or Lana pops out of this thing."

Chloe stepped over and assumed a gunslinger stance with the aerosol can ready. "This is nuts."

"It's the best we can do," Pete said. When Chloe's phone rang, he stopped playing with the lock to listen.

"You're on your way over here?" Chloe looked relieved. "So is Mr. Kent, Lex, but if we can't open—"

Pete grabbed the baseball bat and stood up. With Mr. Kent and Lex joining forces with them, the odds were better. The trouble was, they didn't know anything specific about the enemy. Sharon's father could have a creepy guy army.

"What?" Chloe spoke into the phone, but her gaze snapped to Pete. "Okay, but you'd better hurry."

"Problem?" Pete asked, his pulse quickening.

"We're about to find out." Chloe signed off and dropped the phone back in her pocket. "Lex called Kansas State Water and Power. This facility was on a separate generator when the military was here, and it still is. The power company is going to shut off the juice."

"Bingo!" Pete glanced at the hatch. Without power, the electronic lock would disengage. However, the heavy cover was motorized. "Except I don't think we can lift the hatch without power."

"Lex said that unless it's damaged, it was designed to be opened manually, too. Does balanced with counterweights mean anything to you?" Chloe raised the fly spray can and pressed the nozzle button. The spray was set to mist. She twisted the plastic button to narrow the stream.

"Makes perfect sense," Pete said. The other hatch had been dislodged, disrupting the manual apparatus. Clark had shown him several pictures of the interior, including the elevator platform just below the hatch. The counterweights had to be positioned in the wall behind the ladder.

"Get ready because we'll only have a few seconds." Chloe stepped to the other side of the circular door. She held the spray can in her right hand, leaving her left hand free to lift the hatch.

"Why only a few seconds?" Following Chloe's lead, Pete braced the bat on his shoulder with his left hand. He gripped the rim of the hatch with his right.

"The emergency generator will automatically kick in to take over." Chloe blew a strand of hair off her face, planted her feet wide for stability, and focused on the hatch.

Every muscle in Pete's body tensed. He stared at the digital readout on the lock panel and counted the passing seconds. At forty-two, the digital lock readout went dark.

"Pull!" Pete stumbled back a step as the hatch cover flipped up to rest against a brace. The dark interior below was dimly lit by the red glow from a battery-powered emergency light.

"That was too easy." Chloe stared down into the dark.

"Makes me nervous." Pete's whole body was on an adrenaline alert. He clamped his hands around the baseball bat and flexed his fingers as though getting ready for the pitch.

The emergency power came on suddenly.

Although they were expecting it, the flash of light was startling. They both rocked backward and took a moment to reorient. Neither one was prepared for the sight that met their astonished eyes when they looked back through the hatch.

"Oh, boy." Pete's mouth went dry.

Chloe gasped.

A spindly, naked man sprang out of the elevator and looked up. He opened his mouth as though to laugh, but the orifice stretched into a gaping maw.

Pete and Chloe watched, mesmerized, as the creature clutched the ladder with elastic arms. He pushed off the floor with flattened feet and shot upward toward Chloe. There was little doubt that he intended to engulf her in his enlarging mouth.

"Not!" Chloe aimed the spray can and shot the rubber man in the eye. "Take that, you—freak!"

Pete swung the bat and hit the hideous being in the back. The bat sank right into the thing's mushy, malleable flesh.

"No, no, no, no!" The man let go of the ladder with both hands to rub his burning eyes.

Pete pulled the bat back and swung again. This time he brought it down on the top of the man's misshapen head instead of swinging in from the side. The action drove the naked man farther down the ladder.

Chloe dropped the aerosol can and slammed the hatch closed. The electronic lock automatically engaged.

"Uh—" Pete stared at the red light on the lock panel as he fought to catch his breath.

Clark was still locked in.

"Clark!" Chloe came to the same conclusion. She hit her forehead with the palm of her hand. "How could I have been so stupid?"

"Yeah, well, with Stretch getting ready to chow down on Chloe-to-go," Pete quipped, "we didn't have much choice."

When a loud, grating noise sounded behind him, Pete whirled with the bat ready.

The massive silo lid began sliding open.

Clark stood in the farthest corner of the dark storeroom, staring at the red lock-light on the door. His strength was beginning to return, and the nausea had abated—as long as he stayed clear of the meteor dust.

He had tried shaking Lana awake, thinking she could use his shirt to sweep the potent green residue aside, but she couldn't help. Barely lucid and physically sickened by the sedative, she needed to sleep, and he had left her alone.

But he couldn't delay too long. Every second that passed brought him closer to a confrontation with Sharon or Dr. Farley. He did not think Sharon would risk carrying a meteor-rock, but her father might, and that would end their chances of escape.

Clark breathed deeply. Several minutes had passed since his last attempt to storm the door, and he had become stronger in the interim. His strategy involved speed and every ounce of brute force at his command.

"Dad!" Sharon's shout sounded close.

Clark reached down and pulled Lana to her feet, hoping he hadn't waited too long. If Sharon came through the door, he would run her down if necessary, whatever he needed to do to get out.

"Layton's missing!" Sharon screeched.

"He can't be. Layton never misses a meal." Dr. Farley's voice receded as he passed by. The metallic sound of boots on metal dimmed as father and daughter left the Launch Control Center area.

Clark held Lana close, but he was caught in a dilemma. Dr. Farley and Sharon were between him and the exits, and Layton was loose. Since the installation was a closed system, he didn't want to escape and hide. The scientist could use meteor dust to flush him out.

"But we're going to have to take our chances." With one

arm around Lana's back, Clark tightened his grip on her arms. As he prepared to make his move, the red light on the lock blinked out.

Clark opened the door and pulled Lana through in a split second. He paused in the narrow corridor by the kitchen.

"My head." Lana moaned, and tried to double over.

Clark pushed the storeroom door closed, but it wasn't made of lead and did little to shield him from the dust on the floor. Half-dragging Lana, he stumbled toward the open doorway by the metal bridge attached to the wall.

Beyond the thick wall in the tunnel junction, Sharon screamed. "Get away! Don't touch me, you filthy beast!"

"Back inside, Edgar!" Dr. Farley shouted. "No cigarettes unless—Edgar!"

The power outage had sprung the locks on the cells, and now Layton wasn't the only mutant loose in the compound.

Clark sensed a rumble as the massive generator in the Equipment Building suddenly came on-line. Power was restored a moment later.

Clark's meteor-symptoms subsided as he moved farther away from the storeroom. His ability to speed began to build when he hit the bridge, but he reined himself in to clear the thick wall. A high-speed collision with Sharon, her dad, or one of the mutated men in the narrow opening wouldn't hurt Clark, but neither they nor Lana would survive.

Once he hit the wide tunnel hub, however, he could carry Lana up the elevator-shaft staircase and out the primary access hatch. With his gifts restored, there were no barriers to stop him.

Except the gnarled little man covered with porcupine hair blocking the junction doorway.

The nausea hit Clark's stomach like a runaway locomotive smashing into a mountain. He reeled backward, holding on to Lana and cushioning her fall with his own tormented body.

"Shhhmok!" Edgar took a step inside the opening. The barbed hairs that covered his body were more pliant than they appeared. He wore a pair of baggy shorts and actually looked more like a giant chimpanzee than a porcupine. His angry frown was evident through the brush of fine hair that covered his face. "Now, you."

"Okay, Edgar, okay." Clark held up a hand to keep the meteor-mutant back. He remembered that Dr. Farley refused to give the hairy man a cigarette earlier. "Just stay back, and you can have smoke."

"Yesssssss." Edgar glared, his eyes bright with the glint of insanity. He took a step forward. "Shhhmok!"

The veins in Clark's hands throbbed. Muscle and tendons stretched and twisted in violent convulsions. As he tried to wave Edgar off, Clark realized he had a twofold meteor-related problem.

Dr. Farley had used meteor dust to alter the molecular structure in all his subjects. Max, obviously the last of the six, was a refined, functional mutation compared to his predecessors. Perhaps, as the scientist had learned more about the potent properties of meteor material, he had used less in subsequent subjects. Edgar, being one of his earlier attempts, contained more meteor dust than the shadow had. The effects on Clark were amplified in the narrow confines on the passageway.

Clark could edge backward out of the enclosed space. Once he was clear, Edgar could enter the lab area without causing a violent meteor-induced reaction. But Clark could not leave Lana to an uncertain fate in the passage. Layton had killed for fun. Edgar might kill for cigarettes.

Then Clark recalled Edgar's behavior in the cell. Angered because Dr. Farley wouldn't give him a smoke, the mutant had leaped to the ceiling and stuck there.

Clark gently rolled Lana to the side and positioned himself as a buffer between her and the annoyed mutant. Edgar would have to go through him to harm her.

But Edgar had only one thing on his mind.

Clark felt a guarded sympathy for the impatient addict. Farley had had some kind of leverage over the men who had submitted to his experiments. Homeless addicts and alcoholics were a source of volunteers that wouldn't arouse suspicion, but using their vices to manipulate them was an unconscionable cruelty.

Waving Edgar to go by, Clark braced for the waves of excruciating pain he expected to cascade through his body. "Look in the kitchen, Edgar."

"Good." Edgar hesitated instead of charging past. He smiled and hissed, showing rotten teeth. Then he leaped to the ceiling and scurried past Clark and Lana overhead. The distance didn't completely protect Clark, but the new agony in his savaged body was minimal.

"Lana. Can you hear me?"

Lana stirred slightly, but she didn't open her eyes. "In a minute, Mr. Sullivan."

"Right." Sighing, Clark glanced behind him. Edgar was sitting outside the storeroom door lighting up. *One down.* Rising, he pulled Lana up and hurried through the tunnel.

When Clark finally emerged in the junction, it was immediately obvious that escape was still an elusive prospect.

Screaming in short, shrill bursts, Layton dropped to the ground in front of the closed elevator doors. His hands were still clasped around a staircase railing fifteen feet high and his arms stretched like rubber. They snapped back into their original form when he let go. Still screeching, the elastic man rubbed his right eye with one fist and pounded on the floor with the other.

Because of the meteor dust in Layton's body, the elastic man was an impassable wall between Clark and the elevator.

Dr. Farley and Sharon were in the third cell along the back wall. The door was open, but they were barricaded in by the rudimentary shapeshifter with a limited ability to morph. Shaped like a lumpy rectangle, it had planted itself in front of the cell door. Every time Sharon or Dr. Farley made a move, it lashed out with an arm or leg and shoved them back inside.

"Clark!" Sharon called, her voice frantic. "You can draw Nathan off with chocolate. It's on the cart in the kitchen!"

Dr. Farley looked at his daughter as though she'd gone as mad as his mutant menagerie. Since they had held him prisoner and tortured him with meteor-rocks, it was ridiculous for Sharon to expect Clark to help. But she did, Clark realized. Chloe or Pete must have made a crack about his hyperactive sense of right and wrong.

He had to help. He just wasn't sure what to do. One thing was definite. He wasn't going back into the LCC to get chocolate for Nathan. He lowered Lana to the floor on the yellow swing line by the massive LCC door. She looked dazed, but she didn't fall over.

The chameleon man with kaleidoscopic skin ran back and forth between the cells and the elevator.

"Stop, Cooper!" Sharon yelled angrily. "You're making me crazy watching you."

Cooper continuously swatted at his arms and legs, trying to catch the colorful patterns that flitted over his skin. Clark hadn't realized that the man was literally skin and bones.

When Cooper got too close to the elevator, Layton suddenly shrieked. His head and arms extended outward like a three-dimensional elastic cartoon without the popping eyes.

Clark wasn't laughing. He couldn't get close to a mutant without suffering a meteor-sickness attack, and Layton was blocking the fastest exit out of the installation. If he couldn't remove Layton, he'd have to find another way out.

"Clark!" Sharon jumped back to avoid Nathan's foot. "We've got an emergency system to subdue these animals, but we've got to get out to activate it."

"Is that true, Dr. Farley?" Clark asked.

"Check the storage cabinet by the LFEB door," the scientist said. "There are gas masks there and at other key points throughout the station."

A quick look with his X-ray vision confirmed the doctor's claim. When he heard a faint whooshing sound, Clark glanced to the cell on his left. Hoover's vacant, drugged eyes were now empty and dead. "It looks like Hoover's gone."

"We'll all be gone if you don't do something, Clark!" Sharon tossed her head in indignation.

Clark ignored her as he surveyed the whole area again. Unless they had someone else stashed somewhere else, everyone was accounted for. When his gaze settled on the red-metal-framed glass box by the elevator, Dr. Farley interpreted his thoughts and corrected his assumption.

"That's not the gas release, son. That'll take out everything."

Clark's head snapped around. "A destruct mechanism?"

The doctor shrugged. "Three-minute countdown. Things could get out of control."

Could? The man's cavalier attitude about death and destruction was stunning. The monstrosities he had created would run amuck until they released a knockout gas or brought the whole place crashing down.

Sharon was no better, but the blame was her father's. As Lex had once told him, people were not born bad or good. They were molded by design or example, deliberately or accidentally in a cosmic game of character roulette.

Clark was stricken with a twinge of dizziness when the chameleon man altered course and ran by him. He recovered quickly, and his decision was made without deliberation. Once Dr. Farley and Sharon were free, they could handle the mutants while he got Lana to safety.

He glanced back toward the door where he had left Lana. She was sitting cross-legged, rocking and holding her head in her hands.

Clark was not feeling one hundred percent himself. Between the infested mutated men and loose meteor dust that permeated the whole installation, he had not been completely out of contact with the vile element since Layton had dragged him into the hatch.

"Get ready to run for it, Sharon."

Clark didn't give the girl, her father, or Nathan time to react. He rushed forward, grabbed the blob-man, and tossed him into an empty cell. Sharon and her father were outside before he had the cell door closed and locked. From this point on, whatever happened was out of his control.

"Masks first, Dad." Sharon turned toward the cabinet by the Equipment Building and ripped the doors open. She tossed her father a gas mask and grabbed another for herself.

Clark ran to Lana as Dr. Farley and Sharon raced into the LCC tunnel. Drawing Lana up on her feet again, he slipped an arm around her back and lifted her.

"C'mon, c'mon. Hurry!" Sharon demanded shrilly.

As Clark sped back to the cabinet, he realized he was only

moving at a fraction of his usual speed. He pulled the third and last mask from the cabinet and slipped it over Lana's face. He had no idea where additional gas masks were kept, and he couldn't take time to look. Speed was his only ally, and he had to get clear of the meteor dust.

"Got it!" Dr. Farley's voice was flooded with relief.

Clark held his breath. As he turned to run, the colorful chameleon man stopped suddenly and crumpled. Nathan fell over in his cell, and Clark zipped toward the elevator with Lana in his arms. He suddenly realized that he didn't know whether or not the gas was deadly.

Probably not, Clark thought, when he saw that Layton had not yet succumbed to the poison's effects.

The rubber man was pacing in front of the elevator doors with an odd, gorillalike gait. When he saw Clark, he slammed his fist into the floor, then hauled his arm back and let it fly like a lasso.

Still holding his breath, Clark ducked the elastic arm and jumped back. He glanced toward the connecting tunnel, which was the only alternate route out of the installation, then back at the elastic man.

Layton's malleable bone density was similar to Nathan's. His skeletal legs expanded and compressed as he jumped up and down in frenzied fury by the elevator. He stopped suddenly and resumed his normal form.

Was Layton resistant to the poison? Clark wondered, as Sharon and Dr. Farley raced out of the Launch Control Center. The scientist carried the lead box full of meteor rocks, and they both headed directly for the elevator. They stopped when they saw Layton.

Sharon turned her mask-covered face to stare at Clark with clear-plastic-covered eyes.

Still holding his breath, Clark motioned toward the connecting tunnel with his head. The girl and her father didn't have to worry about meteor dust, but the rampaging elastic man was still a threat.

Sharon shook her head and waved him to leave.

Clark hesitated. Although Layton hadn't harmed Farley in

the past, the rubbery mutant was agitated and cornered. Since Clark couldn't force Sharon and Dr. Farley to follow him while he was carrying Lana, he darted to the tunnel entrance.

The hatch door was closed, but unlocked. He yanked it open and placed Lana on the floor inside. As he stepped out, Layton slid to the floor in front of the elevator doors.

The elastic mutant had finally succumbed to the gas.

Sharon stamped her foot and waved Clark back again.

Since the girl and her father had gas masks and Layton was no longer a threat, Clark had no reason to force them into the tunnel. However, the silo was the only way out for him and Lana.

Clark stepped inside the passageway and pulled the hatch door closed. His tormented body began to adjust to the meteor-dust-free atmosphere, but the healing was incomplete. He felt sluggish as he turned, but did not know if he was reacting to traces of the gas or the meteor dust that seemed to be everywhere.

A Klaxon blared, and the hatch automatically locked.

There was no dramatic countdown to doom uttered in a feminine voice, but Clark suspected that the destruct mechanism had been activated. Focusing his X-ray vision, he concentrated on the door into the junction.

Sharon and Dr. Farley were standing by the elevator. The scientist was near the glass case that contained the trigger. Apparently, he wanted to bury the evidence of his inhumane work and experiments.

The elevator would take Sharon and her father to safety on the surface before the countdown hit zero, but Clark had only one way out. He lifted Lana and sped into the tunnel.

Sharon halted beside her father eight feet from the elevator when she saw Layton standing by the elevator. She was even more startled when she noticed Clark. He was still standing, too, with Lana in his arms as the installation filled with gas.

When Clark nodded toward the tunnel that connected the main sections of the facility with the silo, she shook her head no and waved him to leave. It wasn't that she cared what happened to Clark or Lana. She and her father needed to make a quick, clean getaway once they hit the surface. They'd be long gone by the time Clark found out the silo exit was filled with cement and doubled back to take the elevator.

Clark finally got the message when Layton slid to the floor. He fled into the tunnel and closed the hatch door.

Sharon sighed with relief and glanced at her father. He was frozen in place, with a tight grip on the meteor-rock box, his eyes wide and staring, his breathing labored under the gas mask. Frowning, she looked toward the elevator.

The childlike man sitting in front of the metal outer doors was staring at them.

Why wasn't Layton unconscious?

Sharon glanced back at Cooper, who had fallen outside Nathan's cell. Edgar had collapsed by the storeroom door.

Sharon grabbed her father's arm, but as soon as she moved, Layton's rubbery arm snaked out to push her back.

He smiled.

And she remembered.

Her father had created Layton with immunity to poisons.

Before either Sharon or her father could react, the elastic man bounded upright and smashed the glass covering the destruct panel. He turned the key and pushed the button, activating the mechanism.

Sharon gasped as the Klaxon sounded the beginning of the three-minute countdown.

They had to get in the elevator now!

Sharon was right behind him when her father dropped the meteor box and sprang toward the elevator.

"Get out of the way, Layton!" Dr. Farley's voice was muffled by the cumbersome mask as he ordered Layton to move.

Layton grinned as his arms suddenly elongated.

Sharon's scream was choked off by gas when the mutant's nimble fingers ripped the mask off her face.

Clark quickly covered the hundred feet to the maintenance area that was attached to the silo shaft. The tunnel had been well lit, with not a single bulb missing. The same was true in the empty utility room. Cement from the sixty-foot access tube had overflowed and hardened on a third of the floor. He hadn't thought to ask, but the exit had probably been blocked to keep Layton in.

Although the effects of the sedative were finally wearing off, Lana was still groggy. She clung to him, unaware of her surroundings. The gas mask over her face further distorted her perceptions.

Counting the seconds in his head, Clark stepped up to the hatch that opened into the shaft. He had just over two minutes to make the sixty-foot climb to the silo lid before the old military installation became a pile of rubble.

As Clark had gotten older, his speed and strength had increased and new gifts had manifested. He suspected that as he continued to mature, moving one hundred tons of concrete and steel would be easy.

But he wasn't there yet, and he had just endured his longest exposure ever to meteor-rocks.

With a silent apology, Clark flipped Lana over his shoulder. He held on to her with one arm and opened the hatch. He'd need his other arm free to climb the ladder rungs recessed into the silo wall.

Although the silo shaft was dark, Clark did not look down. The drop to the floor was eighty feet. He was determined to conquer his fear of heights and had made progress, but committing himself to the hundred-forty-foot vertical climb still required an extra measure of resolve.

The seconds counted down.

Recalling the diagrams he had shown Pete, Clark tightened his grip on Lana and felt for the inset metal bars located beside the hatch. When his hand closed over one, he swung out and found capture with his feet on a lower rung. Having to hold Lana made the climb exceptionally perilous. He had to rely on balance to prevent a tragic fall backward.

However, he quickly developed a swift, rhythmic pattern of ascent. Once he was comfortable with the climb, he looked up—and saw stars. The silo lid was open.

Clark knew the cover had been securely in place earlier, which suggested the opening had been automatically triggered when the power failed. Perhaps, once the process was in motion, the full cycle of opening and closing had to run its course.

With less than a minute to go before an explosive firestorm rampaged through the facility, Clark looked up again.

The lid was closing faster than he could climb.

Pete hovered near the moving lid, checking inside the silo every couple minutes, wishing Clark and Lana would appear. He wasn't sure how long he could keep Chloe away. Protecting Clark's secret by diverting the *Torch* editor's attention was a major part of his job description. There was a lot more to being a sidekick than most people realized.

For the moment, Chloe was standing watch over the primary access hatch. Her fly spray was primed to fire, and she was ready to run if the freaky rubber guy showed up instead of their friends. It was going to get crowded soon. Lex would be arriving any minute by car, and the headlights on Mr. Kent's tractor were visible across the LexCorp cornfield.

"See anything?" Chloe asked.

"Not yet." Pete glanced at the huge six-sided cover as it slowly slid back into the closed position. If Clark was going to exit through the silo, he'd better hurry.

They were both convinced that Lana and Clark were down there. Based on the mice and the locked car at the stable, Chloe had deduced that the killer had captured Lana, and Clark had gone to save her.

Except now Clark seemed to be in trouble, too.

Why else would Lana's rescue be taking so long? Pete couldn't help pondering the question, but he really didn't want to contemplate something that was able to give Clark Kent a hard time and get away with it.

Sighing, Pete shifted his handy aluminum head basher onto his other shoulder and stole another peek into the silo. This time he was not disappointed. He could see a silhouette in the lighted hatch sixty feet down. With Lana slung over his shoulder, Clark swung onto the ladder rungs built into the silo wall and started climbing upward.

Slowly.

Pete cast a glance at Chloe.

"There's Lex!" Stepping back from the access hatch, Chloe turned. Lex stopped the silver sports car on the side of the dirt access road and turned out the headlights.

"Why don't you go see if he's got a flashlight, Chloe," Pete suggested. He had one in his car, but he need Chloe gone. "We could use one."

"Yeah, good idea." Chloe half turned back as she headed for the gate. "Either nobody cares that we're hanging around up here, or nobody knows."

Except elastic guy, Pete thought as he glanced down to check Clark's progress. He looked to the side to gauge his rate of ascent against the lid's rate of closure. If Clark didn't speed things up, the lid was going to win.

"Pssst! Clark." Pete kept his voice low so he wouldn't alert Chloe. The sound of concrete grinding along the rails was louder.

Jonathan Kent's tractor stopped out in the field.

Pete knew that if something didn't change in the Clark-silo equation, Clark and Lana Lang would be trapped in the silo before his father reached the enclosure.

On the off chance Clark *was* strong enough to move the concrete lid, his cover as an ordinary, small-town teenager would end if Lex Luthor saw him do it.

"This is how we separate the serious sidekicks from the comic relief," Pete muttered.

He had to do something, but there was no visible control panel he could break to stop the cover's steady advance. Except he didn't have to stop it, just slow it down. The length of chain he had taken off the gate might buy a few crucial seconds.

Pete dropped the chain on the metal rail under the corner of the lid. The steady grinding noise became a tortured squeal as the massive slab jammed.

"Hello?" Clark called out.

Pete leaned over so the shaft would muffle his shout. "Get a move on, Clark! I don't know how long this will hold!"

◆◆◆

Clark moved faster when he realized the concrete lid had stopped moving.

Pete had apparently figured out that he needed a few extra seconds to clear the shaft before the lid closed. Somehow he had jammed the mechanism.

Pete *didn't* know that the silo cover had to be closed to minimize the aboveground effects of the imminent explosion.

As though shot from a cannon, Clark summoned a burst of alien speed. He scaled the remaining interior of the wall with surefooted quickness.

Jonathan Kent darted through the gate just as Clark appeared above the rim of the deep shaft. "Clark?"

"Take Lana!" Clark yelled to be heard over the whine of the heavy silo cover. He still held the limp girl over his shoulder.

Pete dropped the baseball bat and helped Clark's father lift Lana out of the deep hole. As they set her on the ground, Jonathan eased the gas mask off her face.

"What's going on?" Lana's voice was choked, her throat still constricted by the waning sedative. She rubbed her temples, then looked up sharply. "That man! He was eating mice whole—"

"He was a victim of a genetic manipulation experiment Sharon's father was conducting." Clark pulled himself through the narrow space between the edge of the lid and the silo wall. Pete had acted without a second to spare. "Details at eleven. Right now we've got other problems."

"I'll pass on the details, thanks." Lana dragged herself upright. "As it is, I'll have nightmares for a month."

Clark quickly assessed the situation on the ground. The beam of a flashlight bobbed where the drive cut through the trees to the road. He could discern Lex and Chloe's dark outlines in spite of the lingering meteor effects. Particles of the dust still clung to his hair and clothes, exerting a miniscule but steady drain on his physical abilities.

"You have to run," Clark said, relying on the dead-seriousness of his tone to convince them in the dark. "There are explosive charges down there, set to go off in fifteen seconds."

"Go, Pete!" Jonathan barked, then took a softer tone with Lana. "Can you run?"

"From an explosion? Yes!" Lana took off after Pete, stumbling in the dark.

"Clark?" Jonathan hesitated.

"Get out of here, Dad! I'll be okay."

Jonathan ran, catching Lana and checking his pace to stay with her.

Clark had to close the silo lid before the shaft became a giant rifle barrel loaded with a blazing inferno. If the explosion wasn't contained, his father and friends wouldn't be able to run far enough fast enough to avoid severe, and maybe even fatal, injuries from fire and debris.

If he was caught in a blast peppered with meteor-rock particles, his chances of survival weren't terribly good, either.

"Chloe! Lex!" Pete yelled. "Go back!

The flashlight beam stopped then swung as Chloe and Lex turned back toward the road.

A split-second scan revealed the chain that was caught between the edge of the silo lid and the ten-inch-wide rail. Pete's decision to use the lock chain from the gate was impressive, but it had worked too well. When Clark tried to pull the obstruction out, the chain broke.

Ten seconds and counting.

The motorized mechanism that moved the one-hundred-ton lid open and closed over the missile shaft shrieked with the strain of being stalled.

Clark sped to the far side of the cover. He had to get it moving before the mechanism froze. Leaning into the huge apparatus, he pushed. Every muscle tensed with the effort of trying to force concrete, steel, and lead past the links of chain on the rail.

Five seconds.

The bulky cover moved an inch, gears grinding, then three more inches. The remaining gap was less than a foot wide.

Digging in, Clark willed the strength to shove the cover closed.

Three, two—

The silo cover slid cleanly into place as the explosive charges began going off.

As Clark scrambled over the trembling ground to the gate,

his gaze darted to the closed primary access hatch. The elevator took less than a minute to reach the surface after the doors were closed, but there was no sign of Sharon and her father. He would never had left them if he thought there was any chance they'd be trapped. Something he couldn't have anticipated must have gone terribly wrong.

And there was nothing he could do to save them now.

Clark ran with an eye on the flashlight beam ahead and his senses attuned to the changes below. He dared not speed with Lex in the vicinity taking mental notes. Sharon Farley had discovered his ability by cross-checking times. Eventually, Lex might make the same connections and arrive at the same conclusion.

But not tonight.

Clark heard and felt the series of explosions that ripped through the Missile Launch Facility. The ground shook, sinking and buckling as areas below imploded or exploded.

After clearing the gate into the woods, Clark allowed himself a small burst of speed. The blast he most feared was yet to come. When he hit the end of the drive, he slowed to calculate the danger in relation to the people on the road. Lex, his dad, and his friends kept running without hesitation or looking back.

Clark assured himself they were clear just as thousands of gallons of generator fuel ignited in the buried tank outside the Equipment Building sixty feet down.

Caught when an outgassing fissure opened under him, Clark was blasted upward and hurled toward the woods. In the seconds he was airborne, he was able to take in the details of the entire scene.

The forces unleashed by the exploding fuel tank were funneled into paths of least resistance. The primary hatch cover rocketed skyward on a plume of fire, but the silo lid held, keeping most of the destructive blast underground.

Clark envisioned the massive destruction in the compound. Hatches were blown off as shock waves, fiery heat balls, and black smoke raced into every inch of the installation. Everyone and everything within the Equipment Building, tunnel junction, and Launch Control Center were instantly incinerated.

Not knowing they were safely outside the falling debris zone, Clark's father and friends dived for cover.

Clark arched into the woods on the far side of the access road. Branches broke beneath him as he fell, and he landed in a bed of brush and pine needles. Slightly winded because of the debilitating dust, he lay still for a minute, staring up at the stars in the night sky.

The same thought that crossed his mind every time he looked at the wonders of deep space through his telescope struck him again now. He might have been born on a planet orbiting one of those stars, but Earth was home.

"Clark!" Jonathan's frantic voice rose above the subterranean rumble of collapsing steel, cement, and rock.

Clark stood up and brushed himself off. Since no one else could have survived being blasted from one side of the dirt road to another, he hoped no one had seen his unscheduled flight.

"Clark!" Chloe sounded angry, hiding her fear for his safety behind a façade of indignant fury. "Where are you?"

Clark moved quickly and silently, doubling back so his position wouldn't raise too many questions he didn't want to answer. He crept out of the woods by the dirt drive, close to where he had been.

"Over here!" Clark didn't realize his shirt was torn and charred until he waved. His face was probably covered with black soot like his hands and arms. Since the grime disguised the fact that he hadn't been cut or bruised, the smudges worked in his favor.

Jonathan ran ahead of the others, embracing him in a bear hug of relief. He looked knowingly into Clark's eyes as he stood back. "Are you all right?"

"Yeah." Clark nodded. "Tired, but that will pass after I get a shower and burn these clothes."

"Again?" Jonathan arched an eyebrow as the others drew closer.

Clark shrugged with an amused smile. He'd have plenty of time to tell his mom and dad everything later. His mother still had a few days of vacation left, and if his father was on schedule, the back pasture fence was finished. They could all use a day or two to veg.

"Don't ever scare me like that again!" Chloe's eyes flashed as she shook a can of fly spray. Catching his curious glance, she scowled. "Don't ask."

"Okay." Clark grinned. "Pete can fill me in."

"You're the one that needs to report, Clark," Pete said.

Clark glanced at Lana, wondering how much she remembered. "There's not a lot to tell."

Lana frowned and shook her head. "I'm afraid I won't be much help. Except for that funny-looking man at the barn, it's all a blur."

"I'll have to tell my insurance agent something." Lex stepped forward, unruffled and calm.

Rather than let Lex speculate, Clark offered a simple explanation he would not be able to prove, disprove, or dispute.

"You were right, Lex," Clark said. "Dr. Farley was doing some kind of genetic research. His test subject was double-jointed and mentally deficient. Layton killed Howard Stoner, and Lana ran into him at the stable when he escaped. After talking to you, I got suspicious and came here looking for her when she disappeared. I guess Dr. Farley and Sharon were afraid we'd tell someone about their project."

Chloe exchanged a glance with Pete, but she didn't volunteer to fill in the blanks. She knew he'd debrief her in detail back at the *Torch*. She pulled her cell phone from her pocket.

"I'd better call my dad and let him know Lana is safe."

"He must be worried sick!" Lana looked stricken. "I left a note on the door that I was going to the stable, but I probably should have called."

"Don't worry. He'll be so relieved, he'll probably limit the responsibility lecture to five minutes." Chloe smiled as she dialed and turned away.

Lex looked toward the remains of the missile silo enclosure, his brow furrowed. "How did Farley manage to blow up an extensive underground military installation doing genetic research?"

"Dr. Farley's demented patient got loose again," Clark said truthfully. "Lana and I got away while Sharon and her father were looking for Layton. I suppose a lot of things could set off several thousand gallons of fuel stored in a tank."

"No doubt," Lex said. If he suspected there was more to the story, he didn't pursue it. He had what he needed to collect on the insurance policy and recoup the financial loss. "I just hope my car insurance covers flaming debris damage on the Porsche."

"I know my insurance doesn't!" Pete blinked, then gasped and ran to check the interior of the convertible.

Jonathan paled. "The tractor."

"Let's go check it out." Clark was anxious to get home where he could shed the only remaining evidence of Dr. Farley's work, the meteor dust on his skin and in his clothes.

A profound peace and quiet settled over the Kansas country-side as Lex roared off in the Porsche. The gleaming silver paint on the demonstration car was now pitted and scorched, but probably covered by insurance. Pete had offered to take Chloe and Lana home and followed in the blue convertible, which had miraculously survived falling cinders and ash unscathed.

Jonathan gripped Clark's shoulder as they walked toward the cornfield where he had left the tractor. "Looks like LexCorp had nothing to do with Howard's death."

"No," Clark said. "Lex rented the old missile silo site to Dr. Farley, but he didn't know what he was doing. Sharon told everyone that her father was writing a book."

Jonathan nodded as they skirted the field of smoldering brush and debris. "I'll call Lex tomorrow and apologize for almost suing him."

"He'll appreciate that, Dad. Thanks."

"Actually, I should be thanking you, Clark." Jonathan squeezed his shoulder then dropped his hand. "I have no doubt that Lex and Lionel are guilty of many things, but they weren't responsible for this. You stopped me from making a big mistake, one that might have cost us the farm."

Clark just nodded, overcome with affection for his father. "I'm just glad you trusted my judgment enough to listen."

They walked in silence for a few minutes. When Jonathan spoke again, it was a sign that life had already begun to return to normal.

"I'm not sure our insurance covers fire from the sky damage. Could you take a look, son? So I don't waste this walk wondering how I'm going to pay to fix it if it doesn't need to be fixed?"

"Sure." Clark focused his X-ray vision.

The tractor was parked in the field where his Dad had left it, and it appeared to be intact. Clark couldn't detect damaged paint or burn holes, but as long as the old machine ran, his father would be happy.

"We've been needing to get a new tractor for a long time, haven't we?" Clark asked, sounding serious.

"Oh, no." Jonathan stopped short. "It blew up?"

"Joking, Dad. Just joking." Ducking his father's playful punch, Clark laughed. There were far worse fates than being an alien teenager coping with a secret identity crisis.